I0641931

In This Vale of Tears

Gerard Charles Wilson

Gerard Charles Wilson Publisher

In This Vale of Tears

Sixties Series Book 2

Copyright © 2024 Revised 2026 Gerard Charles Wilson

Gerard Charles Wilson Publisher

Mount Martha VIC

Australia

Email: gerard@gerardcharleswilson.com

Website: gerardcharleswilson.com

ISBN 978 1 876262 07 5   paperback

ISBN 978 1 876262 09 9   ebook

Cover illustration Kalhh

Dedication

To those dedicated nuns, brothers, and priests who gave me an excellent
education and a love of reading

Contents

Chapter 1

No going back

UNTIL THAT MORNING, early December 1956, Virginia Pearson had hardly noticed the ticking of the antique clock on the mantelpiece in the lounge. An unnerving silence had descended upon the house, and the ticking now felt like a needle piercing her head. She glanced at the hall door. Her mother was in the kitchen at the other end of the house. At least, that's where she had left her. But no sound came from there. Her student brother had cleared out early to join his mates in the city. Her father had taken her younger brothers to the bay for a walk, despite their protests. Why did they have to do this? What was going on? And why was Virginia all dressed up and sitting alone in the lounge? She rose and walked down the hall to the kitchen. Her mother sat at the table, reading the morning newspaper. She looked up.

'Are you sure you know what you're doing, darling?' she asked, laying the newspaper on the table.

'Yes, I'm sure. I'm just a little nervous about it. That's all.' She tapped the table.

'There is still time to reconsider. Perhaps you should reconsider—give yourself more time?'

'No, it's done. I have thought about it long enough. I have made my decision. There's no going back.'

'If you're nervous, that might be a sign you have not thought about it long enough.'

Virginia looked at her watch. Another five minutes if he is on time.

'No. I'm not putting it off.'

She returned to the lounge room and sat on the edge of the lounge settee. The ticking was now like two needles through her head. She started at the sound of the front doorbell. He was on time. As usual. She opened the door, and Philip Stevenson took her in his arms and hugged her gently.

'What's this summons for?' he said, releasing her. 'It sounds serious.' He smiled and raised an eyebrow.

'Come into the lounge room, Philip.' She took his hand and led him to a single-seat lounge chair. She resumed her place on the lounge settee opposite.

'Where's everyone?' he said, looking around. 'The house is usually full of happy domestic noise on a Saturday morning.'

'Philip, I have something important to say.'

The smile and look of affection faded.

'Where's your ring?' he said, looking at her outstretched hand.

She glanced at her hand and lowered it.

'It's best to get straight to the point. For a long time, I have felt a calling. I think you have known .... It has become irresistible. I am sorry. The last thing I want to do is hurt you, but I have thought enough. I must respond. I would not be honest if—'

'Honest?' he said, rising, his face pale. 'To whom?'

'You, of course,' said Virginia, his unfamiliar expression causing alarm.

'We had dinner at a smart restaurant a week ago. It was your wish. You could not have been more affectionate. We ended the evening with a passionate kiss. What was that?'

'It was my farewell. It was to let you know how much I love you despite what—'

'How much do you love me?' he said, looking down at her.

'Yes, I wanted–'

'Why didn't you tell me then?'

'Because it would have spoiled our last evening together.' She rose and took his hand. 'Please sit down, Philip. Let me explain–'

'What's there to explain?' He shook his hand free. 'Clearly, you have made your decision. You don't want to marry me. That seems to be that.' He took a step towards the lounge room door.

'No, wait, Philip. Please don't go. I want to explain. It's not that I don't love you. I just love–'

'Yes, I know, you love God more. There's nothing more to say, Virginia.' He was now at the front door.

'Wait, Philip. Don't go like this. Be fair.'

'Be fair?' He had his hand on the doorknob.

'Please, Philip, I couldn't bear not giving you an explanation.'

'You have made your decision. Nothing you say could make a difference.' He opened the door.

'At least take your ring.'

'Keep it.'

He closed the door behind him and was gone. She sank onto the settee and listened to his car coughing and spluttering before jerking into life. The Morris Minor skidded in the soft dirt out of the gutter and drove away, the gears grating as he was late with the clutch. She trembled. He had never behaved that way. She had never seen his face so taut and pale. It was entirely unexpected. Dr Philip Stevenson, recently appointed lecturer in the philosophy department of John Batman University, had always radiated affability and self-control, no matter what the problem. Problems were to be worked through rationally, he had told her when she had poured out her difficulties when first confronted with a classroom of sensitive girls. She brushed away a tear.

'What's happened?' said her mother, appearing at the lounge room door.

'He's gone.'

'It didn't go well, then,' her mother said, sitting down and taking her hands.

'No. I don't understand. It was a different Philip. He just wouldn't listen. What am I to do? I can't leave it this way. I must explain. He must give me a chance to explain.'

'What did he say?'

'What? I don't know. I was so shocked. I can only remember his cold expression. Let me think.' She thought for a moment. 'He said there was nothing to explain. I had made my decision. It's just not like him.'

Mrs Pearson hesitated. 'Perhaps it is.'

'No.' She pulled her hands away.

'Perhaps he knows Virginia Pearson would not make such a decision lightly. For him, his reaction was rational.'

'No.'

'Your expectations were unrealistic. Poor Philip has loved you ever since you made eyes at him as a thirteen-year-old. What did you expect?'

'Mother, please, you're not helping. Besides, it wasn't like that.'

'Wasn't it?'

'No, it took a while before he was interested.'

'Listen to yourself, darling.'

'It's not a matter for jesting, Mum. What am I to do? Mother Jerome expects us in three weeks.'

'Give him time to get over the shock.'

SHOCK was not the word for it. Philip Stevenson, Oxford PhD, had to get out of there before he lost all composure. His hands struggled to start the car and put it into gear before it skidded from the curb, adding embarrassment to the shock. He had not expected it for one moment. The dinner and her affectionate manner a week before had given him confidence she was ready to name the day. She had named the day all right, but it was not his day. He wanted to accuse her of deceit, but he could not. She kept putting off the wedding date, saying they must be sure of what they were doing. Virginia was like that. She always wanted things to be perfect, perfectly arranged. But that was a sign she had been struggling, and he had not seen it. No, she had not been unfair as much as he wanted to think so.

As the car swerved and lurched around the road, seemingly not knowing where it was going, he realised he was in no state to be in the busy Saturday morning traffic. He drove to Brighton Beach and parked where he could overlook the waters of Port Phillip Bay. He and Virginia had often parked there for a kiss and a cuddle before they walked hand in hand along the bayside trail. The thought of sitting there in the same car in the same place with the same view forced him out of the car. He trudged along the path until he found a bench that he and Virginia had never sat on. His feelings, stretched taut to breaking point, eased while the embarrassment at his reaction increased. But the easing of his feelings did not help. The opposite. He had to face the cold facts. Virginia had decided. It was contrary to everything he knew about her that she would change her mind. That was it, and he had better take care he did not succumb to pointless hand-wringing.

'Hello, Philip.'

He turned to see Mr Pearson standing behind him. Virginia's brothers were taking the steps down to the beach.

'I don't want to be impolite, Mr Pearson. I'm in no mood for conversation.'

'I understand.' Mr Pearson came round the bench to stand in front of him. 'You have our sympathy. It was a shock to us, too. But you are aware of what Virginia is like.'

'Yes, I know what she is like. She has decided.' He stared before him at the misty blue expanse of the bay.

'I would like to say something different,' said Mr Pearson, 'something encouraging, but I must agree with you. It would be best to put it behind you. Distract yourself with your work. You must have a mountain of work to do with your recent appointment. Who knows, it may not work out. Virginia might be disappointed.'

'I doubt it,' said Philip, rising. 'She would have talked it over with Mother Jerome.'

'Yes, indeed, she has unending admiration for that formidable nun.'

'That formidable nun would not have spared her if she did not judge her suitable.'

'Yes, of course, you're right. But you never know.'

'Thank you, Mr Pearson. I will take your advice and distract myself. Now, if you will excuse me.'

'You are always welcome, Philip. Don't forget.' He offered his hand. 'Let things calm down a bit and then come along.'

'Thank you again, Mr Pearson.' He gave the offered hand a quick, firm shake. He noticed the two brothers on the beach, curiously looking up at him, before he turned to walk back to his car. Even they had an idea of the disaster.

His faithful Morris Minor knew where it was going now. He drove to his flat in North Melbourne, where he bagged all he needed for an extended stay in his Sorrento beach house. It was two months before university resumed, so he had time to blow his top in private. If ever he appreciated the gift of a bachelor granduncle to his favourite grand-nephew, this was it. He wanted to get the hell out of the place. After stuffing his bags in the car, he drove to the university to collect his books and papers. While returning to the car, he heard his name called. It was Father Gorman, chaplain of John Fisher College, the university's Catholic college for men, and chaplain of the exclusive John Fisher So-ciety, with its self-important faith-science project.

'Have you got a moment, Phil?' said the priest, limping toward him, a limp from a war wound. 'We haven't spoken for a while.'

'Yes, Father, I have a brief moment. I'm in rather a hurry.'

'I won't keep you. I just wanted to catch up to see how you were. We haven't seen you since ...' He stopped. 'Are you all right, Phil?'

What was he to say? His glum expression would be evident to anyone, let alone to a dedicated priest uncannily sensitive to the troubled.

'Well, things could be better, Father, but I don't want to bother you with my troubles.'

'Phil, people with troubles, especially here at the university, are my chief concern. That's what I am here for. You know that.' He rested his hand on Philip's arm. 'I don't want to pry, but if I can lend an ear, please don't hesitate to seek me out. My door is always open. You know where I am in the college.'

Philip hesitated. He would hear in the end, anyhow. Everyone would hear in the end.

'Virginia has broken off our engagement. I don't want to talk about it. I'm going down to Sorrento for a break.'

'Oh, I'm sorry,' said Fr. Gorman, after a painful pause and examining Philip's face. 'I thought you were so suited.'

'So did I.'

'I would not have expected Miss Pearson to have doubts at this stage.'

'Me, too. It came as a shock.'

'I imagine she is feeling some pain, too.'

'I suppose she is.'

'She would have a good reason for her decision.'

'She does. At least, she thinks she does. She says she loves someone more than me.' Philip could not help an ironic smile.

Fr. Gorman frowned. 'Do you mean—?'

'Yes, Father, she thinks she has been called, as she puts it.'

'That puts a different light on things.'

'I thought you might say that.'

'I mean, her decision is consistent with the young woman I know—not that I know her all that well. It is my impression.'

'There's not much you can do about it, is there?' Philip gave a sign that he wanted to move on. 'It really finishes the conversation.'

'I can help you understand what it means to have a vocation.'

'Not now, if you don't mind, Father.'

'No, of course not, Phil. My door is always open.'

Thank you. I appreciate your concern.'

'That's what I am here for. God bless you. And don't forget Miss Pearson would understand how hurtful her decision has been.'

Then why did she make it? thought Philip, knowing how unreasonable he was. He was not as zealous in his faith and religious observance as Virginia, but he knew enough to know he was being obtuse. Obtuse or not, nothing was to be done except drive down to Sorrento and sulk in his beach house for a few weeks. He would at least be out of reach of bothersome people with their bothersome questions.

Chapter 2

Submit!

VIRGINIA HAD spent the following weeks after her painful meeting with Philip putting her affairs in order. She returned anything of Philip's to his parents' house. She had no choice. Philip was still at Sorrento, uncontactable. His parents had heard from him just once. He had nothing to say to them or her and did not want to hear from anyone. He wished to be left alone. It was a peevishness unlike Philip. She had to accept it, no matter how much it hurt. There was no time to dwell on it.

She packed up the presents she and Philip received on their engagement and returned them to the givers. All her clothes were packed away or hung protected in her wardrobe, which was firmly locked, the key given to her mother. The expense of her fashion tastes came to mind. Her private things were packed in boxes. It was wise not to give anything away. There was no guarantee she would be successful in her wish to enter religious life. The next eighteen months were to be a period of discernment. Indeed, she might not pass through the postulancy, the first six months of testing, before she received the habit and entered the novitiate. She put her bank account and other financial interests into her father's hands. If the awesome Mother Jerome decided against her, she must be able to reenter civic life without any material disadvantage.

Her preparations, she informed her parents, were prudent. In no way did it reflect doubt about her vocation. Of course not, said her mother, patting her on the arm. She and her father understood her prudence. There remained only visits to her grandparents and aunts and uncles.

On the morning of departure in January, she still hoped to hear from Philip, still hoped he would understand and call to wish her the best. No call came. It was a sign of bitterness, not of understanding. Philip knew what it meant to have a vocation to the religious life. His upbringing, studies, and Catholic circles that she and he had mixed in would leave no misapprehension. His hurt she could understand, but his bitterness she could not. She hoped and prayed he would rise above such unworthy feelings. The family, including her grandparents, accompanied her to the convent in Melbourne's northeast, where she was to be received into the first stage of religious life as a postulant.

After Mass and the impressive clothing ceremony in the chapel, where the young women received their habit of a black dress and black veil, the people and the newly clothed postulants enjoyed a lavish morning tea on the upper terrace overlooking the Yarra River. Then it was time for farewells and the families to depart, leaving the young women to the sisters' supervision. Virginia was well acquainted with the procedures, having spent the last few years teaching at the order's exclusive school in the eastern suburbs. Most of her fellow postulants were tearful as family and friends retired, some mothers with a lace hanky at their eyes.

Among the few without tears was a striking girl, tallish, slim, with long fair hair, an alabaster complexion, and a distant, uncertain expression. She had arrived with a somewhat uneasy couple who departed before the clothing ceremony, seemingly at her urging. A sister kept her company during the morning tea welcome. Afterwards, when the families had left, Virginia could not help glancing at her while the postulant mistress organised them, showed them around the postulant quarters, and took them to their rooms on the upper floor. Others stared. The same thought seemed to be passing through their minds. What was such a striking girl doing entering the convent? There was, oddly enough, a second attractive girl among the twenty or so postulants, not so striking as the fair-haired girl but very pretty—tall and willowy. She was among the most tearful of the group, constantly glancing at two girls of the same age with whom she seemed acquainted and who seemed unworried by what awaited them. The two stared brazenly at the fair-haired girl. At the afternoon tea break, the young women introduced themselves.

The fair-haired girl was surprisingly particular about the pronunciation of her name. 'My name is Aine O'Riordan,' she said in a sweet voice. 'Aine is a Gaelic name, spelled a-i-n-e, but pronounced "Awnya."' She lowered her head after her bold statement, which evoked a whisper from someone. The other pretty girl's name was Jannie de Kam. Virginia had taught several girls from Dutch migrant backgrounds. She recognised a characteristic Dutch complexion and manner in Jannie, who, apparently encouraged by Aine, said in a light accent that her name, though spelled with a 'J,' was pronounced 'Yannie.' Jannie's two companions were Margaret McGuigan and Elizabeth Parker. Miss McGuigan continued to stare at Aine no less brazenly, Virginia noted. Something other than Aine's beauty seemed to attract her attention.

AINE O'RIORDAN stared out of the car window at the Gothic tower reaching high into the blue morning sky. With yet another attempt to sort out her aspirations, she wondered what lay ahead of her in the convent of St Augustine, the motherhouse of the Sisters of the Suffering Savior. The tower seemed to sway as she gazed at it. She trembled and looked away. She looked back again. A face at the uppermost window? She focused, but whatever it was, it had gone.

'Well, here we are,' said Bill Huckerby. He glanced over his shoulder. 'No need to be nervous.'

'No, no need to be anxious, darling,' said Joanne Huckerby. 'It's what you want, isn't it?' She reached over and took her hand.

'I'm not really anxious, Auntie Joanne,' said Aine. 'It's ... I'm not quite sure what I feel.'

'You'll be right once you settle.'

'It's a beautiful spot,' remarked Bill, 'tucked away here in the bush and on a ridge overlooking the Yarra River. You could not have chosen better surroundings for religious life.'

'No,' said Aine, her eyes returning to the tower as Bill parked the car in front of the Gothic-style main building.

A sister hurried to them as they emerged from the car and directed them to the chapel. The postulants had to gather outside the entrance while the families took their place inside. They should make haste because the ceremony would start in twenty minutes. Only families were permitted in the chapel because of the unusually large group of postulants. Friends could join them for morning tea after the ceremony.

'You don't have to wait, Auntie Joanne,' said Aine, fidgeting. 'You have done enough. And you have a long drive back to Binawarra. It's not really fair to have you wait around until after the ceremony. It might be a long wait.'

Bill and Joanne Huckerby were close friends of her parents, who lived in a northern suburb of Sydney. A month before, Paul and Moira O'Riordan had brought Aine to Melbourne for an interview with Mother

Jerome and the postulant mistress Mother Cecilia, but could not attend the clothing ceremony. Bill and Joanne had offered to collect Aine from the train and take her to the convent on the following day.

'We don't mind waiting, darling, if it helps you to relax,' said Joanne, taking her hand and squeezing it.

'No, I'm fine, now that I am here,' said Aine, looking around at her fellow postulants as they arrived at the chapel. She turned her head away when she saw them staring.

'Are you sure?' said Joanne, glancing at Bill.

'Yes, I'm sure. I'm all right now. And all this is unfamiliar to you, too. I don't want you to feel out of place.' She glanced back at the postulant group and noticed a young woman, older than the others, looking sympathetically at her.

'All right, if you are sure,' said Joanne, glancing again at Bill, who nodded.

'Yes, I'm sure. I will be with the other girls,' she said, looking at the mature young woman who now stood with her eyes cast down in contemplation. 'We'll all be in the same position.'

Without further discussion, Aine hugged Bill and Joanne, wished them a safe trip, and joined the postulants as they filed into the chapel. Her agitation eased as she became immersed in the solemnity of the ceremony. The postulants had their habit—a long black dress and black veil—solemnly placed in their hands, and they left the chapel to change. After relinquishing her everyday clothes and donning the habit, she returned with her fellow postulants. Though now bearing the full scrutiny of the congregation, she relaxed a little more. The common habit would shield her against unwanted interest. At least, she hoped it would.

Mass and the clothing ceremony took almost an hour and a half. Fortunately, she had prevailed upon Auntie Joanne and Uncle Bill to leave when they did. Making the Anglican couple wait around so long in the grounds of a Catholic convent would have upset and distracted her. When her fellow postulants joined their friends and family for a late morning tea, a sister collected Aine. She accompanied her while she received a cup of tea and a plate of cupcakes and found a seat near the edge of the broad parapet that overlooked the river below and the sunburnt fields beyond. The sister tried to engage her in conversation to put her at ease, but Aine was not so responsive.

'I'll leave you to sit here and enjoy the view,' said the sister, giving up. 'I have some things to do. You're welcome to have a wander around the grounds. I'll be back in half an hour.' As she rose to go, she added, 'Don't go below. The postulants are not to be there unaccompanied.'

'I will be all right, Sister,' said Aine. 'I don't mind being on my own.'

She drank her tea and ate her cupcakes while she admired the view of the river and the fields in the bright summer weather. Over to her right, the forbidden rocky stairway led down past two parapets bordered by gardens to a clearing above the river. The top of a grotto poked above the lower parapet. She turned to look at the postulants and their families and found people staring at her. She was about to turn away when she saw the friendly face of the mature young woman. The mature young woman seemed on the point of beckoning her, but a family member, apparently her father, took her attention. She rose, put her cup and plate on a nearby table, and made her way around the gathering to pass through an archway in the main building to the grounds at the front.

She strolled around the gardens, admiring the shrubs, plants, and flowers, all the time feeling under observation, a feeling she struggled to resist. It was not the rude staring she usually had to suffer, but something else. She walked along the entrance avenue to the front gates. As she turned to walk back, she thought she glimpsed a face at the uppermost window of the tower, then a face at a first-floor window of the main building. She strained her eyes and focused, but could detect no one. Had she imagined it? Did her fretful, overworked imagination deceive her? Eventually, people walking towards their cars signalled the end of the day's reception. She hurried to join her fellow postulants, unable to shake the feeling that interested parties, whoever they were, were still watching her.

Under the leadership of Mother Cecilia, the postulants spent the rest of the day, broken only by lunch and afternoon tea, being inducted into the convent's routine and shown their quarters. Aine learned that Virginia Pearson was the sympathetic, mature young woman. She put up with the staring, most of it furtive, except for the brazen eyes of Margaret McGuigan, a tallish, solid girl, clearly straight from school. Margaret did not so much as stare as consider her with undisguised interest. The scrutiny became so insistent that Aine tried to give signs she did not like it, but Margaret remained impervious until she became aware of Virginia frowning at her. The schoolgirl met the frown, insolently cocked her head, and turned her attention to Mother Cecilia, who saw nothing of the interaction.

The day of the reception finally came to an end. It had been demanding, even disturbing, and Aine was tired. Learning about the routine was not a worry. The attention she aroused and the constant impression of being under observation by unseen eyes left her unsettled. She climbed the stairs to the first floor with her fellow postulants, entered her cell, and placed her prayer book and rosary on the bedside cabinet. She fiddled with her rosary while listening to the soft footsteps in the corridor and the doors closing. She dressed for bed, knelt, closed her eyes, and bowed her head. A few minutes later, she lay in bed, staring at the ceiling and pondering the day just ended. The dark, the silence, and the subdued moonlight eased her spirits. Her eyelids drooped.

She sat up, clutched the blankets, and looked around. Somewhere, there was whispering. The beams of the half-moon struggling in a ragged night sky shone through the sash window, streaking her long, fair hair. Shadows passed across her. She swung around, rose, and stumbled to the window. A flock of fruit bats glided over the river below, weaving through the moonbeams and shadows of the massive eucalypts along the riverbanks. It must be past midnight. She listened. Now there was nothing. The whispering had ceased. She crawled back into bed, took her rosary, and began murmuring her prayers. Her meditation was taking her away from the anxiety when, of a sudden, she felt pinned down. Whispering came close to her face, close enough to feel the cold breath against her cheeks. There was a tug at her nightdress, then a wrench. She struggled, twisting to the side. The whispering pressed against her ear.

'Submit!' breathed a voice.

'No!'

She put her hand over her face.

'Submit!'

'No!'

'You will.'

The early morning light was creeping into the room when Aine awoke to find herself lying half-wrapped in her blankets on the floor. A burst of magpie warbling in the misty morning chill of the surrounding gum trees broke the silence. There was a sharp knock on the door. She froze and breathed out a response. The footsteps passed on. She got to her feet, steadying herself against the bed. Quickly completing her toilet, she slipped on her long black dress and veil and joined the silent shuffling line of postulants as they made their way from the upper floor to the chapel on the ground floor. The quiet, rhythmical progression of the aspirant religious helped her settle as she took her place and walked in step. But as they made their way along the gusting cloisters of the ground floor, a faint whispering arose and flowed around her, so inaudible as to cause her doubt. There was something, though. Where did it come from?

Now, eyes were on her. She should keep her eyes downcast, but could not resist glancing around. Only the cold sandstone of the walls and cloister columns and the down-turned faces of her fellow postulants confronted her. 'Custody of the eyes,' a soft voice behind her warned. She turned her eyes towards the sandstone paving, reassured. At the end of the cloisters, the postulants joined the novices issuing from their sequestered quarters and followed them into the chapel. As she took her place in one of the front pews, the postulant beside her leaned over.

'Are you all right?' came the same friendly voice.

A glance revealed Virginia Pearson's attractive face and warm eyes. Aine nodded, signifying her gratitude for the sympathetic inquiry. She felt a gentle touch from an elbow. The communal prayers began, and she became so immersed in her meditations that she forgot the happenings around her. The singing of the hours started, and she joined in. The terror of the night and the strange, insistent whispering passed from her mind.

After Mass, the community of sisters made their way to the refectory, where they were to eat in silence. Aine followed her fellow postulants and sat beside whoever happened to be in front of her. When the clacking and clanking of crockery and cutlery distracted everyone, she looked around for Virginia. She hoped she might be sitting next to her. But, no, she sat at the other end of the long refectory table, attending to her breakfast with manners that said much about her. Aine followed her example while she tried to get a grasp on the life she had yet again taken steps to live. The whispering had gone, perhaps into the noise of the refectory, but she still felt that eyes watched her, that they closely observed her. The furtive glances she could not help casting around discovered nothing. Wherever she looked, the community's eyes kept their custody. Even the imposing Mother Prioress and her council of lieutenants sat expressionless at the front table with their eyes directed according to the Rule. Aine's heart sank.

This was the third time since school that she had made a move to discern whether she had a vocation to religious life. Each time, and in a different form, inexplicable anxiety seemed to overtake her. Why? She felt she had a calling. God had reserved something special for her. There had been no desire for the things girls wanted and enjoyed. No interest in boyfriends, fashions, music—all those things that preoccupied the girls her age. Instead, she desired a life devoted to God, Jesus, and the Church, and to do God's will, taking Mary as her model of humility, selflessness, and purity of mind and body. Then why the anxiety? And now, what did the night's whispering and terror mean? This was something new, something deeper, some new obstacle.

Was it a nightmare, though? It had to be, surely. If someone had been in her room, she would have heard the scuffling of feet. She would not have missed the door opening and closing. She would have felt the person holding her down. There was none of that, only the physical pressure of being pinned down. Nothing else. She was not even aware of when the attack stopped, and the person had gone. Attack? Was it that? In the convent? No, what she had feared did not happen. It baffled her. It must have been a nightmare, a terrible, vivid nightmare. She tried to console herself with the thought that it could not have been anything else. But she could not convince herself. She felt a strange unreality, as if dream and actuality were merging, and she could not know which was which.

As instructed, the postulants made their way to their community room when breakfast ended.

Aine took notice of where Virginia sat and took her place beside her. Her friendly presence calmed the flux of her feelings. Virginia gave her a warm look and touched her arm encouragingly as if such a gesture were natural to her. Before long, Mother Jerome, the Prioress and Superior General of the order, glided into the room with the postulant mistress, Mother Cecilia. Mother Jerome gestured to the young women to resume their seats and then took her place in an armchair on the rostrum.

Everything about the prioress radiated confidence and authority. It was what Aine needed. The prioress welcomed the postulants, pleased that the group of 1957 was the largest the order of the Sisters of Suffering Saviour had ever received. It was just as well because young women subject to the influences of their liberal society required the right direction. During their training, a period of careful discernment, the postulants would review those liberal influences. The prioress paused and looked around the room. She let her eyes alight on Aine. A flicker of concern came to her eyes before she moved on. Aine did not see it. She was too preoccupied with the prioress's words as she spoke about Eileen Foley, the foundress of the Order of the Suffering Saviour.

Eileen Foley was an ordinary young woman who devoted herself to Jesus in His suffering and death on the cross. She ministered to the destitute young women of the Dublin Slums. Her humility, selflessness, generosity, and community spirit laid the groundwork for the order's work. Her spirit of love for the needy and downtrodden fired the ever-expanding group of young women joining the order. That spirit was to be the postulants' model. Aine listened, inspired by the purity of Eileen Foley's faith and the selfless life she wanted to lead.

Their community, said the prioress, was based on the ancient Rule of St Augustine to which the sisters owed an interior assent. Such assent was fundamental. Out of their assent arose quite naturally the vows of poverty, chastity, and obedience. Without those vows, the sisters could not commit themselves to the privilege of becoming the loving spouse of that same Divine Master. Mother Jerome rose but signed for the young women to remain seated. The period of postulancy, she continued, was a time of self-examination and breaking away from worldly attachments. Some may find that religious life was not for them. There was no shame in that. It meant Our Lord was calling those to some other life. She paused and looked around at the young faces.

'Before I leave you to Mother Cecilia's care, I must mention the organisational structure in which you will make your vow of obedience. Every four years, the professed sisters of our order elect a Mother Prioress and Superior General. The sister elected is given full organisational authority over our community. The person is designated; the authority comes from God. Therefore, your vow of obedience does not render an obligation to me as a person; it renders obedience to the Lord, whose duties I must fulfil.'

She looked around the room once more.

'Some of you may not be sure what I am talking about. During your formation, indeed, during your religious life, you will hopefully come to understand. I pray you will understand if ever you are faced with a choice between the Church's constant teaching on freedom and authority and views that are gaining increasing prominence in our modern world. I wish you all success in the coming months and pray that the Holy Spirit leads you in the right direction.'

Aine's heart was full, full of the commitment inspired by the prioress's brief. It confirmed her desire to be a religious sister. She pushed aside the doubts and drove out the night's terror and anxiety. As she sat down at the bidding of the postulant mistress, she dismissed the night's fright as a nasty dream and foolish anxiety.

Chapter 3

Margaret and Virginia clash

VIRGINIA AWOKE to the bell that morning, looking forward to the first full day of their postulancy. Having completed her toilet, she left her cell to join her companions, shuffling in silence along the corridor to go down to the chapel for Mass. Aine came out of her room just before her, almost walking into her. A look of nervousness had replaced the distant expression, and she glanced around as they descended the stairs and made their way along the windy cloisters.

'Custody of the eyes,' Virginia whispered, leaning towards her.

Aine looked around at her and then lowered her head. She seemed reassured. Again, Virginia could not help being struck by the girl's extraordinary beauty and the strange aura about her. As they took their place in a front pew, Aine again glanced around her, shifting on her knees and hunching her slight shoulders.

'Are you all right?' whispered Virginia, now responding to a look of panic on Aine's face. Aine focused her intense blue eyes on Virginia and nodded. Her shoulders relaxed, and she bowed her head, closing her eyes.

After breakfast, Virginia found Aine sitting beside her when the postulants took their place in the community room, waiting for the prioress,

Mother Jerome. To allay Aine's uncertain expression, Virginia smiled encouragingly and lightly touched her arm, which seemed to have the desired effect. Virginia's attention, however, was soon taken by Mother Jerome's inspiring address. She listened, enraptured, as the superior general spoke about Eileen Foley, the foundress of the Order of the Suffering Saviour. Eileen Foley was an ordinary young woman, like herself, who responded to the call to devote herself to Jesus in His suffering and death on the cross. Her ministry to the destitute young women of the Dublin slums was how Eileen Foley acted out her devotion.

The power of the prioress's words consumed Virginia. She was hearing about the life she wanted to lead, a life of service to others, the sort of service the great saints, men and women, had given to the ignorant and less fortunate. The dignity, authority, and warmth Mother Jerome radiated filled her with purpose. This imposing woman filled her with zeal to do the work of the community. To be directed, to render obedience to a woman of this sort, would not be a burden. This is what she wanted to explain to Philip. The love of the Gospels, the love of Jesus's female companions, took priority over the love she had for him. Surely, he could understand?

AFTER lunch, Mother Cecilia led the postulants from the cloisters down a steep rocky stairway past two garden-bordered parapets to an open grassy area stretching to a ridge about ten feet above the Yarra River.

'This is your first period of recreation,' she said. 'You are to use your time in accordance with the purposes of the period, all the while reflecting on the morning's instruction. You are to become acquainted with each other, not as seculars—for you are turning your backs on that life—but as fellow religious. Be careful of the ridge near the river. And the steps down to the jetty are strictly forbidden to you.' She then retreated to the next parapet, where she could read her divine office and supervise her charges.

The postulants separated into small groups, some chatting noisily. Virginia looked around for Aine, but the other mature-aged postulants, Rose Lewis and Kay Burgess, took her attention. While Kay talked about Mother Jerome's address, Virginia kept her eyes on Aine, who stood alone by a wooden bench, looking around. It seemed she did not want to be with those laughing and chatting. Some of them stared rudely at h er.

'Just a moment,' she said, interrupting Kay, 'let's include Aine. She's on her own.' With Rose and Kay following, Virginia joined Aine at the bench. 'You're not local, are you? Your parents did not accompany you,' she added in response to Aine raising her eyebrows.

'No, I'm from Sydney. My parents couldn't come, so close friends of theirs brought me.'

'My name is Virginia, Virginia Pearson, and this is Rose and Kay, if you have not remembered.'

'No, I remembered,' said Aine with a shy nod at Rose and Kay. Rose smiled warmly, and Kay regarded her with undisguised curiosity.

'Come on, let's take a stroll,' said Virginia, moving away and giving Aine's arm a short tug. They chatted about the morning's activities and Mother Jerome's address until they arrived near the ridge overlooking the river. Margaret McGuigan and Elizabeth Parker were at the edge, looking down at the dark green waters. Jannie de Kam hung back.

'Go on,' said Elizabeth in a loud whisper. 'You don't dare.' They had not noticed the approach of Virginia and her companions. The threesome turned and furtively looked at the postulant mistress, whose attention was on her breviary. Margaret bent down amid suppressed giggles and picked up some loose stones lying near the edge. With a sly look, she threw a stone into the river. There was a plop as the stone hit the water. She threw another, then another, smirking at her companions and cocking her head.

'Come on,' Virginia said. 'I imagine you're not interested in that childishness.'

While Rose and Kay watched the young women, Aine followed Virginia to a nearby bench.

'It's not wise for the convent to take girls straight from school,' said Virginia. 'Some experience of the world— Oh, I'm sorry.' She glanced at Aine. 'There are, of course, exceptions.'

'I have been two years out of school. I worked in my father's business while I contemplated my future.'

'Really? I thought you were younger.'

'I was a year ahead of the others in my class. My father thought I could start school early.'

'You actually look younger than the girls there.' She nodded at the group still at the ridge overlooking the river. Aine blushed. 'Your father was vindicated if you passed through school without difficulty.' She gave Aine a warm smile.

'I was naturally quiet and studious, not academic, but enough to do well.'

'Are you all right now?'

'Yes, well ... what do you ...?'

'You looked agitated this morning, pale like you had seen a ghost.' She gave a little laugh but then, seeing Aine tremble, hastened to say, 'You truly were upset, weren't you?'

'I was a little shaken by a bad dream. I've probably not settled yet.'

'What sort of bad dream?'

The approach of Margaret McGuigan and her two companions saved Aine from further discomfort.

'Hello, you two,' said Margaret, sitting on a bench opposite. Elizabeth and Jannie joined her, staring at Aine.

'You're from Holland,' said Virginia to Jannie, drawn by her flawless ivory complexion and the shock of honey-blond hair bursting from under the black veil.

'Yes, my family arrived two years ago,' said Jannie, her accent now quite noticeable.

'I had a few Dutch children in my classes, children of migrants. Do you three know each other?'

'Elizabeth and I are friends from school,' said Margaret. 'We met Jannie at the Youth Club. We hit it off. We think the same way.'

'And what way is that?' said Virginia.

'Oh, the teacher saw me throwing stones.' Margaret smirked. 'You don't have to go all timid and silent just because you want to be a nun.'

'No, I don't suppose so. But we'll have to develop habits of discipline to deal with a class of restless students—those of us who go through, of course.'

'The girls in my class will have to watch out,' said Margaret, mimicking the manner of a strict, old-fashioned headmistress. 'I'll be sure to learn 'em habits of discipline.' Her friends tried to suppress smiles while she brushed her hair and veil back over her shoulders.

'I wonder about that sort of class.'

'We had an amazing teacher,' Margaret continued. 'Sister Andrew was always cheerful and enthusiastic. She made our classes fun—more like a girls' club. It can't be that hard.'

'Depends on the teacher's attitude,' Virginia continued. 'Cheerfulness and class order are not impossible.'

'There were other nuns like that,' added Elizabeth. 'That's why I'm here.'

'Me, too,' said Margaret, ignoring Virginia.

'No doubt the girls' club carried the fun over to the youth club for the boys' amusement,' said Virginia.

Aine frowned and glanced at Virginia.

'Not one bit,' said Margaret with sudden vehemence. 'Those stupid boys! It beats me how the girls put up with those ignorant dopes, let alone date them. Yuk!' She shuddered and stood up. 'We had much more fun at school with the nuns.'

'Yes,' said Elizabeth, standing in support.

Jannie, giving no more than a nod, rose, too.

'Many parents want religious sisters to be strict with their pupils,' Virginia continued to prod.

'I'll be strict, too.' Margaret resumed an air of playful defiance. 'I'll be the boss. But I'll let my girls have some fun.' She pulled a face that seemed to mean that she had said enough. 'What made you want to become a nun,' she said, turning to Aine. 'I bet you had plenty of groping boys running after you.'

'No, I didn't,' said Aine, looking away.

There was a brief silence as if Margaret and her friends expected Aine to explain. Margaret shrugged. 'If you don't want to talk about it ...'

'There's nothing to say,' said Aine. 'After school, I worked in my father's business while deciding what I wanted to do.'

The three young women looked at her.

'Aine wants to keep that private,' said Virginia.

'If it's a secret—' said Margaret.

'What did you think of Mother Jerome's talk about obedience and the governance of the order?' said Virginia.

Again, Aine looked at Virginia.

'I hadn't a clue what she was on about,' said Elizabeth.

'She was talking about the justification for authority and the vow of obedience—important matters for those in religious life.'

'I know we have to be obedient,' said Jannie, 'but what was the rest about?'

'She just wanted to say she's the boss,' said Margaret. 'Just like at school, we'll get lines if we muck up.' She grinned at her companions. 'It's no different from school, really. And we'll work out ways to get around it, and have some fun, too. Do you remember the sly digs Collie used to make about the unbearably strict Mother Superior?' she said to Elizabeth. 'Hilarious!' They both giggled.

'And who is Collie?' asked Virginia, tilting her head.

'Sister Columba was our chemistry and physics teacher,' said Margaret, again ignoring Virginia's tone and turning to Elizabeth. 'She was a lot of fun, wasn't she?'

'Does the name Leo XIII mean anything to you?'

Elizabeth and Jannie swapped uncertain glances and looked to Margaret.

'Who's that?' said Margaret. 'My Irish background has not given me much respect for royalty.' She turned to Aine. 'You have a double-barreled Irish name. How far back does it go?'

'My grandparents came from Belfast.'

'Belfast? You'd be full of it, too. Do you know who Leo whatshisname is?'

'He was a pope.'

'A pope?' Margaret could not hide her surprise.

'Pope Leo XIII was perhaps the most influential pope of the last hundred years,' said Virginia, raising a finger. 'His social encyclicals laid out the Church's social teaching in precise detail. Subsequent papal announcements have taken their lead from his work. Mother Prioress's comments on the nature of authority are drawn from that teaching.'

'Oh,' said Margaret, looking to the side and making a face.

'Are you familiar with the encyclical *Rerum Novarum*?'

Elizabeth and Jannie said nothing. Margaret turned to Virginia and frowned.

'*Rerum Novarum*,' continued Virginia, her finger still raised, 'known by its English title, "The Condition of the Working Classes," was a seminal commentary on the clash between the ideologies of capitalism and socialism. His Holiness pointed out that neither ideology could provide the solution for society's ills.'

'Well?' said Margaret, pulling another face.

'You really have never heard about it?'

'What if I haven't?'

'Your Collie did not mention it?'

The unrelenting poking and prodding would succeed in the end.

'She was our science teacher. I was her best student,' said Margaret, her eyes flashing.

'Are you familiar with any of the Church's social writings?' Virginia continued to goad.

There was no response from the three friends. Margaret's playfulness had gone, and she glared at Virginia.

'I wonder why you are here,' said Virginia.

'Keep wondering,' said Margaret. 'It's got nothing to do with you. You're not the postulant mistress, so you can keep your lectures to yourself.' She got up. 'Not only was I the best science student, but I was also the school's dux.'

'You will not resolve your problems by running away to a convent.'

'You're one of us,' said Margaret, chin raised and looking down at Virginia, who remained seated. 'If I don't know about some dead and forgotten pope, I know what equality is. Solidarity and sisterhood are more important than knowledge of some dry historical fact. You deal with your own problems and forget about those you imagine I have.' She walked off, with Elizabeth and Jannie following.

Virginia watched them go. 'I suppose you're wondering why I was lecturing them.'

'Yes, I was,' said Aine. 'Many Catholics are unaware of the existence of papal encyclicals, let alone know what they are about.'

'You're right, of course. But you would think those who want to enter religious life would have a little idea.' She paused. 'Well, have you heard of *Rerum Novarum*?'

'Yes.'

'From whom?'

'My father. He's involved with other men in fighting the communist threat in the workplace.'

'Ah, yes, good for him. Mine too. It's a big struggle. It proves my point, though.' She stood. 'Come on, let's walk. I hope you don't think I'm in the habit of wagging my finger. It's only naughty, irritating schoolgirls who provoke me.'

They walked in silence to the far end of the garden.

'Let's linger here for the moment,' said Virginia, turning to walk along the fence. Aine followed without speaking. They came to a rocky grotto built against the parapet embankment. A statue of Our Lady of Lourdes was high up in a niche. Below, on a ledge midway from the ground, was a statue of St Bernadette kneeling. Virginia stopped and looked up. Her expression gradually changed as she gazed at the statues.

'I asked Margaret and her friends why they were here,' she began. 'The truth is that each of us is faced with the same question.' There was a long pause before she continued. 'That may seem an unnecessary question. One becomes a priest, or brother, or sister because one is religious. But that's an unthinking view. Plenty of people are faithful and virtuous Christians without it entering their heads to join the religious life.' She threaded her arm through Aine's. 'Let's sit down.' They sat on a stone bench facing the grotto, Virginia remaining thoughtful. 'Can I tell what's been occupying my thoughts since I arrived here yesterday?' she said.

'Yes ... of course.'

'I was going along minding my own business,' Virginia resumed. 'I came from a good, loving Catholic family, never questioned my faith, always attended to it; I left school and went to teachers' college, passed my exams, and started teaching; I had close friends and was popular with my students. Everything looked laid out before me. Soon I would get married, have children, and live happily ever after. Then, for some unknown reason, I picked up a dusty book lying on the library shelves at school. It was St Augustine's *Confessions*. Its first paragraph changed my life forever. Are you familiar with it?' Aine shook her head. 'It's about our inclination to recognise God's majesty and inscrutable wisdom. Only sin blinds us to it. God has made us for Himself, and we cannot be happy until we rest in him.

'Reading the *Confessions* was the start of my reading about the role of reason in defending and adhering to our Christian belief. I had help in this—a lot of help.' Philip's cold, pale face flashed before her mind. 'I won't go on anymore about it—and I didn't mean to begin. I'm such a big mouth.' She shrugged and glanced at Aine. 'Anyhow, my reading found its way to papal writings. There, I found my calling to serve God and, in serving God, to serve those who suffer and are less fortunate. That's why I'm here.' She paused. 'Can you see now why I persisted in challenging Margaret and her friends?' She did not give Aine a chance to answer. 'I get so irritated by the superficial and cavalier attitude of—and then, trying to rid herself of the sudden irritation, 'Your feelings about being called came from a different source, didn't they?'

'I'm afraid I have never thought much about it—I mean in the intellectual way you said,' replied Aine. 'My understanding of Our Lord's life and death and the example of His spotless Mother drew me. The perfect offering of one's existence to God ... I could not refuse.'

'You're not familiar with the Church's great philosophers or their arguments supporting the Church's doctrinal teaching, are you—St Augustine and St Thomas Aquinas, for example?'

'No, if you mean reading their works. I know about them as saints, as examples of Christian living. The sisters spoke about them.'

'You know about them the same way you know and admire such saints as St Francis of Assisi, St Therese of Lisieux, St Maria Goretti, and others?'

'Yes, they're among my favourite saints.'

'You know these saints are known mostly for heroically living the Gospels' message and not for any philosophical work?'

'Yes, I suppose you're right. I've never thought about that.'

'You know, too,' Virginia continued, 'that you're contemplating joining mainly a teaching order of sisters despite the order's hospitals and homes?'

Aine hesitated. 'I understand your meaning,' she said at length, blushing. 'I should think more about it. Unfortunately, I let other things get in the way.'

'I don't mean to confront you the way I did with those silly schoolgirls,' said Virginia, missing Aine's meaning, 'but it's something for you to consider. Your commitment to the religious life is obviously strong.'

'Thank you. I haven't had an easy road so far, I have to say. I have been very indecisive.'

'You must expect that,' said Virginia, still missing the signs. 'It'd be strange if you didn't. I don't expect to sail through, either. None of us can be sure we are suited. We are here to find out.' Virginia stopped and considered the pearly, unblemished face looking at her. 'Was that the cause of your anxiety this morning?' Aine's face tensed. 'Is it something more than that? It is, isn't it?' She took her hand. 'Don't worry. We're in this together. If I can ever be of support—a conversation, a kind word—one glance is enough.'

'Thank you, Virginia. You are kind.'

'Come on,' said Virginia, standing, 'I'm too serious again. And I don't mean to lecture, although it must frequently sound like I do. I've always got into trouble for airing my opinions.' She gave a helpless laugh and walked closer to the grotto. 'You know,' she said, looking up again at the weather-worn statue in the niche above them, 'this is what I like about our faith. It's the specific concrete narrative; it's the humanising of some difficult abstract teaching. Before us is the story of the simple, faith-filled peasant girl who received apparitions of Jesus's mother. It's also about the dogma of the Immaculate Conception, something that needs to be understood and explained to bemused outsiders. Let's kneel before this beautiful narrative and pray that the Holy Spirit will guide us through the next six months.' She felt Aine's hand slip into hers.

AINE reflected long on the clash between Virginia and Margaret. She found Virginia's undisguised aggressiveness towards Margaret odd, and the disproportionate challenge unnerving. Without any discernible preamble, she had goaded Margaret with comments and questions that displayed her thorough ignorance of papal teaching. The schoolgirl Margaret, uncowed by Virginia's naked aggression, told her to mind her own business. If she was ignorant of some dead pope—a trivial matter—she certainly knew what genuine solidarity and sisterhood were about. Gathering herself up to her full height and mass, she marched off with Elizabeth and Jannie as her supportive retinue.

It was strange. Virginia was otherwise composed and friendly. Her attractive, open face and bright, confident eyes added extra warmth to that friendliness, despite her sophisticated manner. Margaret and her companions were a little frivolous and cheeky, but it was the first full day of their postulancy. Everyone needed time to settle in. Besides, there were many girls with high spirits, like Margaret and Elizabeth. She had seen enough of them at school. As a teacher, Virginia should know that. She suspected Virginia saw more in Margaret's behaviour than she did. She foresaw continuing friction. Jannie de Kam, though more subdued, evidently admired Margaret McGuigan's self-assured, outgoing manner. Margaret and the pretty, willowy Dutch girl made a strange combination.

Virginia then raised questions about her understanding of a vocation with the Sisters of the Suffering Saviour. Indeed, they were questions about her misunderstanding, but they were gentle and sympathetic in contrast with Margaret. She was grateful for her new friend's support, but it did little to ease the disturbing anxiety she had so far experienced in her search for the right religious order. It occurred to her that her anxiety might have been partly due to a presumption she would have her yearnings gratified in the first religious congregation she applied to.

And there was something else. The last thing she expected when the Huckerbys dropped her off at the convent was the beginning of a warm friendship. But it happened. Her immediate connection with Virginia was like no other relationship she had experienced. It would be a support in the coming months, support she anticipated needing. She feared the strange, ominous sounds, never far away, and the heavy atmosphere would continue to haunt her. The tense clash between Virginia and Margaret, though, signalled something else. The clash amounted not just to a difference of opinion or outlook. No, it heralded a vital, unyielding clash, drawing surprising and uncharacteristic aggression from Virginia. It was a response to Margaret's perverse ideas of religious life, which she expressed with unshakable confidence and mocking impertinence. Fresh out of school, Margaret showed no regard for Virginia's seniority in profession and maturity. Indeed, respect seemed foreign to her. The hints of her Irish nationalism, with which she had unpleasant experiences, also did not augur well. Finally, Margaret's interest in her, an interest unlike the attention she aroused in the others, unnerved her.

Chapter 4

Philip grieves

DR PHILIP STEVENSON parked his car under the rickety wooden carport of his Sorrento beach house, took his bags and books inside, and threw them onto the kitchen table. There, they stayed untouched for the next ten days. He passed his time sitting in a deck chair on the verandah with a whisky, staring at the bay waters, or going for long walks along the bayside beaches. His struggle to understand was far greater than the average undergraduate suffered in understanding the arguments in Immanuel Kant's *Critique of Pure Reason*. And that was indeed a head-breaking struggle.

He understood, of course, that Virginia had ended their relationship after years of intimate companionship to devote herself to her calling, as she put it. They were the facts of the case. But he could not understand how she could do it. How could her calling eclipse so much deep feeling, so much closeness in love and mutual understanding? He always had the feeling they thought as one. He could not avoid the pressing conclusion that she had been playing a deceitful game, that her love was mere appearance hiding a cold, manipulative heart. No, he could never accept that melodrama. Virginia was anything but heartless and deceitful. This paradox plagued his every moment, stirring up a mixture of anger, despair, and grief. Their relationship kept replaying like a sad matinee movie.

The Pearsons and the Stevensons were close. They belonged to the same parish. Their children attended the same schools. Their mothers swapped women's magazines and joined the church and school auxiliaries. Mr Pearson was an accountant, and his father a business executive who had worked his way from the shop floor of a building supply company to state manager. Both had spent time in the army during the War. They supported the fight against the communist infiltration in society and the workplace with overflowing enthusiasm. Virginia was the oldest of the Pearson children, seven years younger than Philip. He hardly noticed them, even when the families came together for dinner or a barbecue. His two younger sisters, closer to Virginia in age, had more to do with her. To the extent he took notice, he saw that she was a pretty young thing with plaits and ribbons who bossed her younger brothers around.

At twelve, she seemed to become aware of him, that he attended university and studied a mysterious subject. 'You must be brainy,' she said to him once. He could not remember her ever addressing him before that bold remark. Her mother told her to leave Philip alone and not be so pert. From then on, she gave him looks meant to show she noticed him. Things changed with the onset of puberty. She dared to do more than speak to him, even after Mass, when the families were chatting. She always wanted to know about his studies, but a playful, sometimes teasing smile accompanied her questions. His studies became a way of talking with him. Her mother again told her not to be so irritatingly pert. On one occasion, when she had asked him if he had a girlfriend, her mother rebuked her for being cheeky. He said he did not mind. And it was true. This teasing, pretty girl of thirteen with playful eyes amused him. Mrs Pearson would not have it. She told Virginia to mind her manners with her elders. When her mother was not looking, Virginia gave him arch smiles and meaningful looks. He still found it amusing.

Such occasions were limited. Philip was in the last year of his honours degree and had no time for social occasions. He saw Virginia occasionally after Mass with the family, but was too preoccupied to pay her much attention, and he did not linger. He only noticed that she was pretty and self-assured at fourteen and not reluctant to tease and smile at him at fifteen, despite her mother's constant correction. Philip's hard work paid off. He earned a scholarship and began preparations to leave for England in July 1949. His parents gave their good friends the news after Mass a few weeks before his departure. He received hearty congratulations from all around. Only Virginia was quiet.

'Is he really going to England?' she whispered to her mother.

'Yes, darling, Philip has received a scholarship. It's wonderful news. His parents are very proud.'

'How long will he be away?'

'I'll be away three years, Virginia,' said Philip, near enough to hear the exchange.

'Three years?'

'Yes, darling, Philip will study for a doctorate.'

'Three years,' repeated Virginia.

She looked at Philip, and then turned her head into her mother's breast. Mrs Pearson put her arm around her and countered Philip's surprise with a shake of her head. That was the first time he understood Virginia's feelings for him were more than arch smiles and teasing questions. He shook it off. A fifteen-year-old schoolgirl's feelings were none of his business. His mother later said that Virginia had just a typical schoolgirl crush. He returned to Melbourne in 1952 armed with his doctorate and ready to take on a tutorship position in the philosophy department at John Batman University. He tried to resist it, but his first thoughts were about Virginia. She was at the end of her first year at the Catholic teacher's college. He asked his mother, among other things, whether she had a boyfriend.

'Oh, she has plenty of boyfriends, I hear,' said his mother, caressing his arm and giving him a meaningful smile. 'She's a popular girl. You'll see her soon enough.'

'Oh,' said Philip, a little deflated.

Soon enough became very soon because Virginia came to visit her mother within the week of his arrival.

'Hello, Dr Stevenson,' said the smartly dressed eighteen-year-old when she entered the living room where he sat reading. She wore the same playful smile. 'I wanted to be among the first, besides family, to welcome you home.'

'Thank you, Virginia,' he said, rising. The pretty fifteen-year-old had grown into a very attractive young woman, as self-assured and outgoing as ever, and with friendly sparkling eyes. 'I'm glad to be home.'

'You must tell me all about your time at Oxford. I'm dying to hear.'

'You see, Philip,' said Mrs Pearson, 'our daughter is just as forward as she ever was.'

'But I'm permitted now, aren't I, Philip? After all, teachers cannot be quiet retiring petals, can they?'

'No, of course not. I'm happy to tell you all you want to know. But I must say a lot of it was hard work—long, boring study hours, I mean.'

'I want to hear everything, even the most boring part. You did not bring a wife back with you, I hope.'

'Virginia!' said her mother.

'No, no wife,' said Philip, smiling.

'A girlfriend, perhaps?'

'Stop it, Virginia. You're embarrassing Philip.'

'No, not even a girlfriend.'

'You just played the field?'

'Now that's a secret.' There were limits to her teasing. He would keep her guessing—and interested. It pleased and relieved him that she still showed interest in him.

'The cost of your secrecy is my imagination running wild. What have you to hide?'

Now, this was flirting, and he liked it.

'If you don't stop your silly talk, darling, I will take you home,' said Mrs Pearson, smiling at Mrs Stevenson.

'Philip doesn't want me to go home just yet, do you, Philip?'

'I suppose it's too soon for you to leave.'

'There.'

Mrs Stevenson ended the flirtation by bidding them all to sit down while she prepared afternoon tea. Virginia dropped her playful manner and asked thoughtful questions about his study and stay at Oxford. He responded similarly. It was a pleasant afternoon tea, and when Virginia and her mother left, Virginia saying she looked forward to seeing more of him, he understood she had invited his attention. Her mother, apparently, too. She later told his mother that Virginia had always liked Philip but was too young to have a relationship with a twenty-four-year-old man. He must keep his distance for the moment. If Philip was interested, he had to be patient, at least until Virginia's twenty-first birthday. In the meantime, she added, Virginia was to engage in the usual social activities of people her age, closely supervised activities.

And so it happened. Philip saw Virginia regularly, always in the company of others, mostly family, but sometimes on church occasions. Her familiarity increased, graduating by the end of the following year to furtive caresses and even briefly holding his hand. He let it happen. She was part of the Catholic Youth Club, attending most of their social gatherings, whether parties or picnics. She accepted invitations to go out from boys her age, but only after her mother and father thoroughly vetted the youth. Virginia jokingly told Philip all about her dates, causing him to laugh at the clumsy manner of some boys. He recognised the clumsiness, he said. She had ways, she told him, of discouraging 'fresh' behaviour, as her mother described it.

By the end of her third year and teaching training, she announced she and Philip were going steady. They would go out together, alone or with others, as they considered fit. Her parents had nothing to say except to remind their daughter of her duties and responsibilities. By this time, Philip was deeply in love and could not see life without her. They had their first passionate kiss late one evening, after a CYC social occasion, while sitting on a bench at Brighton overlooking the calm moonlit waters of the bay. Then, after enchanting him into a delirium of love, she broke the spell, leaving him crushed as if she were exacting some sort of revenge for the insolence of loving her.

After two weeks of running these broken scenes through his head, Philip realised he could not go on like this. When two female students from the English department arrived to console him, he saw the implications and the danger. He packed up, offered the girls a lift, and departed after they declined. They had come to Sorrento to enjoy themselves, not to be with an angry, jilted man. Philip arrived back home to spend a quiet, unobtrusive Christmas with his family. Fortunately, understanding his grief, they left him alone. In January, having fulfilled his family Christmas responsibilities, he packed up, drove to his North Melbourne flat, threw his bags and papers onto the kitchen table, poured himself a whisky, sat in a lounge chair, and stared at the ceiling. Two days later, leaving an empty whisky bottle on the kitchen table, he set off for his office at the university. He came across Fr. Gorman at the same place. It was as if the priest had been waiting to waylay him.

'Good to see you, Philip. How are you feeling?'

'The same.'

'I understand. It is not easy—it will not be easy to reconcile.'

'No, it won't.'

'Would you like to chat about it? We can chat over a coffee at the student union.'

'You must forgive me, Father Gorman. I am in no mood for chatting. I must work through it myself.'

'I understand. I'm available whenever you want to talk. Talking through your grief will help, I assure you. I know from experience.'

'Thank you again, Father. Now I must be going.'

'Wait, Philip. I also wanted to talk about your break with Vic Brennan and his friends of the John Fisher Society.'

'Gosh, Father, that's the last thing on my mind.'

'I consider it serious, Philip. I deplore a break in friendship over religion, and I don't want disruption in the Fisher Society.'

'It's not over religion. I've made it plain, and I've told Vic. It's about politics and philosophy—about his philosophical dilettantism. Unfortunately, the poetical lecturer of the English department does not seem to understand that philosophical disquisition is not the same as analysing a poem. Besides, Vic and his mates are a coterie in the Society. Not all members are part of their exclusive faith-science group, as they pretentiously call it. So, with respect, Father, I would be careful of their free-open-inquiry approach to doctrine.'

'I would still like to talk to you about it, perhaps arrange a meeting with you all.'

'I appreciate your efforts to reconcile our differences, but it won't work. And I don't have time, much less the inclination.'

'Promise me, Philip, you will give it a try.'

'Just for you, Father.'

Acknowledging the priest's best intentions, Philip was glad to get away from him, if at the cost of a promise he did not want to honour. Vic Brennan, with his ignorance of Marxist praxis and his group's growing infatuation with the nonsense of the fraud Teilhard de Chardin, was too much for him to contemplate. At his office, he proceeded to carry out the undertaking formed that morning. He would distract the madness of his grief with work—work, work, and more work. Besides organising lectures, tutorials, and timetables, he must attend to his scholarly writing. That must not be neglected. With a sandwich break in his office and an interruption from a few female students, he worked through until the afternoon, when he left for a departmental meeting. Virginia came to mind during the meeting and the tedious discussions about subjects and timetables. She would be leaving for the convent shortly to change her smart, tasteful clothes for a costume party outfit that would suppress her femaleness. But, of course, that was the intention of the nun's habit. He rang his mother later.

'Yes, Virginia's due to enter this coming Sunday. So you still have a chance to call her, Philip.'

'I won't have time.'

'Don't be silly, Philip. Of course, you have time. You should, even for the sake of good manners. This is not like you, Philip dear.'

'Perhaps it's not. I can't help it.'

'Dad and I know you're broken-hearted, but it's still the right thing to do. Virginia is very upset that she has not heard from you. Please release her with your best wishes.'

'Release her? I'm the one she should release.'

'Please make an effort, Philip.'

'I'll try. What time exactly does she leave?' He noted down the times. 'Please don't tell her you spoke to me.'

'I promise.'

Phillip thought long about it, always firm in his decision not to contact Virginia. But on Sunday morning, he found himself parked in a bushy side street off the road running along a ridge above the Yarra River to the motherhouse of the Sisters of the Suffering Saviour. He had come that far but remained undecided. When he reached the point of whether to continue or return home, he compulsively put the car in gear and drove to the motherhouse, where he parked outside the property and a little way down the road. He slowly approached the long entrance avenue, ensuring no one was around. Glorious singing led him to the chapel. He slipped in the back and squeezed into a corner, crouching a little. He was just in time.

The young women in front of the altar had received their postulant habit and were about to file out of the chapel to change. Philip fixed his gaze on Virginia as she walked with the others, her expression solemn and her eyes directed ahead. They exited through a side door into the convent building. Ten minutes later, the postulants, in their black dress and black veil, filed back into the chapel amid uplifting and joyous singing. Again, Philip fixed his eyes on his former fiancée, now in her party costume. After they reached the front and knelt before the bishop, he had seen enough. He had seen the depth of Virginia's commitment. He had no business there, gawking like an idiot. Almost at a trot, he hurried back to the car and got the hell out of there before anyone saw him.

Chapter 5

Aine and Virginia

THE FOLLOWING weeks, occupied with settling in, learning the convent's routine, and concentrating on the daily prayer and instruction, required the close attention of the postulants. It was demanding but not a burden for Aine's fervour, which she was happy to indulge. Besides, the joy of the daily routine of Mass, Eucharistic adoration, rosary, Bible meditation, and the singing of the hours meant that the whispering and the eyes no longer tormented her. Perhaps the rigour of the formation drew her attention away from their still lingering presence. She did not know; she did not have time to consider that possibility because Mother Cecilia, showing an unnerving insight into each young woman's character, focused her reprimands on their faults. Aine was embarrassed to find herself continually called to attention. In contrast to others who must show their feelings of victimisation, she had no complaint; she was well aware of her tendency to isolate herself in her thoughts. A meek nod was her response to the reprimands.

'What are you going to do, pray tell, when you are faced with thirty restless fourteen-year-old girls?' demanded the postulant mistress of her in the middle of one class. 'Unruly girls will gobble up a timid, indecisive teacher.'

'Yes, Reverend Mother.'

'Then stop daydreaming. Keep your mind on it.'

As a reward for her daydreaming, Aine was given the shared responsibility of organising the kitchen stores, a painstaking, menial task that took much concentration and cooperation. She set to work without a murmur but could not douse the spark of inward rebellion against the brakes on her contemplation. When the kitchen group left their tasks to go to the chapel, her feelings of relief shamed her. It disturbed the consolation she got from losing herself in her prayers. To show she had not yet submitted wholeheartedly to the Rule, she was next given the job of ringing the bell that signalled the community's daily tasks. Again, she accepted the instruction without complaint but felt the heightened pressure of having to concentrate on her surroundings. She had no reason to feel singled out. Each postulant had to suffer the humiliation of their faults and misdemeanours laid bare—all for expiating their faults and reorienting them to God.

Virginia did not escape; she least of all. Mother Cecilia kept on challenging her. Whether it was about religious instruction, the Rule, or the routine of the convent, the postulant mistress called on Virginia to show what she knew—or rather, what she did not know. With barefaced purpose, she questioned Virginia about Church teaching, which was the professional theologian's domain. Even questions of obscure canon law were served up for Virginia's embarrassment.

'See, you don't know everything, do you, Miss Pearson?' Mother Cecilia would say when Virginia failed to give the correct answer. 'A little reflection and humility before you open your too-often-exercised mouth would not be astray. Humility is the way to holiness.'

'Yes, Reverend Mother, I will pay attention.'

'See that you do.'

Despite the reprimands, Virginia had trouble curbing her interference. From time to time, Rose Lewis's face turned deathly pale with no apparent cause, sometimes followed by violent bouts of vomiting. Being a quiet, gentle woman who never complained or showed any disagreeableness, she made light of these occasions, politely brushing aside all concern. Virginia questioned her about its cause, but gentle Rose smiled and told her not to worry. She would get over it.

'There is something wrong with her,' commented Virginia, one day after lunch, as the postulants, some recoiling with their hands over their mouths, watched Rose being sick over the garden outside the refectory.

To Virginia's astonishment, Mother Cecelia took to castigating her. 'I have told you before. You must learn to rise above your dislikes and discipline your body. How will you manage the big things if you cannot overcome small things? You will be helped to conquer your inclinations. Now go and get a bucket of water and clean up your mess.'

Virginia looked in amazement at Mother Cecilia and then at Rose, who nodded and went to fetch a bucket. 'So that's it,' she whispered to Aine. Later, she said to Rose, 'What is it you don't like?' Rose refused to say. 'Then I'll find out.'

Rose was violently ill after dinner for three days in succession.

'You have a dairy intolerance, don't you?' said Virginia, joining her on the third occasion.

'Please ...,' said Rose, unsteady on her feet and trying to put a finger to her mouth. 'Silence.'

'You can't possibly do anything about that,' whispered Virginia, taking hold of Rose's arm. 'I know ... I had a couple of children in one class.'

'Please don't say anything.'

'We'll see, by golly,' Virginia whispered as Rose staggered to the nearby bench.

Mother Jerome appeared in the postulant community room that evening, chatting briefly with each postulant before stepping aside with Mother Cecelia. Over the following days, Rose revived, and colour returned to her cheeks.

'It was the cheese,' said Virginia. 'She could manage everything else except the blessed macaroni cheese dish. The cook seems to have a preference for cheese dishes.'

'Are you sure Mother Cecilia will be happy you went to Mother Jerome?' Kay Burgess asked.

'I didn't. I only mentioned it to Mother Cecilia.'

Virginia did not care about the source of Mother Jerome's information. The result pleased her, and she would disregard the heat her interference would bring. As expected, the wrath of the postulant mistress came down hard on her. The air became so thick with sarcasm and reprimand that one could have cut it away in slabs. She did not miss Margaret glancing with satisfaction at Elizabeth and Jannie.

'It's a little unfair,' said Aine. 'You were just trying to help.'

'Oh, it's all right. I'm aware I'm a little outspoken. I've always had a big mouth. I need to keep in mind that I must listen to others and not come across as so sure of my opinions. It's part of the process of discernment. Our postulant mistress is more insightful than one would suppose.'

'But you're right most of the time. Or so it seems to me.'

'You're too kind,' said Virginia, amused. 'I do make an effort not to open my mouth without being sure of what I'm talking about.' They were standing near the ridge, looking down at the glassy, calm river water. 'But it's not really about the extent of my knowledge. It's about pride. Pride opens the gate to the devil.' She laughed. 'There I go again, preaching away ... but I need to know the temptations pride will lead me to. You, my dear girl, feel for me because you don't know what pride is.'

Aine blushed. 'No, I have my faults, let me assure you.'

'Let's walk a little,' Virginia said.

They walked along the ridge away from the other postulants, most of whom were chatting on the benches. Aine suddenly grasped Virginia's arm.

'What is it? Are you all right?' said Virginia, seeing fear pass over Aine's face as she looked back at the others, the nearest of whom were Margaret and her friends.

'Yes ... yes, it's nothing. I just felt a little unsteady.' She let go of Virginia's arm.

'There's something about you,' said Virginia. 'I'm not sure what it is. And it's not common anxiety you're suffering from. Are you going to tell me what it's about?'

'I don't know myself.'

'Well, what caused that sudden apprehension?'

'Apprehension?'

'Yes, you had a look of apprehension. Come on, Aine, tell me. It may help to talk about it.'

'I looked around and saw Margaret McGuigan looking at us, and for some inexplicable reason, I felt odd.'

Virginia looked back. The group by the benches had dispersed. Margaret and her friends were climbing the steps to the next parapet. They approached an older sister who was tending the rose garden. Virginia frowned and was about to comment on Margaret's brazenness, but then turned and continued walking, holding Aine's arm until she realised what she was doing.

'Has that happened before?' said Virginia, releasing Aine's arm. 'I mean that reaction to Margaret.'

'No.'

'What happened on that first morning?'

'I told you. It was a bad dream.'

They stopped at the boundary fence. Virginia turned to walk back. 'I won't ask anymore. You can tell me when or if you want. You can trust me.' Aine expressed her gratitude. 'No thanks necessary,' said Virginia, wanting to return to her core concern. 'Elizabeth Parker and Jannie de Kam have not escaped Mother Cecilia's reprimands—Jannie in particular. But have you noticed that Margaret, apart from a little scolding, has increasingly gotten away with her perverse behaviour and managed to avoid what most of us suffer? It's as if the postulant mistress has become blind or stumped by her behaviour. I mean, she seems unable to pick Margaret's faults anymore. I really shouldn't be making any comment. But your reaction just then—'

'Margaret adjusts her behaviour depending on who she's with.'

'You're more attentive than I thought.'

'I couldn't help noticing some occasions.'

'Others seem to have missed it—if that's it.' They arrived back at the benches. Virginia sat down, apart from the other young women. Aine sat beside her. 'Is it really true that you had no boyfriends before coming here?'

'Yes.'

'None at all?'

'None. It's as I said. I was always drawn to religious life.'

'But you must have experienced attention—from boys, I mean. They can be insistent, you know. And looking the way you do—'

'I discouraged any attention,' said Aine, looking away. 'It was fortunate my father had a business I could work in. That relieved me of being rude.'

'You don't like people talking about your appearance, do you?'

'No. It's not worth more than passing attention. It's temporary, any-how, whatever it is.'

'Most girls don't think that way. For some, the discovery of their beauty is like an epiphany.' Aine remained silent. 'Well, if you didn't respond to people of the male sort, I certainly did,' Virginia continued. 'I went through the usual routine girls go through and enjoyed it. It was all very innocent, though. My parents made sure I was supervised. I mixed with the boys at the Catholic Youth Club, nice fellows mostly. I went out with a number, but there was always the one I fell in love with early.'

'You fell in love?'

Virginia laughed. 'Don't say that as if you don't consider me capable of it!'

'Oh no, I don't mean that. I mean, I thought, seeing that you want to be a nun—of course, it was silly of me to—'

'No need to explain. And don't take me so seriously. Yes, I fell in love with a wonderful—a girl could not wish for anyone better than my Philip. We were engaged to be married.' She shrugged, her expression and mood changing.

'Engaged? What happened?'

'I told you. I picked up a copy of the *Confessions* and broke his heart.'

It was the first time in those weeks that Virginia was on the point of losing her composure. Aine put her hand on Virginia's arm. Virginia glanced at her hand.

'I had no intention of talking about it,' she whispered. 'That'll teach me to be nosy, won't it? And let things creep up on me.'

Aine smiled and took her hand away.

'Philip took his faith seriously, although not with as much zeal as me—did all the right things in courting me. The day I told him of my decision was the most painful day of my life. If he had only been angry, it would have been bad enough. But he looked at me with cold incomprehension. I tried to explain, but he would not listen. It all took place in my parents' living room. Can you imagine the scene?'

'No, I can't.'

'After staring at me for many painful moments, he left, ignoring my attempts to explain. He would not even take his ring back. He just rushed away.' She paused. 'Discouraging male attention saved you the heartache of deeply hurting someone.'

'I was not conscious of such things.'

Virginia remained silent, wanting to compose herself before continuing.

'But you want to be a bride of Christ,' she said.

'Yes.'

'It's about your maidenhood.'

'My maidenhood?'

Virginia hesitated, captured by the piercing blue eyes and their wondering expression. 'I said Philip did all the right things in courting me. I am twenty-three, and Philip is twenty-nine. There were occasions ... but I wanted ... on our wedding night, you see. It was my special gift to him ... a symbol of our permanent commitment. He understood ... didn't put any pressure on me. Then my heart was stirred by the infinite love of Jesus, a love that demanded as much love as I had to give. Do you see? My maidenhood is a spiritual gift.'

'That hadn't occurred to me,' said Aine after contemplating Virginia's meaning.

'A young woman of twenty-three is ready to think about it, I assure you. Young women should know what they're giving up before they decide on religious life. They need to be tested. There are girls here—they would've done better to have waited a while. Well, you know what I think. Sticking doggedly to religious life without a vocation could cause untold damage to the individual and the community.'

'You're thinking of Margaret, of course.'

'And her friends. There are others, too, but Margaret and company are a serious worry. I doubt they really appreciate the symbolism of a ceremony in which we are presented as Brides of Christ. You can imagine the mocking comments from an insolent girl who doesn't understand.'

'I have thought too lightly about it, too,' said Aine. 'I haven't given enough thought to the significance of—'

'Some of those young women will feel foolish all dressed up in lacy bride's gowns if they have no idea of the symbolism. I hope they were listening to Mother Jerome. I suspect it will only be a joke for Margaret.' She stopped. 'There, I've been gratuitously airing my thoughts again, and being uncharitable this time, which is worse. Mother Cecilia has sound reason to reprimand me, doesn't she?'

'Why do you think Margaret is here, then,' said Aine, 'if she thinks it a joke and treats rules as something to be broken?'

'I'm not quite sure. Margaret is an intelligent young woman, far smarter than her two companions. That, and her temperament, is a dangerous combination. It's a question of maturity, spiritual maturity, if you want. She takes a proper part in all the ceremonies and devotions, but her behaviour in class and outside shows a bewildering clash with the devotional activity. If you ask me, I suspect Margaret does not see any other direction in her life. But I could be wrong. It might be something else.'

'It could be—' said Aine, but stopped.

'I wonder what her family background is like,' murmured Virginia. 'I wonder, too, why she expressed such aversion toward males. She's not so unattractive that no boy would consider her. Well,' she exclaimed, laughing, 'I've got to put a stop to my nosiness and opinion-giving. I'm going to bore even you in the end.'

'Oh no, not at all. I'm interested. You make it obvious I don't think enough about what I'm doing here. I'm too immersed in my thoughts.'

'You're kind and reassuring. But the lesson remains to watch my propensity to lecture like a schoolmarm. Isn't it time to ring the bell?'

Aine looked at her watch, let out a cry, and rushed to the rocky stairway. Virginia watched with a faint smile as Aine, her veil swishing behind her, revealed her blond hair as she climbed the steps leading to the neo-Gothic building with its imposing central tower.

'I wonder what such a beautiful girl is doing here. You seem to have her attention.' Margaret had approached unnoticed with Elizabeth and Jannie.

'One could ask the same of you,' said Virginia, irritated by the insolent smirk. 'Aine has reflected more on that question than you three.'

'The schoolteacher's always ready with her lessons.'

'And you are always ready with impertinent schoolgirl comments.'

'Our postulant mistress seems to see more of your teacher-preaching than my schoolgirl comments,' said Margaret, making it clear she was not to be intimidated.

Virginia, regretting her dig as soon as she made it, determined to avoid open conflict. 'My impression is that Aine is quite spiritually inclined,' she said to end the exchange.

'She seems to have taken to you—and the other way around.'

'We can talk freely with each other if that's what you mean,' said Virginia, frowning. 'I hope I could do the same with everyone.'

'Well!' said Margaret, wide-eyed and inclining her head towards her friends.

The bell rang, echoing down the parapets and across the river. Relieved, Virginia rose and hastened to the steps. This exchange had done nothing to moderate her feelings. Yes, she had to admit, she felt an almost uncontrollable antipathy toward Margaret. She should be careful of where it would lead. But the impudence of that last expression! As she made her way with the other postulants up the rocky stairs, she reflected on what Margaret had said about Aine and the unconscious bond she had formed with her.

From the instant of seeing Aine looking nervously around the cloisters, she saw something different in her. She understood Margaret's frank comment about her appeal to boys. Aine was not just striking. There was an air of the ethereal about her. The slight girlish figure, the pale, spotless complexion, and the long, silky, fair hair would turn most heads. She surely would not have escaped male attention. She must have taken determined steps to avoid it. But it was the meek manner accompanying the appearance that impressed her most. Whatever Aine's education and understanding of Church teaching, it was clear there was a spiritual depth to this childlike young woman.

Chapter 6

Jannie de Kam

DURING THE fourth week of the postulancy, an empty spot appeared in class and chapel. Then it was as if the convent doors were thrown open; in quick time, departures soon brought the number down to twelve. The remaining postulants greeted the sudden absence of each with no discernible reaction. Virginia commented that it was a good thing those girls came to the end of the discernment process with the right degree of resignation.

'With their stint in the convent behind them, they will be free now to dress up, paint their faces, go to dances, listen to pop music, and pursue boys. Normal attrition, the way it should be.'

Then, as if to challenge Virginia's complacency, Jannie de Kam, the quietest of the three friends, showed signs of anxiety. Margaret's quick wit and ability to manipulate the convent routine had impressed Jannie. Jannie, however, did not possess the same ability to slide around the rules. She had an uncanny way of committing her misdemeanours in the full glare of public scrutiny. A feeble explanation for slovenly work in the kitchen or being late for chapel earned her a humiliating chastisement. As these occasions multiplied, Jannie became increasingly unsettled.

One afternoon during a break, Margaret took her to the far end of the gardens, where they were out of sight of supervision.

'She's reaching a breaking point,' Virginia said, drawing Aine's attention to them. 'She should get away from their influence. She doesn't have the temperament for it. I have experience with the Dutch. They like to be routined and organised. Jannie's typical. She can't be herself with Margaret.' Jannie bowed her head as Margaret gestured to her. 'She's crying. Come on.'

'Are you sure? We might make it worse for her.'

'Do you think so? But we can't sit by and do nothing, can we?'

They ambled toward the two girls so as not to draw unwanted attention. Margaret and Jannie stopped talking when they saw them approaching. Jannie brushed her face with her handkerchief and looked away.

'The last thing we need is a lecturing busybody, especially a know-all, as Sister calls you,' said Margaret. She turned to Aine. 'You can stay. You may be of comfort to Jannie. But your friend and her lack of compassion are not wanted.'

'Where did you learn such disrespect for your seniors?' Virginia replied, but regretted it at once.

'My seniors? You forget we're all equal here. If the teacher must know, equality is central to the Gospel message. So there!'

'I'm happy to discuss the Gospel concept of equality with the student, but not now. I'm more concerned with Jannie's state of mind.'

'Of course, not now,' Margaret said, pulling a face. 'If you're worried about Jannie, if you have any compassion, you'd go right back to where you came from.'

'I'll let Jannie decide,' said Virginia, turning to Jannie. 'Jannie, we're all pulled up for our mistakes and character faults. That's all part of the process of discernment. It's not helpful if you let those with a warped attitude to the rules of religious life influence you.'

'I'm not influenced,' said Jannie, pouting.

'You're more comfortable with routine and order. You're putting unnecessary pressure on yourself by following the example of those who see rules as things to pervert.'

'You've gone far enough, I warn you,' said Margaret, lowering her voice.

Aine raised her hand in an appeal for calm. Virginia rested her hand on her arm.

'Jannie, follow Mother Cecilia's directions. Don't struggle against it. She really wants you to succeed. The rules have a purpose. Don't make it harder for yourself.'

'If you have finally finished with your speeches,' said Margaret. Standing at least two inches above Virginia, she stepped between them, forcing Virginia to fall back. 'You should follow Aine's example. Unlike others, she's a model of non-interference and tolerance. I give Jannie what you don't. Friendship. Jannie knows she can rely on me. Don't you, Jannie?'

'Yes,' said Jannie, 'you're wrong about Margaret. And you're wrong about me. It's the unfair treatment I'm getting.' Her breast heaved. A sob escaped. 'And I'm trying my best to do the right thing.'

'You're just making it worse with your interference,' said Margaret, putting her arm around Jannie's shoulder.

'Genuine friendship does not make things worse,' said Virginia, resigning herself.

'My friendship and solidarity with Jannie as she suffers the unfair treatment of a rigid and insensitive authority are what she needs, not your worn-out preaching.'

'Where are you getting all that nonsense?'

'Nonsense, is it? Are ideas of tolerance, equality, and solidarity nonsense? You should ask yourself what you're doing here.'

'You have learned your lessons well,' said Virginia. 'But you should understand exactly how the Church understands the concepts of equality, freedom, and brotherhood. Why have you not heard about those papal encyclicals?'

'Apparently, the nuns did not judge it necessary for my education or my understanding of those key concepts.' She smirked. 'By the way, those ideas are about freedom, equality, and sisterhood.'

'You have no place in this community,' said Virginia. 'You should go elsewhere to pursue your cherished ideals.'

'I'm pursuing Catholic ideals in a community of independent professional women. Talented independent professional women. There could be no better place.' She took Jannie by the arm. 'We've heard enough, haven't we?'

'Yes,' said Jannie, impressed with how her friend dealt with Virginia Pearson. 'I'm all right now. I feel a lot better.'

'I knew you would,' said Margaret, leading her away. She stopped and looked back. 'Aine, I know you want to help. Jannie appreciates it.' Jannie nodded in support. 'You belong with us.'

'I've been routed, haven't I?' said Virginia as they watched Margaret and Jannie walk arm-in-arm along the flower gardens, their black veils and dresses contrasting with the display of colourful roses. 'That young woman is no fool.'

'Routed? No, I don't think so. I'm beginning to understand.'

'Thank you, Aine, but there's more to it than you could be aware of. We may need to be conscious of our own alliance. Margaret is building hers.'

She walked with Aine to the foot of the rocky stairs, where the postulants were gathered in rough groups. She watched Aine climb the stairs to ring the bell. She had her head bent forward and her eyes in front of her as if unconscious of her surroundings. She stopped and glanced back. At the top of the stairs, she walked from sight without again looking at the postulants waiting below for the bell to summon them to chapel.

***

GLANCING back as she climbed the rocky stairway to ring the bell, Aine caught an image of Virginia standing alone among the loose bunch of postulants at the bottom of the stairs. Margaret and Elizabeth had their eyes fixed on Virginia. She reflected on the growing conflict as she tugged on the rope to ring the bell high in the tower. Again, it was not a mere clash between incompatible personalities. Its dimensions seemed primordial—the clash between absolutes, absolute interpretations. She wandered to the edge of the cloisters and sat on a wooden bench. It was approaching, something far below. She put her hand on the bench to steady herself and found it resting on a book, yellow with age. She picked it up. *Pistis Sophia*, she made out in old, faded Gothic print. The next moment, the book was snatched from her hands.

'Give that to me,' barked one of the older sisters. 'None of your business! Can't I leave something unattended for one moment?' She stalked off in a swirl of black linen and turned into a passage off the cloisters.

Shaken, Aine followed Virginia in the loose group of postulants as they arrived at the top of the stairs and turned towards the chapel. She was hardly conscious of her actions. Those strange, unnerving feelings that had accompanied the whispering of weeks earlier were returning. Looking around, she stumbled forward, putting her hand on Virginia's back. Virginia reached around, took her hand, and squeezed it. When they entered the pew, Aine stumbled again, grasping Virginia's hand. She steadied herself, knelt, and bowed her head. She remained that way for several minutes as the community prayers filled the chapel. She looked up. The postulant in front of her turned and gave her a strange, admiring look. Margaret knelt next to Jannie with her head bowed and eyes closed. Then, slowly leaning forward, she rested her forehead on the pew in front. Her head rolled to one side, and she collapsed onto the postulant on her other side. Virginia was up, attempting to drag her to her feet. Ot hers helped.

In the fading distance, down in the cold, moist earth, a faint whispering stirred. She tried to ignore it, attributing it to her anxiety. 'Mothe ...,' she heard again and again as the whispering tapered off in the formation of a word that kept repeating. She struggled to ignore it. The black habits, the burning candles, the altar rails, the dark doors—it was all in constant mingling motion. Someone was pushing and trying to prop her up.

'Take her to the front parlour,' said Mother Cecilia.

They supported Aine, half walking, half stumbling, to the parlour, where they laid her on the settee, with her eyes closed. While Virginia knelt to rub her arms and caress her face, Mother Cecilia stood over her, watching. She opened her eyes and reached out, trying to stand up.

'No, stay where you are,' said the postulant mistress. 'We have called the doctor.'

'I'm all right,' said Aine, again attempting to get up.

'No. Stay where you are.'

'I told Mother about your anxieties,' said Virginia, taking her hand.

'I asked her,' said Mother Cecilia. 'She had to tell me.'

Mother Jerome arrived, sending Virginia to the corridor to wait. The convent's doctor came shortly after. Mother Cecilia returned to the chapel while the prioress joined Virginia in the corridor. The doctor's visit was brief. There was nothing physically wrong with Aine. Stress and anxiety were the cause of her fainting, as he had often found in such cases. Mother Jerome nodded and thanked him for his prompt service. After directing Aine to remain in the parlour, she took Virginia to her office.

'YOU seem to be in the thick of this,' said Mother Jerome, signalling her to kneel in front of her desk. 'What do you think caused Miss O'Riordan to faint?' Virginia hesitated, not wishing to break a confidence. 'I require you to answer, Miss Pearson?' added the prioress.

'Aine has been anxious from the moment she arrived. I'm not sure what it is.'

'So you agree with the doctor?'

'Well, yes, but Aine's anxiety is not ordinary anxiety, as if she were immature or a character defect. It's something else, something that has worried me.'

'Really? Something that has worried you, is it?' Virginia did not miss the irony.

'Yes. It seems more like a spiritual anxiety. Aine looks young, but she's not an immature girl.'

Mother Jerome continued to subject Virginia to her examining gaze. 'I suppose your time as a teacher has given you some insight into girls of that age?'

'I suppose so,' said Virginia, aware she was about to incriminate herself.

'Your experience has judged your fellow postulants and found some of them wanting?' Again, Virginia hesitated. 'Miss Pearson?'

'I must admit I have reservations about a few of them.'

'Reservations?'

'They may not be suited to religious life,' she said, bowing her head.

'You are decided in this, so decided that you have perhaps said something to the postulants concerned—a rebuke, perhaps?'

'Yes, Reverend Mother.'

'You had better tell me why you have arrived at that judgment.'

Virginia related her views about the general ignorance of Church teaching, especially its social doctrine. Some among the postulants were deficient in this respect, above all, those who had come straight from school. There was also a question of maturity.

'It's not your concern, is it?' Virginia nodded. 'These are matters for your postulant mistress. Or don't you consider her competent to deal with them? Perhaps she is also deficient?' There was no sarcasm in her voice; it was merely an open inquiry, which was all the more blaming.

'Oh no, Mother,' Virginia hastened to say, lifting her head. 'It's my personal opinion. I wouldn't dream of challenging Mother Cecilia.'

'Your personal opinion? Your personal opinions are precious, no doubt,' said Mother Jerome, again without sarcasm. 'You have kept these precious opinions to yourself?' Virginia had to admit she had not. 'Perhaps you could curtail your inclination to reprimand your fellow postulants?'

'Yes, Reverend Mother.'

'Did you understand the distinctions I made about the nature of freedom, authority, and obedience?'

'Yes, I have read and studied the social encyclicals of Pope Leo XIII. It was part of my teaching program.'

'Are your fellow postulants aware of the distinctions?'

'Some aren't,' said Virginia, shifting. 'Many people these days do not understand the distinction between the idea of God-given authority and the idea of authority created by the will of the people.'

'Very good, Miss Pearson, you have understood.'

'My fiancé ... my fiancé was ... is an academic,' Virginia could not help adding.

'Yes, I remember, a very admired one, I hear. Was? Is? Do you miss him?'

'I ... I have made my choice, Mother.'

'That's not answering my question, Miss Pearson.'

'I suppose ... it's hard to turn my back ...'

'Of course, it is. Be honest with yourself.'

'Yes, Mother.'

'No doubt you also miss the conversations?'

'The conversations?'

'You had that sort of discussion with others?'

'Not really ... no.'

There were uncomfortable moments while Virginia had to suffer the prioress's scrutiny. 'Miss Pearson, you can return to chapel now.' Virginia rose. 'Please leave matters of discernment to your postulant mistress. And take the time to look into your own heart.'

'Yes, Reverend Mother.'

AINE finished her tea but remained on the settee, looking at the Persian rug under her feet. The shaded parlour in dark antique colours was at the front of the building, facing the public road. The tree-lined crushed-rock avenue from the convent to the entrance gates and the dirt road running along a bushy ridge above the Yarra River were to the left of the parlour. Not a sound came from that deserted area. Patterned translucent glass filled the bottom frames of the long, narrow sash windows. She looked through the clear top frame at the tall eucalyptus's yellow-tinged branches swaying in the late afternoon breeze. The gentle swaying soothed her agitated feelings, granting relief from the fear and incomprehension that had beset her.

As she gazed at the swaying branches in the sun's dying rays, the silhouette of a veiled head and shoulders appeared in the translucent frame below. It remained motionless for a minute. Then it turned to face the window as if trying to see inside. Aine stood, placing her hand on the armrest of the settee. Another hooded silhouette came into the frame. It came closer to the glass. Aine moved to the side and then to the back of the settee. The two profiles drew back from the window so that Aine made out their vague dark forms against the fading light. Quiet whispering followed. The parlour door opened, and Mother Jerome glided in. Aine swung around to face her.

'What is it, child?'

'There's someone outside the window,' said Aine, pointing.

'Outside the window?'

'Yes, that one.'

Mother Jerome went to the window and pushed up the sash. She glanced to the left and right. 'There is nobody there. Are you sure you saw someone?' She closed the window with a sharp push.

'Yes ... yes. They were trying to look inside.'

'It is not usual for anyone to be walking there now. Perhaps you mistook the trees?'

'No, Mother, I saw someone—two people.'

'Well, I'm sure there is a rational explanation,' said the prioress, taking a seat and indicating to Aine to resume hers. 'Now tell me about your anxieties. I have been speaking to Miss Pearson. She is worried about you.'

Aine understood the request was not optional. She tried to explain without embellishment or downplaying what seemed melodramatic and fanciful. The order to submit was left out. It was too embarrassing and somewhat unreal.

'It does sound strange,' said the prioress. 'Is it possible an overwrought imagination may be playing tricks on you?'

'I don't know, Mother. That first night seemed to be a nightmare.'

'An ordinary nightmare?'

'What do you mean?'

'We all have frightening nightmares. Mostly, this is nothing to worry about. Sometimes nightmares, especially if they are frequent, can be a sign of serious stress and anxiety. The doctor suggests you may be under much stress because of your presence here in the convent. Has it occurred to you that religious life may not suit you? This is the third time you have tested yourself. It was a pertinent matter I mentioned during your interview.'

Aine's heart sank. 'Yes, Mother, I have thought of that. But all I can say is that I yearn to pursue the life of a religious. These periods of anxiety do not arise because of my presence here, the enclosed life, or any doubts about my religious aspirations. They come from outside, I mean, they come as something apart from me, something I have no control over.' She found herself struggling to express what she felt.

'Why precisely are you here?' said Mother Jerome after a pause. 'Why do you think you have a religious vocation? There is no dishonour in admitting that you're not being called. Have you thought that God, in

His wisdom, wants you to be a wife and mother, that you could fulfil your religious aspirations equally well in married life?'

'No, Mother, it has never entered my head,' said Aine, her head dropping. 'I am here because I want to dedicate myself to Jesus and to share in his suffering. I want to take the Virgin Mary as my model of holiness, purity of mind, and total dedication to God's will.'

The prioress regarded Aine thoughtfully.

'Miss Pearson has deplored the general ignorance of Church teaching among Catholics. Would you escape that accusation?'

'I don't know. I suppose not. I am here to learn whatever is necessary.'

'Where has your knowledge of the faith come from?'

Aine hesitated. The faith had always been an unconscious part of her existence; it was just there, never questioned and never doubted.

'My family, the school, and my reading about the lives of the saints—'

'The lives of the saints?'

'Yes, Mother.'

'You have never read or thought about some of the Church's philosophers and theologians? Your school results show you have the intelligence to understand.'

'No, Mother, I have never been drawn to that sort of writing.'

'Miss Pearson has. What do you think of that? Does it inspire you?'

'She's naturally interested in that side of the Church. I admire her. She appears more mature than the rest of us.'

'The rest of you?'

'Yes, Mother.'

Mother Prioress held her in her gaze. Aine was on the point of wilting when the prioress rose. She got to her feet.

'I would like you to return to the chapel. I want you to consider what you would give up as a religious with vows of obedience, poverty, and chastity. You are to consider carefully and in detail what it would be like to have a husband and children. I am requesting that of you.'

Aine understood Mother Jerome had dismissed her, and there would be no discussion about her orders. She made her way back to the chapel, perplexed. Surely, she had made it plain enough that marriage was far from her thoughts; she couldn't even think about it. Her mind could not permit such thoughts. Her problems lay elsewhere. As she arrived at the chapel doors, the community was leaving to complete their various tasks. She waited to the side for the postulants to exit. Margaret and Elizabeth gave her a lingering look as they passed. What were they thinking? Virginia's comforting face came at the end of the line. Mother Cecilia emerged and directed her to fall in behind Virginia. The postulant mistress impatiently clicked her fingers when Aine attempted to tell her about the prioress's direction.

THAT evening, Virginia sought her.

'I hope I didn't make things too difficult for you,' she whispered, looking around for Margaret and Elizabeth.

'No. I understand. I couldn't get out of talking about ... Mother cast doubt ....'

They were on the top parapet looking down into the darkness of a moonless night. The resting river reflected the twinkling stars in the clear, cold air. The lights of the rooms along the cloisters gave the postulants in their veils and long dark dresses a yellow ghost-like hue as they walked along the gardens, talking quietly. Virginia took Aine's arm. She glanced over her shoulder.

'Aine, dear girl, none of us can be sure we have a vocation. Let us make a pact. If one of us should have to leave, let us agree to stay in contact one way or another.'

'Of course, I would like that. Very much— Do you think I might be rejected?'

Virginia hesitated. 'Aine, out of all the girls here, you and Rose have the depth of religious commitment that would lead to a religious life.' More hesitation. 'But there's something unusual about you that—'

'Look!' Aine broke in.

At the far end of the gardens, Virginia caught sight of a flowing dark veil disappearing into the shrouded cloisters. 'It's just one of the sisters,' she said, putting her arm around her.

'There were two of them,' whispered Aine.

'Two of them? I ... anyhow, it makes no difference. They were walking in the garden like the rest of us, before retiring.'

When she thought about it, however, the professed nuns were not usually there at that time. And the veil seemed intent on getting out of sight. Aine broke in on her thoughts, telling her that when waiting in the parlour for Mother Jerome, two hooded silhouettes appeared in the translucent glass of the windowpane.

'Good heavens, that does sound strange,' said Virginia. 'Are you sure of what you saw?'

'Yes, no doubt.'

They came to the end of the gardens, where they had seen the veil disappear. 'There's a stairway there that leads to the next floor. It's odd there are no lights on. Come on—'

'Haven't you been up to enough for one day?' called a voice from the other side of the garden.

Aine and Virginia strained their eyes in the dark, eventually making out in the sparse light Margaret, Elizabeth, and Jannie sitting on a bench by the hedge that ran along the boundary fence. Virginia took Aine's arm and turned to walk back along the way they had come. Margaret pursued them along the other side of the garden.

'I know why you want to ignore me,' said Margaret, smirking. 'No doubt you were wriggling under some uncomfortable questioning.'

'You are presumptuous,' said Virginia, stopping and confronting her over the roses.

'Am I?'

'Aine is capable of understanding who she is with, unlike others.'

'Really?' said Margaret, making a face at her companions who had joined her. 'Aine's the one who fainted and had to be carried from the chapel. She's the one the doctor came to see.'

'Just how do you know what happened?'

'You don't have to be Einstein. Aine, this person is not right for you. Your place is with us—in the solidarity of a shared sisterhood.'

'You're fluent in that rubbish. I'm dying to know where you're getting it from.'

'Rubbish? If you mean the idea of solidarity, then it's you who has to wonder what you're doing here.'

'Your rhetoric smacks of the Enlightenment's radical ideas rather than the Gospels.'

'Enlightenment? Well, that's the right word. Aine, really, your anxiety will disappear in our friendship. You'll be freed from the clamping self-doubt this teacher inspires.'

'Just who was your religion or history teacher in your final year?' said Virginia, astounded at what she was hearing.

'The divisions are crumbling. You're losing your influence and power. The equality of the Gospels is overtaking you and your type.'

'I rather doubt your idea of equality is the equality the Apostles spoke of. But you have learned your lessons well. Your tutors can be satisfied.'

'Whatever. Aine, our friendship is always there. Don't forget.' She walked off towards the main area, with Jannie and Elizabeth following.

'Wait!' said Virginia. Margaret stopped, putting one hand on her hip. 'Who were the sisters you were talking to?'

'Which sisters?' she said, glancing at her companions.

'The two sisters who entered the cloisters over there.'

'I have no idea what you are talking about. Come on. Let's get away from this bad influence.'

They walked off, Jannie throwing a worried look behind her.

'Jannie, you're putting yourself under unnecessary pressure,' Virginia called.

Margaret took Jannie by the arm and whispered in her ear. Jannie looked back again and let herself be led away.

'That girl is heading for a crisis.'

'I fear you're right,' said Aine.

'I wonder why Margaret is so intent on getting you out of my clutches.'

'Out of your clutches? Do you think that's what she wants?'

'She obviously wants anyone out of my clutches, but she has a special interest in you. Why?' She paused. 'That's a clever girl who understands the relevant rhetoric, however much she mindlessly reels it off.' She glanced at Aine. 'You're not familiar with the nonsense she goes on with, are you?'

'No, I'm not quite sure what you and Margaret are referring to.'

'Does it sound like the right message?'

'No, there's something discordant about it.'

'Do her invitations have any impact on you?'

'No. I don't want to be unfriendly to anyone, but she makes me feel uncomfortable. Actually, it's not entirely her. It's something about her, something she seems to drag along behind her. I'm not quite sure what it is.'

Virginia looked at her as if searching for clues. 'Come on,' she said, 'let's investigate.'

They entered the darkened cloisters and walked cautiously to the flight of stairs, stopping at the bottom step. The faint light from above struggled to make its way into the stairwell. Virginia climbed the first couple of steps. There was a vague rustling and scraping. She stopped, leaned back, and grabbed Aine's shoulder.

'Did you hear that?'

'Yes, the whispering again.'

'Whispering? What whispering?'

The light above went out, leaving the staircase in blackness. More scraping and rustling, now closer. Virginia fell back on Aine and toppled onto one knee, with Aine clutching at her.

'Ow!'

'What happened?' said Aine, helping her to her feet.

'Let's get out of here,' said Virginia, holding on to Aine and limping. They hurried from the cloisters and walked along the rose garden towards the lights from the main area. Virginia stopped and looked back. She rubbed her knee.

'It's weird, very weird. I don't know whether I fell or was pushed.'

'Pushed? Who would push you?'

'That's a good question. Strange things have happened today, beginning with your episode in the chapel.'

'It started before that.'

'What?'

'When I was ringing the bell, I felt something coming at me up from below—from deep in the earth. It was frightening. I sat on a nearby bench to steady myself. One of the older sisters snatched a book from me that I had picked up from the bench. Then, when I was contemplating Margaret in the chapel, looking at her in prayer, it seemed so discordant .... That thing was still coming at me. A sort of fright overcame me.'

'Is that why you fainted?'

'I think. I don't know what's causing it, though it all seems connected in some odd way. I really don't know.'

'What was the book?'

'It was an old book with a strange title—*Pistis Sophia.*'

'*Pistis Sophia*? What in the world is that? Who was the sister?'

'I don't know. She was gone before I could get a good look at her. She was furious—accused me of interfering.'

Virginia silently pondered the garden at her feet.

'Let's go down to the grotto.'

Aine followed her down the rocky steps into the clearing just above the river, barely lit by the lights coming from above. Virginia took hold of Aine's arm and walked towards the grotto.

'Was it a push?' said Aine, more preoccupied with this action than anything else.

'I'm not sure. I suddenly felt myself falling back. I can't be sure whether I lost my step or was pushed.'

'Surely you would feel it if you were pushed.'

'You would think so, but that's the strange part. I had a sort of sensation as if I was pushed gently but sharply, if that makes sense. In a way, it was to warn me not to come any further. It did not feel like a real push, though.'

They walked in silence until they arrived at the grotto. The white statues gleamed in the dark.

'You know,' Virginia said, after releasing a weary sigh, 'Philip's academic specialty is the history of philosophy. A week or so before we saw each other for the last time, he began discussing the influence of current thinking on some major issues of the time. I don't know why he started on about that. It came out of the blue. Well, we used to talk about those sorts of things endlessly. I will miss that.' She stopped for a few moments. 'Anyhow, he said that discussions that the Church had suppressed in the early part of the century were raising their head again within Church academic circles. These ideas, he said, were incompatible with Church teaching. I expected him to elaborate, but he said we would discuss it again. We didn't talk about it again—he didn't know that would be our last intimate conversation. I felt awful.'

She broke off, immersed in her somewhat disconnected speech. She stepped towards the grotto. Aine followed. A few moments later, she bowed her head in the meagre light and released a muffled sob. Aine's arm came around her. They stood there a while. Eventually, Virginia lifted her head and wiped her eyes.

'There, that's finished now, forever. There's no going back.' She moved forward to the stone kneelers. 'There is something mysterious going on here. Your experiences, the clash I'm having with Margaret, the disappearing nuns, it's like a harbinger—of what, I don't know or understand. Is it connected with Philip's warning? I don't know?' She held Aine's hand tightly. 'Remember our pact, won't you?'

'Of course,' said Aine, 'we will always keep up our friendship.'

'Let's say a prayer,' said Virginia, 'that we will face whatever is to come.'

They knelt in front of the grotto. Several pairs of eyes watched close by, hidden behind the shrubs and bushes on the parapet above.

Chapter 7

The rejection

AGAINST EXPECTATIONS, Aine spent a restful night, waking with the vivid memory of praying with Virginia, the peacefulness their praying brought, and the friendship pact. She rose refreshed—and determined. She calmly accompanied her fellow postulants to the chapel. She sang the psalms with zeal; she lost herself in adoration during the Mass and went to her class with renewed enthusiasm. She returned Virginia's friendly, inquiring smiles to reassure her. Did she dare to think that yesterday's troubles were momentary? A temporary relapse? Could she now devote herself wholly to the formation she desired so terribly to undergo?

As the morning passed without incident or anxiety, she was cautiously hopeful. Perhaps she did not have to reflect on what it would be like to have a husband and children. If Aine had a cautious, hopeful feeling, she could not say the same of Jannie de Kam. The more anxious and unsettled Jannie de Kam became, the more Mother Cecilia picked on her. Each time the postulant mistress scolded her for lack of punctuality, sloppiness in her work, or slow to learn, there would be a warning in the reprimand.

'For heaven's sake, young woman, how will you manage a teaching schedule if you can't get your books together on time?'

'But I'm doing my best, Mother,' Jannie kept pleading.

'You must do better than your best, my girl, if you want to progress.'

It all happened, as Virginia foresaw. Jannie's attempts to keep up with her overconfident companions became too much of a strain. Margaret and Elizabeth did not make it any easier by sympathising after each rebuke.

'I wonder how that girl would have gone without those two,' said Virginia during a break. 'It does no good consoling Jannie over the callousness of the postulant mistress, as Margaret calls it. Jannie must understand Mother Cecilia is like an army sergeant major. We must learn what self-denial is for religious reasons and what self-discipline is for professional reasons. The convent has no place for the intractable private, consigned to peeling potatoes at the back of the kitchen.'

Virginia's analogy with the army private was not without reason. A week after Virginia had her talk with Mother Jerome, Mother Cecilia assigned Aine and her to kitchen duty with Margaret and Jannie, where a crusty old nun waved a wooden spoon around whenever they were slow to act. This move appeared to be a make-or-break test for Jannie, besides putting together people who did not get on. Margaret, however, did not see it that way and whispered comfort whenever the irascible cook pulled up Jannie. Virginia shook her head, resigning herself to the inevitable. The one advantage of this new arrangement was that Margaret ceased her sly baiting.

'It's as I suspected,' said Virginia. 'Margaret has been looking to clash with me since that first confrontation. She has her hands full now—in vain, too, I bet.'

Aine agreed, adding that Margaret's baiting of Virginia was hardly consistent with the life of a religious.

'In her mind, in a perverse way, she's pursuing what a religious should aspire to,' said Virginia. 'Whether from confusion about religious life or conscious and deliberate, I can't say with confidence. I find it difficult to believe it's conscious in one so young. Then again, she expresses ideas you would hear from people a lot more mature. Much is happening that I did not expect to encounter when I entered the convent. You, least of all.'

Aine did not say anything, only relieved her anxieties, and the fainting spell drifted into the background because of the attention Jannie's slow disintegration drew. Despite the encouragement, not only from Margaret and Elizabeth, Jannie could not break away from the influences contributing most to her anxiety. And despite Margaret and Elizabeth's constant efforts to soothe and comfort her, her fretfulness grew. Finally, late one afternoon, it came to a head when Mother Cecilia berated her for not paying attention in class.

'You must give yourself over to instruction. Forget about all else. Abandon yourself and listen. Only when you do this will you make progress. The lives of the saints should be your model. To give you inspiration about what is expected, I want you to say the litany of the saints until you retire tonight.'

That rebuke crippled Jannie. Margaret and Elizabeth tried to lift her spirits during the break. But it did no good. When the bell rang, and the foursome made their way to the kitchen, Jannie began her penance.

'Saint Peter, pray for us. Saint Paul, pray for us. Saint Andrew, pray for us—'

'Sssh, you don't have to say it aloud,' whispered Margaret.

'You don't have to say it until you are free from all other activity,' said Virginia as they entered the kitchen. 'The intention is for you to say the litany to yourself and calmly contemplate its meaning.'

'Stop your interfering for once,' Margaret whispered through gritted teeth.

There was a sharp crack of wood against the benches. 'Silence!' The foursome set about their tasks. Jannie kept on whispering over and over, 'St Peter, pray for us. St Paul, pray for us. St Andrew, pray for us—'

'Stop it,' Margaret pleaded.

The cook heard the whispering. 'What are you saying?'

'The litany of the saints,' Jannie whimpered. 'Mother Cecilia told me to say the litany of the saints.'

'Well, all right then,' said the cook. 'But keep about your business. You others, too.' She sent Margaret to fetch provisions from the storeroom and then resumed her clattering of pots and pans.

Virginia again took the opportunity to tell Jannie she did not have to say the litany until later, and certainly not out loud in public. But Jannie kept up the distracted repetition with eyes rolling and head swaying. Margaret returned to the kitchen as Jannie snatched at a pile of dinner plates to take to the refectory. One slipped from under the pile and smashed on the tiled floor. A tense silence gripped the kitchen while everyone, including Sister Cook, looked at the scattered pieces.

'I can't do it anymore!' Jannie cried. 'I can't do it anymore!' She hunched her shoulders and shook, still clasping the pile of plates. She let out a scream, raised the plates above her head, and hurled them away from her. The scream and the crockery smashing on the hard-tiled floor echoed through the building. The cook looked aghast at the wreckage on her clean kitchen floor and then at Jannie.

'Glory be—!' she exclaimed. 'Here, out of my kitchen!' She grabbed Jannie by the arm and pulled her towards the door. Two senior sisters arrived to investigate. One look was enough. They took Jannie by her arms and marched her from the kitchen. Margaret went to follow. 'You stay here!' ordered the cook. Margaret ignored the order and disappeared through the doorway. A very disgruntled cook raised her hands in exasperation. 'Holy Mother—we'll have to do this ourselves. Pay attention, you two. And not a word.'

Margaret returned after some minutes and cooperated with the preparations. Her obliging manner seemed to mollify the cook, but she steadfastly avoided looking at Virginia and Aine. As expected, Jannie did not appear at dinner, chapel, or the evening's recreation period. Margaret and Elizabeth spent their time whispering and walking among the darkened gardens during the final break, while Aine and Virginia remained with the other postulants. Some whispered comments passed among the group now and then. Then, just before the last bell, muffled pleading drew the postulants' attention to the open gallery of the upper floor. They looked up in time to catch Jannie walking between two sisters. As they turned to pass out of sight, Jannie broke away and came to the side.

'Margaret!' she called, but the sisters led her away.

Margaret raised her hand to wave, but Jannie had already passed out of sight.

'That is so wrong. They have browbeaten her to a breakdown, and now they treat her like a common criminal. And all in secret.'

'Don't be so melodramatic,' Virginia could not resist saying. 'Each of us knows the conditions on which we are here. We are in a period of discernment, not a Girl Guide picnic. Gauging suitability for membership of any association is normal.'

'You're always ready with a lecture, aren't you?' Margaret spat at her. 'And willing to excuse treatment that lacks compassion.'

'And you're showing once again how confused you are about convent life. If you or anyone else thinks this process of learning self-discipline and self-denial lacks compassion, the doors are open for you to leave. There's no jailer here. You're here of your own volition, free to leave whenever you want to join an association more in keeping with the ideals you broadcast. Perhaps the three of you would be more at home in the local theatre troupe.'

She could not resist the last comment; if she now sounded like she was lecturing, it was deliberate. She had to reply to a view of convent life that Margaret never hesitated to propagate. It was her duty to articulate for her fellow postulants what religious life really entailed. But Margaret was not ready to concede any point to the teacher.

'You can stop trying to get me out of here. You won't succeed. And mockery has no effect,' she added, turning away.

At that point, the bell sounded. There was nothing more to be said or done, and the postulants made their way to the study. Sometime after lights out, Aine heard scuffling along the corridor and a door close twice. She sat up and listened. The faint cry of a bird or animal came from the river below. Nothing else happened until about one o'clock. She awoke to the feeling that someone was in the room. She sat up, clutching at the blankets.

'Who's there?'

No answer. She fell back on her pillow, where she remained, breathing heavily. She heard the slightest scuffling of feet. She sat up again, fully awake now.

'Who's there?'

She got up and went to the door. It was shut. She must have been dreaming, she thought, frustrated with herself. She lay down, now staring up into the dark. Her mind passed over the events of the evening. Jannie had suffered a breakdown; Virginia's critical and unyielding attitude toward Margaret was growing, and it somehow seemed connected with her anxieties and imaginings. Imaginings? Were they imaginings? A door closed in the distance. Then the whispering. She sat up again, breathing heavily. No, there was nothing. She took her rosary from the bedside cabinet and lay down again.

AS EXPECTED, the postulants did not see Jannie in chapel the next morning. Nor did she appear at breakfast. Virginia exchanged a glance with Aine as they walked to class. Yes, Jannie appeared to have gone. Aine found it curious that Margaret and Elizabeth seemed unperturbed. They did not exchange sly looks or check for Virginia's censorious expressions as usual. Later in the morning, when the postulants attended to their chores, Aine and Virginia exchanged the same knowing glances. Jannie had gone.

Aine had the chore of cleaning and dusting the parlours and offices that functioned as the reception and business rooms. The postulant mistress warned her that the Convent of St Augustine was the order's motherhouse, so the rooms had to be spic and span. Armed with cloths, broom, and carpet sweeper, Aine made her way to the reception area. She finished one room and went to the visitor's parlour. Immersed in her meditations, she opened the door and walked in with her eyes on the floor. She looked up and stopped with a hand resting on the still-open door.

'Oh, I did not think—'

'That's all right. You can come in,' said Jannie, leaning back in an armchair with her bags beside her. Her clothes were neat, fashionable, and flattering. Her accent seemed heavier. 'I'm not part of you anymore. You must show me the respect you would show a visitor.' In contrast with her clothing, she had a messy, weary look about her, but the frantic, nervous behaviour had gone. She lounged in her comfortable armchair, her luxuriant honey-blond hair nestling around her shoulders and her long, slim legs extended before her. She pouted and raised her chin as Aine stood, deciding what to do.

'I suppose your friend Virginia thinks she has won.'

'That's nonsense. Virginia does not think that way, anyhow.'

'She's got you fooled. You have more in common with us, you know. Margaret and Elizabeth won't betray you. They'll stick up for you, as they did for me.'

'I should maintain silence,' said Aine, not wanting to listen to her childishness.

'But I'm a visitor. It'd be rude to ignore me,' said Jannie with a confidence Aine had not seen until then. 'I'll be gone soon. Surely you can talk to me while I wait to be picked up. Rules should not defeat friendliness.'

Margaret would say just that sort of thing, Aine thought, as she stood at the open door, not yet decided what she should do. It was true that Jannie was no longer part of the convent community. She had a point. Ignoring her would be rude. She turned to shut the door. The door swung away to reveal Margaret standing against the wall, smiling boldly.

'Oh!'

'Soosh!' said Margaret, putting her finger to her mouth. 'I'm just saying a last goodbye to Jannie.'

'See? That's what I mean,' said Jannie, with a deliberately heavy accent. 'That's real charity.'

'Does anyone know you're here?' said Aine.

'No, I just snuck away for a moment. There's nothing wrong with that, is there? I'm saying goodbye to a dear friend.'

'I should not be here,' said Aine, taking up her cleaning equipment.

Margaret rested her hand on Aine's arm. 'Don't be so scrupulous.' Aine recoiled. 'Rules are not an end in themselves. One has to adjust morally to rigid rules.'

'No, I would prefer to obey the rules.'

'Okay, wait. You don't have to go. I've said my goodbyes. I'll go now. Come on.' She led Aine away from the door and closed it. She hugged Jannie, whispering in her ear as she held her. Jannie nodded twice, tears welling in her eyes. 'Now, don't forget,' said Margaret, releasing her. Jannie shook her head. 'Open yourself to our friendship,' said Margaret, turning to Aine. 'It's a true friendship. It's a bond that will carry us along as we follow our special vocation. We all need that.' Then, with one more encouraging glance at Jannie, she was gone.

Aine shivered. Something repellent, something contradictory, hid in Margaret's invitation. Jannie returned to her armchair while Aine concentrated on her work. Five minutes passed while she dusted, cleaned, and swept, Jannie watching her every move. As she swept around Jannie's armchair, she bent down to pick some lint. Jannie's hand slipped under her veil and took hold of her hair.

'You have exquisite hair. Exquisite.'

Aine remained kneeling, not knowing what to do or say.

'You are a beautiful girl.'

'Please let go of my hair.'

'Stunning.'

'Please.'

Jannie let the long strand of fair hair slip from her hand. Aine stood up and brushed her hair out of sight behind her black veil.

'It's such a pity they will cut it off. Perhaps you can keep a few strands for me as a souvenir of my time here. I would like that. You know, you could be Dutch with that fair hair and marble-like skin. You have a real Northern European look. A princess of the north.'

Aine did not respond, suspecting the last phrase originated in Margaret's conversation. It did not seem a product of her mental world. Jannie lounged and stared. A few more minutes passed.

'Is it really true you had no boyfriends?' she said. Aine continued her work, hoping to discourage conversation. 'Unlike Margaret and Elizabeth, who kept away from groping imbecilic boys, I had my experiences.' She paused. 'The morons that followed me around would have gone mad over a girl like you. It beats me how you kept them away.' Aine shot her a helpless glance. 'I suppose you froze them into silence with one disdainful look from that beautiful face.'

'I'll have to go if you keep talking like that,' said Aine, now thoroughly uncomfortable with Jannie's unexpected manner and her hitting—whether by accident or insight—on a few of her experiences.

'You see what I mean,' said Jannie, lounging further into her chair. 'A look like that would have destroyed the dribbly boys that pestered me.'

'I must go. I wish you well. I'm sorry it did not work out.'

'No, wait. I won't say any more. Please stay with me for a few more minutes. My parents will arrive shortly.'

Aine could not resist the plea. She resumed her cleaning.

'Don't you want to know what I'm going to do with myself now?' said Jannie a minute or so later. Aine could not help showing her interest. 'My school results were good enough for further study. Social work appeals to me. Margaret said that sort of work is not so much different from what I would do as a nun. I don't feel so bad now, despite the unfair decision. I'll miss you all.' For a moment, she lost the bold, confident expression. 'You know, deciding who stays and who goes is arbitrary.' She contemplated the floor in front of her. 'The decision may go against you in the end. You never know.' She looked up. 'Come to think of it, I would not be surprised if they pushed you out. You're different, too different.'

Aine stopped what she was doing.

'You're too good-looking, far too beautiful, though Margaret said a girl of your appearance would make a good advertisement for the convent.' She let out an ironic laugh. 'Now I see you with your spotless white apron over the neat black dress, I understand what she means.' She smiled. 'Imagine if they got rid of the two best-looking girls in the group—though, I must admit, I'm not quite up to your standard. What would you say to that?'

'Others have left before you.'

'That's not what I mean.'

At that moment, Mother Cecilia entered the parlour. She looked in surprise at Aine. 'Oh, I forgot Jannie was waiting here. You can finish later, Aine.'

Aine, struck by the kindly tone and the address of 'Jannie,' gathered up her cleaning materials. As she shut the door, she heard Mother Cecilia speaking solicitously with Jannie, whom she had callously expelled. Before she entered the next room, she waited to see if the postulant mistress would leave Jannie to herself. She did not. Fifteen minutes later, as Aine came from the room she had cleaned, Mother Cecilia and

Mother Jerome appeared at the end of the corridor with Jannie and her parents. Aine stopped. Jannie, seeing her, waved. Aine, blushing, turned and headed in the opposite direction.

Chapter 8

Aine fails

AINE'S MIND fed so much on the events around her that she had difficulty processing it all. Jannie's forced departure and the surprising change in her manner, together with her warnings and cryptic comments, were just the latest. She shuddered at the thought that she would not be found suitable because of her appearance. No, Jannie must be wrong. It was a mad idea. A judgment about her suitability for religious life would surely be based on other things. She remembered Mother Jerome's order to consider what it would be like to be married and have a husband and children. The thought caused a deep shudder. She didn't say anything to Virginia for a few days. While everyone digested what had happened, she didn't want to talk about Jannie. The whole episode rendered her anxious and uncertain. A week had passed before she felt calm enough to speak. Virginia had taken her down to the clearing above the river during the evening break.

'I'm not at all surprised at Jannie's changed manner,' said Virginia. 'Her real temperament was being suppressed. Margaret, of course, had to be there until the end. What a nerve she's got.'

'Margaret encouraged her to look into social work as a career.'

'That fits.'

'It was as if Margaret was not seeing the last of Jannie.'

'Really? What makes you say that?' Virginia had been offhand until then.

'She said something to Jannie while she gave her a long farewell hug. It was like she was giving her instructions.'

'Are you sure?'

'No, I'm not. But it was my impression.'

'What are they up to now, for heaven's sake?'

'Jannie also said I'd probably suffer her fate,' Aine blurted out.

'Oh, I'm sorry.' Virginia put her hand on Aine's arm. 'I should have realised how upsetting it is for you. Don't let it get to you. It was probably a flippant comment meant to unsettle you.'

'No, she was trying to do the opposite. She said they would reject me because of my appearance and because I was different.' Virginia's eyes wandered as she listened. 'She asked what I thought about the two best-looking girls being rejected.'

'Oh, did she? She dared to put herself alongside you?' said Virginia, now focusing, the lights from above glinting in her eyes. 'That's vanity for you. Well, I suppose she is quite an attractive girl. Some would even say beautiful.'

'It was a warning.'

'A warning? What sort of warning? You don't mean that the convent will reject you because of your appearance? Nonsense! Ignore her.'

'I thought it was nonsense, too, at first. But there's something about what she and Margaret said, something connected with my experiences that night—'

'It's all utter nonsense,' said Virginia, speaking over her. 'There is no connection. You're not to think about it. You're causing yourself unnecessary worry.' But Virginia was not convincing. She regarded Aine with a faraway look. 'No, no, you shouldn't think about it.'

'But all those things that have happened,' said Aine, disconcerted by Virginia's reaction. 'How do you fit it all together: the noises and whispering at night, the disappearing nuns, the book snatched and—?'

'Oh yes, the book, I had forgotten. What was it called again?'

'*Pistis Sophia.*'

'What a strange title. I must ask Mother Cecilia about it ... the noises and whispering ... what are you talking about?'

Aine gave a broken account of the noises and whisperings, but, remembering she had not told Virginia about the command to submit, left out that detail.

'Goodness. You are sure you do not imagine things?'

Virginia walked to the edge of the embankment and looked down at the darkened water. Aine followed.

'Yes. At least, I'm sure it was not my imagination with some of them. I might have been dreaming at other times. I don't know. They sound real at the time, but I'm not so sure when I think about it later. It's so confusing.'

'Do you know who that sister was?' said Virginia, turning to her. The lights from above again glinted in her eyes, and her cheeks shimmered.

'No. I only caught a glimpse of her. She was gone before I knew it.'

'I can understand why it's unsettling.'

Virginia's thoughts were not entirely with her words, again giving the impression that there was more than she said. It was as if her mind had turned against her prospects. Had she been talking to the prioress? A few days later, Aine asked in a roundabout way if she had. No, Virginia would never speak to Mother Jerome about such matters. What was behind it all, she could not guess. There were possible connections between all

Aine had experienced, but it was at that moment beyond her comprehension. Aine should not give in but pray for guidance. With a squeeze
of Aine's hand, she promised her full support.

Despite her affection and warm support, Virginia had been evasive.
A tone of inevitability marked her words. There was no other choice
but to put her trust in Providence, as she urged. The idea, however, that
she was not suited frightened her. She could not imagine herself doing
anything else. No other way of life had ever appealed to her. She could
never imagine herself wedded to a man. There were aspects of such a
relationship she could not even contemplate. As if to keep those repulsive
requirements vividly before her mind, a discussion arose several days later
about concupiscence and the nature of temptation that Mother Cecilia
had dealt with in class. Some of the younger postulants did not have a
clear understanding.

In an attempt to clarify, Virginia explained that concupiscence had
to do with the desire aroused by our sexual nature. It is a disorder of
our nature that arose after the Fall. Original Sin left us with disordered
inclinations that must be controlled. Margaret broke in, mockingly saying it all meant that the sight of some disgusting boy might excite them.
That was one temptation she would never suffer, she sneered. A furious
dislocating exchange followed, during which Virginia accused Margaret
of immaturity, disrespect, and a perverted attitude to males. Margaret
airily replied that the schoolteacher's finger-wagging and superior airs did
not intimidate her. The schoolteacher might not have become so excited
if she had been as virtuous as she made out with her boyfriends. Virginia
struggled to contain her anger. The postulant mistress intervened, warning that their conflict had gone too far for people wanting to enter the
religious life. She sent them to her study for an interview.

Aine had watched the clash, her mouth open, taking in the air in short snatches. Some preordained disaster played out before her eyes. It was not just the ferocious conflict between two individuals with different views on different paths that unfolded relentlessly before her and her fellow postulants. As she had already sensed, it was a clash of realities with an air of finality about it. The scene drove deep into her experiences of whisperings, of shadows, of the disappearing veils, of warnings from the depths, of the command to submit. She watched the departing figures on the stairs in a daze that had her drifting in and out of real-time. Nobody said anything.

At the bell, the postulants made their way up the rocky stairs in single file. Aine swayed to the side as if the stairs were in motion. She glanced up. The massive solid edifice above them, with its Gothic archways, cloisters, and tower reaching into the cold grey afternoon sky, toppled over them. The trees on either side rustled in a gusty wind blowing up from the unsettled waters of the river, forcing her to glance back unsteadily at the clearing. She stumbled, reaching out for the postulant in front of her. The young woman turned and regarded her with that same admiring expression.

As she knelt in the chapel, she felt all steadiness and stability seeping away. She looked up through the subdued light at the candle-lit altar, at the tabernacle, praying for relief and understanding. The sacristy sister entering the sanctuary, carrying two candleholders, was a jarring distraction. She genuflected at the bottom of the short flight of stairs leading to the altar. As she mounted the stairs, she missed her footing and lurched to the side, dropping one of the candle holders, which rolled over the carpeted stairs and crashed onto the polished wooden floor. Tension gripped the postulants. The sister composed herself and picked up the candleholder. Trembling and fearful, Aine closed her eyes. That night was sleepless, but at least she was spared the whispering and the noises. The next day, during recreation, Virginia whispered to her that she had been warned against forming close friendships.

'You must trust me. You'll be close to my thoughts and prayers. But for the time being, I must follow the rules strictly.'

Aine understood. She understood there was a lot more to it than Virginia said. With an affectionate glance from Virginia, that was the end of it. She now avoided her company, always remaining with the main group of postulants. Aine knew she should not feel hurt, but she did. Margaret made little effort to change her ways. She avoided Virginia but continued her sly, surreptitious ways, maintaining close contact with Elizabeth. She also made efforts to foster relations with the postulants of her age. She repeated her approaches to her under the pretext of Christian charity. It turned her off even more, exacerbating her disintegrating state of mind. Mother Cecilia, incredibly, seemed not to see this blatant political activity.

Two sleep-interrupted nights later, the noises recommenced. A barely audible scuffling came from outside her room around midnight. She hurried to the door. The scuffling stopped a moment. She heard what sounded like quick, light footsteps. She opened the door. There was nothing. Despite feeling wide awake, she wondered whether she really was fully awake. She returned to bed and sat up, listening. About an hour later, with the corridor silent, indistinct sounds came up from the river. She went to the window.

A half-moon left the two lower parapets, and the clearing near the river shrouded in a dark veil through which objects were barely distinguishable. She stared for some minutes, her eyes eventually adjusting. A shadow flitted along the edge of the riverbank, blocking the reflection of the stars for a moment. Then another fleeting shadow. She grasped the windowsill, trembling. Surely, a boat was on the river, floating from the opposite bank towards the jetty. Whatever it was—she could not be sure it was a boat—it passed out of sight below the riverbank. She stood rigid, watching. The chill of the night caused her to shake. She turned aside to grab her dressing gown. When she turned back, three shadows moved out of sight behind the gardens and shrubs near the grotto. She was not dreaming. Who could it be? She remained at the window, but the exhaustion of spirits and the want of sleep forced her to sit on the b ed.

When she came to, the first light of dawn filled her cell. She sat up with a jerk and then hastened to the window. All was calm and peaceful below. The river surface was glassy and green, with a thin mist curling above it. There was no sign of a boat or person on the opposite bank. The warbling of magpies in the distant bush and fields broke the pristine silence. A lone kangaroo broke cover from the bush and hopped towards the river. Then another, and another. They drank for some minutes, raising their heads now and then. They took fright and bolted back into the bush. Three hooded, black-robed figures appeared from the jetty steps and made their way across the clearing and up the stairs. Aine strained to see who it was, but they were too quick and too indistinct in the paltry early dawn light.

They disappeared to the left, towards the stairs where she and Virginia had seen the disappearing veils. She listened at the door. Faint sounds came from the end of the corridor. She returned to the window. The dark shape of a boat made its way through the curling wraiths to the opposite bank. About halfway across, it turned upstream and disappeared behind the trees lining the bank on the convent side. She sat on the bed, bewildered and exhausted. She lay back. The next moment, there was a sharp knock at the door, followed by the morning greeting. She sat up and forced out an answer. It was all she could do to rouse herself, complete her toilet, and dress for chapel. Feelings of despair added to her exhaustion as the faint whispering and the impression of being observed returned, filling the cloisters.

Her distracted state was bound to come under the notice of Mother Cecilia, and she prepared herself. The postulant mistress did indeed take her to task several times, the last time withering in her comments. Then her manner changed, and she ceased reprimanding her. Virginia glanced at her during the class before the noon Angelus. Mother Cecilia took her aside as the postulants prepared to go to the refectory.

'You're not feeling well?'

'No, Mother ... well, I do feel a little tired.'

'Why?'

'I've not been sleeping well. I'm sure I will get over it,' she said, knowing full well the cause of her anxiety and exhaustion would not go away. She blinked some tears away.

'Sit down and calm yourself. I will be back in a minute.'

Aine fought to control the tears. Five minutes later, Virginia appeared. That was enough for the tears to start flowing. Virginia took her in her arms.

'Mother asked me to keep you company. The troubles have returned, haven't they?' Aine nodded. 'Still, the noises and the sound of people in the corridor?'

'Yes.' She hesitated. 'But there is more now.' She related what she had seen from her window.

'Good heavens, are you sure?'

'I'm sure—I think.'

'I don't know what to make of it,' said Virginia. 'It's scarcely believable. Not even Margaret would dare ... well, I shouldn't say ... but it does seem to fit into the other weird things going on.'

'I can't distinguish what's real and what's unreal anymore.'

Mother Cecilia returned, telling Aine she was to see Mother Jerome after lunch. Virginia would keep her company in the meantime. Aine was relieved. She desperately needed the consolation of Virginia's company. After lunch, Virginia accompanied her to Mother Jerome's office. The prioress requested Virginia to wait outside while she ushered Aine into her office.

'Now, Miss O'Riordan, it is time to talk,' said the prioress, pointing to the chair in front of her desk.

Aine feared the worst.

'You understand that I have seen a lot of girls over the years who think they have a religious vocation,' Mother Jerome began. 'Many find they don't. It's something that becomes apparent during this period of discernment, and most candidates see it of their own accord. Sometimes a candidate needs our counsel. There is rarely any trouble, though. You, however, are not the usual case.' She stopped, tapping her fingers on an arm. 'Let me be frank. We could wait a bit, but I do not think the result will be any different. It is evident to all who see you that you have a profound sense of the spiritual, a sense that is rooted naturally in the Gospel narrative. Indeed, your understanding is sharper than that of most young women your age. In normal circumstances, I would say your place is in the convent. Nevertheless, I have a feeling, and I call it a feeling, that you are not being called. In a word, Our Lord is calling you to something else. I don't know what. It is for Providence to lead you in t his.'

Aine had expected it, her heart sinking as Mother Jerome spoke. Darkness waited beyond the convent walls. 'I want to lead the life of a religious,' she said. 'My troubles are telling against me ... but if I had more time to deal with them ... to try to put more order in them.'

'You are not sure whether you are imagining things or not?'

'No.'

'Have you thought seriously about married life, as I asked you to?'

'No, Mother, I cannot, as much as I try.'

'Are you afraid of what's required of you as a wife?'

'It's not fear. The thought fills me with disgust. But it's not just the physical aspect. Virginia said that she wanted to give her maidenhood as a gift. That's the way I feel.'

Mother Jerome contemplated her for some moments. 'Despite my inclination to think that you are called to another sort of life, I will allow you more time for self-examination—for both our sakes. In the end, however, I believe you will have to face it. I will allow Miss Pearson to be with you this afternoon as support. As you know, we do not generally encourage close friendships, but you need to be at rest. It will be temporary, whatever we decide.'

'Thank you, Mother, it will help.'

'Good, now tell Miss Pearson to come in while you wait outside.'

IT DID not surprise Aine that Virginia led her down to the lower level, where they walked and sat at leisure. They chatted about their families. Virginia read passages from the *Confessions*, and they said the prayers they were obliged to say. Aine suspected Virginia had instructions to keep her apart from the others. She wondered about the reasons. It could be to give her a breather. It could be to prepare her for departure. By this time, though, she had resigned herself to whatever happened. She would not feed her anxiety by thinking about it. Instead, she would take advantage of the break and the comfort of her dear friend to prepare herself. Whether she stayed or left, her friendship with Virginia would have to be curtailed. That upset her more than anything. From having no close friendships before entering the convent, she had come to love her new friend dearly.

They spent the evening recess in the company of their fellow postulants. The conversation was light and cautious for her benefit. Virginia directed her comments to the group. Only Margaret and Elizabeth took their usual walk to the far end of the gardens, where they had seen the black veils. They returned about ten minutes before the bell, talking softly. They stopped aside from the group and stared. Aine looked up to see Margaret's thoughtful gaze on her. Margaret turned away. That was odd. She took Elizabeth by the arm, and they walked to the other side of the group, where they sat down. They paid no attention to Virginia, not even when she spoke. Margaret continually looked around the group as if her attention was not entirely on their conversation.

THE STRENGTH sapped from her legs as Aine climbed the stairs. There was silence behind her except for the occasional footfall followed by the creaking and shutting of doors. Silence lay ahead, filling the dark wooden wainscoted hallway to the cells. Her short, jerking breaths forced her to pause. She wiped the moisture from around her lips as she glanced back down the stairs. The postulants were still in the common room. She faced the barely lit hallway, hesitating. Before taking the first step to her room, she closed her eyes and bowed her head.

Once in her room, she checked that everything was in its proper place. Nothing had been disturbed. She looked through the window at the parapets and river below, sparkling in the approaching full moon. Its waters flowed undisturbed. She undressed and knelt to say her prayers. Without being aware, she bent slowly forward until she rested on the bed. She lay across the bed until her shivering roused her. She tried to get up, but her hair was held tightly. She called out, but no sound came from her mouth.

'Your beauty will be your salvation,' whispered the same hoarse voice. 'Your beauty will release the power in you. You will submit—to your power.'

Terrified, Aine tried again to call out but could not speak or move. The next moment, she lay shivering on the floor. A deathly silence pervaded the hoary moonlit room. She struggled onto the bed and lay exhausted, staring at the ceiling. Then pitch-black darkness eclipsed the room's faint light. She sat up. The light switch. She got off the bed and reached for the switch. It was not there. She scratched around the room, trying to locate where everything was, but nothing was in its proper place. She collapsed on the floor. The next moment, she lay on the bed staring at the ceiling while soft moonlight streamed through the window. Her breathing gradually subsided. Her eyes closed. She was drifting off, despite her trembling. A scuffling in the room roused her once more. She sat up to see a figure disappearing into the dark.

'Stop,' she called. 'Who are you?' Nimble and slight of build, she slipped from the bed and went in pursuit. She rushed after the light footsteps of the retreating figure. Quickly catching up, she grabbed at it.

Material came loose in her hand. It was snatched from her, and she was pushed backwards. Losing her balance, she fell on her elbow and side.

'Stop, come back,' she called, scrambling to her feet. 'Who are you? What do you want?' Her slight frame trembled and shook. Now lights turned on, and doors opened. Then Virginia had her in her arms.

'Aine, darling, calm down,' she whispered. 'You're having a nasty dream.'

While people in their dressing gowns pressed around her in the vague yellow light, she stared, with her breast heaving, into the dark at the disappearing figure.

'No, I'm not dreaming. I saw—tell it to come back,' she called out between gasps.

'Take her into her room,' she heard Mother Cecilia say. Once on her bed with a blanket over her, she calmed down. Virginia sat next to her with her hand on her arm. 'It's all right,' she whispered. The warm breath of her words caressed her cheek. 'I'll stay with her until sunrise. It's already past two o'clock.' There was a further indistinct exchange, and then the light went out.

'I'm here, darling,' said Virginia, leaning over her. She kissed her on the forehead. 'Relax. Nothing will happen to you while I'm here.'

Soon she returned to herself, reflecting on Virginia's display of affection. It was the sign. Then acute embarrassment filled her, followed by despair. 'I'm so sorry. I have caused you such trouble. I don't know what's happening to me. I really don't.' She could feel Virginia's hesitation in the dark and then her face coming closer.

'You haven't caused me any trouble. I understand now that you are experiencing something sinister and mysterious. I don't know how you're to face it.' She paused. 'Pray, pray hard for help. Trust in God.' Another pause. 'Would you like to hear verses from the Psalms?' Aine nodded.

'*Adore God, all you His angels: Sion heard, and was glad; and the daughters of Juda rejoiced. The Lord reigns as king, let earth be glad of it, let the furthest isles rejoice!*' She stopped.

Aine waited. 'Please go on.'

'*Death's terrors were near at hand, the terror of the grave was all about me: One cry to the Lord, in my affliction, and He from His sanctuary listened to my voice. Shall I not love Thee, Lord, my only defender? The Lord is my rock-fastness, my stronghold, my rescuer.*' She paused as if waiting for Aine to absorb the message. 'Do you know why I repeated these verses?'

'I should honour God and rejoice in our trust in Him?'

'That's right.'

'I understand. I will try to have courage.'

'Don't lose heart, my darling, whatever happens. You'll always be in my thoughts and prayers.'

Aine felt Virginia's hand come to rest on her bare arm, hesitate, then give her a squeeze. The gesture was her goodbye. Her affectionate words and action were her departing message. She was too exhausted to cry out, though she wanted to. Besides, she should respect her dear friend's effort to calm her. When she awoke, the rays of the mid-morning sun filled the room. She felt refreshed, but it did not take long for the memories to return. She rose, remembering Virginia's last words. Now that Virginia was gone, the wrench from one of the few people who understood shook her. How was she to go on through the day without her? But she should hurry. Mother Jerome and Mother Cecilia would summon her to appear before them. She stopped her preparations and sat on the edge of the bed. A tear appeared on her cheek.

'Come on, Aine, cheer up,' said Mother Cecilia, entering the cell. She helped her to her feet. 'It's not the end of the world. You have your gifts, your own special vocation ahead of you. Now get yourself ready. I will be back to take you to breakfast in fifteen minutes.'

Mother Cecilia took Aine to the visitor's parlour, where she had a table set for her. She should take her time with breakfast, for Mother Jerome would not see her until after lunch.

'When you've finished breakfast, you can take a walk in the front gardens. It's a nice, quiet, calming area. You have a chance to revive and put things in their proper perspective.'

It was, indeed, a peaceful area to walk around. Aine wandered around the beautifully tended but deserted gardens for a while before passing along the crushed gravel entrance avenue. The towering gum trees on both sides gave the impression she was walking beneath an endless archway. She passed through the main gates to the public road beyond. She turned to gaze at the convent building with its high Gothic tower and long, narrow windows along each wing. Moving to the side, she stopped before a plaque fixed neatly to the brick wall supporting the iron gates. The Convent of St Augustine, she read. Virginia and her admiration for that great saint came to mind. She turned away; she must not give in to her tears. Returning to the gates, she stared at the convent complex. The Gothic tower seemed to sway with the gum trees. The feelings she had been trying to suppress welled up within her.

From a window high in the Gothic tower, several pairs of eyes watched a slender female form, dressed in black, no veil, with dazzling fair hair and a face of flawless beauty, slowly ascending like a goddess from the nether regions.

MOTHER Jerome was kind and understanding. She did not tell Aine she was not suited for life in the congregation of the Sisters of the Suffering Saviour. Aine understood. Instead, she seemed anxious to talk about Aine's future with optimism. She outlined the sort of work she should find agreeable. Above all, she said, if Aine kept up her devotions and commitment to the Gospel—the way she had shown during the postulancy—she had no doubt Providence would guide her in the right direction.

'I have no special gift of prophecy,' said the prioress, known for her acute judgment. 'Somehow, though, I think your true vocation is as a wife and mother. Let me add that you will attract attention. You must be careful who you admit into your confidence—' She broke off as if in mid-thought. 'Perhaps it's not necessary to say that. I imagine you will know when you meet the right person.'

Aine, unaware of the break in the prioress's thought, could not comprehend a situation in which she would meet a boy and admit him into her confidence. Nothing approaching those circumstances had ever happened. She nodded in acknowledgment of Mother Jerome's confidence and advice, but had her doubts. Unable to concentrate, she half-listened as the prioress spoke about her future and the lay religious associations she could join. Then her father was on the phone, trying to assuage her feelings of failure. She continued to half-listen while he explained the arrangements to return home. A taxi would take her to Spencer St Station the following day. Of course, she would be staying another night.

The images of the previous night's events came back to her in full force. She shook as she held the phone. The voice, the fleeting figure in the dark, the paralysis, both physical and spiritual—they seemed to choke her. Alarmed, her father asked if she was all right. Mother Jerome took the receiver and explained she was upset and that he should be patient with her. At length, Aine asked for the receiver and composed herself enough to listen to the arrangements for the next morning.

'Where am I to sleep?' she asked after ending the phone call.

'Of course, you will not return to your room,' said the prioress. 'Aine, you are now a guest of the community and will spend the night in one of the guest rooms. A sister has removed your belongings from the postulant quarters. You will find everything arranged in the room allotted to you. Please try to rest and relax for the rest of the afternoon.'

She spent her time quietly but in a state of apprehension. One of the elderly sisters came to keep her company, which provided a welcome distraction. She visited the empty chapel where she said her rosary. In the evening, dinner was served while the rest of the community was in the chapel. She could hear the Gregorian chant. It pierced the walls to reach her ears. She felt something like homesickness. The grief at losing Virginia—then came scraping at the parlour door. She rose at once. No, she thought, it could not happen here. She went to the door, shaking. No one. She returned to her dinner but could not eat. The elderly nun arrived to find her trembling. She tried to console her. But Aine could not be consoled. Mother Jerome appeared. They spoke briefly. The prioress left to return a half-hour later. Aine's father was arranging for her departure that night. That would be best. Aine felt relief. An hour later, the arrangements had been made. It remained for her to pack her things and wait for the car to take her to Spencer Street station.

'Just one last word,' said Mother Jerome as she was about to go to the waiting taxi. 'I will be frank with you. Some of what has happened can be attributed to your dreams, nightmares, or imagination. Part, though, are likely the promptings, temptations, or torments of some evil spirit. Never be mistaken. The devil exists, regardless of the scorn the world now pours on that idea. Our Lord continually rebuked the devil. The

Evil One's special victims are the good and holy; he will find you where you are weakest. Never let your appearance govern your actions. It will be your downfall.'

THE RHYTHMICAL rattle of the train, the lights flashing, the blaring of the horn at railway crossings, and the empty compartment where she sat helped Aine calm herself. Mother Jerome's warning repeated in her head. She knew what others thought of her, but could not see it herself. Opinions about her appearance, whether good or bad, did not trouble her, even when the intrusion aroused sharp feelings. She had had no trouble in turning her back on them. But now, one comment came back to her, by a girl in her class at school: 'You give the impression you don't care about looks because you know and are vain about it.' At the time, she dismissed it as spite.

She had been looking through the window at the houses, streets, and cars rushing by. When the train rattled beyond the houses with their glowing windows and into the dark, her reflection in the window suddenly confronted her. The fresh, young face and long, fair hair so close to her eyes took her by surprise. She turned away.

Chapter 9

Charles Winterbine

Late in the afternoon, Charles Winterbine drove into the prettiest country town he had seen on his getaway trip. Not only did the township of Bendigo, with its rich colonial architecture, appeal to him. The surrounding countryside exercised a peculiar attraction on him. He did not know what it was. There was an odd appeal in the hills, the trees, the fields, and even in the shape of the natural environment. He loved his little seaside village on New South Wales's south coast, but it had never stirred him like the countryside he had just driven through. The following morning, after a good night's sleep, he went to early Mass at Bendigo Cathedral. When he emerged after completing his thanksgiving, the impulse to take his car and go exploring overtook him.

At around eleven o'clock, Charles was driving northwest along one of the main roads out of Bendigo. It was a beautiful day, even if chilly. He went at a leisurely pace. He had all the time in the world. The longer he drove in a north-westerly direction, the more the countryside stirred him. He stopped now and then, got out of the car, and looked around. He breathed in the fresh country air and the force of the environment. It was as if he took up the beauty of the trees, the hills, the fields, and the peaks into his very being. After an hour of driving, he noticed a sign on the roadside pointing to Binawarra. On a second impulse that day, he swung his car into this narrow country byway.

As soon as the two peaks came into view, he slowed his car. On his right, he picked out a strange, grey, rocky platform below the top of the sharp peak above a sheer drop. Further on, on the left, a massive earthy mound squatted over the landscape as if in warning. He stopped the car opposite the sharp peak, got out, and walked a few paces, staring upward at it. He experienced a growing uneasiness as he looked at the rocky platform. Glancing to his left and right, he stepped back to his car, got in, and drove to the earthy sentinel. Despite the sentinel's warning pose, his uneasiness gave way to wonderment, even awe. He got out and stared upward. He climbed through the fence and started across the grassy field.

Making his way around the slopes in a northerly direction, he paused now and then to look around. At length, Binawarra came into view, with the surrounding landscape of trees and farmland. He sat on a rock and gazed at the sleepy township below. He traced the road from where it broke free from the trees and made its way across a creek into the town centre. As expected, few people walked the streets on a quiet Sunday morning. The bluestone Catholic church stood prominent, with its spire rising above the surrounding buildings. What a peaceful scene. He slid off the rock and lay in the thick grass, propping himself on an elbow.

He continued his climb and reached the flat grassy top scattered with rocks. He caught his breath as he looked back at the way he had come and ahead into the distant hills. He wandered around the grassy expanse until, at last, overcome. The course of his thoughts rose above the expressible, and in the pattern of the beauty of the natural world about him, he thought he saw the form of the Almighty emerge. It was not a physical form he saw with his eyes, but a form that emerged as an immaterial presupposition. He fell to his knees and offered prayers of thanks for all the blessings he had received since the tragic death of his parents. When on the point of making his way down to the car, he became aware of the sharp peak opposite with its grey rocky outcrop. He sensed foreboding and caught glimpses of the malignancy that had infested his parental home. He stepped out on the shortest way back down the slopes.

He drove into Binawarra with an inexplicable feeling of belonging, replacing the discomfort caused by the peak. The style of the houses, the layout of the streets, and the undulating ground on which the town stood radiated friendliness and invitation. Wondering whether he imagined these things, he drove down the left side of the large, lush park that formed the town square and parked his car against a row of shrubs and flowers marking the park's border. He strolled to the nearest shops and lingered in front of a charity cooperative. A variety of notices were over the window, and inside, he could see second-hand goods for sale. He checked the job notices for carpentry work.

'Hey, what's a handsome, able-bodied young man like you doing looking at our jobs?' a voice called from behind.

Charles swung around to be confronted by an ample man in his mid-thirties with a big, friendly smile on his florid face.

'Sorry, did I give you a start?' he said, walking up to Charles and patting him on his shoulder. 'My, what a tall fellow you are. I was at the back, attending to the garbage, and came here to see if I had locked the door. Got to be sure, you know.'

'Well, I was a little startled,' said Charles. 'I didn't think there was anyone around.'

'That's right, not on a Sunday. We country folk are at home now for Sunday dinner. Sunday roast, that's sacred, you know. In any case, Bill Huckerby,' he said, holding out his hand.

'Charles Winterbine,' said Charles, taking the jovial man's hand and quivering in response to his vigorous pumping.

'Do you want a job, do you?'

The expression on Bill Huckerby's face said the question was not serious.

'Not really. I am on holiday, touring the countryside. I just happened on Binawarra. It's such a beautiful place.'

'Ah, you'll get along here, cobber. We love our town, and we love to hear people admire it.' He paused. 'What work do you do?'

'I'm a carpenter by trade. But I have been managing some building projects recently—for the local parish.'

'Well, well, you have happened along at the right time,' Bill Huckerby laughed. 'Come on. I can see from your face that you're a good chap. So I'm inviting you home for our Sunday roast. It's lunchtime, and I don't think you've had lunch yet, have you?'

'No, but—'

'Don't worry, young man. You're in no danger. Country hospitality! I have a beautiful wife who, at this very moment, is preparing the most delicious roast leg of lamb, and there is too much for the two of us. Just the two of us, you know. No children. Besides, you can give me a little advice in return for the meal. Bargain?' He gave Charles the most ridiculous wink and drew him along by the arm.

There was no stopping this happy, outgoing man. Charles, too astonished to protest, said he had parked his car behind them. 'Oh, what a dope I am!' Bill Huckerby laughed loudly again. 'Okay, go back, jump in your car and follow me. My car is parked a little further down. You see?'

A few minutes later, they stopped outside a cosy homestead-style cottage with a verandah running across the front and extending halfway down the sides. A vine ran the length of the verandah, forming a patchy, gossamer-like curtain. An abundance of flowers and shrubs filled the gardens, reflecting the meticulous care of their owners.

'Not bad, eh?' said Bill Huckerby, seeing Charles's admiring gaze. 'My beautiful wife and I spend many hours doing all this. It compensates for the lack of children, I suppose. But, then again, they're not there to muck up what we have done!' He smiled, but Charles noticed a sudden, temporary tension in his expression. 'Come on. Come and meet my darling partner in life. She'll be overjoyed to meet you.'

All this effusion and familiarity was a bit unnerving as Charles walked behind Bill up the wooden steps to the front door.

'Hey, darling!' Bill called. 'I've got someone here you're dying to meet.'

'Behave yourself, Bill!' said Joanne Huckerby in an apron, arriving at the front door. 'You are embarrassing the poor boy,' and then to Charles, 'He's a bit overwhelming sometimes. But he always gets excited when he meets a new friend. Come along in. I can see he has chosen wisely. Relax. I'm Joanne.' She led them into the lounge room. 'Sit down, and we'll get acquainted before we have lunch.'

Charles spent a delightful afternoon chatting with Bill and Joanne and hearing about Bill's beloved town. He got to see that this large man, with his outgoing, friendly manner, was more sensible than he seemed at first meeting. No surprise that Bill was the deputy principal of the local high school. The conversation meandered happily through to afternoon tea, with Charles forgetting himself. Then came a tour of the house and gardens. To Bill's delight, Charles said he had never seen such beautiful, well-tended flower plots. As they were finishing their inspection of the back garden, Charles remarked that he should be getting back to Bendigo.

'It's been such an enjoyable afternoon. My sincere thanks, Bill and Joanne, for your warm hospitality, but I must get back to Bendigo before darkness falls.'

'No problem whatsoever,' said Bill. 'Have you got the camping ground number there?' Charles stopped to fish the camping ground receipt out of his wallet, unaware of Bill's intentions. 'Good, I'll call them and ask them to take care of your gear because you will stay the night with us. No, no, no objections.' He was already on his way back to the house.

'He's unstoppable, isn't he?' said Joanne, smiling. 'Now, relax. You're very welcome. There is a sleep-out off one side of the verandah. It's very comfortable.'

Bill returned five minutes later. 'Okay, that's all settled. They'll keep an eye on your equipment as if they were guarding Parliament House.'

Charles had difficulty believing the events of the last twenty-four hours. It was as if someone had thrust him into a different world. He had listened to so much of the history of Binawarra and its people that, on laying his head on his pillow that night, he fancied he had known them forever. What did it all mean? His fervent prayers of thanksgiving and pleas for his new friends went up to heaven.

'GOOD morning, old mate!' was Bill's hearty greeting when Charles appeared in the kitchen the following morning. 'How are we this morning? Sleep well?'

Charles assured him he had never slept better.

'Come on, take a seat. Don't stand on ceremony. We're going to feed you up with a good old-fashioned country breakfast.'

Charles saw from where the appetising smell filled the house. He sat down with his eyes fixed on Bill, standing at the stove, and wrapped absurdly like a canteen chef in a long white apron.

'Good morning, Charles,' said Joanne, arriving in the kitchen and patting him as she passed. 'Breakfast is Bill's specialty. Have you ever eaten fried scones before? Delicious, especially with loads of butter and Golden Syrup. But not good for the weight.' She poked Bill in the stomach and then gave him a kiss. 'That's his Achilles heel,' she added. 'He has to watch his weight. Otherwise, there will be trouble.'

'Okay, Doctor Joanne, it's not surgery hours yet.'

Bill served Joanne and Charles, then joined them with a plate piled high with eggs, tomatoes, sausages, and buttered toast. 'Now, we don't know your plans,' he said to Charles, 'but if you want to see the countryside, you can stay with us—use this house as your base. Drive, go for walks—you'll find beautiful walks around here.'

Charles was ready with his reply. 'I would love to stay if you're sure it will not be any trouble. You don't really know me.'

'Oh, yes, we do,' said Joanne. 'That's settled then.'

'Yes,' said Bill. 'Drive back to Bendigo this morning and pick up your gear. I have to go to school, of course.' Then a pause. 'I have an idea. Joanne will drive you. She can show you the sights.'

The next two days whizzed by, though not much bushwalking was done. While Bill was at school, Joanne took Charles with her on her errands. She showed him the sights of the town while Charles spoke about his work and life in his south-coast village. It turned out that Joanne was keener to show Charles off to everyone they came across than see the sights. In his busy and preoccupied way, Bill happily left the social arrangements with Joanne. He had something else on his mind. On Tuesday after school, he took Charles to the large garage at the end of a cream gravel driveway. As an annex to the garage was a workshop that had seen better days. Was it worth repairing? Bill asked.

Charles, keen to do something in return for the friendship and hospitality, ran his eye over it. It was not as bad as it looked, he said. It was redeemable if Bill did not want to go to the expense of building a whole new workshop. Instead, if he liked, he would do some work on it himself. All he needed was a hammer, nails, a good saw, and the right material. Bill made a poor show of protesting in the face of Charles's insistence, after which he gave in and then beamed. That night, Charles retired early to make a good start the following day. As he left the lounge room, the phone in the hall rang. Bill signalled to Joanne after picking up the r eceiver.

'What's wrong?' Charles heard Joanne say.

'It's Paul,' Bill mouthed at Joanne. 'About Aine ....' Joanne hurried to listen with him.

From the doorway to his sleep-out, Charles heard hushed conversation and movement in the house. Something seemed to be up. He hoped it was nothing serious. He fell asleep thinking about the work on Bill's workshop. At about one o'clock, noise at the front of the house, some whispering, and then the muffled thud of doors shutting roused him, but he soon fell back to sleep. The following morning, he awoke early, washed, and hurried to the workshop without disturbing the house.

For an hour, he worked quietly, clearing a space, arranging the materials, pulling the loose lengths of weatherboard off, and putting them in neat piles. He was surprised that he looked forward to Bill and Joanne's reaction. At length, he stopped. He needed Bill before going any further. No sound came from the house. He wandered down the cream gravel driveway past the flower gardens towards the front verandah, intending to wait there until Bill and Joanne appeared. It was such a pleasant spot overlooking the nearby hills. With his mind still on the job, he came around the corner of the house. He stopped.

On the verandah, leaning against the railing, was an angel. No, it couldn't be. But Charles's consternation at what he thought he saw was so great that his mind kept telling him, against all reason, that an angel was really standing there. The slender figure with an intense expression had long, fair hair falling in wisps around her pale face and neck. She wore a creamy satin gown over a white nightdress. Charles stood and stared at this apparition. He had no idea how long he stood there in that stupid fashion.

Suddenly, the pale face turned and focused her piercing blue eyes on him. He shook as if shoved. The angel's expression changed to apprehension. She stood rigid for a few seconds, closed the gown hanging open around her white nightdress, moved a few steps back from the verandah railing, and then disappeared. Charles stared after her. Without thinking, he walked back the way he had come, still not sure he had not seen an angel despite his mind rebelling against the idea.

Chapter 10

The pale angel

INDEED, IT WAS not an angel. After a restless night, Aine awoke early, utterly drained. She had arrived at Bill and Joanne Huckerby's house at one o'clock in the morning, exhausted and dispirited. Her sleep had changed nothing. She could at least be thankful there had been no nightmares, noises, or strange voices to disturb her. She lay in bed, wide awake, staring through the nearby window at the country landscape. The hills on the southern side of Binawarra were just visible in the early dawn light. A swirling mist shrouded the top of the highest peak that dominated the town. Little by little, the mist dissipated, and the sun flowed across the hills and fields. Despite her exhausted spirits, the increasing brightness in the natural surroundings encouraged her. The warm hospitality of two of the kindest people she knew also reassured her.

Uncle Bill and Auntie Joanne Huckerby had made her welcome from the moment of collecting her from the station. It was a fortuitous coincidence that she ended up in Binawarra, a country town about an hour northwest of Bendigo. There was no better place at that moment for her to seek comfort, relief, and time to recover. Muffled sounds came from the back of the house. The Huckerbys were busy in the kitchen. She had been there often enough with her parents through the years to know their ways. She would not disturb them. The front verandah would give her some sun and fresh air.

As she leaned on the verandah rails looking at the range of hills, her mind returned to the convent. She knew what Virginia would be doing then, that she would be in her prayers. She had promised. She bowed her head and closed her eyes. How would she get over her failure and loss? She lifted her head, opened her eyes, and fixed her gaze on the hills. A tall young man of a dark complexion appeared in the front garden below her as if materialising from the sun rays streaming across the fields. He looked at her as if he was seeing right into her soul. She stepped away from the railing, still looking at him, her hands slightly raised as if seeking protection. The next moment, she was inside, breathing heavily and leaning against the hall wall. Joanne came from the kitchen and breakfast room at the end of the hallway.

'Oh, Aine! What are you doing?' she said, hurrying to her. 'You should still be in bed. You need sleep and rest.'

'I'm all right,' said Aine, her hand on the wall.

'No, you are not. Now, come on. You can rest in the sun and fresh air while I get you something to eat.'

'No, no. I don't want to go out there again.' She looked around. 'Let me sit in the lounge room.'

Joanne hesitated, frowned, and led her into the lounge room. She had her sit on the settee, where she could lean back on a pile of cushions.

'I'll be all right,' Aine repeated, leaning back.

Joanne sat next to her and took her hand. She caressed it. She patted her cheek. 'Is there something—?'

'No, no, I'm all right. I am a little tired.' She put her hand to her forehead and rubbed it. A minute or two passed. 'Who's that tall boy out there?'

'What ...? Oh, that's Charles! Aine, I'm sorry we didn't say anything. We were so worried about you. We only wanted to get you to bed. Have you seen him?'

'Yes, well, I don't know. There's a tall, dark boy out there. He came and stood in the front garden when I was on the verandah. He just stared at me.' She looked wide-eyed at Joanne, then flushed and turned away.

'Yes, that's Charles.' She got up. 'You wait here a minute.' She caressed her cheek. 'Just stay there and relax.'

She hurried to the kitchen, where she found Bill about to pour boiling water into a canteen-size teapot. 'Bill, I want you to go to Charles at once and tell him about Aine. He doesn't know who she is or what she's doing here. They have already run into each other.' Bill was going to say something. 'No, darling, please—explain to Charles before you do anything else. Tell him the truth. Briefly. I'm busy with Aine for the moment.' Bill returned the kettle to the stove, gave Joanne a wink, and headed for the workshop.

CHARLES sat on an old fruit box in the garage. He had both arms draped across his lap and was staring at the concrete floor.

'You're wondering who that beautiful young lady is, aren't you?'

Startled, Charles looked up at Bill and shifted. He rose.

'No, no, sit down and let me tell you about Aine. Aine is the daughter of our dear friends, Paul and Moira O'Riordan, who live in Sydney. Paul and Moira are Catholics. Like yourself. Joanne and I, by the way, are Anglican, from the high end.' He looked around for another fruit box, kicked the closest one toward Charles, and sat on it.

'Aine is their only child, recently turned eighteen. She's always been a sensitive girl, not very outgoing, despite her striking appearance. She's been quite reclusive, avoiding the activities of people her age and devoting herself to her interests. Mostly spiritual things, as far as we gathered. After school, she wanted to enter religious life. We weren't surprised, as we have seen quite a lot of her through the years. There was always this detached spiritual aspect. Paul and Moira were at first upset, their only child, you know, but resolved to aid her. Things did not go without a hitch. No, not by a long shot. She could not decide what sort of religious order she wanted to join. She tried two different orders, but they proved unsuitable. Don't ask me about the reasons and what happened. I'm ignorant of them.'

Charles was stunned. The angel had ideas about religious life, too.

'Unfortunately, the result of all this indecision was a lack of stability in her life. This was a bad sign because she had always been a steady type of girl. Or so it seemed to us. She became depressive—well, it seemed like depression. We don't know how serious it was. All we know is that Aine was unhappy and that Paul and Moira were worried.'

'A few months back, she decided she would try an order of nuns on Melbourne's outskirts, somewhere northeast of the city. We weren't aware of how that was going until last night when we got an urgent call from Paul. You remember—as you were retiring. Mother Superior had rung Paul that afternoon to say Aine was unwell, and it was clearly because of being confined in the convent. Something had to be done. Urgently. Paul asked if it was all right for Aine to leave that evening and come to us. It all sounded mysterious, but, of course, it was all right. Aine's like family. She was delivered to Spencer Street Station in time to get the last train to Bendigo. We drove down and picked her up. Poor girl. She just fell into Joanne's arms. It was not until we approached the hills, just before arriving in Binawarra, that she seemed to calm down. Joanne gave her a nightdress and bundled her into bed.'

Bill leaned across and put a hand on Charles's shoulder. 'There you have it, old boy. It's a sad story about a beautiful young woman.' He smiled. 'Perhaps you can cheer her up.' Bill waited for a reaction. But Charles was lost for words. That delicate pale face with the piercing blue eyes was fixed in his mind. All he could do was look stupidly at Bill. 'Okay, I'll tell you what,' Bill said, smiling. 'Give Aine a chance to get ready, and you can come and have breakfast with her. Meet her properly. You two will get on, I'm sure.'

Charles tried to hide his feelings of apprehension. Bill got up and wagged his finger. 'Give us fifteen to twenty minutes, okay?'

AT THAT moment, Joanne was encouraging Aine to get dressed. She would meet Charles at breakfast. Aine rose from the settee, hesitated for a moment, and then headed for the guest room. Joanne shook her head as she watched her go.

'Well?' she said when she joined Bill in the kitchen. 'In what state is our handsome guest?'

'What can I say?' said Bill, winking. 'Do you want my honest opinion?'

'Out with it, and no nonsense.'

'Well, let's not speak about love at first sight and Cupid firing an arrow into Charles's heart. Instead, let's talk about Cupid gathering his hottest swords and plunging them one after the other in that poor fellow's breast.'

'After one brief meeting? Come on.'

'It can happen! I know from experience! Painful experience has shown how stupid we love-sick blokes can get.'

'Be serious, Bill!'

'I am, I tell you! But how has Aine reacted?'

'He has aroused her interest, for sure. But, in her confused state, she does not realise how much.'

Charles arrived at the back steps soon after. He wanted to see Aine but was nervous. It was beyond his comprehension. He never had any difficulty talking with the girls in his little seaside village. Aine O'Riordan was different. She was very attractive. No, she was more than that. But that was not it. In those few seconds that he looked into those piercing blue eyes, he seemed to look into her soul, and she appeared to look into his. And she wanted to be a nun! His heart pounded.

'Hey, Charles, I'm waiting to serve your breakfast!' said Bill, appearing in the open doorway. 'Come on, mate!'

Charles climbed the short flight of stairs and let Bill lead him into the kitchen and to his place at the breakfast room table. As he sat down, Bill bent over him, and then in a whisper: 'She's a beautiful girl, but she's human, just like you.' Charles looked in surprise at Bill, but Bill winked and attended to the stove.

'Aine will be along in a minute,' said Joanne. 'She's almost ready.'

Bill put a plate of sausages, eggs, and fried tomato before Charles. This would have been welcome at any other time, but now he only stared at it.

'Come on, gobble that down,' said Bill. 'You're going to need it.' He gave Joanne a wink.

WITH mingling thoughts about her dramatic departure from the convent and the young man in the garden, Aine unpacked her bags and showered. She put on the simple white dress she had worn when rushed to Spencer Street Station the night before. She arranged her few things on the dresser, lining up her Daily Missal and rosary beside each other. Auntie Joanne was waiting for her, but she lingered, fiddling with her rosary while her thoughts dwelt on the tall young man who had stared at her. What did he know about her? Had he heard all about her troubles? How she came to be there in Binawarra. He must be acquainted with the story by now. He must be. Auntie Joanne would have told him. It was too painful to contemplate. She could scarcely think about it herself, let alone deal with how others might see her failure. He was Catholic. Perhaps he would understand. But why should she care what he thought? No boy and nothing any boy had done in the past had mattered to her beyond the acknowledgment required by good manners. What was it about this boy she had just met? He was very handsome, she had noticed. She recalled what Mother Jerome had said to her.

Religious life was a calling by God for special service. Not everybody is called. To think that one has a religious vocation only to find out one is not suited is not a failure. Indeed, it must be accepted as God's will. Did Aine not consider that God was calling her to be a wife and mother—that most exalted role only a woman can fulfil? Aine had given little thought to those words, so great was her misery. Love and marriage had never been a serious consideration in her life. For the first time, she realised she was an eligible wife for someone. She shivered, closed her eyes for a few moments, made the sign of the cross, and headed to the kitchen.

AT THE sound of the guest room door closing, Joanne said, 'She's coming, Charles. Now relax.' When Aine did not appear, she went to the kitchen doorway. 'Come on,' she whispered, taking Aine's hand and drawing her into the breakfast room. Charles looked up and received a nervous glance. His face flushed around to the tip of his ears.

'Here, you sit here,' said Joanne, disentangling Aine and forcing her to sit opposite Charles. 'Now, you two can become acquainted properly.'

Charles received another nervous glance. There followed several more glances at Joanne and Bill. Charles saw her rising—he understood—but then Joanne's hand came down on her shoulder.

'You know,' said Joanne, caressing her neck, 'I suspect you two have much in common.' She paused and nodded at Bill. Bill took his cue.

'Yes, you do, a lot, a lot,' said Bill, while placing teacups and saucers on the table. 'Charles gets on well with his parish priest. He's almost like a mentor, isn't he, Charles?' Charles nodded. 'What's his name again?'

'Fr Bertollo.'

'Charles told us how much Fr Bertollo helped him after the death of his parents.' Aine shifted, and her face tensed. Joanne frowned at Bill. 'A good fellow, that Fr Bertollo,' Bill continued unperturbed. 'He helped Charles fulfil his desire to become a carpenter.' He wore a silly smile. 'Now, aren't I lucky? Charles was all the time preparing himself to come to Binawarra to help me out by repairing the workshop. And all for a few nights' board and a free meal. Who says I ain't smart?'

It was a silly flat joke that hardly made any sense, but it had the desired effect. Charles smiled, despite his unease. Aine's eyes brightened a little. She looked down as if she had been rude. Joanne nodded, sending Bill an approving sign, after which Bill gave Charles a fierce pat on the back. 'Come on,' he cried. 'Eat up. You're going to need your strength for the work ahead. You too, Aine. There's toast for you there and a boiled egg.

You also need your strength. Come on, then!' He took the large teapot from the stove and poured tea for everyone. Joanne sat next to Aine, who poked at the toast and boiled egg in front of her.

'That's it,' Joanne said. 'You'll be on top of the world after a good, hearty breakfast. Afterwards, you can go and have a rest.'

Charles could not help giving this fragile young woman opposite him a sympathetic look. It was momentary. But he saw that it got past her barriers. Her lips relaxed, and her face took on a mysterious glow. He contemplated her while she picked minuscule pieces of egg from the shell. She had been through a difficult time, but her angelic face shone above the exhausted spirits. He gave her another look of solidarity. He saw she understood. While Bill and Joanne kept up a good-natured chatter, his attention remained fixed on her. Her childlike face, her delicate features, and her innocent expression rendered the chatter unintelligible.

'Okay, folks, I must make a move now,' said Bill, breaking the trance. 'School is waiting, and the deputy principal cannot be late,' and then to Charles: 'Charles, you don't need anything right away?' Charles shook his head, forgetting he had wanted to consult Bill on some details. 'Well, why don't you make up a list of what you need? I'll drop by at recess to see how things are going.'

Joanne got up to accompany him to the door. The young people rose, too. Joanne tried to encourage them to stay put, but as they were not yet at ease with each other, she let Charles resume his work outside and sent Aine to sit on the front verandah. Charles went to work, but all he did was done mechanically. Aine intruded on everything he did. Her looks, her religious aspirations, her family, his aunts, and Fr Bertollo all jumbled around in his head. And he had met her that morning. It seemed like an eternity ago. He could not come to grips with his feelings, with the way his world had suddenly been turned on its head. First Joanne and Bill, and now Aine.

'My word, you're working hard!' said Joanne, appearing to interrupt the jumble of thoughts. 'But it's time for a break. Can't be working too hard. You're our guest, you know. Come along to the kitchen in a few minutes.' Five minutes later, he was in the kitchen. 'Aine is still asleep,' Joanne whispered and then, putting her finger to her lips, said, 'Here, come with me. I want to show you something.'

She took the teapot from the bench and walked down the hall. At the entrance to the lounge room, she stopped. When Charles came up beside her, she nodded at the lounge settee. The curtains had been closed, leaving the room in soft, subdued light. He came forward out of the sunlight streaming into the hallway from the front door. There on the settee, lying across a pile of soft cushions, was Aine, fast asleep. Her long, fair hair fell across her face, and her lips were parted as she breathed a deep, restful sleep.

'Isn't she a sight?' whispered Joanne, and without waiting for an answer, 'The poor darling, she's dead to the world. She's had such an exhausting time.' She gave Charles a nudge. 'Go and wake her—gently. Be gentle. Tell her morning tea is served on the front verandah.' Joanne was off before Charles could object.

He stood there for a moment and then walked forward. He came within a few steps of the settee and stopped. He looked down at her face with its soft, pale, unblemished skin, her parted lips, and her motionless eyelids and lashes. The image of his dead mother standing outside a jeweller's shop, contemplating an exquisite porcelain figurine, flashed through his mind. He was very young, and his mother cold sober. The expression of longing, as she gazed at that spotless figurine, had fixed itself in his mind. Aine opened her eyes and started on seeing him standing over her. 'Oh!' she said, trying to right herself. But her sleep had been too deep. She closed her eyes and sank back into the cushions.

'Oh, I'm sorry,' said Charles, not knowing what to do. 'I didn't mean to frighten you.'

'No, no, it's all right,' she said, her eyes blinking open. 'I was a little sleepy and didn't know where I was for a moment.' She closed her eyes and sighed.

'Are you all right?' was all Charles could say.

'Yes, I'm right now.'

'Joanne has morning tea for us on the verandah. Are you ready to come? Or do you want to wait a while?' His face burned.

'No, I'll come, of course.' She made another effort to get up. Without thinking, Charles had held out his hand. Aine looked at the hand, hesitated, and then took it. He helped her to her feet, feeling the smooth, slender hand in his and the lightness of her body as he supported her. Once upright, she let her hand slip out of his. 'Please tell Auntie Joanne I will be there in a minute.'

Charles left her standing in the lounge room, her eyes following him as he walked away.

'Well, you have taken your time, haven't you?' said Joanne when Charles appeared on the verandah in a stupor.

Charles mumbled that she was getting ready.

'Getting ready?' She smiled and pointed to a chair on one side of a small table.

A few minutes later, Aine appeared. Her long, fine, fair hair was tied in a ponytail, revealing her delicate face to its best advantage.

'Come on, Aine darling. You sit here. I'm glad you two have got past the formalities.' She passed cups of tea and plates to her young companions. 'Aine, you should tell Charles about your religious—you know.' Aine looked down. 'Now, now, darling, there's no need to be embarrassed. You understand, don't you, Charles?'

Charles felt her anguish. 'Yes, I do understand. I had a similar experience.' He hesitated. Aine looked up. 'My parish priest, Fr Bertollo, who was like a father to me after my parents' tragic deaths, suggested I discern whether I had a calling—to religious life, I mean. I had not thought about it until then. My religious beliefs are important to me, and I set great store by his advice. So, I followed his suggestion. My visit to the seminary was short because the seminary's rector did not think I was suited. He sent me home. Although I had not considered religious life until Fr. Bertollo mentioned it, I was still somewhat disappointed. Fr Bertollo, who seemed unaccountably concerned about my future, then recommended I go 'walkabout' to find myself.' Aine brightened as he told his story.

'I hope you have found yourself,' said Joanne. 'But we are glad you found us, aren't we, Aine?' Aine shifted in her seat, and Joanne, not waiting for a reply, continued, 'This is the best of luck. For both of you. It'll do you both a lot of good to share your experiences.'

Aine and Charles looked at each other a little more steadily.

'Charles, have you discussed this with anyone else?'

'Not really. I did not need to talk to anyone about it until now.' He glanced at Aine. 'Actually, I was never sure that the religious life was what I wanted or that I was suited. Fr Bertollo wanted to help me sort it out. He was good like that.'

'He sounds like a sensible man, your parish priest,' said Joanne.

'Yes, he has been good to me. I have no idea what I would have done without my dear aunties Maggie and Dot, and Fr Bertollo, after my parents' passing. But I would have reacted differently if my heart had been set on a religious vocation and then been told I was not suited. That would have been far worse.'

To his dismay, Aine hunched her shoulders, bowed her head, and suppressed a sob. Joanne hastened to give him a reassuring signal while she put her arm around her. There was a painful period of silence. Charles struggled to understand. At length, he discerned something in Aine's upset other than her disappointment. The upset passed, and Joanne suggested things they could do together. Bill drove up to interrupt the planning.

'Hey, it's willing for some people!' he called. 'Wish I had time to lounge around and have cups of tea. Better now, princess?' he said when he arrived on the verandah. 'Lots of fresh air, lots of good food, lots of exercise, and we'll have that beautiful girl in grand shape again! And here's this great big handsome fellow to help you out!' Not giving Charles the time to react, he continued: 'And how's the work going? The supervisor's here to check things, you know.'

'He's doing very well, thank you,' said Joanne. 'You should see what he has done in a few hours. It'd take you a whole week.' Bill laughed, giving the verandah railing a hard slap. 'And here's the list of materials. So you had better get cracking and not hold up the worker.'

After morning tea, Bill left, assuring Charles he would have everything delivered by lunchtime. And he was as good as his word. Within an hour, there was a delivery from the hardware store and a half-hour later from the timber yard. In the meantime, Joanne and Aine stayed out of sight. Charles, suspecting that Joanne had sent Aine to rest, worked on with her on his mind. By the end of morning tea, she seemed to have relaxed in his company. She was even friendly in her quiet way. What did that mean? He dared not contemplate it. He had trouble enough dealing with his stampeding feelings. The morning had not ended, and it seemed like he was drifting in an eternity of emotion. The morning came to an end, and the angel herself came to announce lunch.

'Auntie Joanne has lunch ready.'

'All right, I'll come straight away.'

She gave him a smile and turned to go back inside. She walked a few steps and then turned to give him a shy look. Charles watched her slender figure until she disappeared through the back door. He tidied up and followed her to the kitchen. Bill joined them not long after. Aine was at ease for most of the lunch, but traces of tension eventually marked her face. Joanne had also seen the change and brought lunch to an end. The two men cleared the table while Joanne and Aine sat in the lounge. With a subdued mood prevailing, Bill returned to school, and Charles continued his work.

An hour later, Joanne, holding Aine's hand, emerged and made for the bench at the end of the garden. They gave Charles a wave but did not come over to him. He busied himself outside the workshop to see what they were doing. Aine glanced his way while Joanne was talking to her. This continued for some time, when Aine bent over and put her face in her hands. Charles dropped his tools. Joanne tried to get her to her feet, but still holding her hands over her face, Aine sagged in her arms. Charles ran to them and took up Aine's limp body.

'Take her to the guest room,' said Joanne.

Charles hurried, with Joanne following. He placed Aine on the guest room bed. She turned her face away, hiding her eyes with the back of her hand, her slender fingers trembling slightly. Joanne sat beside her and caressed her temple. She gave Charles a sign. He returned to the workshop but was in no state to resume his work. A short time later, he heard Bill's car pull up in the driveway.

'Thank you for helping out,' said Bill. 'This is more serious than we thought. That poor child has put herself through terrible stress. I always had an idea of where it would lead. I have called the doctor.' He shook his head. 'Thank you, Charles, for helping out,' he repeated. Then, without saying anything further, he headed to the back door. Charles sat on the saw bench. The doctor arrived in due course. Charles fidgeted and waited. After twenty minutes, the doctor returned to his car and drove off. A little later, Charles saw Bill come out the back door, stop at the top of the stairs while he seemed to be reflecting, and then descend with his eyes fixed on the ground.

'Well, the doctor has been,' he said, shaking his head. 'There is no cause for alarm. Aine is a little run-down. Otherwise, she's quite all right. She has a delicate constitution and should care for herself better. Perhaps there's some female hysteria there, he said. That's it, then. Aine is to rest, relax, eat up and get plenty of fresh air.'

'I'm glad it's not serious,' said Charles. 'She seemed very upset.'

'Yes, collapsing like that is worrisome. Things have been difficult for her, evidently. Perhaps you can talk to her.'

'I would like to.'

'Well, she will rest up for the remainder of the afternoon. Joanne has sent her to her room, hoping she will sleep. So, we'll see how she's going this evening. Anyhow, old cobber, let's get on with the work here. I'm staying to help you. It'll keep our minds off it.'

Charles and Bill worked until dinnertime, only pausing for afternoon tea. They made much headway, almost completing the repairs Charles had planned. Dinner passed in a sombre mood, with Aine keeping to her room. Joanne took a light dinner on a tray to her. When she returned, she said Aine was not in a talking mood, though she looked better. So, it was best not to press her for the moment.

Chapter 11

Aine and Charles

AFTER DINNER, with the washing up done and everything tidied up, Charles made his way down the hall, intending to go to his verandah bedroom. He passed the guest room door but then stopped. After hesitating, he walked back to the closed door and stood there. He knocked gently. He heard nothing. He knocked again and, doing the unimaginable, slowly pushed open the door. He waited and, not hearing anything, put his head around the door. Aine was sitting up in bed with the untouched dinner tray on the bedside cabinet. She stared, wide-eyed. She hastily drew up the blankets.

'Sorry to disturb you. Can I come in?' She nodded. Charles entered the room, leaving the door ajar. 'I hope I don't upset you by coming in.' Aine shook her head, her eyes still staring. 'Can I sit on the bed here?' He pointed to a place at the bottom of the bed.

'Yes, of course.'

'Are you sure you don't mind me being here?'

Aine shook her head again. Charles was relieved to see she meant it. He had no idea what he would say. He sat and tried to raise a reassuring smile.

'You seem a little better now. I hope you are feeling better.'

'Yes, I do. I am a little better.'

'Can you tell me what happened and why you were so upset?'

'I don't really know.' Her hands opened and closed on the blanket. 'So much has happened to me during the last few months. So much. I had to leave Virginia behind with that—' She looked at Charles as if she had said too much and then trembled, putting a hand to her mouth. 'I just got a little tired of thinking about it. I was worn out. Then this sort of darkness came upon me, a penetrating darkness, causing such a dislocation of feeling that the strength sapped from my limbs. You must have seen it. It started at lunchtime ... actually, I felt it coming some time ago when Virginia ... I feared it would overwhelm me ...'

'A darkness?' he said. 'I ... I think I understand. I've also had some experiences .... Who's Virginia?'

With a hand still at her mouth and the other holding the blanket, she looked up at him and shook her head. Charles understood. He looked around the room, his eyes resting on the rosary beside the daily missal. He picked up the beads. 'Would you like to say a decade with me now? It always helps me, especially in trying times.' She nodded, lowering her eyes.

He kissed the little crucifix on the rosary and made the sign of the cross. When they finished, they looked at each other. 'I'll leave you to rest now. I hope I didn't intrude.' He came closer and held out the rosary. He brushed against her slender hand as he placed the rosary in it. 'Can I talk to you later when you're rested?' She nodded.

About an hour later, the phone rang. Joanne came to Aine's room and was startled to find her up and dressed. The tray was on the floor, and the dinner plate empty.

'Is it Mum?' Aine asked before Joanne could say anything.

'Yes, but are you all right, darling?' said Joanne, resting her arm on her shoulder.

'Yes, I'm all right now. I had a talk with Charles, and it made me feel better. I'm tired, but I am better.'

She did indeed appear better, with a different expression, so Joanne let her go to the phone without more ado. Aine spoke briefly to her mother. She said she would like to stay with Auntie Joanne and Uncle Bill for a while. The country air would do her good. Her mother was relieved, assuring her they would come to fetch her shortly. When Aine finished, Joanne took the receiver.

'Moira, just a quick word,' she whispered as she watched Aine enter the lounge room. 'Aine seems all right now. She was rather distressed for a while.'

'We're relieved to hear that,' said Moira. 'She's not a burden, is she? She's not—is she?'

'Not at all. But Moira, there is something. We have a young man staying with us. It appears they like each other.'

'You mean Aine likes this young man?'

'Yes, indeed.'

'But she never so much as glanced at a boy before. You know that. She's always been full of religion.'

'Yes, I know. This boy is different. The two of them are much alike. You would be surprised.'

'Alike? There can't be a second person like Aine, surely?'

'Look, Moira, I won't keep you on the phone. I just wanted to tell you that sparks are flying.' There was a long pause.

'You can't be serious?' said Moira, at last. 'Last night, Aine was shedding tears of despair, and now you say she is interested in a boy she has never met before today?'

'It sounds strange, I know, and it may amount to nothing, but there's no denying it. Aine and Charles like each other. It's all very innocent, of course, like children—'

'But she has always dismissed the attention of boys, sometimes with icy indifference,' Moira insisted.

'Just you wait until you are here.'

'All right. I have no idea what Paul will say about all this.'

'WELL, THE princess is among us again,' cried Bill when Aine entered the lounge room. 'That's the shot. You had us worried.'

Aine flushed at Bill's loud greeting and said she was sorry to have been a nuisance, but she was sure she would be all right now. She gave Charles a look of gratitude.

'Your mother and father are relieved you're all right,' said Joanne when she returned to the lounge room. She sat beside Aine and took her arm. 'So are we.' She paused. 'So Charles was a big help, was he?'

'Why, what's this great big fellow done?' said Bill.

'Well, only Aine can tell us that.'

Aine hesitated. 'He spoke with me for a while, and then we said some prayers.'

'Said some prayers?'

'Yes, he reminded me I should turn to Jesus and Mary in troubled times.'

Joanne and Bill gaped in silence. For once, Bill was lost for words.

'Whatever has happened,' said Joanne, saving the moment, 'we're all very grateful to Charles for his help.' Bill heartily agreed. 'Well, now,' she continued, 'let's put all that behind us and talk about enjoying ourselves. Charles, you've done enough work on the workshop. Bill can finish the rest.' Bill wagged a confirming finger at Charles. 'Tomorrow, I will take you and Aine down to Bendigo, where we'll have lunch and a look arou nd.'

The trip to Bendigo presented a welcome distraction. The young people listened with interest as Joanne showed them around the historical sites. They asked polite questions, at length, discovering they were interested in the same things. They began directing their conversation at each other. At lunch, Joanne was amused to hear them talking in their quiet way, their heads bent forward, listening to the most banal features of the other's life and experience. She led them around Binawarra to see the sights over the following days, but noticed they had little interest in anyone or anything but themselves. After dinner on Friday evening, the phone rang.

'All right. I have heard enough about them,' was the gruff greeting when Bill picked up the receiver. 'When am I going to meet them?'

'Well, things must have reached a serious pass if Miss Florence Barker shows an interest,' Bill shot back. He called to Joanne, 'It's Flo, darling.' And then to Miss Barker: 'You can come around any time you like. You know that. Do you want a special invitation?'

'Well, preferably. That's the proper way to do things.'

'I'll let you talk to the boss,' Bill said with a laugh as Joanne arrived.

After dinner the following evening, Bill announced the imminent arrival of a visitor.

'But I have to prepare you for this guest. She causes a stir now and then because of her manner. Many people find her rude. And she is sometimes a little short. But she's quite agreeable once you get acquainted with her. She has not been in the town very long; she moved here with no apparent reason about a year ago, promptly bought a house, and settled in. We don't know much about her, and she doesn't talk about herself. She'll tell you bluntly to mind your own business if you ask her questions she doesn't like. From what she said to us in conversation, we conclude she was in Singapore when the Japanese attacked and occupied the island. We have the impression she suffered a great deal. People say she was in a concentration camp, but she's never said anything to us about it.'

'So, you will have to exercise a bit of understanding if she is a little short and outspoken,' Joanne added. 'We are sure she doesn't mean any offence.'

Charles and Aine listened to this account of the formidable Miss Barker with apprehension. When Miss Barker did arrive, they discovered that she was not so terrible. She was tall and thin. Her greying hair was tied into a fat knob at the back of her head; she wore no make-up; her clothes were plain and dull: all of which tended to exaggerate a rather severe appearance and make her appear older than she was. But her somewhat stiff expression, Charles saw, belied eyes that softened the more the conversation advanced. Her short, exacting questions and comments were strangely out of kilter with the sensitivity in those eyes. She even drew Aine into the conversation.

'I've never heard you talk so sympathetically to strangers,' Bill exclaimed.

'Bah! Go away with you,' said Miss Barker. 'I am always pleasant and agreeable.' Bill and Joanne responded with a smile. 'I would like you to present those who disagree.'

When Miss Barker rose to leave, she wished Charles and Aine all the best and said she looked forward to their return to Binawarra. Then, without waiting for a comment from the startled faces, she asked Joanne to accompany her outside. They chatted about odds and ends until they reached the front gate. 'That girl is beginning to bloom. You had better prepare for a wedding. Good night.' She then set off on the short walk back home.

ON SUNDAY afternoon, Bill and Joanne accompanied Aine and Charles on a stroll to the hills outside the town. It was not a great distance, but Bill was puffing when they reached the picnic clearing at the foot of the hills.

'I told you you're not fit enough,' said Joanne. 'You should pay attention to what you eat and do more exercise. You're not yet forty.' She looked at the slope Charles suggested they climb. She shook her head. 'You two had better go up there alone. Charles's mountain will be too much for us.' Bill appeared relieved. 'Are you sure you can climb that distance, Aine darling?'

'I think so if we take our time.' She looked at Charles.

'If you think you can do it ....'

'All right,' said Joanne. 'If you're careful, you can go, the two of you. Now, Charles, you will take care of Aine, won't you? If she gets too tired, you must turn around and come back.'

'I'll be all right,' said Aine.

'No, I want Charles to exercise his judgment here. Sorry, Aine. Now, Charles, you understand, don't you? You're responsible for Aine.'

'I'll be careful. We'll climb straight to the top, look around at the views and then come back down.'

'Good,' said Joanne. 'Now off you go and enjoy yourselves.'

Charles led the way, but within a short distance on the uneven slope, Aine stumbled. Joanne was about to shout for Charles to hold her hand, but it was unnecessary. Charles gave Aine his hand, and she took it. He got her over the rough bit and was about to let her hand go, but Aine held on. Joanne and Bill looked on with knowing smiles as Charles and Aine, hand in hand, ascended the slope.

At first, they did not say much. Charles paid attention to how Aine was managing, always conscious of her hand in his. Aine, too, was being careful and answered his concern with a shy smile. Charles stopped when they reached a spot with a view of the town and the surrounding countryside. Aine let go of his hand and sat down on the grassy slope. Charles sat beside her. They took in the view for a while.

'It's beautiful, isn't it?'

'Yes, it is,' said Charles, glancing at Aine, whose expression was so different from the previous Wednesday.

'Mum and Dad used to come here often when I was younger. We would sometimes spend our holidays here. I grew up feeling like Binawarra was a second home. Auntie Joanne and Uncle Bill have always treated me like a favourite niece.'

'They are an affectionate couple. They've made me feel so welcome. Almost like family.'

'Yes, that's what I mean.'

'I know how you feel about Binawarra, too,' Charles continued. 'I had this strange feeling from the beginning. Almost as if I knew the place.' He recalled the peak with its platform of worship as the one exception. But he did not mention it.

'Did you really?'

'Yes, it's like the land, the bush, the town are in me, like the blood in my veins. It's like Binawarra, and its surroundings have a life. It sounds strange, doesn't it?'

'No, I think I understand.'

They were silent again. Aine crept her hand in Charles's without looking at him, as she had done with Virginia.

'Come on,' he said after they had sat in silence for a while, 'we must keep going.' He gently pulled her to her feet. They stood close for a moment, looking at each other. Then they resumed their way. At length, they arrived at the top where Aine rested, the exertion showing on her perspiring face. Responding to Charles's anxious expression, she assured him she was all right. After a brief rest, they walked around the flat grassy area where Charles had been a week before. How much had happened since that time! How his life had changed. Now he was admiring the expanse of God's creation with someone precious.

'I'm surprised I haven't taken notice of this mountain before and its views,' said Aine, as he took her to every side. 'But I am glad I have seen it with you for the first time.'

At that moment, they were looking at the opposite peak with its rocky outcrop. Charles frowned. Aine noticed the change in his expression. 'What's the matter? What have you seen?'

'That sharp peak there with that flat outcrop, as if it were man-made and used for ritual purposes. It gives me a bad feeling ... it ....'

The rocky outcrop was indeed striking, but Aine did not see anything ominous in it—not at first. She took his arm to comfort him, but Charles felt her stiffen and tremble when she turned again to gaze at the peak. That expression of disturbance reappeared. Her eyelids drooped, and she leaned against him. He led her away to the middle of the flat grassy area and was relieved to see the disturbance fading. But the coincidence of her relapse with his vision—

'I'll be all right,' she said, clasping his hand. 'I'm all right with you.'

'You know, Aine,' he said when she had recovered. 'I have never felt happier.' He drew her to him, and she rested her head on his chest. They put their arms around each other.

'I have known you for a few days, but it feels like forever,' said Charles.

'I feel the same way,' Aine whispered. 'I can hardly believe it. I never dreamed—'

Charles did not want the moment to stop. It was the first time he had touched a girl in this way. All the qualities of femaleness that he had in his arms—the softness, the delicateness, and the sweet smell of her presence—they were intoxicating. But there was more than this. Those physical qualities clothed an oppositeness and similarity in spirit that merged with his very being. It seemed, too, that they were consecrating their love at the spot where he had perceived the presence of God a week before. At length, he roused himself. He kissed her on her forehead.

'We have to go now,' he whispered. 'I promised Joanne and Bill I would bring you back safely and in time.'

'Can we sit on the slope for a few minutes more?' said Aine, brushing a hand across her eyes.

Hand in hand, they walked to the crest of the mountain and sat down on the dry grass. The view expanded before them.

JOANNE and Bill had their eyes on the peak when they spotted Charles and Aine at the crest, about to make their way down.

'Charles is clutching Aine's hand,' said Bill, 'as if they were permanently attached.'

'I wonder what has happened,' said Joanne, with heavy irony.

'I don't think we have to wonder, do you? It was just a question of time. That boy fell in a heap.'

'Aine, you look so happy!' said Joanne when the two had finally joined them.

'I am.'

'You don't look like a sad sack either,' said Bill, putting a hand on Charles's shoulder. 'What happened to you two up there?' He gave Charles a ridiculous wink.

'Don't be mischievous!' said Joanne.

Charles and Aine did not answer directly. But then Charles said, 'We walked around for a while, taking in the magnificent views. We said the way we felt about each other. We had a hug and came back down. That's all.'

'That's okay, my boy,' said Bill. 'We know how it is. And we trust you.'

Bill and Joanne let Charles and Aine walk ahead of them back to the house. When Charles turned to see where they were, Joanne called him to go on. She and Bill would walk at their own pace. Charles was happy to follow that direction.

From then on, nothing was to be done with the two young lovers, and they were left to share their feelings. Late on Tuesday afternoon, when the four of them were chatting on the front verandah, a car came into view against the light of the setting sun. Aine, recognising her parents' car, hastened to meet them. Paul and Moira O'Riordan were shocked at what they saw and responded woodenly to their daughter's hugs. Their next shock was to see Charles walking down the verandah steps, arm in arm with Bill, who, in his jovial way, hinted that Charles was the cause of their daughter's change.

It did not take Paul and Moira O'Riordan long to regain their composure and consider the young man who had captured their daughter's heart. Charles was indeed a different sort of young man and responsible for Aine's dramatic change in spirits. Later, when Moira spoke with Aine about her feelings for Charles, it became clear that her desire for religious life had gone. Aine repeated what the Mother Superior had said about her vocation as a mother and wife, and how she did not appreciate what the Mother Superior meant until Charles stood before her on that Wednesday morning. It was a shock at first, also unnerving, but Charles helped her understand. Charles was her life now. Moira believed her, however unlikely and astounding the whole story seemed.

Charles stayed until the following Friday. On the eve of his departure, he rang Fr Bertollo to tell him he would arrive late on Saturday and see him the next day at Mass. He had much to say to him and his aunts. When he asked the priest whether he had any idea that something special would happen on the trip, Fr Bertollo, without showing any curiosity, gave the impression that he did not understand what he meant.

When the time came on Friday morning to leave, Aine and Charles clung to each other while Bill, Joanne, and Aine's parents looked on. Aine tried not to cry, but it was no use. She put her head into Charles's chest and released a few tears. Charles, too, had to wipe his eyes. He said he had to go, but he would only be separated from her in body. She would remain in his heart and in his soul. As soon as he could arrange it, they would be back together again. He traced the sign of the cross on her forehead, kissed her, and said, 'Remember the Southern Cross.' She nodded, brushing her cheeks. The next minute, he was driving down the street with his heart in his mouth.

Aine waited at the gate, alone, until he disappeared in the curve of the road. As she turned from the gate, wiping the tears from her cheeks, she marvelled again at the miracle in her life. Her thoughts returned to the dear friend she had left behind in the convent, to the darkness and infection she had left Virginia in. The tears she had shed in grief were now tears of joy. She had an intense desire to reassure Virginia that everything had turned out well and that she need not worry about her, but rather should worry about herself there in that convent.

While packing on the day of departure, her mind returned to the embrace on the mountain. It was permanent. The memory of her fear, however, as they looked across at the sharp peak marred the bliss of that permanence for a moment. They had come down from their peak, out of the hilly range, changed people. What lay ahead of her was unknown. What it really meant to be in love with a man was not yet visible. She only knew she wanted to be with Charles, to devote her life to him, to be always with him, only him. That Providence had steered her to Charles was beyond doubt. How else could one explain it? To end up at the Huckerby's at the same time as Charles could not bear another explanation.

She thought again and again of Virginia and her committing her maidenhood to Jesus as her gift and of Mother Jerome's opinion that her vocation was as a mother and wife. She understood now that the gift of her maidenhood could be made through Charles. She feared her heart would break when Charles left to return home. The presence of his spirit, as he had promised, and the anticipation of seeing him again shortly must be her consolation. The terror and the strange happenings of the last months retreated into the background now that she had Charles's strength with her.

As she picked up the rosary from the dressing table, she remembered Charles taking them up to join her in prayer. She looked into the mirror and contemplated her appearance for the first time she could remember. It occurred to her that Charles never said anything about it. Did he find her attractive? Without realising it, she started to compare herself, but she remembered Mother Jerome's warning about paying too much attention to her appearance. She glanced away. No, she would never give in to that temptation—to something so impermanent. She packed the rest of her things and went to the waiting car. Her happiness and confidence in Charles's love were so settled that her thoughts on the way back to Sydney returned to Virginia, whom it seemed she had left behind in another age.

IT TOOK little persuasion to convince the parties in Sydney and South Coast that Aine and Charles were ready to wed. The banns were read, and the church and reception booked. The wedding would take place in Sydney at the O'Riordan's local parish church on the north side of Sydney Harbour. But a problem arose for Aine and Charles that neither family noticed. Aine's parents preferred that they settle in Sydney. Mr O'Riordan had business contacts that would give Charles access to Sydney's burgeoning building trade. He had far greater prospects in Sydney. Fr. Bertollo and Aunts Maggie and Dot insisted that it only made sense for the couple to settle in Charles's village, where he had already established his building business.

However, Aine's visit to Charles's South Coast village and Charles's visit to Sydney settled the choice. Aine saw that Charles was entirely out of place in the big city, and Charles saw that Aine did not fit into his village or his extended family. Maggie and Dot would love and fuss over her, but others would pester her. She would not be comfortable. After discussing it, Aine and Charles decided to settle in Binawarra, where they were already known and welcome, and Charles had excellent business prospects. They expected affectionate support from Joanne Huckerby and unceasing efforts from Bill to help build Charles's business. Charles finished his commission for the parish, sold his house, and the couple moved to Binawarra. A little over nine months after the wedding, baby Estella arrived.

Chapter 12

The hooded figures

VIRGINIA SPENT the days after Aine's departure grieving for the loss of her dear friend. Only when Aine's slight figure and innocent, childlike face were no longer there did she truly appreciate how much her presence had meant to her. There was now a gap in her heart that could not be filled. For a while, she felt alone among the others, but she was not the type to let herself wallow too long in self-pity. Fixing her mind on the reasons for being in the convent, she wrenched herself from her grief and adjusted to the change. Kay Burgess and Rose Lewis were a consolation, small though it felt at first. Gradually, she understood they looked to her for leadership. That was curious at first thought. On further reflection, she became aware that Margaret's outspoken character and resolute ways evoked a similar response from the girls who had come straight from school. The small group of remaining postulants split now into two factions. She wondered about its significance.

To her relief, no friction out of the ordinary arose after Aine's departure. Margaret and Elizabeth left off their baiting and remained unusually quiet, even among the other postulants. It was odd. Aine's absence seemed to affect them, too. They evidently had not expected Aine's breakdown and forced departure. Perhaps it was a shock, a miscalculation now regretted. Was she right? How much did they know of Aine's nightmares and the nocturnal visitations? She could be sure about nothing. Time would tell. She turned her mind again to those strange events. Surely, they could not all have been the product of Aine's imagination? But what was real? At an opportune moment, she asked Mother Cecilia if she knew of a book called *Pistis Sophia*.

'Where in heaven's name did you hear that?'

'Oh ... I just heard about ...'

'Well, you can just forget about it,' said the postulant mistress, looking around. 'You have enough to learn and struggle with without bothering with that sort of thing.'

'So it is familiar to—?'

'I said, forget about it. Or aren't you satisfied with my direction? Perhaps Miss Pearson would like to take over the role of postulant mistress? You wanted that from the start, didn't you?'

'No, Mother, not at all,' said Virginia, bemused by the angry reaction.

'Just tell me if you want to take over.'

'No, Mother, I'm sorry.'

'Then get on with your work.' She marched off along the corridor with black garments flapping and flowing in her wake.

Virginia had posed the question as Mother Cecilia inspected her cleaning in the postulants' quarters. Nobody else was present to hear the exchange. Did the absence of anyone in earshot provoke Mother Cecilia's unrestrained response? It was not in the style of her usual reprimand, which was measured, contained, and well-directed. On the contrary, the question had made the postulant mistress uneasy. The refusal to explain sharpened Virginia's curiosity. She should obey and forget about it, but her mind stayed on it. The words were Latin or Greek. 'Sophia' was the

Greek word for wisdom, she thought. And 'pistis'? She did not know. She would look it up in the library.

The rigid routine of the postulants did not offer much chance for private departures. But now, Mother Cecilia's attention seemed focused on her constantly, as if she waited for the opportunity to catch her failing. It would be best to put it aside. Perhaps an opportunity would come. She admitted, too, that her curiosity was a failing in the religious life to which she had committed herself. But no sooner had Virginia made this resolution than another tantalising feature of Aine's experience distracted her. Did Aine really see a nocturnal gathering near the river?

On successive nights after midnight, she rose from her bed and sat at the window, looking through the dark at the clearing and riverbank. She saw nothing. Indeed, the moonless nights prevented her from making out anything distinct. She let it go for a while. Sometime later, she noticed the full moon rising in the early evening. Perhaps it was worth looking again. She did so, not expecting to see anything, only making an effort when she awoke and could not sleep. She was right. She saw nothing. Surely, Aine's imagination, fired through anxiety, created the visions. The interest began to slip from her mind. Then one night, in the light of the waning moon, some indistinct movement caught her attention as she rested her chin on her arms sprawled over the windowsill. She tensed and raised her head. She stood up, now fully awake.

'My God, Aine was right,' she whispered as she focused on the figures fleeting through the shades of the parapets and gardens.

It was just as Aine described. The dark figures, visible here and there, made their way to the riverbank. She could make out some form floating on the river. She strained, but there was not enough light, and the moving shapes dissolved into the shadows. She looked up at the crescent moon moving through the grey, floating clouds. She must hurry. She wrapped herself in her overcoat and tied a scarf around her head. This was something the like of which she had never done. She moved swiftly along the corridor, finding the door at the end unlocked. As she felt her way down the darkened staircase, she thought she heard a noise from above. She froze. No, there was nothing. She came out from the dark stairwell and was relieved to find enough light to show her the way along the gardens to the rocky stairway.

After taking two steps down, she thought she heard a sound again. She stopped and listened. Again, nothing. She proceeded slowly now, uncertain of what she was doing and fearful of ... of what she did not know ... She stopped on the stairway at the second level. Something strange and ominous filled the air, although nothing was to be heard or seen. She continued to the next level. Her fear and uneasiness increased. She did not want to go further. She walked to her left along the garden and crouched behind the thick rose bushes from where she had a view over the clearing and the jetty stairs. A deathly silence hung over the area, lit by the waning moon. She crouched for five long minutes, listening, with her eyes on the shrouded clearing and the river beyond. Then a glint of light over to the left, near the grotto, pierced the edges of her vision. She swung toward it.

Through the bushes and shrubs, she made out a brief flicker. There was something like a subdued moaning or chant for a short while. The flicker disappeared. She crawled towards the light. She stopped, rigid, as silhouettes emerged from the darkness and approached the clearing. Trembling, she remained hidden as she peered through the shrubs and plants. The shadows disappeared. She looked around. Then the shadows were back in the clearing, moving towards the stairway to the jetty. They hurried, bent forward, and without a sound. As they passed her, drawing a frightening aura along with them, she saw five or six of them wrapped in long, flowing dark robes with hoods. Virginia thought of Aine and the terror she had experienced. Now she, too, felt paralysed by fear and indecision.

Some minutes passed as she crouched, unable to move. Then a boat appeared on the river, approaching the opposite bank. It turned upstream when it neared the bank and passed out of sight among the shadows. A minute later, three hooded figures suddenly appeared at the bottom of the stairs and made their way up past her to the main building. She waited, paralysed. At length, she roused herself and climbed the rocky stairs. All was silent as she came out on the top level. The cloisters seemed to be in dark, open-mouth terror as she hurried by them, the dread of ascending the stairs in the pitch dark following on her heels. Where had the hooded figures gone? Shivering, she felt her way to the top. She took hold of the door handle to pass into the corridor. The door would not move. She twisted and tugged at the handle several times. She glanced this way and that. If she aroused attention, it would be the finish for her.

What on earth possessed her to investigate? She should have remained in her cell and reported it instead of being led by her usual nosiness. But something had held her back as she stared from her window at the sinister activities. Sinister, yes, that was it. What she and Aine had seen represented some perverted spirit slithering unchecked through the halls and rooms of the convent. It could no longer be a question of the isolated actions of a few naughty young women in high spirits. There was something deeper here, and reporting it did not seem, for some inexplicable reason, the right decision at that stage. She resisted the creeping regret.

She leaned against the wall and then sank to the floor, where she remained shivering. What could she do, she, the practical, sober-minded teacher, the one always with the solution? She could not stay where she was. She must try something. She stood up and put her hand on the handle. The door gave way. She whipped her hand away and waited. Then slowly, she pushed it open to reveal the poorly lit corridor with the mute doors on either side, disappearing as if into a dark, endless tunnel. Safely in her room, she fell to her knees.

The light streaming in the window woke her. She straightened herself with a start. She looked at her crumpled overcoat and then tore the scarf from her head. The sounds coming from the corridor indicated she had missed the wake-up call. Why had there not been the usual insistence? She hurried. As she took her seat in the chapel with the others, she cast several furtive glances around to see if she attracted any attention. Heads were bowed, as usual. She took a longer look at Margaret. Margaret had her eyes closed as if in deep meditation. Later in the refectory, all seemed normal. Classes and devotions also continued as usual during the morning. Only Mother Cecilia seemed less picky than usual. During lunch recess, she walked with Rose and Kay along the gardens, her mind running over the night's events.

She now better understood what Aine had been through, though there seemed a deeper dimension to Aine's experience than her real experiences. And as she walked in the full light of day without the dark, strange, hooded figures to play on her fears, she began to see things differently. What sort of game were the hooded figures playing? It made no sense. What were these people up to in the convent, roaming around the gardens as if it were Halloween? And who were the dark figures who rowed to the opposite bank? Now, in contrast to what ran through her head as she sat shivering beside the locked door, she had an irresistible inclination to put it down to the maverick activities of Margaret and her ideas about convent authority. But, no, it could not be that. Surely.

Her companions noticed her distraction and asked if something was bothering her. She said she was a little tired. She did not dare talk about it before she had an idea of what was happening. By late afternoon, after the day had passed with little disturbance to the daily routine, she had the odd feeling she had been dreaming. She resisted the inclination. She upbraided herself for her doubt. But as the days passed and no follow-up to the midnight séance occurred, the doubts became more insistent. At the same time, Margaret refrained from her childish behaviour and deliberate baiting and showed signs of adjusting to the life of the convent. And Mother Cecilia toned down her reprimands, dropping the hint that she expected the group, as it now stood, to make it to the formal reception into the novitiate as Brides of Christ. In some ways, it unnerved her that everything was falling into its proper place. It was the prioress who broke the calm flow of events. A week before the solemn ceremony of Reception and Clothing, Mother Jerome summoned Virginia.

'What religious name will you take on entering the novitiate?' said the prioress, without wasting time.

'Agnes.'

'Agnes? Which Agnes?'

'St Agnes, virgin and martyr.'

'You have done the necessary research on the life of this virgin and martyr, no doubt?'

'Yes, Mother, I have chosen the name because of the purity of her faith and the heroism of her witness in the face of the Roman persecutors.'

'You have made it to the end of your postulancy,' said the prioress, barely acknowledging Virginia's reasons. 'Do you have any doubts?'

'No, Mother.'

'You left behind a broken-hearted fiancé. No regrets?'

'No, Mother,' said Virginia, surprised. She did not remember saying anything about her relationship with Philip to anyone in the convent—except for Aine.

'What did your fiancé say about your entering the religious life?'

'Not much. He just walked out—left the house, I mean. He was too shocked and angry. I have not seen him since nor heard what he is doing.'

'Then the affair is still not finished?'

'Affair ... what ... it was not like ....'

'What will you do if you meet him in the future?'

'Meet him ... how?'

'That young man has not disappeared. He is still walking the streets of this city. He may walk into your classroom. We are a teaching order, remember.'

'It would not change anything,' said Virginia, trying to compose herself. The thought of Philip appearing in her classroom had never entered her head. 'Besides, he is an academic. I would not expect to come across him.'

'You would not?'

'No ... no,'

'Most likely, he will marry. What if his children enrolled in your school and you had to meet him regularly? That is the role of a teacher—to talk to the parents.'

'His children?' she said, open-mouthed.

'You have to think of the future.'

'Yes, Mother.'

'Do you still feel the same way about your fellow postulants?'

'Yes, I still feel that a few of the younger ones should have spent time in normal society before testing a vocation.'

'And Miss McGuigan?'

Virginia hesitated, not sure she should say what she thought.

'I require a frank and honest answer from you,' said Mother Jerome, tapping her desk.

'I'm sorry, Mother. I regard Margaret McGuigan differently. In her case, it is a question of a discordant attitude.'

'A question of discordant attitude?'

'She treats the convent's rules as something to be transgressed, or rather, got around. She has a problem with authority.'

'With your authority?'

'I don't have any authority here.'

'You don't? You have not judged her insolent on occasions?'

'I meant I have no authority from the convent community's constitution.'

'I understand your distinction,' said the prioress, nodding. 'I am happy that you understand it, too.' She paused. 'Great changes are happening in our society. I do not think people who are still recovering from the war realise how great it is. We must be careful how we analyse what's happening. Perhaps Miss McGuigan and those of that age are reflecting those changes unconsciously. Perhaps she is more committed to the convent way of life than you have assessed.'

'There's hardly more than five years between us.'

'That may be fundamentally important.'

'Yes, Mother.'

'Miss Pearson,' said the prioress, making it clear she was ending the interview, 'I want you to go now to the chapel. I want you to spend the afternoon in prayer and reflection on the decision you are about to make. I would like you to begin a novena to Our Lady of Perpetual Succour for guidance. During the next nine days, you are to talk to Fr Sheridan. Fr

Sheridan is a simple old priest, a man of great piety. His theology issues from his rosary beads. You are to listen carefully to what he says.'

'Yes, Mother,' she said, preparing to be dismissed.

'Just one last thing, Miss Pearson. Our secular society would consider you an attractive young woman, well-qualified, confident, and under-standing. You are a very eligible young woman. You would not escape the notice of young men of the highest standing, culture, and education.'

'Thank you, Mother.'

'It is not meant as a compliment,' said Mother Jerome with some terseness. 'It is something for you to consider. Carefully.'

Virginia made her way to the chapel, pondering the interview. It seemed Mother Jerome had doubts about her suitability, doubts out of proportion to her conduct during the previous months. Or so it ap-peared to her. She had little doubt about what she wanted. The routine of the convent was not burdensome or oppressive. Margaret's opposi-tion to obedience and self-denial did not bother her. She had experienced none of the trauma and tears that had afflicted some younger ones. But the prioress had reservations. Why?

And why those comments about her social eligibility and her engage-ment to Philip? She was over Philip, she told herself. She had put it all behind her. She had resigned herself to the vow of chastity. As someone who valued clarity in her actions, she found Mother Jerome's unspoken reservations bewildering and unsettling. It unsettled her even more when she learned later that none of the other postulants had been summoned to a similar interview. For once, Margaret did not comment by word or expression. That was curious, too. The only exchange, loaded with tension, came a few days before the clothing ceremony.

'Well,' said Margaret to the group as they sat around on the lowest level, 'we have made it, ten out of twenty-one.'

'It's a pity that Jannie and Aine are no longer part of the group,' said Elizabeth Parker.

'I think they would have succeeded if given a chance,' Margaret whispered. 'I will miss them.'

'I'm surprised Aine O'Riordan had difficulties,' Kay Burgess commented. 'She was more spiritually inclined than most of us. There was something ethereal, something otherworldly about her. You can never tell.'

Virginia wanted to say something, but could think of nothing that would not risk inflaming feelings. She glanced at Margaret. Margaret turned her head towards the river. Her mind seemed elsewhere.

'She was a very beautiful girl,' came the comment from someone, to which there was no reply. A tense silence descended on the group, eventually broken by the question of what religious name each would take.

'I'll be Sister Catherine,' Margaret said with forced gaiety.

'Which Catherine?' asked Virginia. 'There are a few.'

'St Catherine of Sweden.' A slight grin appeared below tensed, watchful eyes. 'Her father forced her to marry a thick, lumbering German prince at thirteen. She made him take a vow of chastity and then accompanied her mother, St Bridget, to Rome.' She laughed to herself while the younger women looked on. 'The pathetic prince died not long after. After that, many rich men pestered her as if money could buy everything. Catherine was a model of female independence.'

'I rather think that her independence was not the point of her saintliness,' said Virginia.

'You don't?'

Virginia did not want to start anything. 'I only mean that there was a greater dimension to her holiness.'

Margaret also appeared to want to control herself. She raised her eyebrows briefly and said, 'And what name will you take?'

'Agnes,' said Virginia, relieved that conflict had been avoided.

'St Agnes, virgin and martyr?' said Margaret.

'Yes.'

'I suppose you imagine that's appropriate.'

Tension gripped the air. Virginia looked at the ground in front of her before answering.

'Yes, at least as a model of holiness and dedication.'

'Do you think a formal bride's gown will suit the idea of a martyr?' said Margaret in an apparent attempt to reduce the tension.

'You don't like the idea of wearing a bride's gown?'

'Well, do you?' Margaret looked around at her fellow postulants. 'It seems a bit silly when we've expressly rejected walking down the aisle to enslave ourselves to one or other dullard at the altar.'

'We will be walking down the aisle to give ourselves to Our Lord and Saviour,' said Virginia, determined to suppress her irritation. 'The Brides of Christ symbolism is appropriate.'

'It doesn't have to be the same way those gullible girls do it, does it?'

'You may be surprised to hear that I agree with you. The ordinary bride's gown has too much reference to the secular.'

'Wonders will never cease,' said Margaret with an airy wave of her hand.

'I would prefer something like the dress the bride of Cana wore when Jesus changed water into wine,' said Virginia, ignoring the pointed sarcasm.

'Well, I would prefer to wear something that highlights the significance of our independent commitment. We are casting off the ordinary bonds of secular life, aren't we? In their place, we're devoting ourselves entirely, without impediment, to our calling.'

Virginia wanted to ask yet again what Margaret was doing joining a Catholic convent. She restrained herself. Perhaps Mother Jerome was right when she hinted she did not truly understand a girl of Margaret's age. But she was not willing to accept that.

A few days later, as the postulants in their bridal gowns processed into the chapel filled with family and friends, Virginia concentrated on the momentous nature of her commitment. Wondering whether her former fiancé was attending did not break her concentration. She knew he would not be there. Only Margaret's whispered comments to Elizabeth distracted her. It had to happen right to the end.

Chapter 13

Philip on the loose

PHILIP EVADED the meeting Fr. Gorman wanted to arrange with Vic Brennan, pleading heavy commitments for the start of the academic year, but he did not evade Vic. Vic forced his presence on him late one afternoon after a tutorial.

'I know you're keeping your head down,' said Vic, after the last student had trooped from Philip's office, 'and I understand.'

'Have you come to gloat or something?'

'Come on, Phil. I know we've had some testy exchanges, but give me credit for a modicum of decency.'

'How decent, then?' said Philip, wondering if the leader of the faith-science group would moderate his superior sneering manner.

'I heard Virginia broke the engagement. I'm sorry for you. I want to assure you this sort of personal matter will not be a subject for discussion in our intellectual disagreements.'

What's he up to? thought Philip. Vic Brennan's cutting, mocking manner in debate formed part of his political arsenal.

'Thank you. That's appreciated.'

'I believe it was unexpected.'

'Yes, I did not expect it,' said Philip, wondering where he had heard about it. 'I don't want it to be part of the student gossip if I can help it.'

'Nobody will hear about it from me.'

'Again, I appreciate it.'

'What's Virginia doing? I suppose she will continue teaching,' said Vic, clearly fishing.

'Yes, I suppose so. Look, Vic, I'm not really in the mood.'

'Sure, Phil, I understand. Truce for a while, okay, and personal matters are out of bounds.'

Vic Brennan left Philip wondering what that was all about. Perhaps he should not be so cynical. Vic played hard, though he thought all he did was defend the truth. As Vic pleaded, he should give him credit for some decency. Well, he would wait to see if he kept to the truce. Much to Philip's surprise, he did. Vic and his faith-science group stayed out of his way for a few months, though continuing to organise their meetings and agitate to bring other Catholic students to their cause, to their superior cause.

Oddly, or perhaps significantly, no philosophy students seemed attracted to the philosophical nonsense Teilhard de Chardin had poured out for decades, his death putting a stop to it in 1955. Ironically, some of the Church's most ferocious critics agreed on this, many calling De Chardin a scientific and theological charlatan. Then a rumour began to pass around that Vic had marital problems. It was common knowledge that Vic had married way below his intellectual class. His friends did not put it that way, but the message was clear. A youthful Vic had recklessly succumbed to a simple girl with nothing to recommend except her considerable youthful charms. Fair enough, thought Philip, that Vic did not want it spread. It was a natural wish to prevent one's marital problems from becoming a topic for the gossipers.

He succeeded in keeping Virginia out of his mind most of the time. His teaching duties and guiding new students in their work consumed his day, and constant invitations to the pub and other social occasions took up much of his time away from the university. The attention from female students and teaching staff increased, to his surprise. Back on the bachelor circuit was probably the cause. The thought that he might be attractive in looks and personality did not occur to him. One female lecturer from the English department said he had matured out of the boyish, studious look of his undergraduate days. That made him attractive, she said, particularly to the female students who grew bolder. She warned him to be careful. Did Philip know anything about naughty Lord Byron? He did not, nor was he interested, but he remained careful, heeding the recent scandal that had shaken the universities. News about Virginia came on a visit to his parents.

'Virginia has finished her postulancy,' said his mother over a coffee after dinner.

'So?' he said, trying to suppress the sudden onslaught of feelings.

'So, she has passed the first hurdle,' said his father.

'All right, she has passed the first hurdle. Good for her.'

'You have to get over it, darling,' said his mother.

'And the best way is to confront it,' said his father.

'I have confronted it—and put it out of my mind. I'm too busy, anyhow.'

'Why don't you come with us to the clothing ceremony when the postulants receive their religious habit on entering the novitiate? It's an impressive ceremony, we're told. You'll appreciate Virginia's commitment and, not as you see it, mull over her abandonment of you.'

'Yes, they all get dressed in brides' gowns. That's an appropriate reminder.'

His parents looked at each other.

'We understand how hurt you are, Philip,' said his mother, 'but it's best to make an effort to reconcile it by accepting Virginia's marvellous self-sacrifice.'

'Yes, you're right. I should accept it,' he said to end another useless conversation about Virginia.

'So, you'll come with us?'

'No. I won't have time.'

On the day of the novitiate clothing ceremony, Philip was again parked in the bushy street off the road leading to the convent. He watched the cars go by, filled with families in their Sunday best. The stream reduced to a trickle, then to none. He looked at his watch. The ceremony would start in five minutes. He drove to the convent and parked on the road outside the grounds. Two nuns were still organising some families at the chapel entrance. He waited on the main avenue, peering around the trunk of a giant gum tree. When the grounds were silent and empty and the nuns inside, he approached the chapel. Assured no one was in the vestibule, he slipped inside and squeezed himself into the same corner. All attention was on the side entrance to the convent building. An organ began playing solemnly.

In their gleaming white brides' gowns, the postulants entered two-by-two, led by Virginia, resplendent in the gown she had bought for their wedding. Just like Virginia to be at the head of the column. He gazed at her regular face, smooth and glowing with a slight blush. He did not know whether he was on the point of screaming out his grief or dissolving into tears of despair. He edged to the entrance without breaking anyone's concentration and slipped out of the chapel. Tears ran down his cheeks as he raised himself to a trot to get out of the place. He sat motionless for a while in the car, with his head resting on the steering wheel and his cheeks wet with tears. At length, he roused himself, turned the car around, and drove off without skidding or grinding the gears. That was it. No one, and nothing, would cause him such pain again.

HE SETTLED into his university routine and social rounds. He left off the whisky and restricted himself to beer. That was safer. Besides, he wanted a clear mind for his research on several papers he was preparing on Aristotle's ethics and politics and their influence on later political philosophers, such as Edmund Burke. Fr. Gorman continued to urge a meeting between him and Vic, but he resisted.

'I'm fully aware it's your job, Father, to reduce the conflict between people,' said Philip, on a visit to Fr Gorman's office to put a stop to the urging once and for all, 'but this is a question of fundamental political belief. There's no common ground between Vic's faith-science group and me. So, it's pointless to argue our positions yet again.'

'I'm concerned about the ill feeling between you.'

'Then let me give you an undertaking that I will keep our discussions polite, should they occur. I hope they won't. I will do my best to avoid such useless discussions.'

'I suppose I should accept that.'

'It's the prudent thing to do.'

'Yes,' said the priest, 'it is the prudent thing to do in the circumstances.'

Philip was about to leave when he hesitated, wondering whether he should appear contradictory by mentioning what had suddenly come to mind.

'Doesn't this faith-science project worry you, Father? Our differences about political issues are one thing, but attempting to reconcile the Catholic faith with modern science is another. The Church's highest authorities have condemned any attempt like it.'

'Is that what Vic and his friends are doing? Or are they searching for new ways to understand the faith? My role is to guide, not to dictate.'

'Well, I won't encroach on your territory, Father. Let me say just this. Teilhard de Chardin, with whom many of Vic's group are infatuated, is no philosopher. And I've heard scientists say he's no scientist. Personally, I think he's a fraud, acting as a philosophical Pied Piper.'

'That's inflammatory language, Phil. You are already breaking your undertaking.'

'You see how pointless these discussions are?'

Philip said no more. He left Fr. Gorman's office, hoping there would be an end to the squabbling. Vic and his friends had not given a similar undertaking. They waylaid him in the student union's cafeteria.

'I hear you've been slandering us,' said Vic, with a malevolent smile, as he and his chief student supporters, Des O'Farrell and Frank Quinn, took up a position at the same table with their coffee and cakes.

'You don't change much, do you?' said Philip, closing his book. 'If you think my criticism of De Chardin and your group's infatuation with him is slander, then I'm guilty. But I suggest your use of the word is poetic rather than accurate in the relevant context. And it's unfair to distort Fr. Gorman's words. He would not have used the word slander.'

'Exaggeration to make a point,' said Vic. 'I don't think Fr. Gorman would be too upset.'

'You've made your point. Let there be an end to it. I'm not interested in another pointless—and frustrating—discussion.'

'They say you're a Thomist,' said Des O'Farrell accusingly.

'That's not entirely accurate, as I have explained before, something an engineering graduate like you does not seem to understand. I subscribe to the tradition of classical realist metaphysics, best developed by Aristotle and Aquinas. What's that got to do with anything, anyhow?

'They say Thomism is obsolete.'

'Who's they?'

'Enrico de Leon, for example.'

'Don't make me laugh. De Leon's new theology is full of holes. I'd be embarrassed to defend that sort of Hegelian fancifulness. You should read Pius XII's letter, *Humani Generis*. De Leon and his mates are a target.'

'Written by Thomists,' said Vic.

'You're out of your depth, Vic.'

'And you're stuck in a rut, Phil.'

'I'll leave you to it,' said Philip, rising and grabbing his book. 'I'm getting off this stale merry-go-round.'

'Ouch!' said Vic. 'Such a mixing of images—'

'Stick to analysing poems, Vic. That's how you earn your money. In philosophy, you and your mates are dilettantes.'

'Perhaps you and your philosophy bored her into the nunnery.'

Philip glared at Vic. 'I thought you wouldn't say anything about that,' he said, realising Vic had discovered the reason for the broken engagement.

'You provoked me. Besides, it's only you who knows the allusion.'

Philip left without further comment. Contempt was easy for the English department's star, who so often resorted to sneering and mockery when his arguments failed or his ignorance became apparent. It was difficult to fathom why he was so cavalier in condemning schools of thought he clearly knew little about. Whatever the case, he would avoid

him and his political agitation. It was up to Fr. Gorman to address the
dangers he and his group posed to the faith. On that score, it was a
mystery why the John Fisher Society's chaplain tolerated the attempt
to reconcile Catholicism with modern science. It was basic, wasn't it,
that the truths of Revelation had a different justification from the truths
found out by unaided reason?

Phil's burgeoning social life helped him ignore the irritations of Vic
and his group. It also helped block thoughts of Virginia. Everyone, it
seemed, wanted to be his friend. Social occasions were available every
night of the week if he wanted to go out. And the women were interested, he was pleased to discover. One female or another, at the mere
suggestion, joined him in the pub. But there were pitfalls. A few months
after the clothing ceremony, Philip found himself, against his will, in a
heavy relationship with an attractive schoolteacher. Ironically, he met her
through the local church. The smell and feel of close female company
was a pleasure. But things took a bad turn. After six months, he saw he
had to commit or stop. If she gave herself to him, which seemed the next
step, he would have no choice. He could not go through with it. The
relationship ended amid weeping and accusations of deceit and betrayal.

His mother severely rebuked him for callously trifling with her affections. How could he lead her on like that? Lead her on? He was not
aware that he led her anywhere against her will. And he must not exact
his revenge on the female race. Revenge? Please, Mother. Whatever his
blamelessness against these accusations, he had to be more careful. Under
no circumstances would he commit to marriage. He had definitely shut
off that path. But another very pretty face and a sweet manner made
him incautious. It was a Catholic girl, a nurse from the nearby hospital,
whom he met at one of the university's watering holes. His family and the
parish gossipers did not know her—or so he thought. After six months,

the temptation was overpowering. Give in or get out because once in, that was it. He got out amid more recriminations. To his astonishment, his mother got to know about it. How did she know? Never mind, she said. He must not play with women's feelings. That was contemptible. She expected more of him. He said nothing and resolved to stay clear of Catholics.

One evening, while at a pub in the city centre with a few colleagues, he got talking with a man of his age, gulping down top-shelf whisky. Philip commented on his discriminating choice. Erik appreciated the compliment, and they embarked on a long discussion about whisky, Philip relating his time in Oxford and the intemperance of some of his wealthy student friends. Erik's close friend Harry joined them. Harry turned out to be a successful fast-talking fashion photographer. Their discovery that Philip was an academic in the philosophy department at John Batman University sparked their interest. The three got on so well that Harry invited Philip to a small, exclusive party to meet his model friends.

'He's cultivating a beautiful girl he has just come across,' said Erik.

'Yes, she has a Dutch background: tall, stunning, with that unblemished ivory complexion you see with some Dutch girls,' said Harry. 'She's a bit flighty but has enormous potential. I just have to control her brittle personality. Anyhow, you'll meet Jannie. She'll be there. Come on.'

Harry and Erik took Phil to a renovated terrace house in Parkville, where he met a mixture of arty types, many in the fashion industry, the type Philip had rarely met, let alone mixed with. They lounged around in an elegant way, smoking, sipping cocktails, whisky, and other spirits. A small number drank beer. Philip was surprised at the warm reception after Harry had introduced him to the gathering.

'This is Jannie de Kam,' said Harry, taking Jannie's arm and drawing her closer.

'Please to meet you, Dr Stevenson,' said Jannie, wriggling and simpering. 'I hope to enrol at John Batman University in social work. So perhaps I'll see you there.'

'You won't have time for study,' said Harry. 'You'll be too busy with a brilliant career as a model.'

'I can do both, can't I? I have a friend who thinks I'm suited to that sort of work—social work, I mean.'

'We'll see, darling.'

Jannie de Kam was indeed a beautiful girl. And she was aware of it. It was not to be wondered at, considering Harry constantly boosted her looks and potential as a top photographic model. Jannie's revelling in the male attention showed a shallow immaturity and insecurity. No matter how much he admired her beauty, she was not his type. He should not be too hard on her, though. She could not be more than twenty if that. If Jannie did not rank as his type, other attractive, more mature girls of Harry's and Erik's acquaintance did. He had a string of short-term relationships with girls from their circle, which broadened to others of a similar outlook. None were interested in a committed relationship. They were out for enjoyment without any break on their desires. It was a libertarian outlook, Philip decided, not that anyone showed an inclination to analyse their behaviour while tumbling between sheets in fits of passion. The only inconvenience for Philip was the occasional prick of conscience. His parents had not brought him up to indulge himself in this way. His mother would be horrified. Virginia had left him gutted of all moral perspective. That justified his behaviour.

'You are aware that Virginia has come through the novitiate,' said his mother in December 1958, when he was on one of his occasional visits, 'and is about to make her temporary vows.'

'Good for her.'

'I don't suppose you're interested in attending next week. It's an important stage in Virginia's religious life.'

'No.'

'Do you want us to pass on your best wishes?'

'No.'

'Philip, darling, you have to get over your disappointment.'

'I am over it.'

Philip saw his father give his mother a little shake of the head.

'I have some news of my own,' he continued. 'I have been appointed senior lecturer. It's mostly supervising the first-year subjects.'

'Congratulations,' said both parents.

IN JANUARY 1959, Philip received news that Dr Joseph Edelman would join the philosophy department to replace a lecturer who had returned to England. He was to share the first-year subjects with him. Philip wondered how he would get on with the new lecturer specialising in analytic philosophy. A cooperative relationship was essential. Philip need not have worried. As soon as Joe Edelman found Philip had an abhorrence of continental philosophy, especially of Hegelian obscurantism, they became best of friends.

'I can forgive you your Aristotelianism if you have as much scorn for German idealist metaphysics as me.'

'I'm glad to hear it. We can cross swords over Aristotelianism when you want.'

The friendship became especially knit when Phil introduced Joe to Harry and Erik and their circle. Harry and Erik evidently liked having a couple of appealing academics in their entourage. Joe behaved like a child in a sweet shop.

'I didn't realise I would have a playboy for a colleague,' said Joe, while discussing the first-year lecture timetable two weeks before term started.

'I'm hardly what you call a playboy.'

'You've got some beautiful women as friends.'

'They're Harry's friends.'

'And you just take your pick.'

'I don't do anything with anyone unless they want to. I'm strict about that.'

'You're Catholic, aren't you?'

'Why do you say that?' said Philip, surprised.

'You've got a conscience.'

'So have you, I hope.'

'I do, but it's not the same. You're plagued with guilt. You know what you do with your luscious girlfriends is against the rules. As a New York atheist, I don't have those rules. People are essentially free and, being free, are open to making their own decisions. But they're also responsible for them.'

'As a libertarian, you fit in well with Harry and Erik's high bohemian crowd.'

'Thank you for the compliment. But my New York accent has some appeal I've experienced.

Philip thought for a moment. 'Is it so obvious?' he said with a helpless laugh. 'I mean, my being a Catholic.'

'To me, it is. As a philosopher, I'm interested in all belief systems. Catholicism has come under my scrutiny, including the rules about sexual morality.'

Philip leaned back in his chair. Joe smiled at him and waited for him to speak.

'You know, Joe,' he began. 'You probably find this funny. I try to compensate for my sins by being especially nice to my girlfriends. That's why some of them find it difficult to break up with me.'

'That's funny—and ironic.'

PHILIP and Joe settled into a friendly cooperative relationship in their work and play. Hardly a disagreement arose between them. Their students gave them excellent reports. Vic Brennan could not hold back.

'Don't you feel a bit of a hypocrite?' he said when he came across Philip in the student union cafeteria.

'You will have to explain, Vic.'

'You tell Fr. Gorman we are compromising the faith, but here you are mixing with the university's most flamboyant libertarian.'

'I'll tell Joe what you think of him. He will be proud of the badge.'

'It still makes you a hypocrite.'

'You're welcome to your judgment, but my behaviour is not an argument against what I think of De Chardin's nonsense and the other Hegelians you seem attracted to. I'll admit, though, that my behaviour disqualifies me from disputes with your so-called science-faith group. Besides, I'm bored with it.'

Vic Brennan had no answer to Philip's confession and left him in peace. Fortunately, Joe remained ignorant of Vic's science-faith apostolate. That would have given ammunition to his inclination to kid and send up the sort of ignorance he said was rampant on all campuses. Philip was obliged to make only one comment, or rather a warning, about Joe's libertarian principles. He became involved with a postgraduate English student at the end of the year. Vic Brennan was her supervisor. He was furious. He accosted Joe in his office when Philip happened to be with him.

'It's got nothing to do with you,' said Joe calmly. 'It's university vacation. I'm not interfering with university regulations or routine. The girl is twenty-one. She's not a philosophy student, though she could do with some training in philosophical method, as is usual with literature students. She can make up her mind about who she goes to bed with. It's got nothing to do with you.'

'The moral tone of the university has something to do with me as a senior lecturer.'

'Then report me,' said Joe, waving his hand.

'Perhaps I will,' said Vic, turning to leave the office.

'Be my guest.'

Vic glared, frowned, and marched from the office.

'You must be careful, Joe. A dramatic scandal over the alleged molestations of a student by a professor has recently shaken the academic world.'

'I am careful. I won't do anything unless it's clear to everyone, not just me, that the girl is willing. Besides, she was a special case. I was in love—for a while.'

Vic did not take up the invitation to report Joe, not that Joe cared or even thought about it.

Chapter 14

The novitiate

VIRGINIA HAD regarded the solid wooden door to the novitiate with much trepidation. The postulants had ample chance to contemplate its heavy, forbidding appearance, for it was at the end of the cloisters near the entrance to the chapel. Was its position deliberate, designed to intimidate the postulants, or merely a felicitous architectural fluke? The emergence of novices, sometimes with swollen red eyes, joining the procession to the chapel suggested its forbidding nature. Whatever the case, now, after nine months of discernment and perplexing events, she proceeded in a single file with her companion novices toward that dark door. At the head of the file walked the tall, stately Novice Mistress, Mother Fortunata, famous through the convent and beyond as Reverend Mother Formidable. The slow, dignified steps and the erect head warned that the fun had finished, and now they would get down to business. She had the manner of a cattle station owner who had rounded up the stray delinquent cattle and was leading them to the holding pens for serious consideration.

In truth, Virginia, now Sister Agnes in full habit and distinguishable as a novice by the white veil, had been under no apprehension about what awaited her if she passed the first stage of postulancy. The postulancy was a period of discernment, the novitiate one of religious formation. That was a euphemism, she thought wryly, for having to undergo the unrelenting process of destroying the self, the personal, and the individual so that the novice came to the act of profession with a will and spirit totally in conformity with the will of God. In the practical, concrete situation, her religious superiors, whose word was law, represented the will of God.

Sister Agnes shuddered in trepidation as the Novice Mistress stopped before the dark door, paused for effect, and then knocked with great solemnity. As the door opened slowly, Agnes realised she was entering the novitiate spiritually naked. In earlier months, every stain and rough point on the surface of her spiritual life had been laid bare in all their ugliness. She could only guess with what relish the novice mistress would go about erasing the stain and smoothing those rough points.

The novitiate was secluded from the rest of the convent, its only known access being the great forbidding door. A high wire fence and a lushly growing hedge sealed the small recreation area off from the rest of the convent grounds. Ironically, the hedge gave the novitiate an exclusive resort appearance. Now, she would learn about the exclusive life of a religious resort. The silent train of novices gliding along the corridor close to the wall came to the novices' community room without delay. It was here that they would spend much time studying, receiving instruction, being reprimanded and, horrors of horrors, taking part in the chapter of faults, the *mea culpa*. There had been much fearful whispering about this last ritual during the previous months—the open confession of one's faults and omissions. Each young woman, including Margaret and excluding gentle Rose Lewis, anticipated that medieval ritual with terror.

The novices filed into the room and lined up along the table in the middle. As they raised their eyes, none could suppress their surprise at seeing Mother Cecilia standing at the side. In response to their unguarded staring, the novice mistress informed them that it would indeed be a surprise to see Mother Cecilia assisting her in the vital task of moulding them into chaste, humble, and obedient nuns. There was a hint of enthusiasm in her voice when she seemed to suggest that all Mother's mental and written records about each of them would be at her disposal. With this short talk completed, they were told to bow their heads and pray. Several minutes later, the rustle of material and the slight sweep of footsteps signalled that someone had entered the community room.

'Please take your seats,' said Mother Jerome, standing at the top of the table with Mothers Fortunata and Cecilia on each side. Running her eye over each, she waited until the new novices settled. 'You have passed through the first stage of your journey in religious life. You may have thought the postulancy was difficult, and now the novitiate even more challenging. I will be blunt: if you think like that, you already show the signs of not having a genuine vocation.' She paused and directed her assistants to take their seats. She walked around the group seated at the table. Agnes could not help, against the spirit of the Rule, glancing at the novice mistress and her assistant. Surely Mother Prioress contradicted the novices' preconceptions and perhaps the views of her solemn-faced assistants.

'Amidst all the rules, instruction, and spiritual exercises,' the prioress said, 'you may have lost sight of the nature of religious life with the Sisters of the Suffering Saviour. Indeed, it's not hard for us sometimes to lose sight of the essentials in our busy lives. Therefore, we must regularly remind ourselves of some simple facts about our foundress, Eileen Foley.

'Eileen Foley wanted to join Our Lord and Saviour, Jesus Christ, in His suffering and death on the cross. But, at the same time, she wanted to follow Jesus' command and example: "Love one another as I have loved you" and "what you do for the least of my brethren, you do for me." She thus had a two-fold purpose in founding a community of religious sisters: first, to draw ever closer to Jesus in His suffering by renouncing the world and the self; second, to devote oneself in charity to the education and development of young women.

'To many in our changing society who regard religious life with increasing incredulity, it seems paradoxical that you are constantly exhorted in your religious formation to destroy the feeling-self on the one hand and to devote yourself in love to your students and their families, on the other. It seems paradoxical to insist that expressing personal feelings and friendships in the convent is to be avoided, while we urge you to be an example of charity to your secular surroundings. The paradox, I will always insist, is as superficial as the reply simple. We empty ourselves so that the love of God, love of our spiritual spouse, fills the void, enabling us to direct the love of the Son to our brothers and sisters, in and outside the convent.'

By this time, Mother Jerome had arrived at the head of the table with her two assistants on either side. She remained standing.

'I told you on the first full day of your postulancy that our order of religious sisters is not as strict and severe as others. My purpose was not to indicate that we are an easier option. No, it is to show the nature of our foundation. We are a teaching order. However devoted we must be to the Rule of the convent and our mission, we must keep in mind the social and cultural conditions of the people at whose service the Gospel places us. There have been many dramatic changes in society in recent years. While holding firmly to all that our Catholic life entails, we must understand social trends and motivations. Our arduous task is to strike a proper balance between the contemplative and disciplinary elements of our religious life and the duty of providing a solid Christian education to the girls in our many schools. My meaning here will become more evident over time.

'Finally, during your life as a religious sister, all manner of objections from members of our liberal democratic society will confront you, even from the parents of the girls in our schools. To demonstrate the saying that a little knowledge is a dangerous thing, a variety of self-appointed theologians, philosophers, and so-called social reformers will challenge you over your beliefs. When confronted with the specious reasoning of the poorly informed, you must remember that our Christian religion is a revealed religion. God revealed Himself to the first apostles in the form of Jesus Christ. They were the witnesses. Their witness has carried unshaken through the centuries to us here today. Never be tempted to regard our religion as reducible to a set of theoretical propositions, making up one or other watertight theory. It will mean the loss of faith. It will mean embarking on a dead-end journey of intellectual despair, a journey that, tragically, many academics are determined to take.

'That is not to say that reason has no place in understanding and explaining our faith. The pre-eminent discussion of the proper place of faith and reason resides in the writings of the greatest of the Church Fathers, St Augustine, whose Rule our convent has adopted. "Believe that you may understand, and understand that you may believe," wrote that great saint. You will study the proper relationship between faith and reason during your theological instruction. For the moment, I will finish by urging you to read St Augustine's *Confessions* during your time as novices.' She paused. 'I will now leave you to the charge of Mother Fortunata. Please kneel while we say a prayer.'

Mother Jerome's talk stayed fresh in Sister Agnes's mind. The talk was brief, but its implications extensive. Agnes wondered if Mother Jerome had perhaps departed from her usual address to novices. Her conversations with the prioress reinforced this impression. Developments in society at large, developments of significance for the governance of the order, seemed to preoccupy the prioress. Her warning about the nature of authority at the beginning of the postulancy also supported this notion. All this was clearly on her mind, motivating her private talks with the postulants and novices.

She noted Mother Fortunata's guarded glances at Mother Cecilia, who seemed to struggle to remain expressionless. After the prioress had left the room, a hasty exchange passed between them before they ordered the novices again to their knees. Was this the first sign Agnes had seen of an underlying conflict within the order's senior levels? She struggled to resist the temptation to reflect on such matters of political significance. In the end, she did not have much choice. The novice mistress's close supervision and the demands of the formation overwhelmed her.

Agnes knew she was in for it. She had been too outspoken, poking her nose into affairs of no concern for a lowly postulant. That was aside from the blazing conflict occasionally ignited in the smouldering antagonism between her and Margaret. But how could she help herself? She had been so used to expressing an opinion as a valued teacher. Her teaching colleagues had applauded her for speaking out on matters no one else had dared to mention. She had dealt with insolent young women like Margaret. Her fellow teachers had respected and admired her. Now she had to shut up. That was part of the game. She had another role in this game. She gritted her teeth and prepared for the worst. The worst came.

When her superiors shared the menial household duties, she found herself at the bottom of the pecking order. She seemed to spend her days sweeping, cleaning, and polishing. They inspected her work minutely for any spot she had missed or any grain of dust not picked up. If they found something amiss, they ordered her to do it all over again. The polished floor of the corridor became her biggest torment. It showed every speck of dirt, lint, and dust on its dark, shiny boards. To make matters worse, doors lined the corridor. One provided an exit to the outdoor recreation area. Each time someone went through a door, a malicious cloud of dust or a flurry of leaves were waiting to follow that person into the corridor. Rarely did Agnes complete a job, just once. If Mother Fortunata found nothing after a preliminary inspection, she would go in and out of doors until her motion had stirred up something. Agnes had to resist uncharitable thoughts about the pettiness of it all. But she did not have to resist too much.

She knew their purpose, and she was sober and practical enough to resign herself to the rules of the game, rules she knew she would inevitably transgress because of her deplorable weaknesses. Like in any game, she would pick herself up after falling and keep going, hoping for incremental improvements. The game, she could console herself, was limited in two ways. First, the discipline covered one part of each day; second, she had to play the game itself, at least the worst part, for six months. At the start of the next school year, she and the others would start their teaching programs. She held this before her mind. The surface pettiness of the novice mistress and her growling with the ample support of Mother Cecilia did not bruise her feelings too much. There was, however, a more important aspect to keeping her composure in most s ituations.

She kept in mind the primary motivation for choosing a religious life. That was simply her total surrender to Jesus as His spouse. On the other hand, the periods of prayer, study, and instruction made up for the iron discipline's pettiness. She could not believe her ears when Mother Jerome urged the novices to read the *Confessions*. Reading and rereading that book would make up for all those times when her feelings rebelled against her treatment. There was also access to papal writings. Mother Fortunata announced that the novices' restricted reading now included papal social writings from Leo XIII onwards. Was this for her benefit? It seemed a strange coincidence that the reading list catered to her interests. No, it could not be so, she told herself. She could not be that important to the plans of the order's superior general.

Agnes's propensity to meddle in her companions' affairs was another reason she settled into her religious formation. And, again, concern for Rose Lewis, now Sister Martha, motivated her meddling. Despite the severe reprimand that followed bringing Rose's dairy intolerance to the attention of the postulant mistress, it pleased her that she had prevented the imposition of such an unreasonable and harmful form of bodily mortification. After all, the idea of learning to subject the body to the will presupposed one's being able to control the body. With allergies and food intolerances, this could not be the case. It was obvious. Clearly, this was an example of discipline carried to the boundaries of charity, a danger to which Mother Jerome seemed to allude.

With that point won, Agnes was dismayed to see gentle, self-effacing Martha sick and vomiting in the third week of the novitiate. She could not believe Martha had been forced to eat the gooey cheese macaroni dish the cook insisted on serving up. There must be some mistake. Her observation of Martha struggling to stop gagging on her meal one evening confirmed her suspicions. What was Mother Cecilia doing? Why hadn't she spoken to the novice mistress about it? Agnes could not help herself.

'So, Sister Agnes, it did not take too long, did it?' said the novice mistress, looking Agnes up and down. 'You would think you had enough to do with your duties and managing yourself. Just what are you doing?'

'The stairs, Reverend Mother,' said Agnes, not disappointed with the reaction.

'Well, let's have a look, then.' At that point, Mother Cecilia joined her and looked on while the novice mistress examined the stairs. 'Dirt and dust everywhere. Just not good enough, Sister. What would be useful to distract Sister Agnes from meddling in the affairs of others, Mother?'

'Perhaps this would help Sister concentrate?' said Mother Cecilia, holding out a toothbrush.

'Now, make sure you clean the stairs until there is no speck to be seen,' said the novice mistress, pushing the toothbrush into Agnes's hands.

Agnes set about cleaning the stairs, hoping the message had got through as on the previous occasion. She did not mind bearing the discipline's stupidity if they spared Sister Martha the trial of eating that disgusting macaroni dish. A few minutes later, Mother Jerome descended the stairs. Agnes's eyes met the prioress for an instant as she hastily stepped aside and cast her eyes down. But there had been enough time to see Mother Jerome look at her and the toothbrush with a hint of a frown. Well, thought Agnes, if the silliness of cleaning the stairs with a toothbrush did not impress Mother Jerome, it would not please her that Martha had again been made to eat the macaroni dish. Her intervention proved ineffective. Sister Martha continued to force the cheese dish down her throat with the inevitable bout of vomiting.

'You should say something,' Agnes had to whisper to her one evening as Martha staggered back from standing over the garden.

'No, please ...,' whispered Martha, her face turning grey, 'no need ....'

'You will harm yourself—'

Martha silenced her with a finger to her lips.

This would be an occasion, Agnes resolved, when the weekly *mea culpa* would serve its purpose. She would confess to breaking the silence and give the reasons to make everyone aware, including the prioress, of Martha's unreasonable suffering. Her pleasure in her bold undertaking was short-lived. Sister Martha rose before her and knelt in their midst, facing Mothers Jerome, Fortunata, and Cecilia.

'Reverend Mothers, I humbly confess that I broke the silence on one occasion through being too weak to bear my penance discreetly. I fear my weakness has got one of my sisters into difficulties. I express my deep sorrow at this failure.'

Agnes looked open-mouthed at Martha and then glanced towards the front. She caught Mother Jerome's admonishing expression before she cast her eyes down. How stupid and embarrassing!

'Sister Agnes, we're waiting,' said Mother Jerome, rousing her from her mortified feelings.

Agnes looked up as Sister Martha resumed her place beside her. She got on her knees, stumbling.

'Reverend Mothers, I humbly confess breaking the rule of silence on five occasions and meddling in matters that are not my business.'

'The continuing appearance of the fault of pride, Sister Agnes, is a sign you have not yet willingly subjected yourself to the formation,' said Mother Jerome. 'You are to exert yourself in your efforts to overcome this fault. For your penance, you will serve your fellow novices at mealtimes for the next week. And you will eat whatever they have left on their plates.'

'Yes, Reverend Mother.'

The punishment did not upset Agnes. It was demeaning to scrape the food off the novices' plates, even though they pushed a portion to the side before eating. But it was unbelievably stupid of her not to realise Sister Martha had specially requested to carry out acts of self-mortification to draw closer to the ideal they all pursued. One evening, Martha made it all the worse by leaving most of the food on her plate while the others left none. She deserved to have her nose rubbed in it. At the end of dinner, on the final evening of her penance, Mother Jerome called her to kneel in front of her team of executives.

'Jesus submitted willingly to the most intense suffering, conforming His will perfectly to that of the Father,' said the prioress. 'In our pathetic little way, we sisters try to join our suffering to Our Lord's. We try to submit our will to the will of the Father. In our fallen nature, we rebel against that submission. The world, emphasising individual rights, looks at our Rule with incomprehension and contempt. We cannot help suffering under that contempt. So, when one of the least of us willingly makes a special effort for Our Lord, we are all edified, aren't we?'

'Yes, Reverend Mother.'

'We should be. See that you benefit from the example when you are privileged to witness it.'

'Yes, Reverend Mother.'

'You are dismissed.'

'Thank you, Reverend Mother.'

Not only did the discipline and punishment bring Agnes into line. Balanced with her pleasurable times of study and reading, she could bear it. Perhaps the realisation that she was not perfect and never would be helped her bear the novice mistress's cruel and often ludicrous reprimands. No, it was Rose, Sister Martha, who made her see she had enough on her plate with her imperfections and selfishness without attending to the faults of others. It was Martha who made her truly understand the purpose of what, on the surface, was cruel and ludicrous. Here was this lowly sales assistant with moderate education and a nondescript appearance, with nothing but a career of menial tasks ahead of her, exemplifying self-effacing humility and holiness. And she did it all with an imperturbable sweetness and serenity.

The example was enough. Agnes could not have suffered a more effective reprimand. She would now take on the yoke and leave the business of correction and formation to the proper authorities. It did not surprise her to see dairy foods disappear from Sister Martha's diet shortly after. The prioress, always prudent, would not allow Sister Martha to harm herself. Neither was she surprised that Martha did not indulge in that sort of self-mortification again. She would be far more discreet in the future. Confident she had learned her lesson, Agnes resolved to shut her eyes and ears to the action around her. In this, she had partial success.

She had been apprehensive that Margaret and Elizabeth, now Sisters Catherine and Hildegard, would carry their tormenting over to the novitiate. It relieved her that the daily routine occupied them too much to continue their needling, and it looked like remaining so. Even during the refectory penance, Margaret refrained from giving the usual signs of her insolence. Indeed, Sister Catherine seemed to have the same determination to survive the novitiate. Only occasionally did Agnes catch her breaking the rule of silence to offer advice or consolation to the novices aligned with her.

Agnes could ignore most of these occasions. One might expect the younger women to have a difficult time initially. Some whispered consolation was not out of place. If Mother Fortunata were like herself as a teacher, she would prudently permit leeway in the rules. As it turned out, Catherine got away with most of her quick whispers of encouragement, whether by good judgment or Mother Fortunata's ignoring it. One occasion, however, evaded the novice's supervision but threatened to provoke Agnes's intervention. All the young women had their turn of tears except Catherine, which impressed Agnes but did not surprise her. One evening during study, when Mother Fortunata had left the novices alone, Agnes heard Catherine trying to soothe the wounded feelings of Benedicta, formerly Kate Armstrong, who was blubbering over her book.

'I know how you feel,' whispered Catherine. 'It's not right.'

'She's so mean,' said Benedicta, whimpering. 'How can she be so mean? What did I do? I try so hard.'

'I know. You try very hard.'

Silence followed for a minute. Agnes struggled to keep her attention on her book. But the expectation of more whispering kept her ears attuned.

'I feel like giving up,' said Benedicta, sniffling.

'No, you can't,' whispered Catherine. 'You can't give in. You mustn't. What would I do if you left?'

Agnes did not understand Benedicta's reply, but her tone signalled the welcome reception of Catherine's sympathy. When the novice mistress returned, silence again fell on the group without Benedicta's blubbering and sniffling. This was not the right consolation, Agnes thought. In the end, it would build up resentment. Margaret's views about authority and unfair subordination had resurfaced. Agnes nearly bit through her lip to stop herself from saying to Benedicta that she should not regard the novice mistress as the enemy, that Mother Fortunata had a job to do, no matter how hard it sometimes seemed. After all, she resided in a convent, pursuing the life of a religious, not in any old job in the outside world. In the end, Agnes's witness to a short exchange between Martha and Benedicta relieved her of the struggle.

'You must be pleased you don't have to eat the cheese anymore,' said Benedicta the following evening. 'That was so—'

'Mother Fortunata changed my diet,' said Martha, putting a finger to her lips. 'I chose to eat the same meals as everyone else.'

'Oh?'

'Mother Fortunata said we should be prudent in our efforts of self-denial. She has our best interests at heart. I was thoughtless.'

'Did ... does she?' said Benedicta.

Agnes was thankful that she had not followed the course of action she was itching to take. In her simple way, Martha had quashed the rising resentment, at least for now. This was as it should be. Henceforth, she, Agnes, would sew her lips shut if that's what it took to stop her interference. Despite being sorely tempted to counter Margaret's influence over the others in the following months, she succeeded. One other serious hurdle, however, arose for her to overcome, and it struck her without warning in a devastating way.

One evening in study, she was poring over *Libertas*, Pope Leo XIII's famous encyclical on freedom. This papal Letter outlined a concept of freedom fundamentally different from the idea that seemed to have the secular world in its thrall. The essential proposition of Leo's idea was that true freedom implied a duty. Yet, as simple as it sounded, Agnes found she had never wholly grasped the arguments. She now read it for the second time, trying to digest every step of the reasoning. She paused now and then in her reading to reflect, just as she had done the first time she had read it on Philip's recommendation. It was vital, he said, that as a teacher, she should become acquainted with Leo's ideas amid all the talk about personal freedom.

They had discussed this important Letter once on a balmy summer night on Sorrento's bayside beach. The occasion was a Christmas party Philip had organised for his political and academic friends at his beachside cottage. They had wandered away from the party at around eleven o'clock to enjoy the slight uneven hush of the summer breeze on the deserted beach. After walking along the water's edge, they sat in the cooling sand. She remembered flicking off her sandals and digging her toes into the sand while Philip put his arms around her, cradling her against his chest. He had that particular way of holding her—she glanced around at her fellow novices, her face burning. She took a quick breath—it felt like a gasp—and tried to concentrate on the text before her. Did anybody notice her discomfort? She cast a look up the table at the novice mistress with her breviary before her. No, no, her thoughts were elsewhere. Margaret was trying to get Benedicta's attention. She fixed her eyes on the text

.

Every sentence brought back that night on the beach in stark images. It brought back the conversation, every word of it, it seemed. She tried to turn it away, but she could not. She was trapped in the study, with everybody waiting for her to lose her composure. At the end of Philip's explanation, they fell silent. He turned her in his arms, her bare knees pressing into the sand while their lips came softly together. Sometime later, she got up and walked to the water's edge. He watched her for a while, leaning on an elbow. The background lights of the street and distant shops twinkled around his face. Then he joined her. She pushed him away half-heartedly. The sound of a small motorboat further along the bay reached them ... the gentle wash of the water at their feet. He led her back to where they had been sitting. She put her hand to her mouth to stop— Shortly after, Philip had proposed, and she had accepted, her joy scarcely containable. Around a year later, she broke the engagement. The incomprehension, followed by the angry expression, the rush from the house— Tears filled her eyes. Her hand hid tightening lips. No, she would not give in. The thought of breaking down in front of Margaret was—

The relief of being alone in her room was short. The full force of her feelings came on her. She cried into the dark, lonely night, wondering what she was doing, all dressed up in those weird clothes. The following two nights repeated the struggle. The crying and her longing, burning body were a losing battle. At all moments, she feared being overcome, and, ripping off her restricting garments, she would race to break free. The image of her sitting and peering through the taxi window at the retreating Gothic tower kept coming to mind. Amid this overwhelming torment, she became aware of being under the novice mistress's observation. The novice mistress moderated her picking. Then Mother Jerome appeared in the novices' quarters, walking by her several times, giving her a brief look as she went about her household tasks. Agnes did not care what they thought. It was all she could do to keep her rebellious feelings under control. Finally, on the evening of the third day, the prioress appeared unannounced in the community room. She signalled for the novices to remain seated.

'We must never lose sight of why we have devoted ourselves totally to Our Lord in the religious life,' she said. 'We have withdrawn from the world. In many ways, it is a hard sacrifice. In other ways, it is a sublime joy. Remember Saint Paul's account of his suffering? He suffered all manner of hardships—beatings, whippings, shipwreck—to serve the Lord. Remember, too, the sting to the flesh the Lord gave him, a sting he thought he could not bear. He did bear it, with God's grace and assurance.' She paused, looking around at the novices. 'During times when we find the way intolerably hard, let us not forget Saint Paul's dedication. Now let's all kneel for the evening rosary, meditating on Jesus's way of the cross.'

It was not a very dramatic intervention, but it was enough to bring Agnes back from the brink. Her heated feelings cooled, and the primary motivations for her life's choice returned stronger than before. But were they strong enough to resist and control her feelings for Philip, the only obstacle that seemed in the way of her choice, an obstacle she had thought she had passed over? She did not know. For the moment, she could go on. She wondered whether Mother Jerome had intervened for her sake. No, some of the others probably experienced similar difficulties.

With that crisis behind her, she found it less and less challenging to ignore Catherine's shenanigans. She only noted that Sister Benedicta had been brought into Catherine's inner cabinet, so to speak, with Sister Hildegard. Two others who had come under Margaret's influence from the beginning—Laura Mulligan, now Sister Julian, and Nora Calwell, now Sister Agatha—looked like an outer cabinet. Agnes resolved not to make too much of that political formation. With her new determination, the months passed quickly. In January 1959, she found herself struggling with a different feeling; she had to contain her enthusiasm because all the novices, except Sister Martha, were preparing for teacher training. To be back in class again would be no burden. Her pleasure increased when she learned her assignment after completing the novitiate would be at a country school for young ladies.

Chapter 15

Aine visits Agnes

IT WAS December 1958. Outside the chapel on the upper level over-looking the parapets and river bathed in the summer sun, groups of family and friends waited for the newly professed sisters to emerge from the chapel. There were politely contained cheers and clapping as the sisters appeared. The people pressed around, congratulating them. Sister Agnes patiently received hugs, kisses, and handshakes from grandparents, parents, uncles, and aunts. When, at last, the excitement subsided and the groups retreated to the chairs and tables set up for morning tea, she looked around. During the next half-hour, between the rapid-fire questions, cakes, biscuits, and sips of tea, she continued to look towards the archway of the main building. Then, at last, a tall, handsome man of a dark complexion, carrying a baby in one arm and holding the hand of a beautiful, fair-haired woman, emerged from the archway. They stopped and looked around. A brief silence came on the gathering as the handsome couple with the baby caught the attention of those nearest th em.

'One moment, Mum, please,' said Sister Agnes to her mother. She walked as quickly as her sisterly dignity would allow. 'Aine, I am so pleased to see you,' she said, embarrassed that she showed more emotion than was proper for a nun. 'You did get my message, then?'

'Yes, Virginia, as you see, we made it. Congratulations! I knew you would succeed. We have been praying for you as we agreed.'

'Thank you, Aine. I had not forgotten. I'm now Sister Agnes,' she said, permitting herself an expression of ironic pride.

'Sister Agnes,' said Aine, 'this is my husband, Charles, and my baby daughter, Estella.'

'I'm pleased to meet you, Sister Agnes,' said Charles.

'I'm pleased to meet you, too, Mr Winterbine.' She looked at the baby now in Aine's arms and ran her hand softly over her head. 'What a beautiful baby. Aine, you must have met your husband shortly after you left us.'

'The day after,' said Aine, a slight blush colouring her unblemished white cheeks. 'We married in December, a year ago.'

'Providence brought us together,' said Charles.

'I want to hear all about it,' Agnes said, giving Charles an inquiring look. 'But first, come and meet my family.'

Agnes's family was curious about the young couple and insisted they exchange their news. There was not much to tell, Aine said. She had met Charles unexpectedly at the house of dear friends of the family, the day after she left the convent. They fell in love and married. There were some questions about where they would live, but in the end, she and Charles chose the country town of Binawarra, where they had met. Binawarra had a cherished meaning for them. Then they were blessed with the arrival of their first child.

'It's strange you ended up in country Victoria,' said Agnes.

'I'm very happy,' said Aine, answering the unspoken question in Agnes's eyes. 'There has been no repetition—' She flushed and glanced at the attentive faces around her.

'Glad to hear,' said Agnes. 'God obviously had his own plans for you.'

'It could not be otherwise,' said Charles.

'Yes …,' said Agnes, giving Charles another curious look.

The conversation became more general while Agnes continued to respond to family questions, mainly about the course of training during the novitiate. She patiently described the work, the study of theological and philosophical subjects, and the teacher training she and the others were undergoing at the nearby girls' school.

'But you hardly needed any teacher training,' said Greg, her younger brother and the only one of her three brothers present for the occasion. 'You had already been through that. So, what was the point?'

'There's always something I can learn about teaching. There is the discipline of the profession, for one thing. Besides, it gave me extra time to study. As a result, I'm a far better and far more knowledgeable teacher now.'

'No doubt, a headship in the future—?' said her father.

'Please, Dad,' she smiled, 'let me first take charge of my class.'

'May I interrupt a moment?' said a familiar voice, breaking in on the conversation.

They turned to see Margaret facing them. Agnes did not miss Aine's involuntary reaction to the imposing form of Margaret in her black habit.

'Of course, Sister,' said Agnes. 'May I introduce Sister Catherine, who has also been professed today?'

'I am pleased to meet you all,' said Sister Catherine. 'I'm sorry to interrupt. I just wanted to say hello to Aine while I had the chance.' She turned to Aine. 'Congratulations on your marriage and baby. We are all very pleased to see how well you have fallen on your feet. Of course, our prayers have been with you.'

'Thank you, Sister Catherine,' said Aine. She introduced Charles and her baby.

'Pleased to meet you, Mr Winterbine,' Catherine said without looking at the sleeping baby.

A brief, polite exchange followed, during which Catherine made the expected inquiries. She listened with an unruffled interest while Aine explained where they lived and that Charles had set up a small building business. As for herself, she was more than happy to be a wife and mother.

'A wife and mother is a worthy vocation,' replied Catherine. 'You are intelligent enough to do more.'

'Thank you. Mother Jerome thought the role of wife and mother would suit me best.'

'Did she?' continued Catherine, without changing her calm expression. 'Mother Jerome is a very wise woman. Her counsel has been beneficial to all of us.'

With that, Sister Catherine wished Aine and Charles all the best, apologised again for the intrusion, and left to join her family group. Agnes curiously noted that Catherine's large family group was staring at Aine.

'She's changed,' said Aine, unaware of the attention. 'She is almost frightening in her habit.'

'Yes, it accentuates her size. She has matured, like us all. Of course, the novitiate formation is designed to mould one to the life of a religious.' Agnes hesitated. 'There can be a change of outward behaviour without necessarily meaning a change from within.' She stopped. 'There, you see, I've not changed if others have. I still must say what's on my mind.'

'What's wrong with that?' said her brother, who had been listening. Like everyone else, he had fixed his attention on his sister's friend. 'I get the impression you're under unwarranted restriction,' he added, with a glance at Aine.

'We're not university students, Greg, toying with the latest views about freedom,' said Agnes. 'We freely live the life of a religious. That means willingly accepting its conditions. If we don't want to accept them, the door is open for us to leave. It is a secular myth that we're somehow held against our will. Immaturity will hold a person prisoner in most circumstances.'

'Well, son,' exclaimed Agnes's father, pointing, 'that's giving it to you. All that blather you boys go on with about freedom—'

'Oh, I hope I didn't sound like I was lecturing,' said Agnes, looking around.

'You did, big sister. It was a nice speech. But I won't provoke you anymore.'

'Student debates are just an excuse to guzzle a whole lot of beer and smoke one's head off,' her father continued.

'Come on, Dad, don't sound—'

'Now, you two, no squabbling today,' said Agnes's mother. 'It's Virginia's day.'

'I didn't mean to set that off,' said Agnes.

'That's all right, Virginia dear,' said her mother, holding father and son in an admonishing gaze. 'It's not your fault.'

The attention returned to what lay ahead for Sister Agnes. Her next assignment, she said, was at St Joseph's Ballarat, which she was eagerly looking forward to. And so, the conversation proceeded until Aine asked to be excused to feed her baby.

'Where are you going to feed her?' said Agnes.

'Charles and I will return to the car.'

'You'll do no such thing. Come on. I'll take you to the visitor's parlour. You can remain here, Mr Winterbine, and enjoy a rest and a cup of tea.'

There was no arguing with Agnes. She picked up the baby bag and beckoned Aine.

'Do you know what Margaret is going to do?' Aine asked as they made their way to the main building.

'Sister Catherine—I have to call her Sister Catherine—will remain at the nearby girls' school, undergoing more teacher training. Actually, she's done very well, a lot better than I thought. The girls seem to like her, and she seems to like them.'

'She did say she would get on with her students, didn't she?'

'She did, indeed. All that's nearly two years ago now.'

'Yes, she was going to be friends with her students, she said, or something like that.'

'Yes, I remember ... we clashed badly then, didn't we?'

'Have there been problems ... did anything happen after I left?'

'There was a little more trouble, but Mother Jerome took us firmly in hand. And then we were so busy. I mean, the demands on our time were so great that we stopped paying as much attention to each other. We just didn't have the time.'

By now, they were in the visitor's parlour. Aine looked around uneasily as she organised herself. Agnes watched on without speaking. When the baby was settled and feeding, she caressed its head and rubbed Aine's shoulder. Aine looked up and smiled.

'You look wonderful,' said Agnes. 'Married life clearly agrees with you.'

'I have a wonderful husband. He couldn't be better. I often wonder about my good fortune and the way it happened. It was as if I left here with a fixed plan to go and get married.'

'You left here without any thought of marriage, didn't you?'

'Mother Jerome saw what I was blind to. It's incredible. She's incredible. I haven't seen her today. Where is she?'

'She's not well. She's suddenly not as robust as she used to be. Nobody is sure what the problem is. She has expressed a wish to hand over the reins to someone else, but nobody else seems suitable.'

'I'm sorry to hear that.'

'Have there been any recurrences of your experiences, you know, the whispers ...?' said Agnes, after a moment's hesitation.

'No.'

'None at all?'

'Well, only on the day after I left. There was this sort of darkness ... and I fainted in my aunt's garden. The doctor came and said I was suffering from hysteria. It was so embarrassing. Nothing since. The turmoil of having to leave the convent and then meeting Charles. It was so overwhelming. Perhaps he was right.'

'Hysteria! I must tell you I saw the dark figures down by the river exactly as you described it.'

'Did you? You see. I didn't imagine it.'

Agnes gave a short account of what she had done and seen.

'Heavens, that's audacious. Weren't you scared?'

'Terrified.'

'And what happened afterwards?'

'Nothing. I stayed up several nights over the following weeks, but heard and saw nothing. For a while, I thought I had scared the people off or made them more cautious. Then, strangely, I started feeling like I imagined it.'

'I know how you felt. So did I.'

'In any case, nothing strange has happened since. I was on the lookout for a while, but then I became so preoccupied. Margaret, I mean Sister Catherine, began to behave differently—I don't know—but now that I'm talking about it again, I remember feeling that something was infecting the convent, a spiritual infection.'

'Yes, I felt that, too.'

'I know.'

There was silence between them as they looked at the feeding baby.

'I must get back now, Aine darling. I'm so glad you came. Please keep in contact. And you can call me Virginia,' she added in a whisper.

'Yes, yes, I want that, too. There's still a bit of me here with you.'

'That's a nice thing to say.' Agnes's eyes filled.

Aine released a hand from the baby and took hold of Agnes's. 'I will leave my address and phone number with your mother. We're not far from Ballarat.'

Not long after Agnes returned to her family, she saw Catherine striding toward the main building with Jannie in tow. What a contrast they made, solid Margaret in her voluminous black habit and tall, slim Jannie now dressed to display her full beauty. Gone was the pretty, immature girl of the postulancy. It would be no surprise to learn Jannie was modelling for one of the great department stores. Strange that Jannie had not yet approached her. Why would she be avoiding her? After half an hour, she noticed them returning to Catherine's family group, where a casually dressed man of around thirty took Jannie's hand. She did not dwell on it. It was time to fetch Aine.

LEFT alone, Aine contemplated her conversation with Virginia. She had scarcely changed. She was more mature and subdued in her manner, but it was the same warm, generous heart. Her mind turned to her meeting with Jannie and Margaret in that same parlour. She looked around, detecting no change. She was sitting in the lounge chair Jannie had occupied. The memory of Jannie taking her hair and holding her on her knees came back to her. There was a gentle knock on the door, and the door opened to reveal Sister Catherine.

'Do you mind if we come in for a moment?' she asked, entering. 'I've got someone to see you.'

Jannie de Kam followed Sister Catherine into the parlour.

'Aine, I'm so glad to see you,' she exclaimed, coming to her. 'I often wondered what happened to you.' She was all smiles and exuberance as she squeezed Aine's arm and patted her on the shoulder. 'What a beautiful baby. But then she's got beautiful parents. I've just seen your handsome husband. Who would have thought?'

'Yes, I know,' said Aine, trying to raise a smile. 'I had no idea what lay ahead when I left the convent. But I'm happy, very happy. Charles is a wonderful husband, and my baby is healthy.'

Jannie was dressed fashionably in a bright floral dress set off against expensive white gloves and white high-heeled shoes. Her slim figure and her full breasts were accentuated. She had let her styled, honey-blond hair grow long. Make-up discreetly enhanced her handsome, regular face with its bright blue eyes. She looked such a contrast next to the large black-clad, heavy-jawed Margaret, who looked older than her twenty years despite smooth, rosy cheeks. Margaret's assured expression with

Jannie's almost frivolous manner was a more striking contrast as Jannie flapped her hands and wriggled while speaking.

'I knew you wouldn't stay single for very long. The miracle is that you were unattached—and unsullied—until then. What a virginal prize your husband won. Then again, he's just as big a prize. Non-virginal, I suspect.'

'I didn't see it like that,' said Aine, noticing that Margaret's composure remained unchanged. 'It just happened the way it did. Charles says Providence brought us together at that point. He's right.'

'Really?' said Jannie, taking no pains to suppress a smile. 'Where do you think Providence is taking you now?'

'I'm happy to be a wife and mother.'

'Marg had always said you were capable of much more. Surely, you'll do something else when your child gets older.' She bent down to have a closer look at Estella. 'If she remains that gorgeous, you'll have your work cut out.' She stood up straight. 'If I were you, I would take myself along to a professional photographer. I know how it works.'

'I'm happy the way things are,' said Aine, shifting a little in her seat. She glanced at Sister Catherine, finding it strange that she said nothing and seemed content to let Jannie do the talking.

'Where are you living?' said Jannie, shifting her attention from the baby.

'In Binawarra.'

'Where on earth is that?'

'Northwest of Bendigo, about an hour.'

'Oh, I might drag one of my men friends up there to have a look at you. He's a fashion photographer, one of the best. He has taken charge of my modelling career.'

'It's not necessary. What have you been doing, besides modelling?'

'Not much until I was discovered,' said Jannie, unable to hide some uneasiness. 'I've been doing modelling—catwalk and photoshoots, things like that. I'll follow Marg's advice and enrol in social work at university next year,' she added vaguely. I owe a lot to Margie's advice and friendship.'

Sister Catherine nodded in acknowledgment.

'Oh, have you visited often?'

'Err, no, I haven't,' said Jannie, glancing at Catherine, 'or only once or twice.'

'She came with my family several times,' said Catherine. 'Well, now, we should leave Aine to finish feeding her baby.'

'Yes, of course,' said Jannie, with the same willingness she had always shown Margaret. 'We'll see you later.'

The very fashionable and attractive Jannie followed Sister Catherine out of the room. What a change, Aine thought. She did look like a fashion model, which did not seem to go with university studies. It was even less a reason to maintain a close friendship with Catherine. These thoughts were occupying her when the door opened again, and Sister Catherine glided in, this time without knocking.

'I've just popped back to say a few things in private to you,' she said, holding up her hand to calm Aine. 'You would, of course, find Jannie changed.'

'Yes, I did, a little.'

'You were wondering why I did not comment on the things that seemed to be preoccupying her?'

'Well, yes.'

'Jannie is still finding herself. I mean her spiritual self. That can take time.' She looked steadily at Aine. 'But you, how are you developing spiritually?'

'I'm still the same with the same devotions. That won't ever change. Charles has strengthened my faith. We strengthen each other.' She turned her attention to Estella, who had finished feeding.

'You told Jannie you were happy being a wife and mother. That is commendable. But don't you think you could do more with your talents?' She paused but went on before Aine could respond. 'Remember Jesus' parable of the talents, or more specifically, about the wasted talents? He was very hard on the man who buried his talents out of fear of losing them, rather than working to increase their worth. Even those who have little will have that taken from them, he said. Remember? Paul spoke about the different gifts of the spirit and how we should use those gifts.'

'What talents do you think I have?' said Aine, irritated by the implicit rebuke.

'Your appearance has a communicative value. You have a personality that attracts attention. You convey your views clearly and compellingly. These are significant assets in communicating the right message.'

'What do you mean? What message?'

'I don't want to tell you what to say. Indeed, nobody can. You must come to a certain stage of enlightenment. Then you will know what to say and how to use your talents to say it.'

'I still don't know what you mean. And being a wife and mother is a worthy role in its own right. Mother Jerome encouraged me to pursue that role.'

'She did?'

'She warned me about placing too much value on my appearance.'

'I would, too. That's not what I mean. Talents are to be utilised to achieve goals, not to satisfy one's vanity. That's Jannie's mistake at the moment. But she will reach a stage of enlightenment under the right guidance.'

'You think I am mistaken, too?'

'I want you to consider what I have said. As always, I only have your best interests at heart. I will leave it at that. You must attend to your baby. I hope we will see you again in the future. As professed sisters, we are now more approachable. Our prayers will be with you.' With a thin smile breaking the seriousness of her conversation, she left the room, leaving Aine again staring after her.

Aine remained that way for some moments before collecting her things and getting ready to go. Once again, she found herself struggling to understand. Then she thought she heard a sound in the distance. She froze with her baby in her arms. The baby bag fell to the floor beside the lounge chair. She looked around the parlour with its old, dark, wooden furniture and subdued colours. Slowly, in the distance, it seemed, some force, some indescribable force, was gathering. The Huckerby garden two years ago. She began to panic. Her knees buckled as the darkness came nearer. She eased herself onto the lounge chair, clutching Estella close to her. Her eyes shut. The next moment, she heard Virginia's voice.

SISTER Agnes arrived in the parlour to find Aine slumped in the lounge chair with her eyes closed and holding on to Estella.

'What is it?' she said, taking her in her arms and holding her gently. At length, Aine opened her eyes and let out a sigh.

'Here, let me hold Estella while you compose yourself,' said Agnes. 'Have you got a handkerchief?'

Aine nodded, handing her baby to Agnes. She wiped her eyes and cheeks and then took back her baby. 'It's come back. I thought it had gone.'

'What?'

'I was collecting my things when I heard a sound in the distance and a sort of whispering with it. Then this darkness came at me, just like when I collapsed in front of Charles.'

'Maybe it's the day's excitement,' Agnes ventured, not very convincingly.

'Maybe because I am here again. There is something about this place. I don't know what it is. I can't help thinking ... I don't know ... I don't want to say anything bad.'

'Something's happened to bring it back, hasn't it? Tell me.'

Aine hesitated. 'Margaret and Jannie came while I was feeding Estella.'

'So that's where they went.'

'It was the same sort of thing Margaret has always said. I must be more than a mother and a housewife. I must develop my talents, but she was vague about what my talents were. She said something about using them to convey the right sort of message, whatever she means by that. It is still the same oppressive way of talking. There was no change there.'

'Whatever is that woman about, excuse me?' said Virginia. 'It's like we have been transported back two years.'

'I don't understand why she is so bothered by what I do. What's it to her? Is she like that with others?'

'She has always had that forceful, determined temperament. Her influence on others has been disproportionate. Sister Hildegard—Elizabeth Parker—is still well and truly under her influence. There are others, too. I don't know whether she has a particular interest in you now. Two years ago, I was sure she wanted to extract you from my influence.'

'It's like there has been no gap in time, despite her different appearance and manner. It's always like there's a distinct purpose behind what she says to me.'

'No doubt, you're right,' said Virginia. 'Margaret has always had a burning purpose. I still have no precise idea exactly what it is or what it has to do with you. She seems so young to be so purposeful about anything other than being holy and obedient, as all good nuns should be. I should stop. I'm going to say uncharitable things.'

'I must go back to Charles,' said Aine. 'He will be wondering where I am.'

Agnes helped her to her feet and brushed her cheeks with her handkerchief.

'There,' she said, 'you look like nothing has happened. Keep up a smile when you are outside.'

'Thank you. I appreciate that.'

As they walked to Sister Agnes's family, they noticed Jannie and Sisters Catherine and Hildegard, who were with Catherine's family group, looking at them. Catherine drew the attention of an older man to them. The casually dressed man, around thirty, still held Jannie's hand and looked bored. He blew puffs of cigarette smoke while he lazily looked around him.

'I don't understand the connection between Jannie, Margaret, and Elizabeth,' said Aine. 'That man holding Jannie's hand seems to be the last sort of man Margaret could tolerate.'

'Should he make a difference?' said Agnes. 'He's probably just accompanying Jannie today.'

'I don't suppose he should, but I can't help—Margaret said Jannie has visited several times.'

'I haven't seen her since she left us.'

'Are you sure?' said Aine. 'I mean, you may have missed her. She came several times with Margaret's family, she said.'

'Perhaps. But it would have been strange if I had not seen her at least once.'

'That's odd.'

'Very odd, if you're right. Your visit has raised all those questions again.'

But those questions receded to the back of Agnes's mind. After farewelling her family and Aine, she turned all her attention to her assignment at St Joseph's and teaching a class of lively young ladies. In January 1959, as the car passed John Batman University on the way through the city to Ballarat, Agnes's thoughts turned to Philip. What was he doing? And who was he doing it with? Had he ever a thought for her?

Chapter 16

Philip and Diana

THE SECOND year—it was 1960—of Dr Stevenson's and Dr Edelman's cooperation still ran without problems. There was one change for Philip, though. While Joe was happy wandering from one dalliance to another, Philip became weary of the shallowness of his short-term relationships. No matter the girl's attractiveness, he missed sensible, thought-provoking female conversation. Sometimes Virginia's voice sounded behind his dissatisfaction, something that irked him. That insistent voice prompted him to wonder how she was doing. She was assigned to a country girls' school, where she was likely changing the school's entire routine. But he dismissed such mean, sarcastic thoughts. He could not criticise Virginia's ability and commitment to her duties. That would diminish him.

The best way to deal with Virginia was to force her out of his mind when she encroached on his wantonness. Instead, he would concentrate on his academic and political interests. This way, the year passed without Virginia's ghost disrupting his life too much. As they prepared for a new academic year, though, he was painfully aware that close, intelligent female company was still missing. He longed to hold beauty and intelligence together, not just a beautiful face and body. Several weeks into

1961, Phil and Joe received an invitation to one of Harry's and Erik's high-bohemian receptions at their tastefully renovated terrace house in Parkville. It was the usual elegant crowd pretending to rough it, but with one exception, at least for Philip. Harry introduced Philip and Joe to Diana Cartwright, who occupied a studio apartment in Carlton. She had recently returned from a stay overseas.

'She's an artist,' added Harry, who gave the impression he had said enough. He left Diana to entertain the boys.

'What sort of an artist?' said Joe.

'Abstract expressionist,' said Diana. 'I hear a New York accent. I've just spent a year in New York's Greenwich Village with a group of artists. So, I am familiar with New York boys.'

'Should I fear unwanted revelations?'

'I won't tell on you. Don't worry.'

Philip was immediately attracted to the bright, intelligent eyes. Diana was around thirty, older, and more mature than most of Harry's girl-friends.

'Do you like what you see?' said Diana, raising an eyebrow.

'I'm sorry. Was I staring?' said Philip, embarrassed.

'You were having a thoughtful look.'

'I'm interested—to answer your question.'

'So am I. Sorry, Joe, I've experienced enough New York boys.'

'Who said I'm interested?

'Now, Philip, tell me all about yourself.'

'It will be a short story,' said Joe, laughing.

'You go and amuse yourself with one of Harry's models,' said Diana, 'while Phil and I talk about deep and meaningful things.'

That was the start of a relationship into which they both eased. Diana was libertarian, but her libertarianism was of the soft, tolerant sort, not of the proselytising loudmouths in the imitation-bohemian haunts of Melbourne. Her passionate interest in all things artistic dulled whatever activist spirit she possessed. Whether it was theatre, dance, music, sculpture, or painting, it filled her conversation. She took a compliant Philip with her to all sorts of music, dance, and theatre performances, after which they indulged in long, languorous discussions over a drink. He did not find it at all boring. Diana gave him engaging lessons in art forms, a change from his immersion in philosophical disputation. He spent hours at her studio apartment watching her paint, often in long silences, only interrupted by her smile now and then. It was so relaxing and free of tension. Some weeks later, as proof of her feelings, she took him home to show her parents. This was a revelation as much about Diana as about her parents. They lived in a restored Victorian mansion in Toorak, Melbourne's smartest and most expensive suburb.

'Gosh,' said Philip, as they approached the front door after alighting from Diana's British racing green MGA on the neatly raked circular gravel driveway. 'You haven't said anything about this.' He stopped and looked around at the manicured lawns and the rock gardens overflowing with plants of many varieties. A fountain spouting and dribbling water over an iron sculpture featured in the middle of the circular lawn.

'Why should I? It's my parents' house, not mine.'

'I think you're being disingenuous.'

'Don't be complicated, Phil darling.'

'Perhaps your studio apartment is subsidised?'

She gave him a self-conscious smile. 'Not entirely. I do sell my paintings, you know.'

Her father was a Queen's Counsel specialising in commercial law. Some of the state's most prominent companies were among his clients. Her mother seemed a business adviser, though he was unsure what sort. They received him warmly, both parents showing a keen interest in him and his academic work during pre-dinner drinks. After drinks, while waiting for dinner, Diana took him on a tour of the mansion, revealing a tasteful, faithfully restored Victorian opulence everywhere. Her prize feature was her well-appointed, beautifully furnished quarters comprising a bedroom, sitting room, and an ensuite bathroom. The colour combination was soft pastel greens and blues. No pink to be seen anywhere. Paintings of hers—unmistakably hers—hung discreetly around the walls.

'You still have a room here?'

'Yes, Mother and Father insisted. They want me to treat this house as my home until I settle downget married. And I do. It's a peaceful retreat. My studio apartment is just a convenience.'

'You're a daddy's girl,' said Philip before he could censor his thoughts. He smiled to dispel any appearance of criticism.

For the first time since they had met, Diana blushed. 'I suppose I am. I'm their only daughter. I have three brothers, all older. My father does support my artistic ambitions, I must admit. He encourages me. But I am careful not to abuse his generosity. As I say, I do sell my paintings. It's not all take.'

'I'm making no judgment.'

'I know, darling,' she said, taking his hand and acknowledging his waggish expression. She quietly closed the door to her room. 'I would appreciate it if you did not talk about my parents' affairs in front of Harry's friends.'

'You don't have to ask, Diana.'

'Don't I? It's as much for them as for me. Some of Harry's friends, not Harry, are political activists. I don't care what the hypocrites say about me, but I do about my parents.'

'I understand—I mean it.'

She hugged and kissed him. 'Come on. Dinner will be served shortly.'

The dinner, served by a maid hurrying in and out of a kitchen in a distant part of the house, passed with the same relaxed affability with which Philip had been greeted. His academic position remained the focus of the conversation without intrusiveness. After hearing Philip's special interest in the natural law philosophers, Mr Cartwright embarked on a discussion about common law and its philosophical foundations until Mrs Cartwright discreetly steered the conversation back to more mundane topics. When Philip and Diana left after a convivial evening— something Philip enjoyed immensely—both parents said how delighted they were to meet him, assuring him of a warm welcome should Diana bring him on another visit.

'Did I pass muster?' he said as they drove through the wrought-iron gates.

'You know you did.'

'I'm glad. Your parents are impressive people.'

'You should be happy. Dad is particular about who his daughter mixes with. He has ways of finding out about people who do not impress him.'

'That admission would put potential friends off, wouldn't it?'

She laughed. 'I usually don't admit it, of course. I tell you because you are, as I expected, considered an impeccable connection—in character, not only in standing.'

'An impeccable connection? I'm way out of their league. Yours, too.'

She laughed again.

'I think we can say we're going steady, don't you?' said Diana one Sunday afternoon several weeks later while Phil watched her as she painted.

'I suppose we could,' he said, roused from his contemplation. Her beauty and appeal had grown.

She put down her brush, wiped her hands, and came to him.

'Shall we announce it in the newspaper?' she said, putting her arms around him. She kissed his neck and ran her tongue around his ear.

'If that's what you want,' said Philip, thinking she was joking. He was never quite sure when she was serious.

'That's what I want. So now let's celebrate our steadiness.'

She opened a bottle of wine, poured two glasses, and gave one to Philip.

'Here's to our steadiness.'

They clinked, drank two glasses, and made love for the rest of the afternoon. Two days later, Philip received a cutting from the daily newspaper declaring that 'Diana and Phil celebrated their steadiness on Sunday by making passionate love.'

Phil was too embarrassed to show anyone at the university, but Joe found out.

'Congratulations on your steadiness,' he said with a broad smile.

'How did you find out?'

'A little bird told me.'

'Don't be stupid.'

'She expects you to be faithful, you realise.'

'You must know, Joe, that I am comfortable with that expectation as a Catholic.'

'How sad and twisted you are, mate,' said Joe, giving him a consoling pat.

From then on, Philip spent most of his time outside the university routine with Diana. Invitations regularly came to visit the Toorak home, where the atmosphere was familiar and relaxed. At Diana's request, he made love to her in her special room.

'It doesn't mean an eternal commitment,' she said later. 'I just wanted to love you in my most intimate place.'

'I don't presume anything.'

'That's not what I mean, you silly innocent boy.'

At last, he took her home to show his parents.

'What sort of relationship is that?' said his mother later.

'We get on together,' said Philip. 'We enjoy each other's company. She's a mature, intelligent, artistic woman who does not make a fuss about things. She suits me.'

'What future is there in it?'

'I'm not looking to the future.'

'I'm worried about you, darling.'

'Not need to be, Mum. Everything is fine.'

IF EVERYTHING was fine with Philip, it was not so with his antagonist in the John Fisher Society. With no warning, news spread that Vic Brennan had left his wife and three children and was living at John Fisher College. Philip made his way to Fr. Gorman's office.

'What's going on, Father?' he said, entering the priest's office and finding him leaning over his desk with his head in his hands. 'What's happened with Vic?'

'I can't tell you much,' said Fr. Gorman, looking up. 'I had no idea he had reached a crisis.'

Philip sought out members of the faith-science apostolate, but nobody would say anything. It was not that the gossip interested him. On the contrary, he was genuinely concerned about Vic, whom he respected despite their intellectual differences. It must be clear to Vic what a disaster divorce was for a practising Catholic. His marriage vows were not meaningless. There were the children to consider. Surely there was a way to resolve his marital problems. Vic stayed low for the following days, only attending to his lectures and then disappearing. Philip eventually tracked him down on his way to John Fisher College. He was uneasy about intervening but would persevere until Vic repudiated his offer of help.

'Vic, wait. I've heard. Is there anything I can do? Talk things through, perhaps.'

'What do you imagine you can do?' said Vic, not stopping.

'Help you assess your decision.'

'That's a bit rich coming from you,' said Vic, slowing.

'What's that supposed to mean?'

'Your life as a Catholic is not what you would call exemplary.'

'I'm not married, Vic. And I don't have children. Think of your children.'

'It's none of your business, Phil. Leave me alone and don't interfere.'

Philip had to desist, but knowing the problems Vic would face in Catholic society, he could not help worrying.

'Why are you expending so much worry over this fellow?' said Joe over a beer at a nearby student pub. 'It's his business. He's a big boy. He's responsible for his decisions. Let it be.'

'You don't understand what divorce means for a Catholic.'

'No, I don't. It's one thing for Dr Brennan to run out on his wife and children. It's another for you to worry about it so much. What a warped and twisted religion you willingly belong to.'

'You will only understand, Joe, when faith enlightens you.'

'Enlightens me? Let me stop there before my brain suffers a short circuit.'

A few days later, Joe strolled into Philip's office.

'What's that sly smile for?'

'I've got a scoop.' Joe sat in the chair in front of Phil's desk and leaned back, putting his hands behind his head.

'What scoop? Tell me before I give in to the urge to slap that smug expression from your face.'

'Victor Brennan is in love.'

'I suppose that's not surprising. It's hardly a scoop.'

'He's in love with a student.'

'No.' Philip rose from his desk. 'How could he be so foolish?'

'It gets worse.'

'How worse?'

'She's a second-year English student in his tutorial group and just eighteen.'

'My God, Vic, have you gone completely mad?'

'Well, if you want to make a fool of yourself, there's no sense in doing it by half. Apparently, the girl is smitten. The only saving feature is that they are very discreet. The relationship started late last year. My source does not know if they've consummated the relationship, but there's no doubt they are madly in love, to use the teenage idiom.'

'Then there is still a chance to pull back.'

Vic did his best to avoid people, but Phil was insistent and eventually cornered him in his office. He closed the door behind him as he entered.

'I thought I told you to stay out of my affairs,' said Vic, collecting his papers and stuffing them in his bag.

'I can't. Have you totally lost your mind, Vic? You must be having a breakdown or something. How could you contemplate starting a relationship with one of your undergraduate students? Can't you see how insane this is?'

'Are you quite finished?'

'No. Someone must make you see sense. You're destroying your life for the sake of a pretty girl. The campus is full of pretty girls with innocent eyes. They are appealing to most thirty-five-year-olds. But it's a surface appeal, a temptation full of disaster that must be resisted. You have to see it for what it is.'

'Are you finished with your hypocritical sermon, your holiness?' He took his bag and made for the door, brushing past Philip.

'Just think about it, Vic. Give yourself time.'

'Close the door behind you,' said Vic, walking briskly down the hall.

Phil closed the door and returned to his office, where he considered the options. He must do something before the situation became irretrievable. He found out who the student was and decided to talk to her. Such a step was full of risk. She might accuse him of harassment. Making the relationship public might inflame the situation. He must await his opportunity. He learned of her movements and joined her as she walked along the south lawn to leave the university.

'Hello, Miss Coghlan, do you know who I am?'

'Yes, of course, Dr Stevenson. Who does not know you on campus?

The self-confidence she radiated was a little off-putting.

'Can I have a little talk with you? It's important.'

'Yes, of course. We can sit on one of the benches here on the lawn.'

'You don't want to go somewhere less exposed?'

'No, I have nothing to hide. And I don't mind being seen in the company of the famous Phil Stevenson. By the way, Vic said you would probably approach me.'

'Well, you know what it's about?' said Philip, a little in awe of her self-confidence.

'You approached me, Dr Stevenson.' She sat on the nearest bench.

'Let me be frank, then,' said Philip, sitting beside her. 'I am concerned about your relationship with Dr Brennan. Do you understand what it means? Do you understand how socially disastrous it could turn out? You are young and perhaps are not fully aware—'

'I'm only aware I'm irretrievably in love with Vic. There's nothing else. Whatever Vic does, that won't change.'

'Think, Miss Coghlan. You are not in a Jane Austen novel. There won't be a happy ending. Dr Brennan will destroy his life.'

'I'm in love with Vic. That's all. There's no crime in that. That's all I have to say, Dr Stevenson. If you will excuse me, I must keep going. I am meeting Vic shortly.'

Phil watched her go. He felt helpless. He had tried and failed, at least for the moment. He trudged back to his office, his thoughts returning to Virginia against his will. How would she deal with such a problem? That evening, he went around to Diana's studio apartment. She was, as usual, pleased to see him.

'I hope you don't mind me wandering in without notice.'

'You are always welcome, darling,' she said, hugging him. 'I can see there's something on your mind. I'm here to soothe your worries away. So, take a seat, and I'll pour you a drink.'

Chapter 17

Agnes's summons

LATE IN 1961, Sister Agnes was summoned from St Joseph's College, north of Ballarat, to an interview with the Superior General of the Sisters of the Suffering Saviour. Agnes looked out the window as the car approached the motherhouse along the deserted bush-lined road. The grey spiky Gothic tower set against the steel-blue sky rose between the trees. Three years had passed. An inexplicable uneasiness seized her.

'It's such a peaceful place hidden away among the trees, overlooking the Yarra,' said Mr Ferguson, a retired gentleman who put his time at the service of the sisters.

'Yes, Mr Ferguson, the order is privileged to have secured this land.'

'The suburbs are spreading, though. I hope it can be maintained in its present condition.'

'Yes, I hope so, too.'

Mr Ferguson glanced over his shoulder at the black-robed figure in the white wimple squeezed into a corner of the back seat. Then, with a smile, he turned to his driving.

'I'm sorry, Mr Ferguson. My mind is not quite with it.'

'I understand, Sister. Summoned by the big boss, eh? I know what that's like.'

'Yes, I suppose you do.'

She did not understand why she should feel uneasy—a sort of nervous unease. Apart from anything else, it was not like her. She had done so well in her assignment to St Joseph's that she had been elevated to assistant headmistress after a year. The lay teachers had told her it was a great honour for one so young. Of course, given her previous teaching experience and excellent record, they expected her to take up her duties without too much trouble. But, still, everyone had to acknowledge her success, even her religious colleagues, without any apparent envy. The general opinion was that a big future in the order lay ahead of her. The system needed talent like hers. Her sympathetic headmistress, Mother Angelica, warned her against responding to the flattery. And she did her best to keep her pride in check. In this, she thought she was reasonably successful, which Mother Angelica acknowledged discreetly. Then why the nervousness?

Sister Martha met her at the entrance and, with a welcoming smile, passed on Mother Jerome's instructions to go to the chapel and wait until called. Mother Jerome expected to see her at eleven o'clock. She looked at her watch. An hour's wait. She bit her lip, glancing at the retreating sister. Then, on reflection, she should be happy to have time for contemplation. It was a week before the schools broke up for the Christmas holidays, and she had been rushing to complete many urgent tasks while struggling to maintain her sisterly dignity. Her religious duties had suffered in her haste. She breathed a sigh of relief as she knelt in a pew before the side altar devoted to Our Lady of Perpetual Succour. She bowed her head.

After some time in prayer, she opened her breviary. On glancing to her right, she saw that the green light of the confessional was on. Why hadn't she noticed when she came in? It was probably Fr Sheridan. Mother

Jerome always delegated him to that confessional. Perhaps he was there for her? No, surely not. Mother Jerome would not have arranged the old priest's presence just for her. She looked around. There was no one else in the cool, silent chapel. She stared at the open page of the breviary for a while before putting it aside. The months before the summons had been so busy that she had lacked the concentration to examine her conscience thoroughly.

As she subjected her behaviour to a close review, she became painfully aware that preoccupation with her success and the good opinion of others had been encroaching on her motivations. Her life as a sister— A vista of pride and selfishness opened before her, the worst of which was her lack of consideration for the feelings and ambitions of those around her. Meaningful looks had passed on occasions between her colleagues, but she had been too preoccupied to give them much attention. Now she was forced to dwell on them. Now she was forced to confront the fault the prioress warned her about. Mother Jerome was no less perceptive from afar.

She entered the confessional, drawing the thick wooden door closed behind her and brushing her black tunic aside. She knelt before the thin wire grille with her head bowed and the stiff front of the veil resting against the wire. After making the sign of the cross, she lifted her head. She recoiled. In the soft shade of the confessional, she saw Fr Sheridan, his head propped up against the back of the chair in which his body seemed untidily slumped. His cheeks were hollow and drawn, his eyes sunken in grey sockets, and his skin stretched thinly over bone and sinew. He looked dead. She could not control her breathing and released a gasp. To her relief, his head turned. He lifted one hand from his rosary and said the opening prayers in Latin as he made the sign of the cross.

Scarcely able to concentrate because of the accusing sight before her eyes, she struggled through her confession. Fr Sheridan was very ill, and here he was still attending to his duties, sitting in a cramped confessional for as long as necessary. After she had recited her failings, she paused for a moment. There was little movement in the priest, just the twitch of one eyelid as he sought to bear his discomfort. How was she to combat her tendency to shine or, more to the point, to outshine others, to draw applause? It overcame her before she was aware of what she was doing.

'Are you sure that's a sin?' said the old priest in a whisper without opening his eyes or changing his expression.

'Eh, yes,' she said, surprised by the question. 'The sin of pride.'

'Where is the pride?'

She described her pleasure in her success and at hearing the praise for her good work. She admitted she was always ready to air her opinions and correct others. She suspected she might be patronising when she corrected their mistakes and opinions.

'Where exactly is the sin of pride in that? Most people think that what you describe is normal. St Paul exhorts us to reprove and correct others when they're at fault, doesn't he?'

Sister Agnes was stumped. She had not expected this simple, pious priest to challenge her. She stammered a reply, trying to reproduce a rational analysis of the sin of pride. But the priest interrupted her and talked about the five sorrowful mysteries of the rosary. He spoke with such emotion about Jesus' surrender to suffering at each point along the way to Calvary that tears filled her eyes. She saw the emptiness of success and praise and the value of a job well done without reference to anyone else's favourable opinion.

'For your penance, I want you to say the five sorrowful mysteries of the rosary, meditating long on Christ's suffering,' he said to finish. 'Then I want you to read St John's first epistle, chapter two, verses 15-17 every day during the next month:'

Love not the world, nor the things which are in the world. If any man love the world, the charity of the Father is not in him.

For all that is in the world, is the concupiscence of the flesh, and the concupiscence of the eyes, and the pride of life, which is not of the Father, but is of the world.

And the world passeth away, and the concupiscence thereof: but he that doth the will of God, abideth for ever.

'Now, I want you to say a sincere act of contrition.'

Sister Agnes resumed her seat, shaken. That dying old man, with whom she had never spoken outside the confessional and not seen for three years, had unerringly focused on her weakness. Mother Angelica had warned her not to forget her religious duties amid her heavy burden of work, work which she willingly took on. And for which she earned admiration and acclaim. She blushed with shame as she understood why she had received a severe penance.

She began the five sorrowful mysteries, trying to surrender to her meditations with all her might. She struggled to beat back the accusing image of students and staff coming to her for help, consolation, or advice. Memories of the students she had forged a close relationship with, despite her efforts to avoid attachments, rose before her mind. There was also Aine, who had visited with her little daughter several times, seeking advice to cope with her strange and insistent torments. All these things she strove to put aside as she meditated on the suffering of the Saviour.

To her astonishment, no sooner had she finished, made the sign of the cross, and kissed the small crucifix dangling from the beads than Fr Sheridan emerged from the confessional. She could not help glancing at him as he staggered with the support of his stick to the altar rails. He let himself fall to his knees, where he stayed several minutes with his head bowed before the Blessed Sacrament. Her eyes stayed on him while she tried to fathom the inner life of someone so holy and humble. The priest struggled to his feet and then, to her discomfort and surprise, staggered over to her.

'Sister, would you kindly help me from the church,' he whispered.

'Of course, Father,' she said, leaping to her feet while becoming aware of the ease and suppleness of her limbs.

'Thank you, Sister, you are kind.'

He put one hand on his stick and another on her youthful shoulder, and they walked towards the back of the chapel.

'Sister, do you have time to take me to the bench overlooking the river?' said the priest when they were outside. 'I would like to wait there until Mother Jerome arranges transport for me.'

'Of course, Father,' she said, conscious she had been told to wait in the chapel.

'Thank you, Sister, you are kind,' he repeated as he settled on a bench. 'It's such a peaceful scene here, don't you think?' He lifted his hand in a poor attempt to wave it in front of the vista before them.

'Yes, Father, it's very peaceful. We are fortunate.'

'You are, indeed, all you sisters, to have such a place for meditation, for spiritual refreshment. I hope it remains unspoiled.'

'Yes, Father.'

'Mother Jerome has worked miracles in guarding the convent. It has been a bitter battle between opposing forces, of which few have been aware. I wonder what will ensue after she has gone. The world seems to be marching toward us from all directions to join—'

He looked at her as if he were appealing to her, as if she had something to do with the world marching towards them, as if she was privy to the details filling his mind. She looked at him, not sure of his meaning, not sure of a response without seeming presumptuous or foolish. He turned his eyes again towards the river and the grassy hills, apparently not expecting an answer. She remained transfixed in indecision.

'I hope Mother Jerome is with us for a long time to come,' she said at last.

'We must keep that in our intentions,' he said. 'We must.'

'I pray so. I can't imagine what it would be like without her,' said Agnes, wondering if his sombre expression was because of the realisation he probably would not live much longer.

'You must keep that eventuality in mind, Sister,' he said, turning his haggard face towards her. 'The reins must not be left lying loose. Those of courage must come forward.' Once again, he seemed to be appealing to her. 'You know good Pope John has called an ecumenical council?' Agnes nodded. 'What do you think about that?'

'I have not given it much thought.'

'Why is that, Sister—such an intelligent young sister as you?'

'Well, I ... there are other things .... That is so far away from us, so far above us and our daily duties ....'

'Is it in the hands of the proper authorities?'

'Yes, Father, I assume—'

'We must pray that it is so.'

Sister Martha appeared, greeting the priest warmly and telling Agnes that Mother Jerome was ready to receive her.

'Thank you, Sister, for your help and company,' the old priest said.

'I'm glad to have helped.'

'Would you accept my blessing, Sister?'

She looked at him, surprised. 'Yes, of course, Father.'

She knelt before him. He made the sign of the cross slowly above her: '*In Nomine Patris, et Filii, et Spiritus Sancti. Amen.*' He leaned forward and put two fingers lightly on her forehead. 'Don't let the fire go out, no matter how hard things may get or how often you fail,' he whispered. 'Jesus and His Blessed Mother will always be with us to help our frail nature. And please pray for me—offer prayers for my impending appearance before Our Lord and Master.' He traced the sign of the cross with his thumb.

'Yes, Father,' she said, getting up and glancing at Martha, who seemed not to have heard or seen anything out of the ordinary. 'I hope you ... will ... keep me in your prayers, too.'

He nodded slowly. He was not yet finished.

'Have you heard of La Salette?'

'The name seems to ring a bell.'

'There are prophecies. Read them.'

'Yes, Father, thank you. Goodbye, Father.'

The priest half-crumpled with a sigh of exhaustion and turned back towards the hills and trees. He seemed lost in his thoughts. She glanced around as she walked away. He did not move. The ravaged face wore a peculiar serenity.

Mother Jerome rose from her desk when Agnes was ushered into her office. She held her hands out as Agnes approached her.

'Well, Sister, here you are,' she said, taking Agnes's hands. 'The country air seems to be doing you good.'

Agnes blushed, aware this sort of greeting was extended to special guests. 'Thank you, Reverend Mother. I'm also happy with my work. That makes a difference.'

'Of course, it does,' said the prioress, moving behind her desk. 'Now, I am sure you are wondering what you are doing here,' she went on, exuding her usual air of authority.

'Well, yes ...,' said Agnes, noticing no armchairs were in front of the desk.

'Please kneel,' said Mother Jerome.

'Yes, Mother,' she said, startled but quickly recovering her sisterly demeanour and going to her knees.

'Do you have any questions, Sister?'

'No, Mother, I'm afraid I really don't know why you have summoned me.'

'No doubt, something important, you think?'

'Well ... I don't know.' Of course, that was not true, and she was conscious of the fib.

'Questions about what you have just seen?'

'Oh, I'm sorry, I ... I realised Fr Sheridan's very sick.'

'He's terminally ill. You will probably not see him again.'

Before she was aware of what she was feeling, Agnes found herself sobbing. She shifted on her knees, embarrassed and angry that she could not control herself. Why was she sobbing? She put her hand to her eyes in a pathetic effort to hide her childishness. What would her teaching colleagues think if they saw her like this?

'Sister, you have a handkerchief?'

Agnes glanced up at the prioress before she tugged a handkerchief from the ample pockets of her black tunic. The prioress seemed unmoved by her breaking down so unexpectedly. Then a second glance revealed sympathy deep in the eyes of that remarkable woman.

'I'm sorry, Mother,' she sniffled as she wiped her eyes. 'I don't know what came over me. I'm not usually—what's wrong with Father? I only ever saw him for Mass and confession, but I'll miss him.'

'We'll all miss him. He is the lowliest of priests, but he has been a pillar of spiritual strength for the sisters. He has lung cancer.'

'I'm so sorry.'

Mother Jerome waited until Agnes had composed herself. Then, she picked up a sheet of paper.

'You have been three years at St Joseph's.' She raised a finger as a sign that Agnes should stay silent. 'You were allocated several subjects at the junior level, to begin with. After several months, with several necessary changes in the teaching roster, you were given organisational charge of the First and Second Years. This was in addition to your unchanged teaching duties. During the year, with the input of your fellow teachers, you revised the junior curriculum. This was not only to Mother Angelica's satisfaction. Your colleagues, both religious and lay, complimented you on the practical and pedagogical improvements. At the start of the following year, Mother Angelica appointed you assistant principal. Again, with all-around consultation, the curriculum and time-timetable were reorganised, this time for the whole school. This, too, met with approval.' She lowered the sheet of paper and looked at Agnes. 'You are to be congratulated for your hard work and success.'

'Thank you, Mother,' said Agnes, glancing at her.

'On the testimony of others, you have worked very hard.'

'It was a job to be done. I liked doing it.'

'Your work on the religious curriculum seems to have borne fruit. Why do you think that is?'

'I tried with a little adjustment to make the key teachings of the faith appeal more to the hearts and minds of the girls. Living a good life is a joy in itself.'

'You thought the catechetical instruction too dry?'

'The teachings of Our Lord should appeal to the heart. Our Lord's parables are full of warmth and human understanding. Nothing can touch the heart more than the story of the prodigal son and the unremitting love of the Father. Catechesis is necessary for knowing the fundamentals of the faith. Appeals to the heart add, perhaps paradoxically, to their understanding.'

Mother Jerome nodded several times and seemed on the point of commenting, but reconsidered. The warmth appeared again in her eyes. 'You have allowed the girls more access to the things of modern society than others have considered wise.'

'Yes, Mother, if you mean books, magazines, and popular music.'

'There are people, Christians, not just Catholics, who view modern music as an evil influence.'

'Not all popular music is bad. The best of it speaks to the adolescent's naturally innocent feelings about love and relationships. One can subject the rest to sober criticism.'

'Oh?'

'I have a booklet which is a compilation of many of Pope Pius XII's speeches and writings on women and womanhood. I use those to discuss popular culture and how girls can be responsible, educated, independent, Christian women. His Holiness stressed that no field be closed to women—'

Agnes stopped herself from rattling on in her usual way. Mother Jerome did not need her lectures. Few women in secular society were as well educated and had risen to an equal position of authority and influence. A great community of religious, schools, hospitals, and aged care homes, a huge school population, honour and respect from parents and religious alike—all these things came under the prioress's purview.

'You are not afraid you will load yourself with too much?'

'No ... no.'

'Why should you break down as you did? This is not usual in our sisters. Nor is it expected.'

'I really can't say, Mother. My feelings, I suppose, have always been near the surface. My enthusiasm—' She stopped as the prioress raised her finger.

'This is general advice for you,' the prioress said. 'You are to approach your work with less intensity, even if that intensity results from diligence and industry.'

'Yes, Mother.'

'Now stand up, bring that chair to the desk, and sit down.' The prioress pointed to a chair against the wall. 'Do you remember what I said more than four years ago?'

Agnes concentrated and threw her mind back to the postulancy and novitiate years. There were several conversations. What could she be referring to?

'What particular conversation?'

'How old are you now?'

'Twenty-seven.'

'One could say that you are at the height of your female powers in certain respects.'

'Oh ... what ... what do you mean, Reverend Mother?'

'You lead a healthy life, and it shows in your countenance. In the judgment of the secular world, you are bright, competent, and successful in your chosen profession. At the same time, you are feminine, cultivated, with warmth and a relaxed dignity. You remain for the world an extremely eligible young woman. Indeed, your veil would not deter the attention of some young men.'

The prioress's expression and tone told Agnes this was not a mere compliment, as it wasn't four years ago.

'I don't really know what to say,' said Agnes. 'I'm committed to the life of a religious. I offer myself to Jesus as thousands of women have done before me. I offer myself as a Bride of Christ,' she wanted to insist. 'I reserve my maidenhood—'

'You are aware the maiden is an archetype in classical mythology?'

'No ....'

'The maiden in Greek and Roman mythology is not necessarily a virgin as we understand it. In some contexts, maidenhood was associated with independence and self-reliance, not with chastity. Indeed, the opposite in that respect is the case.'

'I don't understand.'

'You have not taken your final vows. You are to spend more time meditating on what that means—on what you will give up.' The Superior General of the Order of the Sisters of the Suffering Saviour straightened herself. 'Your assignment at St Joseph's will finish at the end of the term. You are to bring all your administrative matters to a point where they can be handed over to your successor. You will then move back here to the motherhouse to await my pleasure. Mother Angelica has already received my directions.'

'But—' Agnes said, appalled. She stopped. There was no appeal. The vow of obedience—she had lectured others on its meaning. But she bucked internally. Why? Why, when she had done so well? It sounded like she was being punished. It did not make sense. She had to struggle to suppress—

'Mr Ferguson will take you back after lunch. In the meantime, you can join the other sisters in the usual routine of the hours.' She rose and came around to the front of her desk. 'We will now say a decade of the rosary together. You will lead with the first joyful mystery, meditating on Mary's selfless fiat. Lord, Your will be done, not ours.'

Agnes knelt beside the Superior General in front of the picture of Our Lady of Perpetual Succour. In a confused state, hardly able to concentrate on the meditation, she threaded her way through the ten Hail Marys and one Our Father.

Chapter 18

Virginia still in love

THREE WEEKS later, Sister Agnes was again installed in the order's motherhouse, hidden among the trees on a ridge overlooking the Yarra River in a suburb northeast of Melbourne city centre. The peace and charm of the surroundings were no consolation for this Bride of Christ. The heartbreak of ending her work at St Joseph's and packing up her things lingered. She found it hard to hold back her tears of disappointment, as she had when she said goodbye to her teaching colleagues. Her heart sank each time she remembered she could not say goodbye to the girls she had grown close to. What must they think of her? What must they say about her hardness of heart in disappearing the way she did? She struggled to submit herself in spirit to the directives.

As she walked along the upper parapet on the second evening of her return, the one relief was that Mother Jerome had ordered her into a private retreat. She needed peace to revive in spirit and to reflect on her present situation. At this time, it was challenging to face the curious looks of her fellow religious, particularly Margaret—Sister Catherine. From all reports, Sister Catherine received similar acclaim for her teaching and leadership at the nearby girls' school. She, however, had not been ordered into a retreat.

It was ironic, Agnes could not help musing, that the daughter of Irish working-class parents should be doing so well at a school for the daughters of well-to-do upper-class parents, few of whom would have been from the same Irish background. The frustration—she struggled again to suppress it. She stopped at the top of the stairs leading down past the two parapets to the riverbank and listened to the singing of the postulants in the chapel. They were beginning their period of proof before being received into the community as Brides of Christ.

Agnes's mind went back five years to the first day of her postulancy. So much had happened. The vision of Aine standing alone returned. She stood for some moments, staring at the river gleaming languidly in the early evening light. She descended the rocky stairs, each step bringing back that period in ever-increasing lucidity. At the bottom of the stairs, she saw the innocent face of Aine standing beside the bench and staring at her nervously. What a torment that innocent young woman had suffered. While reflecting on those strange events as they came back to her, she made her way to the grotto. She knelt, bowing her head, and recalled the only occasion she had needed Aine's comfort. Here, she gave in to her grief at repudiating the love of the only person she had ever loved in that special way. And now, for the first time in months, the image of Philip's angry, uncomprehending face fixed itself before her mind. The tears seeped through the fingers of the hands covering her face. She could not expel the thoughts she had been warding off for over three years.

What was he doing? Did he think of her as she thought of him? How often? She knew vague and general answers to these questions. Her mother always had news of him during family visits. Philip had achieved his ambitions of teaching at university and was now a senior lecturer at John Batman University, one of Melbourne's oldest and most respected universities. As far as she could gather, he was unmarried and somewhat unsettled. Now she felt the impulse to know more. Desperately, she wanted to learn more. She wanted to hear about him in the intimate terms of their conversations before— She bowed her head and tried to block the thoughts. She could block the thoughts, but she couldn't suppress her grief. Confident she was out of sight and hearing of the rest of the community, she gave in to her feelings. Then, between her gentle sobs, she heard a rustle in the bushes near the riverbank. She jumped to her feet, wiping her eyes and cheeks. Frozen, she stared at the bushes in the fading light. Memories of that night, the night of the dark hooded figures, returned to her. She wanted to run away to the safety of the buildings above, but the urge to investigate was irresistible.

She moved towards the riverbank, not knowing what she would discover. As it turned out, there was nothing to see except the shadowy bushes and foliage down to the river's edge. A noise came from the other side of the high cyclone wire fence to her left. She swung round. A black cockatoo clumsily detached itself from a nearby tree, brushing the branches as it flew away. It disappeared over the river with its ugly squawking fading into the trees. She relaxed. It was only the native animals that lived around the convent property. Exhibiting such ungrounded fear was foolish. She gave her low spirits as her excuse.

As she turned to make her way along the crest of the bank to the rocky stairs, her foot kicked up what felt like a shallow mound of dirt and debris. She lifted her black tunic and looked first at her shoes and then at the mound. In the dim light, she could make out a rough circle of dirt. Or was it dirt? She bent down for a closer look. It smelt odd. She ran her hand over it and then picked up a handful. She brought it to her nose. It was the remains of a fire. Someone had tried to cover up the burnt sticks and grass by spreading earth over them. Besides the burnt wood, there was another smell there. She sniffed some more. It was burnt flesh and bone. Whatever it had been, it had been burnt to a cinder. She straightened, puzzled. Whatever did that mean? Then she remembered the glow between the bushes five years ago as she crouched behind the plants on the next level. That glow would have issued from this vicinity. The painful images of Philip receded as a jumble of new thoughts took their place. Since the clothing ceremony, she had had little time to focus on anything other than her duties.

Now, as each day was reserved for prayer and silent reflection, the memories of those times assumed a starkness she had suppressed. The fearful face of Aine Winterbine took centre place in her thoughts. She went over the strange events, sinking ever deeper into a dark mystery. Who were the shadowy hooded figures? Why was she locked out of the upper floor? Was that some sort of warning? Time and again, her ruminations led her to Aine's belief that an evil force was at work in the convent. Was it still there? There was no reason for it to go away of itself. She could not help glancing around the chapel. Her eyes came to rest continually on Sister Catherine. But as carefully as she examined her demeanour, she could not detect any sign, however remote, that Catherine had anything to do with the dark events. What sort of manifestations would she show, anyhow? As Agnes observed Catherine, all she saw was just another of her sisters taking part in the convent's activities.

Towards the end of her retreat, she was reminded of Fr Sheridan's mysterious comments about opposing forces in the convent and his recommendation to read the La Salette prophecies. After searching all the references and places it might appear, she reluctantly wrote a note to the convent librarian seeking information. The sister, one of the older sisters, frowned before disappearing into a side room. When she returned holding a slim volume, she scribbled a question on Agnes's note. Agnes wrote: Fr Sheridan had requested that she read it. With a distrustful narrowing of her brow, the librarian handed over the slim volume and pointed at a chair beside the library table. Agnes nodded, took the book, and sat at the table.

As she read the prophecy text for the third time, she became aware of her heightened breathing between dry, slightly parted lips. She glanced around at the librarian who sat at her desk, regarding her with interest. She wondered again why she had never heard of La Salette and its prophecies. Here, before her, were prophecies from a Church-approved apparition that threatened the Church and the world with disintegration and destruction if the people did not mend their ways and observe God's laws. Astonishingly, there was a warning about the befouling of convent life. How could it be? Surely not. The Church had always had its difficulties and shameful low points. The symptoms were apparent well before it applied a remedy. But now? Surely the Church had never been stronger. Both the female and male religious orders had never been healthier, attracting vocations at a rate never experienced. Of course, there were problems. But these were procedural problems indicating a procedural remedy. They certainly did not suggest the dire situation of the prophecies. She returned the slim volume to the librarian, no longer wanting to stay under her critical eyes.

The final day of the retreat did not find Agnes calm, relaxed, and reconciled as it was supposed to. It was the opposite; her mind was churning with a mess of warring thoughts. She could scarcely block her thoughts about Philip. But her dismissal from St Joseph's (for that's what it was), her grief at losing her close friends, both staff and students, the mysterious conversation with Fr Sheridan, the fearful face of Aine, and the strange events connected with her, and the terrifying La Salette prophecies—these plagued her. There was something else to destabilise her, too. Fr Sheridan had died in the meantime. The strange part about it, said the prioress, was that he passed away peacefully in his sleep within days of her visit. It had been expected that he would die a slow death, as was usual with lung cancer.

'He said an evening Mass and seemed in good spirits, despite his debilitated state. He was found the next morning lying on his bed, holding his rosary beads. His local superior told me his bed linen was undisturbed, as if he were already prepared for burial. That's something to ponder.'

Fr Sheridan's passing was not a shock. The time and manner of his passing did not have the significance for Agnes that it seemed to have for Mother Jerome. The primary focus of her thoughts was the absence of a confessor and spiritual adviser who listened to her spiritual concerns with understanding. His colleagues from the Missionaries of the Wounded Heart of Jesus, whose Melbourne house was not far away, now took turns saying Mass and hearing confessions. But they were not the same. The counsel of the two priests she encountered during her retreat seemed almost superficial in their understanding of her concerns.

Fr. Hans de Jonge, who was acquiring a reputation for his specialised studies in theology, not only appeared off-hand in his advice but on an entirely different track. In response to her concerns about pride and vanity, he encouraged her to reflect on what precisely those vices were. Was it a question of real harmful pride, or was she justifiably striving for self-fulfilment and taking responsibility for her actions? Everyone would benefit from a sisterhood of responsible, autonomous women, the students, first and foremost. Sister should be careful to avoid a restrictive scrupulosity. She should, of course, avoid rigid selfish pride, one not open to the thoughts and feelings of others. He was dismissive of her concerns about her lingering feelings for Philip. Those feelings are quite natural, and she should not suppress them. Sister Agnes should approach all relationships similarly, that is, with maturity and self-knowledge. Otherwise, psychological harm may follow.

Agnes did not know what to make of that advice. She was inclined to assume she had somehow misunderstood Fr. de Jonge's meaning. After all, he was trained in these matters. Fr. De Jonge did not long occupy her thoughts. His placement in Melbourne was temporary, and he would return shortly to the Sydney house. The issue with Philip took primary importance and was sure to be central to her next meeting with Mother Jerome. One thing had become clear to her. Mother Jerome was not yet confident she had detached herself from the world. And a big part of the lingering attachment was her love for Philip.

'Please prostrate yourself,' said the prioress after Agnes had entered her office.

Agnes lay on the floor in front of the prioress's desk, her arms outstretched, and her nose and chin pressed into the carpet. There seemed an eternity before Mother Jerome spoke.

'Have you learned anything about yourself during this last week?'

Agnes hesitated. 'I realise I'm still somewhat attached to my former fiancé.'

'Attached?'

'Yes.'

'Just attached?'

Agnes hesitated again. 'I'm still in love with him.' Then, to her frustration, a sob escaped. Why couldn't she control her stupid feelings?

'What, then, from here?'

'What do you mean, Mother?'

'The life of a sister is detachment from the world, total devotion to Our Lord in his suffering, and total denial of the self. It is a life opposed to the material values of the modern world.'

'Yes, Mother.'

'Well?'

'It's likely I will never stop loving Philip. But I want to follow the example of St Paul and St Augustine. I love Jesus more and want to devote myself to Him as those great saints and many others have done.'

'Are you decided on this?'

'Yes, Mother.'

'You have not yet made your final vows. There is still time to leave the convent with dignity and lead a life devoted to Our Lord in the married state.'

'As St Paul has done,' said Agnes softly. 'And St Augustine.'

'Many have held it against St Augustine that he left his son and the mother of his son to establish a monastery.'

'We follow the Augustinian rule. I want to live the life St Augustine has prescribed for the religious state.'

'Even if your love for your former fiancé does not diminish?'

'I imagine Augustine's love for his son and mother did not diminish. I could not believe otherwise of the saint who wrote the *Confessions*.'

'You are a young woman of deep feeling. Can you cope with that?'

'I will always do my best.'

'Will your best be enough?'

'I don't know, Mother, but it will not be for want of trying.'

'Are you ready for the sacrifice? Many, even some religious of these times, would be doubtful.'

'I will do my best.'

There followed another long silence. 'Please stand up, Sister, and fetch the chair by the window.'

As Agnes sat in front of the desk, she noticed for the first time that the prioress's face was thinner. Now, prompted to look more closely, she saw that Mother Jerome was altogether thinner and more frail-looking. Fr. Sheridan's words came back to her, and a new anxiety possessed her.

'I have been a little hard on you, but you must understand it has been for a purpose.'

'Yes, Mother—'

Mother Jerome raised her hand. 'It was hard for you to leave unfinished work at St Joseph's.' She picked up a sheet of paper from her desk. 'There's no need to worry,' she said with an understanding smile. 'This, I suspect, will make up for your disappointment. However that may be, the instructions I am about to give you are a privilege entailing a great responsibility.' She paused. 'You are likely unaware that there has been a concerted movement in recent years to improve the academic standard of female religious.' Agnes nodded. 'We pray daily for vocations from young women of your background. With a genuine vocation, you represent the future of our teaching order.'

'Thank you, Mother.'

'It is only as it is. I wish to stress the responsibility your position demands of you. You must understand this responsibility and be willing to take it on.'

'I understand.'

'Hesitate before you make a commitment, Sister. The path may be hard in the coming years. Pray that you are fully aware of what you are taking on.'

Agnes remained silent. There was an urgency in the prioress's voice with which she rarely spoke.

'With the forthcoming ecumenical council, the need is even greater to ensure our sisters are properly informed of new developments in the Church. Already, there is a wide divergence of opinion between respectable theologians and religious superiors on the need for an ecumenical council. I must admit to reservations myself, being aware, as many are not, of theological and scriptural dialogue within the Church. With this in mind, a council of senior nuns has agreed that it is vital that our most suitable sisters pursue formal academic study. You have been selected as one of two students who will enrol full-time at John Batman University for the coming academic year. If you are successful, you will continue full-time study until you graduate.'

The announcement came abruptly at the end of what seemed to Agnes an unusually rambling conversation for the prioress. All she could utter was a lame, 'Oh?'

'Your major study will be philosophy. Your minor studies will be of your choosing, subject to approval, except for commerce. You will enrol in the Commerce Faculty to study economics, accounting, and other such subjects. You must have a basic understanding of the economic principles of human organisations and how a religious order operates. Do you have any questions?'

'No ... yes ... I don't know what to say, Mother. I am surprised and pleased. I had never expected—' She was more than pleased. She was thrilled. To take up formal academic study ... to think that Philip had encouraged her to continue from teacher's college—Philip...? 'You did say that I would be enrolled at John Batman University?' she blurted out, knowing full well the answer.

'Yes,' said Mother Jerome. 'You know someone at John Batman University?'

Agnes had to reveal what she would never tell anyone in the convent community.

'My former fiancé is a lecturer at John Batman University.'

'What in?'

'Philosophy.'

'What's his specialty?'

'I'm not sure ... oh, yes, the history of philosophy was his special interest. He always spoke about the Church's perennial philosophy. There was St. Thomas Aquinas—there were many things I did not understand. I was young then, and Philip is seven years older.'

'It will be your task and duty to understand those things,' said the prioress, raising a finger. 'It will also be the first hurdle for you to pass over. I hope it will not be too high.'

'It will not be,' said Agnes, trying to sound confident.

They spent the following fifteen minutes discussing the preparations for enrolment. Agnes tried to concentrate. She tried to ask the right questions and commit the answers to memory. But she was half taking in the detail. When Mother Jerome suggested she might encounter Philip, she had not taken the suggestion seriously, dismissing it as a hypothetical. She was practical enough not to dwell on such abstract possibilities. Now she was confronted with the brutal reality of the concrete situation. If Philip were not one of her lecturers—a real possibility and the worst outcome—she would at least see him regularly. How would he greet her? What would he say to her? However was she to cope with it?

'There will be many questions for you to ask as you prepare for your studies,' said Mother Jerome, observing her. 'Please be free to arrange times to talk with me. Is there anything else?'

'No ... I don't think so ... at this point.'

'This is a new development in our order. You must be conscious of the great responsibility.'

'I am, truly, Mother. I want to express my gratitude for the confidence you have shown.'

The prioress's manner changed.

'You see, child, you had no reason to be despondent.'

The words were warm and sympathetic, and they brought a lump to Agnes's throat. 'I'll do my best to control my feelings.'

'Less intensity.'

'Yes, Mother.'

'No more questions?'

Agnes hesitated. 'Would it be all right to ask Aine Winterbine to attend the Christmas visiting day?'

The prioress seemed taken by surprise. 'Have you seen her recently?'

'She visited me at St Joseph's with her daughter three or four times. She and her husband live not too far north of Ballarat.'

'How is she?'

'Physically, she is very well. There is no change in her appearance, just as—but she has been suffering the same torments she experienced here. She said they returned after her last visit here.'

'Yes, that would be all right. Please ask her to reserve some time to talk with me—just a friendly talk. Anything else?'

'Are you familiar with a book called *Pistis Sophia*?'

The prioress's expression changed. 'Why do you ask?'

'Aine found a book with that title and asked me about it. I had forgotten about it until this last week.'

'You mean she found that book in this convent, outside the library?'

Agnes described the circumstances of Aine's finding the book to the prioress's increasing interest, even apprehension.

'*Pistis Sophia* is a work belonging to a heretical religious/philosophical movement that developed in the first few centuries of Christianity. The movement, generally known as Gnosticism, is not easy to describe in brief. Your favourite saint, Augustine, battled with the Gnostics. It is best left until you have progressed in your philosophical studies. Is there anything else?' Agnes hesitated. 'There is something else, I see. If it's important, you must tell me.'

Agnes told in detail about her and Aine's sighting of the robed figures in the grounds at night and the boats on the river. Why hadn't she spoken about it before this? asked the prioress, startled.

'We didn't know what to make of it, Mother,' said Agnes. 'But now it seems connected with Aine's experiences and the appearance of that book *Pistis Sophia*. And I can't help thinking that Sister Catherine and her friends are somehow involved. How, I don't know.'

The prioress regarded Agnes distantly for some long, uncomfortable moments.

'I don't want you to mention what you've seen to anyone else,' she said at last. 'Understood?'

'Yes, of course, Mother,' said Agnes, disappointed that the prioress did not share her thoughts.

'Good. Anything else?'

'No, Mother, not at the moment,' said Agnes, but as she stood up, 'May I know who the other sister is?'

'Yes, of course. Sister Catherine. You will be accompanying each other each day. Sister Catherine will major in sociology as well as pursue those subjects in which she excels. Anything else?'

'No, Mother, really this time.'

A smile came to Mother Jerome's lips as Agnes left her office.

Chapter 19

Aine's Christmas visit

AINE WAS overjoyed to receive a surprise invitation from Virginia's mother to join them on their special Christmas visit to Virginia. As much as Charles supported her in her tormented periods, he was baffled, like her, about the actual cause. Only Virginia had shown any understanding of what she was going through, and she had never been far from her thoughts. As the car turned onto the secluded road along the ridge, she fell quiet, waiting for the Gothic tower to rise above the eucalypts. On the entrance avenue, the memory of her final day walking alone between the tall gums came back to her with unnerving clarity. Soon she emerged with Virginia's parents onto the busy upper parapet where the sisters and their visitors were chatting. Aine looked around in a daze as the surroundings brought back more memories. A familiar voice shook her out of it.

'Aine, I am so happy to see you. No more children?'

Margaret had broken away from her family group with a wave.

'Eh … no,' said Aine, glancing at Virginia's parents.

'Excuse me, Mr and Mrs Pearson. Do you remember me, Sister Catherine?'

Virginia's parents remembered her, and some polite small talk passed between them while Aine looked around for Virginia.

'I won't hold you up anymore,' said Catherine. 'May we have a short chat later, after you and Sister Agnes catch up?'

'Yes ... of course.'

'Not with your husband this time?' Catherine persisted.

'No. He had work he could not put off.'

'I will see you later, then. Nice to have seen you again, Mr and Mrs Pearson.'

Aine watched Margaret return to her family group with bold, confident steps, black skirt, and veil billowing as if she had been wearing her religious habit all her life. Virginia's often repeated claim that Margaret did not belong in the convent—either she was wrong, or Margaret was still part of an ongoing puzzle.

'Sister Catherine is less stiff now,' commented Mrs Pearson.

'A very formidable young woman,' added Mr Pearson. 'Will scare the pants off the bubs.'

They ambled on, looking around for their daughter. Suddenly, she was before them. 'I'm sorry, Mum and Dad.' She gave them a quick hug. 'I had a few things to complete,' and turning to Aine, 'I'm so glad you could come. Come on. We've got lots to catch up on.'

She led them to a table and chairs with a view down the slopes to the river and beyond to the fields. For Aine and Agnes's parents, Agnes was Virginia again, talking enthusiastically about the privilege of being sent to university. She would do her best to vindicate the confidence placed in her. The conversation moved on to Aine and her family's life in Binawarra and continued pleasantly until Virginia's mother announced a pause for afternoon tea.

'By the way, dear, I didn't mention it,' said Mrs Pearson, holding a cake wrapped in a tea towel midway between the picnic basket and the table. 'I was concentrating so much on what you were saying about your university course. Philip is now in charge of the first-year subjects. I hope that won't be uncomfortable for you both.'

Agnes stiffened, a reaction her parents seemed to miss, but not Aine.

'It's one of those things we must cope with in religious life.'

'You be careful how you behave. I have the impression Philip is not yet over—' Her mother gave her a meaningful look.

'Oh ... yes ...?'

'I spoke with Philip's mother a few months ago. She said nothing explicit. It was an impression I got. She seemed to hint that he's rather unsettled. She said he has a lot of different girlfriends—'

'That surely says the opposite, doesn't it?' said her father. 'It's more than four years. You don't expect him to be pining indefinitely, do you? Besides, he's not an ugly man. I wouldn't have expected him to lock himself away.'

'No, of course not,' said Agnes, averting her eyes. 'Anyhow, my black habit will be as much discouragement as he needs. It's five years, Dad.'

'Don't be too sure about that. Keep your distance.'

'Yes, Mother.'

'Come on, don't be so serious,' exclaimed her father. 'Philip can handle himself. He's a big boy now.' He turned to Aine. 'Now, Aine, I've been dying to ask about that great big husband of yours. You say he's doing a lot of restoration work in your town?'

While she spoke about Charles's work in the town, she noticed Mr Pearson glancing at Virginia, causing her to blush. She soon composed herself. After her mother had packed the picnic basket away, Virginia suggested taking a stroll down to the lower level. She and Aine wanted to see the places they had shared when they were postulants.

'No, dear, you go alone with Aine,' said her mother. 'They are things for you two to share.'

VIRGINIA and Aine wended their way through the family groups on the upper level. Heads turned as they passed by. When they arrived at the bottom of the stairs, Virginia asked whether the attention still bothered her.

'I try not to notice, and most of the time, I don't. People are just curious, anyhow.' She glanced at Virginia. 'How do you know they weren't looking at you?'

'Me? No, don't be silly. They're looking at you.'

'I'm not so sure.'

'I am.'

They walked to the edge of the embankment and looked silently at the steep drop down to the dark green water.

'We shouldn't stay too long away,' Virginia said. 'I just wanted the chance to talk about your experiences here.' They walked towards the grotto. 'How do you feel about it now?' she said when they had stopped in front of the statue of Our Lady of Lourdes.

'Just the same, I don't understand what was behind it or who those people could have been.'

'No idea at all?'

'No. Do you?'

'I don't know.'

'Have you seen anything since?'

'Not a thing,' said Virginia, pondering. 'But I have been away from the convent for three years. There have been some other things, though.'

'What?'

'First, tell me how things have been going in Binawarra, you know, what you told me about—'

Aine repeated what she had told Virginia during her last visit to St Joseph's. Everything about her life could not be better except when some shapeless evil thing welled up in her mind and left her despairing. There was this inclination to abandon her faith. It was frightening.

'And it's not the same thing or feeling you had here?'

'It's not the same thing,' said Aine. 'The feeling is different, too. It's more despair than terror, although that's also there.'

'Is it like the despair people sometimes feel when they see their sinful behaviour separating them from God?'

'I suppose ... but I have done nothing wrong. I mean big sins, not the usual everyday failings. Those terrible things which separate us from God don't tempt me, but they stalk me ... they stalk me in my mind. Otherwise, I am happy with everything. That's what makes it so puzzling.'

'Let's say a prayer.'

They knelt before the grotto and bent their heads. Virginia took Aine's arm when they rose and drew her towards the riverbank.

'You felt there was some evil force infecting the convent?'

'Yes. It seems absurd, doesn't it?'

'Do you remember Fr. Sheridan?'

'Yes, he was a very holy priest,' said Aine.

'Did you tell him about your experiences?'

'Yes.'

'Do you want to tell me what he said?'

'He warned me about the Evil One, the great tempter. He said Our Lord designated some of us for a personal trial and that I should persevere with my prayers. That's what I have always done.'

'Have you heard of the La Salette prophecies?' said Virginia.

'No, I haven't.'

'They're like the Fatima prophecies, only a lot worse. The world is threatened with catastrophe unless it mends its ways and returns to God.'

'People aren't paying much attention to the Fatima message,' said Aine.

'You're right. The La Salette prophecies foretold the collapse of convent life. Yet, it hardly seems possible when you look around you. The convents seem to be bursting with vocations and optimism.' She pointed towards the main building with its great tower dominating the surroundings. They could see the people at the outer edge of the first level, sitting or milling around in a comfortable, relaxed atmosphere. 'Nothing seems more peaceful.'

'A spiritual malady is not so noticeable amid the signs of welfare,' said Aine.

'Yes, you're right.' She glanced at Aine. 'You're much more confident and mature than five years ago.'

Aine smiled. 'I should hope so. I have a small daughter, a husband, and a household to care for.'

'You see, I'm still that presumptuous know-all.'

They were now near the riverbank. Virginia looked around at the ground.

'What are you looking for?'

'I could have sworn it was somewhere around here, something I wanted to show you.' She unhitched herself from Aine, walked some way

along the ridge, and then came back again. 'For heaven's sake, I can't find it
!'

'What are you looking for?'

'There was a burnt patch of ground around here—burnt sticks and
animal bones,' she murmured. 'I saw it the other night. It's about where
I saw the light coming from, you know, the hooded figures—'

Aine walked along the ridge where Virginia had indicated. At length,
she stopped and bent down. 'Is this it?' She pointed to some fresh bare
earth breaking the otherwise smooth carpet of grass.

'It was a burnt patch,' said Virginia. 'I felt it and smelt it.' She rubbed
her hand around the earth. 'This is fresh dirt. The animals sometimes dig
up the ground.'

'But it doesn't look like that,' said Aine. 'It would be irregular if it
were a bandicoot, a wallaby, or something like that. That looks like a rake
has smoothed it over. The dirt looks like it comes from somewhere else.
Look, the dirt at the edges is different.'

'Good heavens, you're right. Someone has tried to cover it up.'

'Perhaps it was just one of the lay sisters cleaning up. Some gardeners
rake leaves and sticks together, burn them all on the spot, and then clean
it up later.'

'Perhaps,' said Virginia, deep in thought.

'If not, then what do you think it means?'

'That's the big question. I don't know. But if it concerns what we saw,
it is a piece in the puzzle. Come on. We've seen enough.'

AS THEY stepped onto the upper level, they almost walked into Sister Catherine.

'Oh, I've just been along to your mother and father, Sister Agnes. I was wondering if Aine could spare a few minutes.'

'Of course. I should not monopolise her,' said Agnes. 'Mother Jerome would like a few words with Aine, too.'

'You look very well,' said Catherine as they walked to her family group, leaving Virginia to return to her parents. 'Married life suits you. I thought there might be more children.'

That was just like Margaret.

'No, we've been blessed with just the one. We're more than happy with our daughter.'

'Do you want more children?'

'Whatever is God's will.'

'Many wives would regard that situation with less equanimity.' Aine did not reply. 'You're still restricted to the house?' she went on, unperturbed.

'I'm a full-time mother and housewife if that's what you mean.'

'I'm sorry,' said Margaret. 'I only thought you may have considered other interests.'

'No, I'm happy with my family and everything about it. I thank God each day for my husband.'

'You have never considered it strange that you went from the convent where you thought you had a vocation straight into his arms?'

'I've always relied on the guidance of Providence,' said Aine, reluctant to divulge her feelings to Margaret. 'But, I admit, the object of that guidance never occurred to me. So, in that sense, it seemed strange.'

'And nothing else?'

They arrived at the family group, where Margaret introduced her to her parents and what appeared to be a lively contingent of cousins, aunts, and uncles. Margaret seemed to have forgotten her last question. Or was it that the question was meant to hang until she returned to it later, as she had done before? She was half expecting her to take her aside after the introductions to pursue questions that, yet again, seemed to have a purpose. So, she was surprised to find a seat offered to her in the middle of the company, and Margaret settled next to her. Her apprehensions soon dissolved as the familiar Irish accents and friendly welcome made her feel at home.

Mr McGuigan, who sounded like he had stepped off the boat from Ireland that very morning, was typical of the boisterous men she had met in such family groups. He kept the conversation at pace with witticisms and cajoling in an unabashed Irish brogue that had everyone laughing or retorting with similar comments. It soon became evident that he had long assumed the role of the family patriarch. Nobody was reluctant to break in on his stream of comments or cajole and laugh at him, but it was all done in a subtle reference to his approval. The questioning eyes cast in his direction were quick but no less evident to Aine. It was just as clear, too, that underneath his Irish exuberance, Mr McGuigan greatly admired his daughter.

His conversation continually returned to Margaret and her achievements, at least those that Mr McGuigan valued. Aine had wondered what Margaret had been doing during the last three years, something Virginia knew little of. Mr McGuigan now informed her as he listed those achievements, the highest of which was Margaret's teaching success. He clearly did so for her benefit. The eyes of the aunts and uncles critically fixing on her confirmed this as Mr McGuigan worked himself up to a concluding point.

'Fifty years ago,' he said, leaning forward, 'English Protestants still had our family crushed into the dirt of Ireland.' His face turned taut with emotion. The tormented faces of the aunts and the uncles joined him in solidarity. For the first time, Aine saw pain and sympathy on Margaret's face as she looked at her father. 'My grandparents were natives of Belfast, like your family.' He leaned further forward, his breast heaving slightly. 'Were, I said. We were forced to flee to Dublin as refugees in our own land.' He stopped. His mouth worked, and he fixed bloodshot eyes on her. Aine held his gaze. She knew what was coming. 'My grandfather, God bless him, helped out a Protestant neighbour who found himself i n difficulty. Do'ye know how Granddad was rewarded?' He breathed out these words in a stifled, manic manner.

'Mr McGuigan, I know,' Aine said. 'I'm so sorry.'

'Don't be sorry, girl. Remember!' He reached out and put his hand on her arm. 'Protestant thugs arrived one evening—'

'No, Mr McGuigan, it's not necessary—' He grabbed and held her arm tightly.

'They wrenched the baby from my grandmother's arms and smashed its head against the door. They grabbed the fourteen-year-old girl who tried to stop them—' He coughed and exhaled several times sharply. 'They raped her—' Tears were brimming in the eyes of the aunts while the uncles shifted in their seats. 'That girl was my mother ... our mother ....'

'God rest her soul,' said the aunts, sniffling.

'I'm sorry—'

'No, girl, don't be sorry. Sorry doesn't help. Remember! Never forget!'

'There were so many terrible—'

'Look at you, girl! You are pure salt of the Celtic soil. You can't forget. You must never forget that—where you come from and what you must do to exact retribution—to purify the soil of Ireland.'

'Me ... what do you mean ...?'

Aine had heard many stories of unimaginable horror committed during the centuries of English occupation, but no one had yet laid such responsibility on her. Now the circle of Margaret's parents, aunts, and uncles was staring at her.

'You must rise ... like a white Celtic princess—' He stopped, for once searching for words.

'I don't understand,' said Aine. She glanced at Margaret, whose face was flushed with emotion. 'Mr McGuigan, I know terrible things were done to the Irish people, but isn't it time to forgive? My grandparents wanted to leave all that behind them. My parents say it's no good to dwell on the past. It's time to forgive.'

Mr McGuigan began to rise in his chair, but Margaret motioned at him. 'Dad, please don't forget that Aine is our guest here. She understands. Deep in herself, she knows the issues of justice. Her keen sense of justice will speak to her.'

'My sense of justice is speaking to me,' Aine hastened to say. 'Jesus' words to the woman about to be stoned, that's my sense of justice. Revenge is not—'

'Yes, yes, I am aware, Aine,' said Margaret, waving her hand. 'You misunderstand. Besides, I'm familiar with Jesus's justice, justice he applied ruthlessly on occasions.'

'What do you mean?'

'He drove the corrupt moneylenders, the capitalists, from the temple, for one thing—but let's leave that for now. Truly, Aine, I do not need lessons in Scripture. And it's visiting day. We are meant to be spending a happy time together.'

'Yes, please excuse us,' said Margaret's mother, who had said little to that point. 'We're typical of the Irish, aren't we, always getting excited and indignant about something or other? But you, Aine, you would know that, being Irish yourself.'

'That's right, Mother,' said Margaret, forcing a smile and leaving Aine with no chance to reply. 'We can't help it.' She gave her father a sympathetic glance, to which he reacted with a smile and nod.

'Yeah, Bobby, shut up for a while, will you?' said one of the uncles.

Bobby let a smile break the tension on his face. He pointed at the uncle.

'It's time for a cup of tea,' said Mrs McGuigan, getting up. 'You'll stay for a cuppa, won't you, Aine dear?'

'Yes, Mrs McGuigan, but then I must be going.'

The conversation soon returned to the cheerful chatter of five minutes before, while Mrs McGuigan and an aunt prepared the tea and cut slices of tea cake. As the tea and cake were handed around, McGuigan took her husband's head in her hands and kissed him tenderly on the forehead. Aine was familiar with such twists and changes of feeling. She wondered why she was not as demonstrative and outgoing as most Irish people her parents mixed with. Her reserve was more typical of Australians from an English background. Then it occurred to her that Virginia had the sort of intense, emotional, and outspoken temperament usually found among the Irish.

Mr McGuigan resumed his flow of chatter as if nothing had intervened to shake the company to its very core. He indirectly compensated for making Aine uncomfortable by associating her with his daughter's success. It was the usual way, reflected Aine. Such tough, fiery personalities did not openly express their regret. She appreciated it and conveyed her appreciation in her own way, especially because he never alluded to her appearance, at least not how others did. His reference to her being of pure Celtic stock was different, although she did not understand his meaning and purpose. At a proper moment, Margaret brought Aine's visit to an end.

'I'm sure you understand that what happened to my grandmother still strongly affects my father,' Margaret said as they walked back to Virginia and her parents.

'I do understand,' said Aine, keeping up with the confident strides beneath Margaret's black, bustling tunic. 'I have heard similar stories before. It's tragic.'

'He may not have expressed it clearly, but part of the reason for bringing it up was to point to the lessons that must be learned.'

'Oh? What lessons are those?'

'We must learn to be confident, self-reliant. Our goodness must presuppose those qualities.'

'Is that the message for your students?' said Aine, reminded of Margaret's undertaking five years before.

'Yes, I'm at pains to stress to my girls the importance of confidence and self-reliance. Without those qualities, they will risk failing in whatever direction in life they choose.'

'And the humility and self-sacrifice of religious life?' said Aine, also remembering Virginia's response.

'There's no conflict. Besides, I must presume my girls are not likely to become nuns. Most have ideas of marriage and having children. My task is to develop their confidence and independence.' She stopped and faced Aine. 'Don't you understand people will grind you into the dirt if you let them? That's what my father was talking about. That does not conflict with the humility and the self-sacrifice of religious life. How can you be humble and self-sacrificing without being in the position to make a conscious choice about being so? Is it self-sacrifice when you are left with no choice in the matter—when you let the oppressor trample you into the dirt?'

'Is this what your father meant?'

'Yes,' said Margaret, letting a frown pass across her face.

'I suppose you would attribute your vocation to your father.'

'In a way, I suppose, as an instrument. The calling comes from God, after all. You know that.'

'But his thoughts are yours?'

'No, they are not. I choose to listen to him, reflect on what he says, and adopt whatever I find to be the truth. My father's advice is about independence.'

'I didn't mean to antagonise you.'

'You're not antagonising me,' said Margaret sharply. 'I am only concerned with making my thoughts clear.'

'Margaret, I mean Sister Catherine—'

'You can call me Margaret if you like—among friends, you know.'

'Sister Catherine, you've said this sort of thing to me in the past. Is there a reason for it?' They had walked on and now stood at the edge of the upper level. The clearing below was in full view. Aine noticed a familiar figure walking with Sister Hildegard and her parents.

'I want us to be friends,' replied Margaret. 'We have a lot in common. I'm only trying to encourage you to fulfil your potential.'

'But what do you mean by that?' said Aine. She saw Virginia over Margaret's shoulder, beckoning with a quick wave.

'I only want you to strive to achieve what you're capable of, whatever that is.'

'I want that, too. I want to be the best mother and wife I can be.' Margaret looked like she was trying to suppress her irritation. 'Anyhow, I must go now. Virginia, I mean Sister Agnes, wants to take me to Mother Jerome.'

Margaret swung around and caught Virginia staring at them. Virginia turned to her parents, relaxing in their chairs.

'Of course,' said Margaret, frowning. 'Don't forget our common background. That's even stronger than the tie of friendship.'

'Thank you for your hospitality,' said Aine, edging away. 'Also, your parents.'

'No thanks necessary.'

'Is that Jannie down there with Elizabeth Parker?' said Aine, again catching a glimpse of the familiar figure.

'Yes, she arrived late. She wants to talk to you, too.'

'Why?'

'For the same reason as me, of course. We're friends. We have your interests at heart. Aine, don't be so suspicious.'

'I must see Mother Jerome first,' said Aine, backing away.

'Goodbye, Aine. You're welcome to visit me whenever you are down from Binawarra. In fact, I would like you to visit me.' Sister Catherine retreated with the same firm, confident steps.

Chapter 20

Mother Jerome's advice

WITH RELIEF, Aine returned to Virginia, whose warm, open nature was an antidote to Margaret's oppressive company. It was like taking a breath of fresh air after being trapped in a close, stuffy room. Virginia had to laugh at Aine's restrained expressions of relief.

'It can't have been bad enough to put that ugly expression on your pretty face, surely?'

'There was this Irish business ... you have to be from an Irish background to understand ... it's not pleasant.'

'Oh, I think I know what you are referring to.'

'What Irish business?' said her mother.

'Do you think that's behind Margaret's—Sister Catherine's behaviour?' said Virginia.

'Yes, what Irish business?' said her father, rousing himself.

'The English occupation of Ireland, the penal laws and all that,' said Virginia.

'What penal laws?'

'Dad, I will explain later. First, I must take Aine to Mother Jerome.'

Virginia repeated the question as soon as they were out of earshot of her parents.

'I'm not sure how much,' Aine said as they made their way between the admiring glances. 'Partly, at least. It's evident her father has been a significant influence on her thinking. They certainly have a similar way of seeing the world. But there's something else—beyond the Irish thing.'

'What?'

'I don't know. I can't put it into words. She justifies her talk about self-reliance by referring to the horrors the Irish suffered under the English. But I can't help the impression there is something more to it, as I say. She is still seeking a connection with me for some purpose. It's still not clear what it is. It repels me.'

Repels you?' said Virginia, stopping.

'Yes, and I don't know why. She says she's just seeking friendship. How could an offer of friendship repel you?'

'It shouldn't, certainly. I would normally say to someone else that they were imagining things. But you ... you're different.'

'No, Virginia, I'm not. I don't want to be.'

'You are.' She reflected. 'It's got to belong to all that's happened. Come on, though. We don't want to be late for your appointment with Mother Jerome.'

As soon as they entered the visitor's parlour, Aine glanced at the translucent glass of the sash windows.

'Relax,' said Virginia, 'there's nothing to worry about in the middle of the day.'

'I can't help it.'

'Come on, sit down. I'm here with you, too. My personality is a match for any upstart evil spirit,' she laughed. 'Mother Jerome won't be too long, either. Sister Martha has gone to fetch her.' She drew Aine to the same armchair on which she had sat on the day of her departure.

'Will you wait until Mother comes?' Aine whispered.

'Yes, for a minute,' said Virginia, mimicking Aine's tone. She ran her hand over her shoulder and took hold of her hand. 'You know, I'm not supposed to be touching anybody like this.' Aine looked up at her. 'But you're an exception.'

'I'm glad,' said Aine. 'I have no idea why I should feel the way I sometimes do. Charles tries to help when it gets too oppressive—but he's not here now.' She bowed her head.

'Do you remember Psalm 129?'

'Of course. Charles reads it to me when—'

'*Out of the depths I cry to thee, O Lord,*' began Virginia. '*Lord, hear my voice.*'

'Go on.'

'*Let Thine ears be attentive to the voice of my supplications.*'

Mother Jerome walked through the open door. Virginia withdrew her hand.

'That's all right, Sister. You are not feeling well, Mrs Winterbine?'

'I'm better now, Mother,' said Aine, embarrassed that the prioress should see her for the first time in five years in the same state. 'I'm sorry to be so much trouble.'

'You are no trouble, Aine. Sister, you can leave us now. Please shut the door as you go.'

Mother Jerome waited until Agnes had withdrawn, and the door was firmly shut. She then placed a white linen bag on the nearby table and sat in an armchair next to Aine.

'Aine, you look very well, very well, indeed. Now tell me what you have been doing. Tell me all about your family. I want to know.'

Aine began hesitantly, but as Mother Jerome showed increasing interest, she relaxed. Soon, the oppressive feelings had gone, and she delighted in talking about her beloved Charles, Estella and the town they lived in.

As she spoke, she became aware of the prioress's appearance. Virginia had warned her.

'I am not as robust as I used to be,' said Mother Jerome. 'But I am quite healthy.'

'Oh, I didn't—' stammered Aine.

'That's all right, Aine dear. In my position, you learn to guess what people are thinking. In your case, you are more open than others.' She patted Aine on the arm. 'You are happy that I was right about your vocation?'

'Yes, Mother, I could not be more grateful. I love my husband and daughter more than anything in the world.'

'I'm happy I was right, too. You have a fine, devoted husband. He is a very rare man, indeed. Did you consider becoming members of one of the apostolates I mentioned?'

'No, Mother, we're happy to follow our devotions together. Besides, there are those occasions when I am not myself.'

An embarrassing silence followed as the prioress subjected her to one of her searching gazes. Then, without saying anything, Mother Jerome rose and fetched the linen bag from the table. She pulled a book, yellow with age, from the bag and held it up in front of Aine.

'Have you seen this book before?'

'Yes.' Aine recoiled. 'Where—?'

'Where did you see it?'

'I noticed it one day lying on the wooden bench in the cloisters just after I rang the bell ... during the postulancy ... about halfway through ....'

'Did you read anything or look through it?'

'No, I only picked it up. One of the older sisters snatched it from my hands.'

'Who?'

'I don't know. It was nobody I recognised. I didn't see her properly, anyhow. She was gone before I could pay attention.'

'It is not usual for the professed sisters to be near the postulants during the day.'

'That occurred to me, too. I thought it very strange.'

'Do you know what *Pistis Sophia* is, what it refers to?'

'No, Mother, I have no idea.'

'Have you thought about it since?' Aine shook her head. 'Sister Agnes was concerned enough to ask me about it.'

'I realise that.'

'If I tell you it dates from the early centuries of Christianity, that it be-longs to a school of thought—or more exactly, an attitude of mind—that was judged heretical by the Church, what would you think?'

'I would wonder why it was in the convent.'

'Would you wonder why it was there on the bench precisely where you sat?'

Aine had to ponder a question that had never occurred to her. 'I thought I accidentally came across it. The sister exclaimed she couldn't leave anything alone when she snatched it from me.'

'You never thought it could have been left there so that you would find it?'

'No. But why?'

'Did you ever consider its appearance, just where you might be, was perhaps connected with the things you experienced here?'

'No, I didn't. When I think back, I find it hard to separate what was real and what I might've dreamed or imagined. Sometimes it all seems like a bad dream. The older sister was real. The book is real.'

'The book is certainly real. Its contents are all too real.'

'How could it be connected?'

'I am not sure how I should answer that,' said Mother Jerome. 'Can we restrict this conversation to ourselves?'

'Yes, of course,' said Aine, intrigued by the prioress's confidential manner.

'This book, *Pistis Sophia*, belongs to a body of writing that appeared in the early centuries of Christianity. Generally speaking, the writings are fictional stories supposedly about Christ, which the writers called gospels, letters, and so on, imitating what we know to be the true, divinely inspired writings of the Apostles. If someone like yourself, strong in faith, read them, you would find them strange, fanciful, and even laughable. It would surprise you how they could disturb anyone's faith. But unfortunately, people weak in faith are susceptible. That is the first reason a book like this is placed in our reserved section of the library. It is available only to those engaged in the formal study of Church history, those with an appropriate academic background.

'The second reason, more importantly, is that Gnosticism underlies many of these fictional stories. Gnosticism is a manner of thinking that is not easy to define. Let it suffice to say that the Church Fathers condemned Gnostic writings as heretical and defined what writings belonged to the inspired writings, the canon of Sacred Scripture. They also began a process of defining the authentic doctrine of the Church. Thus, we had the Nicene Creed, the fundamental statement of what Christians must believe. Naturally, it is prudent for the convent to place Gnostic writings in a reserve section. A firm understanding of Church teaching should precede their study. Their influence, otherwise, could be pernicious—at the service of both the naïve and malicious. No one among us is presently engaged in such study.'

'But what has that to do with my experiences?'

'Do you know what "Sophia" means and what it refers to?'

'Sophia means wisdom, doesn't it?'

'Yes, it is the Ancient Greek word for wisdom. Pistis means faithful. In the context of Gnosticism, Sophia often refers to the supreme feminine principle.'

'The supreme feminine principle?'

'It is not possible to explain briefly. But, again, it is enough to say that the supreme feminine principle of Gnosticism is diametrically opposed to the Fatherhood of God, whose Son we Christians have accepted as the Redeemer. The Church raised solid ramparts against the heresies of the Gnostics, and they have held well through the centuries, but Gnosticism itself did not disappear as the great temptation to the Christian mind. A Gnostic mentality is behind some modern philosophical schools, those most destructive of Christian thought. There are signs that the supreme feminine principle is gaining its adherents outside the small groups of zealous Gnostic proselytisers. In this respect, this century's so-called women's movements may have this as their primary motivation rather than the vague notion of equal rights. For who really thinks men and women are the same? Now I come to the connection.'

'I speak of the great temptation. I might more accurately speak of the Great Tempter, for the attempt to turn the Christian dogma of the Fall into the suppression of the feminine in the person of Eve is surely as diabolical as the human mind is capable of. Unfortunately, that great temptation has shown signs of its appearance in our foundations. For whatever reason, the devil has laid siege to this convent. It is something I have had to battle for some years now. The manner and place of that book's appearance, typically furtive and elusive, is another sign of the ongoing siege.'

'I had no idea,' said Aine.

'No, you wouldn't. Few people would. Many would not accept what I am saying. Talk of the devil is unsettling for everyone, those who fear him and those who laugh at the idea.'

'Why are you telling me?'

'You ask the right question. You are different. You have the grace to understand, at least this aspect.'

'But what does that have to do with my experiences?'

'The Devil, the Great Tempter, targets the virtuous and the pure of mind. I'm inclined to see your experiences as the result of a very bitter attack by the devil. I warned you about this when you left us.'

'But I don't experience any strong temptation to deny what I know to be true. It's not like that. On the contrary, I feel an oppressiveness, a despair like Our Lord is departing.'

'And if something like the *Pistis Sophia* comes under your eyes while you feel Our Lord is departing?'

'Oh,' said Aine, 'but nothing so obvious would sway me.'

'Aine, my dear child, it is rarely obvious.'

'I still don't understand.'

'I realise the difficulty you have—there is so much you are unaware of. I had not intended to broach this subject with you, but when Sister Agnes told me about the appearance of *Pistis Sophia*, I was alarmed. By the way, you should know there are other works just as malignant as this book. In any case, my purpose in openly talking is to put you on your guard against the wiles of the devil working through others, the wolves in sheep's clothing. The most effective attacks will be unexpected, coming through avenues you least suspect. Second, in your case, it is through prayer, begging Our Lord through the intercession of the Blessed Virgin, that you will persevere.'

'Fr. Sheridan urged me in the same way. Are things so grave?'

'Yes. The prophecies of Fatima are being ignored or, worse still, are dismissed as superstitious nonsense. The Third Secret ... alas, it has not been revealed.'

'Do you know about La Salette?' said Aine, reminded of her conversation with Virginia. Then she realised how foolish the question was.

'Who told you about La Salette?'

'Virginia—Sister Agnes. She has expressed similar worries.'

Mother nodded gravely. 'I will leave it at that,' she said. 'I don't want to upset you, only warn and urge you to be on your guard. Please keep in touch with me to let me know how you are doing. I'm naturally concerned about you, but I also think your experiences may be a barometer.'

'A barometer?'

'Never mind about that now. You will keep in touch?' Aine nodded. The prioress fell again to thinking. 'You have a close friendship with Sister Agnes. She was of great comfort to you. Ordinarily, we discourage close friendships within the religious life, let alone condoning them with laymen. In your case, I will make an exception—on two conditions. First, I don't want Sister Agnes to know I am permitting it. Second, I will leave it to your prudence to decide the extent of your contact. You are as aware as any sister of the commitments of religious life. There are sound reasons for these conditions.'

'Yes, Mother, I'm happy and relieved you approve.'

'Good. I am very glad to have had this talk. Of course, my door is open anytime for you. Don't forget that. And please give my respects to your good husband.'

As they stood up, Mother Jerome turned to Aine and, without speaking, looked over her shoulder at the translucent sash windows. Aine swung round. Nothing. But she had seen the surprise and alarm on the superior general's face.

'I will see you to the door,' said Mother Jerome.

Aine walked back to Virginia and her parents, her mind running through the conversation with Mother Jerome. She could not help but think that much of it made sense, even though Mother sometimes cut her explanation short. The question of 'why' kept coming up. Why was she chosen for these torments? She could not look at herself as the unblemished person Mother Jerome seemed to think she was. To herself, she seemed so fallible, so weak and unresisting. After all, she had often been brought low, sometimes for long periods. She had been incapacitated for almost a year after she had visited Virginia for the first ti me.

'I wondered when you were going to return,' said Virginia, disturbing her thoughts.

'I did not realise I was away for so long,' Aine said, pleased to be back in Virginia's reassuring company.

'You've had a long and intense discussion with Mother, I can see.'

'It's so obvious?'

'Yes. I also had an idea that Mother would bring up the subject of *Pistis Sophia* and your experiences. My mentioning it two weeks ago caused her alarm.'

'I understand why now. It's all so strange and alarming. I hardly know how to digest it all.'

'Ah, Aine, are you ready to go?' said Mr Pearson. People around them were preparing to leave.

Virginia wanted to ask about Aine's conversation, but accepted without complaint that her parents had to go. As they were packing up, Jannie de Kam bounced into their presence, dazzling those around them.

'Oh, Aine, are you going?' she exclaimed, gesticulating. 'I wanted so much to talk to you. It's so long since—'

'I'm afraid so,' said Mr Pearson.

'I'm so disappointed,' said Jannie, her handsome, made-up face twisted into an urgent appeal. When her appeal had no effect, she said, as if illuminated by a sudden inspiration: 'You have to take Aine to Spencer Street Station, don't you, Mr Pearson?'

'Yes, we do,' said Mr Pearson.

'Well, I can take her. I must go back into town. I'll save you the trouble. You live in the Eastern suburbs, don't you? I'll save you time.'

Mr Pearson reacted warmly to the suggestion. Aine was not so keen, but she realised it would save Virginia's parents the bother of driving into town and out again.

'Well, if it's all right with Aine,' said Mr Pearson, 'it's fine with us.'

'It's all right with me,' said Aine as calmly as she could.

'Are you sure?' Virginia glanced at Aine, then at her parents. Her mother caught on, but not her father.

'Of course, she's sure,' exclaimed Jannie. 'What possible objection could she have?'

Virginia and her mother did not reply.

'There's none from our side,' said Mr Pearson. 'It suits everyone, doesn't it? Aine and Miss de Kam will have their opportunity to chat.'

With a fervent goodbye, whispering her undertaking to keep in contact, Aine left Virginia to go to Jannie's car. She glanced around as they entered the main building and saw Virginia through the dispersing people, looking at her just as forlornly as she felt.

Chapter 21

Harry the photographer

'MY, YOU have not changed at all,' said Jannie as they emerged from the convent. 'You look even better than the last time I saw you,' she added, unaware of the contradiction. 'A little maturity in appearance has worked to your advantage.' Aine forced a polite smile. 'I see you're still not interested in talking about it. Hope it's not false modesty,' she kidded.

'I try to remain healthy.'

'Healthy! The men are drooling over your health.'

'I'm married,' said Aine helplessly.

'What's that got to do with it? You think it's compulsory for women to become ugly when they marry? A lot of men think so, no doubt.'

They walked the length of the tree-lined entrance avenue and passed through the front gates. Aine looked around. 'Where's your car?'

'Oh, I'm being picked up. Harry and Erik will be along any minute. Two handsome fellows, if ever you saw. You wait and see. They're both interested.' She tilted her head and gestured as if it were out of her control.

'I was under the impression you would drive me straight to the station,' said Aine, looking back to see if she could spot Virginia's parents.

'What's the difference? Relax. It'll be an experience for you.'

Aine was vexed. She would not have consented if she knew Jannie had invited her to ride with two of her men friends. She should have suspected something. Jannie's flippant behaviour three years before, and her boyfriend at the time, should have been a warning. Perhaps Jannie's different appearance and more mature manner misled her. Gone were the bright floral clothing and high-heeled shoes. Instead, she wore darker colours in a combination of skirt, blouse, and small heels. She was still fashionably dressed but less conventionally feminine. Her manner suited her clothing. No doubt, she was still working as a fashion model. Aine looked back again. What was keeping Virginia's parents? How could she get out of Jannie's trickery? Where on earth were Mr and Mrs Pearson?

'Come on,' said Jannie, 'here they are.'

A luxury car pulled up beside them. In his early thirties, a smart but casually dressed man emerged from the driver's side, looking in surprise at Aine. The passenger, also of the same age and appearance, was similarly impressed. Jannie, smiling, introduced Aine, saying they were to take her to the station in town. To Aine's relief, the men were polite and welcoming. Before she knew it, the car doors opened with a suitable display of gallantry, and she and Jannie were installed. As the car swung onto the road along the ridge, Jannie leaned over and whispered, 'Knocked them out, you did.'

Aine wondered what she had got herself into. She hoped Jannie's remark was not a sign of what would follow. To her relief again, Jannie turned her attention to the men, asking what they had been doing while she was visiting the convent. They had been roaming around the area, where they came across the most delightful weatherboard pub in the middle of the bush.

'It looked like something from the explorer past,' said Erik, who was driving.

'I hope you didn't drink too much,' said Jannie, leaning forward and poking him in the back. She smirked at Aine as she did so.

'Not at all,' said Harry, turning around. 'Don't give our guest the impression we are irresponsible drunks.' He winked.

Before Aine could wonder too much about the wink, Harry turned his attention to her, asking about her connection with Jannie. To her surprise, neither Harry nor Erik seemed interested in the convent connection. Soon, the conversation led to Binawarra and her life there. In contrast to Jannie, who made pert remarks about Aine, Harry and Erik took turns asking inoffensive questions about her and her life in Binawarra. In this way, the time passed pleasantly.

'What time's your train?' asked Harry when they arrived on the outskirts of the city centre. 'But you have more than an hour and a half to wait,' he exclaimed when Aine told him. 'We can't leave you alone on the platform for an hour and a half. Erik, stop at our place. Aine can relax with a cup of tea.'

'No, no, don't trouble yourselves,' said Aine. 'I don't mind waiting. You shouldn't go out of your way.'

'It's not out of their way,' said Jannie. 'They don't live far from the station. You're safer there. You never know who's wandering around the station.'

'No, really—'

'No, no arguments,' said Harry. 'You can relax with a cuppa. Half an hour before departure, I'll drive you to the station. It's only a few minutes from where we live. Easy. So relax. We're not bogeymen, you know.'

Resistance was useless, and Aine resigned herself. Perhaps it was not so bad, she reflected. Indeed, Harry and Erik were not bogeymen. They were pleasant and friendly, not in the least intrusive, all the time treating her with respect. And thank heavens, there was no allusion to her appearance. Eventually, the car pulled up outside an elegant, restored, two-storey Victorian terrace house. She and Jannie were ushered past fastidiously tended gardens onto a brown and white antique-tiled verandah, through a high-ceiling spacious hall, and into the lounge room. She was surprised to see how tastefully it was decorated in light, subdued colours. A variety of tasteful ornaments and plants were around on shelves, side tables, and sideboard. On the wall, spaced pleasingly, was a selection of framed prints and photographs. She was shown to a lounge chair that gave her a good view of the leafy tree-lined road and the classy terrace houses opposite. Erik went to set the tea while Harry excused himself 'for a sec' and disappeared.

'They're clean and tidy for men, aren't they?' said Jannie, who sat opposite her on the lounge settee.

Aine did not know how neat men of that age and background usually were. She nodded vaguely, still looking around her. Charles would be interested in this house and its restoration. A large black-and-white photo of a young woman's face caught her attention. The big dark doe-like eyes below a forehead covered in blond wisps peered out at her.

'You like what you see?' said Harry, entering the room holding a camera. He put it on the ornate sideboard near the entrance and sat in the armchair beside her.

'Yes, my husband is making a specialty of restoring period houses. There's none of this sort in Binawarra, though.'

'He's quite welcome to come and have a look,' said Harry. 'We had it restored by experts. Expensive, but you can see the results. Perhaps he would get some ideas.'

'I'm sure he would,' said Aine. 'He has picked up a lot of techniques and information from studying the buildings themselves. There are examples of Colonial, Italianate, and Gothic Revival styles in Binawarra, though nothing quite as rich as you find in Bendigo.'

'I see you know something about Australia's residential architecture.'

'Really only what I have learned from my husband's work,' Aine said, surprised she was at ease with these two easy-going but correct young men. 'He often talks about it with me.'

The conversation centred on the architectural qualities of early residential Australia for a while. Aine noticed that Jannie's manner became less flippant as the conversation advanced. She leaned back in her armchair, letting her slender legs, bent slightly sideways at the knees, stretch in front of her. They were elegantly moved aside when Erik placed a Wedgwood cup and saucer on the small table beside her. She made sensible comments as she sipped her tea and brushed her hair now and again as if to emphasise her point—and her presence. She really did have the manner and appearance of a fashion model. Her stay at the convent now seemed so strange and incongruous. Whatever brought her to imagine she might have a vocation?

Seeing Aine's interest in the house and its style, Harry began an account of how and why he and Erik bought it as an investment and what they did to restore it to its former glory. Then, without warning, he broke off, leapt to his feet, and invited her to view the rest of the house. Jannie's encouragement quickly overcame Aine's shy reluctance, and she allowed Harry to show her around while Jannie and Erik remained in the lounge room. Harry kept to the point, attentive to her interests and comfort. During the tour, she learned that he was a fashion photographer and that Erik was a solicitor. The house reflected their success.

'That's how I came to know Jannie,' Harry said when they returned to the lounge room. 'I saw her potential. Jannie's got a good reputation for keeping to schedule, too,' he added somewhat irrelevantly and with an expression that seemed to attach much importance to this quality.

'It's my Dutch background,' said Jannie. 'Erik's Dutch, too,' she added.

'Well, it's a long time ago now,' said Erik. 'My grandparents came long before the wave of migrants in the fifties. I don't even speak the language.'

'I'll have to teach you.'

'Do you mind if I take a photo of you?' Harry picked up his camera from the sideboard, fiddled with a few knobs, then came forward, bent down, and aimed the camera at Aine. She recoiled from the flash.

'You might wait for permission,' said Erik.

'You don't mind, do you?' said Harry, moving closer.

'Of course, she doesn't,' said Jannie. 'Not many girls would have such a famous fashion photographer wanting to take their picture.'

'Not really,' said Aine, blinking. There was another flash. She looked away. 'Hold that expression.' Another flash. 'Now look at me.' Shuffling of camera shutters followed, but without the flash.

'See that bonsai on the table beside you?' Aine looked to the side. 'Bend toward it—with your eyes on it. That's it.' More shuffling of shutters. 'Turn back to me. Now put your right hand across your tummy. Relax, relax. Now touch your chin gently with the bent index finger of your left hand. Naturally, at ease, natural, natural.' Another flash. 'Stay there.'

'Why are you doing this?' asked Aine, feeling foolish and dropping her hand. She had followed his instructions out of politeness, thinking each photo would be the last. Another flash.

'It's my interest, my job.' He moved back a pace and then came forward. 'Relax, I've nearly finished. Just one last—turn your head to the side but keep your eyes on me.' Aine turned her head, but Harry was not satisfied. He came forward again. 'Keep your eyes on me.' She was looking into his eyes. 'Do you mind?' He gently placed his hand against her cheek and pushed so that her head turned. The unexpected touch shocked her, and she drew back. 'Excellent! Stay there.' The shutters shuffled several more times.

'She's a natural,' said Jannie.

'Striking,' added Erik. 'Very striking.'

'Yes, you're absolutely right,' said Harry. 'You know,' now turning to Aine while fiddling with his camera again, 'your sort of look is becoming increasingly fashionable—that slender, fragile appearance with the far-away, bewildered expression. The time of the bummy girls with all the smiles is passing.'

'Well!' laughed Jannie, 'where do I fit into that?'

'About halfway, but don't worry, darling,' he said as he put the camera on the sideboard, 'you'll get more than enough work as long as you look after yourself. It's not just about looking good, although you're gorgeous, of course.'

'I'm glad of your support,' she replied in a nonchalant tone. 'I really don't care.' Her bottom lip quivered.

The sudden vulnerability did not escape Aine, revealing perhaps that Jannie's confidence and studied flippancy were at least partly a veneer. But then, as Jannie resumed her confident showy manner, it occurred to her that the quivering lip may not be a sign of hurt but something deeper.

'Here,' said Harry, drawing a business card from his shirt pocket and handing it to Aine. 'Give me a call next week. I can get some work for you. I know a few magazines that will go for your looks.'

'Thank you,' said Aine, taking the card and looking at it, 'but I'm really not interested. I have enough to do with my family. Thank you, anyhow.' She put the card on the table beside her.

'There's no harm in considering it,' said Harry, unmoved by the refusal. 'It would not interfere with your family.'

'It's time to go,' said Jannie, standing up.

'Oh,' exclaimed Aine, looking at her watch, 'I was forgetting—' She looked around for her bag. How could she forget the time?

'It's okay. You've got half an hour,' said Jannie, picking up Harry's card. She gave Harry a look, which drew a nod. 'I'll take you in my car. I want some girl talk with you.'

'Thank you for your hospitality,' Aine said to Harry as he held the door of Jannie's Mini open.

'It was a pleasure,' he replied. He gently pushed the door shut. 'Think about it.'

'They're very nice, aren't they?' said Jannie as they set off, leaving Harry looking after them.

'Yes ... they are nice.'

'These are men with class and style.'

'They were friendly and polite. I'm glad of that.'

'Aine darling, not all boys are stupid and gross.'

Aine glanced at her.

'That was the one thing I disagreed with Margaret about,' Jannie continued. 'You must know how to handle men, know their weak points.' She paused. 'Then again, Margaret's not exactly a raving beauty.'

'You have kept up your friendship with Margaret and Elizabeth?'

'Yes,' was Jannie's delayed response. 'We're friends ... she supported me ... it was difficult. I have not forgotten. I won't forget. There was pretty cruel treatment.'

'You seem so different.'

'You think so? I don't know if that's true.' Jannie kept her eyes on the road ahead.

'There's a big difference between a nun's life and a fashion model's life.'

'I have to earn my money some way. Modelling came my way co-incidentally. I was sort of discovered. Harry discovered me through an acquaintance. Well, of course, you must have the looks for it. I knew I did. I took advantage of a fellow's interest in me, a fellow with the power to benefit me. Well, I did like him, too. You can sometimes manipulate our society's vast inequalities to the advantage of the disadvantaged.'

'Oh? Do you think you belong to the disadvantaged?'

'We all do—women, I mean.'

'I don't feel disadvantaged.'

'You just don't realise it. You will when the inequalities are brought to the forefront of your consciousness.'

By this time, the station car park was a few blocks away.

'You haven't responded to my question,' said Aine.

'I am responding,' said Jannie, after a moment's thought. 'The way I earn my money does not reflect my real interests. I'm still studying, you know. There have been a few false starts, but with Margaret's advice, I've fixed on an arts degree at John Batman University. I've just finished my first year. There's no stopping me now.'

'Margaret will start at John Batman University next year.'

'Yes, I know. Incredible fluke, isn't it? We'll study and pursue our interests together, after all. I'm doing sociology, too. You see, that's where we are alike.'

'Oh, I see,' said Aine, not entirely convinced.

There was silence as Jannie turned into the station car park and manoeuvred the car into a parking space.

'Do you really see, though?' said Jannie, taking up where they had left off as they walked to the terminal.

'I suppose ...,' said Aine, embarrassed that Jannie had guessed her doubts.

'I'm serious now.'

Jannie stopped beside the wrought-iron fence running along the interstate platform and took hold of Aine's arm. A train blew and hissed not far away, preparing for the long trip to Sydney. She had to raise her voice.

'Men think I'm scatty. I let them believe that. It gives me an advantage. And if they're so stupid as to let my shapely legs and pretty face mesmerise them into thinking they have a chance of spending an afternoon making love to me, that's their fault and my advantage. I will use that advantage if they have all the cards and I have none. Think about that. Think about the power this card has. It's just one tool you can manipulate.'

'You've become very cynical,' said Aine, ignoring Harry's card, which Jannie was dangling in front of her face. She resumed her way towards the terminal's entrance, leaving Jannie standing.

'You think that's cynical?' said Jannie, hurrying to catch up. 'I call it realistic. I call it seeking justice.'

'Is it right to deceive and manipulate people?'

'People—who have all the power, privilege, and advantage?'

Aine found it difficult to respond to this horrible perverse misrepresentation of human society.

'My husband treats me like a princess. And sometimes, I don't think I am worthy.'

'If he didn't treat you like a princess, what could you do about it?'

'I have to get on the train now.' She stepped into the carriage. 'My husband is always conscious of his duties, of what's right and wrong.'

'Okay, let's not argue,' said Jannie, with an expression that said she had won the point. 'I want to be friends, and friends want to help each other.'

'That's what Margaret said.'

'We both want to be friends. Don't be so suspicious. Here,' she said, holding the card in front of her again, 'take it. There's no harm in that. It is a terrific opportunity for you to earn something for your family. You should utilise the talents God has given you. Surely, I don't have to remind you of the parable of the talents.

'Margaret again. It's not clear what talent you both think I have.'

'You certainly do. Don't be cute. Come on, take it.' She opened Aine's bag and poked the card into it. She grabbed her in an embrace. 'Keep in touch. A small difference of opinion doesn't mean we can't be friends.' She released her. 'You don't know how much we have in common.'

Jannie waited on the platform as Aine made her way to her seat. The train's brakes were released with an enormous hiss, and the train started to roll. Jannie kept pace beside it, staring at Aine with a strange, lost look. Aine, again, did not know how to respond. A faint smile was all she could raise as the train gathered pace and outran Jannie, who skipped into a trot but then stopped and stood on the spot, staring. This strange end to their meeting capped off a day of joy and discomfort. She extracted Harry's card from her bag and looked at it on and off for the next half hour. She screwed it up and put it back in her bag.

Chapter 22

Philip's shock

BETWEEN THE hurry of preparing for university enrolment and making the mental adjustment to where she would be in a few weeks, Sister Agnes's Christmas conversation with Aine kept on intruding. As much as Agnes wanted to push the strange events surrounding Aine into the background, her visit insisted on bringing it all back in sharp relief. Her mind struggled with a vague scenario that she could not order with satisfaction. She had gone over it again with Aine, but Aine could no more enlighten her about its causes than she could. They felt some evil spirit hanging over the convent. Margaret and Jannie also encroached in this distraction.

Now working as a fashion model, Jannie turned up, showing herself as attached to Margaret as ever. Although no less brittle, she had undergone a dramatic change since the postulancy, now outgoing, flamboyant, and coquettish. Already a very pretty girl, she had polished that beauty through her work as a fashion model. She turned heads. It had given her a confidence she had not possessed. Besides her modelling work, she attended John Batman University in her first year of sociology, in which she intended to major. She attributed her success in work and study to Margaret's sympathy and support. For reasons still unclear, she strove to ingratiate herself with Aine. At the end of the visit, she insisted on taking a reluctant Aine to Spencer Street Station for her trip back to Bendigo. The change in Margaret had also been great, at least outwardly.

As postulants, Margaret had made it her business to torment her at every opportunity, often slyly inciting others to join in. But from the start of the novitiate, she had unilaterally instituted a ceasefire without resolving the issues of their conflict. Either she was too preoccupied to challenge her, or she had reasons related to her supposed agenda, whatever that could be. To enhance the uncertainty, Margaret and Jannie seemed to vie with her for Aine's attention. This had every appearance of a resumption of Margaret's political activity with its place in her supposed agenda. And now she had to consider something new. Because of the sequestered postulancy and novitiate period, followed by an assignment to a country school, she had enjoyed little contact with the sisters whose lives and duties centred on the motherhouse. Of course, she knew the sisters by name, and that's as far as it went with most of them. Whereas Margaret gave every sign of being on familiar terms with them all, especially those with whom she had been through the novitiate.

The atmosphere of the motherhouse differed distinctly from St Joseph's, as she expected. After all, St Joseph's was a country boarding school with day pupils from Ballarat and nearby country towns. A school of lively girls, more interested in pop stars than in religious principles and duty, would make a difference. That was not the significant difference, however. Amid the silence and dedication of a community of religious sisters, a creeping furtiveness and underlying suspicion were worming their way. Strangely, she could not pinpoint its origin. The same lines of rigid veiled heads with eyes cast down in the chapel and the refectory came under her scrutiny.

The slow change in Mother Jerome did not ease her discomfort, either. The Superior General had lost none of her mental sharpness or organisational competence. She had raised the question of her inevitable replacement, but the general view seemed that nobody as yet possessed the required qualities. Now, there was a slight stoop in a figure that had lost weight. The indefatigable aura she had radiated for many years had gone. At the end of the day, Agnes sometimes thought she struggled. Only her indomitable spirit saw her through. Agnes hoped she saw it worse than it was.

The adjustment to the prioress's routine was also significant. During the postulancy, Mother Jerome seemed to leave each sister to her delegated task. For example, there had been little interference in Mother Cecilia's routine. Only at the end of the first year of the novitiate did she occasionally appear in the novices' quarters as if to check things. Was it a coincidence that Agnes had never again received the penance of cleaning stairs with a toothbrush? No one else, for that matter, had ever again suffered that nonsense. Now, Mother Jerome appeared everywhere. That was no less the case with the enrolment preparation. Discussions over subject descriptions in the university handbook were frequent. She and Sister Catherine had to give good reasons for their subject choice. They had to sketch a preliminary three-year plan, understanding that they would proceed only if their results were satisfactory.

While reflecting on these matters, Agnes kept alert for signs of the hooded figures and fires at night. That sinister activity, she decided, was consistent with the furtive atmosphere of the convent. When she awoke at night, she sometimes sat at her cell window, peering through the dark at the river and clearing below. She saw nothing, no sign of human activity. She checked for burnt patches in the grass near the riverbank. She found nothing. Again, she had the unnerving feeling of having imagined it all.

As the weeks passed and enrolment day approached, these concerns retreated into the background. Not just the demands of preparation overtook Agnes; her excitement and enthusiasm in anticipation of the year of study filled those preparatory activities. Of course, there was also the coming meeting with Philip. Her stomach twisted each time it came to mind. Did he know she would be enrolled in his department? Her mother occasionally spoke with Mrs Stevenson. Likely, he knew. So what? She would be all dressed up in the armoury of her black habit. Nothing could be more of an incentive to stay clear.

IT WAS a bright sunny day, perfect Melbourne weather with the early autumn breeze just lapping around the city edges when Mr Ferguson arrived at the front of the Convent of St Augustine to pick up his two charges. Sisters Agnes and Catherine had been stationed on the front porch for ten minutes, barely speaking. They did not ignore each other. It had been so long since they were alone in each other's company, and their past antagonism must have been as much at the forefront of Catherine's mind as hers. They struggled with a few comments about the weather before they gave up. Mr Ferguson's car coming through the front gates provided a welcome escape.

'Well, Sisters, this will be a new experience for you,' he said as the car drove along the ridge with the river sparkling up at them from far below. 'Mother Jerome assures me you have all your directions—your list of dos and don'ts—so it remains for me to say that if I can be of any help, please don't hesitate to ask.' He glanced over his shoulder. 'As a university man, I am handy in dealing with young uni upstarts, you know.'

'Thank you, Mr Ferguson,' said Agnes, appointed as the senior of the two sisters. 'I'm sure there won't be too many difficulties.'

'Don't be too sure, Sister. Unfortunately, manners are not high on the list of some young agitators these days.'

'Agitators?'

'It doesn't take much to inflame the ideas and sensitivities of the radical groups on campus.'

'What did you study?' asked Agnes after some time in silence. It was odd she had never stopped to wonder what this friendly retired gentleman had done in his life.

'Engineering. At the very same university, you young ladi—sisters will be attending.'

'Has John Batman University changed much since you were there?' asked Agnes. She glanced at Catherine, who seemed to be paying attention without wanting to join in.

'Outwardly, very little. But the atmosphere and activities have changed a great deal in recent years. I visit chums there.'

'In what way?'

'It's difficult to say what it is exactly. Political disputes and a bit of larrikinism frequently broke out on campus during my day. The difference now is the lack of good-natured fellow feeling in the conflicts and pranks. You know, the attitude with some is that if you disagree with me, you are morally corrupt, and your opinion scarcely legitimate.'

'The same attitude in communist countries …?' said Agnes, more for the conversation than to start a debate.

'Precisely. No discussion at all.'

'You would find a good conversational partner in my father, Mr Ferguson.'

'I don't doubt it. Most Catholics share the same view about communism.'

'Where did your ancestors come from, Mr Ferguson?' Catherine piped up.

'You mean those who settled in Australia?' said the retired gentleman, surprised at the question.

'Yes.' She leaned a little forward.

'England. I don't know too much about them, though. It's something I should turn my mind to, I suppose. My generation has tended to turn their backs on the past—that sort of past, I mean.'

'Were they convicts?'

'That much I do know. No, no convicts. Both sides of the family came from villages in Surrey, in the south of England.'

'Surrey?' said Catherine calmly. 'Have you ever heard of the penal laws?'

'The penal laws? No. Is that something connected with the convicts? Excuse me, Sister, we engineering students were not history buffs.'

'The English used the penal laws to delegitimise the people of Ireland and Catholics in England.'

Mr Ferguson cast two quick looks into the rear vision mirror. 'You'll have to tell me about that sometime, Sister.'

Agnes half-looked at Catherine. Catherine glanced at her and then turned to look out the window. Fortunately, thought Agnes. She diverted the conversation by asking about the university routine.

'I'll show you all those things—student union, library, and so on—after you have formally enrolled,' said Mr Ferguson cheerfully. 'There's an Irish Club, too, if Sister Catherine is interested.'

'Ferguson is an Irish or Scottish name,' said Catherine. 'Perhaps your folk originally came from Celtic countries.'

'That's a thought, Sister. I might investigate those clubs, too,' he said, jovially.

Sister Catherine smiled and looked at Agnes with as much goodwill as she could muster. That's certainly a change from the old Margaret, thought Agnes. A genuine effort to make up for her terseness—not that Mr Ferguson was aware—that's to be encouraged. It also eased the discomfort between the two former antagonists. They spent the rest of the journey discussing the order in which they would complete the enrolment formalities. After completing the tedious enrolment process at the end of the morning, Mr Ferguson left them sitting on a bench on the university grounds' front lawn to have lunch, saying he would be back later to show them around the library and student facilities.

'Everything has gone without a hitch,' said Agnes after they had sat eating for some time.

'Yes, that's fortunate.'

'Mr. Ferguson has been very helpful.'

'Yes, but it won't be necessary to bother him after we've filled in all the necessary forms.'

'That will be up to Mother Jerome, I suppose. He's very generous with his time.'

'He is very generous,' said Catherine. 'I only mean it's unnecessary to burden him with more than he has to do. After all, he's quite an old man.'

'Not that old, but you're right. We must not burden him.'

'It is five years since we entered the postulancy,' said Catherine after some silence.

'That's right. It is indeed five years.'

'Is that enough to make a point?'

'None of us has made her final profession,' she said in reply to Catherine's bluntness. 'All of us must have confidence we're doing the right thing.'

'There's still the same number of us—since the novitiate, I mean.'

'Yes.'

'It seems to me that five years is enough time to erase all those little inequalities between us,' Catherine persisted.

'That's the idea of religious life—apart from the hierarchical structure of the order's governance. Equality in the religious life refers to the personal, the individual, not to the functions we fulfil. Mother Jerome made that point on the first full day of the postulancy. Do you remember?' Agnes could hear herself lecturing.

A long pause followed. Margaret looked around the sun-drenched lawn. Young people in groups roamed everywhere.

'Yes, I do remember.'

'Sister Catherine!' they suddenly heard. 'Sister Catherine, it's me, Gillian.'

A young woman had disengaged herself from a group on the main pathway and was hurrying toward them. How come Sister Catherine was at the university? She exclaimed with pleasure when she learned Sister had enrolled. Catherine maintained her sisterly dignity while remaining friendly and welcoming, just as she did with Jannie and the members of her convent faction. She gave generous encouragement to the girl's plans to study for a science degree.

'I have you to thank for that, Sister,' said Gillian. 'I would not have persevered without your help.'

'That was my role as your teacher.'

'You can be happy you have a satisfied former student,' said Agnes when Gillian had returned to her group.

'I get on pretty well with my students, provided they are serious about their work. They have my full support if they're serious.'

Agnes was inclined to ask what criteria Catherine used to judge the right kind of seriousness, but restrained herself. She still did not trust herself to keep her mouth under control if she ventured there. Fortunately, Catherine cooperated. She did not seem inclined to pursue the subject. They relaxed into silence, content to eat their sandwiches after the busy morning. Mr Ferguson returned on cue and led them through the afternoon's program. During their tour of the library, the student union, and the different lecture localities, Agnes took notice of the reaction they caused. Most of the young people gave them curious but cursory looks. Some from Catholic backgrounds gave them respectful nods, some even greeting them with the correct address. The occasional sneering look and muffled comment came their way. Mother Jerome warned them of possible unpleasant experiences. Agnes hoped the reception would not be any worse in the following days because it did disturb her a little.

The comments themselves did not trouble her. She could hardly make them out. Rather, the unprovoked antagonism with which those students regarded them disturbed her. She had not encountered much of this blatant prejudice before entering the convent. Her almost exclusive Catholic environment had protected her against the extreme sectarianism her father had spoken about. Surprisingly, Catherine did not notice the scruffy young men scowling and sneering under their breath—or ignored it. In this, Agnes did not do as well as her companion, which irked her. Finally, with all preliminaries completed, they returned to the convent to catch up on their religious duties. The following day would be more stressful, and Agnes prayed it would work out.

MR FERGUSON accompanied Agnes to the principal lecture theatre to ensure she had a seat in the front row near the entrance. She would be out of the direct view of the students, he said, and not exposed to the pestering of those in front of her. She could also slip in and out of the theatre with minimum notice.

'Everything okay now?' he asked after she had taken a seat a few places in from the aisle.

'Would you mind staying a little longer, please, Mr Ferguson?' She expected Philip to stride through the open double doorway at any moment.

'Of course, Sister, I understand. It takes a little time to adjust. The students will get used to you.'

She continually checked her watch as Mr Ferguson chatted about the university and his experiences from more than forty years earlier. He did not notice her agitation and seemed unaware of her disjointed responses. Then, at last, Philip strode through the doorway, followed by an officious young man and a young woman. He glanced up at the lecture theatre at the tiered rows of students, then, noticing her in the front row, respectfully nodded before continuing to the lectern on the rostrum.

'You'll be right, Sister,' said Mr Ferguson as the student chatter died. He disappeared through the double swing doors.

He did not recognise me, thought Agnes. Or he did not get a good look. Mr Ferguson must have obscured her. Or perhaps he did. Perhaps he did, and that was the only acknowledgment she would get. Perhaps he was over her. Yes, surely her mother was wrong. It was so long— That would be best, anyhow. That would be easiest. He began talking about the lecture and tutorial program while his assistants walked up the aisles, distributing two sheets of paper. One detailed the lecture program and tutorial times for the first term, while the other provided a background reading list. She was in his tutorial group! He must know it was her. But why had he put her in his group if he thought she was only worth a cursory nod? She looked at him sideways, knowing that her veil would obscure her face.

He looked around the theatre as he spoke, his mind concentrated on his subject, as was his typical manner. He even looked in her direction a couple of times. She had not seen him for five years, but he had not changed much, at least to look at. He was not as neat in his dress as he used to be. Indeed, his pants and coat appeared worn and baggy under his academic gown. His hair was longer and untidy as if he did not care. He had not put on weight. If anything, he seemed a little slimmer. For a man in his mid-thirties, he still looked good. As he moved on to talking about the first term's lectures on Plato and Aristotle, Agnes calmed down. She had managed the first contact. That was a relief. Things would only improve, and she could concentrate on why she was there in that lecture theatre.

She followed his summary of the course topics by referring to the handout. At length, her full attention was on philosophy and not on the lecturer. Or perhaps his familiar way of explaining things relaxed her into listening as she used to. Eventually, she looked up from the handout to see him look in her direction. His eyes narrowed as he focused on her. He stopped mid-sentence. His mouth opened a little. He shuffled the papers on his lectern as if he had lost his place. He glanced at her and then once more.

'It's a nun, not a penguin!' someone called from several rows above Agnes.

A cautious titter flowed around the theatre. That seemed to shake Philip out of his distraction. 'Quiet, please,' he called. 'Believe me. You will have the opportunity to show what smart-alecks you are.' He pointed in the direction of the comment. 'You, in the row, there ....' The lecture theatre fell silent.

That was just like Philip, Agnes thought. No one would push him around, certainly not some callow youth fresh out of school. But if he could calmly deal with insolent youths, he could not maintain his composure after sighting her. He continued his explanation, now in an edgy way, stammering sometimes as if he could not keep his mind entirely on what he said. Glistening beads of perspiration appeared on his forehead. Agnes wondered if anyone else saw what she saw. Probably not. Nobody else could be aware of what was happening between them. In the end, his uneasiness distracted her so much that she could not concentrate. The words on the sheet before her became blurred in the apprehension of what he would say later.

The session finished, and he invited questions. With those few questions dispatched, he made ready to go. She kept her eyes down while she collected her pens and papers to put in her briefcase. A ruckus surrounded her as the students made their way out of the lecture theatre. She looked up. Several students were talking to him. She got up and waited for most of the students to pass before stepping into the aisle.

'Virginia!'

This was it. She stopped, and he came up to her, dodging the last of the students exiting the theatre.

'It's Sister Agnes, Dr Stevenson.'

'I didn't know it was you. I wouldn't have put you in my tutorial group if I had known.'

'Oh?' Her face burned to the tip of her ears under wimple and veil.

'I was only aware that a sister had enrolled in first-year philosophy. I, eh, leave the details to others. Sister Agnes appeared on my list. Because I'm the only Catholic in the department, it is easier for a religious to be in my classes.'

'I appreciate that,' said Agnes, unable to look him full in the face and wondering why he felt the need to explain himself.

'But it's probably better that I put you in another group.'

'Yes, it would be.'

An uncomfortable silence followed.

'I wondered when I would see you again,' he blurted out as she turned to go. 'I expected I would some time—'

She walked on.

'No, wait!' He grabbed her arm.

'No, Philip, please.' She glanced at his hand.

'I'm sorry,' he said, releasing her arm. 'I didn't mean—but what do you expect? You think I'm looking at a nun? You're Virginia Pearson, dressed up in that ridiculous costume. If you think I will call you Sister whatever, you're mistaken.'

These were words with a five-year delay. This is what she had expected when she broke the engagement. She hurried out of the lecture theatre. Fortunately, Mr Ferguson appeared.

'Ready to go, Sister?' he said cheerfully. 'Oh, hello,' he continued, seeing Philip a step behind her. 'I'm here to collect Sister Agnes. Ferguson, engineering graduate.' He held out his hand. 'Dr Stevenson, no doubt. Yes, I've checked the teaching staff.' He smiled broadly.

'How do you do, Mr Ferguson,' said Philip. 'I won't keep Sister long.' He glanced from one to the other in an uncertain way. Agnes looked up at him, her eyes pleading. 'I just wanted to add a word of advice for Sister. Sister, I recommend you pay close attention to the books on metaphysics.

Understanding the metaphysical framework of Plato's and Aristotle's thought will help understand the works of St Augustine and St. Thomas Aquinas.'

'Thank you, Dr Stevenson,' said Agnes, casting her eyes down. 'I appreciate the advice.'

'If you've got time, Sister, read Fr Copleston's book on Aquinas,' Philip went on, still looking from one to the other. 'It's one of the best, unimpeachably orthodox.'

'Thank you again, Dr Stevenson. I appreciate your advice.'

'You're welcome.'

She felt his eyes on her as she walked beside Mr Ferguson. She felt him follow at a distance as they walked to meet Sister Catherine on the south lawn. She felt him stop at the border of the lawn area, prudently keeping out of sight of her fellow sister. She felt him walk despondently back to his office in the main building. But in her mind, she did not see him take a half-filled bottle of the best Irish whisky from his cupboard and pour himself a generous glass. Nor did she see his bohemian artist girlfriend arrive half an hour later in her usual long floral dress and headband. She had never known Philip to have a liking for whisky. Indeed, he had never been more than a moderate drinker.

The grand silence came as a relief. She could retreat into herself after an exhausting day. Attending the first lecture sessions was stressful without dealing with Philip. The worst scenario imaginable had occurred—the delayed accusatory episode. There seemed to be no gap between his angry look of incomprehension more than five years ago and his angry words in the lecture theatre. It was as if a shutter had come down on the convent period, and she now had to defend herself for her cruel, insensitive action. Her feelings were running so hot that she could scarcely separate the mental image of the lounge room scene and the reality of her kneeling in the chapel, trying to pray. What would she do? How was she to deal with the next meeting, the second lecture?

PHILIP spent the evening by himself, trying to overcome his feelings of stupidity and shame. The sight of Virginia in his lecture theatre was a shock. It was a shock of the surreal. The woman he had loved since she was fifteen, sitting there dressed in that fancy dress costume, was so unexpected that he lost grip on his surroundings. No wonder one of those snot-noses just out of school seized the opportunity to entertain his friends. He had behaved the way he feared he would five years earlier when Virginia unexpectedly announced her dropping out of society to enter a convent. But he could not run from the lecture theatre full of students and speed off in his Morris Minor. He had been rough and rude with her. It was low behaviour, not like him. He hoped it was not like him.

What would he do? How would he handle it now? Her presence was a fact he had to adjust to. Whatever he did, he would not be rude and rough again. She did not deserve it. Even hidden in rolls of black fabric and that absurd white wimple, she radiated elegance and class, someone who demanded his respect, demanded everyone's respect. He resolved to apologise and treat her like any other student. He must put their personal and historical connection behind him. That's what the situation demanded; he would not be childish about it. Diana arrived late in the evening and set about comforting him on seeing his upset. She could not know her affectionate caresses, rather than comforting him, filled him with guilt.

Chapter 23

Philip apologises

TWO DAYS later, Agnes sat on a bench in the shade of a tree not far from the entrance to the lecture halls. Mr Ferguson had left her to enjoy the sunny morning air, and Catherine had made off as soon as they arrived on campus, making little attempt to hide her eagerness to go her own way. She took the lecture notes from her briefcase and began reading through them. Two days of wrestling with the problem of Philip had resulted in her determination to persevere and not respond to his anger and resentment if it should continue. She attended the university to study—for nothing else. But the resolution formed that morning before leaving the convent was very shaky, fifteen minutes before the second philosophy lecture. The feelings of unease and apprehension were returning. She became aware of someone standing in front of her.

'Can I disturb you?'

'Of course.' She shuffled the sheets of paper and went to put them in her briefcase, but held on to them. She looked up at Philip.

'I want to apologise for my behaviour the other day. Your appearance was so sudden and unexpected that I—no, no excuse. My behaviour was unforgivable. You have my promise that there will be no repetition.'

'Thank you, Philip, I ....' She wanted to say so much that she understood, that she appreciated his resolution, but she could not. She would not say anything personal.

'I have left you in my tutorial group,' he continued. 'If I shifted you suddenly to another group, questions would be raised, at least among the staff, if not among the students who witnessed my stupid behaviour. I assume you would rather not have it known you were once engaged to your philosophy lecturer.'

'Yes, yes, I suppose .... That's prudent.'

'Don't hesitate to ask any questions about the course.' He had several folders and a book cradled in one arm. He picked up the book and waved it around. 'You are assured as much of my help as any other student. While you are enrolled in our department, you will be Sister Agnes, philosophy student.'

'Thank you, Philip.' She bowed her head, not knowing if she could keep her composure. Then he was gone. She looked up. He had disappeared among the students who now filed into the lecture theatre amid loud chatter. She must hurry to secure the front seat. Settling, she restricted her eyes to her papers, notepad, and pens. She glanced toward the rostrum. Philip was talking in a relaxed manner with his two assistants while referring to papers on the lectern. She recognised the familiar stance, the familiar gestures. Several boisterous young men passing in front of her broke in on her observations. Broken phrases in crude language filled the air around her. She looked up as they turned into the aisle. They were smirking at her. 'What a waste!' one mocked as they thumped up the steps. At the same time, tapping resounded in the speakers. Philip looked at the youths who took their seats in the back row. He waited until all students had settled.

'Before starting on the series of lectures about Plato's forms,' he said in an even tone, 'I have something fundamental to say about the enterprise of doing philosophy. Some of you, we know from experience, will not understand what we are on about in the department of philosophy and will fail because you have not understood.' A tense silence overcame the hall. 'The philosophical enterprise is about investigating what is and what is true. People make all sorts of claims about what is and what is true. As you will see, Plato seemed to think that what is and what is true come together. Our task is to review the arguments for the different schools of thought. Whoever one is, whatever one represents, whatever vision one adheres to, our task here is to review the arguments—nothing el se.'

A murmured comment came from the back of the lecture theatre. Those closest looked around and then at the sister in the front row.

'Adolf Hitler ran an argument eminently representative of a major fallacy,' Philip continued, unruffled. 'It's called the genetic fallacy. The argument runs thus: You are of class x, 'x' representing any class at all. Therefore, your statements are wrong. The Nazis claimed the theory of relativity was false because Einstein was a Jew.' He paused. 'What are we to think of a person who makes such a claim?' He looked toward the upper rows as if waiting for a retort. 'Anybody who fails to understand the genetic fallacy is not likely to make the grade and should seriously consider changing their enrolment.' He waited. A few seconds later, he began the lecture.

Agnes scribbled her notes for a while, not knowing what she wrote until she read them later. She wondered that it made sense. Then her feelings cooled. Philip could not stand bullying in any form. He would defend anyone being picked on. At the end of the lecture, she thought he might say something, but he stood talking with some students, not giving any sign he wanted to hurry away. She dawdled from the lecture theatre, not really disappointed that he did not come. She should be happy with the outcome of their first two meetings. The situation she had feared for so long had resolved itself. He had been resentful at first, but then came to his senses and now treated her as any lecturer should. That meant the elimination of the one major obstacle to her studying.

As it turned out, Philip was not the only one Agnes knew on campus. She had forgotten until Vic Brennan, senior lecturer in the English department and highly regarded poet, strolled over to her before starting his first lecture.

'Hello, Virginia, fancy seeing you here,' he said with a welcoming smile.

'It's Sister Agnes, Dr Brennan.'

'No need to be so formal, Sister. We are well enough acquainted to be at ease, don't you think? Indeed, looking at you, I suspect there has not been much change in Virginia Pearson behind that black disguise. I can't imagine there would be.'

'I would rather maintain the relationship of lecturer-student if you don't mind, Dr Brennan.' She glanced around at the attention she was drawing from the bustling students. 'There has been an important change.' As with Philip, she pleaded with her eyes.

'Don't worry, Sister. Your secret is safe with me.'

'I appreciate it.' She glanced again at the surrounding students, hoping he would now return to the lectern.

'I imagine you gave my friend in philosophy a jolting surprise after seeing you in his lecture.'

'You have to ask your friend.'

'He had no idea you would be there, did he?' said Vic, much amused.

'You have to ask him.'

'Come on, Virginia, relax. Surely, not all conversation is barred between those of the big bad world and you.' He smiled again in the same welcoming manner.

'No, of course not,' she said with a hint of a smile.

'That's the girl.'

'Please, Vic—'

'He didn't know, did he?'

'What does it matter?' said Agnes, curious about his insistence.

'It matters because he would have given some sign. He could not have helped it.'

'I don't see why.' She did not believe herself.

'Your brutal blow knocked him off balance. His way of life changed. Your reappearance would disturb him. But, Sister, we cannot dally in conversation any longer. We'll talk later.' He turned to go but stopped. 'I have a special tutorial group of talented first- and second-year students. It's extra material for your enjoyment. Not examinable. You're welcome to join.'

He strode to the lectern and proceeded to give the sort of engaging lecture she had attended in the past. She could scarcely concentrate. What did Vic mean? What kind of life did Philip lead? Surely Philip was strong enough not to let himself go.

IN THE following weeks, she settled into the four subjects she had chosen without too much stress. In addition to philosophy and English, she had taken history and economics. English and history were no burden. She had majored in those subjects at teachers' college and now covered material and books familiar to her. She enjoyed getting back to reading her favourite nineteenth-century authors. Vic's special tutorials provided, as he predicted, extra enjoyment. Economics challenged her—she did not want to say it was boring—but because the purpose was to give her a rudimentary understanding of the ways society organised itself economically, she decided she would go for a percentage pass. It was probably not the right attitude, but Mother Jerome had stressed philosophy as the primary object. Rationalising in this manner, she threw herself into the study of philosophy.

In contrast to her fellow students, she liked the philosophy tutorials best. Never shy of saying her piece, she certainly would not be the shy retiring violet in a group of kids fresh out of school. But it was Philip who made the tutorials easy and enjoyable, and not just for her. In the first tutorial, he took steps to reduce the tension between the unfamiliar sight of a religious sister and the students just out of school. Her fellow students soon relaxed in her company and regarded her as just another student to the extent it could be expected. With the breakthrough of the first tutorial, which put everyone at ease, Philip moved on to the material covered in the lectures. He provided additional background reading lists for those who, he said, had enough time and interest to read more deeply.

'This is if you are interested,' he said. 'These passages will take you beyond our introduction to Plato's key ideas. You'll only be examined on the material we cover in the lectures.'

Agnes studied the additional lists and found he had indeed arranged them to broaden their prescribed work. It was very clever. She entertained the thought for an instant, just an instant, that Philip provided the lists for her benefit. Whatever the case, she could not get enough of it, the more demanding and difficult, the better. After a few weeks, she became aware that her mind had shifted from the convent's environment to the university's. The convent became a place to study, rest, and sleep.

'You seemed to be taking well to the responsibilities of studying full time,' said Mother Jerome several weeks into the term.

'Thank you, Mother,' said Agnes as she sat in front of the prioress's desk. 'I am conscious of what is expected of me.' That sounded a little sanctimonious, so she added: 'But I do like what I'm studying, especially philosophy. It's no burden, really.'

'No trouble?'

'No, Mother,' she said, understanding the allusion. 'It belongs to the past. I'm treated like any other student.'

'Really?'

'He always refers to me as Sister Agnes. He never talks to me personally or outside the tutorials.'

'Are you happy with that?'

'That's as it should be.'

'Be careful you don't let your enthusiasm run away with you. Your daily life has to be steady, your interests evenly distributed, and your religious duties attended to.'

'Yes, Mother.'

Agnes was troubled that she and Catherine fudged Mother Jerome's instruction to seek each other out when neither had lectures or tutorials. Catherine gave signs she was aware of the disobedience. Her excuses to be off by herself, or rather with the students and staff in sociology, appeared weak and unconvincing, and she gave them uneasily, as much as the supremely confident Catherine could be uneasy. Agnes decided to let the small misdemeanour ride. After all, their routines did not coincide, and their interests, as usual, diverged. More importantly, Agnes wanted time to work through the course material thoroughly. Within a couple of weeks, she had a comfortable routine of spending time in the library and then taking a break on a bench on the spacious front lawn not far from the library.

It was a pleasant spot, a little out of the way of where most students gathered and partly hidden by the shrubs and trees that had outgrown the garden. Hidden as she was, she observed the university's comings and goings unnoticed. From here, she had her first glimpse of Philip away from the lecture theatre and tutorial room. One Thursday afternoon, a little after four o'clock, she saw him with several men and women she assumed were colleagues. They did not appear finished for the day, as none had briefcases or the paraphernalia that lecturers walked around with. Then she remembered she had been to a nearby pub with Philip and some friends. She pushed the memories out of her mind. But in the days following, when her routine permitted, she went to the bench at four o'clock. She excused herself by saying she needed a break. She could not help it if it coincided with Philip's activities. Besides, just curiosity and nothing else prompted her.

She did not see him again until a week later, on the same day and at the same time. He was again with others, not all the same people, though. A slim, attractive woman of around thirty dressed in the popular bohemian style—long dress and headband—was of the party. She walked beside Philip as they chatted among themselves. Agnes kept her eyes on her. The woman took Philip's hand and kissed him on the cheek. Agnes looked away. A week later, she sat on the same bench at the same time. The same woman walked with him. Agnes watched her every move and gesture. She had no doubt; she was his girlfriend. A week later, she sat on the bench against her will and better judgment, waiting for them to appear.

They appeared with the woman, talking animatedly to the other three as they walked. They stopped for a moment. They were now laughing as the woman seemed to be explaining something. As she gestured amid the laughter, she turned to Philip, took his arm, and caressed it. There was more laughter. Then the woman happened to glance over Philip's shoulder. For a moment, it did not seem to register what she saw. Agnes turned away, embarrassed that she was caught staring. She could not resist a glance. Now Philip was heading towards her after gesturing to the others to go on. She collected the books and papers on the bench beside her.

'Waiting to be picked up, are you?'

'Yes.' How did he know that?

'Revising a few things?' He shifted.

'Yes.' She fiddled with her papers.

'You've taken to this course, haven't you?'

'Yes, it's very interesting.'

'That's because we are examining arguments for the existence of immutable principles of knowledge and the good. It suits the perspective of Catholic belief, doesn't it?'

'Yes, I suppose it does.'

'You can understand now how Augustine and Aquinas drew on the Greeks—on Plato and Aristotle, I mean.'

'It's mostly new to me,' she said, aware of the double allusion to their past conversations. 'I imagine I'll understand better over time.'

'Of course, you will.'

An awkward pause followed. Agnes shuffled her papers and books, making ready to go.

'You're doing very well, you know.'

'Thank you. Your friends must be waiting for you.'

'That's okay. They're in the pub and won't be going anywhere in a hurry. We usually go for a drink at this time ... sometimes dinner later.'

He paused. 'I would ask you to join us if I thought you were allowed.' He smiled.

She returned a weak smile, unable to say anything. He flinched.

'I knew you would take to the course—always thought you had an inclination for this sort of study. So many students don't have a clue, you know.'

'A certain maturity is required,' she said. 'I'm ten years out of school. That makes a difference.'

'You're right.' He nodded. 'That discernment is just like you, Virginia. I'm sorry—habit— Excuse the pun.' He laughed self-consciously.

'That's all right.'

'A few of your fellow students say you have helped them to understand the material.'

'I'm happy to be of help.'

'Your enthusiasm and confident air help.'

Confident air! She got up, brushing her black tunic straight with two firm strokes.

'I'm interested. That helps.'

Sister Catherine, approaching with Jannie de Kam, drew their attention.

'Here's Sister Catherine to meet me,' she said, her eyes appealing. Philip gave her a nod.

Jannie greeted her gushingly, all the time glancing at Philip. 'We have met before, Dr Stevenson, at Harry and Erik's place,' she said after the introductions. 'Do you remember?'

'Yes, of course,' said Philip. 'You're Harry's fashion model.'

'Last time, that flirt, Erik, hogged the conversation, talking to your girlfriend,' she laughed nervously.

'They're just friends.'

'I hope they are!' said Jannie. 'He's mine.'

Philip acknowledged the relationship politely and then excused himself, saying his friends were waiting for him.

'I will see you next tutorial, Sister,' he said, with an expression Agnes understood as directly as he had understood her appeal. 'I wish you a good afternoon, Sister Catherine, Jannie—'

They watched him stride across the lawn.

'He's an impressive man,' said Jannie, 'popular with the students. You have luck being in his tutorial group.'

'He's an excellent lecturer,' said Agnes, wondering how she knew she was in his group. 'How are you doing in your course, Jannie?'

Now that her male audience was no longer there, Jannie became less engaging. She shrugged, saying it was all right. But Margaret helped her spirits along. That was a big incentive to stick to it. Agnes restrained herself from posing questions that came to mind. The conversation dwindled. That was not unwelcome. Mr Ferguson would be waiting for them, and she had little to say to the flighty Jannie. She glanced at Catherine. She seemed just as reluctant to keep the conversation going.

'We must be going now, Jannie,' said Catherine. 'See you tomorrow.'

'Okay, Marg,' said Jannie, looking around. 'Have you seen Aine recently?' she added as if the question had just come to mind.

'Not since the Christmas visit,' said Agnes.

'You don't know that the Harry and Erik mentioned picked up Aine and me that day and took us to the city?'

'No,' said Agnes, unable to hide her surprise.

'Yes, we spent some time at their Parkville terrace before I took her to the station.'

'Oh,' said Agnes, striving to contain her surprise and curiosity.

'Yes, Harry's convinced Aine has a big future in the fashion industry. Harry's a fashion photographer.'

'What does Aine think about that? Does she know what he thinks?'

'Yes, of course! He took a whole lot of photos of her. What do you expect with someone like that?'

'What does Aine think?'

'She was pretty willing—had no objection at all to Harry. She was a lamb in his hands.'

'We have to go now,' said Catherine, interrupting. 'We can talk about this again.'

'Harry offered to promote her to several agencies and fashion magazines—that face, you know. She's considering it.'

'How do you know?'

'I rang her, of course. Besides, Harry wanted to know, too.'

Catherine seemed preoccupied on the way back to the convent. That suited Agnes. She, too, had little inclination to talk. And Mr Ferguson seemed prepared to indulge them. She wondered if the same things were running through Catherine's mind. She said almost nothing when she and Jannie came across her and Philip together, but she did stay alert, coldly scrutinising Philip, far from the same manner as Jannie, who seemed compelled to deploy her considerable female charms whenever a male appeared. Did Catherine suspect anything? Did she see any sign of their former relationship, signals she could not control? She did not think so. She hoped not.

There was also Aine. When Jannie said that Harry, the photographer, was pressuring Aine to accept work in the fashion industry, Catherine seemed just as surprised. That was curious; one would have expected Jannie to pass that information on to Catherine, given her keen interest in Aine. But then Catherine cut the conversation short. They did have to leave. That was true. But her manner seemed hasty. No doubt, there were things meant only for Jannie's ears. The former relationship between Catherine and Jannie seemed well and truly re-established—if there had been any slackening in the first place. She now had an inkling there had been none.

As the car approached the climb to the ridge along the deserted dusty road, a depressive feeling began to weigh on her for the first time, a sort of sluggish resistance. She had tried to ignore the feeling, but now it had arrived at the surface of her consciousness. The disturbing contrast between university life and convent life bothered her. Her mind lingered more than was proper on the lectures, the tutorials, and the constant vision of young adults, colourfully dressed and behaving as if the usual social restraints had dissolved.

Sometimes she had to leave the front lawn because of the uninhibited scenes nearby. But until now, that had not made any difference to the way she regarded convent life. On the contrary, she was mostly relieved to be away from the university's social disorder and back in the quiet, ordered life of the convent. The feeling of sluggish resistance had caught up with her and was unnerving; it took the whole evening to drive out. It was not until the last community prayers that her feelings returned to what was proper—or had the appearance of returning.

Back in her cell, she knelt beside her bed and said her prayers, reaffirming her commitment to her calling. She got into bed with the last prayers said, and her commitment reaffirmed. But sleep did not come. Philip's look of understanding appeared every time she attempted to relax her mind. As much as she tried, she could not dismiss what that look meant, indeed, what their exchange of looks meant. Philip did not look at her as a religious sister. Her severe black medieval habit, the instrument to cut oneself off from the secular world, did not make the slightest difference to his—to the way he regarded her. Indeed, he had mocked her habit from the first moment he saw her. Her mother and the prioress had warned her that a religious habit would not perturb some men. Some men? Philip was not 'some men.'

She lay in the dark, staring at the ceiling. The light from the waning moon scarcely penetrated her cell. Her room was on the right-hand side of the main building, where the tall eucalypts partially blocked the light of the sun and moon. The short wing of the novices' quarters had the same effect. It contrasted with the postulant quarters where the rooms were bared to the moonlight and gave an unobstructed view of the river and the bush beyond. Again, her thoughts shifted to those dark events of long ago.

She remembered her panic and terror when locked out of the upper floor. The experience was so disjunctive—so out of the realm of her everyday experiences—that she wondered again whether it was real. She had to tell herself it all happened as she remembered it. The hoods, the light near the grotto, the boat on the river— Now the memories of events so dark and strange began to weigh on her. She tried to shake it off, but it pierced what seemed to be hours of fitful sleep.

She flicked the light on to see the time. One-thirty. She got out of bed and sat at the window. She spread her arms on the sill and rested her head as she had done five years before. The windows of the novices' quarters were dark and still, belying the turbulent atmosphere there. To her left, she made out the rocky steps leading down to the river twinkling in the meagre moonlight. The clearing was obscured. The grotto to the far left disappeared in a greyish-green haze. She stared at the river for some time, mesmerised by the twinkle.

She sprang to her feet, her eyes fixed on the clearing. Breathing in gasps and with her heart pounding, she peered into murkiness. She was mistaken, surely ... the sleeplessness and exhausted feelings ... she imagined it. But there it was again, two fleeting shadows, and another, moving to the left. Then two hooded figures coming from the stairs. She could not be dreaming. As she had done five years before, she had the mad inclination to investigate. But, no, the memory of the terror stopped her. She continued to peer. There was nothing for some minutes. Then, far to the left, near the grotto, a light flared for an instant. Now it was gone as if it had been snuffed out—as if everything had been snuffed out. She awoke with her head on her hands. The dawn light was creeping over the slope.

Chapter 24

Aine visits Agnes

HARRY'S BUSINESS card stayed in Aine's bag for some weeks. It was not that she forgot about it. She was aware of it there like some sly little animal crinkled in a nocturnal sleep. Her first inclination had been to throw it away and forget about it. But for some odd reason, she could not bring herself to do it. So, she left the card in its crinkled state in the depths of her bag until the day it came out and went straight into the bin. She was so sure of this sequence of events that she did not even mention to Charles what had taken place in a very elegant terrace house in an expensive suburb of Melbourne. Harry's card, however, sprang to life in late February 1962.

'Aine, it's me, Jannie,' said an excited voice when Aine picked up the phone one evening.

'Oh,' said Aine. 'I was not expecting—' That was a fib.

'Of course, you were. Not even Aine O'Riordan would be determined enough to turn her back on Harry's offer.'

'It's Aine Winterbine, Jannie,' said Aine, embarrassed that Jannie should see so easily through her.

'Yes, of course. But what about Harry's—?'

'I gave my answer. I don't want to. I'm happy enough with my life in Binawarra.'

'You were coy. Very alluring, but I'm a girl, too, you know.'

'Jannie, really, there's nothing more to say.' The implication that she would resort to the sort of coquettish behaviour Jannie seemed to be perfecting was objectionable.

'What did that handsome husband of yours say?'

'What ...? nothing ....'

'Oh, you haven't told him, have you? You little devil.'

'Please, Jannie, I didn't say anything about something so unimportant.'

'Oh, yes, pull the other one. What if I send some of the photos up to you? You and your husband will see how stunningly you photograph.'

'No, Jannie, don't. Don't send anything.'

'Come on, Aine!'

'Why are you so insistent about this?' said Aine, in an effort to turn the conversation back on Jannie.

'What a dumb question! I've already told you. I'm your friend. I want to help you reach your potential.'

There it was again: Margaret's talk about her potential. The conversation then began to go around in circles. Eventually, Jannie had to give up, saying that she would let Aine think about it some more. Harry said he would be patient. He knew it was a big decision for her. It was understandable that she and her husband needed the time to think. But he was convinced that she had a big future. Aine said it was very nice of Harry to say that, but it would not change her mind.

'Very nice!' exclaimed Jannie. 'Harry's not interested in being nice. You're his discovery. He's interested in having your beautiful face on the cover of the best fashion magazines. You're wrong if you think Harry's just flattering you.'

Aine, fearful of provoking another round if she replied, brought the conversation to a close. Jannie resigned herself but threatened to be on to her again. That was no idle threat, thought Aine as she put the receiver down. Her hand remained on the receiver for a moment. What was she to do? Charles was outside with Estella when the phone rang. She had no option now but to tell him everything. When she stepped into the workshop, and Estella came running to her, she saw that Charles's mind was not on the phone call. Then it occurred to her that he may not have heard the phone ring. She would wait for him to ask—no harm in that. But he did not ask, and he gave no indication that he had heard the p hone.

That decision made her uncomfortable because now she was keeping something from Charles. And she had never done that before. Was it truly keeping something from him? Nothing was settled, and she did need some time to weigh it all up. After all, it only concerned her at that point. When she got to the point of seriously considering the proposal, that would be the time to talk to Charles. Despite arguing herself to this reasonable conclusion, she continued to feel uncomfortable. She tried to put it out of her mind. She did her best, but it would sneak back at the most unexpected times, most often in the form of Harry.

Harry's quick and resolute manner had impressed her. He went about his work in the same careful, confident way as Charles. That reassured her. Then his polite, easy-going manner had also put her at ease. She did not think it false. Jannie had confirmed this impression, and Jannie was not likely to mislead her in this. No, all things considered, she thought Harry was sincere and his offer genuine. He really did think she had potential. But the potential in what? Was it the same potential Margaret had been talking about? It was odd for her to think about her appearance in terms of potential. She knew about vanity and appearance and had always been careful not to succumb to flattery. But appearance as work potential was something else. What skill was there in posing before a camera? Whatever Harry's conception of her potential, she was sure Margaret and Jannie did not view it in the same way or the same context. Once again, she did not know why she thought this. It was more an intuition than a carefully reasoned analysis that led her to this view.

Several weeks passed without her thoughts developing in any direction about Harry's offer and the motivations behind it. Her happy life with Charles and little Estella distracted her from unproductive thoughts in the long run. However, there was one pleasing aspect in this process: no anxiety. That was curious. More importantly, she was also free from the terrible torment that occasionally arose to leave her despairing. Perhaps with age and maturity, she was getting over it. With her thoughts running into a dead-end about Harry and Jannie and their proposals, her thoughts returned to Virginia.

She wondered how she was faring at university. She wondered how she had dealt with meeting her former fiancé. It would not have been easy despite her claim that she was over him. She remembered that incident at the grotto. She could still feel Virginia's gently sobbing body in her arms. She had felt the depths of feeling in the otherwise confident, mature young woman whom everyone, except Margaret and Elizabeth, liked, admired, or respected. It was not likely that Virginia would have forgotten Philip entirely. Then how would she have dealt with it? Had she been careful as her mother had advised?

The more her thoughts about Virginia superseded the pointless wondering about Harry's proposition, the more she felt drawn to making the trip to Melbourne to see her again. Mother Jerome had expressly allowed her contact with Virginia to continue. In this, she understood a recommendation to maintain contact to comfort or even help Virginia. Perhaps it was the other way around. This time, as she usually did, she discussed her proposal with Charles. Charles was all for it. He was sure Mother Jerome's permission was meant to achieve some good for both. He reminded her that she had been free from her troubles for nearly three months—since her last trip to Melbourne—and suggested that visit with Virginia may have been beneficial in the way Mother Jerome had anticipated.

SISTER Agnes took her place on the bench on the south lawn of John Batman University. She glanced at her watch. She was in good time. She opened her folder and began going over her notes from the last philosophy lecture. But she could not keep her mind on it. She continually glanced towards the southern entrance. After a few minutes, she put the lecture notes aside and waited. Then, with a surge of joy, she saw what she was looking for.

Aine had mounted the short flight of stairs leading to the concrete path that ran through the middle of the south lawn. She hesitated and looked around. She was too far away to catch her attention, so Agnes was content to observe her as she made her way along the path. A few students were sitting on benches, and others were entering or leaving the university. Each of these looked around as the tallish, slender young woman, dressed sedately but attractively, passed by without paying any attention to the curious stares. She wore a broad-brimmed sunhat, making a striking contrast with the elegant dress. She had on white cotton gloves, which accentuated the contrast as she touched and adjusted her hat and long fair hair. Virginia stood and waved.

'You're looking well—and smart.'

'Thank you. I thought I should dress well for a visit to the university.'

'I think you have a very wrong idea about university fashion,' Virginia smiled.

'Do you think so?'

'You'll see plenty of scruffy students before you leave the university today. Come on, sit down. It's a comfy spot, and we won't be bothered.'

As if somebody had deliberately conspired to contradict Agnes, a group of male students had halted and were staring, making comments to each other.

'Don't take any notice,' she said. 'They'll go away eventually. Now tell me how things are in the country.'

Agnes was right. The boys moved on after a few moments, allowing Aine to talk more easily about her activities.

'What about the troubles?' said Agnes, after there had been much general talk about their activities.

'There's been nothing since the Christmas visiting day, you know, in the convent parlour. I've never felt more relaxed. I've been happy with Charles, but often not relaxed. It's strange in a way.'

'Perhaps it's just part of maturing and becoming more confident?'

'That's what I thought.'

'Jannie told me a fashion photographer was interested in you.'

'Interested in me?'

'I mean for work as a model. Jannie seemed to think you were interested.'

'Do you see Jannie?'

'Yes, regularly. She and Margaret are often together. It's a peculiar relationship, I think, for their surroundings: the exuberant fashion model and the formidable nun. It continually gives me the feeling we're in a time warp.'

Aine briefly related how Jannie had tricked her into accepting the lift with Harry and Erik, who took them to their house in Parkville. But it was not so uncomfortable in the end. Harry and Erik were pleasant young men who did not make her feel uncomfortable. As for the idea of her working in the fashion industry, all the enthusiasm was on the side of Jannie and Harry.

'That Jannie,' said Virginia, 'I fear that she's no more stable than she was during the postulancy. I wonder what she's up to.'

'She says she's just helping me as a friend.'

'To reach your potential, no doubt.'

'That's right.'

'Margaret.'

'That's what I thought.'

'How interested are you in the photographer's offer?'

'I told Jannie and Harry I was not interested. I stressed my lack of interest. Harry is pleasant and shows me nothing but respect, but it's not about him. I cannot reconcile the idea of exploiting my appearance.'

'Did you say that?'

'Not in those words.'

'I don't think they would understand.'

There was a short pause, both reflecting.

'How did the first meeting go with Philip?' Aine asked cautiously.

'I was waiting for that question. You had eyed me suspiciously when the subject came up on Christmas visiting day.'

'Your mother seemed worried about how you would deal with it.'

'That's what mothers are like. Anyhow, the first meeting was awkward. I didn't know what to expect exactly.' She went on to relate that Philip had been nothing less than a gentleman towards her after the initial display of anger.

'Is that all?' said Aine. 'I thought it might've been more difficult. He must have been shocked to see you there in the lecture theatre.'

'He was, but he got over it, as I said. He's my philosophy lecturer, and I'm just another student. Besides, he has a girlfriend, quite an attractive girl, but not at all like me, like I was, I mean.' Aine could not hide a doubtful expression. 'You don't believe me?'

'I'm surprised it has been so easy for you both.'

'Well, that's the way it's been. We don't have any personal contact. I see him in lectures and tutorials with all the other students.'

Again, as if someone was deliberately conspiring against Virginia, Dr Stevenson suddenly appeared from the direction of the lecture halls, making his way over the lawn towards them.

'Oh, that's him! What does he want?' she appealed to Aine. 'And you can't hide what you're thinking.' They waited in silence until he reached them.

'Hello, Sister Agnes, I had an idea that I would find you here,' he said, giving Aine several glances.

Virginia made the introductions.

'Pleased to meet you, Mrs Winterbine. I hope you enjoy your visit to the university. And I apologise for interrupting your conversation. I'll just be a minute.'

'It's no trouble, Dr Stevenson,' said Aine. Philip's interest was for Virginia alone.

'Thank you,' he said, handing Virginia a sheet of paper: 'This is a list of additional references. They're from a second and third-year course I occasionally give. Although our first-term lectures cover essential concepts found in the writings of Plato and Aristotle, the focus is on Plato's ideas, with Aristotle's criticism of Platonic forms introduced to give you an idea of possible objections. The references on the list will expand your understanding of Aristotle's major ideas if you are interested. I think you will be.'

'Thank you, Dr Stevenson, I appreciate it. I will look at them.'

With another apology for interrupting their conversation, he was gone.

'You see? He treats me like any other student.'

'Oh, yes, like any other student,' Aine could not help saying. 'With a special list? I think he would have stayed longer if I weren't here.'

'He would give this list to any student with my interests. It's an established list.'

'Make a special trip to give you a list on his personal paper?'

'That's irrelevant,' said Virginia, glancing at the sheet she still held before her. 'He probably gives talks outside the university. He has a good reputation. And he was probably on his way somewhere.' She folded it and put it in her briefcase.

'I fear you protest too much,' said Aine.

'Stop quoting Shakespeare at me,' said Virginia, amused. 'It doesn't suit your image at all.'

'What image is that?'

'You know, mysterious and ethereal. That's what your fellow postulants said.'

'I'm not mysterious nor ethereal. That's nonsense. It's the way some people see me—my unfortunate appearance.'

'The way people see you, your unfortunate appearance—is that it?'

'Yes.'

Despite their amusement, they were touching on sensitive points and so returned to talking about their everyday lives. Virginia spoke long and with enthusiasm about her university course. But when she was at pains to emphasise that Dr Stevenson was treating her like any other student during tutorials, she saw an ironic smile reappear on Aine's pretty face and could not, in turn, suppress a smile.

'Don't look like that,' she said. 'It's true.'

If Aine had been reflecting on her friend's behaviour, Virginia was no less busy scrutinising Aine. Aine was always neatly and tastefully dressed. But her style was usually simple and unadorned. Now she was dressed up with the full display of heels, gloves, earrings and bracelets. She really did look a picture with that winsome straw sunhat to top it all off. Did she seriously think she had to get dressed up to visit the university? It was a strange misapprehension if it were true. And then there was a certain new confidence to go with the raising of dress style. She could not help feeling there was more to it than Aine was admitting—or wanted to admit.

At midday, she took Aine to the student union, where she could eat in comfort and continue their conversation. After finding a table as far removed from the centre of activity as possible, Aine went to order a sandwich. Virginia watched her weave her way through the tables and the growing crowd of noisy students. Heads turned as she went, most apparently from surprise at seeing someone so out of harmony with her surroundings. Whether Aine had to deal with any comments or unwanted attention, she could not know. She walked in her usual aloof manner, ignoring what was happening around her. A young man appeared on the other side of the table, blocking her view of Aine. He stared at her.

'Is there something you want to say?' said Sister Agnes.

'I'm sorry, I've never spoken to a nun before, although I've seen plenty of you around,' he half-stammered. He fidgeted with a folder.

'Is there something you want to say?' Sister Agnes repeated to encourage him.

'I feel I must say something— I can't watch you walk around here without alerting—'

'You want to tell me that the Catholic Church has perverted the message of Christianity?' she went on to help him out.

'That's it—you know—'

'The Catholic Church is unbiblical. Is that what you want to say?'

'You're a political organisation concerned with power, not the message of the Gospel.'

'Do I look like a politician?'

A combination of a politician, spy, and military figure,' he said darkly.

'I must be a very dangerous person,'

'Most people do not realise how pernicious your proselytising is.'

Aine arrived back at the table and sat down next to Agnes. She gave the young man an inquiring look. He flushed, his tongue now numbed.

'Get out of here, you pathetic idiot,' said another young man, bumping the first, causing him to stumble against the next table. 'Go and spread your crap elsewhere.'

The biblical young man righted himself and, with several fearful glances at the much bigger student, crept away.

'He was not bothering us,' said Agnes, recognising one of the students who had stared at them earlier.

'I couldn't care less. I'm more concerned with those who haven't woken up to you.'

'I thought that may be the case,' said Agnes, struggling to suppress a smirk. 'I would kindly ask you to postpone communicating your views and leave us to have our lunch undisturbed. I have my friend with me who is visiting from the country.'

'She's why I am here,' he said, glancing at the wedding ring on Aine's finger and losing a little of his bold manner, 'to stop you from spreading your poison.'

'You mean spreading the message about Christ's love for the world.'

'Yeah, the message to suck in innocent people, to delude them.'

'All that sounds very dramatic, but—'

'I'm not deluded,' said Aine, not bothering to look at him. 'I don't need your help in deciding what I think.'

Agnes had to stop herself from smiling as Aine's short, indifferent manner left the student deflated.

'What are you—the indoctrinator or indoctrinated?' he sneered at Agnes.

'Perhaps the same question could be asked of you. But I rather think you are the indoctrinated.'

'How are you, Mrs Winterbine?' came a loud greeting in a thick Irish accent, the owner of which was Bobby McGuigan, who was approaching with several students in his wake. Aine acknowledged the greeting with an uncomfortable nod.

'Hey, lad,' said Bobby McGuigan, landing a heavy hand on the student's shoulder, 'you're not bothering my friend here?'

'Your friend?'

'Mrs Winterbine is a good friend of my daughter's. Purer Celtic stock you could not find anywhere.'

Frowning at the gratuitous remark and ignoring the students, Aine introduced Agnes to Mr McGuigan. Agnes was not blind to the reason she did this.

'We have not met, Sister Agnes, but I know about you from my daughter.'

'And I about you from Aine, Mr McGuigan. I did not expect to see you at the university.' It was a not-very-subtle attempt to satisfy her curiosity.

'I'd believe that, Sister. Students and unionists have common cause.'

'In that respect, your friends seem to be waiting on you,' she said, nodding at the students behind him. They were shifting sullenly and glancing at Aine, who maintained an icy expression.

'How long will you be here?' said Bobby McGuigan to Aine.

'I will be returning to Binawarra after lunch when Vir ... Sister Agnes goes to her lecture,' said Aine, barely looking at him.

'I'll catch you later,' he said, his eyes narrowing a little as he glanced at Agnes. 'I think you would be interested, as an Irish lass, in what we—'

'Mr McGuigan, I am Australian.'

He regarded her in a patient, patronising way. 'Don't ever be fooled into thinking you are. You're a white Northern girl. I'll see you later. Come on, fellas.' He marched off with the students following. The d-eflated student glanced back at Aine several times. Aine, the corner of her lips tensed, watched them without saying anything.

'I see what you mean,' said Virginia after Bobby and his boys had settled at a table not far away.

'What?'

'That Irish business and the influence on Margaret. Or is it rather Celtic?'

'I wish he wouldn't involve me,' said Aine, not responding to Virginia's question. 'I'm conscious of my Irish background, and so are my parents, but the last thing we want is to stir up Irish discontent. My father has said that life's hard enough without dredging up the troubles of Irish history.

'I had no idea that people of Irish ancestry were so preoccupied with it.'

'I know. You have to be from an Irish background. I think most Australians have no idea of the harshness of the penal laws the English used to suppress us.'

'You've given me a different insight into Archbishop Mannix's actions.'

'I suppose you would think differently if you were brought up in a family of English ancestry.'

'Undoubtedly.'

They lapsed into silence while Aine ate her sandwich.

'Are you going to meet Mr McGuigan later?' asked Virginia, after staring at the rowdy, gesticulating Irishman who seemed to have his student friends hanging on his lips.

'I'll try to avoid it, not only because of the Irish thing. I find him overwhelming, like a lot of Irish men. My mother and father are the quiet sort.'

'I hope you succeed.'

'Do you think we can return to the lawn?' said Aine, pushing her half-eaten sandwich away. 'It's too noisy here.'

Virginia readily agreed. She understood that it was not only the noise that was bothering Aine. The growing attention of male students who came to have a look was worse.

'Aine, wait! We're coming.' Jannie was making her way between the students and tables, with Margaret following unhurried, not far behind.

'I didn't know you were coming to Melbourne,' she exclaimed. 'You should've contacted me.' She sat at the table, making a place for Margaret. Virginia noticed the usual expressionless demeanour Margaret now adopted in Jannie's company, apparently happy to leave the talking to her, though remaining alert to what was going on.

'It's only a short visit,' said Aine.

'It doesn't matter. There'll be time for a short talk, won't there?' She glanced at Virginia.

'I'll be with Virginia until she goes to lecture. Then I intend to go straight to the station to catch the train.'

'Good, I'll take you. What time's your lecture?'

With a helpless glance at Aine, Virginia had no option but to give the time that Aine was free. That being decided, Jannie switched to Harry's offer, giving Virginia a clear idea of the sort of pressure she was putting Aine under. As steadfastly as Aine rejected the idea, Jannie insisted that she consider it. And when Jannie suggested she give Harry a call, Aine became agitated.

'Your father's over there, Sister Catherine,' said Virginia, to take the heat away from Aine.

'Yes, I know.'

'Why's he with those socialist fanatics who are always pestering me?' said Jannie, distracted momentarily.

'He said that unionists and students have common cause,' Virginia could not help commenting.

'*Rerum Novarum* supports the existence of unions,' Margaret replied.

'That's true,' said Virginia, regretting her hastiness. 'But as with all economic and social activity, the role of the unions must remain underpinned by the laws of God and acknowledgment of His Church. *Rerum Novarum* provides no justification for socialism.'

'That depends on what you think socialism is. The Gospels' principles of fairness, equity, and brotherhood are central to most notions of socialism.'

'If it's a question of political organisation,' said Virginia, conscious of the boldness and fluency of Margaret's reply, 'the Church does not in principle favour any particular form of government. The essential task of any government is to acknowledge God's laws and His Church, as I say. Atheistic socialism is diametrically opposed to anything you'll find in *Rerum Novarum*.'

'You have gone quickly from unions to atheistic socialism,' Margaret commented. 'My father remains Catholic.'

'I did not mean to impugn your father's motivations. I just wanted to make clear what *Rerum Novarum*'s approval of unions entails.'

'It should not be thought that political organisation for rights, freedom, equality and fraternity equates directly with atheism,' said Margaret, maintaining her calm.

'You're quite right. It doesn't necessarily follow, but that wasn't my meaning.'

'It seemed to be.'

'I'm sorry if I gave that impression.'

Sister Catherine did not respond to the apology. She rose, beckoning Jannie, who stood up as if in attendance on her. She wished Aine well, saying she hoped to see her again shortly. Aine could not say when she would be in Melbourne again. Undeterred, Catherine said she looked forward to hearing how she was going and whether she was not yet ready to strike out. Aine said she did not know what was meant by striking out, but assured Catherine that she was still happy with her family duties and could not foresee any change to that. Catherine greeted that assurance with a slight incline of the head and an almost imperceptible raising of her eyebrows.

With an invitation to Jannie to follow her, she made for her father but stopped several paces short of the table, evidently waiting to catch his attention. She did not have to wait long. Bobby McGuigan's boisterous manner of talking and looking around soon had his formidable daughter within his vision. He sprang to his feet, leaving his student companions staring bemusedly after him. He walked with her a few paces away from them. Jannie shrugged and, to the delight and undivided attention of the students, sat at their table.

'Do you think Margaret has much changed?' said Virginia as they watched Margaret and her father talking together.

'Outwardly, she has changed. She's very self-controlled now. She was not like that. But I think she's still the same on the inside. You said that during my Christmas visit, remember?' She pushed the plate around with the half-eaten sandwich. 'None of us changes much on the inside, I fear.'

'You fear? I don't suppose you're thinking of me?'

'No, Virginia, not at all. I was thinking of myself—my self-deception. Perhaps Margaret's sceptical look was justified.'

'Don't take any notice of her. She's in the act of advancing her agenda.'

'What agenda?'

'I still don't know. Look, she's finished with her father and leaving Jannie with the men.'

They watched her make her way out of the eating hall, apparently blind to her surroundings.

'She seems to stick to the Rule pretty well,' commented Aine. 'Her manner with you and Jannie—that was not the case six years ago.'

'Yes, she does mostly, at least outwardly. I must confess that we both fudge it a little while at the university.'

'Interior assent to the Rule is the essential quality of keeping to the Rule, isn't it?' said Aine, more to herself than to Virginia, 'and that a mere exterior adherence is a stain?' She glanced at Virginia.

'Yes. But I shouldn't say anything more if I want to obey the Rule.' She held out her hands with a helpless expression. 'There, you see, it's already too late.'

A minute of silence passed as they focused their attention on Jannie.

'She really is an attractive girl,' said Aine.

'And she knows how to use her attraction. By the way, I have not until now heard you comment on someone's appearance. So, you do think about it.'

Aine blushed. 'I hope I've never given the impression that I do not notice—'

'Well, you have.'

'I only meant to say that appearance is not important and should not make a difference to your self-examination or your relations with other people.'

'You're speaking about yourself?'

'Oh, well, I meant generally,' she said, flustered. 'Appearance is superficial, no matter what the viewpoint.' She began to wilt under Virginia's searching gaze. They turned their attention again to Jannie, who had her male audience hanging on her every word.

'She seems so different from the girl we knew in the convent,' ventured Aine.

'Seems. I have a feeling something was already wrong before she entered. You know, she had hardly been in Australia for two years. She still had that accent, most of which she has now lost. There must have been a jarring rupture culturally, something that could leave many people lost.'

'I think I understand. There's that Irish thing that clashes with our identity here.'

'I have never really considered that. I've never had that alien feeling.'

'But you identify with things English—with the English ascendancy,' said Aine.

'Yes, but it's a general cultural identification. That's because English-ness is at the foundations of Australian society.'

'And not Irishness?'

'I don't know. If I listen to you, I feel I have missed out on something.'

Jannie drew their attention by standing, throwing a furtive look in their direction, and leaving the table. She stopped as Mr McGuigan called after her. She stood listening for a few seconds and then resumed her way.

'She seems to have gone away with some purpose,' said Virginia. She looked at her watch. 'It's time I got ready for my next lecture.' She stood, collecting her folders and briefcase.

Aine rose, too, picking up the sunhat she had placed on the chair next to her. She positioned it carefully on her head, ignoring the attention that she at once aroused. 'I'll walk as far as the lecture halls with you,' she said. But as they made their way to the exit, they heard Bobby McGuigan call out.

'Oh, no, I don't want to talk to him.'

'Then politely excuse yourself.'

'It's not that easy.'

'Of course, it is. Pretend he's that student you froze into silence.'

'He's not a student. It's different, anyhow.'

'Aine, I can't help you.'

They looked back to see Bobby McGuigan pushing his way through the students, many of whom were preparing to go to lectures.

'Aine, come and join us for a while,' he called before he had reached them. 'We've got things to talk about,' he added, out of breath when he was with them.

'I don't think I have time. I don't want to risk missing the train.'

'Nonsense, girl, there are plenty of trains. Besides, Jannie will take you to the station.'

'My husband will be waiting for me at the station.'

'What time is your train?'

'Three-thirty.'

'You have plenty of time.'

'I would rather keep going, Mr McGuigan.'

'I think it would cause Aine too much anxiety if she lingered, Mr McGuigan,' Agnes interrupted. 'Perhaps next time she comes to Melbourne ...'

'Do you think so, Sister?' said Bobby McGuigan. 'There's nothing to get anxious about. She's with her own here.'

'Nevertheless, I don't think she should be harried—'

'Harried?' Bobby exclaimed. 'You're living up to your reputation, Sister.'

'My reputation?'

'Please, Mr McGuigan, I will find the time when I am next in Melbourne,' said Aine, glancing from one to the other.

'Okay, girl, I'll keep you to that,' he said, keeping a wary eye on Agnes. 'Margaret will keep me informed.'

He left them without acknowledging Agnes to return to his student friends. Agnes noticed three men of the same age and appearance had joined the students.

'Do I have a reputation?' she asked when they were out in the fresh air.

'Anybody who knows you knows you're not afraid to express your opinions,' said Aine, looking behind her.

'Is it that bad?' said Virginia, amused by Aine's artlessness. 'I thought I had made some progress.'

'It's not bad at all. It's one of the reasons I like you. You are honest and solicitous with everyone.'

'Including Mr McGuigan?'

'Yes, you were polite and nothing else. He had no reason to take exception. You were just thinking of me. He's so taken up in his ... whatever it is ... that he could not see how I felt. You did.'

'Thank you, Aine. That's why I love you.' She smiled. 'I should not speak such things.'

'Mother Jerome would understand. She knows our friendship is not harmful.'

'Do you think so? She has warned me about my emotions.'

'Did she?'

Virginia could see that Aine did not want to continue the subject and had her suspicions why. By this time, they had arrived outside the lecture halls. 'You know, Aine,' she said, 'Philip always said that my outspokenness was one of the reasons he liked me. He was always guaranteed to get an honest opinion. Now I have to guard against that tendency to follow the Rule. At moments like this, I feel most keenly that the religious life is a life against nature.'

'I understand,' said Aine, much sympathy in her voice.

Virginia felt the inclination to take her hand and embrace her, but kept herself under control. 'I know you do.' They stood facing each other, preparing to depart. 'You know, we've been speaking for a few hours, but you've not said exactly why you arranged to meet me.'

Aine brushed her hair, pulled at her white cotton gloves, adjusted her sunhat and sunglasses, fiddled with her silver bangle, and looked around. 'I just wanted to see you. Apart from Charles, you're the only one I can talk freely with—who understands me. Charles understands me differently, too.' She avoided Virginia's gaze.

'I hope I've provided the comfort you wanted.'

'You've provided comfort that nobody else can give.'

At that moment, Dr Stevenson came up beside them.

'Good afternoon. You're off to a lecture, Sister Agnes?'

'Yes, Economics. Aine's on her way home.'

A short exchange followed, during which Virginia gave her full attention to Dr Stevenson as he attempted to make a joke about her studying such a subject. She blushed at the intimate allusions. Then he was on his way to give a lecture, wishing Aine a safe trip back to Bendigo. Virginia glanced at Aine after he had disappeared into the nearby lecture hall.

'Are you sure there's nothing more ... between you?' said Aine.

'Yes. A little expected embarrassment does not mean anything.'

With their goodbyes repeated several times, and the inclination to hug each other resisted, they went their separate ways. Virginia stopped at the entrance to the economics building and looked back. She saw Jannie catch up with Aine as Aine was about to enter the path through the middle of the south lawn.

Chapter 25

Harry works on Aine

THE ECONOMICS lecture was more tedious than usual, forcing Virginia to exert herself to keep her mind on the material. Running through her note-taking were the meetings with Jannie and Margaret, then Mr McGuigan, and finally Philip, with Aine's presence and reaction overlaying each episode. What puzzled her the more she thought about it was Aine's unexpected visit to Melbourne. It was to see her, ostensibly. There seemed to be something else there, though. But what? Aine made it clear that she did not want anything to do with Margaret and her father. That was plain. Although she showed, on the surface, little inclination to develop the friendship Jannie wanted, she gave a glimpse now and then of an odd, equivocal attitude towards her. Was that through a natural sympathy for anyone with problems? Or something else? As she left the lecture theatre with her mind on these matters, Philip fell in with her.

'How did it go?'

'What? ... I mean, I beg your pardon,' she said, surprised to see him but glad he was there. 'Oh, you mean the economics lecture?'

'Yes. Somehow, I cannot see you among all those economics students studying the laws of supply and demand or whatever else—'

'It's more than that, as you must know,' she said, finding herself responding readily to his light-heartedness.

'Why on earth did you choose that subject? That's not you at all.'

'Mother Prioress wanted me to include it.'

'Ordered you, more likely.'

'Yes, but strict obedience is part of the life. You must know that, too.'

'Yes, I do. Sorry for the prod. You're allowed to give me a rap over the knuckles with your hardest ruler whenever I overstep the mark with my juvenile comments.'

'I'll remember you said that.'

'Do. Where are you going? To the library?'

'Yes.'

'So am I. I'll walk with you. Is that all right?'

'I can't stop you from taking the same path.'

He laughed. 'You haven't changed, Virginia, have you? Oh, there I go forgetting—hang on a minute.' He stopped, glancing around. 'Come over here.' They were at the beginning of the path leading down along the side of the south lawn towards the library. He walked to a bench at the side. She followed but did not sit down. 'Look, at the start when I saw you in that habit— well, you know what happened. Despite what I said, I accepted that it signified your commitment and that you had changed and adapted to the life—but after all these weeks of being with you in tutorials, I see you haven't changed that much.'

'Philip, please, this doesn't serve any purpose. I'm committed, as you say yourself.'

'Don't worry. I accept that. You won't have any difficulty with me. I just wanted to say that I simply cannot call you Sister in private. You will always be Virginia Pearson to me. That black habit doesn't hide it anymore. You'll have to keep out of my way if you don't want me to—'

'I can't force you to do anything. I merely hope you'll respect my choices.'

'I do. You have nothing to worry about,' he repeated. 'I've adjusted finally. It's a fact of life that relations form and dissolve, sometimes with a lot of heartache. Life goes on. I accept that.'

This was just what Virginia did not want to hear. She wanted to say how sorry she was and that her affection for him had not dissolved. But she must not. She must not do anything to re-establish— She tried to think of something to say, but the feelings rising within her had to be controlled. She saw him looking at her, awaiting a response. She must get away from him. His expression changed, thoughtful at first, then a flicker of surprise.

'I don't want to dig up the past,' he resumed, 'but there's something I've always wanted to know. Do you remember that night on Sorrento beach?'

'Philip, it's best we don't go there.' She found herself doing what she had resolved to avoid—what Mother Jerome had told her to avoid. 'I must go.'

'No, wait. Just one question and no more.' She stopped after several steps, knowing she should flee rather than listen. 'Did you make your decision before or after that night?'

'After. Several months after.'

'After we became engaged?'

'Of course.'

'How ...?'

'It started when I read St Augustine's *Confessions*. I told you that. Now I must go.' She could not bring herself to walk away.

'I suppose I should be consoled that it was one of the great philosophers of Western Civilisation,' he commented. He seemed to come to himself as he looked at her. 'I'm sorry to upset you. I didn't mean it. Wait a few moments. You don't want people to see you like that.'

Was it so obvious? She put her briefcase down and sat on the bench. She sighed and bent her head.

'Do you have a handkerchief?' He pulled a clean handkerchief from his trouser pocket and went to dab her eyes.

'No,' she said, pushing his hand away. 'I must go.' She flicked a finger across both eyes but remained seated, looking at the folder in her hands. She hoped there was no one around to see what had happened. Several students had walked by, chatting loudly. Fortunately, they appeared not to pay attention to them. She hoped that Philip's calm manner and his keeping his distance covered the raw emotion that had overcome them. Indeed, he seemed to have positioned himself so that she was hidden from the direct gaze of passers-by.

'I thought you said your friend was on the point of leaving to catch the train,' he said, after a painful silence, and apparently to put the conversation on an even keel.

'What do you mean?' she said, looking around. She got to her feet.

The path to the library along the side of the south lawn was on a gradual incline. The lawn was at chest level where they stood, giving them a view through the shrubs and flowers across the lawn.

'Over there, that little crowd watching your friend and Jannie de Kam go through their paces.'

'Going through their paces!' she could not help exclaiming. All thought of her upset with Philip retreated as she looked, shocked, at the scene on the other side of the lawn.

A man around Philip's age was taking photos of Aine and Jannie, using the leafy gardens as a backdrop. She guessed he was the professional photographer Jannie had wanted to call, the one Aine wanted nothing to do with. Not only had the photographer come, but Aine, in the face of her protestations, had submitted to be photographed! How long had they been at it? The small crowd of onlookers seemed to suggest quite a while. She and Philip watched in silence as the photographer directed the young women into various positions and poses while he snapped from different angles. As they continued watching, they saw that Jannie was helping Aine follow the photographer's instructions. She would strike a pose and stand back while Aine copied it. The muffled exclamations of the photographer's approval drifted across the lawn.

'They certainly are good-looking girls,' said Philip at length. 'I'm not surprised your friend has aroused a professional photographer's interest. She has that look.'

'What look?' Virginia said helplessly.

'That detached look with the intense blue eyes. It's an alluring combination. That photographer has seen it. I'm told he's among the smartest and most perceptive around.' He paused. 'I'm amazed she spent some time in the convent, even more than I am of Jannie de Kam.'

'Do you know the photographer?'

'Don't you remember? I knew Jannie de Kam by reputation but only met her formally at Harry and Erik's place. Harry's the photographer.'

She remembered. It was his girlfriend who knew Erik.

'Your friend is striking, but she's not my type,' he said, seeming to read her thoughts. 'That distant, aloof look does not engage me. It's too cold and unresponsive. I like the soft open heart of a girl who can't help showing her feelings.'

'You would be surprised at the depths of Aine's feelings and spiritual life,' she said hastily to cover her feelings.

'I can't see them at the moment.'

'This is not like her.'

'A girl who looks like that will always have trouble ignoring the flattery. That won't help her spiritual side. And she's not getting help at this precise moment.'

Philip did not know how cutting his comments sounded. How could he know? He did not know Aine the way she did. But then, there was Aine, letting herself be photographed. Something was going on inside Aine that she had not seen.

'We're not the only ones interested in what's happening,' said Philip.

Sister Catherine stood at the entrance to the path through the south lawn. Expressionless, she was observing the same scene.

'Oh, I've arranged to meet her in the library,' said Virginia. 'I can't linger any longer.'

'What's wrong with meeting her here?'

'No, no, I'll meet her as arranged. Please, Philip, let me go on alone.'

'I understand. I won't bother you any longer.'

He sat on the bench and watched Sister Agnes hurry into the library. A minute later, Sister Catherine passed by without so much as a glance. She moved forward with confident strides, engrossed in thought and with the same expressionless face he had already observed. This was a formidable young nun who already had the department talking about her cleverness. He waited—against his better judgment. Ten minutes later, the two sisters emerged from the library. As they turned towards the university's southern entrance, Sister Agnes looked in his direction. Her fresh young face, framed incongruously in black and white, lingered just a moment before turning away. He got to his feet and trudged back to hi s office. Sometime later, he rang Diana to say he would not see her. He had some urgent work to prepare. He walked home alone, his bottle of Irish whisky waiting to keep him company for the evening in his sparsely furnished bachelor flat.

While staring at the walls, glass in his hand, he ran over the meeting with Virginia. Her responses showed she still had feelings for him, but they were feelings she had to suppress. Her commitment to religious life was unchanged, and she was prepared to struggle against any interference or outside influence. What was he to do? It would be unfair to take advantage of her. And it would not work. He would only make her university studies difficult, if not impossible. He must not do that. The only choice was to maintain distance and avoid personal contact outside the tutorial meetings. That was his resolve. He hoped he could follow through.

AINE let herself drop onto the seat, holding her hat and breathing heavily. She had just made it. She took a deep breath and waved at Jannie, Erik, and Harry, who stood on the platform. As the train pulled out of Spencer Street Station, she watched their smiling faces and waving hands retreating slowly. Jannie's radiant face sharply contrasted with the earlier occasion when she had acted so strangely. She sat back and leaned her head against the back of the seat. She stared through the window up at the autumn sky.

It had vexed her when Jannie, with Harry not far behind her, juggling his photographic equipment, caught up with her. 'You're beautiful when you're angry!' Jannie laughed after they had her cornered. Harry stopped Jannie's teasing, saying they should not joke about her understandable caution. After that admonition, Jannie wisely let Harry do the talking . He reassured her he would not do anything to discomfort her. He only wished to show the style of photos he wanted of her if she would allow it. They would be for promoting high-fashion house products, nothing at all vulgar or tawdry. That did not suit her distinctive looks. He had several fashion magazines to give her an idea of what he had in mind. He led her to a bench on the lawn, where he patiently explained how the photos were set up to convey a particular aura and mood.

She had intended to give him just enough time to be polite. After all, she could never fault his manners. He was always considerate and kind. But as he advanced in his explanation, she became interested. Even more, she became fascinated by the creative effort that went into the photos. This gave her a different perspective on fashion photography, both for the photographer and the fashion model. There was a lot more to it than she had thought. It was not a simple matter of posing and smiling sweetly into the camera. Then Harry fished an envelope out of his bag. It contained large prints of the photos he had taken of her at Christmas. He explained why he thought she was suited. She had to admit that it all made sense and was far from the superficial, exploitative work she thought it was. Half an hour passed before she knew it, so interested did she become in Harry's explanation.

'You see, there's a lot more to it than you think, isn't there?' he said as he slotted the photos back into the envelope.

'Yes, I must admit there is.'

'Jannie's very attractive, but her real talent is speaking to the camera lens. I'll show you.'

In the meantime, Jannie had replaced her clothes with an expensive fur-trimmed winter coat over an elegant dress that fell halfway down her calves. Quality dark leather shoes with high heels were on her feet. Harry positioned her in front of a garden rich in shrubs and ornamental trees. He explained how to arrange the coat and project the mood he wanted. Now Aine saw a different side to Jannie. With a confidence Aine had not witnessed before, Jannie struck a fluid sequence of poses, during which Harry clicked away, making encouraging comments.

'Sit quietly on the bench so as not to soil the clothes,' he said to Jannie when he had finished. 'Don't move.' Jannie silently followed his instructions. Then turning to Aine, 'You see?'

She did see. She said she found the process far more interesting than she expected. It was a simple, honest response, but Harry took it to mean much more.

'Look, come on, try the coat on. Come here, Jannie,' he said, vigorously beckoning her and preparing his camera. 'Jannie's a little bigger, but it should fit.'

Before Aine knew it, Jannie had put the coat on her. There were exclamations of how well it suited her.

'Now wait a minute,' said Harry, looking at her. 'Come here, Aine.' He directed her to the bench. 'Jannie, the shoes.' Again, before she could protest, Jannie had pulled her shoes off and slipped on the expensive leather shoes. 'Stand up,' he said, giving her a hand. 'Beautiful! How do they feel?'

'Surprisingly comfortable.'

'They're a perfect fit,' said Jannie. 'Everything's a perfect fit. We've almost the same size.'

'The hat,' said Harry.

Jannie drew a fur-trimmed hat from a carry bag. She positioned it on Aine's head. From then on, in a whirl of instructions and encouragement from Harry and Jannie, Aine was photographed in various discreet poses and subtle expressions. She was surprised to find how relaxed she remained and how easily she responded to Harry's encouragement. She did not feel uncomfortable, either, when people gathered to watch.

'You know, you're a natural,' said Harry.

'What about photos with some makeup?' said Jannie. Without waiting for an answer, she sat Aine down and expertly added lipstick and eye makeup. 'There,' she said, standing back. 'Wait, one last thing.' She brushed Aine's cheeks.

'Sensational,' said Harry. Another round of clicking and directions followed. 'There, that's not too painful, is it?'

'No, it wasn't painful,' she agreed, giving him an indulgent smile.

'That's the girl.'

With his eyes still on her, he nodded at the watching people. With that point made, he began packing up his equipment while she returned to the bench to take off her coat and put on her shoes. Jannie approached Harry and whispered in his ear. He hesitated momentarily, glanced at her, but then shook his head. 'That's enough for today.' Jannie faced her with a silly expression and shrugged. She sidled over to the bench with the same silly, embarrassed expression, picked up the shoes, brushed her stockinged feet, and went to put them on.

'Wait,' said Harry, 'haven't you got other shoes?'

'Of course,' she said, putting the shoes carefully beside her and rummaging again in her bag.

'I want you to take the dress off, too.'

'I'll be back in a minute,' she said to Aine with a weak smile. 'Don't go anywhere.' She headed off with her bag towards the student union.

'I have to look after the clothes,' Harry said.

Aine remained on the bench, observing him as he packed up his equipment with care and precision.

'You're very dedicated to your work,' she commented when he had finished and came to sit beside her.

'It's my life. My work is my life.'

'Don't you have time for other things?'

'Of course. I don't mean I don't do anything else. I'm not a hermit. Far from it. I mean, everything revolves around the creative process of photography. My mind's hardly off it.' He regarded her for a moment. 'I'm glad you're more relaxed in my company. You can trust me, you know. There's no ulterior motive. I genuinely see potential in you. You're different in a way that photographs well. I saw it the first time I laid eyes on you. If you allow me to promote you, nothing will interfere with that task.'

'I don't know what to say,' she said, seeing he expected an answer. 'I don't really understand the potential you're talking about. I can't understand the way others see me.'

'I know. That's part of your potential. It's part of what gives you the photographable expressions. You're honest in front of the camera. There's more to it, of course, something inexplicable, something I don't understand.' He smiled. 'It's what I don't understand—what others don't understand—that I try to capture.'

'I'm just an ordinary person. What you say about me sounds fanciful.'

'Ordinary person!'

'Yes. I can't help the way I look.'

'Please, no more,' he laughed. 'But leave that aside. I'll tell you what I want.'

He explained he would choose the best photos to show clients. He was sure he could secure lucrative work for her. In the meantime, she should discuss his plans with her husband. If Charles wanted to know more, he should call him. It was important that they both fully understood the goal he wanted to work toward. Jannie arrived back at that point, and a few minutes later, Erik, whom Jannie greeted excitedly.

AS THE train rattled on into the growing dusk, Aine turned these scenes over in her mind. Not the least anxiety accompanied her thoughts. Harry and his strictly professional manner of going about his work and explaining his plans put her at ease. Her mind lingered on the somewhat furtive and manipulative way he and Jannie led her on, but she dismissed any suspicion of ulterior motive. She dwelt for a moment on the impression that Jannie's role exceeded that of mere help to a friend and a professional photographer but dismissed that suspicion, too, as unfounded. In any case, time would tell if something else motivated Jannie. In that unlikely case, she would take action and do whatever the situation required. All in all, she concluded, there was little reason to worry about Harry's plans. She could now tell Charles about it. When she stepped off the train into Charles's waiting arms, he looked at her in surprise.

'What's the makeup for?'

'Oh, I forgot. Charles, darling, there's something I want to tell you.'

On the way back to Binawarra, she explained how she had met Harry and what he was proposing. Charles listened intently.

'What do you think?' she said when she had finished.

'If it's what you want to do, you'll have my support.'

'No reservations?'

'None, if you have none. I know nothing about this sort of thing. I trust you if you think it's all right and it's something you want to do.'

'It's not that I want to do anything. Nothing has happened. I'll wait and see.'

'All right, it's your decision as long as it doesn't cause you any anxiety.'

'I don't feel at all anxious. I may have got over it at last.'

'I hope so,' he replied, looking askance at her.

She sat back in her seat as the car passed between the two peaks, signalling the entrance to their little country town. For once, she did not notice the strange, sharp peak on their right. Instead, she was happy and relieved that Charles showed no concern about where Harry was leading her.

THAT SAME evening, after dinner and recreation, when the grand silence had started, Sister Agnes knelt in front of Mother Jerome's desk. She had her head bowed, waiting for the prioress to say something. A long period of uncomfortable silence passed. Then, at last, she glanced up. Mother Jerome was observing her with interest. The prioress raised her eyebrows.

'What do you expect me to say?'

'I don't know.'

'You mean that Sister Agnes, usually so confident and ready to explain herself, does not know what she should do in this simple matter? Nor does she know what I should say.'

'I was hoping you could give me advice.'

'Perhaps this is something so fundamental that I, or anybody else, cannot advise you. It's something, perhaps, that you must resolve yourself.'

'You do not agree that I should change tutorials, give up philosophy, or even discontinue the course?'

'For what reasons would you take that action?'

'To take me out of the way of temptation.'

'Think, Sister. Is it really a question of temptation?'

'Well, I thought—'

'On your account, Dr Stevenson has not proposed anything sinful.'

'No! Not at all.'

'He has remained perfectly respectful?'

'He has become very familiar.'

'Sister, for heaven's sake, you were engaged to him! You broke that engagement. Do you think the man is made of rock?' Agnes responded with a sob she could no longer suppress. She clasped her hands. Mother Jerome waited until she composed herself. 'Sister Agnes,' she went on, 'this is about your vocation—whether you have a vocation. I have said many times, and I repeat, that it is no indignity to find that you do not have a vocation. You can live a virtuous life as a wife and mother. I have the impression Dr. Stevenson would make a good husband.' She stopped. An unbearable silence prevailed again. At length, Agnes thought she heard a short sigh. 'At this stage,' the prioress resumed, 'you must be honest with yourself and the community.'

'I want to devote myself to the religious life, to the Suffering Saviour,' said Agnes, struggling to control her feelings. 'I want to follow the great examples of St Therese, St Ignatius, St Vincent de Paul, and many others. They are my model. I don't want to give up.'

'Then you must deal with your relationship with Dr Stevenson. Be honest with yourself.'

'I have no relationship with Philip.'

'You will always have a relationship with Philip. You will have to manage.' She paused. 'As long as you remain a sister of this order, I will not permit you to change your existing routine. Is that clear?'

'Yes, Mother.'

'Now dry your eyes and attend to your business.'

Chapter 26

Troubles on campus

SISTER AGNES left Mother Jerome's office hurt and puzzled. Mother Jerome had mixed tenderness and understanding with firmness when she could not control her feelings. Now it was as if she was restraining herself from bundling her out of the office with the invitation to grow up. Agnes had never been exposed to her impatience, and it shook her. She struggled to control her feelings as she hastened to the chapel for Compline. Later, alone in the seclusion of her cell, she reflected. Philip's behaviour was, as Mother Jerome had pointed out, not unexpected, and she had reacted in a silly, girlish way. It was behaviour that one would expect from a love-sick fifteen-year-old. Fifteen. Indeed, that was her age when Philip, the oldest son of family friends, at last took notice of her. It was after two years of working her smiles and teasing on him. Her mind returned to that time, a period of innocent hope and expectation until he finally submitted. How ironic that she had loved him long before he returned her feelings. That just added to her feelings of guilt.

The memories took hold, and she struggled to drive them from her mind. She knelt beside her bed and again reminded herself of why she was in the convent. She meditated on Jesus' invitation to the rich young man, the invitation to sell all, reject the world, and follow the Saviour. It was the Gospel passage that must influence every religious vocation. Slowly, her resolve returned. Whatever the hardships, whatever the lapses in her strength, she told herself boldly, she would renew her determination to persevere. Once in bed with the lights out, though, sleep would not come. It was one thing to immerse herself in a meditation designed to motivate her; it was another to deal with the concrete circumstances of Philip's presence. The Rule was empty if interior assent and love of the Rule did not match the outward display of adherence. It was equally true that prayer and meditation were meaningless without resolute action. She must avoid Philip outside tutorials and lectures.

There were only two places where she would run into him: outside the lecture theatre and on the lawn where she took a break. She determined to keep clear of those places. But having once isolated the circumstances and resolved on her action, she still could not induce sleep to block the recurring images of Philip and his question or the places where she had spoken to him. So, she lay there staring at the walls mottled by the clouds passing over the waning moon, eventually falling into a half-stupor filled with Philip's bodiless presence.

A short shaft of light across the ceiling roused her as if shot up from below. She struggled onto an elbow and listened. She went to the window and stared at the clearing far below. Without being entirely conscious of her actions, she put on her coat and made her way along the silent corridor, down the stairs and outside. Her bare head, with its short wispy brown hair, strangely did not feel the chill of the autumn night. She continued down the rocky stairs to the clearing and, without halting, headed for the grotto. As she approached, she saw a group of hooded figures standing in front of the grotto, where a bright orange flame flickered around their silhouettes. She crept forward, fearful of disturbing them.

Now she heard them singing a mournful chant, their heads tilted upwards as if fixed on the statue of Our Lady of Lourdes. She inched closer. Then a bright light shone from the niche. She looked up. She stumbled backwards. In the niche where the statue usually stood was Aine dressed in a brilliant long white dress with her bare feet visible. She stood looking serenely over the heads of the hooded figures into the distance. The hooded figures bowed and then turned to Agnes. She inhaled in gasps as she looked into the dark, empty spaces where faces should have been. Then, stumbling further backwards, she turned and ran—and ran and ran.

Agnes woke to the sound of the bell echoing along the corridor. She answered the greeting, falling out of bed. With prayers said, she went to the window. The sun's early morning rays were bathing the river and surrounding bush in a warm yellow light. A slight mist hung over the dark water. It was a scene of undisturbed peace. She hastened to prepare herself for chapel, all the time reflecting on a dream that seemed so real, as real as the experiences of five years earlier. In the end, those experiences had felt like a dream, something she knew was not right. She had truly witnessed those hooded figures. What did this confusion of impressions mean? It was just like Aine's experiences. And it had followed her compulsive reflection on her problem with Philip. She tried to forget it as the chapel rang with the sweet female singing of the faith's ancient psalms.

Later that weekend, she made her way to the lower level with her breviary. She had no plan to linger at the grotto—at least, that's what she told herself. But as her wandering brought her there, she stopped to reflect. She lowered her breviary and then closed it as she looked around. At first, nothing seemed different. On further examination, she noticed a broken chain of flowers hanging over the side of the niche where the statue stood undisturbed. The remnants of flowers and leaves lay below the niche among the roughly piled rocks forming the grotto's lower part. She picked up a handful, turning them around in her hands. They were from the front gardens.

She stepped back, looking around—for what, she was unsure. She ran her eyes over the grassy area in front of the grotto. It was trodden flat without being damaged or broken anywhere. That was odd. Usually, the traffic of hard heels would dig up the grass, exposing the earthy brown wounds. She contemplated the statue. There were two notches in the rocks on the left. She gathered her skirts. 'That's not a very dignified sight,' a voice came from behind as she tried to stabilise herself on the first notch. She turned to see Catherine, Hildegard, and Benedicta approaching. The comment had come from Catherine. She was all triumph.

'Oh, I just wanted to look at the flowers there,' said Agnes, trapped precariously on one side of the grotto and forced to give a stupid reply.

'There are often flowers there,' said Benedicta.

'I was curious what they were,' said Agnes, as she clumsily stepped down.

'They're probably from the front garden,' said Catherine.

'I believe you're right.' Agnes brushed her black tunic and picked up the breviary she had laid on the rocky kneeler. 'My curiosity got the better of me,' she added before she understood what she had admitted to.

'That often happens—to us all,' said Catherine.

Hildegard and Benedicta continued to observe her as if in attendance on Catherine.

'I'll continue my reading elsewhere,' said Agnes, moving away.

She opened her breviary and walked towards the clearing. She had to resist the temptation to look around. When she came to the clearing, she sat on a wooden bench. The inclination to look was too strong. A furtive glance did not reveal her fellow sisters. Where had they gone? Much shrubbery grew around the crest of the riverbank. So, they could be anywhere. To prevent succumbing again to her curiosity, she rose and walked to the ridge that dropped sharply to the river. To her right, below her, was the narrow jetty. It occurred to her that she had never been there. They had been strictly forbidden to go anywhere near it during the postulancy. She had maintained that prohibition even when there was no mention of it after her profession.

She descended the wooden stairs, noticing they were in good repair. So was the jetty. She walked to the end and looked down into the glassy green water. She looked across the river. Now being much closer to the opposite bank, she had a clearer view of it. From her cell window at night, it appeared as a dark, mysterious boundary. Now she could see that the bushes by the river sheltered a dirt track running along the bank. That was curious, as she had never seen anyone walking there during the day. Over to her left, the track ran up into the fields beyond.

As she turned to walk back to the jetty stairs, she thought she caught sight of someone or something bright between the shrubbery and small gums near the river to her right. She focused but saw nothing. Then, for an instant, a head popped up out of the brush, a head with short-cropped dark hair. She hurried up the stairs and towards the grotto, curious and afraid. But nothing. She lingered at the grotto, thinking about the image of the head with the dark hair. Then, while returning to the clearing, she caught sight of Sisters Catherine, Hildegard, and Benedicta making their way, single file, up the rocky stairs. Surely, there was no time to return to the stairs unobserved if they had been among the foliage near the river. Had she seen what she thought? Why and for what purpose? Once again, she could not avoid the feeling that she had imagined it, or that her eyes had deceived her.

AGNES strove to control her edginess as she walked from the library to the lecture halls. She expected Philip to fall in with her at any moment and resume the same close questioning of the previous week. But he did not appear. Her unease hardly lessened as she took her place in the front row. She was early, and there were few students in the lecture theatre. That was the penalty for being unwilling to wait outside. She perused her notes. The noise and chatter of students grew as the theatre filled. Still no Philip. Several minutes after the scheduled time, he appeared and hastened by without acknowledging her. It was better this way, she told herself, but she remained unsettled. At the end of the lecture, she was one of the first to leave the theatre. He did not follow. She went to the library, where she avoided her usual place. For her break, she found a bench near the library entrance. Late in the afternoon, on the way back to the convent with Mr Ferguson chatting in his friendly manner and Catherine, as usual, immersed in her thoughts, she was satisfied she had succeeded in her task. But she was not happy about it.

In the following philosophy tutorial, she discovered why she had so easily kept out of his way. Philip was determined to avoid all personal contact with her. He maintained his relaxed manner but addressed her formally with the merest eye contact. It was a change in manner towards her that only she would notice. At the end of the tutorial, he said he did not have time to linger.

'If anyone has any problems they want to discuss at length,' he said, 'please drop along later or make a time now.'

The tactic was well executed. Any personal approach had to come from her. He had relieved her of the fear of raw personal contact, and she appreciated it. It was the prudent thing to do. It was his responsibility to her as a student. But the tactic was not primarily the outcome of his sense of responsibility. She knew Philip; he did not want to upset her. So once again, the realisation that she had the situation she wanted did not eliminate her unease. The following two lectures were the same; he came a little late, hastening by without looking at her. At the beginning of the following tutorial, it was evident he would continue in the same distant manner. Now she saw a problem she had not anticipated. The term was coming to an end, with her final essay due shortly. She would have to talk to him soon. The worry about how she would approach him distracted her, and she found it difficult to keep her mind on the discussion.

'Sister, you have not added much,' he said halfway through the tutorial, bringing her mind abruptly back to the discussion. 'Do you have concerns about your essay topic?' Before she could stammer a reply, he turned to the others. 'Is there anyone who has questions about their essay topic?' Everyone had worries. 'Okay, we will discuss the topics in the second half of this tutorial. At the end of the tutorial, as everyone was on the point of leaving, he said, 'Sister Agnes, can you wait? I won't keep you more than a minute.' They waited until the last student had exited. 'Are you happy with your essay topic and your progress?

'Yes, Philip, I, eh ....'

'That's good,' he said, pretending not to notice her embarrassment. 'If you keep up your standard in tutorials and the previous essay, you'll do very well. So, there's no need for concern.'

'Thank you.'

'Come to me if you have any questions. Don't hesitate. That's what I'm here for.' He paused. 'Now, there is a second reason I asked you to stay. One of your fellow students has personal problems more in your line than mine. It's affecting her study. Would you mind talking to her? I don't want her to give up.'

'Of course, but why—?'

'She did not want to impose. She wanted me to ask you first. I recommended she talk to you. You would understand. She's waiting outside.'

It was a good thing the student was waiting outside Philip's office. She did not know how she would have behaved if she had dwelt on the short exchange.

'Sister, I hope you don't mind—'

'Of course not, Anne. Let's go somewhere quiet to talk.'

Anne was from a Catholic family in the eastern suburbs and had attended an exclusive girls' college. This was something Agnes had experience with, as Philip well knew. That experience told her that if Anne had a serious problem, it would likely be one of two: boyfriend troubles or, more problematic, issues with her parents. Anne burst into tears when they sat on a bench on the front lawn.

'Tell me,' Agnes said gently.

'It's my parents ...' Anne hesitated and sniffled.

'They're separating?'

'Yes.' More crying. 'My father has already left and—'

Agnes took her hand and caressed it. This issue was one of the most demanding she had been obliged to deal with as a teacher in a Catholic school. Sticking faithfully to the Church's teaching and discipline meant there was rarely a material solution if a reconciliation was not possible. Increasingly, girls from well-to-do families had to cope with family break-ups. The religious transgression added to the grief and heartbreak of seeing the family fall apart. This was the graver problem for a girl strong in faith because remarrying put the parents' souls in jeopardy. Between sniffles and sobs, Anne told a familiar story. Her father was to blame. She listened patiently, offering comforting words at appropriate moments. When Anne had exhausted her tearful story, Agnes tried to console her.

'It may not sound like much comfort to say that everyone has to face serious problems at some time or another,' she said. 'But it's true. For everyone, not just Catholics, it becomes a moment of truth. That truth is the right way to deal with the problem, especially when there is no satisfactory solution.'

The child facing the shame and grief of a father abandoning his family faces the same issues as a parent with a son leading a life of crime or a daughter selling herself. The law of charity should guide one. There can be no abandoning loved ones or dependents. As Agnes continued to expand on this theme, she noticed the nervous young man from the student cafeteria staring at them. Anne saw him, too.

'What's he looking at?'

'Don't pay any attention to him. It has nothing to do with you. He's concerned about my presence on campus.'

'Why?'

'He thinks the Catholic Church is corrupt, and I'll be a bad influence here.'

'What an idiot!' She stood up and stared furiously at him. The young man walked on, glancing back at them.

'He's harmless enough,' said Agnes. 'We must be patient with people like him.'

'He's a fool. I have no patience with stupid boys.'

'As hard as it is, Anne, you must never lose sight that your father is your father. You must strive to understand why.'

'And my mother! She just doesn't deserve it. She has supported him all these years. So now he's successful, he's gone. It's cruel! He's a bastard— Oh, excuse me.' She burst into tears again.

Agnes took her hands and held them. When Anne had settled again, Agnes took up the same theme, encouraging Anne to maintain her love and care for both parents, offering support wherever possible without relinquishing her principles.

'You can love and support your father without approving his actions. You must continue to pray that he will see the wrong he's doing to your mother and you. The charitable way you deal with his desertion should lead him to understand the wrong he has done.'

'And my mother?'

'Your mother especially needs your love and support. You will not support her by losing courage. Be positive. She'll be feeling terrible. A child must understand that a parent is a person with the same feelings as their children.'

Sister Catherine arrived on the scene, casting a questioning look at their clasped hands. After seeing from Anne's expression that she had no objection to telling Catherine, Agnes explained briefly.

'I sympathise,' said Catherine, sitting on the other side of Anne with an expression of understanding Agnes had seen bestowed on Jannie. 'That's the way some men behave, unfortunately. Your mother has committed her whole life to a man who has trampled on her without the slightest regard for her sacrifice.'

'Anne must never forget that her father is her father,' Agnes said, 'and it's responsibility, not sacrifice, in a parental relationship.'

'I don't mean she should forget him,' said Catherine with surprise. 'I only mean Anne's mother would have been better off if she had been less vulnerable.'

'We must not diminish the father's responsibility to care for his family. That's the point.' Agnes saw that Anne was giving all her attention to Catherine.

'Of course not. Neither should we overlook the situation of the mother. There is a lesson to be learned by all women from such failures of male responsibility, something that happens all too often, it seems. As I encourage all my students, I would encourage Anne to ensure she fulfils her potential and achieves independence. That does not diminish the responsibility of Anne's father in any way.'

'It sounds like you are setting mother against father,' said Agnes, frustrated that she could not adequately answer Catherine's comments without launching into a tedious explanation of the marital relationship.

'Not at all,' said Catherine, again exhibiting mild surprise. 'A partnership of two independent people would be more stable than one based on the subservience of one of the partners.' Anne's eyes widened.

'You think a traditional family structure implies subservience? A partnership of a man and woman will not succeed unless based on the moral responsibility of both people.'

'I don't see how that conflicts with my view.'

'Your view entails a different understanding of the structure of family life. If society relieves the man, husband, and father of his responsibility in nature, by law or custom, then you will cripple the family in years to come.'

'In nature?' said Catherine with raised eyebrows. 'I don't know what you mean by that.'

'You don't? Surely you do.' Agnes, conscious their debate was in front of an impressionable young mind, found it difficult to believe Catherine was in earnest. An incomplete explanation of the Church's beliefs about the nature and duties of marriage and how society should provide for them, risked distorting Anne's understanding.

'As I said,' Catherine continued, waving her hand, 'I'm not relieving the man of his responsibilities. My concern is with the woman.' She turned to Anne. 'I hope your problems, as troubling as they are, do not deter you from continuing your studies. That would be adding tragedy to tragedy.'

'That's what Sister Agnes said,' said Anne. 'No, I certainly won't. You have both convinced me of that, and I thank you.' She rose. 'I must go, but I feel better. Sister Agnes, I really appreciate your comfort,' and to Catherine, 'thank you, too, Sister. You have given me something to think a bout.'

'We have seen off a satisfied customer, I believe,' said Catherine, without looking at Agnes.

'I hope so.'

'I must go, too,' said Catherine, dismissing the subject. 'I have a meeting shortly. I'll see you at the usual spot this afternoon.'

Within a minute of Catherine's departure, the young man, who had set out to correct Agnes's Catholic errors, approached, carrying his Bible.

'Let's introduce ourselves before you talk,' said Agnes before the young man could open his mouth. 'I'm Sister Agnes. And your name ...?'

'Basil,' he said, coughing nervously.

'Basil who?'

'Etheridge ... Basil Etheridge.'

'Here, sit down, Basil,' said Agnes, tapping the bench. 'Now, you want to correct my errors as a Catholic, don't you?'

'Yes,' said Basil as he sat on the bench.

'Then let's have a friendly exchange. It's only right that we listen to each other's beliefs, right?'

'I know what you believe.'

'Let's see if that coincides with what I actually believe.'

Basil reluctantly agreed, saying rather artlessly that it was his mission to reveal the truth to people like Agnes.

'What do people usually call you, Basil or Barry?'

'Barry.'

'Good, Barry, let's start.'

Agnes began with the Apostle's Creed. She had to suppress her amusement as Barry struggled with the surprising coincidence of their beliefs on fundamental points. He repeated the points of agreement each time as if he suspected some language trick, so shocking was the evidence of that agreement. And when he found points of departure, he repeated these triumphantly, but at the same time gave the impression he understood those points did not in themselves condemn the papist church. Agnes saw that Barry's enthusiasm covered a keen, sensitive mind.

'There are a lot of other things—the concocted doctrine and political apparatus,' said Barry, grasping for evidence to support tackling the black-gowned enemy, an enemy that now appeared inconveniently sympathetic.

'I have a question for you, Barry,' Agnes continued. 'What came first, the Church or the Bible?'

'What sort of a question is that? The Christian Church is based on and proceeds from the Holy Scriptures.' He tapped his Bible. 'No Bible, no Church.'

'My question has to do with your *Sola Scriptura* belief as opposed to the Catholic position of Bible and Tradition.'

'That's easy. The Lord condemns tradition in the Scriptures. That's just where you are most obviously heretical.'

'You're right that Our Lord warned about the influence of human tradition. But other verses speak of a different sense of tradition. For example, St Paul says—'

'Hey, you little creep, still spreading your poison,' said the same belligerent student leading a contingent of Bobby McGuigan's student friends.

Barry froze.

'He's with me,' said Agnes, standing. 'He's not bothering me at all. Please leave us alone.'

'We don't want either of you spreading your foul propaganda,' said another student.

He snatched the Bible from Barry's hands and ripped pages from it.

'Hey, you can't do that,' said Barry, jumping to his feet and making a fruitless grab.

Two others took hold of Barry, pushed him roughly back and forth between them, grabbed his Bible, and flung him into the gardens to howls of delight. They threw the Bible on the lawn. The other students gathered around and began urinating on it.

'Stop that,' cried Agnes, running to help Barry out of the garden.

'We're not in school, Sister,' said one, provoking the laughter of the others.

'You're a disgrace!'

'Is this a disgrace, too?' said the belligerent student, turning towards her and exposing himself. Agnes looked away, scarcely able to control her anger and disgust. 'Don't look away, Sister. It's natural—nothing dirty about it.'

'You're a contemptible bully,' she said, helping a dazed and dishevelled Barry onto his feet. 'Are you all right?'

'He needs to visit the garden again,' said one of the students who approached, doing up his fly.

Agnes stood in front of Barry. 'I'll go to the university authorities,' she said, her face reddening. Barry cowered behind her.

The students looked at her, bemused. 'Get that garb off and join the real world,' said the belligerent student. 'You must be aching for it.'

'You're nothing but spineless bullies!'

'Come on,' said the leader, nodding at several people who had stopped, 'it's time to go.' And then to Agnes: 'I warn you. We won't let you and your propaganda have a free ride here.' He leered at her and then ambled off towards the main buildings with the others in his wake.

'Are you all right?' Agnes repeated, brushing the dirt and bits of plant from Barry's clothes.

He sat on the bench, bewildered and wordless, staring in front of him. Agnes picked up his Bible and brought it to him. He looked at it for a moment and then took it.

'Have you got something to wipe your hands on?' he said, taking a clean handkerchief from his pocket.

'It's all right. I'll wash them shortly.'

'Thank you for sticking up for me.' He wiped the Bible and checked the damage.

'You can't let them get away with this.' He gave her a helpless glance. 'Have they done anything like this before?'

'Yes, whenever they see me, but nothing like this.'

'Why do they pick on you?'

'They're socialists, godless communists. They pick on anyone like me. They're well known for it.'

'Are you sure? Could that be the reason alone?'

'I'm sure. And it is.'

'Who are they?' said Agnes, remembering Jannie's mocking comment.

'The Fourth Club. There are several socialist clubs on campus. The Fourth Club is the most extreme by far. Trotskyists. Club! It's more like a mafia cell.'

'You've got to do something about it, Barry. You can't let them bully you. It'll get worse if you don't do anything.'

'What?'

'Go to the university authorities. What faculty do they belong to?'

'Arts, of course. They're all history, philosophy, and political studies students. A lot of the lecturers agree with them. I wouldn't get anywhere.'

'What do you study?'

'I'm in Arts, too—economics, politics—the same as them. That probably makes me more vulnerable. I challenge their stupid economic theories.'

'Philosophy?'

'No.'

'I'm doing economics, too. First year.'

'Oh,' he said, 'I'm doing third year.' He looked at the ground. He released a sigh.

'Do you have friends who'll support you?' Agnes put her hand on his shoulder, but took it away again.

'I belong to a Scripture group. They keep out of the way of those thugs, too.'

'Do you have a girlfriend?'

'No ... I must go. Thank you for, eh ...'

'Barry, we're on the same side in this matter. Please come and talk to me anytime. We don't have to talk about religion. Tell me how you get on.'

He nodded, rose, and then walked off, collecting the few torn pages still lying around.

Agnes hastened to the library toilets, where she vigorously rubbed the soap into her hands to wash away the ideological putridness with the faecal matter.

'Your father's student friends arrived after you left,' she said to Catherine on the way to meet Mr Ferguson. 'They viciously assaulted a poor, defenceless boy I was talking to.'

'Friends of my father's?' said Catherine. 'I don't know if you can call them friends. That's too much said.'

'He seemed on friendly terms with them that day.'

'That was a political meeting between unionists and students. What are you saying?'

Agnes realised she could not pursue her thoughts without sounding offensive. 'Are those students from the Fourth Club in the habit of assaulting people who disagree with them?'

'I don't know. I hardly know them.'

'Your father knows them well, doesn't he?'

'Maybe he does. That does not mean I know them.'

'I had the impression—'

'That's right. It's an impression.'

Agnes decided there was nowhere to go with her questioning, and they both settled into the usual mode of returning to the convent. Mr Ferguson chatted to Agnes while Catherine gazed through the window, her mind obviously a thousand miles away.

Chapter 27

Worldly friends

IT WAS DIFFICULT for Agnes to accept she had made it to the end of the first term and was now sitting in her final philosophy tutorial. All her work had been done with her enthusiasm and enjoyment undiminished. She was disappointed that Philip would not give the second-term lectures on Descartes' *Meditations*. Whatever her struggles in coping with his presence, he was an engaging lecturer and tutor, always making the material come alive, even the most obscure arguments. When he brought the session to a close and the students were packing up, he asked her to wait. Just a few formalities to discuss, he said.

'Anne, do you want to talk to Sister?' he said, reacting to a suppressed 'Oh!'

'Just a few words,' said Anne, looking appealingly at Agnes.

'I won't keep her long,' said Philip, shuffling papers on his desk. 'It's lunchtime. You can meet in the Union cafeteria, so you don't have to wait around here. Is that all right with you?'

'Yes, of course,' said Agnes, surprised at his presumption.

'I'm sorry. I hope I was not presumptuous,' he said when they were alone. 'You know what I'm like when something's on my mind.' She waved aside his concern. 'Sit down,' he went on. 'I won't take long. I've read and marked your essay. It's outstanding work, showing a thorough understanding of Plato's arguments for the forms and their relationship to his moral thought. You also brought in Aristotle's objections to the Platonic forms. Your essay is mature work at a good academic level. For a first-year student, it is, without dispute, deserving of a high distinction. Congratulations.' He sat back, contemplating her. 'It seems the two religious sisters are outstanding students,' he said, unsure how to proceed.

'Oh?' said Agnes, shifting.

'Yes, on reports, your companion is very clever,' he said with an ironic smile. 'We, lecturers, do talk to each other, even to those of another department.'

'Yes, of course.'

'What I wanted to say,' he continued, looking away. 'I have taken the precaution of having my first-year colleague second-mark your work, someone with no religious commitment. He agrees with my assessment.'

'Precaution? What do you mean?'

'It's a long story, but I will keep it short. I've been skirmishing with the socialists and anarchists on campus for some time. It's not open warfare yet, and I don't want it to be. To be brief, I don't want to give them any reason to accuse me of favouring you above the other students.'

'Why would they think that?'

'Why do you think?' The academic reserve had disappeared. 'They know I'm Catholic and can present a competent philosophic defence of Catholic teaching. And you, well, they can see from a mile away what you are. Two and two make five for these people when it comes to religion.'

'But that's impugning your integrity. Surely, they will allow you some sense of responsibility. Nobody would dispute your reputation.'

He gave another of those looks that made her uneasy. 'Virginia,' he said, shaking his head, 'you've been too long out of circulation. In fact, in many ways, you were never in full circulation. You have never experienced the real embittered anti-religious bigotry that drives some people. These people are not interested in my reputation. They are only interested in views that are incompatible with their ideology. I'm a bourgeois flunky that must be defeated at all costs, which will inevitably happen, according to them, as they bring me into conflict.'

'I must admit I'm not fully aware of such things,' she said, the scenes of Barry's pummelling returning. 'I thought people here would respect the sincerely held—'

'Sincerely held!' Philip snorted. 'They're ignorant of what sincerity is. Anyhow, I just wanted to alert you in case something is said.'

'Do you expect trouble?'

'I don't know. I have been warned. Anyhow, that's not worth dwelling on now. You have done very well, and that's all that matters for you.'

'Thank you for telling me. I should know these things,' she said, preparing to go.

'Just one more thing—' He hesitated, searching for the right words. 'You've had a chat, no doubt, with Vic Brennan?'

'Yes, but it was a short exchange. He only alluded to—'

'Well, good—'

'And you've never spoken about him with me.'

'Yes, well, we agreed not to discuss each other's private lives.'

'I appreciate it. I assume, meaning me?'

'Yes, but not only you.' He hesitated again. 'But there's something I should mention—indeed, ask for your help. Of course, this is in strict confidence.'

'Of course, you have my word.'

'Vic fancies himself in love.'

'You mean with someone other than his wife?'

'Yes, but there's more. The woman, or rather the girl he's in love with, is one of his students, a second-year student.'

'Patricia Coghlan?'

'Yes. How did you know?'

'It was an informed guess. She is often in his company and has that student-crush look. Surely Vic would not take a student crush seriously.'

'Well, he has. And I have the impression that eighteen-year-old Patricia Coghlan is not your typical student-crush type. This is a young woman who sees what she wants and will have it.'

'Why are you telling me this, Philip?'

'Both Vic and Patricia told me to mind my own business when I pointed out the disastrous consequences of such a relationship. Vic went further and abused me as a hypocrite. As sinful as my ways are, I told him adultery was—' He looked at Virginia. 'Well,' he continued as if trying to compose himself, 'I thought you might have a word with him. Your manner will be more effective in getting through to him.'

'I don't know whether I could or should,' said Virginia, hardly able to look Philip in the eye. 'He may resent my interference—the interference of a student.'

'He won't see you as a student. He knows you and knows you would not speak gratuitously. Besides, your habit will give the right context.'

Agnes hesitated. 'I will consider it.'

'Thank you. It's worth a try. You will be more effective than you assume. You've been of help to Anne, for example.' His manner had lost all reserve.

'I hope so.' She began to edge away.

'I thought you would be.' He walked with her to the door. 'You always had a way with people. You were always a popular girl.'

'Thank you. I must go.'

She hurried down the corridor, breathless, down the stairs and outside into the fresh air. He could not stick to his undertaking, and she, she feared, could not stick to hers. Thankfully, the term was at an end. As she made her way to the student cafeteria, she realised she had not seen his bohemian girlfriend for a while. Perhaps in avoiding Philip, she had avoided her. She found Anne busily chatting with two girls who gave her a friendly welcome. Like Anne, they were from Catholic ladies' colleges but older and more mature.

'I thought Dr Stevenson would keep you for ages, Sister,' said Anne cheerfully.

'No, he had a few comments about my essay and other things. That's all.'

Anne introduced Agnes to her friends Barbara and Carmel. 'He's been such an excellent tutor,' she said. 'It's a pity we won't have him for next term's lectures or tutorials.'

'Not the tutorial?' said Agnes, in surprise.

'No, didn't you know?'

'No, he has said nothing about it.'

'He told me when I was discussing my essay with him. I thought he told everyone.'

'No, he has said nothing to me,' said Agnes, glancing at Anne's companions. 'Did he say why? It's not usual for tutors to change.'

'He said it was a question of timing. He swapped with another lecturer but would have us again in the third term. It's a real pity. He's so helpful and understanding, and I am used to him. They shouldn't make changes like this. It's upsetting.'

Fortunately, Anne's preoccupation with the tutorial change blinded her to any betrayal of Agnes's feelings. Philip was the best tutor she had in any subject, she continued. He was very sympathetic, even helping her find solutions to her problems. She indicated Agnes with a grateful nod.

'He's not what you would call a really handsome man,' said Barbara, 'but he's very, very attractive.'

There was hearty agreement among the three girls, who seemed to be monitoring Philip's activities on campus.

'I'm sorry, Sister, we shouldn't be talking about these things in front of you,' said Anne.

'That's all right. I taught in a girls' school,' she said, hoping the subject of Philip was at an end. But then she added before she could censor the thought: 'I was a girl once, too.'

The girls stared at her. The normally composed Sister Agnes shifted a little.

'I can believe it,' said Barbara, who appeared more worldly than Carmel. 'You're not that much older than me.'

'Sister turns twenty-eight this year,' said Anne. 'I call that a lot older.'

'Twenty-eight?' said Carmel. 'You look a lot younger. Are you really that old, Sister?'

'Who told you?' said Agnes.

'Philip,' said Anne. 'I asked once when I was talking about you. I was curious. I think I embarrassed him, too. He let it out before he knew what he was saying. It was on your enrolment forms, he said. He told me not to repeat it.'

'Oh,' said Agnes, noticing how Dr Stevenson had become Philip.

'Then you are twenty-eight?'

'Not quite, but it's not something sisters talk about or want to discuss.' The girls stared at her again. This time, Agnes met their gaze. 'A religious sister's life is willingly away from the secular world. Such things as age and appearance are out of the boundaries of the spiritual world we endeavour to remain in.'

'But you're at university now,' said Barbara.

'You must have heard it said that the religious is in the world but not part of it,' instructed Agnes.

'I think you were an attractive girl before you left our world to be in your spiritual world,' Barbara persisted.

Now the girls were going too far, and Agnes had no choice but to extricate herself as tactfully as possible.

'Come on, Barbara,' said Anne, 'no putting Sister under pressure.'

'I'm sorry, Sister, if we sound inquisitive,' said Carmel. 'You must admit it's natural to be curious about a nun's life.'

'You're still doing it,' said Anne.

'Well, I do have something far more interesting to tell you about Philip. He's broken it off with his bohemian girlfriend.'

'Really?' said the other two, eagerly leaning forward. 'When?'

'Just recently. He didn't tell anyone. But he couldn't hide it from his close mates.'

'He broke it off?'

'That's what I'm telling you.'

'With a girl like that? Gosh!'

'Yes,' said Barbara, lowering her voice. 'There's a whisper there's someone else. If there is, nobody knows who.'

'Where are you getting this from?' Carmel.

'I'm not telling.'

'You don't know,' said Anne.

'You'll see,' said Barbara. 'A friend went around to his flat and found him paralytic one night.'

'Where are you getting all this?' Carmel repeated.

'My contact.'

'Who are you going out with now?'

'Excuse me, girls,' said Agnes, collecting her things. 'This is not for me. Anne, perhaps we can meet at another time?'

'Oh, I am so sorry, Sister,' said Anne. 'I came across Barbara and Carmel by chance. I really want to talk to you about you know what.'

'Yes, I'm sorry, too, Sister,' said Barbara, getting up. Carmel rose, too. 'We're going. We were on our way somewhere else, anyhow.'

'Please wait, Sister,' said Anne. 'I'll be back in a jiffy.'

'Now there's a chance for me,' Agnes heard Barbara laugh as they moved off. She watched them to the door, her heart pounding. The thought she would have to cope with this sort of situation had never occurred to her. She must work out a way to avoid becoming entangled in their conversations. What was it about her demeanour that seemed to give them licence to have such a conversation in her presence, as if she were one of them? She fervently hoped there would be no more talk about Philip when Anne returned. It was too much to hear about his broken romance and drunkenness. His drunkenness? Although he liked his beer as much as any man, she had never seen him drunk. Barbara was typically indulging in melodrama.

'I'm terribly sorry, Sister,' Anne repeated as she flopped onto her chair. 'I was not expecting to meet Carmel and Barbara here.' Agnes gestured for her not to worry about it. 'That talk about Philip, Dr Stevenson, delayed them.' She raised her eyebrows and looked Agnes in the face. Agnes endeavoured to look indifferent. 'Aren't you the slightest bit interested in what we were saying about him?'

'It's not that I'm not interested,' said Agnes, with a slight cough. 'It's the sort of conversation I don't—'

'But you talk to me about my parents' marriage.'

'That's entirely different.'

'I suppose it is,' said Anne, sighing. 'But you seem to know so much about the feelings involved.'

'I grew up in a Catholic family with three brothers. I'm only human. I taught at a girls' school. These were my experiences before entering religious life. That gives one insight into relationship problems.'

'I understand.' Anne shrugged. 'But you seem different from other nuns, I mean. In a way, you're just like us, but in a habit.'

'I'm human, as I say,' said Agnes, realising she would get an answer to some of her questions.

'It's more than that. Carmel and Barbara felt it, too.'

Agnes tried to ignore the thought that Philip had said the same thing. 'A woman is not different because she wears clothes that give witness to her beliefs.'

'No, I understand that. But you're still different. Carmel said you had such a pretty, warm face underneath that veil. She said she had no trouble seeing you in modern slacks and a top with short, wispy brown hair.'

'She said all that in that short time?' said Agnes, trying to make light of it, but conscious she was losing the battle on all fronts.

'What colour is your hair?'

'If I tell you, will you stop talking about me?'

'I promise,' said Anne, blushing.

'It's brown.'

'Dark or light?'

'Anne!'

'Just that—and I won't ask anymore.'

'Light brown. Now, are we going to talk about what you brought me here for?'

'Is it wispy?'

'Anne, I'm going now.'

'Okay, okay, I'll stop.'

Anne kept her promise and updated Agnes on her parents' separation. As Anne spoke, Agnes understood she was not seeking advice but talking to ease her anxiety. She did her best to share the feelings of a daughter suffering the breakup of her parents, whom she loved equally, giving comfort and encouragement when needed and offering advice she considered appropriate. Thankfully, the painful subject of divorce did not arise this time. Anne seemed to hope there might be a reconciliation.

'My mother will take him back,' she said to conclude. 'He doesn't deserve it, but she still loves him. Why is it that women are the ones to get kicked and then have to forgive?'

'It's not always the man who strays,' said Agnes, rather unconvincingly, for in all cases she had experienced, it was the man shirking his responsibilities.

'Mostly,' said Anne.

'Men often let work dominate them these days. They shouldn't. It's wrong to let work pressures affect their family life. But one should not forget that there are two people involved in marital problems. Men fail in certain ways; women fail in other ways. Sometimes, the woman may have virtually ended the relationship long before the man leaves. That's why I advise you to try to understand why your father has gone. I'm not saying he's excused—that can never be the case—only that there can be reasons you have not seen. Your father is evidently not a bad man.'

'No, he's not. What sort of failures on the woman's side do you mean?'

'I'm a little out of my depth here,' said Agnes cautiously. 'Perhaps if you reflect on how you've behaved in relationships with boys. What are the things that annoy them?'

'I haven't had a real boyfriend yet.'

'No? I'm surprised. I assure you it will happen—an attractive girl like you.'

'Thank you, Sister.'

At that moment, Agnes spied Barry walking through the cafeteria with Bible in hand. 'Do you mind if I have a word with that young man there?'

Anne watched, intrigued, as Agnes hurried to intercept the rather dowdy student she had glared into retreat. There was a short exchange, and then the dowdy student followed Agnes, apparently reluctantly, to the table where she introduced him. He was invited to sit down, but he made excuses, vaguely saying he had a meeting to go to. Despite his vague excuse, he stood there, his mouth working indecisively.

'Is there something you want to say?' said Agnes.

'Yes, yes, there is.' He ran his hand over his mouth. 'I want to thank you for supporting me—with the administration, that is. I didn't expect it. You're taking risks.'

'Risks? Barry, you can't let it go on. You mustn't let them bully you.'

'I hope it doesn't cause you trouble.'

'You mean from those boys.'

'Yes, and they're not boys. They're thugs. You'll know it if they decide to give you a hard time.'

'I will deal with that when it happens. But, anyhow, I was assured they would be warned.'

'They won't take any notice. They'll get around it. Thank you anyway. I appreciate it.'

'You're welcome, Barry. Please say hello anytime you like.'

Anne gave Agnes a questioning look when Barry had departed.

'Would you do me a favour?' said Agnes.

'What?' said Anne, warily greeting the question.

'Barry is a nice young man deep down. Unfortunately, he's a little lost on campus. Would you mind saying hello to him when you see him, even have a tea or a coffee if the situation presents itself—just offer a little friendship?'

'He's such a nondescript—'

'He's just like you, with feelings that can be hurt.'

'Oh,' said Anne. 'One good turn deserves another, I suppose.'

'We all need comfort. I'm not asking any more than a friendly hello.'

'What if he wants more?'

'I'm sure it would be a long time before he reached that stage if he ever did. He is very religious, you know.'

'I don't want any bible-bashing from a fundamentalist.'

'You'll be able to control the conversation and the contact, let me assure you.'

'Are you speaking from experience, Sister?'

'I must mind you in future,' said Agnes, pretending to be severe.

'I think you are.'

'You'll do me that favour?'

'Yes, Sister. Because you've asked me. Because you think of other people. I appreciate the comfort you have given me.'

'You're a good girl, Anne. I knew I could rely on you.'

As they walked out of the student union, Anne said, apparently as an afterthought: 'You're so attentive to the feelings of others. Aren't you concerned about Dr Stevenson? Obviously, he's got personal problems.'

'He's our lecturer. It's not our place to interfere there.' She hoped she did not sound as evasive as she felt.

'But it must be a concern. We've been close to him for a whole term. I feel I know him well, well enough to worry about him.'

'Really?'

'Yes. And it's not just that he has been with us. He has a sympathetic character. You know, the way he referred me to you for help.' She paused. 'He's a bit like you, the same attentive character. He projects self-confidence, but behind that, there is this vulnerability. There's a rumour he has had some broken relationships. Doesn't that arouse your sympathy as you look at him during tutorials?'

'Of course, I sympathise with anyone feeling sad,' said Agnes, looking straight ahead.

'Yes, of course, you do,' said Anne, looking around. 'Sorry to go on about it. I'll see you later, Sister.' She went on her way as if she had not a care in the world.

Agnes changed her destination. Instead of going to the library, she hurried to the chapel in the nearest Catholic college. Behind a thick sandstone pillar, only several paces away from a statue of St Anthony of the Desert, she put her head in her hands. Several hot tears dripped into her cupped palms.

PHILIP Stevenson loaded the last of his things into his Morris Minor. He checked to see if he had everything needed for a three-month stay at his Sorrento beach house, separated from the busy world of the university. He needed a break from the demands of his lecturing duties, but more to the purpose, he needed a break from Virginia. He could not cope with her presence. It was not just his love for her. That was unchanged, and he could do nothing about it. That ridiculous party costume made not the slightest difference. But it was just as much the moral judgment her presence radiated. It was unnecessary to say his relationship with Diana was wrong. No, not a word. He knew how she thought, how heroically she stuck to her principles.

It made no difference that he and Diana were consenting adults who shared a genuine love. The relationship was wrong in itself. It was a perversion of the original contract between male and female, a contract on which a healthy society was built. He could hear her saying it. His faith told him that. His reasoning about the proper order of nature should tell him that. He had spoken to her about the observable order of the world, an order from which an enduring moral code emerged. He could hear his own words, words so long pushed to the background, coming back at him from Virginia. It was no longer possible to ignore her. How was he to tell Diana?

'Your Catholic faith has at last broken the surface,' she said after he told her he could not continue their relationship. 'I half expected it from the beginning. There's no other woman, is there?'

'Am I so transparent?'

'In a way. You've been kind and courteous, as if careful not to damage me. It was more than the affection between two people who love each other. It has been a sincere friendship, despite all our differences. You love me but cannot commit entirely.'

'No. I'm afraid not. But it is not strictly true that there is no other woman. I was once engaged. She broke the engagement. I am still not over it.'

'That's being honest.'

'It's the truth. It's not your fault. I truly have much affection for you.'

'Yes, I know,' she said, smiling. 'It's not me. It's you.'

'Something like that.' He returned the affectionate smile.

'Are you going back to her?'

He reflected before he answered. 'She's committed.'

'It would seem pointless, then, would it not?'

'There is more to it than I have said. It's complicated. I would rather not talk about it.'

She considered him a moment. 'All right, I won't press. But let's not stop seeing each other. We can see each other as friends—close friends. We enjoy so much together.'

'Is there any point? I have nothing to offer you.'

'Let me decide that.'

'Anyhow, I am leaving Melbourne for two or three months. I have research to do for a book I am writing.'

'Then come and see me when you get back. Promise?'

'All right. I promise.'

She hugged him, kissed him on the cheek, and he departed.

Chapter 28

At Binawarra

ON A MILD autumn day with the sun shining brightly in a cloudless sky, Jannie, Harry, and Erik approached the town of Binawarra. It was late morning, and the fields, shaded by rises, ridges, and gum tree clusters, still glistened in the dissipating autumn dew. It was a peaceful scene along the deserted country road, and the boys relaxed while listening without responding to Jannie's excited chatter.

'I can't wait to get to Binawarra to see Aine,' she said.

'You won't see her until tomorrow,' said Harry at the wheel.

'We'll be there early enough. We'll have time.'

'No, I don't want to bother them until tomorrow. The situation is delicate. Keep a lid on your eagerness. You could spoil everything.'

'No, I won't,' she pouted. 'You're too finicky.'

'It's better to be sure. It's her husband I worry about. Your exuberance and flighty manner may put him off.'

'My flighty manner! *Alsjeblieft meneer*, my manner usually attracts men if you haven't noticed.'

'I've noticed, darling. And speaking Dutch even gets me going. But this is different. That woman and her husband don't think the same way as most people.'

Erik, who sat in the front with Harry, gave her a sympathetic look. She relented. She put her hand over the seat. Erik took it and kissed it.

'Okay, I'll be patient,' she said, leaning on the neat pile of clothing, taking up the rest of the backseat.

'Hey, keep away from the clothes,' said Harry, glancing in the rear-view mirror. 'They're in order. I don't want any risk to the shoot.'

'I'm not touching anything,' she said, drawing her arm away. 'You can't see me, anyhow.'

Harry did not dignify that lie with a reply. Erik turned and gave her a smile. She settled down, and there was silence for a while.

'That's an unusual shape,' said Harry, taking his foot off the accelerator. Erik and Jannie craned their necks.

'You're right,' said Erik.

The car slowed to a stop. Harry looked up at the sharp peak that seemed part of a chain of hills. A broad rock platform jutted out about a quarter of the way down. He stepped out of the car, followed by Erik and Jannie. They stared up in silence. Harry looked around. He pointed at the massive grassy hill rising above the sharp peak a little further down the road on the opposite side.

'Those strange peaks look like a gateway to the town, which can't be too far from here.' His gaze lingered on the road that rose and disappeared mysteriously between the peaks. 'I wonder.'

'What?' said Erik.

'The surroundings ... the rocky ledge ... the sun shining directly ....'

'No, you can't be that mad.'

'What are you talking about?' said Jannie, already showing restlessness. 'Let's keep going.'

'No, Erik, look over there.' With his finger, Harry traced a rough line through the air, starting at the rocky ledge. 'There's a ridge running off

to the left. It must come down to the road somewhere up there. Come on.
'

'What?' Jannie repeated.

'Don't ask questions,' said Harry. 'Just get in the car and put yourself in the mood.'

'You're mad,' said Erik.

'What mood?'

'Make yourself desirable.'

'Desirable? How do you mean?'

Ignoring the question, Harry drove towards the treed gap between the two peaks. 'Ah, here's what I expected,' he said, swinging the car across the road into a clearing. 'Wait here until I check.' He walked along the bush border and found the entrance to a track along the ridge. He went about twenty yards along the track and then hurried back to the car. 'Come on, you two, there's a track. I'll drop dead if it doesn't lead to that platform.'

'You and your harebrained ideas,' said Erik, getting out.

'You're not planning to do a shoot up there, are you?' said Jannie with a mixture of caution and excitement.

'It's perfect for the swimwear. You wait and see. Now get into one of the swimsuits and put your coat on. We'll take a few more in the bag.'

'It's too chilly.'

'Not up there. The peak protects the ledge from the wind, and the sun is blazing down directly onto it. So, it'll be warm if anything.'

'Well, okay. But you don't imagine I will change in front of you two, do you?'

'Don't be silly. You'll have your coat around you, and we won't look. I promise your modesty will be preserved. Now get ready. Erik, turn your head until I say so.' Erik walked away from the car and picked at the bushes. Harry busied himself with his equipment, carefully separating the items he wanted to take. When he had completed his preparations, he joined Jannie, who had changed on the other side of the car. He opened the coat, which she had clutched shut. 'Good. That's a good choice.' He closed it again. 'Now listen. I want you to be careful when we're on the track. Walk between Erik and me. I don't want you scratching your skin on the bushes. Okay?' Jannie nodded. 'What's in the bag?'

'My make-up—and other things.'

'Okay. Now get yourself into the mood.'

'How ...? I don't know what you mean?'

'Erik, you can look now ... what? Of course, you do. Think of something pleasant and soothing. You know. Recite something in Dutch—poetry or something like that. I find you irresistible when you are in your Dutch mode,' he said absently as he again checked his equipment.

'Irresistible?'

'Come on,' said Harry. 'Don't get too excited.'

They had walked some way along the track in silence when Jannie said: *'Min de stilte in uw wezen, zoek de stilte die bezielt.'*

Harry, who was in front, stopped. 'That's nice. You sound different when you speak Dutch, like you have a different voice.'

'It's still my first language, you know.'

'You still have an accent,' said Erik from behind.

'English is a foreign language. Everything's foreign here.'

'You do pretty well then,' said Harry.

They resumed walking.

'What did it mean?' said Harry.

After some hesitation, Jannie began: 'Love the silence ... in your being; ... seek the silence ... that animates. There! It's by a well-known Dutch poet, Adama van Scheltema. I remember it from school.'

'Very deep—and appropriate.'

'There's more, but I've forgotten it,' Jannie murmured, now lost in her thoughts.

When they arrived on the platform, Erik exclaimed while Jannie looked around, still engrossed in thought.

'Sensational, isn't it?' said Harry, unloading himself. He and Erik swapped admiring comments about the surroundings while Jannie placed her bag on the ground and took off her coat to reveal her lithesome, full-breasted figure clad in a colourful one-piece swimsuit.

'I remember some more,' she said, brushing back her long, honey-blond hair several times. For once, the admiring gaze of the two men escaped her.

'Min de stilte in uw wezen,
Zoek de stilte die bezielt,
Zij die alle stilte vrezen,
Hebben nooit hun hart gelezen,
Hebben nooit geknielt.'

She finished with an air of self-congratulation.

'You have a sweet voice in Dutch,' said Harry. 'Doesn't she, Erik?'

'Very.'

'And not in English?'

'It's different,' said Harry. 'Your accent gives it a different aspect—a charming one, of course. Well, what does it all mean?'

'Let me think,' said Jannie. 'It's not always easy to translate literally from Dutch to English.'

'Love the silence in your being,

Seek the silence that inspires,

Those who fear all silence,

Have never read their hearts,

Have never got to their knees.'

She looked eagerly at them, the incongruity of the beautiful fashion model with her hands on her hips after reciting poetry in a foreign language, high on a rocky platform in the middle of the bush, appearing to escape her. The two men regarded her, startled.

'Well?' she said, a little impatiently. 'It rhymes in Dutch.'

Harry shot a conferring glance at Erik. 'If it hasn't got you in the mood, it certainly has us.'

'In the mood? For what?' She smiled.

'Come on, let's get to work. You should be careful about making yourself irresistible. Take off your shoes.' She slipped off her shoes, and he gently manoeuvred her into the position he wanted.

For the next ten minutes, while Erik looked on, Jannie followed Harry's directions as he clicked from different positions.

'Great. Have a short break and then put on the black piece,' he said. 'It's not too cold, is it?'

'No,' said Jannie, as Erik draped her coat around her shoulders. She returned his gesture with a sly smile. 'I'm not cold at all—if anything hot.'

'Be careful,' Harry said, walking away.

Erik and Jannie missed the hint and continued to chat in low tones while Harry reappraised his equipment and its settings. He laid a large white towel near the edge of the platform. He glanced cautiously over the edge and adjusted its position. When he had arranged all to his satisfaction, he ambled over to Erik and Jannie. Erik now held Jannie in his arms with her back against his chest.

'You've done well,' he said. 'You're always professional.'

'Thank you, Harry darling,' she replied, projecting indifference, but her eyes beamed at the praise and attention of the two men.

'Of course, you must have the looks to go with it.'

'And I've got them?'

'You know you have. You're gorgeous, and you know it. Sometimes I must remind myself that you are not as scatty as you make out.'

'Do you think I'm scatty, Erik?' she said, turning in his arms.

'Come on, Jannie, back to work,' Harry said, snuffing out any reply. 'Put on the black cossie. Refresh your makeup. Some bright red lipstick.' When Jannie had adjusted her make-up, he said: 'Erik, hold the coat for her—and don't look. I want her to maintain her mood.'

'I will be the perfect gentleman,' said Erik, holding the coat as if it were a curtain. 'See, I'm looking the other way. Okay?'

'It's all right. I'm still in the mood,' said Jannie, giggling. 'Hold the coat a bit more around me.'

Harry released a low whistle when Jannie stepped from behind the coat in a jet-black one-piece swimsuit from one of the high fashion houses. 'We could not have chosen a better person to model it.'

'Thank you, Harry,' said Jannie, cutting a pose. 'You're not often so complimentary about me.'

'Don't get excited. I'm just giving credit where credit is due. I have not realised until now how well your figure suits swimwear. Your skin, too, unblemished with still a little colour from the summer.'

'You've never recommended me for swimwear before.'

'That's my mistake.'

'Did you hear, Erik? Harry's actually admitting a mistake!'

'Yes, raise the flag and sound the trumpets. Harry's human, after all!'

'Okay, you two, cut it out. Sarcasm doesn't suit either of you. Come here, Jannie.' He took her hand and led her to the towel. 'I want a series of photos, some close-ups, on the towel with the precipice in the background. Understood?' Jannie nodded. 'I want you close to the edge, but be careful. Keep your mind on it. I don't want you falling.'

'You're really so sweet, Harry, so attentive,' she said, sitting on the towel and moving nearer to the edge.

'Stop being cute. Concentrate.'

'I'm in the mood, ready to go. Such sweetness and attention ...'

For the next fifteen minutes, Harry and Jannie followed the same routine; Harry issued instructions, and Jannie responded, though Harry was now far more precise and reflective. There was a series of photos with Jannie sitting or kneeling in different positions. Harry checked the light and background after each snap. Then followed a spontaneous series in which Jannie lay on the towel. As Harry rattled out a quick succession of clipped instructions, Jannie writhed and twisted fluidly from pose to pose, expression to expression.

'Wonderful,' Harry said, clicking. 'How you ever ended up in a convent beats me,' he commented as he changed position.

Jannie went rigid. 'I'll walk away if—' She got up on an elbow, her eyes brimming.

'Now, now, I'm sorry,' Harry said. 'I didn't mean anything.' He stroked her arm. 'I only meant to encourage you. You're doing so well. Don't spoil it.'

'Don't you spoil it,' said Jannie, resuming the supine position and closing her eyes. She breathed in deeply.

Harry tenderly ran his hand over her cheek and scooped up the tear that broke from one closed eye. 'Come on, forget what I said. Let's start again.'

It took a few minutes to get Jannie back into the same mood. 'Wonderful, terrific,' said Harry, marvelling at the sharp change in mood. 'You're a real professional. I mean it.' He moved in for close-ups. 'We're nearly there. This is for all those men—' He bent over her as she lifted her chin and looked dreamily past the camera lens. 'Great,' he whispered. He clicked several times. He lowered his camera but remained bent over her. He kissed her on the lips. The kiss brought her out of her dream-like state.

'Oh, have I done that well?' she murmured without changing her position.

'You have. Sensational. You're running hot.'

'I am.' She exhaled with a sigh and ran her hand over her forehead. 'I've finished.'

'Oh, I could keep going.'

'I know. Don't overdo it. And be careful. I warn you.' He threw a glance over his shoulder in Erik's direction.

Jannie smiled languidly, making no attempt to sit up. Harry contemplated her.

'What makes Erik so different?'

'What do you mean?' she simpered.

'I've seen you endlessly play the tease with all manner of men. I've seen them run up against a brick wall in the end. How has Erik got past?'

'Has he got past?' she said naughtily. 'Perhaps it's his Dutch background. He looks so Dutch.'

'Cut it out. Erik doesn't speak a word of Dutch.'

'It's still there. I feel at home ...'

Harry contemplated her again—in silence. He bent over and kissed her on the cheek. 'I'm warning you. Be careful. You're running hot, and I don't want you doing something you'll regret.'

'You're so gallant, Harry. I've never seen this side of you,' she said with a smile. 'Even an apology.'

'Jannie, you're on your own now.' He stood up. 'Come on. I've finished. Pack up your things. We're going back to the car.' He helped her to her feet with care and ensured she was well away from the edge of the rocky platform before letting go of her hand. He left her with Erik while he packed up his equipment. He checked the program he had set himself, noting on a clipboard those tasks he had completed during this improvised session. Eventually, he was ready to go.

'Come on, let's go,' he said, glancing at Jannie and Erik. 'What have you been doing?' Erik was holding Jannie, who was still wearing the black swimsuit. They looked at him in surprise. 'I'm ready to go. Get a move o n.'

'Why don't you go?' said Erik. 'We'll follow in a minute after Jannie gets her things together. We'll be right with you.'

Harry looked at them, clearly vexed. 'Jannie, I don't want you damaging the clothes.'

'Don't worry, Harry. They're safe.'

'See to it,' he said. Twenty minutes later, he put his equipment in the car and returned the swimsuits to the neat pile on the back seat. He ran over his program again. Five minutes had passed before Erik and Jannie emerged from the track into the clearing.

'Here's the swimsuit,' said Jannie, smirking. She held it in front of her. 'Like new.' With the other hand, she opened her coat to reveal the slacks and top she had been wearing that morning.

'Splendid,' said Harry, taking the swimsuit and examining her face.

She smiled at him. 'It's cooled down a bit?'

'There's more to you than I thought,' he said with a laugh. 'Now get in the car and stop being so cute.'

'Do you think I'm cute, Erik?'

'More than I can bear.'

'Get in the car, I said, you two.'

HARRY drove slowly around Anzac Square, all three taking in the scene. When they passed the old bluestone church on the square, Harry turned into a parking space.

'Perfect,' he said.

'What's perfect?' said Jannie, still scanning the shopping precinct. 'This is the most charming little country town I have ever been in.'

'When Harry says something is perfect, he means for his photography,' said Erik. 'Look at that music rotunda in the park. It's been restored.'

'The church, the church is perfect,' murmured Harry.

'Why is it perfect?' asked Jannie. 'I hope you don't want me to pose in front of it. I won't do it.'

'I don't mean you, Sister Jannie.'

'Oh, I see. And don't call me that.'

'I'm sorry,' he said hastily. 'It was just a joke.'

'It's not a joke. It's a deep wound.'

'So I gather. I won't make any more reference to—'

'I'm happy with two apologies from you,' said Jannie. 'But you've got to get Aine to agree to your plan, and then you must persuade her to be photographed in front of her church.'

'I'm aware of that.'

'Let's take a walk around the park,' said Erik.

They got out of the car, Erik and Jannie looking around the square, and Harry staring at the church. He made a frame with his hands and ran it around the church.

'Can't you forget it for a minute?' said Erik. 'Come on, Jannie, let's have a look around.' Without waiting for an answer, he took her hand and headed for the music rotunda.

Harry got his camera and light meter out. After taking several readings and adjusting the camera, he took up a position beside one of the bluestone posts holding the wrought-iron gates. He brought the viewfinder to his eye and focused on the Gothic-style arch that was the entrance to the bluestone church. As he tried to picture how Aine would appear in the frame, the woman herself exited the church, holding a small child's hand. He lowered the camera. She was dressed neatly and modestly as usual, with a black lace mantilla draped over her head. The contrast between the mantilla, her pale complexion, and her very fair hair was striking. She had not seen him because the little girl kept her attention. He raised the camera again, his breathing heightened. She heard the click and looked up. The post and the gate obscured her view of him, so holding the little girl's hand, she descended the small flight of stone stairs. He kept clicking.

'Oh, Harry, what are you doing here?'

'We've come to see you.'

'How did you know I was here?' she said, taking off the mantilla.

'I didn't. We parked there, and I just had to take shots of this charming church. Jannie and Erik are over there.'

'Yes, I see them now,' she said uneasily. 'This is my daughter, Estella,' she added, seeing Harry's attention taken by her daughter.

'A beautiful little girl,' said Harry. 'Your husband is dark.'

'Yes.'

'You are a pair, indeed.'

'What do you mean?'

'I mean, what anyone would think if they saw you together.'

'How long are you staying?'

'Tonight and Saturday night. We'll return to Melbourne on Sunday. We did not intend to contact you until tomorrow.'

'Why have you come?'

'You know why.'

'Just for me?'

'Not entirely. I wanted to do some shoots with Jannie. I had an idea that the surroundings here would be suitable. We did some shots of her on that peak outside Binawarra.'

'Which peak?' said Aine, clutching Estella's hand.

'The sharp one, you know, the one with the rocky ledge. Why, what's wrong?'

'You went up there with Jannie?'

'Yes, why, what's wrong?'

'Nobody goes there. It's not a place to—'

A yell from across the park rang out. It was Jannie running towards them.

'Please don't say anything to Jannie,' said Harry.

Jannie arrived, gushing. 'This is your daughter, of course. My, she has grown. Still beautiful ... my, my, so much beauty in the one family.'

'Don't overdo it, Jannie,' said Harry. 'You're making Aine uncomfortable.'

'I'm not, am I, Aine?' She crouched, taking Estella's hand. 'How are you, Estella? I'm Jannie. Remember me. We've come to visit your mummy.' She looked around. 'Where's your handsome daddy?'

'At home,' said Estella, showing little sign of shyness.

'He's working,' said Aine. 'He's got urgent work for the town.'

'Why are you here?' Jannie said, standing up and looking at the church. 'It's not Sunday.'

'Father hears confessions on Friday afternoon.'

'Confession! What have you to confess? I'm the one who should be in there.' She laughed half-heartedly. Her bottom lip trembled a little.

'We all do the wrong thing at one time or another—me as much as anyone else,' said Aine.

An embarrassed silence followed as the three, bemused, regarded Aine.

'I've got something to show you, Aine,' said Harry, fidgeting. 'Come here.' He walked to the nearby car and fished a magazine from his bag. 'Take a look at this.'

Aine, with reluctance, came to his side and looked at the double-page spread he had flicked open. 'Oh, I didn't know—' She looked at a full-page photo of herself. A side caption described the coat, hat, and shoes she had worn on the lawn at John Batman University.

'No, I know you didn't. I wanted to see if I could take good photos of you under less-than-satisfactory circumstances. It worked.'

'I don't know what to say.'

'Say you like it.'

'I have no objection.'

'No objection!' exclaimed Jannie. 'You look fantastic. Tell her, Harry, the reaction so far.'

Harry gave a brief account of the praise she had received from colleagues, agents, fashion houses, and magazine editors, as if there could be no other possible outcome of her appearing in the magazine.

'Look,' he said, to clinch his argument, 'this magazine is *Fashion Today*, one of the best magazines in the region. You make it here; you make it anywhere. You have a future. A bit more training and experience, and you will be incomparable.'

'We can work together,' said Jannie. 'It would be terrific. We have so much in common, much more than a dress size.'

'I don't know what to say,' Aine repeated, looking askance at Jannie.

'Can I have a word with you in private?' said Harry after a moment's reflection. 'Would it be okay if Jannie and Erik took your daughter for a walk? We can sit on the bench over there. It won't take long.'

Aine felt reluctance but also thought she could not refuse such a polite, inoffensive invitation.

'I took a risk, I'm aware, in submitting this photo to the magazine without your permission,' he said when they were seated, and Jannie and Erik were ambling with Estella to the far end of the park. 'I apologise for that. But I could not do it in any other way. A refusal was likely if I asked you beforehand. I just had to prove a point. I hope you don't mind.'

'Well, it's done now.'

'Legally speaking, you can still object. It would cause me enormous trouble, but it's possible. I must be honest.'

'No, Harry, I wouldn't cause you unnecessary trouble. I think you're sincere.'

'That's a vote of trust,' he said. 'I can't tell you how relieved I am to hear that.'

'I wouldn't have anything to do with you if I thought otherwise.'

'I know.'

There was a moment of silence, a break in the conversation. Harry again appeared uneasy. Until then, he had seemed confident in his actions and organisation. From his expression, the feeling passed quickly.

'There's one other thing before we go any further.' He took a folded envelope from his pocket. 'This is for you.'

'What is it?' she said, holding it unopened before her.

'Go on, open it,' he smiled. 'It's not a death notice.'

She opened the envelope. 'Oh!'

'That's your payment for the photo session and the modelling.'

'So much money? I hardly did anything. I was just myself most of the time.'

'That's it precisely. It's not the amount of work. It's the quality of your work. As I said, you're a natural with the right sort of look.'

She stared at the cheque. 'Harry, I appreciate all you've done and are trying to do for me. Sincerely, I appreciate your disinterest. But it's not your motives or the money that's at issue. It's whether I want to do this—whether it's proper to do it.'

'I understand,' said Harry. 'Jannie has helped me to understand. It's not how I think or how most people think in our business, but I respect it. So let me promise not to do, or even suggest, work that would conflict with your principles.' He opened the magazine to the page with her picture. 'Look at this. Is there any possible objection you could have to this? You're dressed tastefully and elegantly. Your pose is discreet and subtle, projecting and enhancing the quality of the design and materials you are modelling. There's nothing tawdry about it. In fact, it's the opposite, promoting propriety and elegance rather than the other way around.'

Aine looked long and hard at the picture. No, there was nothing she could object to. It was as he said: tasteful and elegant—and proper. She would have no objection to owning and wearing that coat and hat. But then, as she gazed at the photo, it seemed to undergo a subtle change. A photo of herself with all the memories of that day on the university lawn, swimming around in her head, was no longer before her. Instead, she was looking at a young woman beautifully dressed, with elegance and poise and an expression of innocence and mystery. It was striking, she had to admit. She glanced at Harry. He was waiting for her reaction.

'You are very persuasive, Harry,' she said with a sigh.

'I'm telling it the way it is. No tricks, no traps, no ulterior motive, just the way it is, and the way you are.'

'What next, then? You evidently have something in mind.'

'I have a selection of clothing for the summer season. All smart and elegant. High quality. Perfect for you. I want to do a shoot with you. Three outfits. The rest is for Jannie. Jannie's already done some of the swimwear. That's not for you.' Harry spoke quickly and a little haphazardly, taking short, quick breaths. He had made the breakthrough. And they both realised it.

'When and where?'

'That's something I'm yet to decide. I'll scout around this afternoon.'

He arranged to call her late that afternoon. In the meantime, she should put the whole plan to her husband. Charles must be entirely happy with any arrangement. Of course, he was very welcome to attend the shoot or put any questions to him. Aine nodded her agreement, still with an air of reluctance. With those preliminary arrangements made, they turned their attention to Jannie, Estella, and Erik, who were walking back towards them.

'You have a very pretty daughter,' commented Harry. His mind appeared not wholly on what he was saying. 'It's not always the case that a beautiful parent has a beautiful child.'

'Jannie's very attractive, too,' said Aine, also not entirely with it. 'She seems to have blossomed these last few years.'

'You mean she was not like that in the convent?'

'Not really—in appearance, I mean.'

'She doesn't talk about the convent. She's very sensitive about it.'

'Is she really?' For all Jannie's exuberance since leaving the convent, she never gave much sign of what she was really like inside.

'What happened?' said Harry. He could not hide his curiosity.

'She had some difficulties.'

'What?'

'If she hasn't told you, I should not say anything.'

'She said the convent time is a deep wound.'

'A deep wound?' The vision of Jannie screaming and smashing the plates on the tiled kitchen floor would never fade. It had been an enormous struggle for her. And now this forced, flippant manner and her deliberate deception of people.

'I'm still here,' protested Harry.

'Sorry, I was just reflecting on that time.'

'I know you were. I wonder what it is about convent life that it has had such an impact on both of you.'

'Both of us?'

'Yes, indeed,' he replied. 'And what do you make of the friendship with that nun, Margaret? I can see what two singular attractive girls have in common—like you and Jannie. But what does Jannie have in common with that rather dour forbidding nun?'

There was no time for an answer. Jannie had arrived and was eager to hear what they had discussed and if they had arranged something.

LATER that afternoon, a tall, attractive young woman and a fashionably dressed young man carrying photographic equipment caught the people's attention around the shopping square as they headed toward the music rotunda. The young woman seemed oblivious to the attention while the photographer focused on his destination. Soon, a small group was standing at a respectful distance, watching the fashion model and photographer at work. Several people were bold enough to suggest to the photographer that he was fortunate to have the unique music rotunda as a background. Harry agreed, adding to the townspeople's delight that he was lucky to have happened on such a beautiful country town. Jannie said nothing, content to look pretty and smile indulgently at the admiring faces. When she had returned twice to the nearby hotel to change into another outfit, Harry halted the shoot.

'That's enough, here,' he said. 'You can have a rest now. Mind the clothes,' he added when he saw her heading for the nearest bench.

'Yes, slavedriver.'

Harry stopped what he was doing and glanced at her. He finished packing up and joined her on the bench.

'Is there anything wrong?'

'What could be wrong?' she said, looking the other way.

'You're not going to start objecting to my ways now, are you?'

'What ways?'

'I don't mean anything. It's just my way of working. We always work well together.'

'Do we?'

'You know we do. I've been the one to recognise your ability. You've had a lot of work through me—and a lot of money.' She replied with an expression of distaste. 'What's wrong, Jannie? Tell me.'

'There's nothing to tell. Just tell me what you want to do next.' She continued to look away.

Harry contemplated his hands, fiddled with the camera bag, and looked around.

'Here comes Aine's husband,' said Jannie, her expression changing.

Harry stood up, preparing to greet the tall man approaching them. 'Mr Winterbine, I am pleased to meet you at last,' he said, offering his hand.

Charles first greeted Jannie and then returned Harry's greeting. 'I've dropped along to say hello, and to assure you that you are welcome. Have you found accommodation yet?'

Harry assured Charles they were comfortably accommodated in the hotel on the square. Jannie sparked up and supported Harry in his praise of the town and its hospitality.

'I'm glad to hear that. Are you able to join us for dinner tonight?'

Harry thanked Charles for the invitation but politely declined. He still had a lot of work with Jannie to do before calling it a day. Jannie would be dead tired by the time they finished. Erik, their companion, had already excused himself through fatigue. But if Charles and Aine were free the following night, he would like to invite them to dine at the hotel.

'No, I insist you join us tomorrow evening,' said Charles.

Harry gracefully accepted the invitation, and they settled on a time. Harry inquired whether he and Aine had discussed his proposals. They had. Charles left it to Aine to decide whether it was for her. He had complete confidence in her judgment.

'That's wonderful,' said Harry. 'Would you and Aine mind if we did a shoot tomorrow afternoon here in the square?'

'I imagine Aine has no objection.'

'Good, I'll call later to confirm that with her.' He paused. 'By the way, can you suggest suitable places for us to use as a background—a rough bushy area to serve as a backdrop?'

Charles made several suggestions, including the picnic spot below the peak just outside the town.

'Which one?' said Harry. 'The sharp one or the other.'

'The one with the level top. There's an attractive approach from the picnic area, this side of the range. The creek is also close by.'

'That's good. We've already done a shoot on the other peak,' said Harry before he realised what he said.

'Yes, Aine told me,' said Charles, frowning. 'Nobody goes there usually.'

'Really?' said Harry, glancing at Jannie.

'Why?' said Jannie.

'The young people even avoid it. There's something dark and eerie about it.'

'Now you tell me,' Jannie said, turning to Harry.

'I didn't know that beforehand. Besides, it was all right. We didn't feel any eeriness. The sun shone brightly on it. It was a great spot for my purpose.'

'For your purpose, maybe,' said Jannie. 'I did feel different up there.'

'You did very well, the best ever. You were flying.'

'A little too high, I fear.'

Charles heard this exchange with interest but said nothing. Harry absorbed Charles's reticence and glanced at Jannie. 'It was probably a place you weren't used to. Anyhow, it's done now, and we won't be going up there again. Charles, I'll follow your suggestions.'

Chapter 29

A tender moment

HARRY EXCLAIMED with delight as they came out onto the picnic area from the bushy, dirt track leading from the main road out of Binawarra. It was perfect for what he had in mind: a broad grassy area with bush on all sides, a creek close by streaming with water from the recent autumnal rains, and a treed vista of the peak rising high above them.

'It's much more inviting than that other peak,' said Jannie.

'Do you think so?' Harry was again lost in his preparations and not paying attention. 'I don't know what you're talking about.'

'Aine and Charles certainly do.'

'Female imagination,' he said offhandedly.

'*Ach, meneer moet altijd gelijk hebben,*' she sneered. [*Oh, sir has always got to be right.*]

He swung around to her. 'What has got into you? And what's with the Dutch all of a sudden? Are you in a state of regression or something?'

'*Omdat ik daar zin in heb,*' she pouted. [*Because I feel like it.*] 'And Charles is certainly not female, in case you haven't noticed.'

'Come here, Jannie. We've got to settle this before we go any further. I'm not going to waste film on a foul mood.' He took her by the hand

and led her unresisting to a nearby picnic bench. 'Sit down and tell me what's eating you.'

She sat, put on her best pout, and looked defiantly at him. He regarded her. His expression softened. 'You know,' he began, 'I can see why you photograph so well as I look at you this close. You have such good, healthy, regular facial features—and those deep blue eyes.' The pout weakened. 'I suppose that's a Dutch look.' The pout went. 'It's stupid of me not to realise there's this other dimension to you. Tell me about Holland. When did you come out to Australia?'

'We arrived—we came to Australia in 1954—late 1954, the beginning of the Australian summer. I was sixteen,' she said, seeing Harry put aside his camera.

'That's a critical time for a young person. If I think back to when I was sixteen—did you speak English?'

'A bit—school English.'

'It must have been strange.'

'You couldn't know how much,' she said, shaking her head. 'Holland was just recovering from the war and the terrible things the Nazis did. They shot many men in our area as reprisals for the actions of the Dutch underground.'

'Really?'

'Yes. People have no idea here what we, my family, lived through.'

'The Japanese—'

'That was far away. We lived through it, in the middle of it. Neighbours were shot dead in front of your eyes. No Japanese patrolled the streets of Melbourne.'

Harry caressed her arm, and her expression softened.

'Do you miss Holland?'

'Yes, I do. It's so different here.'

'Friends?'

'Especially my friends and family.'

'Tell me about it.'

Harry let her talk, only interrupting to ask questions. She spoke about her village in Brabant, about village life, about her school, family, and friends. She sometimes spoke joyfully, at other times wistfully or sadly.

'I understand now why those verses about silence remained in your head,' he said when she paused to reflect on the images running through her mind.

'Yes, you're right,' she murmured. 'The stillness of the countryside under a thick blanket of snow ... it's like a ... *openbaring* ... a revelation.'

'I'm beginning to understand. I sometimes see a mood through the camera lens, something beyond the image.' He reflected. 'But why go to your knees, you know, that last line in the poem?'

'That's the point, isn't it?' said Jannie. 'In the depths of silence, within, you find God—the divine. That's the way I have understood it.'

'I'll never regard you in the same way,' said Harry, with no attempt to contain his wonder. 'There's a whole life in you that people wouldn't know existed.'

'I'm glad you understand,' she said after a few moments.

'I've met your parents a few times, and I have to admit that until now, they only appeared as people with funny accents.'

'It's unfair and stupid of people not to realise that another language holds a world of thought and feeling. My father's a very successful businessman, much more than a funny accent. In Dutch, he can express himself much better than most Australians in English. It's stupid that people only hear the accent while ignoring his success.'

'I'm sorry.' He took her hand. She did not resist. 'Do you want to call off work for the day? We can come back tomorrow.'

She considered the question. She let out a sigh, then leaned over and kissed him on the cheek. 'Thank you for your sympathy and understanding. That means so much to me. No, I will get myself into the right mood. I'll be all right now.'

'Are you sure? I mean it. You can leave it for today.'

'No, I'll be all right. Give me a little time to concentrate. Get your things ready.'

'Jannie, you're a real professional,' he said, getting up. 'Have you got that from your dad?'

'My mother and father have always given me an example of duty and the benefit of an efficient organisation. It's a Dutch trait.'

'Do you see yourself as Dutch or Australian?'

'Whatever I think, I am Dutch. I can't help it.'

While Harry prepared his camera, Jannie checked her outfit, adjusted her makeup, and combed her hair. Finally, she had a brief look at the following outfits to anticipate hair and makeup requirements. Now she patiently waited while Harry surveyed the surroundings, showing his usual precision and fussiness in choosing and setting up the scene. Soon they were at work. Half an hour passed quickly and with little superfluous conversation, as Harry directed and manoeuvred her through three casual outfits, the last two shot by the fast-flowing creek.

'Let's take a break,' said Harry, putting his camera in the bag as if he was determined to give his full attention to Jannie. 'You've done very well, as usual. It makes it easier when there's nobody around, too.'

'I'll get out of this outfit and put my coat on,' said Jannie, walking to the car.

Harry watched her as she went about her business. He was not interested in catching glimpses of her in her underwear—he had seen enough models changing clothes—he was more intrigued by the methodical way she organised herself.

'Why haven't I noticed before how well organised you are?' he said when she had joined him on the bench.

'You're always occupied with your preparations,' she said. 'Besides, I have taken your compliments about my professionalism to be about that.'

'Yes, you're right. I'm self-centred—my best and worst quality. Do you want something to drink? I've got lemonade with me.'

They had a drink in silence, each lost in his thoughts.

'That mountain is so inviting,' said Jannie. 'Not like that other one.'

'Do you think so?' said Harry, roused from his meditations and looking up at the peak.

'It would be easy to climb up there,' she commented. 'What about a few shots from there?'

'That's a big climb,' he said. 'You'll be tired by the time you get there—in no condition for photos.'

'I suppose you're right. But it's so inviting.'

Harry got to his feet. 'You don't mind if we give it a miss? There's only a little more to do, and then we can get back to the hotel.'

'That's okay. It was only a thought.'

'You're a good girl,' he said, massaging her neck.

She closed her eyes and let him continue for a minute or two. 'That's nice,' she whispered.

They went back to work, again near the creek. It was not long before they were walking back to the car, chatting about the work they had completed. At the car, Jannie put her arms around Harry's neck and hugged him.

'Thank you,' she said into his ear, 'for putting up with my moods.'

'I'll be more attentive to your feelings,' he said, holding her. 'I don't want to spoil our friendship.'

Jannie laid her head on his shoulder.

THERE was already a little group of people looking on as Jannie attended to Aine's makeup. Aine, holding a black clutch purse and dressed in a grey three-piece suit with a swing skirt, cropped jacket, and white gloves, waited without moving or saying anything.

'Just a little,' Jannie said. 'We don't want to hide that beautiful face.' She stood back. 'There, that's enough. Just discreet enough to make a difference. You make that suit come alive. Stunning.'

In the meantime, Harry had finished his preparations and joined them. He shook his head as he looked Aine up and down. 'Who's going to say I'm wrong about this? Put the mantilla on.' He adjusted the black lace mantilla and brushed her hair into the form he wanted. 'Okay, Aine, you know what to do?'

'Yes, I think so.'

'Okay, just be yourself. Don't try to act. I want your natural expressions. Go on and don't take any notice of me—except for my instructions.'

Aine passed through the wrought-iron gates and mounted the stairs to the bluestone Gothic archway. She turned and moved into the positions and poses Harry had discussed with her. She repeated these moves twice more with some variations. The little group of onlookers had grown by this time.

'Wonderful,' said Jannie when Harry told her to take a break. 'She's wonderful, isn't she, Harry?'

Harry murmured his approval while he checked his camera and his schedule.

'How do you feel about it now?' she asked Aine. 'You couldn't possibly have any objections to this elegant suit. It's the sort of suit President Kennedy's wife has made famous.'

'No, they're beautiful clothes. I couldn't wish for better.'

'With those clothes, you'll be promoting elegance and propriety,' said Harry, looking up from his camera.

'Harry's right,' said Erik, who had joined them. 'You'll make people melt with envy.'

'What has that to do with elegance and propriety?' said Jannie.

'Nothing, I suppose,' said Erik. 'It was just a compliment.'

'Humph!' said Jannie, stroking Aine's hair and brushing her jacket.

Erik held out his hands and raised his eyebrows. Harry shook his head and put his finger to his lips. Erik shrugged and moved away.

'Aine! What's happening here?' a loud, friendly voice called.

'Oh, hello, Uncle Bill and Auntie Joanne,' said Aine.

'You look absolutely stunning,' said Joanne Huckerby. Where is—?'

'We're Aine's surrogate parents in Binawarra,' said Bill to Harry.

Aine made the formal introductions, explaining Harry's work and his proposal.

'Mr and Mrs Huckerby,' said Harry, warmly shaking hands with them, 'Aine's being far too modest. The truth is that she has a great future in modelling if she wants to go into that field. We're in the middle of a fashion shoot for next summer's collection.'

'Absolutely stunning,' Joanne repeated, looking Aine up and down. 'What woman could ignore such elegance? How much will it be?' she said, turning to Harry.

'Hang on, hang on,' Bill continued jovially. 'Let's not get too excited. Our pockets are not deep. Hey, young fellow, you should go elsewhere with your expensive clothes.' He gave Harry a ridiculous wink.

'Behave yourself, Bill,' said Joanne.

'You're too beautiful,' said Bill in a loud whisper to Aine.

'You see what I mean,' said Harry. 'You're made for it.'

'Where's Charles?' Bill interrupted, looking around.

'He's at home looking after Estella,' said Aine. 'He has some work to attend to.'

'You should have asked us to mind Estella,' said Joanne. 'Charles would not want to miss this.'

'I didn't think—'

'Do you mind, Mr and Mrs Huckerby, if we continue?' said Harry. 'I want to take advantage of the sun in its present position.'

'Of course not, young fellow,' said Bill. 'Take no notice of us.'

'Thank you, Mr Huckerby. Jannie, will you get Aine ready?'

While Jannie accompanied Aine to the nearby hotel, Harry chatted to the Huckerbys, putting questions to Bill about Aine and Binawarra, with Bill only too keen to provide prolonged answers. It was not too long before Aine returned in her new outfit, with Jannie beaming beside her. 'Doesn't she look terrific?'

'Wonderful,' said Joanne.

There were now flattering comments coming from all sides. Aine, dressed in a blue cotton shirt-waist dress with full skirt, white gloves still on, and fair hair tied loosely behind her, smiled happily at Joanne.

'You really like it? Do you think it's okay for me to do this?'

'Why not? I can't see any reason why not,' said Joanne. 'If they want you to do it, and you can, why not? You're so beautiful, darling.'

'Thank you, Auntie Joanne.'

Harry interrupted them and led Aine and the entourage across the road to the music rotunda. There, Aine went through a similar routine while the growing crowd looked on. More than happy with the results, Harry sent Aine, again accompanied by Jannie, to change into the third and last outfit. They soon returned with Aine wearing a burgundy silk A-line-style dress and overblouse. There were black gloves on her hands and a cute pillbox hat on her head.

'That's Jackie Kennedy!' someone called.

'Do you think so?' said Harry, trying to sound offhand but pleased with the recognition.

'Aine looks better,' another said.

Aine smiled shyly, unable to hide her pleasure.

'You're looking much more relaxed now,' said Harry.

'I am relaxed.'

'Comfortable with the idea?'

'A lot more now.'

Without more ado, the group moved to the old weatherboard courthouse on the square, where Aine followed Harry's instructions again. Towards the end of the shoot, a tall, severe lady in her forties happened on the scene, frowning at the activity. Some of the people moved away.

'What's going on here?' the lady asked Bill Huckerby.

'Flo, you've missed it all!' said Bill, turning to her.

'What's going on?' Miss Barker repeated.

Joanne pushed Bill aside and gave Miss Barker a brief account of what she was seeing. Miss Barker waited, her narrowed eyes fixed on Harry.

'I thought you were off today, Flo,' said Bill. 'We didn't expect to see you.'

'I'm just making the last preparations for Saigon—' She still had her eyes on Harry.

'Saigon? I thought it was Sydney.'

'I meant Sydney,' said Miss Baker, hurriedly correcting herself. 'I've just been reading about the fighting in Vietnam. Introduce me to that young man.' She pointed accusingly at Harry, who had finished shooting.

'Miss Barker, this is Harry—'

'I am Miss Barker, young man,' said that formidable lady, speaking over Joanne. 'You will call me Miss Barker.'

'Yes, Miss Barker,' said a bemused Harry, caught putting the camera into its bag.

'I trust you will always be open and honest with Aine. You take advantage of her, and you'll have me to answer to.'

Blinking, Harry looked around at the silent group as if seeking an explanation for this strange, unexpected personage.

'Miss Barker, it's all right.'

'Leave this to me, Aine,' said Miss Barker, moderating her tone. 'Well, young man?'

'Miss Barker, I can assure you Aine has been and will be treated with the greatest respect,' said Harry, recovering. 'I hope Aine and Charles will testify to that.'

Miss Barker looked around with much deliberation. 'Where's Charles?'

'He's looking after Estella, Miss Barker,' said Aine. 'He also has some work to attend to. He'll be along shortly.'

Indeed, just then, Charles was approaching on the far side of the square, holding Estella's hand. Aine waved eagerly. He soon joined them, making admiring comments about Aine's clothes and appearance. Harry said he was very pleased with Charles's reaction. Charles's approval and cooperation were essential to the plan to promote Aine's career in the fashion world.

'A career in the fashion world?' said Miss Barker, making it evident she understood Harry's not-very-subtle meaning. 'Are you sure this is what you want?' she asked Aine. 'I have never heard you utter a word about it before this. Peace and solitude seemed more in keeping with your inclinations.'

'I think you have an incorrect idea about modelling work,' said Harry.

'Do I, Mr. ...?'

'Call me Harry.'

'I'm not sure that I do, Mr Harry. I wasn't born yesterday.'

'Fashion modelling is a diverse field, Miss Barker. I have recommended Aine model in the high-end, high fashion. It suits her look and personality. You can see what she is modelling at this moment.'

Miss Barker subjected Harry to one of her withering looks, making that victim wince. 'I'll keep an eye on what's going on. Don't forget. Good day, all.'

The group, including onlookers, seemed paralysed as Harry watched Miss Barker retreat across the park.

'For heaven's sake, what was that?'

'Don't worry, young fellow,' said Bill, clapping him on the shoulder. 'She's not as fearsome as she seems. But don't get on the wrong side of her, anyhow. She's fiercely protective of Charles and Aine.'

'She does not need to worry, I assure you.' He began packing up, his mood now much subdued.

Chapter 30

Jannie reflects

AINE THOUGHT she had every reason to be content with the day. Harry had lived up to all he had promised—and more besides. He had conducted himself as a thorough gentleman, ensuring that her wishes were respected in every detail. Like everyone else, she was full of admiration for the style, cut, and material of the clothes he had selected for her. It was a privilege to wear such quality clothes, clothes that were far beyond their means. If this were the clothing she would be modelling, she had no reason to turn her back on the path he had outlined. Surely. The one dampener on the day's proceedings was Miss Barker's abrupt treatment of Harry.

Aine was aware of Miss Barker's odd way of scrutinising her surroundings and her propensity to speak her mind without embellishment. But today, she seemed unusually severe, unusually cantankerous about what seemed entirely unobjectionable. Auntie Joanne and Uncle Bill certainly saw nothing objectionable. Indeed, Auntie Joanne's enthusiasm was irrepressible. Did Miss Barker see something nobody else saw? Aine was also aware of Miss Barker's almost unfailing insight into people's motivations. Still, reflecting hard and long on the circumstances, together with Harry's behaviour, she concluded that Miss Barker was too cautious on this occasion. Uncle Bill was right about her fiercely protecting Charles and Estella, and her as if there was danger at every turn.

The evening dinner with Harry, Jannie, and Erik confirmed her opinion. It could not have been more pleasant. As she suspected, Harry and Charles found they had interests in common. Harry spent much time questioning Charles about his restoration work and exclaimed over his knowledge of Australia's residential architecture. Their exchange was so interesting that Jannie and Erik listened without any sign of boredom. A tour of the house and the gardens in the fading light preceded the dinner.

'This garden is going to be something to behold when it's finished,' said Erik when they had finished their tour.

'We both work in it for our pleasure,' said Aine. 'It will take years to finish, but it will be worth it in the long run. It'll be our little Eden.'

Only the religious objects around the house seemed, on occasions, to leave the guests, even Jannie, a little bewildered.

'You have more crucifixes and holy pictures here than at the convent,' Jannie whispered to Aine after looking around the house.

'Do you think so? You exaggerate, surely.'

'There's a lot here.'

'I don't notice anymore.'

'Anybody who enters your house will be hit in the face by it all.'

'Jannie, you exaggerate!'

'Harry's speechless.'

'Don't be silly.'

Aine's light exchange with Jannie over the religious objects highlighted yet another feature of the weekend. She had come to see another side to Jannie. The exuberant, deliberately scatty behaviour had made way for an even-tempered spirit and a genuine concern for her as she followed

Harry's demanding schedule. She could not fault her attentiveness to her feelings and the shoot's detail. Jannie had joked that she was Harry's assistant, but Harry really could not have done without her precise preparation, intelligent direction, and warm encouragement.

During the evening, she seemed subtly to unite with her in solidarity, in contrast to her past, when she had switched to her coquettish role at the first sign of male presence. The coquetry always seemed a competitive thing, too. But that evening, Jannie ignored the two handsome, successful young men who accompanied her. Surprisingly, she appeared to have developed indifference, even coldness, toward Erik, even though they had seemed to be an item until then. There was, in fact, a distinctly reflective quality to Jannie's demeanour. The unexpected change was again apparent the following morning when she and Charles met Jannie in the church vestibule after Sunday Mass.

'Have you been to Mass?' said Aine, surprised, for she had not seen her in the church.

'Yes, of course. I'm Catholic, remember.' She laughed evasively.

They moved outside to the front path, with Jannie expressing her admiration for the charm of the bluestone Gothic-style church. Despite Jannie's chatty offhand manner, Aine had the impression she was there for a purpose, not just to attend Sunday Mass.

'Charles, do you mind if I go for a walk with Aine?'

'A walk?' said Aine.

'Yes, I'd like to have a chat with you, you know, a girl chat. I would really appreciate it.'

Charles, who was holding Estella's hand, seemed this time more attuned to the reasons for Jannie's request. 'Why don't you come home with us now for morning tea?' he said. 'You and Aine can go for a walk after that. There are picturesque tracks near our house, running along the creek and range.'

Jannie could not have looked more pleased and said she was ready to go. 'Let me take Estella. I want to make friends with this pretty little thing.'

Jannie was good to her word. She kept up a constant chatter with Estella as they walked the short distance from the main square to the Winterbine house near the foot of the hills on Old Melbourne Road. When they were almost home, Charles remarked that five-year-old Estella was unusually responsive to Jannie. Jannie replied that they were children together. That light-hearted response set the tone for the conversation, during which Jannie's manner with Charles was unaffected. Her new manner contrasted with her suggestive comments during the Christmas visit to the convent nearly three years before. They had bordered then on the objectionable. Now her manner was friendly and restrained, lacking the self-centeredness of that time. She seemed prepared to sit and chat about them and their family life as if that had been her purpose in coming there. Aine had to remind her that Harry and Erik would be wondering where she was.

'Let 'em wonder,' she said. 'It'll do them good. They expect people to wait on them all the time. Besides, they'll figure out where I am. They are many things; stupid is not one of them.' Relieved of those thoughts, she seemed satisfied, and her fierceness faded while her thoughts turned to the walk. After discussing several possible routes, they set off to the bridge over the creek. Aine expected Jannie to embark immediately on the matter she wanted to discuss. But Jannie did no such thing. Instead, she continued to speak about Aine and her family, asking questions about the most mundane domestic subjects as if they were of the first importance.

'Is this all you want to talk about?' Aine could not help but ask. 'I thought there was something particular you wanted to speak about.'

'There is something, but I don't know what it is,' said Jannie, twisting as she walked and grabbing at the long grass stems along the route. 'I just felt I wanted to talk to you.'

'Well, I'm here to talk when you're ready.'

'It sounds stupid, I know,' said Jannie, pursing her lips and then sighing. 'And this time, it's not deliberate.'

They walked in silence for a while. Jannie looked at the hills, but her mind seemed directed inwards.

'I don't understand how you could make yourself appear deliberately stupid,' said Aine. 'You're such a beautiful girl. It's not as if you lack attention or need to compensate.'

'I know you don't. And I know you don't care what people think about right or wrong behaviour. I do care what people think, and I don't know why I'm different.'

'This weekend, you've not done that—I mean, put on an act.'

'Yes, put on an act,' murmured Jannie. 'This weekend has been different. Something has happened to me. Harry said something that made me reflect. And entirely to my surprise, he showed he has a heart.'

'But you have told me that Harry can be trusted.'

'You can trust Harry with the things he has undertaken to do for you. It's like a business contract. He won't break a business contract. He's ice-cold about decisions that concern his professionalism and craft. He won't do anything to harm that. It's all self-interest. Whether he cares about you personally is another matter.'

'But he has been nothing but a gentleman.'

'That's partly self-interest and partly his idea of beauty. He abhors crudity and vulgarity and that sort of thing, especially when he's confronted with someone like you. His manner of seduction is impeccably well-mannered.' She laughed a little bitterly. 'Until now, I would have said he'd soon turn cold towards you if you did not work out—politely, of course.'

'Up until now?'

'Yes. He suddenly showed he does have a heart. It took me completely by surprise. In a way, this weekend with him has turned me upside down.'

'What about Erik?'

'Yes, what about Erik? They're both self-centred. I didn't need any warnings, but Harry ... what he said ....' They continued to walk in silence until they came to the picnic area below the great grassy hill. 'This is where it happened,' said Jannie. 'This is where Harry revealed he has a heart, where I was sure he just had a camera. He was very tender.'

Aine looked around. This place also had cherished memories for her. She wanted to ask Jannie what happened, but restrained herself. She would not be intrusive. She would let Jannie tell her if she wanted to. But Jannie was not inclined to go into it. They sat on a nearby bench, Jannie lost in her thoughts and Aine waiting.

'I wanted Harry to climb that mountain with me,' said Jannie, looking up at it. 'It looks so inviting. But he said that he did not have the time. Pity.'

'That's where Charles and I said we loved each other for the first time.'

'Really?' Jannie's mood changed. She leapt to her feet. 'Come on, then. You can take me. I want to see where you did it.' She was already on her way.

'Are you sure? It's a big climb,' Aine called after her.

'If you could do it, so can I.'

Aine saw there was no dampening her resolve, and she set off after her. With Aine taking the lead, they climbed in silence, going up across the hill one way and turning to come back the other way. To Jannie's cries of joyful wonder, Aine pointed out where she and Charles had stopped to rest that first time. They stopped, too, while Jannie took in the view and the significance of the location. Then they were off again. At last, they came to the top.

'Where were you when it happened?' said Jannie.

Aine walked to the middle of the grassy area, where there was a stone marker. 'There, we stood there and embraced for a moment before Charles told me he would love me forever.'

Jannie stared at the marker. 'How did you feel?'

'After all the turmoil at the convent, I thought I would burst from happiness. I still get that feeling when I think about it. Our coming together in that way seemed to have the hand of God in it. This place has a religious aura. Charles felt it, too.'

'A religious aura,' said Jannie, gazing around. 'Why didn't that happen to me? I left in the same state of turmoil.' She stared at the marker. 'Why?'

Aine had no answer. She put her arm around Jannie before she knew what she was doing.

'What happened then?' Jannie asked, responding to the comfort.

'We said prayers in thanksgiving for our good fortune in finding each other. Then we went back down. Auntie Joanne and Uncle Bill were waiting for us. We didn't want to worry them.'

'Prayers?' Jannie muttered despondently. She turned away from the marker and walked to the side of the hill with Aine following. She stopped to look down at the smooth rocky platform jutting out from the sharp peak. 'What's so eerie about that?' she said, after contemplating it awhile and becoming aware Aine wanted to move on.

'I don't know. Charles was the first to see something sinister about it. Then I saw it, too.'

'What?'

'Something indefinable.'

'You're imagining things. It's just a peak with a rock platform.'

'I don't think so. Our physical surroundings often have a distinct aura, like the top here. That peak has the opposite aura—like something dark and—'

'And people say I'm fanciful! We were there, the three of us. We felt nothing odd. There was just us, with our human behaviour. You're imagining things.'

'We would never go there. Nobody goes there,' said Aine with a slight shiver.

'Someone goes there. There is a track leading up to it, a worn track.'

'I've never heard of anyone going there. Come on, Jannie, let's go back.'

Jannie followed a few paces behind until they came to the crest on the town side. 'Wait a minute,' she called. 'Let's have a rest here for a moment. I need to catch my breath.'

'This is where Charles and I sat before we made our way back down,' said Aine, sitting beside Jannie.

'I want to understand what you have with each other, what causes you to say what you do,' said Jannie, but she did not attempt to follow up with pertinent questions. She stared in front of her. 'What started it this weekend were the Dutch verses that came back to me from my school days in Holland. They had completely gone out of my mind until Harry asked me to recite some poetry in Dutch. He said I sounded different in Dutch.' She recited the Dutch verses. 'Do I sound different?'

'I have no idea what you said, but Harry's right. There is a different quality to your voice.'

'What?'

'I can't say exactly.' She concentrated for a moment. 'Perhaps your voice is sweeter.'

'Sweeter! *Goede hemel*, that's what Harry said! What is it with you two? Dutch is supposed to be a hard-sounding language.'

'It did not sound hard to me.'

'Do you want to know what it means?' Aine nodded, and Jannie repeated her translation. 'You understand that, don't you?'

'Yes. They're appealing thoughts.'

'That scary woman said your inclination is for silence and solitude.'

'Yes, that's right, Charles, too. But that does not mean we want to avoid company,' she added defensively.

'What do you think the last sentence refers to?' Jannie said, repeating the last sentence.

'It refers to the Transcendent, to God, to knowing God in the silence of your inner being.'

'That's what I thought. Harry didn't see it.'

'Your thoughts now seem to contradict your general behaviour—at least, what I have known of you.'

'Perhaps I am in contradiction. Perhaps I am a great big contradiction.' Her despondent tone returned.

'The solution is to resolve that contradiction,' offered Aine. 'Be yourself.'

Jannie tugged at the grass beside her and nodded. She appeared to want to say something, but kept nodding as if accusing herself of some grievous fault.

'Why does Margaret continually encourage me to seek my potential?' said Aine, seizing on Jannie's frank and open mood.

Jannie stopped tugging at the grass for a moment. She pulled several faces and began pulling at it again. 'I told you. She likes you. She wants you to live a fulfilling life. It's the same concern she has for me.'

'Does she have anything to do with Harry's plans? Is there some agenda?' She would risk being explicit.

'You're very suspicious, aren't you?'

'Does she?'

'Whatever plans or agenda Margaret has, she has them for her friends. No, she has nothing to do with Harry. She's only met him a couple of times. They're not at all alike. Harry's in my world. In my world,' she repeated.

'I can't help thinking there's more to it,' said Aine.

'You should ask her. Besides, as far as Harry is concerned, you have all the information you could want now. He has been completely open. It has nothing to do with Margaret.'

'Have you seen Margaret frequently since leaving the convent?' Aine had come this far. Now she would pursue the issues Virginia had raised.

'I've seen her off and on. Why?'

'Did you see her while she was in the novitiate?'

'What's this got to do with anything? I don't remember. Margaret's a friend, just like Virginia Pearson is a— Wait a minute. This is that meddling Miss Pearson, isn't it?'

'We both wondered,' said Aine, mortified that her purpose had become apparent.

Jannie stood up. 'Aine, I like you very much. I hope I have demonstrated my genuine affection. I can't say the same about your friend. Come on. It's time to get back to the boys.'

'Jannie, I'm sorry to upset you,' said Aine, getting to her feet. 'Yes, you have been kind and helpful to me this weekend. I'm very grateful.'

'I'm happy with that,' said Jannie, hugging her. 'Don't say any more now. Just show me the way.'

They made their way down the mountain in silence, this time not stopping to reflect on the significance of Aine's special locations. As they made their way across the picnic area with Jannie still deep in thought and paying no attention to the place of her epiphany, Aine once again offered her apologies for upsetting her.

'Don't worry about it,' stressed Jannie. 'It was a small thing in the scheme of my mad world. Things happen that suddenly send me to the depths. That was one of them. It's not your fault. It's like there are demons in me.'

'Jannie, I wish you would stop all those things, that behaviour that gives people the wrong idea about you.' Aine caressed her arm.

'You sound anxious about me,' said Jannie, stopping. 'Are you?'

'Of course, I am. I have a glimpse of what you're really like. Take away the barriers.'

'That you are concerned about me means more than what you say.'

'Virginia said ... that's what Virginia was trying to say to you in the convent. She wanted you to face yourself as you are. Virginia has the softest heart.'

'Without the influence of Margaret?'

'Without the influence of anyone, not just Margaret.'

Jannie frowned, a painful frown, and resumed walking. Aine kept in step, glancing at her. When Jannie seemed on the point of speaking, they ran into Charles, coming along the dirt track, almost at a jog.

'I was a little worried,' he said, looking relieved. 'Two attractive young women alone in the bush—you've been away quite a while. Harry and Erik are at home, waiting.'

'Sorry, darling,' said Aine, taking his hand. 'We lost track of time. We climbed your mountain.'

'Really?'

'Your mountain?' said Jannie, her despondency broken by curiosity. 'Why is it Charles's mountain?'

'I climbed it on the first day I arrived in Binawarra,' said Charles. 'Bill Huckerby gave it that name after I had spoken about it.'

'Everything's connected in your life, isn't it?' she commented to Aine. 'In contrast, my life seems like a lot of loose threads.'

Charles threw an inquiring glance at Aine, whose expression signalled that he should not inquire further.

'I hope you have entertained the boys,' said Jannie, evidently wanting to be free of the subject.

THE THREE occupants of the car remained silent as they drove up between the peaks on their way out of Binawarra. Each glanced around as the car descended to follow the winding road leading to the highway back to Melbourne. Jannie turned and kept the peaks in view until the bush and the turn in the road eclipsed them. Harry and Erik discussed the weekend, commenting on the town and its people. Harry boasted about his success in winning Aine over. He said nobody could doubt that she was a hot property with a big future. A girl who could so easily and so stunningly model the high end of fashion would not miss. Erik's endorsement of these judgments kept Harry expatiating until Jannie asked him to talk about something else.

'Why?' said Harry, getting her in the rear-vision mirror. 'It's been a terrific weekend, a total success. You, especially, have never been better—gorgeous, professional, intelligent. What more do you want?'

'Yes, you've been great,' said Erik, leaning over the front seat to take her hand.

She brushed his hand away. 'I suppose it's a let-down after so much that's happened.' She looked out the window, unwilling to meet the eyes of either man.

'If you consider how well you did,' said Harry, 'it must cheer you up.'

Jannie gave no reply, and the boys turned their minds to other things, avoiding the subject of Binawarra. They did not see Jannie's face falling, her mouth tightening, and her eyes closing. They did not see the first tears rolling down her cheeks. By the time they got to the highway, Jannie was sniffling. Now the boys were alerted. Harry strained to get her in the rear-vision mirror while Erik turned around.

'What is it?' said Harry. 'What's wrong?'

Erik tried to take her hand again, but she pushed him away. They drove on, an oppressive silence gripping each. Then came the sobs. The boys looked at each other. Finally, Harry pulled into a roadside stop.

'Jannie, what is it? You've got to tell us.'

After a long pause, she said: *'Ik voel me zo alleen.'*

'Say it in English,' Harry appealed.

'Verlaten,' she said.

'We don't know what you're saying,' said Harry, barely able to contain his exasperation. 'Erik, tell her to say it in English.'

'Ik voel me verlaten,' she repeated as if she did not hear him.

'She says she feels lonely ... and abandoned,' said Erik, looking straight ahead.

'I thought you didn't understand a word of Dutch,' said Harry, his exasperation worn all over his face.

'I lied,' said Erik. 'I do understand a few things. I just don't want anyone to know.'

'You're mad, too.' He faced Jannie. 'Why on earth do you feel alone and abandoned? I thought we had become closer this weekend. We care about you—genuinely. Whatever happens, we care about you. We do, don't we, Erik?' Erik nodded. But Jannie did not respond. The sobbing had subsided, but the tears continued to trickle from her eyes.

'*Ik wil naar huis,*' she said at length.

'Erik?'

'She wants to go home.'

Harry tried to console her, but nothing he said made a difference. Jannie stared out the side window and repeated that she wanted to go home. He gave up. They resumed their way in silence, Harry throwing looks of incomprehension at Erik, who returned each with a shrug. After a while, they began chatting about mundane matters, occasionally glancing around to see any improvement. There was none. An hour and a half later, they dropped Jannie off at a neat, gleaming white house with lush gardens and manicured lawns in an eastern suburb of Melbourne.

'I'll be in contact this week,' said Harry as he got Jannie's bags out of the boot for her.

'All right,' said Jannie, without interest.

'Well, that's better. Now we can understand each other.'

'Can we?'

'We're friends, Jannie, close friends. Don't spoil it.' She said nothing and went to pick up her bags. 'No, I'll take those.'

'No need,' she said. 'I'll do it.'

'All right.' He saw the determination on her face. 'I'll open the front gate for you.' While opening the gate, he commented in an apparent attempt to cheer her up: 'I've never noticed those things before.' He pointed to the green shutters on the window and the red clogs hanging on the wall beside the front door. 'They're a nice touch.'

'You've been here several times.'

Jannie walked to the front door without looking around. She heard the car start and then drive away as her mother opened the door.

'You look tired, *lieverd*,' her mother said in Dutch while watching Harry's luxury car drive up the street.

'I'm all right,' Jannie replied in Dutch. 'Just a little bit weary.'

'I hope that slick young man has not worked you too hard.'

'No, Mamma.'

'He hasn't been mean?'

'No, quite the opposite. Harry's never been nicer.'

'Be careful, *schat*. Your father says that behind that polite, cultured manner is a very hard businessman.'

'I know Harry's limitations, Erik's, too. By the way, Erik can understand Dutch. What a pathetic man.'

Not waiting for a reaction from her mother, who stared blankly, she went to her room, where she unpacked her bags and put everything away in its allotted place. Then, satisfied that all was in order and the room's neatness maintained, she took a photo album off her shelf and flicked through it. She stopped at a photo of her standing beside a snowy, frozen canal in her village in Brabant. She remembered the precise time and place as if it were yesterday. It was the winter before the family left for Australia, and she and her best friend had been skating all morning and enjoying the pestering of those stupid village boys.

AFTER putting Estella to bed, Aine joined Charles for their evening prayers. After prayers, they sat in the lounge room with their usual reading. Charles flicked through the Sunday paper while Aine read a novel, a Regency romance. But she could not concentrate. Her mind was too full of the weekend.

'How do you feel about everything, Charles darling?' she ventured at length.

'More to the point is how you feel about it,' said Charles, lowering the paper.

'No, I don't want to do anything you're not keen on.'

'Aine, darling, I have no reason to object. Harry's been open. He gave me assurances and said I was always welcome to come with you. If you're happy with the arrangements, I am, too. The decision is yours.'

'It all went well. The clothes were so beautiful. Harry's manner was impeccable. I have no reason to distrust him.'

Chapter 31

Agnes's torment

DESPITE THE challenge and enjoyment of the philosophy lectures and tutorials, Agnes was relieved when the term ended. The contact with Philip, and the sparks it struck, threatened again to race out of control. Away from the university and in the convent's peaceful seclusion, she was left alone with her thoughts, some of which she struggled to block. Philip was on his own; it had nothing to do with her. If he had broken romances, that could be for any number of reasons, anyhow. She should not flatter herself that he carried a torch for her and that she was responsible, even if indirectly, for his broken life. No, it was too stupid to contemplate and juvenile into the bargain. These confused and self-deluding thoughts washed around in her head for several days before she settled. Then the summons came from Mother Jerome. As anxious as she was about undergoing cross-examination by that demanding woman, at least Philip must drop down the list of items for possible discussion. Her neglect of the Rule on campus played on her mind while she made her way to the prioress's office.

'Well, it's a while since we spoke,' said the prioress, more affably than at the earlier meeting. She picked up a sheet of paper. 'I have your results in front of me.' She raised her eyebrows and looked over her glasses. 'We have a scholar on our hands,' she said, smiling. 'Congratulations.' She pushed the sheet across the desk.

Agnes perused the grades—two high distinctions, one distinction, and one pass. This satisfied her. 'Thank you, Mother.'

'You are not the only one,' the prioress went on, clearly pleased with herself. 'Sister Catherine has had similar results, the only difference being that Sister did not score below a distinction. But then she did not have to study a subject she had no interest in or aptitude for.'

'I'm happy, Mother,' said Agnes, especially since the prioress had acknowledged the handicap she had placed on her.

'And Dr Stevenson?'

'I am managing. I have taken precautions,' she said in response to a question posed in passing.

'See that you do. All that is up to you.'

'I understand. I will continue to take precautions.'

'I am reorganising your convent duties for the next term,' Mother Jerome went on, waving the subject of Philip aside with a flick of the hand. 'You will no longer be helping with relief teaching. Instead, I am assigning you to work with Sisters Bridget and Martha. Your time will be divided between them, mornings with Sister Martha and afternoons with Sister Bridget. That's when you are not at the university, of course. You will report to Sister Bridget this afternoon.'

Agnes left the prioress's office, trying to control her rebellious feelings. Once again, it seemed that doing well had earned a punishment. Instead of giving her wider teaching responsibilities, the prioress had downgraded her to menial domestic tasks on the one hand and to deadening administrative paperwork on the other. The self-effacing Sister Martha supervised the vegetable gardens and other sundry domestic duties while Sister Bridget functioned as the order's bursar. The motherhouse's most uninteresting room was the bursar's office, which bulged with files and loose, floating paperwork. It seemed out of place in a convent. That was a ridiculous thought, she had to concede, as her mind tried to suppress an aversion she knew was unreasonable.

More relevant was her term in first-year economics, giving her an insight into the sort of organisation required for a religious order. The relevance of economic thought to her life as a religious had never entered her head. It did now. Perhaps the need in the community for expertise in economics motivated Mother Jerome. That answered the question of the purpose, but the ultimate question still remained: why her? She would major in philosophy and history with English as a minor study. That prepared her for teaching and overseeing the Christian foundations of the order's educational establishments. All her abilities and inclinations rendered her suitable for proceeding in that direction. She could not resolve the question. By the time she appeared before the bursar, her practical nature had taken over, and she was reconciled to her new duties. To her surprise, it was not as bad as she had imagined.

Sister Bridget was a small sparrow-like woman who hopped unperturbed around her office, poking at piles of documents, picking at files, and disturbing reams of paper. At first, she seemed merely to be shifting elements in an overwhelming administrative chaos. But as the days passed, Agnes began to see a method in her managerial madness. The aspects of the economic and financial management of the vast structure of the order resembled a set of spinning wheels that had to be kept spinning. As Agnes followed the bursar's direction in preparing papers, filing others, and checking still others, she saw how competently the little sparrow managed the wheels. Then out of the chaos arose an ever-clearer picture of the balancing of income against outgoings, the care and stabilisation of property holdings, equipment and other capital acquisitions, account reconciliations, forward planning, and other such economic and financial matters. The visit from the order's accounting firm was a revelation. The experience and enlightened skills of Mammon were a necessary tool for maintaining the order's existence.

Although entirely different, her work with Sister Martha instructed her as much, perhaps more so. Rose Lewis, former Coles salesgirl and now Sister Martha, the least important in one sense, had always been a model of sisterly humility and goodwill. She was such a 'living example' of the Rule that Agnes did not always want to pay close attention to her. From afar—it was always from afar regarding the lay sisters—humble Sister Martha was, in a way, a constant reminder of her faults.

She was less than comfortable on the first morning that she reported. She anticipated the court of Martha's holiness and humility would roundly condemn her poorly supervised ambition. The uneasiness soon dissolved. Martha greeted her with joy and affection, as if she were welcoming a long-lost friend. She explained what needed to be done and then set about the work, showing the endless patience and affability a beloved family member would give. She did it all without the slightest awareness of the purity of her behaviour. At all times, Martha ensured that she and Agnes strictly adhered to the Rule. This was an example of the love of the Rule that the novice mistress had spoken about. As the three weeks of term holidays passed, Agnes became painfully aware that she needed this exposure to Martha to bring her back from the university campus to the religious life of the convent. Mother Jerome read Agnes like a book. Then, a few days before the start of term, a letter arrived addressed to her in a hand she recognised.

'You'll tell me if it is anything important, won't you, Sister?' said Mother Jerome, handing it to her.

'Of course, Mother. It's from a student in my philosophy tutorial. She's had trouble coping with the separation of her parents.'

Agnes had an intuition that it concerned something else. Her intuition was correct. A copy of the most recent Fourth Club Newsletter had come into Anne's hands. An article about her and Philip splashed across the front page.

'You should know about this,' wrote Anne, 'before lectures start next week. I'll talk to you then.'□

BLATANT BOURGEOIS CLASS PATRONAGE

'All independent thinking people know that religion is the tool of the bourgeois class to keep working-class people in their place. That people still wander unimpeded around the university, submitting impressionable minds to their tactics of indoctrination, is to be deplored. The independent socialist mind, however, must never lose courage in the class struggle. We must always have the courage to speak out, no matter what consequences issue from the privileged bourgeois class.

'It's no secret that a first-class papist holds a senior position in the philosophy department of John Batman University. It is no secret because Dr Philip Stevenson is ever ready to defend and justify the elephantine institution that has been responsible for history's most determined reign of murder, manipulation, and class oppression. The record shows that Dr Stevenson is ever ready to defend the Spanish Inquisition, that gory, blood-soaked gang of criminals who conducted one of history's greatest reigns of terror. Millions of women died in a holocaust of flames just because they were female.

'Duly honouring the great democratic principles that the Fourth Club subscribes to, we raise a voice of protest against a policy that allows students to wear the emblem of that oppression. We cannot stand by paralysed in inaction when Dr Stevenson effectively uses his position to advance his class oppression.

'For some time, students have raised questions about the cosy arrangement Dr Stevenson has with a particular Catholic nun. For what purpose did Dr Stevenson ensure that the nun was in his tutorial group? For what purpose did Dr Stevenson provide individual help and study sheets to this nun? Suspicions are not without basis. And why has Dr Stevenson been seen talking exclusively to that nun outside the lecture and tutorial room? These are questions that need to be asked and answered. Is the answer in the fact that the nun has scored the highest marks in her term exams?

'Why should Dr Stevenson get away with a blatant attempt to disadvantage students who have not been indoctrinated or forced to take the opiate of the working class? We leave that question to the independent minds on campus to answer—and to take action. It's no good to have a philosophy if we don't act on it.'

Sister Agnes had never read so much childish nonsense and in such juvenile prose. No one would swallow it, surely. Anne had asked the students in their tutorial group whether they agreed with the Fourth Club story or provided the information. All called it rubbish and denied ever talking to the fanatics who made up that demented group. Dr Stevenson gave no one an advantage. He was scrupulously fair. Besides, the best student in the tutorial was obvious. Agnes had no option but to show Mother Jerome the letter and newsletter. The prioress scanned the article and the letter and handed them back to Agnes with a dismissive gesture.

'This won't be the last time you have to deal with this sort of thing, Sister. You must prepare yourself to cope with it. Charity in everything, first of all. Secondly, you must make sure your history is correct. The

Inquisition is a favourite topic for those who hate the Church. It was not nearly as bad as they make out—nothing compared with atheistic communism's show trials and labour camps—and must be examined within society at the time. After all, the cultural context is the great weapon usually employed by these people to attack the Church's objective moral teaching. As for millions of women burned at the stake as heretics, this is one of their favourite fantasies. The treatment of witches had more to do with the remnants of pagan belief and pagan modes of punishment than with the Church, whose clergy were rarely responsible. The number killed is in the thousands rather than the millions, and women were often the instigators of the persecution. You must arm yourself against this slander, Sister. You are, after all, a history major.'

Sister Agnes took herself away from the prioress's office, not at all sharing her confidence and equanimity. It was one thing to deal with intellectual arguments against the slander of those socialist fanatics. It was another to deal with what they would actually do. They had treated Barry like so much dirt beneath their feet. He had warned her of the consequences of crossing their path. Philip had warned her of trouble. As soon as she returned to campus the following week, she set out to find Philip. To her dismay, a scribbled note pinned to his door stared at her, saying he would be back at the start of the third term. She hastened to the department office to learn whether he could be contacted. No, he could not be reached. Sister should direct her inquiries to the replacement tutor.

Agnes wandered, stunned, around the corridors, trying to come to grips with the news. She felt threatened. Who could she turn to? Philip acted as her ally and protector. But he had gone. Feelings of hurt and desertion arose within her, but she checked them. He had no duty to her, and she had no reason to expect special treatment from him. Catherine was, of course, the last person she could go to. No matter how much she tried, she could not put their past antagonisms behind her. Indeed, how 'past' were they? Catherine now behaved with prudence, but an undercurrent of antipathy and guardedness flowed through their contact—and an attempt to keep her at arm's length. Besides, Catherine had a connection with the Fourth Club, at least through her father, regardless of how tenuous. Suddenly, Agnes felt alone on campus, very alone. Then she thought of Philip's arrangements. She made her way to Dr Edelman's office.

'Don't take any notice,' he said, returning the article without reading it. 'This sort of adolescent polemic is part of the university. You have a legitimate grading in this department. That's all you need to worry about. Concentrate on this term's lectures on Descartes, Sister. I'm sure you'll find it just as interesting as Plato.'

'I'm not just worried about the marks,' said Agnes, unwilling to say what she feared.

'What?' he said, not understanding for a moment. 'Oh, no, no, Sister, plenty of anti-clerical people roam around the university, but the only pain they will cause you is verbal. So just shut your ears to it if you don't want to join the fray.'

Agnes was not convinced. The images of Barry's brutal assault and the desecration of the Bible were still fresh. She left Dr Edelman's office, realising she would no longer be at ease as long as the socialists targeted her. She made for the library, sure that it was the safest place to be between lectures and tutorials. They could not pester her there. After spending an hour reading background material on Descartes, she relaxed. But then, one of the socialist students installed himself at the desk in front of her. She looked on as he put his folders and books on the desk. Her anxiety receded as he attended to his books. She returned to her reading and note-taking. Five minutes later, the belligerent student stopped to chat with his friend. At first, they spoke in quiet tones. Then they raised their voices enough for Agnes to hear the lurid conversation. She could not endure it. She packed up to leave.

'Ah, Sister's leaving. I hope we did not say anything offensive. That would not be right, would it?'

Agnes made her way to the busy catalogue area, where there were a few desks. The belligerent student followed her. She sat at a desk and took out her book and notes. He began checking the cards in the catalogue drawer close by her. She looked at him, unable to concentrate. He remained there for five minutes, going from drawer to drawer, perusing cards, with an occasional glance in her direction. Agnes had to keep her eyes on him, prepared for anything he might do or say. But after five minutes, he smirked lazily at her and then strolled towards the entrance. A half-hour passed. Just when Agnes felt enough at ease to give her full attention to her reading, the first student appeared at her desk.

'Doing some background reading on Descartes?' he asked.

'Please don't bother me.'

Without changing his inquiring expression, he leaned towards her and made a disgusting proposal in equally disgusting terms.

'How dare you!' she said, rising.

'What's wrong, Sister?' he said, raising his voice a little. 'Not feeling well?'

Several students turned to them. Agnes knew she was trapped. She could do nothing without causing herself a lot of trouble and discomfort.

'You're a bully,' she hissed, gathering her book and notes together.

'I don't know what you're talking about. I was just trying to be help-ful.' He threw a look of incomprehension at a nearby student, who returned a knowing smile.

She hurried to leave the library, glancing around as she passed through the door. He came ambling after her as if he had no precise purpose. Where would she go? She stopped at one of the benches below the lawn, fearing her distracted manner would attract attention. She sat down, preparing for another assault. But the student walked past her without glancing at her. Ten paces on, he shouted. His friend, standing near the lawn, waved. They disappeared in the direction of the student union. Agnes was numb, realising this signalled things to come. She berated herself for not considering the obvious tactic.

'Hello, Sister, I've been looking for you,' said Anne, arriving from the library. 'Is there anything wrong? You look so pale.'

'No, no ... well, I've just had an unpleasant experience.' She could not suppress her shocked reaction to behaviour the like of which she had never experienced. Philip was right. Her whole life had sheltered her from this sort of people.

'What? Tell me?' said Anne, sitting beside her.

'Two of those students from the Fourth Club cornered me.'

'That's what I wanted to talk to you about. Come on, let's go to the Union cafeteria.'

'But they're sure to be there,' said Agnes, relieved to some extent by Anne's presence.

'It doesn't matter. They won't do anything there. Those slimy crea-tures won't do anything while I'm with you.'

'Don't be too sure,' said Agnes. 'They have no regard for a Catholic religious.'

'Come on, Sister. Your habit makes you vulnerable. And you can't retaliate. I can—the way girls can. You'll be even safer if Carmel and Barbara are there, too.'

Agnes decided she had no other option if she wanted protection. With some doubt and misgiving, she accompanied Anne. They came across Barbara and Carmel sitting well away from the Fourth Club group, who, in their usual way, talked noisily at a table covered with empty cups and food scraps. The two who had verbally assaulted Agnes were there. They looked around as Agnes sat with the three girls, a look of surprise covering their faces.

'That's them, isn't it?' said Anne.

Agnes nodded.

'What?' said Carmel.

Anne gave a brief account of the newsletter.

'Those creeps,' said Barbara. 'They're always here. You'd think they wouldn't have time to write those childish newsletters.'

'Tell us what happened in the library,' said Anne, 'and I'll tell you what I have found out.'

'What creeps and cowards!' exclaimed Barbara when she had finished. 'They only pick on people who can't retaliate.'

'They're getting at Philip through you,' said Anne. 'I've found out there have been some clashes between Philip and them—a sort of running battle. Philip makes fun of all that stuff about free love, freedom from authority, banning private property, and the rest.'

'It's not the one group,' said Barbara. 'Don't get them mixed up. The freethinkers and free-love people—the libertarians—have big differences with the socialists, though those revolting socialist creeps are also about free love. Yuck!'

'Whatever,' said Anne. 'Sister has to realise she's not their real target.'

'I'm not so sure about that,' said Agnes.

'You've heard about Gemma Greene, surely?' Barbara persisted. 'Just finishing her master's degree in English. You would hardly come across a bigger grub. Yuck. I don't know how she does it—boasts about it, too. She's a ringleader of the freethinkers, their star, in fact. If she doesn't get pregnant or catch some horrible disease in the end, I'll be surprised.'

'She's a convent girl, too,' Carmel added.

'I think it's more than that,' said Agnes, and she related the incident with Barry. 'They warned me they would not let me get away with it. Barry warned me, too.'

'Who's Barry?'

Anne pointed out who Barry was to the amusement of Carmel and Barbara. She was quick to put a stop to any mockery by mentioning Agnes's request.

'What will you do if they do it again?' said Carmel.

'I don't know exactly. I'll try to avoid them, I suppose. That's all I can do until I think of something more effective.'

'Stick with us whenever you can,' said Anne. 'They know we won't sit by and take it. They don't want too much attention to their bullying, either.'

'We'll give them attention,' said Carmel, looking furiously at them.

'Yes, but be careful who you take on,' said Barbara, persisting with the topic of Gemma Greene, one that clearly fascinated her. 'Nobody has a more poisonous tongue than that slut. She's the radicals' pin-up.'

Agnes was grateful for the fulsome support offered by the three girls, although she had doubts about their confidence. Barbara seemed worldly enough, but whether sufficiently sophisticated to deal with those boys remained a question. Furthermore, she did not want to have the girls mixed up in her problems. With these reservations, she decided to do her best to avoid places and times where the socialists could torment her and to keep the three girls' company whenever the occasion suited.

As it turned out, the strategy was partly successful. A week passed before three members of the Fourth Club managed to corner her in the library. Knowing what to expect, Agnes packed up and left her library desk. The boys followed her for a while, uttering their disgusting invitations whenever out of earshot of others. But they enjoyed limited success and had to retreat when she went to the information desk or sought help from library staff. When they repeated this mode of torment several times, with a similar lack of success, they left her alone in the library. Seeing the chagrin over their failure, Agnes had no doubt they would try something else. She was not disappointed. The aural assault changed to a visual one.

Some narrow passageways led through the labyrinth of buildings that made up the campus of John Batman University. Agnes could not avoid these paths as she went to lectures and tutorials. Her tormentors chose this as their point of attack. They stationed themselves at favourable points, and under the cover of the others, one would expose himself as Agnes came from the opposite direction. Evidently, they notched up a comprehensive victory over the purveyor of religious superstition from their gleeful shouts on these occasions. But as distasteful and insulting as the act was, the boys did not expose something entirely unfamiliar to her. For a start, she had three heedless younger brothers. She had found the verbal assaults far more intimidating. Her response of lowering her eyes and walking straight on dealt adequately with this new tactic. It did not discourage the students, though, who clearly gloried in their lewd behaviour and kept at it whenever propitious conditions presented themselves, fortunately not often.

Anne and her friends also helped her to cope by making good their promise of offering protection. They gave Agnes a copy of their lecture and tutorial programs and arranged times when they would be in the library or student union. And much to her surprise and pleasure, they seized on another tactic. Several weeks into the term, Agnes arrived at the student Union to see Barry sitting with the three girls. When she joined them, they acted as if it were the most ordinary event in the world to have that studious young man in their company. Barry's expression said he was wholly at ease. The tactic revealed itself when he made ready to go

.

'Come on, Barry,' Carmel said, 'we'll walk with you.'

Barry, scarcely able to contain his pleasure, followed the two girls. When they came near the loudmouth Trotskyites, Barbara, with lavish display, put her arm through Barry's. She gave that bemused contingent a sneering look as they passed by.

'I shouldn't laugh,' said Agnes, unable to suppress a smile at the tactic's effectiveness.

'You should,' said Anne. 'And I can see you have some satisfaction in seeing it.'

'It is unseemly of me.'

'You said you were only human, Sister.'

'That's true. Perhaps Barry may feel used.'

'No, we told him we supported you and wanted to do something. We suggested we show solidarity whenever those creeps appeared. He was a little reluctant and unsure at first, but he agreed when we showed we were serious and not making fun of him. He complimented us on a cunning counter-offensive. Don't you think he has changed a little?'

'Yes, yes, there is a noticeable change. He seems happier.'

'You were right. Deep down, he's not bad. If I—we—have made a difference, I'm happy, too.'

'You're a good girl, Anne.'

'Don't say that.'

'I mean, you're thoughtful, charitable. That's what I mean.'

Anne looked at Agnes. 'Why is it that I feel comfortable with you? It's like you're just another of the girls, but in funny clothes,' she said, repeating her previous comment with more emphasis. 'I'd like to see you in everyday girl's clothes. Perhaps it's that, as much as religion, that gets under their skins.'

Agnes brushed the comment aside with an embarrassed smile and prepared to go to her next lecture.

Chapter 32

Gemma Greene

DURING THIS time, a welcome distraction from Philip and the social-ists' campaign came—welcome only in the sense that the problem was not hers. On her return to campus after the term holidays, she noticed a change in Jannie de Kam. She was also aware that Jannie was spending more time with Catherine. At first, she did not pay much attention, attributing the change to her unstable disposition. As the days passed, the ups and downs in Jannie's behaviour flattened to leave her appearing worried and bewildered. She asked Catherine if anything was bothering Jannie. It was nothing more than the usual trials and tribulations we all must overcome in our lives, was the clichéd answer. The attempt to fob Agnes off only made her more curious, and when she caught Jannie on several occasions in deep conversation with Catherine, she became more than curious. Jannie had some nagging problem, and Catherine was giving her the benefit of her individual style of counselling. When she found Jannie in tears late one afternoon with Catherine at their usual meeting place, Agnes could no longer hold back.

'You're worried about something,' she said. 'Is there anything I can do?' She had taken them by surprise, so intent had they been on their conversation. Jannie started. For a moment, there was fear in her eyes.

'No,' said Catherine, irritated by the sudden interruption, 'we're dealing with it.'

'Something's bothering you a lot. I can see it.'

Jannie put her handkerchief to her eyes and turned away.

'You're interfering?' said Catherine. 'We are dealing with it.'

'That's not the impression I have.'

'Sister,' said Catherine, raising her chin, 'you're unaware of the detail. It's a matter she wants to share only with her closest friends. Outside interference is unwelcome and will only make things worse.'

Agnes could feel her blood rising. That smug, pompous—how irritating that Catherine could be! Agnes felt inclined to push the chin back into its place. Resisting the temptation, she resolved to seek Jannie out when she was not under Catherine's supervision. A few days later, she came across her sitting alone in the student union, ignoring the attention she usually thrived on.

'Do you mind if I sit with you while I wait for my friends?' she said, taking her place beside her. Jannie's head jerked up as if she had been disturbed in some guilty act. She shook her head. 'You have a problem you can't find your way out of, don't you?'

'I know you want to help,' said Jannie, 'but you can't. It's better you leave me alone.'

'You're pregnant, aren't you?'

Jannie's head jerked up again, and she went to say something, but her head dropped forward. 'I have cried so much there are no tears left.' She hesitated. 'How did you know?'

'I spent four years teaching girls. I dealt with a lot of problems nobody else wanted.'

'Schoolgirls pregnant?' was all Jannie seemed capable of saying.

'Every girl was a separate drama. You know who the father is?'

'Yes, I know who it is.'

'You have little choice but to marry him. That's the best solution. It will be too painful and difficult to go through the pregnancy and give the baby up.'

'Are they the only choices?' said Jannie, opening up. 'And what if the father doesn't want to get married?'

'Jannie ...'

'It's not as bad as that. It was a moment of affection that overcame both of us before we knew it.'

'Can't that be the basis for an enduring relationship?'

'He doesn't love me enough. I don't love him enough.'

'Jannie, you're responsible for creating a human person. Young people often get into this situation, where their sense of responsibility should hold them back. If it doesn't, they must face an even greater responsibility. You can't get away from it.'

'Speaking from experience, are you?' she said, adding: 'I've never been that calculating.'

'It's not calculating. It's having a sense of moral responsibility.'

'You sound like you did five years ago. It's not helpful.'

'Jannie, I'm sorry if I sound like I'm lecturing. The situation is serious. There's a life involved. You need to treat it seriously and show moral courage. Showing moral courage will be a comfort and consolation in the long run.'

Jannie stared at the ground in front of her. 'What do you say to the idea that I have a responsibility to myself, to my happiness, to my self-fulfillment?' she said, looking up.

'You can't mean that.'

'What if I did?'

'It's corrupt, selfish thinking that can only end in unhappiness. Jannie, it will destroy you from within.'

'Will it?' Jannie stood up, now with a purpose. 'You sound like you have experience in such things. Anyhow, I must go.'

'No, Jannie, I don't—please don't.'

'I appreciate your attempt to help. But you have said all you need to say. I must work it out myself now. Tell Catherine I will be at the usual place.'

Agnes, sad and helpless, watched her walk away. Her attempt to help did not work, she had to admit once again. There was a barrier she could not overcome—or even perceive clearly. Was Jannie getting that talk about self-fulfilment and independence only from Catherine or someone else? Then again, whatever the source of the rhetoric, Jannie had a mind of her own, capable of seeing the truth. Catherine arrived, glancing around.

'If you're looking for Jannie, she said she would be at the usual place,' said Agnes, answering Catherine's expression.

'Where's that?'

'I don't know. She said the usual—' Agnes understood Catherine was testing her. 'You know where it is.'

'You've been interfering again, haven't you?'

'I cannot stand by and listen to all that deluded talk about self-fulfilment and independence. You shouldn't, either. You're putting her on the wrong track.' It had been building up, and she could no longer hold back.

'You're your usual presumptuous self,' said Catherine, showing a premature crease at the corners of her mouth. 'Once again, you've probably done more damage than if you had held your tongue.'

'You're going too far—in all respects.'

'I can't stand by, as you can't, while you engage in harmful behaviour.' She moved a step forward, looking down at Agnes. 'We're no longer the teacher and the girl fresh from school.'

Agnes stood up, gathering her folders and picking up her briefcase. She would not let Catherine's imposing figure intimidate her. 'We mustn't stand here arguing. I'll suffice with the comment that the Church's teaching on pre-marital sex and pregnancy is unambiguous. It is teaching that is entirely rational, given what's at stake. Care should be taken when discussing freedom, independence, and self-fulfilment.'

'You can't help yourself, can you, Sister? You must wag your finger at everyone. Even if you don't see it, others recognise that I am capable of managing problems myself.'

'I have never doubted or denied your cleverness.'

'One thing you don't have, and I do, is a close friendship with Jannie.'

'Then, all the more reason to be prudent, Sister.'

'The message is not getting through, Sister.'

'I assure you it is.'

Catherine regarded Agnes calmly. 'Besides, who said Jannie is pregnant?'

'She did.'

'She imagines she's pregnant. It's not at all sure. So your advice could be disastrously premature.'

Agnes was caught without a reply. She just assumed—

'Well, well, well, if it's not that glorious Virginia Pearson,' a loud female voice called, interrupting the two sisters.

Agnes and Catherine turned to see a tall, attractive young woman dressed ostentatiously in the bohemian style making her way through the crowd of students. Many stood aside on seeing who it was. Catherine looked at Agnes, who had long expected this meeting.

'This is Gemma Greene,' said Agnes, happy for the interruption. 'Gemma is a former student. Gemma, this is Sister Catherine.'

Catherine nodded politely and said in her usual forthright manner, 'Greene? Are you from an Irish background?'

'Sorry, Sister, pure English stock. No ally in me. Besides, I don't recognise such cramping divisions.'

'Don't you?' said Catherine with a superior twitch of her eyebrows. She gave Agnes a quizzical look and excused herself.

'Imposing woman,' said Gemma, offhand. 'Probably wields the cane with the fury of an Irish harridan. Clever, too, I hear. But can't you just smell the Irish radical a mile off?' She grinned as if she thought she had thrown out a challenge. 'Such an unpleasant smell.'

'I've heard she has a good relationship with her students,' said Agnes, attempting to douse that line of interest.

'Well, what a shock it was when we returned to school in 1957 to learn that the young, vibrant Virginia Pearson, engaged and all, had entered the religious life,' said Gemma, ignoring the comment. She sat down, inviting Agnes with a nod to do the same. 'We were all absolutely floored.'

'Others enter the religious life,' said Agnes, sitting to lessen their visibility.

'Come off it, Ginny,' Gemma laughed. 'Tight, withered women, fearful of their sexuality, enter religious life. Not the Virginia Pearsons, not those bursting with their animal attractions.'

'Please don't call me that,' said Agnes, lowering her voice. 'Ginny' had been the girls' nickname for her. It had also been Philip's term of endearment. Fortunately, neither he nor anyone else had used it until now. 'I am, after all, a religious sister.'

'Ginny, you're a vibrant young woman who has clothed herself in black delusion.'

'Perhaps it's you who is afflicted by delusion,' said Agnes, knowing she should offer resistance if she did not want the articulate Gemma Greene to steamroll her.

'Don't give me that. The fantasy of religion won't stand up to the scrutiny of human reason.'

'You're right if you think human reason cannot fathom the depths of Revelation.'

'That's not what I meant. Be careful, Ginny, I'm no longer that obliging girl who hung on every word from the lips of the popular, lovable Miss Pearson, who most of us had a crush on.'

'I'm well aware of your academic progress—and your reputation.'

Gemma laughed again. 'Good. I hope you are. You should be. Let me tell you of the delicious—'

'Please don't.'

'I had great affection for you, you know. You're the only female I fell in love with. When I regard you now, there's—' Agnes did not answer. 'What are you studying?'

'Philosophy, History, English and Economics.'

'Economics? Why on earth? Now don't tell me. It was an order from on high.' Agnes did not answer. 'No matter, that's not the point. Dear Ginny, your Christian mythology will not survive a year of philosophy.'

'You think not?' Agnes had sat long enough to be polite and now made moves to go.

'It won't work, you know. You're not the type. You're too full of life and energy and intellectual curiosity. Your mind will not survive the cramped, boring, soul-destroying life of the religious.'

'You are of the opinion, no doubt, that religious life is reducible to a psychological state.'

'Psychological and sociological. It's not an opinion. I know so.'

'Gemma Greene is far more confident of such things than that smart, willing girl I used to teach.'

'I had my epiphany when I realised that all rules are arbitrary, and nobody has the right to intrude on my personal sovereignty.'

'They're high-flown words for self-indulgence. And you are smart enough to recognise it.' She stood up. 'I must go.'

'No, that won't work, Ginny. All acts are self-indulgent. And so they should be. All else is delusion—by self or by those wanting the power over others.'

'Sister, wait!' Agnes heard Anne's voice calling.

Anne arrived breathless, with Carmel and Barbara following. All three looked dumbfounded at Gemma Greene, who smiled affably.

'Yes, Ginny, don't go. We've not finished catching up. Come on, girls, sit down. Ginny, introduce me to your friends.'

Agnes would not risk inflaming Gemma's wit and cleverness. She sat and made the introductions.

'Ginny, you forgot to say you were my teacher,' said Gemma, with mock severity.

'Really?' said Anne. 'Sister really was your teacher?'

'My favourite teacher. Ginny was the girls' favourite teacher. I was in love with her.'

'Is that what the girls called her?' said Carmel while Anne and Barbara stared.

'Of course, she was known formally as Miss Virginia Pearson. "Ginny" was a far more appropriate name among the girls. She was no more than a few years older than most of us seniors.'

'What a surprise,' said Barbara, regarding Agnes with renewed respect.

'Yes, we don't know much about Sister,' said Anne. 'She won't talk about herself.'

'Well, here I am to answer questions,' said Gemma with a naughty grin.

'I should go,' said Agnes.

'No, Ginny, don't worry,' said Gemma, reaching out and taking her arm. 'I wouldn't say anything that would make trouble for you. I have too much respect and affection for you.'

'What did she look like—I mean, without the habit?' said Carmel.

'Everything about her was appealing—looks, manner, personality. It was an attractive combination.'

'What colour hair?'

'Brown, light brown.'

'I must go.' Agnes saw where the conversation was leading but remained seated.

'She was engaged, you know,' said Gemma, as if reading Virginia's thoughts.

'Really?' said all three girls together. They looked at Virginia, who now appeared nailed to the spot. 'Did you ever meet him? What was he like?'

Gemma did not answer. She fixed her gaze on Agnes, who was desperately trying to appear calm but appealing with her eyes. 'We never knew who it was,' said Gemma. 'One moment, we heard she was engaged; the next moment, it seemed, she had disappeared into the convent. We were all broken-hearted.' She still had her eyes on Agnes. 'I imagine her former fiancé was, too.' She stood. 'Must be going ... people are waiting for me. Ginny, it was great to see you again. Fancy ending up at the same university! What a coincidence. It's a pity I'll be off overseas next year. But we'll talk again.' With a friendly wave at the three admiring girls, she was off. Whispering followed her out of the Union cafeteria.

'I can't believe you taught the notorious Gemma Greene,' said Carmel.

'Yes, why didn't you say?' said Barbara.

Virginia tried yet again to explain the limits she had freely chosen to put on her life. She enjoyed the company of the girls, but there were conversations she should not participate in. Besides, she did not know if Gemma would be happy to make that information public.

'Well, you know now,' said Carmel. 'She was so sweet to you. But she can be a real bitch, people have said.'

'She may not want me to talk about her school days.'

'She doesn't care what people think of her,' said Barbara.

'I would rather not talk about her, given the change in her outlook.'

'Was she very different at school?' said Anne.

'She was a very sharp, intelligent girl, but a little sensitive. I am surprised to see her project such a hard image. It's difficult for me to accept she has changed so much on the inside.'

'I could use another word,' said Carmel. 'She's the most promiscuous woman on campus and boasts of it. She boasts of having ... well, you know ... important men, before they ... well, try it on her ... if you know what I mean.'

'That's sad. She's only damaging herself,' said Agnes. 'Anne, we must make a move if we don't want to be late for the lecture.'

Anne remained thoughtful until they were outside and on the path to the lecture halls.

'Why do you think Gemma Greene has changed so much?'

'I don't know for sure. It was common knowledge that Gemma had trouble with a distant father and a demanding mother. I only mention it in connection with your parental problems. You must not let it dominate you and determine your behaviour. One must try to understand why parents behave the way they do. They're just as human as you.'

That evening during Compline, the meeting with Gemma Greene came back to Agnes. Nobody who knew Gemma would be surprised that she had gone on to postgraduate study. Nor should anyone forget that a brilliant but sensitive girl who felt abandoned was at significant risk. So it saddened her when Barbara, with furtive delight, confirmed that she had gone wild. Still, more worrying at that moment was the trouble Gemma might cause. What did she know about her? Was she aware Philip had been her fiancé? Judging from her sly manner, she was inclined to think so when one of the girls asked her.

She had worried about the repercussions if knowledge about their former relationship came out. That would have been trouble enough, but with the accusations the Fourth Club trumpeted about favouritism, it had potentially become far more troublesome. Perhaps it was time to make it public. If she and Philip said nothing now and it was revealed later, they would accuse Philip and the department of a shocking cover-up. Motives would be sought. And what would they manufacture about her? How she wished Philip were there. Why did he go away right now? There was also Gemma's unsettling prophecy that her religious life would end in ruin. That should not worry her, though, given that Gemma had dismissed the faith she grew up in as mythology. But it did worry her. Gemma, sharp and insightful, had cheerfully foretold her failure. It was vexing—and unnerving.

SHE AND Catherine returned to campus the next day with an uncomfortable silence prevailing in the car and on the walk across the lawn. At the junction of the paths to the library and the lecture halls, Catherine left her, saying she had extra tutorials and seminars in the sociology department that would keep her busy all day. Agnes was relieved. She could barely cope with her presence. She wandered towards the library, her mind returning to the Gemma Greene problem and what she could reveal. Steps must be taken to avoid her and the enticement the meeting would bring. Of course, that did not prevent Gemma from telling people, for the fun of it, that Philip had been her fiancé. It tormented and frustrated her that she could not work out a solution to the problem. She caught sight of Jannie sitting on a bench, clasping her folders and books to her breast and looking at the ground in front of her.

'I thought you had seminars in the sociology department.'

Jannie looked up, blinking. 'What ...? No, there's nothing until later.'

'But Catherine said— Were you waiting for me or someone else?'

'No.'

'You don't know what to do, do you? I mean about your condition.'

'Please let me be. I don't want to talk about it. Your solutions are no solutions.'

'Jannie, I'm always available to talk,' said Agnes, taking that as confirmation she was indeed pregnant. 'You know what I think, but you must also know I have much sympathy for you. I know what it's like to face a distressing situation.'

'Do you? Thank you.' There seemed no life left in her. She got up. 'I must go now. I have to do something.'

'I pray that you do the right thing.'

Jannie did not answer. Agnes watched her shuffle across the lawn to the southern entrance.

AGNES'S strategies for avoiding the socialists and Gemma Greene bore results for a while. The socialists had some success, but not enough to cause more than a minor irritation. She was confident she could avoid Gemma without much trouble. After all, the whole term had passed without coming across her. Once again, as if there was a relentless conspiracy against her, she ran into Gemma, hurrying from the library's reserved section.

'Ginny! What a coincidence! I'm hardly ever in the library these days. I'm really glad to see you. Come on, let's have a drink. I want to chat about the past without anyone else present. And I promise I won't say anything rude.' Gemma's overwhelming personality would not allow a refusal, and Agnes followed her out of the library. In any case, a cup of coffee and a chat would not be a bother. There was another motivation, though, now that she could not escape. Gemma may be susceptible to a former teacher's advice, one she had declared affection for. She should at least try, however futile it may turn out. When they came to the lawn, Gemma turned onto the path leading out of the university.

'Where are you going?' said Agnes, stopping.

'You don't think I'm going to the student union, do you? Come on. Nobody will disturb us where we're going. I promise to preserve your dignity—more than in the student cafeteria.'

Thus reassured, Agnes walked beside Gemma while she gaily chatted about the past. They crossed the road outside the university entrance and headed for the pub nearby.

'We're not going there, are we?' said Agnes, looking at the pub she and Philip had visited.

'Don't worry. Satan's not there at this time of the day, so there's no occasion of sin. I promise you we'll be left alone.'

'No, Gemma, there's a limit. This is absolutely forbidden to me. I'm returning—'

'Okay, okay, you win—for the sake of our chat. There's a cosy Italian coffee lounge around the corner.'

When they had settled with their coffee, Gemma reminisced about her convent days, eliciting smiles from Agnes, who marvelled at the lucidity of her memory.

'You remember everything so clearly,' Agnes said when Gemma stopped to take a breath.

'As if it was yesterday.'

'You sound like you enjoyed your school days, a period spent with Catholic sisters, for the most part. There were only a few of us seculars.'

'On balance, yes. I have no trouble admitting that. There's no inconsistency. Looking back, I realise it was an entirely female atmosphere. It was an institution run by a bunch of women at a high professional level. It was very special, even unique. Male presence, just their presence, changes everything.'

'What were the drawbacks, then, if you liked the sisters' professional level?'

'I liked the young girl atmosphere. I liked the professional organisation of the nuns. But I discovered later that the institution's religious routine and philosophical assumptions were stifling and sometimes brought out the very worst in the female. That vitiated the good part to a certain extent and will mean the institution's downfall in the end.'

'You shouldn't take the human failure as the failure of the essential nature of the convent.'

'A nice distinction, Ginny,' said Gemma. 'The convent has not affected your analytical skills. But you mistake the issue. The essential nature is oppression.'

'The essential nature is the provision of truth. The truth about God's creation will set you free. You should know that.'

'Yes, I've heard that a million times. Unfortunately, there's no truth to know. That's Christianity's big con.'

'It makes me sad to listen to you speak like that.'

'Don't be sad, Ginny. I have a wonderful time enjoying myself.'

'Your misuse of God's abundant gifts saddens me.'

'God's gift! My intelligence is the result of random physiological happenings. I have been lucky to have more brain cells than most and to have the proportions of my body a little better put together than most. All the result of nature's whimsical selection. It's an explosive combination, as many a youth will tell you. No need to be sad.'

'You have a responsibility not to harm others.'

'Ginny, save me the lessons,' she said with good humour. 'I've heard it all before. Repeating it won't make any difference. It's not me doing harm, besides. Now forget all that. I want to reminisce with one of the sweetest people I have known, the teacher who had such an influence on my life. I'm now totally disregarding your fancy dress. Virginia Pearson is now in front of me.'

There was no stopping her. Agnes let her have her head, taking a mental step back to observe a former student bound to shake up the world somehow. But, despite Gemma's engaging and entertaining reminiscences, Agnes excused herself in due course, saying she had a lecture to attend.

'You know what I would like to do?' said Gemma. 'I would like you to slip into slacks and a jumper, like the ones you used to wear, and come with me on a drive along the coast all the way down the peninsula to Sorrento as we did on those excursions. Wouldn't you like to do that?'

Agnes knew exactly what she was referring to. Those joyful, rollicking excursions with a bunch of high-spirited girls not much younger than herself were among her most pleasurable memories of those days.

'Hah! I've got you thinking. Come on. I can rustle up some casual clothes for you.'

'Gemma, you're incorrigible.'

'That's me.'

'I have to go, Gemma.'

'Come on, no one will know. We'll have fun. People will see how cute you are. You can get back into that fancy dress later.'

'No, Gemma, I must attend lectures.'

'Hmmm,' she said dreamily, 'I almost had you.'

'No, you didn't.'

'Ginny—'

'Please don't call me that, Gemma.'

Gemma still had that faraway look as Agnes stood up. 'Do you know what day it is?'

'Of course.'

'I mean, what happens on this day, Thursday, the twenty-first of June?'

'If you're not referring to today's feast day, I've forgotten.'

'I'm certainly not referring to a Church feast day, but to a feast day celebrated from the beginning of time. You don't know?'

'No, what?'

'The winter solstice, of course. Ginny, I'm surprised you don't know. In Europe, it's the summer solstice or midsummer's night. You know Shakespeare's glorious comedy?'

'Of course, a time of lightheartedness and frivolity—'

'A lot more than that as young bucks lustfully eyed the maidens around the bonfire,' said Gemma, laughing loudly.

'I must go.'

'I'll come with you,' said Gemma, reluctantly getting up.

'There's no need, Gemma. I can find my way back.'

'Your naivety is endearing, Ginny. Come on. No one will bother you if they see who you're with. Keep clear of that outrageous Gemma Greene, they'll say!' She laughed loudly again.

'You see. Basically, you're considerate.'

'Basically?' Gemma smiled a little wistfully. She accompanied Agnes in silence to the university's entrance, where she stopped. Her expression softened.

'Whatever you are now,' said Agnes, getting in before she could speak, 'I will always remember that sharp young girl with the good heart.'

'Won't you reconsider? The winter solstice is the time to forget past grievances. It's the time to show friendship and love as nature reaches its full descent before beginning its rejuvenation in light. We'll go down to the peninsula. There are some spots where some friends gather wrapped in the arms of Mother Earth as she begins to rise again, filling us with her spirit.'

'You're not serious. I mean, about this sort of nature—'

'I'm serious about gathering with friends and celebrating our connections in and with nature. Come on, you'll feel it. We gather in a circle and watch the fire rise, slowly shedding its light around. We chant about the providence of nature, and we feel the spirit of the earth rising up within us.' Gemma's brash, confident manner had deserted her for the moment. 'A little time out in friendship with other women is not so much different from your life of ritual, is it?'

'A lot different,' said Agnes, scarcely able to contain her amazement. 'You don't take all that nature worship seriously, do you? How does that reconcile with your rejection of God and truth?'

'You would find out. The autonomy I claim intellectually is perfectly reconcilable with the spirit of nature. The spirit within is perfectly autonomous. And that spirit is female. It transcends theory. You have a lot to learn, Ginny. I'm giving you a glimpse of the future.'

'I can't believe what I'm hearing.'

'You're too young in spirit to take it in. You must drink the milk before you can have the full richness of the food that lies ahead. Tonight would give you a glimpse of that feast.'

'No, Gemma, not now, not ever.'

'We'll see. We'll see what happens as your philosophy lectures take apart your Christian mythology piece by piece.'

'You seem to subscribe more to mythology than I do.'

'That comment merely shows how little you understand. Human mythology is the key to understanding the spirit. It's the sublime literature of the spirit.'

'You're right. I don't understand. Now I really must go.'

'It would've been a good night, Ginny. You would've liked it as much as those school excursions.' Agnes gave her a curious look. 'Hah! You got a peek,' cried Gemma.

'Goodbye, Gemma.' She walked away.

'You'll become Virginia Pearson again,' Gemma called after her. 'At the end of the year, I'll see that glorious girl who made hearts flutter.'

Virginia walked on. She dared not look back. When she had mounted the stairs leading up to the pathway through the lawn, she gave in to the temptation. Gemma stood outside that pub with one hand on the door handle. She waved when she saw her.

FOR some time after lights-out, Agnes lay in the dark, eyes wide open. Eventually, she rose, put on her gown, and sat by the window. It was cloudy with little moonlight. Through the dim haze, she could just make out the river curling around the bottom of the property. If her suspicions were correct, something would happen. Time passed slowly, but sleep did not come. Whether it was because of her unsettled mind or the anticipation, she could not guess. Then, around midnight, she heard the faint tolling of a bell. It seemed to come from across the river. Five minutes later, an object appeared on the river. 'I'm right,' she whispered. She wrapped herself in her winter coat and made for the stairs as noiselessly as possible. On the ground floor, she hurried to the big wooden door and reached for the handle.

'Sister! What on earth are you doing at this hour of the night?' Mother Cecilia called.

Staggering, she swung around. 'I thought I saw something by the river,' she stammered, embarrassed to be seen out of her habit and wearing the silly nightcap. She wrapped her coat tighter around her.

'And why do you think you have to investigate?'

'I wasn't sure what it was.'

'You are not making much sense, Sister. Please return to your room.'

'But I—'

'You will leave this to others,' Mother Cecilia ordered. 'How dare you take it upon yourself. You still have a lot to learn, Sister.'

Agnes returned to her cell, thwarted. Why was Mother Cecilia walking around at that time of night? She took her position at the window again, her senses on heightened alert. But apart from a hazy movement on the stairs and a faint glimmer by the river, there was nothing else. In the early hours of the morning, sleep overcame her. Next thing, the bell echoed through the corridors, leaving her in a benumbed stupor to prepare for chapel. That evening, she responded to the expected summons.

'What do you mean by wandering around the building at night?' said Mother Jerome, whose expression did not match the demand.

'I thought I saw something on the river.'

'That's what you said to Mother Cecilia, and like her, I don't find that an adequate explanation. So make me understand.'

'It was undoubtedly a repetition of what I had seen before. It was a boat on the river, presumably with people to make a rendez-vous with others from the convent. I wanted to get in a position to confirm my suspicions.'

'Go on. There must be more.' Now there was a flicker of interest in the prioress's eyes.

'I've never been able to establish a connection between all those events. I suspected there was a link, but I had no idea what it could be until now. You spoke, too, of indistinct problems in the convent. Nothing made sense until now. And I don't know whether I'm right, anyhow. Today is the summer solstice, a time, someone told me, for women to come together and be wrapped in the arms of Mother Earth. Why was Mother Cecilia up at that time of night?'

Mother Jerome looked at her as if she were not entirely present. 'Mother Cecilia is the novice mistress. She needs to be up at all times,' said the prioress, but then vaguely looked past her. 'I would like you to keep this to yourself for the moment. Don't say anything until I call you. Is that clear?'

'Yes, Reverend Mother.'

Chapter 33

Agnes's dark moments

SISTER AGNES drifted into a dark downward spiral after her meeting with Gemma Greene, who gaily forecast the disintegration of her religious beliefs. She did not know whether her former student was the sole cause or a combination of events. Perhaps the onset of the cold, grey winter months affected her. But, no, she had never had any trouble with the winter, and she gave that up as a cause of her inexplicable depression. Depression? She could not remember ever experiencing depression. Instead, a foreboding mixed with weariness and dryness of spirit gripped her. She tried to deepen her meditation, returning to those biblical passages and the lives of the saints that had always inspired her. It did little good. Nothing dispelled the foreboding or the drying-up spirituality. Not even the opening paragraph of St Augustine's *Confessions* had its usual inspiring effect. She tried to console herself with St Augustine's account of his struggle against temptation and his search for God. To no avail. Agnes did not feel the turmoil of struggle. It was the opposite; it was a catatonic dryness. This thought passed through her mind while wryly acknowledging her perverse exaggeration.

Her philosophy lectures and tutorials maintained her interest but did nothing to ease the greyness of her feelings. In contrast to the first-term lectures on Plato and Aristotle, the lectures on Descartes' *Meditations*, engaging though they were, presented such a disjunction between ordinary life and abstract thought that she felt pushed further down that spiral. For how could you realistically dismiss the material evidence of our senses, even for the sake of an abstract activity that aspired to clear up other pressing philosophical problems, as Descartes suggested? How could you suspend belief in the room you sat in, in the fire that warmed you against the cold winter outside your room, and in the book you held in your hands? It led to a dead-end road whose cul-de-sac presented a wall of madness. At least Plato and Aristotle's starting point for their speculation was man in all his concrete forms.

It intrigued her that her fellow students did not have the same trouble understanding Descartes as they had with Plato. Did that say something about the clarity of Descartes' arguments or their depth? Whatever the case, she understood her task was to examine the arguments and assess them. This she set about doing clinically. And so, her first essay on Descartes' arguments about certainty and scepticism brought on the first of several events, slight though some of them were, that left her shaken. After handing out the assessed essays at the end of a tutorial, Philip's replacement tutor and lecturer on Descartes, Dr Joseph Edelman, asked her to stay on for a moment.

'You've done very well,' he said, pointing with much emphasis. 'You have kept up an excellent standard.'

Agnes thanked him, pleased she had satisfied the standards of a lecturer, outspoken about his atheism. The finger heralded, she suspected, a sting in the tail.

'Never fear I will penalise you because I think some of your views are fantasy,' he said with a knowing smile.

'I'm sorry. Did I give that impression?'

'Not entirely. But it's worth saying you should not judge us—I mean all us terrible atheists—by what Trotskyist numbskulls do on campus. I'm a friend, too, of your patron in the department.'

Agnes reddened. 'I hope I do not display such prejudice, Dr Edelman.'

'Sister … a bit of kidding. Don't take me so seriously. But let's get one thing clear: I wouldn't waste a jot of contempt on that scurrilous rag put out by those lunatics if there's a sneaking fear troubling you. Philip's a man of intellectual integrity, whatever else I think of his metaphysical position.'

'I'm sorry, Dr Edelman. I'm … we are not used to kidding. And I'm not offended. I'm just not used to—'

'That's all right, Sister. This is not what I wanted to say.' He waved his hand and looked away for a moment. 'As you know, I read your first two essays. Excellent, they were. Now I notice a big difference between the mood, so to speak, of those first-term essays and this second-term essay. You wrote the first with passion and excitement, and the second with a cold, clinical, almost distasteful approach. It was as though you were handling something that stank.'

'I had more affinity with thoughts of Plato and Aristotle.'

'And Descartes—what are the feelings?' She hesitated. 'Sister, don't be afraid to say what you think. Saying what you think is the point of this conversation.'

'Descartes' writings struck me more like a verbal game rather than a genuine attempt at deepening our knowledge and wisdom about human existence.'

'Well put. You're not the only one to have a go at Descartes for that reason. Some people—I'm not one of them—think the whole of philosophy took a wrong turn with Descartes' *Meditations*.' He raised his eyebrows. 'I am wrong in thinking you're inclined to agree with that view?'

'I don't know enough to make that judgment at this stage.'

'Or is it because you're afraid of where your clear-headed reasoning is leading you?'

'What ... what do you mean?'

'Are you handling something that stinks or something that is leading you inexorably where you think you mustn't go?'

'You think I'm afraid of the conclusions Descartes' arguments are leading to?'

'It's even more fundamental than that. Are you perhaps afraid of the unrelenting process of reason, afraid some of your beliefs may not stand up to it?'

'My specific criticism of Descartes so far is about the misuse of reason. Perhaps your judgment is outrunning the evidence.'

'Very good, Sister. You're keeping up, but for how long?'

'What's the point of this?'

'The point is this: I'm a philosopher who thinks the obstacles littering a closed mind should not hold back the philosophical enterprise, which is the application of our reason.'

Agnes regarded him defiantly.

'You're a young woman with a sound mind. As your philosophy tutor, I want you to use it.'

'Nothing I have written or said so far seems to have been held up by the obstacles you have mentioned.'

'Not yet. That's why we are having this talk. You've been fair to Descartes, but only just.'

'You have given me a High Distinction,' she said, consulting her essay.

'Only just. You made a fair attempt to include all the positive elements of his argument, but it was grudging and defensive.'

'If you are right, I'm not the only one who does that.'

His expression softened. 'Look, I don't mean to put you on the defensive. I want to be positive—show you the gate is open if you want to walk through.'

'The gate is open?'

He looked at her as if not sure of how he should proceed. 'What's your name—I mean, your real name?'

'That's not relevant to anything.'

'I'm sorry. There's a point.'

'If there's a philosophical point and you won't misuse that information ...?'

'I promise.'

Realising he could find out quickly enough, she said, 'Virginia Pearson.' Indeed, he may know already.

'Let's say Virginia Pearson is a clever young woman who had a promising academic path ahead of her,' he said with a look of satisfaction. 'At a certain moment, she took a turn away from that path, picked up a religious name with all that's attached to it, and by fortuitous circumstance came back on that academic path. I would like that clever Virginia Pearson to be courageous and mature enough to go where her mind is leading, even to the extent of passing through the gate where she leaves the religious name behind—together with all those other things.'

'There is a string of assumptions in what you say,' she dared to say.

'Those assumptions can be defended. Your religious beliefs will find it difficult to bear the scrutiny of human reason. I would hate to see you end up in the neurotic intellectual paralysis that others in your line have found themselves. It would be such a waste.'

'A waste?' she said, frowning and shifting in her chair.

'A waste of a clever young mind,' he emphasised, pointing. 'That's all I have to say, Sister, other than looking forward to your next essay. Be free, of course, to come to see me whenever you want. I hope I have not kept you too long.'

'Thank you for your concern,' she said, straightening herself. 'When will Dr Stevenson be back?'

'Sometime towards the end of the second-term holidays, I'm not sure when,' he said, a trace of embarrassment appearing on his face.

'Where has he gone?'

'Do you have a special interest?'

'It's none of my business, I know,' she said, meeting his steady but unsuspecting gaze. 'I was only curious because I heard other students talking about him. You know the rumours that spread, and things happen.' She stood, preparing to leave his office.

'Oh, yes, the rumours! I'm aware that Phil's girlfriends are of interest to the female students. You can tell your fellow students Phil took leave to catch up on some research. There's absolutely no girlfriend involved this time. I know for sure. He'll be back as scheduled.'

She walked to the door. 'One of the students thought he was involved with Gemma Greene,' she said, again on impulse and aware of the fib.

'You can tell that student Gemma Greene will never have her way with Philip Stevenson. I'll tell Phil of your concern for his Catholic soul,' he added, smiling.

She bade him a good day, regretting her impulsive questions, hoping she had left him with the misapprehension that only Philip's soul concerned her. But she could be happy about nothing else. Everything else, though seemingly inoffensive, left her uneasy. She would survive whatever Descartes would present regarding reasoning—nothing she had read had made her doubt her beliefs—but her tutor displayed unshakeable confidence that she was vulnerable to what would follow. He had seeded another insidious doubt in her mind, and she had no choice but to wrestle with it. It was a nuisance. And Dr Edelman's motives? She did not want to think about it.

The question, however, nagged her at the perimeter of her consciousness. No, no, she must be wrong, she told herself firmly when it became too insistent. After all, she was wrapped in such unsensual clothing. Surely that would put a worldly man like Dr Edelman off. Thoughts of her pre-convent days and her relations with young men flowed back. She was liked. She knew men found her attractive, not in the same way as an incontestable beauty like Jannie de Kam, and certainly nowhere near the ethereal heights of Aine Winterbine, but appealing, nevertheless. She remembered the attention. Again, she was forced to entertain thoughts not at all wanted at the surface of her consciousness.

She observed Joseph Edelman in the following tutorials, but he gave no hint of that sort of partiality. Without the relief she wanted, she pushed that suspicion out of her mind, feeling she had been unfair to someone who now only seemed eager to do his duty as a teacher, however wrong-headed his motivations. The days passed with these thoughts flowing through the mechanical activity of attending lectures and tutorials and preparing essays. She used the tutorial assignments as an excuse to avoid the company of Anne and her friends outside regular class times. Their high spirits and conversation did not help her efforts to rise above her black mood. The one relief was that the Fourth Club now left her alone. The thought occurred to her that they might be leaving her alone because of Catherine's presence, whom she sought out more often in a determined attempt to stick to the Rule. She dismissed the suspicion as baseless and a manifestation of their unfortunate antagonism. Even so,

her renewed efforts to keep Catherine's company precipitated the next jolt
.

Agnes's tactic to keep track of Catherine had been to wait for her close to her lecture hall and tutorial room. This worked well. Catherine could only make excuses if she had a genuine reason to stay behind in the Sociology Department, for it was usually her companions in sociology that she sought. In the unusual event that one or both had an unexpected delay, they would meet at an agreed place in the library. One afternoon, a discussion about the time for a special English tutorial delayed Agnes. Once the time was fixed for this 'extra special' tutorial on heroines in the nineteenth-century English novel, with a 'mystery' guest, she hurried to meet Catherine at the appointed place. As she expected, Catherine had not waited. She checked that she was nowhere in the Sociology Department. With feelings of exasperation, she headed for the library. But she could not find Catherine anywhere.

Taking out her books and lecture notes, Agnes settled at a desk to wait. Her mind, however, stayed on Catherine's unusually flagrant transgression. It was not like her, always having that knack of worming her way around the rules, deceiving all and sundry. Even when heavily involved in Jannie's affairs recently, she had managed to keep up the wobbly pretence of sticking to the Rule ... Jannie! Jannie and her problems had not occupied her for some time. As she ran her mind over their last meeting and her clash with Catherine, an intuitive connection between Jannie's disappearance more than a month before and Catherine's unusual transgression flashed through her mind. Jannie had taken time out from study to deal with her problems, Catherine had said. She should be back by now, surely. Agnes packed up her books and notes and hurried from the library.

She walked briskly, stopping herself from breaking into a run, hoping and praying her intuition was wrong. For this would herald a new phase in her relationship with Catherine. As she came around the hedge into view of the benches on the lawn, she stopped, breathing heavily. 'Oh, no, she couldn't have,' she whispered. As a confirmation of her terrible premonition, Catherine was at ease on the bench, chatting with Jannie. She approached slowly, not because she wanted to sneak up on them but because she had gone weak in her legs. Her mind cut out her surroundings, leaving her to focus on the two women. Catherine's imposing bulk, accentuated as usual by the black habit, projected more than ever a rock-like immovability; Jannie's handsome face shone with newfound confidence. As she got nearer, she could not help fixing on the trivial thought that Jannie seemed to become better looking with time. Jannie could now class herself as a genuine beauty without fear of ridicule.

'You could not have,' said Agnes, standing before them.

They looked up at her, not much moved by the sudden interruption.

'Couldn't have what?' said Jannie, barely looking at Agnes.

'You should be careful of making assumptions before you go any further,' warned Catherine.

'How could you overthrow all that you have been taught?'

'Overthrow? I've overthrown nothing,' said Jannie, barely glancing at Agnes. 'I've only acquired a deeper understanding of what it all means.'

'This is your doing,' Virginia said to Margaret.

'You are entitled to your thoughts,' said Jannie, standing up at her full fashion model height, so she looked down at Agnes. 'From now on, I want you to treat me as an independent, self-sufficient woman. Otherwise, I will ignore you.' She sat down. 'Neither you nor Margaret or anyone else, for that matter, will tell me how to act, what to do, or what to say.'

Catherine's smug, knowing expression and the implied responsibility for what she saw before her would usually cause Agnes's blood to rise. But, again, she focused on the trivial aspect of Jannie's clothes. Until now, Jannie's clothes had exuded a tasteful flamboyance aimed at compensating for her insecure feelings and unstable personality. That tasteful flamboyance had gone; a quiet confidence in subdued colours and elegant cut had come in its place. Agnes could not stop the tears on her cheeks.

'For heaven's sake, control yourself, Sister!' said Catherine. 'Find out the real situation before you give an embarrassing display of your emotions.'

'I will pray for you and the innocent you have—'

'I told you not to make assumptions,' Catherine said, speaking over her.

'I can't help the conclusions you drew from your unwanted interference,' said Jannie. 'You're upsetting yourself for nothing.'

Agnes stumbled away, half shielding her face with a folder. She made her way to the path leading to the library. There she sat on a bench and bent over the open folder, pretending to read. When nobody was looking, she pulled her handkerchief from deep in her pocket and wiped her eyes. She could hardly think; she had nothing to say but the obvious against an act so self-evidently wrong. How could she ever understand it? So she remained there, staring at her lecture notes and letting the jumble of thoughts take possession of her mind.

At length, it occurred to her that Catherine had not followed her as she should have. That was a relief; she could not bear looking into her smug face at that moment. Many connections formed as the spike of her helpless revulsion and outrage eased, and her mind brought order to her reflections of Jannie's actions from the convent days onwards.

They were beginning to explain .... Her mind flashed to something she had seen not long before her confrontation with Catherine and Jannie. She snapped the folder shut, collected her briefcase, and headed for the Sociology Department.

Being on the move helped her deal with her emotions. And it helped her focus. Where had she seen it exactly—a splash of colours catching her eye as she searched for Catherine? She walked the length of the hall, past the lecturers' and tutors' offices and the seminar room, but did not see it. Perhaps she had missed it in her distracted state. She retraced her steps to the entrance and started again, carefully this time. There it was on the wall beside the stairs, the rainbow-coloured poster that had caught her eye earlier.

*

The Aquarian Company
Harmony and understanding!
Come, be the first companions in the journey to the New Age.
Winter Solstice will be celebrated on 21 June 1962

*

Contact details were under the announcement, giving a room number in the department and an address in a nearby street. Virginia stared at the brief notice. Ordinarily, she would have attached little importance to it if she had even bothered to stop and read it. It would have appeared as yet another notice of the many student clubs and associations making their home on campus to satisfy young adults' unstable and searching inclinations. But for some reason, the bold lettering and the colours stayed like a snapshot in her mind. She remembered Gemma's invitation to join an exclusively female company to celebrate the winter solstice. She summoned the boldness to go to the department office to ask whether they had any information on the Aquarian Company. The office secretary seemed to find nothing unusual in the request and answered that such notices had nothing to do with the department. Sister should note the contacts. She returned to the notice and jotted down the information. The room was on the second floor.

After some hesitation, she mounted the stairs and made her way along the corridor, counting off the numbers. About halfway down was an open door where the correct number should be. She glanced warily into the room. She recoiled, turned, and hurried away. Leaning over the desk, talking excitedly, and looking at a poster were Gemma Greene and a man about Philip's age, both dressed in the familiar bohemian style. Fortunately, they had been too immersed in their conversation to have heard anything. She returned to the entrance and checked the name against that room number on the staff list. Later in the library, she checked the name in the student handbook. He lectured in, among other things, the sociology of religious organisations and primal cultures. The following day after the English tutorial, she asked Anne to make inquiries for her.

'Whatever for?'

Agnes, caught without a reply, said she was interested in the clubs on campus. Fortunately, that seemed a satisfactory answer, and Anne hurried away, saying she would do her best. It suited Agnes that Anne had her mind on other things then. Indeed, she had for a few weeks been keen to go off by herself. There could only be one reason. While waiting for whatever she could dig up, Agnes was left to contemplate and deal with Jannie's terrible choice, her independent choice as a woman. As anticipated, she was now in a new phase with Catherine, who would encourage Jannie never to slacken in her journey to independence and self-fulfilment. The car trip to the university each day became painful, with both women refusing to look at each other. Mr Ferguson struggled to get a conversation going but had to give it up.

'It's not much fun driving you two in anymore,' he said to Agnes, whom he seemed to consider more approachable. 'You should work out whatever is bothering you.'

Agnes was mortified to find her problems with Catherine so visible and apologised for their rudeness.

'I'm just as concerned about you as I am about the lack of pleasant company,' Mr Ferguson said. 'I'm old enough to understand some personalities do not get on, but something more is happening here.'

It was another blow to her heart. Someone else was warning her. She was losing touch. She suspected she did not even see all she struggled with. A few days later, Anne brought some coherence to her thinking. She had done her best to get information about the Aquarian Company but had not been too successful.

'It was strange,' she said. 'The lecturer asked about my motivation, and I just said it seemed interesting. When I asked for written information, a brochure, or something, he said it would serve better if I attended one of their meetings. Reading about it from handouts would not convey the core meaning of their activities.'

'He gave you no idea of what it was about?'

'Well, vaguely. He said the movement was spiritual, about promoting harmony and understanding between all peoples, no matter who they were. I must have looked as if I didn't understand, because he then said that the world was passing from one age to another, that people would learn to put the causes of wars and disharmony behind them, and that they would experience inner enlightenment. It all sounded very mysterious.'

'Mysterious?'

'Yes, he seemed to imply there was some hidden mystery or secret to be learned about the world or us. But then he changed his manner and said the group had a lot of fun together, and I was sure to make a connection.'

'Are you—I mean, did it appeal to you?'

'No, it sounded weird. He sounded weird. And I have other things to do.' She shrugged. 'Oh, yes, there was something else. He said modern industrial society had lost its connection with nature. As a result, people had lost sight of their place in the harmony of the cosmos. For one's sanity, one had to reconnect with the earth as the giver of life. That was enough for me. I excused myself.'

'Did he mention anything about individual autonomy and self-fulfilment?'

'No. But I didn't give him a chance to go on.'

'Does Aquarius mean anything to you?'

'Only as something in astrology. And you?'

'No, I know nothing about astrology.'

Despite the paltry information, Agnes saw a connection, tenuous though it may be, between the Aquarian Company and Jannie and Margaret. She tried to gather more information at the library, but the search was tedious, and she did not have time to spend on it. In frustration, she left it in her head as a question.

Chapter 34

Diana rescues Philip

HOPING TO put these matters out of her mind, Agnes arrived some days later for the special tutorial on the heroine in the nineteenth-century English novel. It was in Vic Brennan's office and arranged for his first- and second-year group. The nineteenth-century English novel was her favourite literary sort, so this tutorial promised to be a welcome distraction. As she settled in her chair, prepared to be entertained, a familiar voice came from outside in the corridor. The next moment, Gemma Greene breezed into the room with Vic, drawing a gasp from the other students. She tapped Agnes on the knee as she walked by to take the seat offered to her. With a brief introduction praising the high standard of Gemma's postgraduate work, Vic handed over the session and took a seat opposite Patricia Coghlan, who gave him an affectionate eye.

'Before I start,' said Gemma, with an arch smile, 'I want to say that the best teacher I ever had sits in this room.'

There was a moment of surprise and confusion as the students looked at Vic and then around the room, some eyes coming to rest on Agnes.

'Sister Agnes?' said Vic.

'Yes, Sister Agnes was my teacher in my final year of school.'

'I didn't know that,' said Vic. 'I'm surprised you said nothing, Sister.'

'Nuns don't talk about themselves,' said Gemma. 'And certainly, Sister Agnes would not put herself forward.' The students looked at Agnes with renewed interest. 'Miss Pearson, as she was then, did not teach in a dry monotone. She led. She made classes a journey of discovery. And that's what I'll do now—adopt Miss Pearson's very effective method.'

Agnes, wondering about Gemma's purpose, was relieved when she launched into her presentation. She spent the next ten minutes reviewing the role of the heroines in several of the period's best-known works, including Jane Austen's Elizabeth Bennett in *Pride and Prejudice* and Emma Woodhouse in *Emma*, Dorothea Brooke in George Eliot's *Middlemarch*, Becky Sharp in *Vanity Fair* and Estella Havisham in *Great Expectations*. It was a spellbinding performance, demonstrating a biting wit, keen insight, and a thorough knowledge of the plot of each novel. Even before Gemma returned to the same group of novels and heroines, Agnes could see a theme emerging.

Gemma considered each heroine for her individuality, independence of spirit, and self-sufficiency. As *Pride and Prejudice* and *Middlemarch* were the set texts for the first-year students, Gemma came to concentrate on the roles of Elizabeth Bennett and Dorothea Brooke. She led the students through a discussion of these two characters, focusing on the three qualities. Agnes was content to add her comments, but that did not seem enough for Gemma. Increasingly, she appealed to her to assess her fellow students' views as if it were her duty to resolve all differences. Wishing to avoid a clash, Agnes expanded on the group's analysis, pointing out what she thought had been missed. But Gemma was not satisfied.

'What do you say to the claim that Mr Collins, that pompous clerical bag of wind in Pride and Prejudice, brought into focus the inequities in Regency society and Elizabeth's reaction to them?' she said, looking at her. 'Was this not an unassailable demonstration of the independence Jane Austen thought all women should possess, and was denied to them?'

Agnes was pushed into a corner. Gemma had exaggerated her point to provoke her. Gemma was well aware of her thoughts about this scene. She had no choice but to state what she had said in class six years earlier.

'To interpret Elizabeth's rejection of Mr Collins's proposal, however arrogant and pompous, in the context of the so-called inequitable position of women in Regency society is to miss, or even misrepresent, Jane Austen's point of view and what she was attacking here.'

'The so-called inequitable position of women,' Gemma repeated with a sequence of exaggerated expressions. 'Well, I do declare—'

'Each of Jane Austen's six novels, together with the unfinished novels and letters that survive,' Agnes began reluctantly, 'demonstrate that Jane Austen did not challenge the fundamental structure of the society she lived in. Neither did she reject the Christian religion. She was quite devout. In both the secular and religious contexts, she accepted traditional ideas on the differences between men and women, which played out with fallible fidelity in her society. Jane Austen's concern was to focus on human frailty. The focus was on virtue and vice. Mr Collins was a failure in moral terms, not in social structural terms. We meet the same moral failure in Mrs Elton in Emma and Mrs Norris in *Mansfield Park*. One could call Mrs Norris the most heartless woman in the nineteenth-century English novel.'

'Well, that's unequivocal enough. So we have a debate, don't we?' Gemma said with an appreciative nod. Vic also nodded, which drew a glance from Patricia.

A vigorous discussion followed, with all students taking part initially. As the discussion progressed, taking in all of Jane Austen's works, the conversation became restricted to Gemma and Agnes. Although Agnes held her own, even against the biting wit, she suspected Gemma was playing with her. Gemma did not take the lead; she followed Agnes, providing textual evidence against her assertions. Agnes also knew that Gemma was not saying too much about Jane Austen's final novel, *Persuasion*. That was tactical; *Persuasion* supported her view more than any other of Jane Austen's novels. Gemma must know that.

'Of all the novels,' Agnes said in due course, '*Persuasion* must surely provide the irrefutable evidence that Jane Austen's concern was with man's virtue or lack of it. In this case, the focus was on constancy and faithfulness to a beloved. Anne Elliot remained constant in her love for Captain Wentworth even when all seemed lost.'

There seemed to be some hesitation in Gemma. 'Has anyone else read *Persuasion*?' she said, looking around. Two students raised their hands. 'What precipitated Anne Elliot's display of constancy?'

'Lady Russell, Anne's *de facto* guardian, persuaded Anne that she was too young and Captain Wentworth was unworthy of her,' said Agnes when the other students did not answer.

'Did not Anne admit to Captain Wentworth that she regretted succumbing to Lady Russell's persuasion when she and Captain Wentworth eventually came together?' said Gemma in an unusually subdued tone. Agnes was about to reply, but Gemma spoke over her. 'Wasn't it rather a question, Sister Agnes, of Anne Elliot's reluctance to make an independent decision, free from the influences around her, especially that of an abused or incompetent authority, one that drew its legitimacy from accepted and unquestioned tradition?'

'That was Anne's characteristic respect and Lady Russell's failure, a failure of—' Agnes stopped. A lump came to her throat.

'You're too great an admirer of Anne Elliot's constancy to the exclusion of—' Gemma, too, halted in the progression of her thought. She looked at her watch. 'Well, we've had a worthwhile discussion, haven't we?' There seemed to be a feeling in the room that something penetrating had been said but missed by most. Vic looked at Gemma, then at Agnes. 'There is certainly a lot to think about on this question. It's something students of Jane Austen will argue about for years to come. Thank you for your attention.' The students clapped in appreciation, a few staring at Sister Agnes.

Vic rose, giving a gushing thanks to Gemma for her brilliant exposition. As the gathering was breaking up, Gemma asked Agnes to stay.

'Do you mind, Vic?'

'Of course not. I have other things to do.' He left the room with Patricia on his heels.

'Are you all right?' Gemma asked when they were left alone. 'You're not too upset?'

Virginia's eyes brimmed, and she sat down. Gemma shut the door.

'Did you deliberately organise this tutorial to torment me?' said Agnes. 'I can't believe you would do that.'

'I'm not a nice person sometimes.'

'What interest do you have in this? Why go to all this trouble?'

'Just the interest that a former student has for a former teacher whom she still has great affection for. I don't want to see you waste your life, one with so much promise.'

'It's none of your business.'

'I know. I'm a busybody. I make appalling, gratuitous comments all the time. I upset a lot of people—deliberately. I glory in the brilliant manner in which I upset people.'

'What happened to you, Gemma? You were never like that.'

'But I don't want to upset you,' said Gemma, taking her hand. 'I want you to re-establish your engagement with your Captain Wentworth and reward your constancy.'

It was too much for Virginia's worn-down heart, and she bent forward, putting her hand to her mouth. Her breast heaved. Gemma put an arm around her and drew her forward. Virginia felt her veil's stiff, starched rim press against Gemma's cheek. Apart from Aine's comforting embrace, it was the first time someone had put an arm around her in a gesture of affection since ... since Philip.

'Apart from anything else, you're too soft for the hard religious life. You can't deny your feelings,' Gemma whispered.

Virginia lifted her head and disengaged herself. 'I know you mean well,' she said, wiping her eyes, 'but there's a lot you don't understand. Please leave me to deal with it.'

'You'll have to deal with it eventually,' said Gemma. 'He'll be back next term.'

'What—?'

'Don't worry, Ginny. Your secret is safe with me. I would never do anything to hurt you.'

'There are others who would,' said Agnes, standing.

'Who do you mean?' said Gemma, a frown indicating a change in feeling. 'Who's doing what to you?'

'There are some people ... but that was to be expected.' She breathed in to regain her composure.

'Who and what? Tell me.'

'Gemma, I appreciate your concern, but please cease your actions. They're misguided and misdirected.'

'You can rely on me,' Gemma called after her as she left the room.

Agnes was not surprised to hear Vic call her back after the following tutorial.

'You seemed upset, Virginia, very upset, after Gemma's presentation. Is there something wrong? Gemma can be too subtle sometimes, but she upset you, didn't she?'

'It's nothing to worry about, Dr Brennan. And would you please address me with my religious name?'

'I'm sorry, Sister. It's difficult to make the change. But let's get back to the point. You need to tell me if you have any worries or difficulties that affect your studies.

'As I say, it's nothing. I will cope with it. I have been a little tired recently.'

'Yes, you look tired. What are they doing to you at that convent?'

'Please, Vic, it is nothing.'

'Is there a problem with Phil?'

'Nothing more than the discomfort of the presence of one's former fiancé. And I must thank you for not talking about it.'

'Phil and I agreed personal matters were off-limits.'

'He has not said anything about you—except for one thing.'

'I can guess what.'

'He asked me to talk to you.'

'It's pointless, Virginia, besides being personal. Phil should first correct his less-than-exemplary behaviour before wanting to correct mine.'

'He is motivated as a friend,' said Agnes, reluctant to hear about Philip's girlfriends. 'He sees, as I do, tragic consequences. Have you fully considered how society will view leaving your family for a girl half your age?'

'You mean Catholic society. I have already experienced the charity of those who differed with me over the threat of communism, particularly those zealots in Santana's group.'

'They are the practical consequences, as important as the moral transgression. Vic, your conscience will eat away at you.'

'Look, Virginia. I will be polite. Of course, it is your duty as a religious sister to advert to transgressions of the faith, but having listened to your thoughts and warnings, I ask you not to concern yourself with my private matters—at least not talk to me about them.'

'All right, Vic. I respect your wishes. Besides, you don't really need to be told.'

'Thank you, Virginia.' He hesitated. 'Has this anything to do with your feelings for Phil?'

'That's private—' said Agnes before realising she had checkmated herself.

'Just so,' said Vic. 'Let me finish by saying you have done exceptionally well, even standing up to the brilliant, irrepressible Gemma. I expect you to finish with a high distinction.'

A couple of days later, Patricia Coghlan joined her on her bench.

'It was an interesting debate you had with Gemma Greene,' she said, sitting down without invitation and without using Agnes's name and religious title. 'It was a pity it ended so abruptly.'

'I am happy you enjoyed it,' said Agnes, not wishing to engage with this overconfident young woman.

'I am irretrievably in love with Vic,' said Patricia, not deterred from her purpose. 'I don't care what you or anyone else thinks about it. That won't change, even if Vic does not love me. But fortunately, he does love me, whatever the consequences. Do you know what it's like to love someone wholly, helplessly, and shamelessly? I think you do.' She got up and strode away, her head in the air.

PHILIP Stevenson lay in a deck chair on the verandah of his beach house. He gazed unseeingly at the blue wind-rippled waters of Port Philip Bay. It was sunny, and the coolish spring breeze flowed around his face. But the rejuvenating spring air did nothing to change the lowness of spirit or alert him to the feverish heat of his temples. Suddenly, Diana was standing before him.

'What ...?' he murmured, struggling to sit up.

'Good heavens, what have you been doing to yourself?' She put her bag down, knelt beside him, and took his hand. She felt his forehead. 'You've got a fever.'

'What are you doing here?' He closed his eyes, giving up the effort to sit up.

'Joe asked me if I knew where you were. He had not heard from you.'

'What's he worried about? I'll be back in time.'

'That's just what he is wondering. Term holidays end in a week.'

'In a week? No, that can't be right.'

'It certainly is.'

'What are you doing running his messages, anyhow?'

'Let's get you inside first. You're not well. Come on. Cooperate so I can get you to your feet.'

Diana helped him inside and, taking one look around at the upheaval and the empty bottles, took him into his bedroom. She made him sit on the side of the bed while she tidied the sheets and the blankets.

'When Joe said he had not heard from you, as he expected,' she said, easing his head against two pillows, 'I was alarmed. It's not like you to deviate from your arrangements without a sound reason.'

'No, it's not, is it?' He sighed.

'Now, first things first. I'll call the doctor. Where have you got his number?'

'On my desk.' He waved towards the lounge room.

With a bit of difficulty, Diana found the doctor's phone number among his papers and rang from the nearest public telephone. She insisted he come immediately to deal with a possible case of pneumonia.

'Well, young lady,' said the aging doctor, after a brief examination, 'you're right. He has pneumonia. He needs bed, a clean diet, no alcohol, and antibiotics. Who's here to care for him?'

'I am.'

'He'll need a least a week in bed and then quiet time to recover.'

'Don't worry. I will look after him.'

'Good. I'll come back in a week.' After writing a prescription and handing it to Diana, he wagged his finger at Philip. 'No alcohol, Phil. You won't be so lucky next time. It's fortunate your young friend came when she did.'

Philip raised his hand as a sign of surrender. 'Thank you for coming, Dr Robertson,' he whispered. 'I am indeed fortunate Diana came when she did.'

When Diana returned, after seeing Dr Robertson off, she said, 'Young lady, young friend? That's flattering for a 30-year-old.'

Philip smiled. 'He's right. Thank you for coming, Diana.'

'It's what a close friend would do, Philip darling. Now, I will ensure you're rested and fit before returning to your classes. I'll give Joe a call.'

She fixed him a cup of tea and a hot lemon drink made from a shrivelled lemon she found at the back of the refrigerator. The local chemist filled the prescription, and Philip was made to swallow the first dose. Her attention then turned to the house, which took a couple of hours to put in order.

'You didn't have to do that,' said Philip weakly. 'It's embarrassing, too.'

'You're excused. You're not yourself. That must have been some woman to reduce you to such a state.' Philip could only shake his head. 'Don't worry, darling,' she said, softly running her hand over his face and wiping a tear away. 'Most of us suffer heartbreak at the collapse of a relationship, at some time or another.' She caressed his arm. 'But you're not to think about it now. You must rest and regain your health. That's the priority.'

She checked the linen cupboard for sheets, blankets, and pillows. They were there, neatly arranged.

'I will leave you for a few hours, Phil, to fetch a few things. Now, don't move from your bed. I will set a pot of tea and put a plate of biscuits on your bedside cabinet. You have no excuse to move while I'm away.'

'Really, Diana, I don't want you to go to all this trouble. I can't—'

'Keep quiet. I'll be back in a couple of hours.'

She returned after a few hours, as promised, first checking that Philip was in bed.

'I've been obedient,' he said when her face appeared around the door.

'Good. I will put the groceries away and make up the spare room, after which I will make you something substantial to eat.'

They settled into a routine. Philip stayed in bed, letting Diana attend to him. He slept a lot, apologised a lot, and frequently declared he felt painfully guilty. She brushed it all off with the same reply. She was his friend, his intimate friend, and she only did what a trustworthy close friend would do. No conditions, no obligations. She left him alone when he made it clear he did not want to talk. Understood was that the subject of the 'mysterious committed woman' was banned. She had brought painting equipment with her, and she set herself up on the verandah where she painted scenes of the bay while Philip languished in his bedroom.

'You're very domesticated for a little rich girl,' he said on the third day of convalescence.

'Happy to see your mood has lightened.' She caressed his forehead. 'The fever has gone, too.'

'You dress in the bohemian mode, but I increasingly have the impression it's just style. The anarchy of bohemianism is missing.'

'You're right,' she said after a moment's thought. 'I like the fashion. It suits me, at least at this time in my life. I keep Harry and his friends at arm's length, so they don't find me out, not that Harry and Erik entirely fit the mould. They're mostly in it for young female flesh, especially Harry.'

'That's harsh.'

'Harry's very personable, great fun, but it's true. As for being domesticated, I like order in my world. It's more efficient that way. I can devote more time to my art.'

After five days, Philip could no longer keep to his bed. With her approval, he joined Diana on the verandah and watched her paint as he had done at her studio apartment. They hardly spoke, Diana often bestowing a smile on him.

'You remain so calm,' said Philip in the second week of his recuperation, 'and cheerful. My mother would say I had trifled with your affections.'

Diana laughed. 'Would she? That says a lot about her.'

'She accused me of trifling with someone's affections several times in far less culpable circumstances. She's right, considering how much you have let me into your life.'

Diana put her brush down and stared at the bay.

'First, you are right. I let you into my life. I am not a twenty-one-year-old. At thirty, I hope I am mature enough to make decisions after sober consideration. Second, I don't subscribe to your or your mother's Catholic way of thinking about relationships—at least on particular points. You have not betrayed me.' She paused. 'Phil darling, you don't seem to understand what an attractive man you are, not just in looks. To be truthful, I don't understand how your mysterious woman has rejected you. She's Catholic, I assume.'

Philip hesitated. 'It's complicated. I can't talk about it because I can't reconcile it. I must work through it. I will tell you when I have worked it out.' He hesitated again. 'After all you have done, willingly, I now value your friendship even more than before.'

At the end of two weeks, Diana packed up her things to return to Melbourne.

'You're well enough to be left alone,' she said while they sat on the verandah with a last cup of tea. 'Don't neglect yourself. You will work through it. Promise me.'

'I'll do my best.'

'Philip, let me tell you something personal. I have experienced heartbreak, too, like most. I was betrayed so brutally in my early twenties that I thought I would not survive, so broken was my heart. I did survive with the resolution that I would never commit myself in that way again. I realised later that my love was the desperate, selfish love of youth. Mature love is different. You will get over your heartbreak. Don't lose heart. In the meantime, you have my friendship, which you can rely on.'

Chapter 35

Under attack

AGNES DID not have time to ponder Gemma's concern for her, Vic's moral transgressions, or the bold insolence of his eighteen-year-old girlfriend. Other worries overtook her. During this time, political posters appeared on campus about troubles in Vietnam, which seemed to capture the attention of the radical groups. Bobby McGuigan appeared with various groups of students. Did the same issue bring these people together? And the reason the Fourth Club had been leaving her alone? It tempted her to ask Catherine what her father was doing on campus and why that obscure Asian country interested him and his entourage. However, given their fragile relationship, she decided against it. There was no point, anyhow, in starting a conversation about a topic that would probably fade from the excitable attention of the socialists. But then, as if on signal, attention to her revived.

At first, the comments following random meetings with her tormentors seemed opportunistic, considering they only came when she was not in Catherine's company. Even the couple of unzipped flies seemed merely opportunistic. It was usually the same two students, one from her philosophy year and the other, a second-year politics student, the belligerent one. They appeared to have a penchant for this manner of tormenting her. But the harassment in the library became more determined. When the second-year politics student exposed her to a lewd act with a girl behind the library shelves, it was clear they had launched a new offensive. She took precautions. The sorts of things they would get up to were limited in the library. Her precautions seemed to check them. She realised, though, that these bullies put few limits on what they would do.

The philosophy lectures were safe. There she sat under the lecturer's eyes in the front rows. Two students from the Fourth Club attended the lectures irregularly, and they sat up at the back. So, she had good reason to feel safe. But not long into the lecture following the lewd act, a vile, stifling smell arose around her. With her hand to her mouth, she looked around. Students moved away. Sniggering came from the back. The smell was overpowering. A glance under the now deserted seats revealed nothing. She gagged. The students' eyes were now on her. Some were laughing, others frowning. Dr Edelman came to her as she moved into the aisle.

'What's going on?' he said, but when he got near, he put his hand to his mouth and bent down. 'Dog poo. Sister, go and sit over there,' he said, grimacing and pointing to an empty row in front of his lectern.

'It's on my habit. I must leave.'

'Wait one moment,' he said, looking around at the students. 'I'll take you—' His face darkened. 'Calder, get out!'

The attention turned to a student who sat alone a couple of rows up from Agnes.

'What? I'm just sitting here listening with my friends,' said Stephen Calder, lounging in his seat. 'I'm vitally interested.' More sniggers from above. He glanced at his mates in the back row.

'I'll give you ten seconds to get out,' said Dr Edelman. 'There will be repercussions.'

Stephen Calder got up, waved at his friends, and came down the aisle, bathing in the attention. 'Dog poo is not the only thing that stinks here,' he said, looking at Agnes. 'Ideas that stink of corruption and oppression.'

'If you appear in one of my lectures again,' said Dr Edelman. 'I will start official proceedings against you. Your full record of bullying and intolerance will become visible.'

'Weak-kneed liberal,' said Calder as he wandered out of the lecture theatre.

Dr Edelman handed the supervision of the lecture over to one of his assistants and then took Agnes to the staff quarters.

'I'll ensure you have your privacy here,' he said. 'Please wait until I get back. We need to talk.'

Agnes was grateful for his kind, understanding manner. That was at least some compensation in this war against her. She went to the restroom and set about sponging her tunic. As she took up the folds and held the soiled part under the warm running water, she felt the oddity of her dress. When she put on her religious habit during the moving clothing ceremony, she did so eagerly, treasuring it as a symbol of her complete commitment to Jesus and his Gospel of love. It had marked the culmination of her proving period, and she was proud to have reached that stage. As a spouse of Christ, she had set out on her journey of witness and charity. The rough black serge rubbed between the fingers of her young hands; it seemed so ridiculously incongruous. 'What am I doing in this?' she murmured, but then rehearsed the response that inspired those in religious life.

Blessed are ye when they shall revile you, and persecute you, and speak all that is evil against you, untruly, for my sake.

Be glad and rejoice, for your reward is very great in heaven. For so they persecuted the prophets that were before you.

The poetic Beatitudes. She sighed, wondering whether the prophets had to contend with dog poo thrown at them. She scrubbed away, now hardly conscious of what she was doing. Eventually, she was satisfied she could do no more to wash away the smell. Drying it as best she could, she returned to the staff room, where she sat alone to wait. Her mind was blank, and her body numb. She did not have to wait long.

'Are you all right now?' said Dr Edelman, throwing his lecture notes on the nearby table. 'Has this sort of thing happened before?'

'I've had trouble. We expected some misunderstanding.'

'Misunderstanding!' he exclaimed, taking the seat beside her. 'There's no misunderstanding. Those young thugs know exactly what they're on about. If their harassment is getting too much for you, you must get your superiors to make a formal complaint to the university authorities.'

'I would rather not. It may inflame them even more. I'll try to keep out of their way.'

'I will complain. I don't want one of my best students affected.'

'Please don't do anything, Dr Edelman,' she said, glancing at him. 'I'll not let it affect me. I have enough untroubled time to compensate for the little irritation they're causing.'

He was not convinced but would nevertheless respect her wishes. 'Well, if you don't allow me to do anything about them,' he continued, 'I'll make sure you're not disadvantaged. Come along. We'll cover the second half of the lecture in my office.'

Agnes was of two minds about going alone to his office, but told herself not to be stupid. He was just doing his job as a man dedicated to his specialty. The next hour did nothing to increase her unwelcome suspicions. Although he spent much longer than was reasonable compensation and went into greater depth than the public lecture, he did not deviate from his task. She left his office, relieved and castigating herself for her hysterical suspicions. But in the next tutorial, she found that the castigation may be premature. He asked her to stay behind to discuss her essay topic.

'You know, I like the name Virginia Pearson much more than Sister Agnes,' he said when the other students had gone. 'It's a pity you had to give it up.'

'It's a sign of religious commitment,' she replied after hesitating.

'Now, don't get defensive,' he said, smiling. 'It's just a comment about your name. I'm saying no more than before about your religious commitment. If I can help you out of it, I will. That will entail more than a passing comment about your name.'

'Please don't concern yourself with my religious vocation, sir,' she said. 'I have taken vows,' she added, conscious of the gratuitousness of the comment.

'Vows? Ah, yes, the vows. Poverty, chastity, and obedience. I don't understand how a reasonable person could commit to that. It's beyond me, that's for sure. Anyhow, we'll see how you'll go with your essay on Descartes' ontological argument for the existence of God.'

After discussing her essay topic, which did not seem necessary, she left his office again in two minds. Was he just teasingly pleasant, or was there something else behind it? She did not have time to ponder the question because she found Anne waiting for her at the end of the corridor.

'Can you come with me?' she said. 'Barry's got information about the Aquarian Company.'

'Barry—is he the one?' she said, happy for the distraction.

'Barry and I have something in common,' she said, blushing. 'His parents broke up when he was ten. I understand how terrible it would've been for him.'

'You have been talking about it?'

'Yes, we understand each other, incredibly.'

They found Barry waiting at a table in the Union eating hall. The change in his manner and clothes was more than evident.

'I'm glad you two have become friends,' Agnes said as she sat on the opposite side of the table, leaving Anne to take her seat beside him.

'Thank you, Sister. I acknowledge it was your doing. Perhaps I should apologise ...'

'No need, Barry, Sister understands,' Anne broke in before Agnes could reply. 'Tell Sister what you know about the Aquarian Company.'

'Well, I'm not acquainted with that university club, but I've had some experience of what's behind it.' He related how a few years after his parents' divorce, he got mixed up in all sorts of strange company, including a group interested in magic and the occult.

'Magic and the occult!' Agnes could not help exclaiming. 'Do people take that seriously?'

'You had better believe it,' said Barry. 'There's far more to it than people realise. Fortunately, I only dabbled in it. It involved secret inner knowledge and energy, and using it to influence things—something like that. It's dark and secretive. The idiots I got mixed up with gave the impression they hadn't a clue what they were getting into. So I drifted away from them with others interested in ancient esotericism and astrology. That suited my state of mind.'

'Esotericism? What's that? I've never heard of it.'

'Neither had I,' said Anne.

'Is it widespread?'

'I don't know exactly. As with the occult, I accidentally came across it through another boy at school who had a terrible home life. His father used to bash him and his mother. I think that's what the Aquarius club is involved in—esotericism. The name refers to the Age of Aquarius. The Age of Aquarius is supposedly a period of peace and harmony that will follow the upheaval of the Age of Pisces, the divisive Christian period that is ending. According to its adherents, it will unite all religions and form one gigantic religion and establish a one-world government. It's a sort of promise of redemption through inner enlightenment that opposes the Christian idea of redemption from sin.'

Seeing the rough concurrence of Barry's revelations with comments from Gemma, Margaret, and Jannie, Agnes threw questions at him, but Barry held up his hands. 'I didn't stay with those people long enough to learn more about it. They did nothing to dispel my torment. It was the opposite. I was succumbing to a dark, despairing depression. I then happened on the enlightenment of the Gospels and the message of the Lord. A friend had managed to drag himself away from the influence of that dark, secretive world, and he succeeded in dragging me away, too.'

'How?' said Agnes. 'What was the appeal of a fundamentalist Protestant group?'

'I had no idea how my friend's group fitted in with Christianity generally. Like others, I had until then contempt for all its forms. His unconditional friendship was the start, but the constant reading and propounding of the Gospel texts got me in. Something not only contradicted the message of esotericism but brilliantly countered its dark atmosphere. Since then, I have wanted to spread that light against the darkness. Esotericism is meant to be about the inner divine life of the individual. It's a fraud. The inner life is in the Gospels.'

Agnes stared in silence. The young man's zeal and perseverance in the face of so much bullying impressed her. Her present feelings and frame of mind accused her.

'Yours is an inspiring story of conversion, putting many lukewarm Catholics to shame.'

'Thank you,' he replied modestly.

'You see, there's more to Barry than people think,' said Anne. She put her hand shyly on his arm.

'There certainly is,' said Agnes. 'I'm happy I caught a hint of it in the beginning. Perhaps Barry now thinks a little better of our Church.'

Barry hesitated, shifting in his seat. 'I appreciate your kindness and understanding. I'm grateful for the introduction.' He gave Anne a look of embarrassment. 'But that's you personally.'

'I'm a representative of the Church,' said Agnes, with the disturbing feeling she was pretending.

'Barry needs more time to think about it,' said Anne.

'But Barry,' Agnes insisted, 'there are facts of history you can check.' She then rattled off a series of dates and milestones relating to Church councils.

'Sister, please give Barry a chance,' said Anne, interrupting her.

Agnes stopped in mid-sentence. 'Oh, I'm sorry. Did I sound a little insistent?'

'Barry just needs more time.'

'Of course, of course,' said Agnes. 'I was not conscious of how I might have sounded.' The thought mortified her that she had been pushy while Barry tried to be amicable.

'That's all right, Sister Agnes,' said Barry, 'no offence. It's your job to proselytise. It's what I do, too.'

Agnes watched Anne and Barry walk from the union eating hall, chatting happily. She felt terrible. Did she hunt them away with her pushy manner? And proselytise? Did she sound like she was proselytising? She only meant to engage him in a little conversation about his views. Anyhow, why should she worry? She had gratuitously given out information about the Church many times without dwelling for a moment on how people may react. She always aimed to state the truth as she saw it and defend it. So why did she worry now? It had been such a little thing, a question of history, not faith. She took up her things, her ample black habit weighing on her, and headed for the library. She was negotiating the path bordering the front lawn when a familiar voice disturbed her thoughts. Jannie was sitting on a nearby bench, beckoning her.

'I want to show you something,' said Jannie when she arrived at the bench. 'I've been waiting for you.' She flicked open a glossy fashion magazine and held it out in front of Agnes. Agnes's eyes widened. 'Beautiful, isn't she? Utterly incomparable. Harry's work. Virginia, there's a message in this if you want to open your eyes.'

Agnes turned to the handsome, suntanned face, wearing an expression of imperturbable confidence.

Chapter 36

The problems converge

AGNES STRUGGLED amid exhaustion and disconnection to reach the end of the second term. With all assignments and exams at last completed, she was relieved when she awoke on the first day of the holidays without the task of running the usual gauntlet to attend lectures. She needed rest. Apart from anything else, she needed time to overcome the disturbing feeling of her last meeting with Jannie de Kam. That handsome face full of meaning as she proudly showed the photos of Aine had been unnerving in the extreme.

Fortunately, there was now the relief of the gentle, self-effacing Sister Martha each day, who brought stability to her life. The bird-like antics of the busy bursar also provided, as the days passed, a holdfast amid everything else in her life that seemed in flux. Besides the calming influence of the two contrasting sisters, her daily routine isolated her from most of the community. She hardly saw Sister Catherine. Even the expected summons from Mother Jerome passed by without the usual anxiety. Mother congratulated her on her outstanding results without the testing preamble that had marked her other meetings.

'I must note that you have achieved a Credit in Economics,' she said, smiling. 'Have I uncovered an unsuspected ability there?'

'I forced myself to concentrate on the material,' said Agnes, which was only the truth.

'Well and good. Keep it up,' said the prioress. Then, with a short comment that her duties would be unchanged for the rest of the year, Mother Jerome dismissed her. As Agnes reached for the door handle, she heard: 'You are aware that the Second Vatican Council begins in a few weeks?'

'Eh, no, I had forgotten.'

'You will be responsible for compiling the reports—you alone. So devote time to how you will organise all that.'

'Yes, Mother,' she said, surprised at the news and its manner of conveyance, 'will there be much to organise?'

'I don't know. There are different ideas about what this Council means. Some believe it will be a waste of time; others think it will be wrapped up in two weeks; others fear what it will unleash, and some look forward to it as an opportunity for change. The last, a clever minority, is not subtle about it.'

'What is your opinion, Mother, if I may ask?' said Agnes, coming several steps back into the room.

'You may. I am a little nervous and uncertain about it.'

'May I ask why?'

'I would rather wait before expressing my thoughts,' said Mother Jerome, whose face appeared gaunter than ever. 'You will learn in due course. We will be discussing it. That is one of the reasons you are studying philosophy.'

'Is it?' This was news.

'Yes, but don't spend time on it now. You can return to your duties—and Sister, there will be no study during the holidays. You are to take a break. You appear tired and worn. I have warned you about that.'

'Yes, Mother.'

Agnes's head was too full for entertaining thoughts about the coming Vatican Council, and she was only too happy to follow the prioress's instruction. After a week of rest and forcing aside her worries, her thoughts returned to those sources of concern. What had happened to Jannie? There was such a change in her. Agnes suspected it was more than Sister Catherine's influence, as powerful as that was. What had got Jannie over the scruples of ending a pregnancy, enabling her not only to rise above such an appalling act but to assume such solid confidence in herself when flirting and flightiness had characterised her behaviour until recently? Whatever the influences and causes, Catherine took responsibility for the change. And then there were the photos of Aine in the fashion magazine. It looked like Aine had also succumbed to Catherine's advice and manipulation. Had Aine seen Catherine without her knowing it? No, it could not be. Surely, if Aine had made the trip to Melbourne, she would have seen her before she saw anyone else.

But the more Agnes considered it, the more she doubted. She had to face the bare fact of the magazine photos and the dramatic change in Aine's appearance. It simply did not look like her. She was beautiful, stunning, as she had always been, but a different character marked her beauty. It was not the Aine she knew. Was it really a question of change, she kept on wondering, or was it the cleverness of the photographer that had created the fashion look he wanted? The look! It was a depressing thought that a girl so pure-minded could be brought down, brought into a world whose brittle superficiality she had recognised herself. She prayed fervently that it was not so and that Aine would not be lured further into that world.

Agnes's preoccupation with Aine had at least one pleasing effect. She could establish emotional distance between her and Philip and the other torments at the university. With a clearer mind, she could take steps to deal with those problems. To avoid the Fourth Club's ambushes, she asked Mother Jerome to arrange permission to study in the library of Magdalene College, the Catholic women's college on campus. The prioress greeted this request with approval and made the arrangements that day.

'Good,' said Mother Jerome, who especially came to the vegetable garden to inform her. 'It's good to see you taking decisive action to deal with the problem instead of wallowing in your hurt feelings.'

'Did I appear hurt, Mother?'

The prioress did not answer, merely raised her eyebrows before returning to her office. Agnes glanced at Martha. She gave Agnes a smile and gently rubbed her arm. Oh, how much Agnes depended on Martha's gentleness and simple soul! Martha's example had more meaning to her about the good life than the two terms of philosophy she had completed. With her silent encouragement and example, Agnes's state of mind improved, and her spirits brightened. She not only enjoyed her work with Martha but also looked forward to it each day. She wondered what went on in the head of that simple, humble sister who seemed to achieve peace and serenity in work whose narrowness and restriction she could not bear to contemplate. She could not help asking how she did it.

'It's the Rule,' Martha said. 'It's the total abandonment to and love of the Rule. The Rule is our way of showing our love for Jesus. It's a mistake to think of it as something restricting or oppressive. Correctly seen, it is liberating, especially as it ties all the sisters together in community. Mother Jerome said that about the Rule during the first meeting with the postulants. Do you remember? She's right. I can't imagine what would happen if the Rule suddenly disappeared.'

Agnes wondered why she kept on asking the same question. Was it because she did not understand how a rule could be liberating? Or was it that she was not prepared to accept the answer? The idea that a strict rule could be liberating contained a neat, attractive paradox in a literary sense. That certainly was not the way Martha viewed it. The Rule for her was genuinely liberating. The question for Agnes was whether the literary device was more appealing to her than the idea's supposed truth. Whatever the case, having improved in strength and spirit, she felt more prepared to face the final university term and all that came with it.

As it turned out, the peaceful days with Martha in the gardens and kitchen had soothed her into a false sense of security. Towards the end of the final week of the university holidays, Martha took advantage of the balmy spring weather to prepare the vegetable gardens for sowing. She and Agnes spent the day weeding, turning the soil, and cleaning up. Late in the afternoon, Agnes was at the edge of the garden plot, overlooking the slope leading down to the river. She had paused in her work and was enjoying the view over the water and bushy hills when she noticed several sisters talking with two young women in the clearing below. Her first reaction was to force her attention away from something that did not concern her. But as she turned away, a flicker of recognition forced her to turn back. A slim, elegant girl in summer slacks and blouse, with sunglasses, a broad-brimmed sunhat, and colourful bangles on her wrists, was looking at the sisters. Beside her, and with her back to Agnes, was a more subdued but smartly dressed young woman with her long, honey-blond hair tied in a ponytail. The ponytail bobbed as she talked. The ponytail—Jannie!

'My God, it's Aine, too! What was she—?'

Agnes's sudden exclamation brought Martha hurrying over to her. With her hand over her mouth, Agnes pointed toward the clearing. Sister

Martha craned her neck to see who it was. She gave Agnes a look of incomprehension. Agnes took several breaths and pointed.

'It's Aine Winterbine with Jannie de Kam,' she whispered out of frustration.

Martha put her finger to her lips and signed that it was none of their business whatever Aine and Jannie were doing there. She smiled sympathetically and returned to what she was doing. Agnes could not move. Why were they there? Aine made some familiar gestures and stepped back a little. Then Agnes caught sight of someone sitting in the long grass on the other side of the river. It was a man. He was pointing a camera with a telephoto lens. Aine raised her hand at him. He jumped to his feet and signalled urgently, to which Jannie gave him a calming wave. But he insisted. Aine hurried to the jetty. With some words to Catherine, Jannie followed. Agnes found her feet.

'I'll be back,' she called to Martha.

'No, Sister!'

No, indeed! Someone in trouble must override the rule of silence. She hurried from the garden along the top level. By the time she reached the stairs, Jannie and Aine were already boarding the boat alongside the jetty. Agnes stopped. The boat on the river! Jannie was rowing to the opposite side with Aine in the stern, her head bowed. A dreadful feeling overcame her. She prayed Aine had not forgotten, as Jannie had forgotten. When the boat reached the opposite side, Jannie steered it to the left, and they disappeared in the bend of the river. She was roused from her thoughts and hurried down the stairs. Then she saw Jannie and Aine emerge from a grassy hollow and walk to the man. He put his arm around Aine, who still had her head bowed. Aine took off her hat, letting her long, fair hair fall around her face. She did not resist the comfort of the man. They walked up the slope toward the bush. Agnes realised they would be out of sight by the time she reached the clearing.

'What were you doing with Aine and Jannie there?' she demanded, blocking Catherine and her companions on their way up.

'I beg your pardon,' said Catherine. 'It was a chance meeting if you must know.'

Sisters Hildegard and Benedicta stood behind her, giving no sign of intervening.

'Chance meeting, my fat—' Agnes stopped herself. What was she saying? She had not used that expression since her childhood.

'Sister, calm yourself,' said Catherine with unbearable composure. 'Jannie brought Aine and her photographer friend here to take photos—for fashion purposes. Jannie thought it suitable. We simply happened to be there at the same time.'

'You don't expect me— What upset Aine?'

'Upset Aine?' Catherine repeated, turning with a mystified expression to her companions. 'Aine was not upset. On the contrary, she gave the impression our praise and congratulations had pleased her.'

'Pleased her! Then why did she leave so suddenly?'

'Suddenly? She and Jannie returned to their work, I imagine. What's behind this—and your manner?'

'You're as slippery as a snake.'

'I beg your pardon. Would you please move aside? I'll remind you it is silence now.'

'Who are you to preach about the Rule?' said Agnes, helplessly realising that she was transgressing all manner of convent rules.

'Please move aside.'

'Taking Aine to the same sort of disaster as Jannie?' Virginia said as Margaret passed by her.

'And what is that for my information?' said Margaret, stopping.

'Breaking her marriage vows!'

'I will ignore that offensive accusation,' said Margaret as her companions squeezed by them. 'Jannie and Aine are responsible for their own choices. I only ever encourage people to be responsible.' She turned to continue her way.

'Responsible for wrongdoing,' Virginia called after her.

Margaret stopped and came down a few steps. 'You have told me many times that I am not suited to convent life and should seek my life's purpose elsewhere. You would not dare deny me the right to question your suitability. Your recent actions raise serious questions about your suitability. Your emotional, sometimes hysterical, outbursts are not compatible with convent life. You appear tired and worn, as if you are on the point of a breakdown. You should reflect on your presence here and do the right thing for the sake of yourself and your fellow sisters.'

'You would be tired and worn if you were continually harassed,' said Virginia, barely holding back the tears of frustration. 'How do you escape it? Why do they leave you alone?'

With a twitch of contempt disturbing her otherwise composed face, Margaret looked at her for a moment. Then, shaking her head, she resumed her way. Virginia was already weeping before she reached the top of the stairs. With her face turned away from the building, she hurried back to the gardens, where she sought shelter among the shrubs at the far end. Martha came to her and put her arm around her while she gave in to her helplessness and frustration.

She had no way of knowing that Mother Jerome, with the worrying problem of one of her favourite sisters on her mind, had gone to her office window on the upper floor to ponder that problem. Agnes had no way of knowing that Mother Jerome had observed the whole incident, beginning with Aine's arrival on the opposite bank with the photographer and Jannie de Kam, to her clash with Catherine on the rocky stairway. But she did expect the incident to be reported and a summons to follow. The summons did not come. On the morning of her return to university for the final term, Mother Jerome, Prioress of the Convent of St Augustine, Superior General of the Sisters of the Suffering Saviour, with a staff of hundreds servicing schools and nursing homes throughout Oceania, a cultured woman of vast authority, came to Agnes while she was waiting for Mr Ferguson on the front porch.

'Your task is to concentrate only on your university work, Sister,' she said. You are not to let anything else disturb your thoughts. You must be conscious of your duty and nothing else.'

'Yes, Mother,' said Agnes, a little bewildered.

'Good, you have done well with your studies. With similar success this term, you will be continuing. Keep that in mind. Your studies will be needed in the future.'

'Yes, Mother.'

Agnes knew it was meant to be encouraging, whatever purpose exactly was behind Mother Jerome's words that morning. And it did raise her spirits. She made a brave effort on the way into the university to strike up a conversation with Mr Ferguson while Catherine looked through the window with the usual bored expression. But those spirits were dashed at the first philosophy lecture. Dr Edelman announced with much regret that Dr Stevenson would be absent for a couple of weeks more and flippantly added that there would be no excuse for any disturbance to the students' study schedule. The lectures would be rearranged so that Dr Stevenson would lecture through the second half of the term. Agnes was not surprised that the first question in the following tutorial was about Dr Stevenson's absence.

'It's a private matter,' said Dr Edelman.

'Is he getting married?' asked Anne.

'To relieve the tender feelings of all Dr Stevenson's tender admirers,' he said, smiling, 'no, he is not getting married. No more questions on that topic, please.'

'It's a mystery,' said Anne, outside in the corridor after the tutorial. 'Have you got any idea what's happening? It's strange that he should be away for so long.'

'No, how would I know?' said Agnes, struggling.

'I thought Dr Edelman would— He seems to like you.'

'No, he's said nothing. Besides, he treats me like any other student,' Agnes said, flushing at the flagrant lie.

'I don't mean anything by that,' said Anne, 'but he does.'

'Don't be silly.'

Dr Edelman came into the corridor and called over the students' heads: 'Sister Agnes, would you have a few minutes, please? Anne, I won't keep her long.'

'Don't worry. Your secret is safe with me,' whispered Anne. 'I won't wait. I'm meeting Barry for coffee. Come and join us when you're finished.' She was gone before Agnes could reply.

'I want to make sure you're prepared for this term's work,' he said when she had taken a seat. 'Or more to the point, I want to ensure you're not bothered by extraneous matters.'

'I'm all right, Dr Edelman.'

'No, you're not. And none of that long-suffering behaviour. You're not in the convent here.'

'Please, Dr Edelman ...' She was now familiar with Dr Edelman's outspoken temperament.

'No, no, don't try that stuff on me. You've just come back from three weeks' holiday, and you look tired. What do they do to you in that convent?' She did not answer. 'You've lost weight, too.' She still did not respond. He regarded her closely. 'Let me speak frankly—'

'You are always frank, Dr Edelman,' she broke in, 'and it shows your concern. I thank you for that. But there are things about my life you don't understand and will never understand. So it is best that you don't worry about my life outside the university. I'll continue to apply myself to the best of my ability.'

'I'm still going to say what's on my mind,' he said after a thoughtful pause. 'Make no mistake. My first concern is for you as my student. I want you to do well, as I want for all students. However, in your case, I'm dealing with someone whose mind is attuned to the philosophical enterprise. You have an able philosophical mind with a practical bent. Some of us are attracted to an abstract mode of thinking; others are drawn to the practical side, always linking speculation with the everyday concrete world. Phil Stevenson is like that. You are, too. It's a legitimate approach, an approach I want to nurture. But I see someone before me who is tired and nervous. Why?'

'There's no point in going into it, even if I was willing to talk about it.'

'Why?'

'No, Dr Edelman ...' She suspected he knew something.

'If part of the problem is those Trotskyist thugs tormenting you, you must say so. I really can't do anything unless you permit me to raise the issue.'

'I can deal with that. I have taken steps this term.'

'If, on the other hand, your mode of life—your vocation, as you call it—is coming under assault from within, then you must acknowledge that. It's just wrong and unhealthy to ignore it. If you try to live a life fundamentally opposed to your good reason, you'll make yourself sick. I've seen it before with intelligent people who imagine they have a religious vocation. You're showing signs.'

It was ironic that Dr Edelman had hit on what she was facing: that she had, in a confused way, doubts about where she was going. But he was wrong about an important point: it was not because of an intellectual assault on her faith. After two short terms of philosophy, she had more reason to conclude that the compass of human reason was very limited. No, it was not that. Something in her did not want to give up the purpose of being in the convent. On the other hand, something else was leading her away from it.

'Dr Edelman, you are kind, and I know you mean well, but I must insist—'

'You and Phil look the same—both tired and nervous,' he said in exasperation. 'At least Phil has an excuse with his bout of pneumonia.'

'Pneumonia?'

'Yes, well, I said I was not at liberty to say anything. But I suppose you're an exception. I trust you'll keep it to yourself.'

'Is he all right? How serious ... pneumonia is serious, isn't it?' She shifted in her seat.

'It was just a touch, fortunately. He'll be okay. He's been working too hard and neglecting himself, locked away in his cottage down the coast at Sorrento—probably visiting the whisky bottle a little too often. He'll be back shortly. The doctor wants him to spend longer recuperating, but I bet he's not cooperating. As wrong-headed as you, he is. What is it with you bright Catholics?'

Agnes was desperately relieved to hear he was all right, and there was no hint of a connection between Philip and her. But Sorrento—where she had spent so much time with him.

'I hope he gets better quickly. The students miss him. I must go now,' she said, standing.

'Reflect on what I have said, Virginia,' Dr Edelman said, getting to his feet. 'I'm here always to talk things over with you.'

'Please don't call me that.'

'I'm not a Catholic, Virginia,' he replied. 'I don't see a religious sister in front of me. Instead, I see an attractive, personable young woman under that terrible black costume. She's trying to get out but is afraid of the open door. She's withering before my eyes.'

'At least not in front of other students,' she said in resignation and wearied by her flaring emotions.

'I promise.' He watched her go to the door. 'By the way, your essay on Descartes' ontological argument was very professional—deserved the High Distinction.'

'Thank you,' she said, halting in the doorway.

He gave her a knowing look. 'The failure of such a well-known argument for the existence of God doesn't bother you?'

'No. The Church has never depended on any abstract theory to justify its existence. Besides, St Thomas Aquinas acknowledged its deficiency.'

'You sound like Philip.'

She did not reply, leaving him looking after her.

THE BENEFITS Agnes had enjoyed during her time with Martha in the serenity of the vegetable gardens were thus cancelled in the first days of her return to university. Drawn helplessly again into the spiralling descent, she summoned what remained of her strength and set herself to attending lectures and tutorials. Between lectures and tutorials, being careful that no one saw where she was going, she sneaked away to Magdalene College library. There she had found a desk hidden by the shelves at the far end of the room. In this way, she went mostly unnoticed, sometimes even by the students who came into the library. Her efforts to escape notice, tedious though they were, brought one consolation. During this time, she could follow Mother Jerome's instruction to concentrate only on her studies. Losing herself in her reading and research forced that wearing, undefined problem to the outer limits of her consciousness during the day.

It was not until a few weeks later that her new routine was disturbed. She found Stephen Calder and his two philosophy friends following her. 'So that's where she's got to,' she heard Calder say. Seeing him enter the library a few days later was no surprise. But even Stephen Calder could not get away with this trick. The library staff was on to him at once. He did not even have time to see her, so quickly was he escorted out of the library. She later learned that he received a severe warning for unauthorised entry into the women's colleges. He was wise enough not to attempt that sort of assault again. That was one little victory for her, at least. She was well aware, though, that the frustration of failure would spur him on to bigger things. So she must remain ready. Several days later, Anne cornered her after the tutorial.

'Where are you always going, Sister?' she said. 'Are you trying to avoid us?'

'No, Anne, I'm maintaining the routine of a religious sister.' Again, she sounded as though she was lying. The spirit of the religious life seemed to be ebbing away, leaving her in an empty shell of routine, rituals, and schedules.

'It looks like it. Is there something wrong?'

'No, why?'

'You don't look well,' said Anne, who did not appear happy.

'I'll be all right. It's a tight schedule for us sisters. The end of the year is approaching, anyway.'

'I need to talk to you. Do you have time?'

'Yes, of course.'

'My father has got a girlfriend, a young girlfriend, not much older than you,' Anne blurted out tearfully when they had settled at a table in the student cafeteria.

As Agnes listened to a long, disjointed tale of betrayal and disgust, she realised her feelings differed significantly from those she had felt the first time Anne had spoken about her father. Then, she did not have to pause before launching into explaining the Church's teaching about marriage. Now her heaviness of spirit and confusion of mind were so oppressive that she felt paralysed. Only her occasional sounds of sympathy kept Anne from noticing the change she felt.

'He's a childish bastard,' said Anne, in conclusion, making no effort to apologise for her bad language. 'Sister Catherine was right about one thing.'

'As horrible as it all appears,' Agnes said, her heart sinking at yet another sign of Catherine's influence, 'you must be understanding. People make mistakes. None of us is perfect. Pray that he understands in the end what he's doing.'

'I can't accept what he's done to my mother. She doesn't deserve it. She's broken-hearted.'

'Your mother doesn't deserve it, I know. Often, innocent people have to suffer for the mistakes of others. Pray that she has strength during this trial.'

'Pray! Pray! Why should she pray? It doesn't get her anywhere,' said Anne fiercely.

'She can't give up. She mustn't give up. All of us must trust and hope that it will turn out for the best.'

'I would like to kill him!'

'No, Anne, lack of courage won't cure anything. One wrong won't solve another.'

'Poo!'

Agnes was relieved to see Carmel and Barbara approaching. Never had she looked forward to their exuberant presence so much. Her relief was well-founded, for, giving her a friendly greeting, they began an engrossing account of the boyfriend troubles of a mutual friend, news which distracted Anne from her problems. Agnes had an excuse to withdraw. Before she could make her excuses, Carmel started on a subject that kept her seated.

'Phil Stevenson's still not back, is he?' she said to Anne.

'We've heard something,' said Barbara before Anne could answer.

'What?'

'He got sick because of a bout of drinking. Apparently, he can throw it back when he wants.'

'But nobody I know at the university has ever seen him drunk,' said Anne.

'That's because he avoids mixing with the students—unlike others.' She winked at Anne and then glanced at Agnes.

'Does anyone know why he's hitting the booze?'

'None of his colleagues knows,' said Barbara. 'Some suspect it has to do with a woman. Then, again, no one has ever seen him serious with a girl. He's had a string of girlfriends since being on staff here, but none serious, except perhaps for his bohemian artist girlfriend, who he has dropped. Joe Edelman reckons he would know if it was a woman. He says he's been working too hard, you know, too much stress, and then the drink.'

'Do you know Dr Edelman?' said Agnes.

'Yes, I know him,' said Barbara with a sly smile. Anne frowned and shook her head. 'Anyway,' Barbara continued, 'Joe is sure it's not women trouble. Others are not so sure.'

'Intriguing,' said Anne, 'romantic, too, if he's carrying a torch for someone after all this time.'

It was too much for Agnes. She rose, excusing herself. Anne tried to detain her, apologising for a conversation that would not interest her, but Agnes was firm. 'I have some reading to do for the next philosophy essay.'

'Thank you, Sister, for your comfort. I really appreciate it,' said Anne, laying her hand on Agnes's arm.

That small gesture seemed to Agnes to have great significance. Anne would never have dared such a familiar gesture in the first term. What had happened ... and why was it so significant? More analysis, more to weigh on her mind. Like other unwanted thoughts, she forced it out of her mind by taking refuge in her books at the back of Magdalene College library. The pressure of unsought-for meetings, however, continued to increase. The following week, she found Gemma Greene waiting for her after her English tutorial.

'Got you, at last!' she said, taking her arm. 'Come on, Ginny, we're going to have a drink and a chat?'

'Okay, but not in a hotel—please,' said Agnes, surrendering without a struggle.

With an impatient wave, Gemma took her to a cosily furnished room in the English Department.

'We won't be disturbed here,' she said, pointing at a comfortable armchair. 'Now, why have you been avoiding everyone? I've been looking everywhere for you. And don't give me any nonsense.' She put the kettle on as she spoke.

'I need to have time to myself.'

'If it's because of a crisis of belief, then I'd be glad to hear it. I'm here to help you along the track of unbelief until you get out of your dark hole.'

'Gemma, you can't help,' said Agnes. 'I don't want you to help. If it is as you say, I will work through it myself. You must respect that. Besides, it's not about the sort of self-deception you seem to have in mind. It's not as clear as that.'

'Okay, we're getting somewhere. It seems you've passed beyond the boundary of self-denial.' She put the cup of tea on the table in front of Agnes. 'But if your obvious stress has another source, we need to speak about it. I've just learned what those Trotskyist animals have been doing to you. They're boasting about it, you know. You must do something. Animals understand one thing: the torment they hand out. I can help you. I can call on people who'll be just as ruthless.'

'No, Gemma, don't. I'm managing. If you can't find me, they can't either. There's only a little way to go until the end of the year.'

'They'll ground you into the dirt if they get a chance,' said Gemma, relenting. 'They know the meaning of total war, let me assure you. But

I can't make you do anything. If you want help, I'm there.' She paused. 'But it's not just them, is it?'

'No, it's not just them. And don't ask any questions. If you want to be my friend, don't put more pressure on me.'

'Dear Ginny, you must be feeling awful to be talking like this.'

Agnes bent her head a little, determined not to give in to the tears that seemed ever on the verge of flowing. 'Everyone has their trials.'

'Your religious talk is failing you, Ginny.'

'Please, Gemma, don't—'

'Philip will be back next week.'

'How do you know?' said Agnes, raising her head.

'Much of what goes on in certain quarters in this university does not escape me. That reminds me, you're a real duffer, aren't you?'

'What do you mean?'

'Asking whether Phil had bedded me. Outrageous!'

'Did Dr Edelman tell you that?'

'He didn't say you were asking for yourself, but he appeared to find something odd about your question. He was fishing. Don't worry. I didn't tell him anything. I just laughed at the idea. Phil's not my type, and I'm not his. Phil has relationships by default.'

'What do you mean?'

'I'm not sure.'

Gemma moved away from the subject of Philip. Whether it was because it was too difficult for her or she lost interest, Agnes could not guess. In any case, she was grateful that she had eased off and talked about her plans to study at Oxford University. The cup of tea and the pressure-free conversation that followed succeeded in distracting her.

'Try and stay relaxed,' Gemma said as they parted near the front lawn. 'Remember, I'm ready to help if you want help. Just sing out. In the meantime, I'll keep an eye on those disgusting pigs.'

Chapter 37

Harry's photo shoots

AINE HAD not felt so relaxed in years. It was a constant wonder. Contrary to her expectations, and despite her reluctance, the entry into the fashion world had been smooth under the beneficence of Harry, the photographer, and Jannie's indispensable backup. She had experienced nothing but pleasure in the work, respect, and amiability from the colourful types forming Harry's busy entourage. From the moment of the breakthrough in May, she had dropped her resistance and let talented Harry guide her along the track he was marking out for her. Nothing changed in his manner; she still could not fault him for his organisation, charm, and willingness to cater to her needs. The most important of those needs was Charles's acquiescence. In this, Harry left nothing to chance. Ten days after the Binawarra visit, he was on the phone with Charles.

'Mr Winterbine, the photos of Aine are ready. You'll be very proud of your wife. I would like to arrange a time to come up to Binawarra and show them to you at your convenience. There are important matters to discuss.'

Charles could not repel such a polite, respectful request. 'He's a pleasant, enticing fellow, that Harry,' Charles remarked to Aine when he had finished arranging Harry's visit. Aine took that as a vote of confidence, permission to forge ahead. When Harry arrived ten days later—altogether a discreet delay, thought Aine—he did nothing to dispel Charles's favourable opinion of him.

He declined the invitation to stay in their guest room, saying it would not be right to let business intrude on their young family. Instead, he would book into the local motel. Aine found that choice considerate and understanding. Harry arrived for dinner on a Saturday evening, holding his bag of business in one hand and a bouquet in the other. After a relaxing dinner, during which Harry showed himself interested in all aspects of the Winterbines' life in Binawarra, he waited until Aine had cleared up and put Estella to bed before asking permission to unpack his b ag.

'May I lay them all out on the table?' With permission granted, he arranged the large prints in order. 'Come on, don't stand back. Take a close look.'

Charles and Aine pored over the photos, the surprise showing on their faces as their eyes shifted from one photo to another. Harry took a strategic position behind them.

'I look different,' said Aine in a whisper.

'Yes, you do,' agreed Charles.

'Different from what?' said Harry, stepping forward on cue.

'I don't see myself like that.'

'Like what?'

Aine could not give a ready answer.

'It just doesn't look like Aine,' said Charles. 'I mean, I recognise her naturally, but the feeling the image conveys is not Aine.'

'Charles, modelling is about projecting an image that suits the clothing modelled. It's a lot like acting. The best models act the part.'

'But I just followed your instructions,' said Aine.

'That's your uniqueness,' said Harry, with a visible effort to temper his smugness. 'You have a natural manner in front of the camera. The image you cast on film is striking. It's an image for now, perhaps a little before now.'

'I don't really understand,' said Charles. 'But you are the professional, so I imagine you know what you're doing.'

That was the opening Harry was looking for. He spent all the time necessary to explain the details of the photos and how successfully Aine had performed, giving the best possible projection of the quality and cut of the clothes. He also spoke of his clients' excellent reaction and their request to use the photos in their next magazine promotion. The use of the photos brought on an eager explanation of the modelling business. That included remuneration. Harry gave every appearance of assuming that the generous payment for Aine's looking beautiful would seal their approval for his next project.

'It seems a lot of money,' said Charles.

'A high-quality product costs more than an ordinary one.'

'A high-quality product?'

'Charles, do you think your wife is beautiful?' said Harry, hurrying to cover the unfortunate phrase.

'Of course, but it's the inner beauty I love.'

'That's what I mean, the inner beauty that shines in the camera lens,' said Harry. 'That's the nature of business—to pay more for a beautiful, unique person.'

Harry kept his eyes on Charles and appeared relieved that he merely nodded in response to his explanation of the beauty his lens strove to discover in its subjects. He glanced at Aine and then back at Charles.

'Well, Harry, I have no objection if you're wondering,' said Charles. 'It's up to Aine. I have confidence in her. She would not do anything she had reservations about.'

Aine was back at the table, looking at the photos. While she listened to Harry offering more explanation and reassurance about his plans, she looked closely at herself. She was looking at the fine, elegant clothes, at her posture, her poise, at the expression on her face, the long fair hair, at her slim legs and the quality shoes with the delicate heels. She recalled the feelings she experienced. An odd longing to be back in such clothes welled with her. It had been like a temporary ascent to a purified material world. Embarrassed by that ridiculous thought, she became aware of Harry at her side.

'I can see you like yourself in those clothes,' he said. 'And so you should.'

'May I keep one of these photos?'

'Take a couple.'

Late the following morning, Sunday, when the Winterbines were attending to the Sabbath duties, Harry set out on the trip back to Melbourne. He pondered his success as he drove without hurry up the incline out of Binawarra and passed between the two brooding peaks. He had been confident of getting Charles on board with his plans—his charm mostly won out—but there was always some doubt. Charles and Aine Winterbine were definitely not the usual sort that got mixed up in the high-powered, high-tempo fashion industry. Anyhow, he had won through. That was the main thing. No need to worry about it anymore. Perhaps, he continued to muse, he had no reason to worry about Charles in the first place. He was explicit about leaving the decision in Aine's hands. Very trusting of him, for sure. Most fellows would be wary of letting a girl who looked like Aine Winterbine loose among some of the unscrupulous— In fact, he was more worried about that risk than Charles seemed to be.

He fell to surveying the precautions he should take to limit the influences, to keep her quarantined. Despite her appealing naivety and endearing virtue, Aine was human, after all. His mind focused on Aine herself, on her uniqueness. He stopped the car and drew the large prints from the envelope on the passenger seat. He shuffled through them, picked the best, and laid it in view. He glanced on and off at it for the rest of the journey back to his elegant, faithfully restored Victorian townhouse in Parkville. Installed in the lounge room with the best Scotch whisky in his best crystal tumbler and his feet up, he shifted his gaze between the view of the leafy street in the fading afternoon sun and the three framed black and white prints of a beautiful pale face framed by the purest silken fair hair.

AINE'S next shoot was in Melbourne, in Harry's studio. Harry had insisted Charles accompany her so he could view the action for himself. It pleased him to observe how tedious Charles found the lengthy process of changing clothes, adjusting make-up, and setting up the scene. Charles would now likely accept his offer to have a taxi pick Aine up, drive her down to Melbourne, and then back again after each session. Apart from the tediousness of the shoot, the day proceeded without hitches.

'I'm glad to see how relaxed you are now,' said Harry as he accompanied Charles and Aine to their car.

'I know what you want and what to do,' said Aine. 'That makes a difference.'

'Good. You're quickly becoming a professional, like Jannie.'

'She has a lot of support, I see,' remarked Charles.

'I'm lucky to have an excellent team,' said Harry. 'Aine won't lack attention.'

'Where is Jannie?' asked Aine.

'Jannie's away on a break.'

'Is she coming back—to be with you?'

'Be ... be with me?' said Harry.

'I mean, is she still going to be working with you?' said Aine, wondering about his reaction to her simple question. 'I hope she is.'

'Oh, yes, of course. I'm sure Jannie will be back to take care of you for the next project. She wouldn't have it any other way.'

'I suppose Erik will be glad to see her.'

'Erik? I suppose he will.'

Charles was already at the car's wheel, and Harry held the door open. 'Where did she go?'

'To visit her family in Holland.'

'That was sudden, wasn't it? She never mentioned it to me.'

'I think one of her aunts or uncles was sick. Yes, it was sudden. She went to visit. Besides, she was missing Holland—a bit homesick. She had not been back since she and her family arrived in Australia. She can afford it now.'

'Oh,' said Aine, her curiosity about Harry's discomfort left unsatisfied. She eased herself into the car and gave him a smile. That brought pleasure to his face. He signalled to wind down the window.

'I'll be in contact about the shoot and the next project. Okay?'

She nodded and gave him a little wave as Charles brought the car away from the curb. She turned once to wave again and saw him standing still, watching as the car merged with the heavy Melbourne traffic. He was a handsome man, she decided. She was now entirely at ease with him. It was curious that such a handsome, worldly man had succeeded where every other male had failed, except for the very unworldly Charles.

AS HARRY had forecast, Jannie was back to take control of the next studio shoot. She elected to come herself and fetch Aine, a plan Aine tried to dissuade her from.

'It will be a lot of trouble for you, surely,' said Aine when Jannie had rung to make the arrangements.

'No, no, not at all,' said Jannie. 'It's my job. You've got to be relaxed and at ease for the camera.'

'But I'll just be sitting in a taxi.'

'Besides, I want to see you, you gorgeous girl. Harry has been telling me how successful the last shoot was. You'll have your photos in one of the best magazines, too. And I have a lot to tell you.'

Jannie arrived at the door the evening before the arranged day.

'I didn't expect you until tomorrow,' said Aine, standing aside to let her pass. She had a look around outside before shutting the door.

'We need to get an early start tomorrow morning,' Jannie replied, breezing into the lounge room. 'Where's that handsome husband of yours?'

'In the workshop.'

'And your pretty daughter?'

'In bed.'

'Already?'

'It's after eight. Five-year-olds are in bed at that time,' said Aine, detecting a change in Jannie's demeanour. And the accent was back, more pronounced than ever.

'Oh, take no notice of me,' laughed Jannie, taking up position on the lounge settee. 'Children are about as far away from my thoughts as anything could be.' There was a slight twitch at the corner of her coloured, nicely shaped lips. 'Now look at you!' she exclaimed. 'Aine Winterbine hardly looks older than eighteen and already has a child of five. Amazing.'

Aine smiled and sat down, waiting for Jannie to get to the point, for she had something on her mind.

'Plans for any more?'

'That depends upon the will of God.'

'Does it really?'

'Of course.'

'You have some say in it, you know.'

'You're not here to talk about babies, are you?'

'I would hate to think an unintended pregnancy would ruin the future that awaits you.'

'No pregnancy would be unwanted. Surely, this was not your purpose in coming early.'

'Relax, not so formal and suspicious. I came to chat with you, as an old friend. We parted friends last time, didn't we?'

'Did you enjoy your stay in Holland? You've been in the sun, I see.'

'Yes, utterly enjoyable. I had a lot of time to think about where I was going and whether I wanted to continue in that direction.'

'Were you pleased to be back? The last time we spoke, you seemed to have some homesickness.'

'Yes, in a way. The village I left was no longer the same. I was sad at first, but then I realised it would never be the same. And then I formed a new connection, a connection that was a release from the problems I imagined I had.' She stopped. 'Do you remember telling me I should be myself and stop putting on an act?' Aine nodded. 'Well, that was the best advice anyone could have given me. It turned out to be the key, although I wasn't aware of it at the time. I was such a stupid little flirt. But, you know, Aine,' she continued, leaning forward, 'you can't really be good to anyone unless you are good to yourself. That's the mistake of the convent. They want you to erase the self before you can help people. That's wrong. It's tragic.'

'Erase the self?' said Aine. 'But that's not quite what is meant. Erasing yourself in the religious life is to abandon oneself to the love of God. It means merging in love with the love of Christ. It's a way of life that's special.'

'Then why did you fail, a person like you?'

'A person like me? I'm not sure what you mean by that.'

'Don't you just?' Jannie irritatingly raised her eyebrows.

'I simply did not have a vocation. God's will was otherwise for which I am eternally grateful.'

'Really?'

'Yes, I say a prayer of thanksgiving every day that Charles and Estella have come into my life.'

'But it's your life, not theirs.'

'Jannie, what are you getting at?'

'I'm sorry if I'm upsetting you. I'm only saying it's not necessary to deny yourself everything.'

'I'm not getting upset, and I'm not denying myself everything. I have all I want. And as far as work goes, I'm following the course you advised.

Isn't that enough? Is there more you think I should be doing? Speak plainly, Jannie.'

Jannie hesitated. 'I'm sorry if I sound a little pushy,' she said. 'It's just that I had a liberating experience in Holland, an experience I would wish for everyone, especially those I love. You're one of those.' She looked at Aine. Aine did not respond. 'I suppose you can only understand if you have that experience yourself.' Aine still did not respond. 'Let me leave it then,' she went on with a sigh. 'At the moment, I want to help you in your work with Harry.'

'I'm grateful for all your help,' said Aine, relieved Jannie would spare her the liberating experience. 'Harry has a high opinion of your ability.'

'Did he say that?'

'He doesn't have to.'

'You have got to like Harry, haven't you?'

'Yes, I like him. He's very kind to me—encouraging.'

Jannie searched Aine's face. 'Harry's a very charming man. I hope you see his limitations.'

'What do you mean?'

'Men will be men, and I don't think, as beautiful as you are, you have had lots of experience in that direction. Believe me. Harry has his own seductive manner.'

'Jannie, you've already said that. And I find this sort of talk objectionable. I'm married and love Charles more than anything. I don't think for one moment about Harry in—like that. And he doesn't regard me like that. He has been kind. He has also been open about his intentions, as you said he would be.'

'Okay, Aine, I'm sorry. I'm still too used to thinking about myself and all the men prowling around me. But you are warned. I will have a shoulder if things turn out differently.'

'I won't need it. If there are any changes to the present arrangements, changes that affect my family, I will give it away immediately.'

'Would you do that—so lightly give away the promise of a brilliant career?' A faint smile of disbelief encroached.

'You say it's a brilliant career.'

'All right, Aine, I won't speak about it anymore—for the moment.' The smile lingered. 'I've been stupid in the past but, I hope, not self-deluded.'

Aine frowned at Jannie. 'What does it matter to you, anyhow?'

'Well, well, I've never seen you so aggressive,' said Jannie. 'The lady does protest too much, perhaps.'

'I'm sorry. I don't mean to sound that way,' said Aine. 'The thought I could do—'

'You shouldn't get upset about a mild observation. That's all it was. There are more important things to consider.'

Thankfully, Charles arrived to interrupt the unpleasant conversation. 'I wondered whose car that was,' he said, offering Jannie a hand. 'I thought you were coming tomorrow.'

Jannie's explanation for her early arrival was readily accepted. Charles seemed more concerned about where Jannie would spend the night. He would not hear of her booking into the motel on Melbourne Road. Jannie accepted the offer of accommodation after a proper number of refusals. Aine then left Charles to entertain her while ensuring all was in order in the guest room. When she returned, she found Jannie chatting with Charles, expressing interest in his work and asking pertinent questions.

'You know, Charles,' Jannie said, when the subject seemed exhausted, 'you're a lot like Harry. There's the same passionate devotion to your work. There must be the same skill level if the town council has commissioned you for so much important work.'

'Yes, he's very skilled,' Aine found herself saying before she realised there may be a point behind Jannie's comment. But, no, Jannie's expression had no other content than the sincere interest anyone would show.

EVEN before the car drove between the two peaks the following morning, Jannie was chatting about her holiday. Instead of the irritation she felt the previous evening, Aine found herself relaxing as she listened to Jannie's vivid description of the Dutch landscape and the style of life that arose from that unique natural environment.

'It's hard to imagine a country so endlessly flat,' said Aine when they were on the outskirts of Melbourne.

'But it's broken beautifully by waterways, lines of poplars, villages, and farm settlements. The dykes and the natural dunes on the coast keep the water from flooding the land.'

'Aren't people afraid of what might happen if the dykes broke?'

'Yes, it's a constant worry. Around ten years ago, there was a major disaster in the province where I spent most of my time during my visit. Eighteen hundred people drowned when a fierce storm broke through the dykes.'

'Goodness!'

'The sea has been a friend and enemy to the Dutch through the ages. The Romans and traders from Germany erected an altar to the goddess Nehalennia on the coast of Zeeland to offer prayers before making the treacherous crossing over to the coast of Britannia.'

'How do they know that?'

'They found the remains of an altar and temple near the modern coastal resort of Domburg. That's where I was recently, such a beautiful area ...' Her voice tapered into a murmur.

'You must have enjoyed yourself,' said Aine, struck by the different mood.

'Utterly, as I said.' She gave her a sly smile. 'Not a man in sight!'

'Did you meet new people?' said Aine, who had the impression Jannie wanted to hear that question.

'Yes, I happened on this delightful little girl while walking around the dunes. She invited me home to meet her parents.' Jannie laughed. 'She thought I looked sad, the dear little thing.'

'You mustn't have expected such an invitation.'

'She thought I was Catholic. She was right, of course—about being sad, too.'

'Very odd.'

'I suppose it is. A lot of odd things have happened this year. Her concern touched me.'

'Were there others?' said Aine, giving her the right cues.

'I ran into a group of people obsessed with the environment. They were fascinating and taught me many things I didn't know. It was an eye-opener. We had a lot of fun, too.' She hesitated and cast several cautious looks in Aine's direction. 'There was a summer festival, a lot of dancing, singing, and drinking—'

'Oh,' said Aine, glancing at her.

'There were no boys, at least not in my group, just a lot of girls together, being ourselves, having fun. No pressure. It was a real change.'

'Oh,' Aine repeated, observing Jannie's meaningful expressions.

'You are not familiar with those sorts of activities, are you?'

'I don't suppose I am.'

'You don't know what you're missing out on.'

'Don't I?'

'No.' She smirked.

With a few meaningful glances, Jannie left the subject. When they were near Harry's studio, she remarked, 'You haven't been told what you'll be doing, have you?'

'No. Harry said it would be a surprise, a pleasant surprise, something I would love.'

'One of Harry's surprises,' Jannie commented, raising her eyebrows in her typical way. 'But he's right. You'll love it. Harry knows already how to please you.'

'He knows how to please you, too, doesn't he?'

'I'm afraid so ... well, knew ... maybe ....'

While they stood in the lift to Harry's studio, Aine ventured: 'I get the feeling something is going on when you talk about Harry, something you're not saying.'

'Do you?'

Chapter 38

Harry's promise dissolves

THERE WAS no time to pursue the subject. The lift opened into Harry's studio, and the man himself was already talking before they stepped out. After a warm greeting and taking Aine's bag, he apologised for a slight change in the schedule. He had hoped to get on to Aine's shoot immediately, but an urgent request had come in the meantime.

'I have a client who wants some swimwear shots for a campaign in spring. You okay with that, gorgeous?' he said, turning to Jannie. 'We've got to take advantage of that luscious tan, too.' A knowing smile was Jannie's answer.

Harry installed Aine in a comfortable chair with refreshments close at hand while Jannie looked over Harry's schedule. Soon, Jannie was emerging in different one-piece swimsuits, posing and posturing in response to Harry's directions. It was the first time since that day on the lawn at John Batman University that Aine had the opportunity to observe Jannie in action. Even with her limited experience, she understood how professional Jannie was. She watched and listened as Jannie, in smooth, fluid movements, changed position and expression to Harry's flow of instructions. Her attention heightened as he moved in for close-ups in different lying positions. She strained to hear his whispered directions.

'What a gorgeous girl you are,' Harry said near the end of the shoot.

'You don't have to keep saying it,' said Jannie, changing position and hardly moving her lips.

'I thought you liked it,' said Harry, without interrupting his clicking.

'I do.'

'Well, what's up?' He came closer.

'Aren't you going to kiss me?'

'Do you want me to?'

'Yes.'

'You don't.' He stood up, adjusted his camera, and then the lights.

'My lips are no longer attractive?' she resumed when he came in close again.

'What are you playing at?'

'Playing at?'

'Stop that girl stuff. I haven't the time or patience.'

'Sorry, master, don't you love me anymore?'

'Of course I do. More than ever.'

'Then kiss me.'

'Keep your mind on it, will you?'

'You don't want to kiss me in front of Aine, do you?'

'Come on, get up and change. We're here to do a job.'

'You would rather kiss Aine.'

'Stop it,' he said, going to the lights.

'Yes, Harry darling.'

Aine watched Jannie disappear into the changing room, then observed Harry at his equipment table, preparing for the next batch of photos.

'How are you? Comfortable?' he asked, coming over to her. 'We're nearly finished.'

'I'm all right,' she said with a smile. 'Where are your other assistants? There were people everywhere last time.'

'I don't need them until later. Jannie is worth three of them, anyhow. You like the swimwear.'

'Jannie looks very attractive in them.'

'She should do. She's got the looks for it, and they are top-shelf. They're not for you?'

'Not really. I don't go swimming.'

'Really? You don't enjoy swimming?'

'It's not that alone.' Aine was embarrassed for the first time about her views on modesty. She liked the swimsuits and wanted to maintain a friendly manner with Harry, but she could not deny her principles. It was a dilemma she wished to skirt around. Fortunately, Harry showed no inclination to pursue the topic, and Jannie appeared to put an end to it

.

'Come on,' said Harry when they had finished, and Jannie was back in her clothes, 'let's have lunch before we begin on Aine.'

Harry took the two ladies to a first-class restaurant. On seeing the rich decor, Aine hesitated. 'I really can't afford such a place,' she said as the waiter held the chair out for her. 'Especially without Charles.' A sly smile appeared on Jannie's face.

'You're my guest,' said Harry. 'Besides, they give me a good deal for bringing beautiful women to their restaurant.'

'Let him shout us,' said Jannie. 'He can afford it. We're his meal tickets, don't forget.'

'You're my friends and colleagues,' said Harry, frowning. 'We're in it together.'

Jannie did not respond, airily taking the menu the waiter handed her. Aine acquiesced. She should be gracious in the circumstances. Harry first explained the menu in detail to Aine, leaving the waiter looking down his nose at him. Then he passed on to the subject of his work, which appeared inexhaustible. In this way, the lunch passed agreeably,

'I'll see you two later,' said Jannie as the waiter inquired whether they wanted dessert and coffee.

Harry paid little attention to Jannie, giving her a slight nod while asking if Aine wanted dessert. Aine watched, bemused, as Jannie hurried from the restaurant.

'She's preparing the set,' he said and resumed describing the desserts on offer.

After much deliberation, two desserts were ordered with coffee. Harry sank into a mood of desultory musing about his life, keeping up a monologue only broken when his faraway look focused a moment on Aine's response. Aine found the style of ordinary, intimate comments about his life intriguing, perhaps more for the glimpse they offered into his private thoughts than for the unexceptional musings themselves. Harry roused himself at length from his public ponderings, made excuses for his blabbering on and boring Aine, and then called for the bill, which he paid in crisp new pound notes. Back at the studio, Aine was surprised to see how much Jannie had done. One of Harry's assistants had also arrived in the meantime.

'Evening gowns,' said Harry, again switching subjects without a beat, 'you're going to model evening wear, the like of which you have never seen before.'

Harry was right. Never had Aine seen, let alone worn, such beautiful clothes. She was in awe as Jannie helped her change. For a moment, she forgot she was undressing in front of someone.

'I'm a girl, too,' said Jannie.

'I'm not used to this,' said Aine, again feeling awkward at being wedged between the need for assistance and the possible compromise.

'You're a funny girl sometimes. It's just your underwear you'll be in. Okay, I'll look away until you have the gown on.'

But it was no use. Aine did not want to risk spoiling the garment. So, to Jannie's murmurs of approval, she let Jannie help her until she was satisfied.

'But my bare shoulders, I didn't realise—'

'You'll have a variety of shawls and veils for the photos,' said Jannie, maintaining a business-like manner. 'Now sit down while I do your hair and make-up.'

Jannie was meticulous with this part of the operation and had to hold off Harry twice when he called out.

'Now for your shoes.' She slipped finely crafted silver high-heeled shoes on Aine's slender feet. 'Stand up.' She draped a black translucent shawl around Aine's bare shoulders. 'Perfect. Harry will also take a few with a veil.'

Aine stepped back into the studio amid the exclamations of Harry and his assistant. Harry remained standing in front of her, shaking his head. From then on, it became a repeated routine until late in the afternoon. Aine could not help being pleased and reassured by the admiring comments of Harry and his assistants.

'The shots of you with the veil will turn out best,' he said when Aine was again in her own clothes. 'You wait and see. It will be elegance and a peerless beauty mixed with an unfathomable mystery. The dark, see-through veil around that glowing, pale face with the eyes—my clients will swoon over them. Every debutant and every girl attending a university ball will want to look like you.'

'Do you think so?' said Aine.

'No doubts.'

'I don't see myself as others see me.'

'You have to bring the two visions together to form the one confident person,' said Jannie.

'No,' said Harry, 'she may lose that unique aura.'

'You mean you want her to remain the little subservient Miss?'

It was an abrupt comment delivered with a faint, uncharacteristic sneer.

'No, that's not what I mean,' said Harry, glancing at the equally surprised faces of Aine and the assistant. 'I mean that Aine has a distinct personality, and it shows to advantage in her posture and expressions. It's got nothing to do with subservience.'

Jannie seemed to realise she had gone too far. 'I didn't mean to upset anyone.'

'What's eating you, anyhow?' said Harry. 'Not jealous, I hope.'

'Certainly not. I want Aine to succeed as much as you, probably more.'

'Then stop the comments. You're spoiling it.'

Jannie tried to recapture the pleasant atmosphere that had prevailed before her comment and was partly successful, for Harry resumed his affable manner, which was to his great credit, thought Aine. A forgiving nature was one of the best qualities a person could have. Jannie said goodbye to her in the studio and left Harry to accompany her to the taxi. As Aine settled in the taxi after a final goodbye to Harry, she looked back on a hugely enjoyable day with people she liked very much.

'I LIKE Jannie now,' she said to Charles that evening after dinner as they relaxed in the lounge room. 'I've gotten to know her a lot better.'

'She's changed,' said Charles, after listening to Aine's account of the day's happenings. 'She has more confidence in herself. I have the impression something has happened to her.'

'Do you think so?' said Aine, contemplating the suggestion. 'She said she had a liberating experience in Holland.'

'Liberated from what?'

'I don't know.'

'I would be curious to hear.'

Aine did not see any meaning in Charles's expression and continued to reflect on the day with Harry and Jannie. 'It seems wrong to be earning money from wearing beautiful clothes and being in the company of such friendly, considerate people.'

'Does it?' said Charles, looking away.

'You sit there while I tidy up,' said Aine, again missing the expression. 'I've been the one to enjoy myself today.'

She kissed Charles on the forehead and went to the kitchen. Charles sat listening to the sounds from the kitchen before picking up the local paper.

AS IT turned out, Harry arranged for Aine to come to Melbourne around once a month, always by taxi, for Jannie did not repeat her offer. With such a schedule, there was not much disruption to their domestic situation. Moreover, Harry continually consulted Charles about the convenience of having her away for the day. He always enjoyed hearing

Charles acknowledge that the arrangements satisfied all parties. Besides, the generous payment for her work was now making itself felt, naturally assuaging any reservations about the nature of the work. The first change to the schedule came at the beginning of summer. Once again, Harry consulted Charles about the change, or rather, an addition to the plans.

'Now and again, I hold an exhibition of my work,' he said one evening after making a special trip to Binawarra with Jannie. 'I would like to do a series of tableaux with Aine as the model—actually the central feature of the tableaux.'

'You did not have to come all the way to Binawarra for that,' said Charles.

'Yes, I did,' said Harry. 'I want you both to agree to it. It's something new, and it will mean Aine staying overnight in a city hotel, of course. We need to speak about it, and you need to be under no misapprehension of what is involved. Jannie is with me because the tableaux are her suggestion. She'll be setting the scene with my oversight. A normal high-class model's fee will be paid for her time and talent. This is the sort of work models do. And Jannie is right: Aine's perfect for the tableaux she has suggested.'

Harry and Jannie gave a long, detailed explanation of the tableaux and the requirements for setting up each scene. There would be four, each depicting one of the seasons. The whole day would be needed to set the many varied props in their proper place and proportions, and fit Aine into it all.

'There'll be a lot of adjustment throughout the day before Harry can start shooting,' said Jannie.

'I'll have to examine the prints overnight to see how successful it's all been,' added Harry. 'It may be necessary to make adjustments the next day.' For a moment, he looked unsure of himself.

Charles posed a few pertinent questions about Aine's accommodation and meals.

'I'll be looking after Aine,' said Jannie, showing as much enthusiasm for the project as Harry. Indeed, it seemed to Aine that she was the more fired-up of the two. 'I'll make sure she's safe and comfortable. I'll guard her with my life.'

'I hope that's not necessary,' said Charles, releasing a smile.

'Of course not,' said Harry. 'Don't overdo it, Jannie. Aine will be looked after, Charles. She'll be in one of the best hotels, meals, and service a button push away.'

'How do you feel about it, darling?' Charles said to Aine.

'I have no objection if you don't.'

'It's up to you. It's your work.'

It was clear to the three onlookers that Aine had no objection. And so it was settled. Jannie would call Aine when she was ready to set up the first tableau, which would be spring. Having gained Charles and Aine's agreement, Harry showed no wish to linger.

'You're not going to drive back to Melbourne at this hour?' said Charles. 'You can stay the night here. We can accommodate both of you.'

Harry would not hear of it, no matter how much Charles insisted. It was no trouble to make the drive, and when Charles said they would not be back in Melbourne before midnight, Harry replied that he often retired after midnight. 'I do some of my most creative thinking after midnight, Charles.'

THE FIRST call from Jannie came the following week. She had assembled most of the requirements for the spring tableau but needed to schedule a day with Aine to order the plants and flowers.

'Do you know what the main inspiration will be for these tableaux?' she said when Aine arrived late in the morning at Harry's studio. Of course, Aine had no idea where her inspiration came from. 'It's partly classical and partly Celtic. I'll be drawing on Greek, Roman, and Celtic myth, as so many artists in the past have done. The ancients had a close connection with the seasons and the earth as the life-giver. Are you familiar with ancient myth?'

Aine was familiar with myth from her time at school. She had done Latin for a couple of years, and one of her teachers had read Greek and Roman legends to the class. She remembered the story of Daedalus and Icarus, which, for no apparent reason, she felt compelled to relate to Jannie. Daedalus, Icarus's father, had made wings of feathers and wax so that they could escape the island of Crete and King Minos. Daedalus warned Icarus not to fly too high, or the sun would melt the wax. But Icarus, in his excitement, flew higher and higher, forgetting the warning until the wings disintegrated, and he fell to his death.

'What about Celtic myth?' said Jannie, showing not the slightest interest in Aine's brief retelling of the doom of Icarus.

'Just those stories I came across in the books on Ireland that passed around the family, which is not much.'

'Margaret knows a lot about Celtic myth.'

'Yes, I had that impression. Her father's influence, I suppose.'

'Why do you say that?'

'Just a few comments he made to me. I wondered that a person like Mr McGuigan would be interested in Celtic myth.'

'Perhaps it's the other way around—the influence, I mean,' said Jannie pointedly.

'You may be right, although it's odd that she should be so concerned about it now.'

'Did you know that "Aine" is a goddess in Celtic religion?'

'No, I never heard that.'

'Yes, she's a moon goddess connected with fertility and the summer solstice.'

'Margaret told you that?'

'Well ... yes.'

'My parents told me that Aine is the Gaelic form of Anne,' said Aine, not seeing any significance in Jannie's comments. 'I was named after St Anne, the mother of the Blessed Virgin Mary. I'm sure my parents have no idea of the mythical background of my name. It would not have motivated them, anyhow.'

Harry arrived, and Jannie dropped the subject, returning to her preparations for the tableau. Harry warmly greeted Aine and then looked over Jannie's work. After a long conversation about what was needed and awaited for the tableau, Harry took Aine to a nearby tearoom.

'You should eat something now because there'll be a lot of intense work later,' he said when they were seated and served. 'You know, Jannie is very creative,' he continued. 'There's much more to her than you would expect at the first meeting. This new thing about ancient myth has really grabbed her. She's turning it into a creative moment.'

'Has she said much to you about it?'

'About myth and the earth goddess and all that sort of thing?'

'Yes.' She had the impression it did not occupy his thoughts much.

'Yes, since she arrived back from her holiday in Holland. Apparently, she met people interested in that sort of thing, too.'

'That holiday has changed her.'

'Yes, it has,' said Harry, not concentrating entirely on the subject. 'She's more focused than she used to be. But she was always well organised. She'll have a good administrative career once the looks go. I mean, when she's too old for modelling work.' He gave her a self-conscious smile.

'You don't have to be embarrassed,' said Aine, surprising herself that she should be so familiar with him. 'I understand youthful female looks are not eternal. My mother and others have warned me of the impermanence of physical appearance. It's what's underneath that's important.'

'Did I look embarrassed?' he said with a guilty smile.

'A little.'

'It was a little tactless. I must have sounded mercenary, too.'

'Not at all. It's your work. And I don't take this sort of work seriously. It's been your encouragement that has led me on. Without that, it's doubtful I would be doing it.'

'Really?'

'Yes, of course.'

'I'm privileged.'

'You have treated me well.'

'I hope I continue to do so. You must tell me whenever there's something you're not comfortable with, as I said in the very beginning. I'm not as mercenary as some people think.'

'I know. It's your job,' she repeated. 'People must confuse that with how you are as a person. You've been kind to me. That's not mercenary.'

'You're open and honest. That could be fatal in this industry.'

'As long as you remain the same, I'm safe.'

'I have a high rule to live up to.'

'You recognise it as a rule?'

'You have made it one.'

'It's not I that has made the rule.'

'Then who?'

Aine hesitated. Why did she hesitate? 'The rule of kindness and generosity is written in the scheme of things.' She suppressed her exasperation with herself.

'Written in the scheme of things? Where on earth did that come from?'

'Decent people treat others kindly. That thought should occur to anyone not blinded by selfishness.'

'Oh, I see. I keep forgetting you and Jannie were in a convent. It was part of the instruction, wasn't it?'

'The major theme of the Gospel accounts of Jesus' life is love for one's fellow man. It forms scriptural teaching about charity. But the scriptural or religious teaching merely confirms what people have called natural morality through the centuries—what appears to human reason and sensibility as right.'

'You explain it well, like a lesson you had.'

'Of course, it was part of the study routine, but it's not a lesson you would only have in a convent if that's what you mean. It's fairly straightforward, isn't it? Isn't it reasonable?'

'Yes, it's not difficult if I can understand it,' said Harry. 'I wish you hadn't told me.'

'Why?' asked Aine, suspecting his meaning.

'Because I don't like being confronted with rules or moral arguments that seem to make sense. I'm very self-centred, you know, and don't have any inclination to change. I'm sure Jannie has said that.'

'Then you are kind despite yourself.'

'I won't have any more tête-à-têtes with you. You make me look at myself too much. It's not pretty.'

'You exaggerate terribly,' said Aine, smiling.

He focused his bright, intelligent eyes on her across the small table until she blushed. 'My momentary discomfort has been royally rewarded with that smile. But, come on, we must get back. Jannie will now be wanting help.'

They walked back to the studio in silence, with Harry looking thoughtful and Aine glancing at his thoughtful expression.

'Where's Erik?' she asked when they were in the lift.

'Erik? He's at work, of course.'

'I had the impression Erik was Jannie's boyfriend.'

'So did I—the first one, in fact. I mean the first serious one.'

'Really? What happened?'

'I don't know. She suddenly went off him. I don't know why.' He cast a nervous look at her and then peered at the floor numbers as they lit up. He seemed relieved when they arrived at his floor.

There were continual signs of something between Jannie and Harry. Aine was curious about when it started. Did it begin on that weekend at Binawarra? The question remained in her head while Harry threw himself into his work, stationing her comfortably to the side to watch the interaction. He and Jannie worked well together, each anticipating the other. Cooperating generously, he did not question Jannie's concept of the scene. Flowers and plants and bushes in pots arrived regularly. As the scene started to take shape, he became fulsome in his praise, going no further than recommending adjustments to the original idea. Aine was relieved Harry had taken her for an extended morning tea because any notion of eating and drinking seemed to have vanished. She was happy to see plates of sandwiches delivered at around two o'clock.

'Excellent, Jannie,' said Harry, biting at a sandwich while he examined their work from different angles. 'Terrific. It's another talent you have.'

Jannie, who sat next to Aine, holding a steaming mug at her mouth, nodded in acknowledgment of the praise.

'It's time to start putting Aine into the scene,' continued Harry, still without looking at her.

That was just what Jannie had in mind. So, after a quick lunch, she had Aine take off her shoes and socks and, cradling her milk-white feet in both hands, examined them.

'Look at this,' she called to Harry.

Still contemplating the work already completed, Harry backed over, stuffing the remains of a sandwich in his mouth. He turned and looked down at the slender feet cupped in Jannie's hands. He reached down and ran his hand gently around them, uttering sounds of approval. Aine withdrew her feet.

'I'm sorry. I forgot.'

'He's just admiring your feet,' said Jannie. 'The form of the feet and the texture of the skin are important to the tableau. You'll be barefoot in all the shots.'

'You have beautiful feet,' said Harry, 'perfect for what Jannie has in mind.'

'I'm not used to—'

'I know,' said Harry, 'I apologise. I'm used to doing such things with the models.'

'It's just work,' said Jannie, opening her make-up bag. 'What colour?' She turned to Harry after taking out several small bottles of nail polish.

'Bright red.'

'I agree.'

Aine watched her go to work on her feet, feeling once more wedged between her principles and what appeared, at least to Jannie and Harry, quite unexceptionable behaviour. Usually, she would never have taken off her shoes in such a situation, let alone let a man run his hands over her bare feet like that. That sort of caress was reserved for Charles. But the nature of the work, her implicit permission to adjust her appearance, and the growing affection she had for both people made it different. This was no longer the case of a male pestering her, something she was never in two minds about and had handled efficiently, if not politely, sometimes. The dilemma kept presenting itself, a dilemma she was not facing up to.

Jannie spent a long time on her toenails, meticulously cutting, filing, and painting. She finished by rubbing cream over her feet so that they glistened faintly. Then she worked on her hair, which did not take as much time, for it was meant to hang loosely. After that, Jannie took her to the dressing room, where she handed her a gleaming white silk tunic that fell halfway down her calves. This time, she was left alone to dress. 'Come out when you have it on—and no shoes,' said Jannie, hurrying back to Harry. When she appeared, Harry and Jannie gave her a cursory look of approval and then began experimenting with different positions in the unfinished tableau. This process seemed endless as they discussed Aine's pose and position and the necessary adjustments to the background. They were unconscious of the extended periods they had her in the same pose.

'You can have a break now,' said Harry more than an hour later. 'You're looking tired. I'm sorry if you were uncomfortable.'

'It's surprisingly tiring,' said Aine, grateful for the break.

'It's not as easy as it appears,' said Jannie. She came behind Aine and began rubbing her neck and shoulders.

'That's relaxing,' said Aine, closing her eyes. 'My neck aches a bit.'

'Here's a cup of tea,' said Harry.

'Thank you, Harry,' said Aine, opening her eyes and taking the cup. She sipped the tea, and her eyes closed again. After a minute or two, she realised something was different in the rubbing. She opened her eyes and swung around. Harry was standing behind her.

'I'm giving Jannie a break,' he said. Jannie was sitting to the side with a cup at her mouth.

'I would rather not,' she said, getting up.

'Okay,' said Harry, stepping away, 'I was just trying to help—nothing else.'

'You're annoyingly scrupulous,' said Jannie. 'Harry's rubbed hundreds of tired, aching necks.'

'You don't have to exaggerate,' said Harry, frowning. He made off to the kitchen.

Aine could not find the words for a response. But, despite feeling her reaction a little scrupulous, as Jannie said, she knew she should not allow Harry to touch her that way. Harry returned a minute or so later, holding a mug.

'I'm sorry,' he said. 'I'll make a greater effort to pay attention to your needs. Please continue to tell me if something is bothering you, no matter what.'

Aine nodded and tried to smile. That was enough response for Harry, and he resumed talking about the tableau. The discussion, the props adjustment, and Aine's positioning continued until late afternoon.

'We're going to stop now,' said Harry eventually. 'Aine, you're too tired. It's starting to show in your movements and expression. Wait a moment,' he added as Aine stepped off the platform, 'I want a few shots of you to get an idea of how it will come up in the film.'

Aine stepped back onto the platform, awaiting his instructions while he fetched two cameras from a nearby table. As he returned, he was already clicking, using each camera alternately. Aine stood looking at him. She raised her hands in an inquiring gesture, but he did not respond. She looked at Jannie, who was smiling. 'What?' formed on Aine's lips. Harry gestured vaguely to move to different positions, which she attempted to do. Then he had finished.

'A few loose, impromptu shots,' said Jannie while he was putting his cameras away. 'You'll be surprised at how some of those shots turn out. They're like trophy shots for him.' She glanced at Harry, but he had not heard.

'I'll look at the black and white ones tonight,' Harry said cheerfully, joining them. 'Jannie, you can take Aine to her hotel for a rest. I'll see you both tonight at dinner.'

Aine was pleased to be left alone after Jannie deposited her at the hotel room door. The day had been stressful despite the lack of physical activity. She suspected the situation and the burden of the dilemma had wearied her. She lay on the bed, intending to stay there for a short rest before turning her mind to resolving the dilemma. And she must ring Charles. Soon, she had drifted off and was awoken by an insistent knocking at her door.

'Fell asleep, did you?' said Jannie, waltzing into the room. 'I know how you feel. It can be very stressful. People don't realise how much.'

'I feel better now.'

'And then there's always Harry to add to it.'

'What do you mean?'

'Harry's very particular personality is what I mean,' she said. 'And don't start telling me again how kind he is. Go and have a shower.'

Aine was happy to leave the subject alone and went to shower and dress. Not long after, they arrived at the restaurant to find Harry seated, looking out over the Yarra River. He had the uncertain expression of someone interrupted while engrossed in thought as their greeting broke in on him. But the candid moment was gone, and he became his usual cheerful self. He seemed to understand Aine's weariness and kept the conversation light over a sumptuous dinner, mostly recounting inoffensive experiences from his childhood. When this source dried up, he turned the conversation to Jannie, asking questions about her holiday in Holland. Jannie spoke rather superficially about her excursions around the former island of Walcheren. Surprisingly, for Aine, Harry showed no interest in what seemed an interesting topic. Who, for example, was Jannie with all this time? Didn't he want to know?

'It's still early,' said Harry after paying the bill. 'Let's go for a walk along the river. A walk in the fresh air will help Aine with her beauty sleep.'

They walked in silence for a while, each enjoying the quiet, fresh night air and the city lights glistening in the dark, undisturbed water. Jannie threaded her arm through Harry's. When they turned to walk back, two men appeared from the shadows, making indistinct comments aimed at the young women. Jannie ignored them, but Aine, frightened by their sudden appearance, drew closer to Harry.

'They're pretty harmless,' he said as they retreated into the shades of the surrounding trees. 'I think they've had a few. Take my arm if it makes you feel better.'

'Had a few what?' said Aine, now seeing Jannie had her arm through Harry's. She felt safer that way, too, and linked her arm with his. It would be just until they left the river.

'A few drinks, you silly thing,' Jannie laughed.

'You can't blame them for expressing admiration for two beautiful women,' said Harry, glancing at Aine. Aine looked away.

'Jannie, do you think you're beautiful?' said Harry, after looking at Aine until he caught her eyes.

'I know I am.'

'That's not very modest, is it, Aine?' Aine did not answer. 'Do you think you're beautiful, Aine?' he went on unperturbed.

'I don't think about myself like that, as I have already said.'

'But why?'

'Such talk is proud and immodest to her.'

'That's not all,' said Aine.

'Why shouldn't I acknowledge nature's gift to me?' said Jannie. 'That's not being immodest. And what's wrong with pride?'

'Well, what have we here?' said Harry, stopping. 'Two beautiful Catholic girls from the same convent: one thinks her beauty is God-given and she should be proud of it; the other, obviously from other religious reasons, thinks she should deny it. Whose view is correct in your religious terms?'

Jannie laughed. 'You're right, Harry. I hadn't thought about it like that before. Harry, the theologian!'

'You have not accurately expressed the Catholic point of view,' said Aine. 'There's no real conflict in acknowledging God's gifts and genuine modesty. It's the narrowing selfishness in pride—'

'Come on, Aine, I'm only joking,' said Harry. 'Let's not be so serious about it. I accept your moral views without question. I show that, don't I ?'

He was right; his actions spoke volumes. She smiled and nodded. Jannie seemed inclined to prolong the subject, but received a signal from Harry and desisted. As they branched off the path along the river to walk back into the city, Harry left it to Jannie to return Aine to her hotel.

'Have a restful sleep, Aine. It'll be hard work tomorrow.'

Harry had gone some paces when Jannie released Aine's arm and went after him. She whispered something in his ear.

'I'm always good to you,' Aine heard Harry say as he turned and gently held her arm.

'I know,' said Jannie and kissed him on the cheek. She watched Harry walk away, then came back to Aine. 'Come on. I'll take you back to your hotel,' she said without looking at her.

Chapter 39

Jannie takes control

HARRY SPREAD a bundle of prints out on the dining room table late that night. He looked closely at each. Then he arranged them in order of quality. The photo of Aine looking into the camera lens with an unguarded expression headed the series. Her lips were a little parted as if she was going to say something, and her eyelids drooped a fraction to give her that ethereal look she sometimes had. This time, though, that ethereal look was focused on him. He remembered the exact moment. He pored over the photo for some time. The following morning, he rose early and went directly to the dining room. It did not take him long to decide he was right. That was the best photo—of Aine as she was. To think she had bestowed that look on him.

'What's got your attention?' said Erik, wandering into the room, holding a teacup.

'Have a look.'

Erik bent over the photos. 'She certainly is different. You can pick them, I have to admit. I feel more inclined than ever to take up photography.'

'You'll have to have more than an inclination.'

'You can teach me. I'll become your pupil.' He sniggered and gulped down his remaining tea.

'Get lost, will you? This is serious.'

A half-hour later, now ready to depart for work, Erik passed by the dining room door again. 'You're still not looking at that girl, are you? She's married, you know.'

'One in a million,' Harry murmured, hardly heeding Erik.

HARRY'S last words to Aine were not idle. As soon as she arrived at the studio, she became captive of a process that had her dressed and painted meticulously—nothing would be left to chance—and then positioned in the centre of the tableau, now complete with various fresh shrubs and flowers. An extra assistant had arrived for the menial tasks that cropped up. The two changes from the previous day's preparations, apart from the meticulous facial make-up, were a different white silken tunic, bordered with green symbols, and a thick garland of colourful flowers on her head.

'Do these figures on my dress have any significance?' Aine asked when she could get Jannie's attention away from all the other things.

'Figures?' Jannie said. 'Whatever you want them to mean.'

Aine found the reply unsatisfactory but did not press for further explanation. In any case, there was no time to linger over such matters. Harry now had control of her as he clicked and repositioned her continually. Despite the intensity with which he threw himself into the task—clicking, reassessing, conferring with Jannie, adjusting the props—he never raised his voice or spoke roughly to her. He was all gentleness. Perhaps it was because she understood his directions and moved into the correct pose and position, assuming the right expression as soon as he spoke. He was encouraging between instructions, and that made it easier, of course. He called a brief break mid-morning for a cup of tea, but even then, he discussed the next phase of the shoot, which entailed merging her with the flora in the tableau.

'All Jannie's idea,' he said with a shrug.

'The idea of the earth's renewal by Mother Nature after the dying-off symbolised by the winter solstice is of absolute importance,' Jannie stressed.

They continued until lunch, with Harry and Jannie becoming voluble in their praise of Aine and the expectation that the shoot would be a resounding success.

'The shift to holding the flowers was exactly what I needed,' said Harry. 'It had the right joining of purity in nature and purity in person.'

'In the personification of nature through Aine, you mean,' said Jannie. 'That's the point.'

'What point?' said Harry.

'That nature is a living thing like us. The match of the pristine flowers with Aine's pale, flawless face and neck—that's what gives it the meaning.'

Harry regarded Jannie closely as if not quite understanding. 'That meaning is the important thing in all this, is it?'

'Yes, of course, I've been telling you that. What were you thinking?'

Harry hesitated. 'I was thinking in terms of beauty in nature and beauty in the person, as represented by Aine.'

'That's not my idea,' said Jannie. 'You've missed the point.'

'What meaning will there be in the summer tableau?' said Harry.

'Fertility, Mother Earth and the goddess of fertility.'

'As an image, I assume.'

'More than that.'

'I'm not quite with you on this,' said Harry. 'I'm still inclined to view the exercise in the context of beauty.'

Aine listened with close interest to this exchange. For the first time, she had a distinct idea of the different attitudes of her two friends. That confirmed her confidence in Harry, that there was a straightforward motive in his actions, whereas Jannie had a higher purpose, a purpose that reminded her of Margaret. It passed through her mind that Margaret may have something to do with Jannie's new confidence. That thought did not linger because Harry called a halt for lunch. As she went to the dressing room, she saw Jannie conferring with him. When she joined Jannie again, Harry had gone. 'On a message,' said Jannie, anticipating her question.

'I think we can wrap it up now,' he said breathlessly to Aine when he returned around forty minutes later. 'Jannie thinks we have enough shots from all possible points and poses, and so do I. Since we have enough time, she suggested we tackle a shoot I had scheduled for two weeks' time. It won't take too long. I've got everything arranged—picked up the necessaries. Will you be happy to stay on a little longer?'

'I suppose so,' said Aine, 'but I must tell Charles.'

'I've already rung him,' said Harry. 'He's quite happy about the arrangement. The taxi will arrive a couple of hours later. That's all.'

'If Charles is happy about it ...'

The location of the shoot for summer accessories was once again Jannie's idea, Harry confided, as Jannie set about changing Aine's make-up and preparing a different selection of clothes. It did not take long to have Aine dressed and made up, and the equipment packed in Harry's car. As they set off, Aine asked where they were going.

'That's a surprise,' said Jannie.

Harry's expression told Aine he had no idea what the surprise would be. Around half an hour later, Aine recognised the area they were driving through.

'This is the country around the convent.'

'It will be perfect for what you have to promote. Never fear,' said Jannie, to dampen further discussion until they arrived.

Aine was unsure where they had stopped, as they had entered the area from an unfamiliar direction. They gathered their equipment and stock and made their way along a farmhouse fence. When they came through a bushy, hilly area out onto open, undulating ground with an expanse of long grass, Aine recognised where she was—on the other side of that river. Coming around a shallow rise, they walked into full view of the convent building with its Gothic tower dominating the ridge.

'Why have you brought us here?' said Aine.

'It has a great background for the promotional shots Harry wants,' said Jannie.

'You're right,' said Harry, looking around. 'The sun is in the right spot, and the lush green grass with hills and bush in the background gives an excellent choice of shots. Very outdoor and recreational.'

'Don't be so suspicious,' said Jannie.

Aine had to be satisfied with those explanations, however much she suspected something more behind it. At least Harry was above all suspicion in this. His mind was evidently on nothing other than the photos he wanted of her wearing a range of summer jewellery, hats, sunglasses, and footwear. He began the same meticulous routine, organising her clothes, position, and pose. Soon her suspicions retreated into the background as she attended to his instructions.

'You're doing very well,' he said, between a change of hats and sunglasses. 'You are beginning to anticipate me. That's what makes Jannie such a good fashion model.'

'I can't get used to your praise,' said Jannie before Aine could answer. 'You used to be a lot harder on me.'

'You needed training. Besides, I see you differently now.'

Jannie smiled knowingly at Aine as she positioned herself in response to Harry's gestures. When they moved further down the sloping land towards the river, Aine became suspicious again. And anxious. Harry took a few shots of her by the river, with the convent in the background. The worry that she may spoil the shots because of her looking around increased her anxiety.

'I'm sorry,' she said. 'I keep on moving.'

'No, don't worry,' said Harry eagerly, 'I'm capturing some very different expressions. The convent is a stunning contrast, too.' He stopped. 'It's making you nervous, isn't it?'

'Yes, it is.'

'Why?'

'I'd rather not say.' She looked around for Jannie. But Jannie had disappeared. 'Where's Jannie?'

'Haven't a clue,' he said, appearing just as surprised as Aine. At that moment, Jannie appeared in a small rowboat from around the bend in the river. 'There she is, full of surprises, as usual.'

Jannie rowed into the bank where they stood. 'Come on, Aine, climb aboard as you are. Harry will get some shots of you in the boat. There's nothing so romantic as a boat on a river.'

There was no resisting the invitation, especially as Harry responded with enthusiasm. She let him help her on board, where, on Jannie's guidance, she took up a position in the stern, looking nervously at the boat, the river, and the tower. With Jannie keeping the boat steady, Harry shot her in different poses and in various spots on the water. They returned to the bank twice more, where Aine distractedly put on a different combination of hats, jewellery, sunglasses, and shoes. As Harry was finishing the third series of photos, Jannie exclaimed: 'Look, Aine!' Aine looked up to see Margaret waving at the edge of the steep bank.

'Do you mind if we stop and have a few words?' Jannie said to Harry. 'Must you?'

'I would like to. It's boring for you, I know. I'll take you back to the bank, where you can wait. We won't be long. You can take some pictures from the bank.'

Harry gave in to this false compromise and submitted to being deposited back on land.

'Did you plan this?' said Aine as Jannie turned the boat around and rowed toward the jetty she was so familiar with.

'Don't be so distrustful. Besides, you should be happy to see an old friend. Where's the harm?'

'You could've told me.'

'I didn't say I planned it.'

'You've done this before, haven't you?' said Aine as Jannie manoeuvred the boat alongside the jetty. She could scarcely suppress her trembling as the vision of the boat on the dark river floated before her eyes.

Jannie did not answer, pretending to concentrate on mooring the boat securely. Margaret arrived and held out her hand to help her onto the jetty.

'What a pleasant surprise,' she said as she let go of Aine's hand and offered hers to Jannie. 'I've been wondering how things were going. Come on. I've got a few familiar faces to show you.' She led the way up the stairs and onto the clearing. Sitting on the bench that Aine and Virginia sat on six years before were Elizabeth Parker and Kate Armstrong, or as they now were, Sisters Hildegard and Benedicta.

They greeted Aine warmly, exclaiming over her fashionable clothes and appearance. It had been so long since they had seen her. They wanted to know all the news. Margaret punctuated Aine's broken account of her life with various knowing and approving comments. All the time, Aine looked around her. The tower rose in the fading afternoon sky and seemed to waver; the main building with the yawning gaps between its cloister columns frowned down on them, and the rustle and murmur of the trees and bush along the property's border continually came at her. She lost track of what she was saying. Fortunately, Jannie connected the sentences and kept the conversation flowing.

'I knew you had something more substantial to do with your life,' Aine heard Margaret saying again as she looked up at the tower spiking into the sky.

'Where's Virginia?' she said, thinking of her dear friend.

'I'm not sure,' said Margaret. 'Sister Agnes is in the building somewhere, I suppose. This is a good spot for fashion photos, I imagine.'

Aine's discomfort with the surroundings and the incongruity of the chance meeting froze her lips, leaving Jannie to complete an enthusiastic account of her success. The swaying of the nuns' veiled heads accompanied the hollow-sounding praise interspersing Jannie's enthusiasm. The silhouetted hoods in the translucent glass—the whispering—the dark spirit—she stepped back a little and looked across the river. Harry sat near the bank, pointing his camera's long lens at her. She waved at him. He lowered his camera and looked. Then, gesticulating, he jumped to his feet and rushed to the water's edge. Margaret's face darkened.

'I think that man wants your attention,' she said to Jannie.

Jannie glanced at Harry and then at Aine. 'Sorry, we have to go, Marg.' She put her arm around Aine and led her away.

'We understand,' called Margaret. 'It was wonderful to see you, Aine, even better to see you have struck out on a journey of independence.'

The words rang in Aine's ears, but she could not speak. She nodded with a slight turn of the head, grateful that Jannie did not argue with Harry but at once acted to extract her from the oppressive environment of Margaret and the convent. She struggled to regain her composure as Jannie rowed across the river to where Harry waited, his arm outstretched and his camera dangling on the strap around his neck. When Harry put his arm around her while Jannie packed up, she did not resist. By the time they were in the car, driving back to Harry's studio, Aine had calmed.

'We got some good shots,' said Harry. 'You did well, Aine, very well.' But he did not say anything to Jannie about her jaunt with Aine across the river. He seemed too satisfied with the shoot's success to attend to anything else.

Chapter 40

Joe's dismay

GEMMA'S INFORMATION proved correct. Philip was present for the following tutorial. The fuss made over him by the other students, especially the girls, kept his attention spread evenly around the room. It meant she could hide the shock and sadness at seeing him looking so unwell. What a change from the Philip she knew, and what a difference from the beginning of the year. He was pale, even greyish, and his features drawn. He, too, had lost weight.

'Stop the questioning,' he said. 'It's not as if I'm on my deathbed. I'll recover.'

'How come you got pneumonia at this time of the year?'

'Is pneumonia restricted to seasons?' he said. 'Stupidity, I suppose,' he added, not waiting for an answer. 'Too much work and not enough rest.'

'And too much of something else,' someone said.

'Cut it out,' he said wearily. 'Come on, let's get down to work. My private life is no one's business here.'

Despite the sadness caused by his appearance and despite the unspoken problem, Agnes's spirits rose now that he was back. He avoided addressing her directly, but his presence was enough. It gave her a feeling of solidarity and shared perspective. His thoughts had been so much her own for so long, and perhaps because there had been no tapering off, just that heartbreaking, abrupt end, a large residue remained.

'Sister Agnes, can you spare a few minutes?' he tried to say casually after the following tutorial. 'Is everything all right? I mean with your study.' he continued after the students had left his office.

'Yes, Philip.'

Her use of his Christian name appeared to jolt him.

'Was Joe Edelman okay?'

'Yes, he was kind and helpful, although forthright.'

'Yes, he's not reluctant to air his views, but he's a good chap, clever in his field, and will help whenever he's needed.' He tapped his desk a few times and wrung his hands. 'Virginia, you look tired.'

'Nuns have a lot to do. It's not an ordinary life.'

'I'll say—' He coughed. 'I just wanted to say I'll give you whatever help you need. Don't hesitate to call on me. There is nothing to be uneasy about. That's my job as your tutor.'

'Of course, Philip, I have always known that.'

'You get a different perspective from me. I know the sorts of problems you'll be confronting, things Joe Edelman is not aware of or understands.'

'I know. Thank you.' She paused. 'I'm sorry to hear you've been sick.'

'It's nothing.' He waved his hand.

'Pneumonia is not nothing. You don't look well.'

'I'll get over it.' He gave her a quick, uncertain smile. 'People exaggerate.'

'Dr Edelman said you were busy with research work.'

'Yes, it's that book I started, you know, when we were together before—' His greyish colour deepened for a moment. 'It's about the history of ideas if you remember.'

'Yes, I remember.' He had spoken at the time with such enthusiasm about his project. 'It's taking a long time.'

'Yes, well, things interrupted me—my academic duties—but that's the way with academics. It's a big project, besides.'

'Yes, of course. I hope you made progress.'

'Not as much as I had hoped. But I'll get there—eventually.'

'I wish you all the very best with it.'

'Thank you.' He seemed at a loss for something more to say. 'That's about it, I suppose,' he said, his mind not entirely with his mouth.

'I'll be going then.'

'Oh, I don't mean to push you out.'

'That's all right, Philip. I must go, anyway.'

He walked her to the door. 'Remember: don't hesitate to come to me if any questions or difficulties with the course material arise.'

'I won't, Philip.'

'Goodbye, then.'

'Yes, goodbye.'

She walked away from his office feeling she had regressed to the cautious phrasing she sometimes adopted with Philip when she was a teenager. That evening, Philip remained on her mind as he was then. As she entered the chapel with the other nuns the following morning, she again experienced that feeling of unreality. What was she doing all dressed up in black with row after row of stiff bowed heads? She had again that almost uncontrollable urge to wrench the black costume from her body and put on regular clothes, clothes a young woman in her twenties would wear. Her wardrobe at her parents' house, full of smart dresses, skirts, blouses, and slacks hanging in a neat row, came to mind—clothes she had paid good money for. She thought of Virginia Pearson in those clothes and the admiring looks she once received.

The rest of the day was spent struggling out of the daze of unreality, the second time she had to engage in this struggle. She kept reminding herself why she had joined the religious life, why thousands before her had entered the religious life over the centuries, how great saints arose from monasteries and convents as stunning examples of holiness and the Gospel message. She eventually succeeded in driving out the feeling but was left with dry reality, the only bright spot being, perversely, the return of Philip.

The improvement in her feelings endured over the following days. She ignored the significance of the improvement, happy only that her dark mood had faded, for she could do nothing in the paralysis of that mood. Her thoughts returned to Aine, who had been at the edge of her mind but desperately ignored. To understand what Aine had been through at the convent and the possible influence Margaret and Jannie now had, she resumed searching the university library for information on the Age of Aquarius. She had a breakthrough, finding a book on neo-paganism and the re-emergence of Gnosticism. What she read utterly astounded her. It was as Barry had related. How many did this nonsense suck in? The section on rituals and when they were performed caught her eye. They seemed to be mainly drawn from the pre-Christian Celtic religion.

As she ran her eye over the dates of the rituals, she saw that some coincided with Aine's episodes. Indeed, the night she had followed the hooded figures coincided with a pagan feast between the equinox and the winter solstice. The next pagan feast day was October 31st, the eve of All Saints Day for the Church. The Church had created the Christian feast to replace the Celtic feast of Samhain. Samhain celebrated death, the end of summer, and the coming rebirth of nature. All Souls Day was only a few days away. If her speculations were correct, there would be activity around the clearing and the grotto.

On the evening of October thirty-first, she sat at the window of her cell, preparing for a long wait. Close to midnight, her patience was rewarded, and her speculations justified. Suddenly, out of the gloom of the rocky stairway, three hooded figures appeared fleetingly. Others could have followed. Because of the cloudy night and the angle of vision, she could not see clearly, but she was sure the figures, joined by others from the river, headed for the grotto. There was again a flash of light around the grotto, and then darkness.

The excitement of being right and the relief of an explanation for the mysterious events encouraged her to investigate. Wrapping herself in her coat, she crept in the faint light of the corridor to the stairway. She halted at the top, listening for movement in the building. She began to descend the stairs but stopped where the stairs turned. The great wooden doors were locked. She crouched and waited. It was a wise precaution. Moments later, Mother Cecilia appeared. She pulled on the door handle and then retreated out of sight. Agnes returned to her room to consider what to do. The following afternoon, while reading her daily office, she made her way to the grotto. Remnants of flowers were among the rocks and scattered around on the grass. There were a few burnt twigs here and there and a roundish patch of grass that was a little withered and discoloured. She caught a whiff of a strange sickly odour.

'I'M GLAD you informed me,' said Mother Jerome that evening. 'I need to be alerted to this sort of thing.'

'What's to be done? What will you do?' asked Agnes, amazed that the prioress took the news so calmly.

The prioress was hesitant. 'I would like you to keep this to yourself, as I've asked you.'

'It seems ominous.'

'I know you want action, but you are not to concern yourself with it. There is enough on your plate.'

'But these sisters, whoever they are, are perverting the life of the convent.'

'Several others and I have been aware of a malignant undercurrent in our congregation,' said Mother Jerome after some consideration. 'It has been difficult to find the rotten point. Indeed, it remains elusive. As for Gnosticism, neo-paganism, the occult, and esotericism behind it, these movements, all related in one way or another, have flourished underground since the French Revolution. It was only last century that their adherents broke cover—with caution. Their sworn enemy is the Catholic Church.

'In their unrelenting efforts to destroy the Church—the enemy of freedom as they understand freedom—they will shrink from nothing, even going into the heart of their enemy's institutions, pretending to be fervent adherents. Because their movements and ideas are still not common currency, I have played their game, waited, observed, and made counter moves when it seemed their ideas were at play. Until now, they have not touched many sisters. Those touched are not blatant, but occasional signs of succumbing appear. These strange and daring events are a manifestation.'

'It's horrifying,' said Agnes. 'How could any female in her right mind be attracted?'

'At the heart of this neo-paganism is the Goddess, Mother Earth, the female deity, and whatever else neo-pagans want to call it or the idea. This has an irresistible attraction for some women. Women connected with the so-called women's rights movement, the suffragettes, were heavily involved in goddess worship. This is not generally known.'

'Goddess worship, surely not? Surely any sane woman these days will not be attracted to this sort of—'

'Sister, there's a lot more to it than I'm saying, not least the political aspect. The idea of the inner divinity and the self-legislating individual is seductive and has grave implications for the organisation of society. But, I repeat, I don't want you to bother yourself with it. Your plate is full, and you are already under much stress. When the time comes, we will talk about it.'

'If you say so, Mother.'

'I say so.' She paused. 'Let me remind you we spoke about the La Salette prophecies.'

'Father Sheridan's recommendation to read them was uncanny.'

'You will remember that the corruption of female religious orders is foretold, that many orders will be riven with unnatural lust.'

'Is there a connection?'

'To start with, ritual prostitution relates to the worship of the female deity. And unrestricted sexual activity is the pathway to enlightenment in the divine feminine.'

'I can hardly comprehend it. Surely, this could not be true.'

'I understand your reaction. But, fortunately, this modern form of Gnosticism is as far from the thoughts of most young women as anything could be.' She stopped and looked at Agnes. 'Come now, Sister, enough said about this sordid business for the moment. Leave it to stronger and wiser heads to deal with it. Your moment will come all too quickly.'

'Yes, Reverend Mother.' She thought for a moment. 'What about Sister Catherine? What about her talk of self-fulfilment and the influence she seems to have on Jannie and Aine?'

'You will leave Sister Catherine to me. Your characters are too different. I think you may misjudge your fellow sister.'

'No, Mother, there is too much—'

'No, Sister, you are to leave her alone.'

'What about Aine?' she persisted. 'She's getting involved with people and things completely out of character for her.'

'Again, Sister, you are to leave her alone. Mrs Winterbine must overcome her trials, which are upon her. You must not forget that the Evil One targets the pure of heart more ferociously than anyone else. We must continue to pray that your friend overcomes her present trial.'

'So you recognized that she's straying?'

'She is under severe temptation.'

'And Sister Catherine seems to be more than encouraging it,' Agnes could not help saying. She had never questioned Mother Jerome's judgment before this moment. But in this case, for some unaccountable reason, the prioress seemed blind to the gamut and purpose of Catherine's actions.

'There's an end to it, Sister. Your task is to decide whether to become Virginia Pearson again or settle into religious life. That decision is before you.'

'I understand, Mother,' said Agnes, her nose roughly rubbed into her undefined problem.

'You may go now.'

Agnes bowed her head. 'Thank you, Mother.' She rose.

'You are aware the Second Vatican Council has started?'

'I had not been paying attention, Mother.'

'There was dissension from the beginning. I fear those holding the dam against the destructive undercurrents are being pushed aside.'

'Philip said something like that to me before—'

'Before you broke the engagement and entered the convent,' said the prioress. 'Yes, that speaks volumes about your Dr Stevenson. In any case, one of the lay sisters is collecting reports from the different newspapers and compiling the material that has arrived via Church channels. It will be waiting for you in January.' She rose. 'Goodnight, Sister.'

After Agnes had left her office, Mother Jerome returned to her desk, pondering. Eventually, she picked up the yellowing copy of *Pistis Sophia* and flicked through it. Putting it aside, she picked up a new book, delivered in a brown paper package a few days before. She turned to the preface that she had read that first day. 'With the repeal of the last Witchcraft Act in England in 1951, adherents of the three-millennia-old goddess religion are now free to worship unhindered by unjust laws,' the first sentence read.

DESPITE Mother Jerome's disturbing revelations, Agnes's dark mood retreated. But the coherence of the revelations and connections, dispelling much of her confusion, merely brought her back to being edgy. Only Philip's lectures and tutorials, and his presence, eased that edginess during the day. From Dr Edelman, he took over the themes of the third term lecture series, 'Some Ideas of the Enlightenment.' Dr Edelman, with characteristic gusto, had concentrated on the arguments of the British empiricists that would destroy any idea of a transcendent God and an objective scheme of morality. All morality was reduced to a question of will, individual or communal, with drastic implications for society and its organisation. He seemed entertained by Thomas Hobbes's solutions to the problem of organising a viable society of innately selfish and violent individuals.

Notwithstanding his zeal and upbeat manner, he did nothing to improve her state of mind with the attempted destruction of all those features of life she held dear. Surely the other students reacted the same way. What was left after the demolition, if not nothingness and despair? Though lacking gusto but not quiet determination, Philip devoted his lectures to the failures in the metaphysical and epistemological arguments of his colleague's most admired philosophers.

'It's an irony,' he said at the beginning of his lectures, 'that the Anglo-Saxon thinkers across the Channel crucially influenced the architects of what should be called the French Enlightenment. The French *Philosophes* really had nothing original to say. The much-admired Voltaire is only remarkable for his poisonous tongue.'

For Agnes, that was a good start. Philip continued his gentle, ironic style of attack during tutorials, engaging the other students as much as herself. He kept his distance, appearing uncharacteristically scrupulous. It amused her despite herself. His obvious intention was to relieve her of the discomfort his presence might cause. If he only knew.

'Sister, may I have a word?' she heard Dr Edelman calling in the corridor after a tutorial sometime later. She followed him into his office.

'Well, you're looking a lot better, I'm pleased to say,' he said. 'Oh, I get a smile, too! I'm privileged.'

'Dr Edelman, you did not ask me in to swap pleasantries. And please stay away from the personal.'

'Ah, we are loosening up, too—another privilege.'

'Please, Dr Edelman—'

'Call me Joe—'

'I'll be going if this is all you have to say,' she said, trying to remain expressionless.

'Virginia, you pulled that one no doubt on many a pesky youth before you escaped from the world.'

'You have something to say about the course, I know. Please say it.'

'Phil looks better, too.'

'Dr Edelman—'

'I'll go on if you call me Joe.'

'Please, Joe, go on.'

'Well, well,' he said. 'Okay, if you're going to spoil my teasing, I suppose I must get on with it. I hope this is not a sign of disrespect.'

'You can't have it both ways, Dr Edelman.' Indeed, she was now so used to his open manner and underlying friendliness that she was inclined to be less formal with him, despite herself.

'Touche! Your spirits have really improved. Perhaps you'll relax and open up a bit more.'

'Your conversations always end up being about my religious vocation and its irrationality,' she said, realising he was right. 'If you must know, I was quite a normal girl before I made the free, conscious decision to become a religious sister. I had a normal social life with friends, including boyfriends. That's as far as I am going. So there's no point in probing for more.'

'It's what you were like in your social rounds that intrigues me.'

'It shouldn't. I was an average girl, like thousands you would meet.'

'An average girl—an attractive, personable one that boys would fall in love with?'

'As I said, it was all normal. The same sort of story most girls at the university would tell you. You're exciting your curiosity for nothing.'

'I wonder.'

'Unlike most girls, I felt a deep calling to devote myself to God,' she continued. 'It was the calling of Jesus in the Gospel: self-denial in conforming one's will to God's will and truly acting out the message of charity. This is clearly something you don't understand, and because you don't understand, you can find no good rational reason for the choice. It seems to me there's a fallacy in your thinking. I could give many analogous arguments to prove my point—an otherwise intelligent person who cannot understand the processes of mathematics, for example.'

'Very good, Virginia, but the rationality of mathematics is demonstrable.'

'Demonstrable by a third party, you mean? Besides your argument appearing regressive, many intelligent people throughout history have provided compelling arguments for the rationality of Christian belief and, just as important, have argued that faith and reason complement each other. Your claim that I will succumb to reason and jettison my faith because of the alleged irrationality of Christian belief is falling on deaf ears. That's not to speak of the fallibility of the philosophers we are reading and the question-begging nature of their idea of reason.'

'At least I have prodded you into argument, and you're no longer sitting there like a long-suffering saint.'

'An essential element of the religious life is avoiding the personal, particularly in contacts with seculars. Transgressions fall under disciplinary rules, you should know.'

'Seculars!' exclaimed Joe. 'It sounds like I have a disease.'

'You may find humour in it, but I'm in earnest,' she said, unable to suppress her amusement.

'You can't be serious,' he said. 'Avoiding the personal and contact with seculars—it's not normal—it's mad.'

'Dr Edelman, there's something about you I don't understand,' she said, 'something that appears equally unnatural.'

'Oh, yes, what is that if you insist on being personal?'

'You seem to be at your most enthusiastic about arguments and philosophers who aim to debunk all idea of a transcendent God, a scheme of objective morality, and an ultimate purpose in life,' she said, ignoring the dig. 'That would cut most people adrift in despair and meaninglessness. What is your reason for being so happy about such doomed and chaotic circumstances? It seems against the nature of the normal person to be overjoyed about despair and meaninglessness.'

'You're referring to my lectures on Thomas Hobbes,' he said with an appreciative nod. 'Indeed, that is why I asked you in. It was to congratulate you on the excellent essay on Hobbes's "state of nature." You went beyond the scope of the lectures and provided a lively argument against his materialist position. But, before answering your little speech, I must say you give the impression of having thought much previously about these issues.'

'I used to discuss with Ph— with someone interested in philosophy long before I entered the convent,' she said, frustrated with herself for the slip.

'It shows. It was some Catholic, no doubt, for you argue naturally from a classical realist position like my good but deluded friend Phil.' He stopped, frowned, and looked thoughtful. 'It's liberating to face up to the reality of human existence,' he went on. 'It's liberating to be freed from the illegitimate authority that others of equal worth—we are all of equal worth—have imposed on society. It's liberating to know that we are responsible for our own scheme of morality and political organisation. No authority is legitimate if there's no general agreement and acceptance about its structure. What's against nature in that?'

'Leaving aside the assumptions you're making about the world, why are you happy that the individual must make the best of the very worst circumstances, and all for no particular point? Surely, the happiness felt in those circumstances is the very worst of delusions.'

'Indeed, Virginia, you have found your tongue.'

'I have always expressed my opinion, Dr Edelman. We're at the end of a year during which I devoted much time to these matters. I should now reply to some of your criticisms.'

'Okay, I seem to have done my job. But to reply to your objection, even if there is ultimately no point to existence, happiness is worth pursuing, isn't it?'

'Why, though? And then we are back to the same question: what constitutes happiness? Catholics happen to differ with you on this question, as we do on what constitutes state and society. The argument is far from finished as you and others seem to think it is.'

'Oh, no, not another excursion into Leo XIII's social writings. Spare me!' At that moment, Philip entered Joe's office. 'Speak of the devil. Here's our resident expert on papal ideas of state and society appearing on cue!'

'What are you talking about?' said Philip, looking distracted. 'I'm sorry to interrupt, Joe. I need a few moments with Sister when you've finished. Do you have time, Sister? It's only a minor matter, which I keep forgetting about.'

'Of course, Philip, I won't be long.'

'Of course, Philip,' repeated Joe when Philip had gone. 'What's Philip done to deserve that familiarity—?' He gaped. There were long, painful moments while they looked at each other. 'Great Scott, you're the one, aren't you? It's been you all the time.'

'The one what?' said Virginia, realising her fatal mistake.

'The second reading of your essays, Philip's moodiness, the drinking bouts, his absence, the similarity in thought, you both looking tired and ill, it all adds up. How could I be so dull?'

'Whatever you're thinking,' said Virginia, rising, 'I beg you to keep it to yourself. I must go.'

'I assure you of my confidence,' he said, appearing in awe of his conclusion. 'The girls were right. A woman is at the heart of it—a nun into the bargain.' He paused, reflecting. 'I'm beginning to understand, too, how hard this must have been for you. I would have been less jesting if I had known.'

'I thank you, Dr Edelman. You've been generous with your time.' She walked to the door.

'Wait a minute,' he said, following her. She stopped. 'I wanted to say this before. A branch of my family established itself in Italy. They escaped the Nazis through the avenues that your Pius XII worked out. We're eternally grateful for that. Others may be mounting a campaign against him. We will not be part of it. Your secret is safe with me. Of course, my offer to help in any way remains.'

'Thank you, Dr Edelman.'

Virginia walked slowly to Philip's office, attempting to weigh up the implications of what had passed. Then she realised she did not know what conclusions he had drawn precisely. There were things he could not know.

'My mother made a special request to be remembered to you,' said Philip as soon as he saw her. 'She wants to drop by the university for a chat when she's in town.' He stopped. 'Is there something the matter?'

'Dr Edelman knows.'

'Knows what?'

'I don't know exactly, but he knows there's something between us. Philip, you must do something. Please. It'll come out eventually.'

'Is there something between us?'

They both knew it was not a question but more of a statement. She warned him again. The brief respite Virginia enjoyed with Philip's return was at an end. A tidal wave was forming over her.

Chapter 41

Pushed to the limits

FROM THE hollows of a deep sleep, Virginia could hear it—could hear its insistence. She struggled to the surface. Her eyes popped open in the dark. To her left, a faint light penetrated through the window. She breathed in and struggled onto an elbow. The scuffling had stopped. Far away across the river in the bush, an animal cry rang out, echoing through the surrounding hills. She fell out of bed and turned the light on. Her cell door was ajar. She shut it, flicked off the light, and returned to bed. The following night, around one o'clock, a scratching at her door awakened her. Her sleep was less heavy than the night before, and she sat up at once, listening. It stopped. She went to the door and opened it. Nothing. Just the corridor lit by one blinking, failing globe at the corridor end. Was she dreaming? A little shaken, she returned to bed, not to be bothered again that night. Then, on the third night, in the gloom of the early hours of the morning, she became conscious of someone or something pressing her into the bed.

'Get off,' she murmured. 'Get off. You're hurting me.'

'Go, leave, get out!' said a hoarse voice in her ear. A cold breath caressed the side of her head.

She writhed and struggled. There came a release when she was at the end of her strength. She lay some time in an exhausted daze before falling into a fitful sleep, with formless beings floating around her bed. When she awoke in the early dawn light creeping through the window, she sat up, bolt upright, recalling the night's horror and her powerlessness against the overwhelming strength of—what was it? But as she said her prayers and went to chapel with her fellow sisters, she had the feeling she had been dreaming, that same unnerving feeling. Her memories of the night were fading. No, she told herself, the pressure was real. Something was holding her down. It was real. Aine said the same. The vivid horror seemed like a bad dream in the light of day. Was it a harbinger of some sort? She resolved not to succumb to this sort of fear campaign, imagined or not. She would prepare herself for the next occasion, be it the following night or the nights after that. She did not know what she would do except confront whoever it was. She would at least determine if she was dreaming.

She was not bothered by another visitation until the following week. That night, she slept lightly until after twelve. Now wide awake, she lay in her bed, listening and thinking. She thought she heard a sound in the corridor. She got up, put on her dressing gown, and sat beside the door. No further sound from the corridor. With her head resting against the wall, she closed her eyes. She seemed to be floating, and then there it was again. She opened her eyes as if awakening from a deep sleep. The door swung slowly open. She remained sitting against the wall, waiting. She looked up at a dark, indistinct shape.

'What do you want?' she said, not moving.

'Go, leave. You are not wanted,' said the same voice. 'Go while you have the chance.' Cold breath flowed around her ear.

'Who are you?' she cried, grabbing at the voice.

She felt cloth, but no body, no arm, no head. The cloth was wrenched from her hands, accompanied by a muffled cry. She lunged again but grabbed hold of nothing but material. She held on tight. Whatever or whoever it was, it dragged her to her feet and out into the darkened corridor. The fabric was torn from her hands as she was pushed backward. She fell heavily on the corridor floor and listened to the soft patter of departing feet. Out through the door at the end of the corridor, down the steps, and along the upper level, she ran after something indistinct. Now chasing down the rocky stairs, she made out the robed and hooded shape. At the clearing, it disappeared. She shivered and began climbing the rocky stairs. At the top of the stairs, she found herself at the corridor door. She pulled at the handle. The door was locked. She sank to the floor, leaning back against the door. Then she was lying in the corridor. Exhausted. With the first light of the day, she awoke to find herself on the floor in her cell. During the day, she struggled, as she had before, to keep hold of the experience, but it continued to fade.

While suffering these visitations, she revised the term's work and sat for exams, allowing her to ignore the experiences for a time. She had to postpone worrying about evil spirits, real or unreal, until after the exams. If she thought of anything unconnected to her study, it was Philip. When he had asked her, with pointed irony, whether there was something between them, she had answered that they were once engaged, and if that information became known, it would cause him trouble. He should know that.

'There's nothing for you to worry about,' he had replied. 'I've covered myself and you. Besides, what you did years before starting at university is nobody's business but yours. The same rule applies to you as applies to everyone.'

She hoped he was right, but had grave worries that he underestimated what the Fourth Club was capable of. They had been unmerciful. She could not imagine what they would cook up for a senior lecturer who had suppressed an earlier relationship with one of his students. Halfway through the exams, Philip sought her in the library.

'Would you come to my office when you have time?' he said with a frown, acting as if he had bumped into her.

When she arrived at his office an hour later, the frown was still there. He shut the door.

'Why didn't you tell me?' he said with an impatient flick of the hand.

'Tell you what?'

'Those thugs, those cowardly thugs— Why didn't you tell me they were bothering you? Well, it was more than bothering. It's been a campaign of persecution!'

'Who told you?'

'What does it matter who told me?' he said, throwing his hands in the air. 'Joe and Gemma both thought I knew. How on earth could they think that? I had no idea. Those thugs have been laughing about it?'

'Philip, I've been able to handle it. Please don't get upset.'

'Upset! I'm furious, furious with myself first of all, and furious with them, and a little angry with you for being unwise at the very least. It's a wonder it hasn't affected your studies.'

'It's all right, Philip. It's something we were prepared for, something that I must handle as a religious.'

'Virginia, for me, you are a student. It's my duty to see that the students are unimpeded in their studies. This has been a clear case of victimisation. I'm obliged to act.'

'No, Philip, don't. You'll make it worse.'

'They left your fellow sister alone. Do you know why?'

'No.'

'Whatever the reasons, I have a duty of care for all students, including you. Causing conflict in bourgeois society is their duty. That's what they want. The breakdown of bourgeois society is the path to their new society. If they get away with picking on you, it'll give them the green light to ratchet up the campaign, in particular against the Church, which they hate with an incurable passion. They see the Church in you. Don't be so naïve.'

'Please don't do anything about it until after the exams, when I'm not around.'

'All right, I'll leave it until the end of the year. But then I'm going to act formally. It'll mean discussing it with Mother Superior.'

'Whatever you decide, Philip. You have your responsibilities, as you say.'

'Yes, I have.' He regarded her with a painful expression. 'I suppose it's my fault to some extent for running away for a couple of months.'

She knew what he meant. 'I must go now, return to the library.'

'All right.'

'Thank you for your concern,' she said in little more than a whisper. 'Whatever the circumstances, it's appreciated.'

He nodded. 'All essays have been assessed and exams marked,' he continued, trying to brighten. 'I can tell you unofficially that you are among the top five students. Joe's in full agreement with me about your ability. Your work has been outstanding. Congratulations.'

'Please thank Dr Edelman. He was always helpful.'

'He was helpful when I should have been.'

'Don't blame yourself, Philip. Thank you again.'

'There'll be an end-of-the-year social evening for philosophy students in early December. I hope you can come.'

'I'll have to see.' She hastened from his office. She could not bear it any longer.

A FEW days later, Jannie came across Agnes and Catherine as they were walking along the pathway through the front lawn. Agnes was surprised to see her at that time of day. Catherine and Jannie usually arranged to meet elsewhere when she was not around.

'I had to make sure I caught you early,' said Jannie. 'I've got tons of things to do later.' She opened the magazine she was carrying. 'I wanted to ensure you saw Aine's latest photos.'

Agnes and Catherine looked at the colourful double-page spread of Aine in casual summer clothes.

'Stunning, isn't she?' said Jannie.

'I'm happy to see her success,' said Catherine.

'Brilliant success!' said Jannie. 'Harry's mapping out a big future for her. He says she has the looks of the future.'

'Is Aine happy with everything?' said Agnes.

'Very happy.'

'There's no recurrence of the episodes she had during the postulancy?'

'None at all. That's all behind her. She's very relaxed with Harry. He knows how to deal with her?'

'Deal with her?'

'Yes, he's attentive to all her needs. He talks to Charles, too, to make sure he's comfortable with the arrangements.'

'Arrangements?'

'You're full of pointed questions, as usual, Virginia,' said Jannie. 'But ask as many as you like. They will all be satisfactorily answered.' She had once again that smug, confident look—and that accent. 'Harry arranges for a taxi to bring Aine from Binawarra and take her back again. I'm there all the time, too. I act as Harry's assistant. I don't work when Aine is present.'

'That's very generous of Harry,' said Agnes, 'and very well organised, I must admit.'

'At last,' said Jannie. 'Perhaps Aine can be an example for you?'

'What could you mean by that?' Agnes glanced at Catherine, who, as usual, said nothing when Jannie was speaking to her.

'I'll leave you to work that out.'

'I will always be happy to hear an explanation.'

Bobby McGuigan's broad Irish accent rang out across the lawn. The three women turned to see Catherine's father approaching with several men.

'Hello, gorgeous,' he said to Jannie, with his friends gawking. 'You look better every time I see you, girl.'

'Thank you, Bobby,' said Jannie graciously. 'I suppose I'm becoming more mature.'

'Is that what you call it? Good morning, Morrigan, my esteemed daughter,' he said with a playful glint in his eye. He kissed her on the cheek.

'Morrigan?' repeated Virginia.

'Well, if it ain't our little English friend, Sister Virginia.'

'My ancestors go back several generations to colonial times, Mr McGuigan. I think I can safely claim to be Australian. By the way, it is Sister Agnes.'

'It depends upon your cultural affiliations, doesn't it?'

Agnes realised again that Bobby McGuigan was not as ignorant as he sometimes appeared. But she was loath to get entangled in the Irish question. 'Morrigan is one of the Celtic goddesses, is she not, Mr McGuigan?'

He glanced at Catherine, who frowned and gave a quick shake of the head.

'Well, Sister Virginia, you surprise me. You do know something about the ancient land of the Celts. Morrigan is the greatest of the Celtic goddesses.'

'You mustn't take that as an indication, Mr McGuigan. I only came across that information recently.'

'You'll benefit from having more knowledge of Ireland's history and the English oppression.'

'I'm sure I will. But what brings you to the university? Union matters, I suppose?'

'The unions and students are in common cause against capitalist oppression, as I explained. We will raise our voices against capitalism, imperialism, and colonialism wherever it raises its ugly head.'

'And what particular group is the victim of these oppressors at this particular point in history?'

'Vietnam. Ever hear of it, Sister?'

'I confess I know little about that country. I'm certainly familiar with East Germany and Poland. There's a wall—'

'You will hear of it. It'll become the battleground of the fight against the world's oppressors.'

The arrival of members of the Fourth Club interrupted the exchange. They did not notice Agnes until they had greeted McGuigan and his companions and gawked at Jannie. Belligerence at once appeared in their posture.

'Mr McGuigan, your student friends could certainly advise you on the nature of oppression. Sister Catherine, I must keep going. I'll leave you with your father and meet you later at the appointed time.' She moved off.

'You shouldn't confuse the fight against oppression as oppression itself, Sister Virginia,' he called after her.

She stopped. She should keep her mouth shut. 'Can you explain why your student comrades consider me the oppressor and not your daughter?'

'Perhaps it's a question of attitudes, Sister.'

'Dad, please ...,' said Catherine. She took him by the arm.

He had answered her question. Indeed, he had responded to several questions. Catherine's expression told her she realised it, too. She continued her way to the library, concentrating her thoughts not on what Bobby McGuigan said but on her failure once again to hold her tongue and maintain her dignity. But he irritated her as his daughter irritated her. They brought out the worst in her. She was not settled long in the library when Anne arrived at her desk.

'Hello, Sister, you look a bit flushed. Is there anything the matter?'

'No, no, just the walk to the library. It's a warm morning.'

'The exams are nearly over,' said Anne, disregarding the answer. 'Can you have lunch with Barry and me? I may not see you again until next year.'

Agnes only had one exam to do, so she readily accepted the invitation. When she arrived in the student union eating hall, she found Anne with Carmel and Barbara—and no Barry.

'We thought we'd say hello, too,' said Carmel. 'We're finishing today.'

While the conversation lingered on the year's study and final exams, Agnes waited in nervous expectation for the inevitable talk about Philip.

'Philip Stevenson's looking a lot better,' said Barbara.

'Yes, he's cheered up enormously,' said Anne. 'The tutorials are so interesting, aren't they, Sister?'

'Yes,' was all Virginia could say.

'The drinking bouts have stopped, too,' Barbara went on. 'But my contact says the problem is a girl and always has been. He was wrong, he admits.'

'I wonder who it could be?' said Carmel. 'It's nobody at the university. We would know, surely. He wouldn't be able to hide it.'

'My contact won't comment about it at all. I'm not sure he knows, anyhow.'

The contact was Dr Edelman. Agnes was relieved and grateful that he kept his word. But it was bound to come out, at least the fact that they had been engaged. Other conclusions would follow. Now she felt sick at the realisation that her young friends would think her two-faced.

'He won't be able to keep it a secret indefinitely,' said Anne to confirm her thoughts. 'Whoever it is and whatever it is, there's a problem in there. Otherwise, he wouldn't have been drinking as he has.'

'A married woman?' Carmel ventured.

'Possibly,' said Anne. 'But that's not likely it. He's no Goody two-shoes, but I don't think he would get involved in adultery. What do you think, Sister?'

The question came at the worst moment. 'Yes, you're right—I mean about breaking vows—he doesn't seem the type—'

'Are you still hot, Sister? Is it hot in here?' said Anne to her friends.

'It's a bit warm. We can move elsewhere if Sister is uncomfortable.'

'No, no, don't move. I'll be all right.'

'I'd be hot if I had to wear all those clothes,' said Barbara.

'You get used to it.'

Barry arrived to be warmly greeted by Anne. Fortunately, Barry distracted the girls from the subject of Philip, and the conversation moved on to less spicy and controversial topics. As Agnes observed the interaction between Anne and Barry and the change in Barry's appearance and manner, she thought she had achieved something worthwhile that year. Barry and Anne had much in common. Towards the end of their lunch, their conversation stopped on the boisterous entrance of McGuigan with his student and union friends.

'Calder and his union mates,' Barry said with disgust.

Agnes hoped they remained too preoccupied to pay attention to them, but someone in the group eventually spotted them. Words and laughter rang out, after which Calder rose and came over to them. McGuigan called after him, but he paid no attention.

'Well, if it isn't our little fascists cooking up schemes to spread their oppressive poison.'

'You'd know what oppressive poison is,' said Barry.

'Go away and leave us alone,' said Anne, glancing at Barry.

'Don't interrupt when your lord and master is speaking,' Calder sneered, 'you little fascist tart.'

'A psychopath like you wouldn't know what decency was,' said Barry, standing up and leaning toward him. 'There's more decency in Anne's little finger than in the whole of your corrupt body and mind.'

'Barry, don't—there's no need,' Anne pleaded.

The conflict had spiked so quickly that it left Carmel and Barbara staring, looking from one to the other.

'Mr Calder, would you please leave us alone?' said Agnes, rising. She motioned to Barry to sit down. 'I have been urged to lodge a formal complaint about you. Your enrolment will be in jeopardy if I do so.'

Calder hesitated. He leaned across the table and brought a finger close to Agnes's face. 'Someday, we'll put an end to the influence of twisted, frustrated Gorgons like you.'

'Will you murder thousands of nuns, brothers, and priests, as you did in Spain?' said Agnes, refusing to step back.

'There'll be the inevitable casualties in the conflict that resolves the class war. The people, the workers, will welcome death to the oppressors.'

'That's the best excuse a psychopath has at his disposal these days,' said Barry, who had remained standing. 'What are you and your thugs meeting for?' he continued. 'Don't tell me. It's Vietnam. That's the new one. You won't be happy until you subject the Vietnamese people to the merciless, murderous dictatorship of Marxist ideology, will you? You're already planning the re-education camps, no doubt.'

'See your class losing grip on the deceived, do you, you little creep?'

'You won't succeed this time,' said Barry. 'The world is too awake to the poisonous, deceptive talk of madmen like you. The savage dictatorship of the proletariat in the Eastern Bloc and Russia must surely be enough. Nobody could be deceived again. Your brutal dictatorship will not be a reality in Vietnam.'

'The reality of the new order will come not only to Vietnam, you disgusting little superstitious worm.' He reached out to grab Barry, but a hand on his shoulder stopped him.

'I have such trouble controlling your enthusiasm, don't I?' said Bobby McGuigan. 'You're not antagonising the lad, are you, Sister Virginia? Now, that would not be charitable, would it?'

There was a pause.

'Sister Virginia?' said Carmel.

'Oh, I'm sorry, Sister. I can never get it right,' said Bobby. 'Virginia is your real name, isn't it? Virginia Pearson, wasn't it—while you were teaching at St Brigid's—when you became engaged? It was one of those academic blokes, wasn't it?'

'I did not expect you to be looking into my past, Mr McGuigan,' she replied, seeing the malice in his eyes. She was now under her companions' scrutiny.

'These things have a way of coming to the surface, Sister.'

'It is almost six years since Morrigan and I entered the convent. Our past life is just that. It's what lies ahead for me and Morrigan that's important.'

For a moment, the boisterous Dubliner seemed lost for words. She had struck home with a dig that suddenly came to her lips.

'Come, Steve, let's leave these people to their lunch,' said McGuigan, turning in an indecisive manner. 'We'd hate to give them indigestion with food too strong for their guts.'

'You'll keep,' said Calder, pointing at Barry.

'Gutless bullies don't scare me now,' said Barry.

Calder tried to stare Barry down, but Barry held his ground, leaving Calder no option but to retreat with no advantage. The three girls paid no attention to the contest, or the threat, or to the men who were walking away. Neither did they notice Barry's newfound confidence. Instead, they looked in wonder at Agnes.

'Who broke off the engagement before you entered the convent?' said Barbara.

'I would rather not talk about my pre-convent private life,' she said to the expectant faces around her. Barry was now aware that McGuigan had divulged something important. 'It's not just my wish, but part of the Rule under which we sisters choose to live.' It was a weak and evasive answer that would not satisfy their curiosity. 'I must go now.' She rose. 'Please be assured, I enjoyed your friendship and conversation during the year. I hope my companionship has been appreciated as much as I have appreciated yours, especially yours, Anne. If I don't see you again this year, I wish you a merry Christmas and an enjoyable holiday break.'

The three girls murmured their return wishes, still in wonder at the possibility that had arisen. Barry expressed his thanks again for the introduction to Anne. Agnes then hurried from the student eating hall and was preparing to take the longer path around the buildings to avoid the narrow passageways when Anne caught up with her.

'Sister, wait,' she said, taking her arm. 'We were too stunned to say anything. But we now realise what we may have done to you— And you may think you have deceived us. Please don't feel that way. We understand. The three of us want to say we're sorry if we made it difficult for you. We won't say anything if it's what we think.'

'I appreciate that,' said Virginia. 'I would never deliberately deceive you. Besides, whatever you're thinking may not be true.'

'If you were engaged to Dr Stevenson, it's true, all right. It must be terrible for him—and for you.'

'I must go, Anne. Thank you.'

'Bye, Sister. I hope to see you next year.' She stood there, watching the slightly stooped figure hurry away to the library.

IT WAS late in the evening when Anne and Barry left the university library and ambled to Barry's car parked in a side street nearby. They walked hand in hand, talking happily about their study and what they would do after graduating. Barry was two years ahead of Anne, so the work issues were far more pressing. Anne stood close to Barry while he searched his pocket for the car keys. He pulled the door open and waited for her to step in. In the protective shade of the overhanging branches of the large oak tree under which the car was parked, Anne put her arms around his neck and kissed him.

They were lingering in the embrace when Barry was ripped away from her. She looked on in horror as a man in a hood and dark clothing set about bashing him. Taken unaware, Barry could do nothing but hold his arms up against the pummelling. Anne jumped on the man's back. He shook her off violently and kicked her as she lay on the ground. Barry regained his senses and came at the man. But the slim, studious youth was no match for the man's strength and ideological viciousness. While Anne screamed, Barry struggled against his assailant's superior might until felled. The dark figure looked at his bleeding and unconscious victim in the dirt and grass. Then, with several kicks to the head and a backhander to Anne, he disappeared into the darkness of the trees along the poorly lit street.

VIRGINIA felt a tap on her shoulder as she knelt in the chapel. She looked up to see Mother Jerome beckoning her. She followed the prioress outside.

'Dr Stevenson rang this morning. He wanted to speak to you.'

'Oh?'

'He was ringing on behalf of a fellow student of yours. Anne. The message is that Barry, Anne's Barry, is in hospital.'

'Oh, no,' said Virginia, 'surely not? Surely, he wouldn't—?'

'Your friend, Anne, is, to use Dr Stevenson's words, distraught and despairing. It seems she has no one to confide in except you.'

'Her parents are in the middle of a painful break-up.'

'Dr Stevenson has asked permission to fetch you.'

'Oh,' said Virginia.

'I will allow you to offer comfort to your friend. I will consider it in the context of your university activities. Mr Ferguson will take you in. You will return in the afternoon. As Sister Catherine is not required at university today, nor is she available, Sister Martha will accompany you.'

'Yes, Mother, thank you.'

Anne fell into Agnes's arms when she appeared in Philip's office, big sobs shaking her small frame.

'He nearly killed him,' she said when she had calmed a little.

'It was a severe bashing,' said Philip, replying to Agnes's inquiring look. 'He's bruised and suffering from a concussion. A couple of days in the hospital, and he'll be allowed home.' He made sure Sister Martha was comfortably seated.

'How could anyone be so cruel and heartless,' wailed Anne. 'What has Barry done to deserve this?'

'Who was it?' said Agnes.

'Stephen Calder, the same one who—you know—the dog poo.'

'Are you sure?'

'Yes. He's a monster,' cried Anne.

'It's ideology, Anne,' said Philip. 'Calder is a new type on university campuses. Fuelled by rigid ideology, their sick minds and characters no longer see limits to what they call political action.'

'Why would he bash Barry just because he has a different view?' Anne sobbed, hardly listening to Philip. 'Everyone has their views. That's what we're at university for, isn't it?'

'In their own words, they want to smash opposition as soon as it arises.'

'It doesn't make sense.'

Philip looked at Agnes and shrugged. Agnes tried to convey that all Anne required was comfort. An analysis of the political aspect could wait. He understood.

'I'll leave you for the moment,' he said.

Agnes nodded gratefully. While Sister Martha looked on, Agnes consoled Anne. She said Barry depended on her, and he would be bruised in body and mind. Comfort and understanding were what he needed.

'Does he?' said Anne.

'Yes. I see how much he feels for you. He'll be upset that he could not protect you.'

'But he didn't have a chance. That monster didn't give him a chance.'

'He'll be looking for your reassurance.'

'Really? Barry's my first boyfriend. I don't really know ... thank you, Sister.'

Agnes glanced a little self-consciously at Sister Martha. Sister Martha smiled and nodded.

Philip returned shortly after. 'I've rung the hospital. Barry's much improved and can receive visitors.'

'I want you to come, too, Sister,' Anne pleaded.

'Of course, I'll come.'

'Thank you, Dr Stevenson, for your help,' said Anne. 'I don't know what I would have done without your help—and Sister's, too.'

Philip drove them to the nearby hospital. He accompanied Anne and Agnes to Barry's ward and returned to Sister Martha, who remained in the waiting room. Anne burst into tears at seeing Barry's bruised and bandaged face. He winced as she hugged him.

'Oh, I'm sorry. I didn't mean to hurt you.'

'You're not hurting me,' Barry gasped. 'I've been waiting for you to come.' A tear appeared on his cheek. 'I'm sorry,' he said, turning his head.

'Oh, oh, Barry,' said Anne, looking at Agnes.

'It's all right, Barry,' said Agnes, putting her hand on his arm. 'You're very tender. Anne's here to cheer you up.'

It was all the direction Anne needed. From that moment, she spoke gently, encouraging him and making plans for what they would do during the Christmas holidays. At length, he brightened.

'Thank you again, Sister,' Anne said.

'Yes, thank you, Sister,' Barry said. 'I appreciate your bringing Anne to see me. I have a lot to thank you for, especially considering the first—'

'No, Barry, that's all in the past.' She rose. 'I'll leave you for the moment. I must talk to Dr Stevenson.'

'Thanks for leaving us alone,' Anne said. 'You'd make a good mother. I don't understand how—'

'It's not the time, Anne. Barry needs your attention.'

'Of course.'

Agnes slowly returned to the waiting room, turning over in her mind what Anne had said, something that had not been said out loud before. Her eyes came to rest on Philip's face as he engaged Sister Martha in polite conversation. She had a sudden inclination to cry. Philip looked at her.

'Is there anything wrong?' he said, coming to her.

'No, no, I've left them alone to talk. He was badly hurt, wasn't he?'

'Yes, yes ... he was. It could have been serious if he had fallen on a hard surface. The grass cushioned his head. Virginia, this man is a monster. He must be stopped.'

'Philip, please don't call me—' She glanced at Martha.

'I'm sorry. I'm going to take action now the year's finished.'

'Be careful, Philip, you don't make things worse.' They had reached Sister Martha by this.

'Is everything all right?' said Sister Martha, looking from one to the other. Agnes gave a short account of Barry's injuries and improved state of mind. 'That's good to hear. Sister,' Martha continued. 'We will have to leave shortly. Mr Ferguson will be waiting.'

'Yes, yes, of course, I lost sight of— I'll say goodbye to Anne first.'

'I'll go with you,' said Philip.

'I'd like to stay longer,' Agnes said as they went to the ward.

'Why don't you? Surely this is the time when your presence is justified. Anne's obviously dependent on you. I hadn't realised how much of a connection you've made with her.'

'It's not that simple,' said Agnes. She was reverting to her old familiar manner with him, but she could not stop it.

'I don't understand. The situation demands an act of charity.'

'But from me? Am I the only one to provide comfort and consolation? And should I forget all my other duties?'

'Steady on, Ginny, I—'

'Oh, stop it, Philip. Don't—' she said, stopping. 'Don't make things difficult. I can't live two lives.'

'I'm not asking you to— Okay, I understand,' he said, raising his hands a little. 'Please overlook my lapses. This business with Barry—it's just outrageous.' He paused. 'How do you expect me to act when I see all those qualities that made me fall in love with you?'

'We can't talk like this. We mustn't.'

They walked the rest of the way in silence. Agnes had enough presence of mind to remain encouraging and ask Anne to keep her up to date on Barry's condition.

'Just drop a line in the post,' she said. 'You have the convent address, don't you?'

'I will, Sister,' said Anne, 'and thank you again. You don't know how much I appreciate your kindness and understanding. I couldn't do without it.'

Philip and Agnes returned to Martha in silence.

'Dr Stevenson is a nice man,' said Martha when they were leaving the city centre.

'Yes, a fine young man,' said Mr Ferguson, who appeared on good terms with Sister Martha. 'I met him on Sister Agnes's first day at university, didn't I?'

'I'm sorry, I can't remember, Mr Ferguson.'

'Yes, a fine, fine young man,' Mr Ferguson repeated. 'Good Catholic lad, I believe. That's what we need these days, isn't it, Sisters? Good Catholic men.'

Agnes felt Martha's eyes on her. She looked out the window.

'You are right, of course, Mr Ferguson,' said Martha.

Chapter 42

Virginia breaks

WITH THE exams completed, fewer people roamed around the university grounds. Small groups of inebriated students lolled about in the evening, the outcome of the university clubs and colleges having their end-of-year bash. If Dr Stevenson, senior lecturer in the Department of Philosophy, imagined he could give in to his grief and frustration without being noticed, he was mistaken. The rumours circulated about the bottle, or bottles, of Irish whisky unashamedly in full view in his office. Other rumours, challenging the credulity of the university population, were about him being desperately in love with an unattainable woman. The candidates covered a variety of married women, high and low, plebeian and aristocratic. Philip had to laugh into his glass of double whisky every time Joe Edelman told him of the latest. As yet, none had picked that he was afflicted with the most outrageous and impossible love. Those few who knew kept confidence, but he was now so drunk so often that he didn't care anymore.

'Why me, Joe?' he asked one evening in his office when the level in the whisky bottle was dropping at an alarming rate. 'Let me sound as pathetic as I can. What did I do to deserve this?'

'Don't ask me to explain fate, mate,' said Joe, who had long given up matching Philip glass for glass. 'It would've been easier if you'd told me at the start of the year.'

'You reckon?'

'I do.'

'I had got over her, I thought.' He draped a leg lazily over the corner of the desk. 'I was just living my boring life, minding my own business, with plenty of nice girls to choose. Who'd want a sweeter and classier girl than Diana?' He leaned forward. 'Joe, I treated them well.' He wagged his finger at him. 'I treated all my girlfriends well. Very well. If I'm going to sin, I have to make up with acts of charity.' He waved his hand.

'You need a psychiatrist, not a bottle of whisky. And you make an undignified drunk.'

'And then she came and just sat there in my lecture theatre.'

'Why can't you put an end to it? People come and go all the time. That's life. Go back to your classy, wealthy girlfriend. She adores you.'

'I've known her all my life, from when she was a toddler in ribbons. She's screwed into my mind, and I can't get the screw out without my mind falling apart.'

'You need help, mate—badly. Your images are terrible. I'm reporting you to our colleagues in the English Department. I'll be along to Vic Brennan tomorrow.'

'My memories of her are like a photo album you keep opening year after year.'

'If you don't stop it, I'm going. You'll send me around the bend, too.'

'Okay,' Philip sighed, 'enough of the stupid talk. I'll get over it again with the help of my Irish friend.'

'Good boy. Let's behave with the dignity worthy of philosophers and go into town for a big feed. You need to soak up the whisky.'

As they left the university grounds, Joe said: 'You know, the socialist clubs are having their big bash tonight.'

'Where?'

'The usual pubs close by. I would be inclined to join in if it wasn't for your well-known papist stance.'

Philip stopped and staggered. 'Wait, Joe,' he said after a few moments. 'Don't go away. I'll be back in a minute. Forgot something.'

'Phil ...'

Philip, breathing heavily, looked around his office. He grabbed a sheet of paper from his desk. He opened several drawers, pulling a brown paper bag from the last and stuffing it into his pocket. A minute later, he was back with his friend. 'I've got what I want. Come on, let's join your socialist mates. It might be fun, a worthwhile distraction for you in your interminably dull academic life.'

'What are you up to? I don't like the look of this. Besides, they're not my mates.'

Philip had a quick look around the first pub they entered. 'No, let's try the next.'

'What are you looking for?'

'Gemma's usually at these occasions, isn't she?'

'Yes. She enjoys mocking the people she loathes, especially the ones who see her as a chance.'

Philip had a quick look around in the next pub. 'Yes, this company will give us more fun. There's Gemma, too.'

'I'm glad of that.'

'Go and order some drinks. I'll be back in a minute.'

'What are you up to?' said Joe, now alarmed.

He followed Philip to the nearby park and watched, perplexed, as Philip looked around in the grass.

'Good, just what I want,' said Philip, taking the brown paper bag and a sheet of paper from his pocket. He bent down, scooped something from the ground, and put it in the paper bag. 'Let's go,' he said, holding the bag out in front of him.

'I hope you don't intend to do what I think.'

'Just stand back and enjoy it.'

'No, Phil, no, this is really risky. It's not worth it.'

'It certainly will be.'

He stopped as he entered the pub. Then, he walked straight to the bar, grabbed Stephen Calder by the shoulder, and swung him around.

'Well, if it isn't the very paradigm of the socialist coward.'

'I wouldn't take on what I can't handle,' Calder sneered after recovering from his surprise.

'The Marxist creep always looking to bully the weak,' said Philip, giving Calder a sharp push on the shoulder while holding the paper bag behind him. The pub fell quiet. The people behind Philip took a step back.

'Don't push too far. There are witnesses all around,' said Calder.

'That's right, you psychopath, hide between people and circumstances.'

'You're drunk. Go back to your papist office.'

'Come on, Phil,' said Gemma, taking him by the shoulder. 'This is not you. Leave me to deal with creeps like Calder.'

'Yes, you deal with me,' said Calder, leering at her.

'No, Gemma. This is my business. Everybody stands back and lets scum like this have their way. This time I'll give him a little of his own medicine.' He reached into the paper bag, pulled out the small paper parcel, and smeared its contents roughly over Calder's face and front.

The unexpected action caught everyone by surprise. Calder let out a yell with several expletives and fell back a few paces while people moved away. Retching, he frantically wiped the dog poo from his face. Philip's mocking laughter only made it worse. Calder came at him. They went into a clinch, their faces inches away from each other.

'You're full of bravado when it's a defenceless nun. It's a little different when someone's prepared to give it to you.'

'Outside, you papist scum!'

'Good, I'll go down, but I'll take you with me.' Calder hesitated. 'Scared?' Philip taunted. 'You contemptible toad, the dog poo's a suitable match for your character and ideals.'

Calder let go and moved outside. Philip was not out the door when Calder grabbed him, swung him to the ground, and began swinging. Philip had to collect several blows before he could fight back. A short, furious struggle followed before university colleagues intervened. When both men were on their feet, it was clear that Philip had gotten the worst of it. He staggered a little. Joe grabbed hold of him.

'I'll meet you at the administration.' He steadied himself against Joe.

Calder, with a split lip, spat blood on the ground. 'This is just one battle. You lost, but you will lose even more in the future.'

'Thug .... That's your style ...,' said Philip, slurring a little. 'What you call "the people" is not a reality; it's an excuse for violence and domination.'

Calder spat again and then moved away, with several members of the Fourth Club following.

'He needs to go to casualty,' said Gemma, holding a battered and staggering Philip on the other side.

AGNES was in the community room during afternoon recreation when Mother Jerome entered.

'May I interrupt, Sisters?'

'Of course, Mother,' said Martha.

'Would you please join me outside, Sister Agnes?'

The prioress did not say anything when Agnes had joined her on the upper parapet, merely signalling for her to walk alongside her. Lines of concentration creased her thin, ascetic face. When they arrived at the end of the walkway and were near the stairs leading to the corridor on the second floor, she stopped and looked out over the slope.

'I have often looked over this view when pondering some difficult issue.' She paused. 'Your friend, Anne, rang.' She raised her hand. 'At first, she would not talk to anyone except you, only saying it was extremely urgent. The call came through to me. I had to give her an undertaking that I would give the message in its entirety to you, which I am about to do.' She hesitated.

'Yes, Mother, I'm listening.'

The prioress pointed to a nearby bench. They sat down.

'Dr Stevenson, it seems, was in a fight and has been knocked around quite badly.'

'No, no,' said Virginia, standing up.

'Sit down, Sister.' She waited until Virginia had resumed her seat. 'It seems he will get over the bruising and scratches. It's his frame of mind that your friend Anne is worried about. Self-destructing is the way she described him. That's the message in its entirety, except that she begs you to come and talk to him. He will be in his office all afternoon, Anne assured me.'

'I must go,' said Agnes. 'I must.'

'Sister, I know how you must feel about this. I assume you are in some way connected with this occurrence.'

'Yes, Mother, I am. Dr Stevenson threatened to do something about the people bothering me.'

'I don't need to know more. Sister, you know that intervening in Dr Stevenson's life is against every rule and convention of convent life. You are mindful that although we are under the strict rule of charity, that does not necessarily mean that a person must take up that obligation to a particular person in particular circumstances to the exclusion of other duties and commitments? Dr Stevenson has many other neighbours: family, friends, colleagues.'

'I am Dr Stevenson's particular neighbour in these circumstances. There is unfinished business that I must finish. No. I must go.'

Mother Jerome looked ahead of her, blinking several times. She clasped her hands lightly.

'I will arrange for Mr Ferguson to come and collect you. When will you be ready?'

'I'm ready now.'

Mother Jerome accompanied Virginia to the car when Mr Ferguson arrived.

'You are on your own, Sister,' she said. 'I hope the mission of mercy is successful. It is early afternoon. You have time to complete your mission and return before Vespers.'

'Thank you, Mother. Thank you for your consideration.'

Mother Jerome watched as one of her most promising sisters departed. It would be tragic for the order to lose someone of Virginia Pearson's character and abilities. Few women combined such strength of character and ability with such warmth of feeling. All the signs pointed to the world being on the brink of a social explosion. If the order were to negotiate the turbulent waters ahead, women like Sister Agnes—strong in her faith, confident in her ability, dedicated, familiar with the world, and unafraid of it—would be needed to step forward. The world is going to need the right sort of female leaders.

SISTER Agnes did not know what she would say to her former fiancé, who was pining for her. All she felt was the urgency to speak to him, explain why she had entered the convent, and give reasons for accepting the reality of a religious vocation. Her decision was not a rejection of him. On the contrary, although she could not say it, she loved him as much now as when he left her in anger and frustration nearly six years ago. A religious vocation meant choosing God, Jesus, and solidarity in his redemptive work. It took priority over everything else. Fortunately, Mr Ferguson understood there were exceptional circumstances for his summons at such an unusual hour, and he left her in peace. As they approached the outskirts of the city centre, she forced herself to concentrate. But as much as she was free to rehearse her ideas, her mind was all confusion by the time Mr Ferguson pulled to a stop outside the gates at the southern entrance.

'Mr Ferguson, I expect to be no more than an hour. I'm sorry you must wait.'

'Think nothing of it, Sister. I have all the time in the world. I'm happy I can be of service.'

She was hurrying along the pathway through the front lawn, lost in thought, when a familiar voice called.

'Sister, I'm so glad you're here. I knew you would come,' said Anne, running up to her. 'He's still in his office. Please talk to him. He badly needs it. People are saying he's suicidal.'

'Suicidal? Surely not … he's not the type.'

'He needs you badly. Sister, perhaps this is not the time to say it, but you and he belong together. I don't know why you're— You would make a wonderful wife and mother.'

'You're right, Anne. It is not the time.'

Agnes halted outside the closed office door. Her heart was in her mouth. She felt like that teenage girl so desperately in love—what was it? —fifteen years ago. She knocked.

'Come in. The door's open,' she heard.

She opened the door to reveal Philip sitting at his desk, head down and writing vigorously. He continued for a few moments before looking up.

'Virginia, what are you doing—?' he said, standing. His face was scratched, bruised, and slightly swollen around his left eye.

'May I come in?'

'Of course, of course.' He rearranged the armchairs in front of his desk and waited until she was seated. He sat in the other, facing her. 'What brings you here?' he said, fidgeting. 'When you didn't turn up for the philosophy social evening, I thought that was it until next year.'

'Well … I heard you were in a fight.'

'Did you, all away out there in that closed-off convent? Remarkable.'

'I was told you were in a bad way.'

'Oh, well, you know, I got the worst of it. But Calder would be sore, too. That fellow needed a beating, although I didn't quite achieve that.

Maybe next time.' He tried to laugh, but the effort was painful. 'Who told you, by the way?'

'Someone.'

'Someone? Who could that be? Let me think,' he said, continuing his attempt to make light of it. 'Anne was here around lunchtime, fussing and wringing her hands. Lovely young girl. I didn't think she was so upset about it, though. Of course, it was her, wasn't it?'

'Yes, it was, Philip. You shouldn't be so dismissive. People are worried. It's no joke.'

'What? I got a little drunk and found it hard to control my anger about how Calder and his mates picked on you. He's an animal, a contemptible, cowardly animal. He deserves far more than he got.'

'It's serious, Philip, for you, I mean. It'll have a bearing on your position here. It's not like you to act that way.'

'I know,' he said, sighing and waving both hands in surrender. 'You're right. It was a bit juvenile. You're right to give it to me. I was just busy explaining myself to the Head of Department. I've been drinking too much. Joe has got stuck into me.'

'And the absence from the university, the pneumonia—?

'I know, Virginia, I know all too well. Trying vainly to beat Calder to a pulp brought me face to face with it.'

'You must face things. I must face things.'

'I know. You're right. I must get over it at last. I know what you'll say about a religious vocation and commitment and all that. I will accept it. I must.'

'It's not that I have no feeling for you, Philip.'

'I know, you have a greater feeling for—' He waved his hand in resignation and looked away. He tried to smile. 'I promise I'll be different next year.'

'You'll make a good husband—for the right sort of girl.'

'You've seen that, too. You don't change, Virginia. Although you are not right about—'

'It's only what your mother would say.'

'My mother! Virginia ... Sorry ... You're not my mother.'

The conversation continued in this manner until she was satisfied that his frame of mind was sound, that he had resigned himself to their circumstances, and that Anne had exaggerated.

'I must go now,' she said. 'I'm glad things aren't quite as bad as Anne said.'

'She brought you in to save me from myself?' he said, smiling.

'Yes, something like that.'

'It's a wonder you were allowed to come.'

'Mother Jerome made an exception.'

'She must have considered it serious, too.'

'Yes, she must have.'

By this time, they were standing next to the door. She looked up at his face and the sorrowful smile of resignation.

'Things will be all right now, Philip.' His bruised and swollen face had her trapped. 'It must hurt,' she murmured.

He did not reply. He looked into her eyes. She reached up and stroked his swollen cheek. He slowly raised his hand, giving her time to take her hand away. She did not. He took hold of her hand and ran it across his lips. With the touch of those warm lips, the doors that had been on the verge of shutting for so long now closed over the last six years. Philip pulled her gently back into the office and kicked the door closed. Suddenly, she was aware of the unreal sight of her veil lying on the office floor. In all that followed, it was the strange sight of the veil on the floor that was imprinted on her mind.

'No, Philip, not here,' she said, pushing him away as she pulled the wimple back over her bare head and glanced at the veil.

'Then where?'

'I don't know.' She was reeling from the kiss.

'Will you come with me?'

'Yes.'

'Will you allow me to organise things?'

'Yes.'

'Then wait here.'

She sank into an armchair, staring before her and breathing heavily. She glanced at the veil on the floor but could not stir herself to pick it up. Minutes later, there was a soft tap on the door.

'Virginia,' she heard Joe Edelman whisper, 'open the door. It's me, Joe. I have instructions from Phil.'

'Wait,' she called. She arranged her wimple, picked up the veil, and, after securing it, opened the door.

'I know what's happened,' he said, slipping past her and shutting the door. 'No need to say anything. When you're composed and feel up to it, Phil wants me to take you to your parents' house, where he will meet you.'

'My parents' house?'

'You will need clothes and other things.'

'Yes, of course,' said Virginia. She did not have the presence of mind to plan too far ahead. Only the enormity of what she was doing filled her mind. What would her parents say? She resumed her seat. Several more minutes passed in silence.

'What about Mr Ferguson?' she said, straightening and turning to Joe.

'No need to worry. Phil told Ferguson he was no longer required, with the message you would explain in due course.'

'In due course,' said Virginia with an ironic smile. 'All right, I'm ready to go. How do you want to do this?'

'Go to the front entrance of the university and wait until I fetch you. Phil said it was your normal routine.'

'That's right. That's where Mr Ferguson picks us up.'

'But don't make as if you're in a hurry. Do your best not to attract attention.'

'Yes, Joe, thank you for your help. My mind can't entirely grasp the madness of what I am doing.'

'I understand. This is a radical step for you.'

'It's not quite what you were hoping for, is it?'

'No, but it has happened this way. Now, give me at least ten minutes.'

'No, make it twenty. Someone might detain me on the way.'

It was a good thing she had extended the time. She was halfway along the path through the south lawn when she heard Anne call.

'Wait, Sister. What happened?' she said, catching up. 'Tell me. Is Philip all right?

'He's fine, Anne. Just a bit regretful about what happened. He appreciates your concern, but there was no need for such worry, he said.'

'But he looked terrible. His face was swollen and scratched, and he looked really upset.'

'He was upset because he let his anger get the better of him.'

'Why are you leaving so soon?' she said, looking around. 'He needs you.'

'He's all right. Anne, I must go.' She resumed her way.

'Are you sure?' said Anne, walking with her.

'Yes, I'm sure.'

'Why are you in such a hurry?'

'I'm not in a hurry. I have to meet someone at the entrance. I don't want them kept waiting.' By this time, they were at the steps leading down to the entrance gates. Joe was parked in full view. He jumped out to open the door when he saw her. 'Goodbye, Anne. Merry Christmas.'

'Why is he picking you up, Sister? What's going on?'

'Not now, Anne.' She must say something to deter Anne from imagining the worst. 'I will tell you later. Don't worry. Everything is all right. Philip is all right. There's no need to worry. You'll learn soon enough. Dr Edelman is doing Philip a favour.'

'Doing Philip a favour? Are you—?'

'Not now, Anne, please. I will tell you later. Please keep this to yourself.'

'All right, Sister. Or should I say, Miss Pearson? I hope so. You and Philip belong together.'

'I could not stop her from guessing what I was doing,' she said as Joe drove away.

'It doesn't matter. You're doing nothing wrong. People will learn shortly, and most will not care. In fact, many will congratulate you for breaking free.'

'Dear me, Joe. That shows just how little you know about the life of a Catholic religious. I am creating an enormous scandal for the convent, the Church community, and my family.'

'It can't be that bad, surely?'

On arrival, they found Philip's car parked outside the house. Virginia alighted and hesitated. 'Joe, I want you to come in, too, if you don't mind. It will help you understand my predicament.'

'Of course, but won't I be out of place?'

'You and Philip will help my parents understand.'

'I don't know how at this stage,' said Joe, uncharacteristically subdued, 'but I will be of assistance if I can be.'

They met an agitated Mrs Pearson at the door, who was about to say something but stopped on seeing the senior lecturer. She led them into the lounge room, where Philip hastened to say he had already briefly explained, but was leaving a full explanation to Virginia. Virginia introduced Joe to her mother and father. She stressed the support Joe had given her in her studies and his assistance in her present crisis. Her mother, clasping her husband's hand, looked from one to the other.

'Please, Mother, say what you wish to say. Philip and Dr Edelman are both involved in my difficulties.'

'But, darling, has it really got so far? Do you understand what you are doing?'

'Yes, Virginia,' her father entreated, 'you must know this action—running away—will have serious repercussions on your relationships and work prospects.'

'If I will permit me, Mr and Mrs Pearson,' said Joe, 'Virginia, apart from anything else, has been under severe pressure. I regret that I did not understand how severe.'

'That puts a different complexion on things, of course,' said Mr Pearson after Philip uttered the same regret and recounted the persecution by bigoted students.

'Why didn't the university authorities do something?' said Mrs Pearson.

'That's my fault,' said Virginia. 'I asked Philip and Dr Edelman not to do anything. I thought I could cope with it.' She noticed the attention her mother paid to Joe.

'Well, it has happened,' said her father. 'What do you propose doing now?'

'I will take Virginia to my beach house in Sorrento to recover,' said Philip, receiving a nod from Virginia. 'I give my word there will be no irregularities. We will discuss where we go from there. Virginia will decide what she does about the convent. For the rest, I promise we will avoid all scandal.'

'I trust you are doing the right thing, darling,' said her mother, glancing at Joe.

'I hope you remain prudent about your future work prospects,' added her father, 'if you insist on breaking with the convent. You should plan for possible repercussions.'

'I will collect my clothes,' said Virginia. She had noticed Joe gazing around at the religious objects in the lounge room.

'I will help you,' said her mother.

SHE WAS now back with Philip, back in his arms, back in the old familiar places. The mild sunny December days, the walks along the beach, her bare feet in the chilly water of the bay, the favourite restaurants and hotels, they were all back as if they had never been away. The carefully chosen clothes that hung neatly and silently in the darkness of her wardrobe for so long were taken from their hangers and brought into the light. She was surprised to find many of them still in fashion for the likes of a conservative young woman. The slacks, sandals, dresses, and blouses—it was as if they had never been off. She flushed at the comments that she looked so young for twenty-eight. People marvelled that she had not changed in six years.

Amid the frantic pursuit of catching up on lost time, Virginia and Philip stopped for a moment of rest on Sorrento beach one bright sunny morning, on that same spot where she had trouble controlling her feelings years before. She was resting in Philip's arms, her feet dug into the sand, enjoying his embrace, when she spotted a familiar figure approaching from the Sorrento pier.

'Well, it had to happen, didn't it?' said Gemma Greene.

'What are you doing here?' Virginia sat up straight.

'You both look such a picture—made for each other.'

'Gemma has some friends close by in Portsea,' explained Philip. 'She's often down here.'

'What was it, the collapse of faith or Philip's arms?'

'It wasn't a collapse of faith.'

'You can never guarantee that,' said Gemma, sitting down in front of her. 'You just imagine it's love.'

'The psychological explanation won't do, Gemma. My year of philosophy has shown that human reasoning is prey to all sorts of traps. The reasoning that has brought you to some of your conclusions is specious and inadequate. The effect has been the opposite of what you prophesied.'

'Bravo!' exclaimed Gemma. 'The girl has found her voice. There'll be no sisterly self-effacement now, will there?'

Virginia flushed. 'I'm merely answering your comments, comments you've been making since the second term.'

'I agree,' said Philip. 'It's difficult to understand how a young woman of your intellect and background can swallow all that verbal fluff.'

'Oh, it's obvious what you think, Philip. You're beyond redemption. But this smart girl here, I still have hope.'

'There's no hope if you think your sort of life will draw me in.'

'You never imagined you would muster the courage to escape the convent prison.'

'You have it all wrong, Gemma. Apart from your misconceptions and assumptions, leaving the convent is entirely different from the moral surrender you are hinting at.'

'Moral surrender!' she laughed. 'I don't mean you'll adopt exactly my lifestyle. You do not possess the temperament for such flamboyant leaps into freedom. On the other hand, there's a diversity of freedom for you to embrace.'

'Spare us that undergraduate drivel,' said Philip.

'The summer solstice is almost upon us,' said Gemma, ignoring Philip. 'Now there's the opportunity to join us—many women together. No men.'

'You're wrong if you still entertain the idea I wanted to go with you for the winter solstice. I can't believe you take all that female deity stuff seriously.'

'You must understand what I take seriously.'

'The Church Fathers recognised what Gnosticism was all about,' said Philip. 'They rightly took active measures to rid the Christian Church of that irrational tangle of myth, Eastern mysticism, and philosophy—bad philosophy. I'm confident the Church authorities will deal with neo-Gnosticism in the same way.'

'You speak like a man, Philip. And you're suffering from overconfidence. This is the way of the future. Virginia, the female deity is not a transcendent being. That's a creation of the male mind. The female deity is a symbolic idea, representing an inner power, an immanent power. It's the symbolism that unites the many strands of female thinking.'

'What bosh,' said Philip.

'You're on the brink of discovering the real power within, the greatest liberating power you would experience,' Gemma continued, ignoring Philip. 'Don't worry, no need to abandon Philip. He'll respect your independent character even more.'

'It's useless to talk to me this way,' said Virginia. 'You misunderstand me if you think your ideas have any appeal at all.' She shook her head. 'I don't understand you. You call my ideals delusions. Rather, a diabolical delusion afflicts you.'

'The devil seems to be playing havoc with you,' said Gemma, all smugness.

'The devil tempts us all. Sometimes we give in to temptation. We have the promise of forgiveness, of making things right. Gemma, you have forgotten that "hope" is one of the theological virtues. Giving in to one temptation does not necessarily mean total surrender to the devil.'

'You've escaped the convent walls, but not yet its emotional and psychological imprisonment. The devil is another creation of the male mind to keep poor little nuns in check. Once you understand that, you understand the devil is the gateway to freedom.'

Virginia did not answer. She stared thoughtfully ahead of her.

'Hah! I've got you thinking.'

'You don't know what I'm thinking, Gemma,' said Virginia, refocusing. 'I make mistakes. I pray I will never succumb to what has you in its spell.'

'The spell of freedom. Poor Ginny.'

'The ancients, Gemma, made a distinction between wisdom and cleverness,' said Philip, taking advantage of a lull in the exchange. 'You're a clever woman, but you are not wise. While you're a poor philosopher, you have a brilliant literary mind. No doubt, one day, that literary mind will produce something many people will want to read. It's possible—no, probable—that you'll reach an international audience and acquire international fame. But it will not be because of a compelling rigour of thought. Your thoughts are philosophically old hat, too much the uncritical regurgitation of Sydney's Professor Patterson and the Thrust libertarians. No, it will be because of an array of stunning images and their evocative juxtaposition.'

'Thank you, Philip. I'll take that prophecy as a compliment.' She turned to Virginia. 'Ginny, despite your undeveloped stage, I love you as much as I ever did, right from when you were my teacher. Now don't look apprehensive. I love the male body more than most females, more than is good for me. I love you with the disinterested love only a woman can show. So I'm going to give you a special present. I will play the part of Salome and bring you, not John the Baptist's head, but Herod's on a plate.' She rose and brushed the sand from her clothes.

'Gemma, don't do anything silly,' Virginia replied, hesitating before she understood. 'It's not worth it.'

'Of course not, my darling. But you must understand that Herod's type, those who persecute and kill the innocent, only understand one language—their own language. We'll talk again. Bye, Philip. I much respect you despite all. You're what's known as a good man.'

'She makes it sound like an insult,' said Philip as they watched her depart.

'She has a way of perverting the good in reaching out for the good,' said Virginia, resting against him. She felt his arms go around her. She closed her eyes. A minute later, she opened them.

'Is there something wrong?'

'No, no.' After several minutes, 'I will have to confront what I have done, Philip.'

'Yes, Ginny—but not yet.'

'No ... not yet.'

AT THE end of the first week of her escape, Virginia found herself alone with Joe Edelman on the verandah of Philip's beach house. They had just waved him off on his way to the university to deal with department matters.

'Look after her, Joe, would you?' he had said. 'I'll be back this afternoon.'

'It will be my pleasure.'

'You have been very kind, Joe,' Virginia said when they were seated in their deck chairs with a full view over the bay's smooth blue waters.

'It's only what you deserve after my clumsy, embarrassing manner with you during the year. You were right. That short chat with your parents in their Catholic house opened my eyes. That's apart from confronting the shame of the undeserved pressure I put on you.'

'You couldn't know. And you were always a gentleman.'

'Thank goodness for that, at least.'

They were silent for a minute or so.

'I suppose you will get married soon.'

'Philip and I have decided to take up where we left off, but we will take it easy. As much as I am relieved about resolving my problems, I realise there is much to do before we can plan a wedding.'

'I'll be careful now that I don't say anything stupid. Your parents made it clear that you just can't say to your superior that's the end of it and leave.'

'Well, I could, but it would cause problems for Philip and me. Big problems. I fear Philip has not yet faced that realisation.'

'I think he does from our chats, but wants to prolong this honeymoon period if I can put it that way.'

Virginia smiled. 'Your wit was amusing, Joe.'

'Now you will admit it?'

'Yes, I'll admit it now.'

'You sometimes found it difficult to keep a straight face?'

'Yes, but I realised you were teasing—in a nice way.'

'It was just to get behind the sisterly manner to find the real you. I did not realise I was adding to the pressure. I'm sorry.'

'Well, it's over now—and no need to keep saying sorry.'

'Yes, it's over now, and I see what you really are without the black suffocating habit. I can see what Phil fell in love with.'

Virginia glanced at him. 'I have my faults.'

'It was just an observation, Virginia.'

'I know, Joe.'

Chapter 43

The nightmare

AINE WATCHED Harry and Jannie drive off into the darkness of the hills with one hand holding Estella's and the other in Charles's. 'It was generous of them to bring you home,' said Charles, turning to go inside.

'Harry felt guilty about holding me so long. He wanted to make sure I got home safely. Jannie came along to keep him company. They seem to do everything together.'

It was another of those few occasions that Aine withheld something from Charles, and it made her uncomfortable. The truth was that Harry had refused to let her go home alone after the upset at the convent.

'It was kind of them,' Charles repeated. 'Jannie seems to be blossoming,' he added.

'She has changed since the Holland visit ... you know, she had that liberating experience.'

'Whatever it was, she seems more mature, more confident, and more appealing. A handsome woman and a grating personality are a bad combination.'

'Charles, you surprise me—your unaccustomed frankness.'

'Do I? Jannie has the sort of personality that makes itself felt.'

'You're right, though. Jannie is more appealing. It's a good thing, for she revels in the attention.'

Charles's surprising frankness and the oddness of his comment did not linger. Her mind returned to Harry's observation that she and Jannie had differing attitudes about their appearance. Which was proper? Jannie correctly claimed nothing was wrong with being proud of nature's gifts. But, on the other hand, it was not right to be vain about it, at least according to Christian virtue. Harry seemed to hint that she, Aine, thought one could not be proud of personal beauty without being vain. But that was mistaken. One could be proud of nature's gifts, in the sense of being grateful, without being preoccupied with it as something superior. Was Jannie vain?

Vanity did not motivate Jannie's previous flirtatious ways—insecurity, yes, but vanity, no. And now, with her newfound confidence and maturity, vanity did not seem to play a part at all. Jannie appeared to accept the fact of her beauty without fuss. Perhaps Jannie's views were sounder, after all, and she should review her stand on her own appearance. Really, there was nothing wrong in admitting nature had been kinder to her than others. Only one should not exploit or misuse one's appearance. Perhaps she should not be so scrupulous about Harry's continual praise.

That was one of two thoughts about Harry that occupied her. The other was that she had become so relaxed in his company that she no longer experienced the least anxiety about going to his studio. Harry had passed a test that no other male had passed except Charles. The visit to the convent with Jannie and the recurrence of those strange sounds and feelings had left her in a confused, anxious daze. At first, she was unaware it was Harry's arm giving her comfort. She was just grateful for it. And Harry released his arm when she recovered. He simply showed his disinterested care for her. She found herself looking forward to the next trip to Melbourne.

After a discreet period, Harry rang to ask if Aine was all right and still happy with the present arrangements. He expressed his gratitude again for Charles's cooperation, saying he understood that the occasions in Melbourne might sometimes be disruptive to family life. He was confident, however, that the rewards would compensate for the disruption in due course. Charles made the same unaffected reply to this sort of guarantee. He was only concerned that Aine did what she wanted to do, which seemed to put Aine and Harry at ease. In the meantime, Harry would give Aine a well-earned break. He would have the present shoot placed in an appropriate magazine and finalise the details of her next visit. He anticipated it would be in the first or second week of December. Aine would be kept up to date.

In due course, a selection of photos of the summer accessory shoot arrived at Binawarra with Harry's usual professional comment. His favourite shots were of Aine standing by the riverbank and in the boat on the river. Aine was surprised to see he had taken them while she was looking at the convent buildings. He had captured her mysterious look 'in all its stark enticement.'

'In all its stark enticement?' said Charles, studying the photos. 'That's a strange way to describe it. But these photos look more like you than the others. You are anxious.'

It struck Aine that where Harry had seen a mysterious look, Charles had correctly seen her anxiety. But she did not attribute any significance to the different reactions. Charles merely expressed his view as her husband, Harry as a professional photographer whose concern was mere appearance. Later, Harry showed his care in the right way and at the right time. The issue of the photos and the next shoot in Melbourne faded into the daily life of the Winterbine household. Only now and again, Aine thought of Harry and his charm, friendliness, and consideration. She heard nothing from Jannie until Harry had finalised his plans. Then it appeared that Jannie had an even bigger say in the arrangements. What it would be exactly was too difficult to explain over the phone, said Jannie. Aine should prepare for another overnight stay in Melbourne. She would be brought back to Binawarra the following afternoon. It was only left for Charles to express his satisfaction with the plans, which he did.

WITH an air of studied self-possession, Jannie opened the taxi door as it pulled up at the curb of one of Melbourne's most exclusive hotels.

'I've been waiting for you,' she said as she helped Aine out. 'I had an idea you would arrive about now. Good guess, eh?' She paid the taxi driver, ignoring the mumbled reply from Aine, who looked up at the imposing façade of Hotel Queen Victoria. 'Come on. I'll take you straight to your room and leave you to settle in. We want you to rest so that when we go to work, especially this evening, you'll be at your irresistible best.'

Aine was glad of the rest but a little overwhelmed by the luxury of the surroundings and the hotel staff's attention. They did not leave her to rest until they had delivered plates of fruit and sandwiches, various soft drinks, and a selection of chocolates to the suite. It was a pity they had gone to so much trouble, she thought, because she did not feel at all like eating. She looked forward to another session with Harry and Jannie, but her nerves again took hold of her.

'You have had nothing to eat or drink,' said Jannie, frowning when she returned about an hour later. She took an bottle of lemonade and poured a glass full. 'Here, drink this. You need to be fresh and full of vitality.'

Aine drank the lemonade, thinking it a bit strange that Jannie should insist. It had a slightly bitter taste for lemonade, but her mind did not linger on it, for Jannie took her to a conference hall two floors up. Here, a hive of activity confronted her as the hotel staff arranged tables and chairs and set them for what appeared to be a dinner. At one end of the hall, people were assembling a tableau on a stage in the same style as Jannie's spring tableau. It bore her imprint. Throughout the activity, Harry moved frenetically, giving orders and making adjustments. Jannie waited with Aine near the entrance until Harry was free to provide them with his attention.

'I'm so glad to see you,' he said, running over to them as soon as he caught sight of Aine. 'This evening will be a culmination of all I've been arranging. As a first step, I mean. It'll be a sort of coming out for you.' He took her hand and shook it, then raised it to his lips. 'Sorry, you have to indulge me in this. I'm so excited.'

'That's all right, Harry. I see you're busy.'

'Well, I'm glad. After all this time, you'd think you'd be at ease with me.'

'I am.'

'That's what I want to hear.'

With Jannie following, he led her to the end of the hall, where two women were busy carrying out his final instructions. Jannie left them to give directions to the women.

'This tableau is of summer, as you probably see,' said Harry, standing back and surveying the product with a critical eye. 'Jannie's creation again. She does a terrific job, doesn't she?' He stopped and went to

Jannie to deliver some instructions. 'Yes, this is the second tableau,' he continued, returning to her. 'Jannie had the brilliant idea of setting up the shoot for the summer tableau to coincide with my yearly dinner for my best clients. People have been asking about you; it was Jannie's idea to show you at your best, situated as the fertility goddess amid nature's abundance. Brilliant.' He broke off and went to someone organising the hotel staff. After vigorously pointing and saying a few words, he returned to her side. 'The fertility goddess, along the lines of Celtic myth, do you know anything about that? Jannie said you have an Irish background.'

'Yes, my grandparents on both sides came out from Ireland; no, I don't know much about Celtic mythology. I've never associated Celtic myth with being Irish.'

'Jannie says it's the best background to place you in to show the power of your beauty. That mysterious, faraway look, the slender figure, and the milk-white skin tone—it drives into the scene in an energising way. At least, that's what Jannie said. I agree with her.'

'Did Jannie say that?'

'Of course. I could never come up with anything like that. I know a lot about the creative process of photography, but next to nothing about classical mythology. This time the creative idea is all Jannie's.'

'It's not real, though.'

'What's not real?'

'Well …,' she hesitated, embarrassed. 'The idea of the energising goddess.'

'Of course not. It's a myth, a creative idea, that's all. Whatever made you say that?'

'Jannie seems to take it all seriously.'

'No, she's too practical to take anything like that seriously. She said it herself: she's utilising classical myth for creative purposes, like the

Renaissance painters. Come on. I want to start experimenting with positions and poses.'

Aine was relieved Harry had nothing to do with the tableau's creative process other than offering suggestions. She followed him, preparing to submit to his instructions. They spent the next two hours experimenting and making adjustments to the tableau made up of various plants, shrubs, flowers, bowls, and baskets of fruit and vegetables. Harry was aware that Aine needed a break now and then, which she was grateful for.

'That's it,' said Harry, late in the afternoon. 'I think we've got it. But Aine, you need to rest. I want you to look your best for the performance. Are you happy with what we've decided on? With the music and Jannie's reading, it will last around ten minutes.'

'Yes, it's straightforward,' said Aine, pleased Harry was satisfied with her.

Jannie accompanied her to her room, poured a glass of lemonade, and selected sandwiches from the platter. 'Here, you need to keep your fluids up—to keep that skin glistening.' The lemonade had that slightly bitter taste again. She closed the curtain over the windows with a view of the Yarra parklands. 'I'll be back in an hour to help you dress.' Aine did not feel sleepy, nor did she need any sleep. Nevertheless, she fell into a deep sleep and had to be shaken awake.

'I'm glad you had a good sleep,' said Jannie, pushing the curtains back. The evening had come, and the city's lights sparkled around the windows. 'This evening will be full of intense joy.'

'I had such odd dreams,' said Aine, stretching her arms into the air.

'What about?'

'I was standing above a room full of people. They were shouting at me, cheering me. I felt I had this tremendous power over them.'

'What's odd about that?' said Jannie. 'You should be happy it was a pleasant dream.'

'It was pleasant, in a way. It kept on repeating.'

Showing no further interest in Aine's dreams, Jannie sent her to the bathroom to freshen up. When she returned, she found Jannie bending over, examining a black silk dress with a purple border of symbols. 'Come on, put this on.' After some adjustments and a close examination, she had Aine sit while she did her hair. This took time as the style was purely Celtic, Jannie said, and required plaiting several strands of hair. She applied makeup lightly and stood back to appraise her work. 'Wonderful, the people will not know what they're looking at. Now your hands and feet.' Soon, Aine was ready. Jannie placed her in front of the full-length mirror. 'What do you think?'

'I can't believe it's me.'

'You have to get used to knowing that's you.' She poured some more lemonade. 'Here, one more before we go up. You need to keep up your fluids.'

Aine drank the lemonade with the bitter taste, deciding now it was not at all unpleasant. Jannie led her with an overcoat draped over her shoulders, a scarf around her head, and sandals on her feet via the fire escape stairs to the conference room. They entered through a side door in a dimly lit part of the hall. Aine gasped at the brilliance of the scene. People dressed in elegant evening wear filled the room: the men in black dinner suits or tuxedos with white jackets, the women in long evening gowns. Silver cutlery and white china were meticulously arranged on the tables, and bottles of wine were lined up imposingly. Flower arrangements flowed discreetly around slim red candles, spreading an arcane glow. Raphaelite prints decorated the walls. It seemed like an army of black-clad waitresses with white caps and aprons were serving the people standing around, chatting. Jannie ushered Aine behind the stage, which was in darkness with partitions hiding the tableau.

'They don't have a clue what's going to happen,' she said. 'I'm sure they think the stage has been partitioned off for the night.' She helped Aine off with the overcoat and scarf and made some last adjustments. 'Good, you look perfect. We're almost ready to go. Just wait a moment.' She disappeared and returned with two glasses. 'Here, take a sip of this.'

'What's this?' she said after tasting it.

'You've never had champagne before?'

'No. I don't drink alcohol.'

'Don't worry. It's like a delicious lemonade. A little bit won't hurt. It'll help you relax.'

'I'm already relaxed,' said Aine. It was true. She felt a little light-headed, and her edginess had gone. She sipped the champagne, surprising herself, for she usually put any alcoholic drink aside that, on rare occasions, came her way. Jannie was right. It tasted like a pleasant, though sharp, lemonade.

'Good,' said Jannie, observing her closely. 'It's the best French champagne. It would be a miracle if you didn't like it.'

'You look sensational,' exclaimed Harry, appearing and looking resplendent in a black dinner suit, gleaming white shirt, and black bow tie. 'You're going to knock 'em out.' Aine beamed at the compliment. 'What are you drinking?'

'Jannie gave me a little champagne.'

'Harry, we're ready to go,' said Jannie, interrupting. 'I'll set myself up and then start the music. You can help Aine take her cue.' She disappeared around the front of the stage.

'Here, give me your glass,' said Harry.

Aine took a long sip and handed him the glass. She held out her hand to him to steady herself as she slipped off the sandals. Harry took her hand and watched the sandals slide from her pretty feet. A brief, intense moment followed as they looked at each other, Aine's hand still in his. He pulled her to him and held her in an embrace, their faces and lips inches apart.

'I'm in love with you,' whispered Harry. He met her startled expression and then kissed her on the lips. 'I would cover you in kisses if it wasn't for the makeup.'

'No, Harry, you mustn't,' said Aine, making no attempt to disengage herself.

'Mustn't what? My love is a reality. I can't deny it. I can't resist it—neither can you.'

'No ... we mustn't.'

'I know you feel something for me. I've been feeling it. It's irresistible. I'm willing to do anything ...' The music started. Harry looked torn between holding her and obeying the cue. She hung unresisting in his arms, dazed and shocked. 'Come on. We have to complete the job. We'll talk about it after.' He led her to her position at the bottom of the short flight of stairs leading onto the stage. 'You'll do well. My love goes with you.'

With those last words burning in her ears, Aine ascended the stairs and took up the agreed pose on stage. The partition withdrew, and a blazing spotlight enveloped her. She heard a suppressed gasp around the room. She could not have imagined what they were looking at: an unblemished pale beauty, barefoot, with her fair hair tied in plaits and woven around her head, the delicate leafy garland on her head, the black silk dress with the purple border motif. Jannie had brought a figure to life out of the most ancient of myths.

As Jannie weaved her poem of Mother Earth's abundance between the rising and falling music, Harry's declaration of love lingered in Aine's head, provoking shock and pleasure. The forbidden feelings retreated as a strange power overtook her body. The power grew in unison with the poem of the energising earth goddess drenching creation with summer's fertility. She was locked in a bright aura, seeing nothing but the images of the growing energy in her body. To the side, Harry's adoring encouragement came to her as she moved fluidly through the poses and positions she had learned. Her spirit rose above the stage, the people, and the room into another realm where she felt an unearthly power, giving her conquest of Harry, Jannie, and the room full of elegant people.

The agreed poses soon became a restraint. So, she first extended them with improvisations and then moved into a series of entirely new movements that became more like a dance. Her arms rose and weaved, her body bowing and twirling, with baskets of fruit, then with swaying palm branches, then with a cluster of vegetables— It seemed to go on in an endless ecstasy of ascendance. She became aware Harry had stopped his encouragement and Jannie her reading. When the music came to an end, she twirled around and around and came to rest in a half-kneeling position, with her arms extended towards the audience and her head raised towards the heavens. A deathly silence gripped the room. Thunderous applause broke out.

'My God, where did that come from?' said Harry, helping her to her feet.

'I don't know,' said Aine, her breast heaving, her spirits still soaring.

'*Ongelooflijk!*' [unbelievable] cried Jannie, who now stood on the other side of her. 'You're glowing as I've never seen before. You've found the inner spirit, the goddess, the pathway. And so soon.'

'What are you on about?' said Harry, distracted for a moment.

'It's the imagery of success,' said Jannie after some hesitation.

'And what success!' he murmured, refocusing his adoring gaze. He took Aine's hand and drew her forward with a flourish of his arm. 'Behold the face and figure!'

'Behold the future woman,' intoned Jannie, but her words were lost in the din of applause and admiring chatter.

Aine acknowledged the clapping and bowed, feeling the rush of power from her dominance of the room.

'Come on,' said Harry, taking her hand. 'I want to introduce you to some important people.'

An enslaved Harry led Aine around the room for the next half-hour, confronting her with more attention and praise than she had ever thought possible. Where did she come from? What had she been doing? Amazing, stunning, and unequalled were the comments coming from all sides. She hardly grasped what was happening amid the tumult of her elevated feelings. Then she found another glass of champagne in her hand, which she sipped as she went. Eventually, Harry brought the introductions to a close.

'We'll let Aine have a brief rest and a chance to change,' he said to the people crowded around her. 'She'll be back later to show a different side to her beauty.'

He motioned to Jannie to wait a moment while he had a few words with Aine outside. Jannie, who had been close by during the tour around the room, raised her eyebrows and nodded once. Then, with her spirits in the heavens and the power and conquest still coursing through her body, Aine let Harry lead her to a cosy niche of armchairs beside a large window overlooking the Yarra glittering in the city lights. He took her in his arms. She did not resist, letting her head rest for a moment on his shoulder.

'You have known how much I love you, haven't you?'

'Have I?' She looked into his eyes, not quite focusing on them.

'I think you love me, too, at least a little.'

'Do I? I suppose I do, in a way. You've been good to me.'

'I never had any intention, I promise. It just happened.'

'I know. It just happened.'

He kissed her on the lips. 'You're no longer resisting.'

'No, I'm not, am I?'

'What do you feel?'

'I don't know ... I think I need to rest awhile.'

'Of course, it's been stressful. I'll take you to your room.'

'No ... no, I would like to be alone for a few minutes ... to gather my feelings.'

'You can't go by yourself.'

'You can come down in half an hour,' she said as if she did not hear. 'I'll be ready for you then.'

'Are you sure?' he said, looking at her in surprise. 'Are you really sure?'

'What ...? I suppose so. I feel so overwhelmed.'

'Of course, I'll get Jannie to accompany you.'

With brief words of encouragement and congratulations, Jannie left her to herself. Hardly aware of her surroundings, Aine drifted around the room, finally coming to the window overlooking the Yarra. She gazed down at it. It seemed closer and darker, the city lights now extinguished in its glassy surface. Fortunately, Jannie said nothing, nor stayed behind to organise her. She had to be alone. She was lost in a tangle of feelings through which Harry's embrace and words of love ran.

She did not know how long she stood there before she began shaking, slightly at first, then violently at length. Her face was on fire. She ran to the bathroom and splashed cold water over her painted face. She bent over the sink, the water dripping from her face. 'My God, what have I been doing?' She vomited. She splashed water on her face again. Leaning on the side of the sink, she stared at the sick oozing around the plug hole, broken by drips from her face. She turned the tap full on. 'What have I been doing?' she repeated as she walked haphazardly around the room, her mind trying to review all that had happened that afternoon. So much of it had mingled with the haze of those soaring feelings.

'Oh, oh, oh,' she repeated. 'What have I been doing?' She stopped. 'Harry!' She looked desperately around the room. She grabbed her bag and emptied the contents of the drawers into it. She took her clothes from the hangers, preparing to change. 'No, no!' She stuffed them into the bag, put on her shoes, and rushed from the room, leaving the door wide open. She waited for the lift to arrive, jabbing continually at the button. It opened to reveal Jannie hurrying out, deep in thought. Aine jumped in and pressed the ground floor button.

'What are you doing?' said Jannie, jamming her foot between the closing doors.

'I'm going.'

'Where?' She got into the lift.

'I'm going.'

'What's happened? You were flying to the heavens just now.'

'Rather to the underworld.'

'Wait, Aine. If it's the things Harry said, give him the chance to explain. He thought—'

The doors opened, and Aine rushed out. Jannie followed, calling to her. On seeing Aine approaching in a hurry, the porter opened the door of a waiting taxi. Aine got in and went to pull the door shut. Jannie held it.

'No, Aine, don't go like this. Harry will be devastated. He will be able to soothe—make up for whatever is bothering you.'

'No, Jannie, it's all finished. Harry can't say anything that will change that. Besides, it's not what Harry's done.'

'Then what is it?'

'Let go of the door.'

'No, I won't let you go until you tell me what's happening.'

'What did you put in the lemonade?'

Jannie hesitated. 'Just a little gin, just enough to calm you. You're not upset about that, are you, such a little bit? It's nothing. You weren't even affected.'

'That's not the main thing.'

'Harry had nothing to do with that.'

'I know. Please, shut the door.'

'Then what's upsetting you? Tell me.'

Chapter 44

The flight

DURING THIS time, Harry arrived in Aine's room. He looked aghast at the empty space. He stumbled over the furniture to the window and caught sight of Jannie below at the open door of a taxi. He rushed from the room and arrived outside the hotel just as the porter took the door from Jannie and shut it firmly.

'What in the blazes is happening?' he said, running up to Jannie as the taxi drew away from the curb.

'She won't tell me.'

He ran, stumbling beside the taxi. 'Stop! Stop!' Aine turned her head away and tapped the driver's shoulder. 'Let me explain!' The taxi swerved out into the traffic and accelerated.

'I'll take this taxi,' Harry called to the porter as another taxi pulled up beside them. 'Follow the taxi that just left,' he ordered. 'Don't lose it, whatever you do.'

The two taxis weaved their way out of the city and headed in tandem towards the northeastern suburbs. As they left the built-up area and made their way through the trees in the dark, Harry muttered to himself: 'Where the hell are we going?' It wasn't long before the two taxis had negotiated the road along the ridge and turned into the Convent of St

Augustine. The sharp Gothic tower framed high against the starlit sky looked down on them as they drew to a stop.

'What are we doing here?' Harry mumbled as he watched the door of the taxi in front fly open, Aine run to the large wooden doors and begin pounding.

'Let me in,' said Aine to the surprised lay nun who opened the door. She pushed past her.

'You can't—'

'Keep the door shut!'

'But ...,' the lay nun stammered.

'Shut the door!' said Aine, pushing the huge wooden door shut with a bang.

'That's all right, Sister, I will handle this,' said Mother Jerome, descending the nearby stairway.

'Mother, I need your help, please, please— ' cried Aine.

'Calm yourself, Mrs Winterbine,' she said, taking Aine's hand. 'Sister, will you detain the gentleman until I return. Put him in the second parlour. Offer him coffee. And ask Sister Martha to wait on me.'

Harry ran to Aine's driver, heading for the front doors and carrying Aine's bag with his arm raised. 'Leave,' Harry said, taking the bag and pressing a ten-pound note into his hand. He banged on the wooden door. 'I want to see Aine, Mrs Winterbine,' he shouted, pushing past the unresisting lay nun when she opened the door again.

Mother Jerome led Aine to the parlour where she had confronted the departing Jannie five years before. Aine looked around.

'Aine, please sit down and tell me what brings you here,' said Mother Jerome. 'You have no reason to be fearful. Somebody will be with you all the time.'

'I have betrayed myself and all those I hold dear,' she said, falling to her knees and clasping her hands. 'I have been absent from my husband for almost a year.'

'Absent?'

'Absent in mind and spirit, if not always in body.'

'Does the man I can hear have anything to do with it?'

'In a way, but he's not the problem. I'm the problem.'

'Does how you're dressed have anything to do with it?'

'All to do with it.' She tugged at the black silk dress and rubbed her face with both hands as if trying to wipe away dirt. 'I have succumbed to the very danger you warned about.' She hesitated. 'That voice belongs to a fashion photographer who had been preparing me for—'

There was a knock at the door, and Sister Martha appeared as it opened. She looked with pleasurable surprise at Aine but remained at attention in front of them. Mother Jerome nodded almost imperceptibly.

'Oh, Aine, it's so nice to see you,' said Martha, coming forward and bending down to embrace her.

'Sister, please stay with Aine while I see to the gentleman we can hear.'

The sight of Martha and the memories of her simple, unaffected ways were perhaps the most cutting accusation Aine could face. The tears of shame that had threatened on the way to the convent began to flow. Martha helped her to her feet and held her in a consoling embrace without saying anything. Harry's voice, which had been echoing in the hall, fell silent.

'Mr …?' said Mother Jerome, appearing in the entrance hall and frowning at the shouting and gesticulating gentleman. She dismissed the lay sister who had gestured her helplessness in dealing with the male intruder.

'Harry, call me Harry,' said that gentleman, having been brought to attention. 'Where's Aine— Mrs Winterbine—what have you done with her?'

'You don't have a surname, sir?'

'No— none that I want to reveal.'

'Very good, Mr Harry, will you please follow me. And keep your voice down. Shouting won't achieve anything, and you must respect your surroundings.'

Harry followed to a cosy parlour and fell onto the armchair indicated to him. He turned his flushed face toward her.

'Would you like a cup of coffee, Mr Harry?'

'No ... no, thank you. I want to see Aine. I must know why she suddenly left the dinner—why she left the brilliant reception. I want to know what has upset her,' he said in a rush, somewhat intimidated. 'I demand to know. She owes it to me.'

'Perhaps if you tell me what happened, sir?'

With his eyes rolling, Harry related the success of the evening in a solipsistic manner until Aine took flight without apparent cause.

'You imagine you have feelings—an interest in Mrs Winterbine?' said the prioress, expressionless.

'Imagine? I don't imagine! Yes, yes ... I never planned it. I even tried to resist it. I can't help it. She's like no one I have ever met. It's not just her appearance, either.'

'Doesn't the fact that she is married mean anything, sir?'

'Lady— Madam—'

'Call me Mother Jerome. It is an ecclesiastical title and has no significance for you other than that.'

'Mother Jerome,' said Harry, 'I only know what I feel. That's the reality.'

'The reality, sir, is that if you think that justifies coveting another man's wife, you entertain an entirely different morality from Mrs Winterbine. That can never be a basis for a successful relationship. I gather you don't want to make the person you love unhappy.'

Harry stared at that formidable nun as if he did not quite comprehend. 'Feelings are feelings. People fall in love and naturally want the object of their love. It's either Charles's bad luck or mine.'

'It does not bother you that you may break up a family?'

'It's the price of love.'

'How can you guarantee you will not tire of Mrs Winterbine as you tired of others?'

'Aine is different—besides, I'm not going to sit here arguing. My apologies, but none of this is your business. I want to see Aine. I'm not leaving until I see Aine.'

Mother Jerome regarded him, her lips rounding a little. 'I will take you to Mrs Winterbine on two conditions. First, you do not touch her; second, you leave as soon as you have both said your piece or as soon as she requests it. She will be staying here for the night. Whatever happens after that is your business—and hers.'

'All right, I'm a fair person, however else you may judge me.'

Mother Jerome held up a calming hand as she ushered Harry into the parlour, where Sister Martha was consoling Aine. 'Mr Harry has promised to go as soon as you have said your piece, or you want him to go.'

'There's nothing to say,' said Aine, avoiding Harry's desperate eyes. 'I made a terrible mistake. It remains for me to try and right the wrong I've done.'

'What's wrong?' Harry held out his hands. 'What are you talking about? Your behaviour has been impeccable. If anyone has done anything wrong, it's me.'

'You don't understand, Harry. You will never understand. No, put an end to it. It's doomed. It'll be for your good. Go to Jannie. She cares for you far more than I ever could.'

'Jannie ... how did you ... that's finished ... I love her, but not the way I love you.'

'Then you must understand I can't love you the way you want. Besides, you are not my problem.'

'But you said you loved me. How can you go back on that?'

'I was in a delirium—of evil.'

'A delirium of evil! What in blazes are you talking about?'

'No, Harry, it's useless. Go now. You've done me no wrong. You've always been kind and gentlemanly, and I appreciate that. It's the spiritual world I've gotten mixed up in that's evil.'

'What spiritual world? I don't understand. Please, Aine, I love you. I want to know what you're talking about. I'll do anything. I'll become a Catholic. I'll take instruction—just tell me. Don't let it end like this—with me not knowing what's happening. Why have you become so hard?' Tears appeared on his cheeks.

Aine softened. 'Harry, I don't want to hurt you ... I have ... I have affection for you—as a friend. It has never been anything more than that. Be happy with that. I can't give any more. Please go. I must right the great wrong I have done to my husband. I must repair my spiritual life. Please, Mother, will you take Harry away? I can't bear it any longer.'

'No, Aine, please ... don't do this ....' He released a sob.

'Come, Harry,' said Mother Jerome, 'it's useless to insist now. Remember your undertaking.'

'How can you turn so hard and rigid in the space of an hour? It's like I'm talking to a different person.'

'She's upset, Harry,' said the prioress. 'She accuses herself of betraying all that is dear to her. You cannot expect her to be otherwise.'

'It's like a delirium of evil has now overtaken you and turned you into stone,' said Harry, ignoring Mother Jerome. 'Where did it come from?' He glanced around, and his expression changed. 'It's this place, isn't it? You and Jannie cannot get over this terrible place. It still has you in its grip— in the grip of a— of a— ' He turned his head side to side, searching for the right words. 'You're enslaved to—whatever it is. It didn't occur to me until now, but that's it. That's what I've been careful about all these months.' He got on his knees. 'Aine, please, I'll get you out of it, I beg of you ... I'll make you happy, whatever it takes ... you just need to get out o f it.'

'Please, Mother Jerome, I can't bear— ' She put her hands over her face.

'Sister, take Mrs Winterbine to the community room and bring coffee to Mr Harry.'

Sister Martha, who had remained expressionless, rose and helped Aine to her feet. With her hands still over her face, Aine was led out of the room. As the door shut, Harry toppled over onto the floor. He rolled onto his back, put his hand over his eyes, and moaned. Even the self-composed prioress had to give expression to her sympathy as she looked at the handsome young man in a black dinner suit lying on the floor, moaning and rocking from side to side.

'Come, Harry, some dignity. Not so melodramatic. It's not the end of the world.'

'Some dignity! Melodrama! I see the results of months of hard work evaporate before my eyes. I see the woman in my arms, less than an hour ago, looking into my eyes with love in hers, vanish. She has now gone cold, breaking my heart. How can I remain dignified?' He got into a sitting position, clasping his knees.

'You've been drinking, Harry. Things will be different in the sober light of day.'

'Yes, I was drinking the best of French champagne to celebrate, toast after toast—' He crawled to the nearby armchair and hauled himself onto it. 'Aine could swim in French champagne in the end ... I don't understand ... however will I see things differently?'

'You just said Mrs Winterbine's new mood is like a delirium of evil and that the convent is exercising an evil influence; she made a similar claim about this evening. It seems you have opposite ideas of good and evil. This is not the basis for a relationship. Mrs Winterbine sees that clearly. You would never be happy with her. You will realise that in time. Forget her and go back to your dinner. Your guests will be wondering where you have got to.'

'Let 'em wonder. I don't care anymore. I want my melodrama.' Sister Martha arrived with the coffee and put it on a small table beside Harry's armchair. He reached out eagerly for the cup and took a few sips. 'You could have better coffee,' he said, smacking his lips.

'Your taxi is waiting, Harry,' said Mother Jerome when he had finished. 'It's best you go back to your guests. You will achieve nothing here. You can contact Mrs Winterbine when you are more yourself.'

'I suppose I can,' he said, brightening. He put the empty coffee cup back on the table. 'I've never been really in love before this.' He got to his feet. 'She did say she has affection for me, didn't she? Perhaps that's a start. Perhaps it's not hopeless.'

'I will accompany you to the taxi,' said the prioress.

On the porch outside, Harry turned to her: 'It's not like me to lose control in such a stupid way. I've never faced this situation before. I'm sorry.'

'Then you may have more regard for the feelings of the young women you meet.'

'I'm always respectful of the young women I meet,' he said, straightening.

'Just one last word, Harry,' said the prioress. 'Mrs Winterbine acts according to a moral scheme you don't understand, perhaps will never understand. You should respect her views and be sober enough to realise that persisting is useless. You do not strike me as an unreasonable man.'

'I hope I'm not.'

'Then forget about her.'

'I can't.'

'Good evening, Harry.'

Returning the farewell, he walked to the taxi, his back bent and shoulders hunched. As the taxi turned around the drive, Mother Jerome saw him look up at the Gothic tower.

Ten minutes later, Mother Jerome entered the community room where Aine sat with Martha, sipping her tea. 'I took the liberty of ringing Mr. Winterbine to tell him where you were. It was best I spoke to him. He might have got the wrong idea if you had spoken.'

'Wrong idea? How more wrong could I have been?'

'That's precisely what I mean. You would have upset him more than necessary. Sister Martha, would you please leave us? But stay close at hand.' She waited until Sister Martha had left the room. 'Aine, in the end, you withdrew from the temptation. Be careful not to make it graver than it is. You must consider your husband. You don't want to hurt him unnecessarily, do you?'

'No, I don't, that least of all.'

'Some things can remain between you and God—your state of mind, for example.'

'I realise Charles had an idea of what I was getting into. I thought I could follow Harry's plans without entering his world.'

'And you found you couldn't.'

'It was what went with the success. Jannie and Margaret, I mean Sister Catherine, spoke about the freedom and independence I would enjoy if I pursued a career. I discovered that my success brought an overwhelming feeling of power, which Jannie eventually called the freeing of the inner spirit. That feeling had been developing, and I had tried to ignore it. But this evening, it broke out. I was in ecstasy—like it was something due to me. Jannie said I had freed the inner spirit. I felt mastery over Harry as he held me in his arms— He mistook that for love. His kisses thrilled me in that way.' She bent her head. 'Oh, I feel so sick as I recall it.'

'What brought you out of it?'

'I don't know. The alcohol had affected me a little, but not enough to account for the soaring spirits. So, it wasn't the gradual sobering. Something began to rebel within me. The high spirits and feeling of conquest were an illusion, an illusion that would destroy everything I had and lived for. I was so appalled that it made me physically sick.'

'By the Grace of God, you were drawn back.'

'What is it, Mother Jerome? What is this thing inside me that torments me in one way or another? Thinking I was free from it ended up being the worst torment.'

'It's the primeval temptation, the promise of unlimited power, the temptation that Eve succumbed to. St John spoke about the Pride of Life.'

'Why me? Why the torment?'

'That is one of the mysteries of life. I can't answer that. That is between God and you. I told you the devil gives priority to the innocent and pure of mind.'

'I feel far from innocent and pure.'

'That's part of the Evil One's success. Beware.'

'What's going to happen to me?'

'You must not despair, and you must stop thinking about it tonight. You are exhausted. Sister will take you to your room for the next two nights. She will always be close by, so there's no need to be anxious.'

'Two nights?'

'I asked your husband if he was happy for you to stay two nights. There is something I would like you to help me with. He had no objection.'

'Help you with ... what ...?'

'We will discuss that tomorrow. Now is not the time.' She walked to the door and called for Sister Martha. 'One more thing before you go: you said that your affection for Harry is that of a friend. Be careful you are not deceiving yourself.'

'My feelings for him differ from my feelings for Charles,' said Aine after a few moments of consideration. 'I hope I'm not deceiving myself.'

'Sister, will you take Aine to her room?' Mother Jerome said to Martha, who appeared at the door, 'and make sure she is comfortable for the night. She must be able to contact you if something is worrying her.'

'Yes, Mother, certainly.'

'Good night, Aine. It would be appropriate if you offered prayers for your deliverance this evening—the five Joyful Mysteries.'

'Yes, Mother, good night.'

HARRY arrived back at the hotel conference hall to find everyone enjoying themselves, unaware of his terrible drama and the collapse of his ambitions. He did not have to wonder about the reason; he expected Jannie to have taken matters into her hands and offered some plausible explanation for his absence. He was right. She had told the guests Aine was not well, and he had taken her home. They milled around him as soon as he appeared, offering their congratulations for the splendid dinner and the stunning show. They looked forward to more of the work of Harry's incomparable new beauty. Jannie brought him a glass of champagne, patted him on the back, caressed his shoulder, kissed him on the cheek, and told him to relax. Later that night, when the guests had gone, and Harry could barely stand, she took him to the room Aine had vacated. The future international supermodel put him to bed, kissed him on the forehead, and turned out the light before leaving.

A faint sound roused Sister Martha around one o'clock in the morning. She looked up from her rosary to hear footsteps and a door closing, from where she could not tell. She walked along the corridor to the stairway landing, looked down into the darkness, but finding all quiet and in order, returned to the chair she had placed outside Aine's room. She resumed threading her way through her rosary.

Chapter 45

Seeking Virginia

A LAY SISTER woke Aine at half-past six and informed her that Mass was at seven o'clock if she wished to attend.

'Thank you, Sister, I will attend,' she said, drawing herself up and looking around. The memories flooded back.

'You will be served breakfast in the visitor's parlour after Mass, Mrs Winterbine. Please tell me if there is anything I can do for you.'

'Thank you, Sister, there's nothing. Where is Sister Martha?'

'She went to bed at about five o'clock. She will be with you later in the morning.'

'You mean she stayed up until then?'

'Yes, Mrs Winterbine.'

'Thank you, Sister. Oh, Sister, is there confession before Mass?'

'Yes, if you hurry, you will catch Fr O'Brien.'

Aine dressed and hurried to the chapel, where she found the same sister waiting.

'Father is waiting for you, Mrs Winerbine,' she whispered. 'Please follow me.'

She took her to the confessional at the back of the church. Aine was conscious that she might be holding up Mass and began her confession in a hasty, confused manner.

'Please take your time, Sister,' said Fr O'Brien. 'Mass can wait.'

Fr O'Brien helped her put into words the sins her blindness had hidden from her for so long, sins so naked now that she could scarcely speak of them. Ten minutes later, she emerged, feeling the relief of the sacrament. It was now a matter of her resolve and making up to Charles for her neglect. Seconds later, Fr O'Brien also emerged and hastened past the silent rows of black veils to the sacristy. Mother Jerome's skilful arrangements, of course. She was pondering the significance of this and all that had happened over breakfast when there was a knock at the parlour door. Before she could say anything, Margaret slipped in, shutting the door behind her.

'Aine, I had no idea you were here with us.'

'I found myself in a little trouble and sought help from Mother Jerome.'

'What sort of trouble? Nothing serious, I hope. An overnight stay—?'

'I'd rather not speak about it.'

'You can confide in me. You know that, Aine.'

'This is a private matter, Margaret—Sister Catherine.'

'Please call me Margaret. We're friends. And I want to help if you're in trouble.'

'I would rather not discuss it.'

'It must be something out of the ordinary if you're here overnight. Has it got to do with Sister Agnes?'

'No, I have not seen Virginia in months.'

'Nobody has seen her for quite a while—and there are rumours.'

'What sort of rumours?' said Aine, realising Margaret was fishing.

'I'd rather not say.'

Sister Martha entered the room, smiling. 'I hope you had a good night's sleep, Aine,' she said. 'Oh, hello, Sister Catherine. What are you doing here?' She fussed around Aine, seeming not to expect a reply from Margaret, who now wore that familiar disgruntled expression.

'I slept very well, thank you, Sister,' said Aine. 'But you're the one who needed sleep. I can't imagine you got much.'

Martha said she had as much sleep as she needed and then chatted on, forcing Margaret to retreat without obtaining what she came for.

'Mother Jerome wants to see you in her office at ten o'clock,' Martha said when Margaret had left the room.

'Thank you, Sister. Have you seen Sister Agnes?'

'No, I have not noticed her. Do you need anything else?'

Mother Jerome was engrossed in thought when Aine knocked on the open door of her office shortly before ten o'clock.

'Come in, Aine, and please shut the door.' She rose and came around to the armchairs in front of her desk.

'Does this have something to do with Virginia—Sister Agnes?' Aine asked as she sat opposite the prioress.

'The rumours are already doing the rounds, I see.'

'There's something wrong, isn't there?'

'Who mentioned it?'

'Sister Catherine, but she only said there were rumours.'

'Where did you come across Sister Catherine?'

'She came to the parlour while I was eating breakfast.'

Mother Jerome resumed her thoughtful expression. 'Yes,' she continued, 'I will be straightforward because I need your help. Your dear friend has, like you, reached a crisis. She went on a visit to the university and did not return.'

'Oh, no, she couldn't— That's not like Virg— '

'Sister Agnes has had a very challenging year. Those less robust in spirit would have succumbed well before Sister did.' The prioress then recounted the circumstances of Virginia's disappearance. 'Yesterday, I found out where she is. This is the fortuitous side of your difficulties. I would like you to accompany me when I go to talk with her. I am confident you can reach her where others can't.'

'Reach her?'

'You have experienced much together. Hearing your difficulties might help clarify what she is going through.'

'Does she know you're coming?'

'No. Dr Stevenson would not wait around if he knew. He has already taken precautions. Are you ready? We will discuss things as we go.'

Fifteen minutes later, Sister Martha arrived outside the front porch at the wheel of the convent car.

'We are going down to a house at Sorrento, on the Mornington Peninsula,' said Mother Jerome as Sister Martha steered the car out of the circular driveway onto the entrance avenue. 'It will be a long drive, so we can spend time reviewing what has happened to you, both during your period at the convent and during the last year.'

Aine glanced at Sister Martha, who, as usual, gave the impression she heard nothing. Then, with Mother Jerome beside her in the back seat, she related, in just above a whisper, what had happened, starting with the period of postulancy. Mother Jerome listened, frequently asking for elucidation. She was especially interested in Margaret and Jannie's activities during the past year.

'We must pray for your former colleague,' said the prioress. 'Miss de Kam has evidently succumbed where you drew back. Do you understand, Aine, that what you and she have been exposed to is something new and unheard of for the ordinary person, something that will grow in the coming years?'

'No, Mother, I am completely ignorant of it, other than what I experienced.'

'It is truly a diabolical spirit that sees the Church as its most deadly enemy. Where we offer thanks to God for giving you the grace to draw back from the seduction, the promoters of this delusion will accuse us of locking you up in a prison of our illegitimate power. We cannot conceive of where it will lead at this moment.'

'I thought my experiences were about me.'

'No, they certainly weren't. It is not widespread, but its determined, often fanatical adherents are coming together from various theoretical and so-called spiritual movements. It threatens to break out from these groups to achieve a general acceptance of its chief principles.'

'I don't understand.'

'That's because you have been sheltered from most influences until now. Your task now is to shut yourself away from those influences. Your experiences are a warning.'

'Yes, Mother.' After some minutes of silence: 'Do you think Harry is aware of these things, of this movement?'

'No, I am persuaded your judgment of him is correct. He is a considerate man who leads a loose, immoral life in some respects, without stopping to examine it. We must also pray that men like Harry will reconsider their lifestyle and return to what good men know to be manly virtue. Our Christian society will not survive without such men.'

'I'm glad you agree with me—about Harry, I mean.'

'Don't deceive yourself, Aine,' said Mother Jerome. 'That appealing young man is part of your temptation.'

'I fervently hope not.'

They drove on in silence until they were nearing the beach resorts at the end of the Peninsula.

'I will go by myself to talk to her first,' said the prioress. 'Then I will let you speak to her alone. I don't want you to encourage or discourage her from returning to the convent. Sister must make up her mind. She will be seeking comfort, understanding, and reassurance from you, her friend.'

'Yes, Mother, I will do my best,' said Aine, feeling guilty about neglecting her friend.

Sister Martha turned into a side street opposite the bay beach. With a few more turns, she was requested to slow down. They were on a road up a slope leading away from the beach.

'That should be the house,' said the prioress, pointing to a neat white weatherboard cottage on a corner block. 'Do drive on a little, Sister.' As they approached the house, they could see a woman sitting in a deck chair on the verandah, looking at the gleaming blue water of the bay. Her light brown hair was short but neat, and she wore a modest summer dress. 'Stop here, Sister, thank you.' The young woman on the verandah was preoccupied, for she paid them no attention. Mother Jerome entered by the side gate and followed the path to the front of the house.

Chapter 46

Virginia's choice

THE NEED TO do something about her irregular position would not stop bothering Virginia, even during the most relaxed times of being back with her beloved Philip. There was so much to attend to. It had been more than two weeks since she had taken flight. Philip kept postponing confronting the problems, wanting to squeeze the last bit of pleasure from this glorious interlude before they could no longer avoid facing them. While these thoughts were yet again running through her head, as she sat on the verandah staring at the Bay's glimmering waters, Mother Jerome suddenly materialised from around the side of the house.

'Oh, Mother Jerome,' she said, getting to her feet. She looked around, brushing her dress and stroking her hair.

'Calm yourself, Sister. I am here to talk with you, not to reprimand you.' That imposing woman ascended the short flight of stairs to the verandah. 'If you provide me with a chair, we can begin.' With a look of resignation, Virginia fetched a chair from inside. 'I'm glad you look more relaxed and healthier than the last time we spoke.' She looked around. 'Dr Stevenson not at home?' She sat down, calmly arranging the ample folds of her black dress.

'No, Mother, he is visiting a university colleague with a beach house nearby—university business. He will be back at any moment.'

'Good, that will make things easier, to begin with. Now, Sister, let's take things as they are. No reprimands, no accusations. Prudence will be our guide. You are here, but you are an intelligent woman and must know you cannot stay indefinitely in this irregular situation. You risk giving scandal not only to the convent but also to your family and friends.'

'Yes, Mother, I'm only too aware, though it's not as irregular as it appears.'

'No?'

Virginia shook her head, slightly easing the prioress's expression.

'Be that as it may, I am not here to judge you on such matters. Those are issues for later. There are two choices before you. You can return to the convent and undergo the repercussions of your actions. Or you can go about cutting your ties with the Order of the Suffering Saviour.'

'You mean you'll take me back? Not that I want to go back,' she hastened to add.

'Until recently, the order would have considered your transgression too great to tolerate. However, as I have said before, fundamental changes are operating in the world, including radical changes in public attitudes. So, we must look carefully at the circumstances we find ourselves in. Few sisters in their training ever had the burden you were under this year. It would be imprudent, not to mention unfair, to apply the rules made for other circumstances rigidly. We should, therefore, start with the most basic of all questions. Has your breakdown been the cause or the consequence of a loss of faith?'

'No, Mother, it certainly is not that. If anything, I now find less cause for uncritical confidence in human reasoning.'

'Good, that is the first hurdle passed. Tell me, then, what has resulted in your being here.'

'It's been a great deal on my mind,' said Virginia, 'because it's not like me to act as I did. Amid my torment was the unbearable burden of my love for Philip and the way I hurt him. I couldn't bear to see him destroy his life because of me.'

'You could not bear to see him destroy his life because of you?'

'No, I couldn't— I just could not do it.'

'That's a great act of charity, isn't it, Sister?'

'What do you— ?'

'Abandoning your life's goal for the sake of another person.'

'Please, Mother, do not make it sound praiseworthy. It's not.'

'No?'

'I love Philip deeply. I always have, and I suppose I always will. My selfishness is in there.'

'All right, supposing you choose Dr Stevenson, there are two more options before you. Firstly, you can remain where you are, here, and cut ties with the order. In that case, unfairly, you might judge, a certain ignominy is attached to your action. People will say you ran out, broke your vows, and conclude you turned your back on the Church. You may find it hard to find employment in the Catholic education system. Deplore the unfairness of it in your case, but unfortunately, that's the reality.'

'It is unfair, but I realise you are right. And the second option?'

'You can return with me now and undertake the standard steps to leave the order with dignity. Your breakdown need not be mentioned. You would receive an excellent academic and teaching reference from the order. In addition, you would receive help to continue your university studies.'

They were distracted by the sound of the side gate shutting. A few moments later, Philip and Joe Edelman appeared. With face set, Philip took one look and mounted the verandah stairs, leaving Joe staring.

'It was only a question of time before the hounds tracked us down,' said Philip. 'Good afternoon, Reverend Mother Jerome. Here to claim the escapee?'

'No, Philip, don't— '

'I'm sorry, Virginia. They took you away from me once before.'

'Dr Stevenson, I understand your feelings, but there is a certain reality about the present circumstances,' said Mother Jerome, her voice firm and steady. She glanced at Joe.

'What is that reality?' He sat in the deck chair beside Virginia while Joe backed away, out of sight.

Mother Jerome explained the options.

'If you go back, Virginia, you'll never come out again.'

'Dr Stevenson,' the prioress intervened, not giving Virginia a chance to respond, 'I give you my solemn undertaking that I will not try to persuade or coerce Sister Agnes one way or another.'

'Sister Agnes?' said Philip wryly.

'Virginia Pearson is still a professed sister, under vows, of the Order of the Suffering Saviour.'

'And you say you won't coerce her?'

'I can't avoid stating features of the reality of the circumstances. I undertake not to add anything else. If Sister returns with me, I will only suggest that she go into retreat to consider her decision, isolated from the community. That is more of a safeguard for you than any other arrangement. She will come under nobody's influence. That's my solemn undertaking. If she chooses not to examine herself in retreat, she will be left to continue her duties until the formalities are completed, and she can leave the convent in the normal confidential way. You would be advised when you could pick her up.'

'Mother's right, Philip,' said Virginia. 'It's best for all parties concerned that I leave the convent in the proper way. I couldn't bear harming your career.'

'No, Virginia, you'll never come out if you go back. Take my word for it. Forget about my career.'

'Trust me, Philip. You can't doubt my love for you now, not after what has happened.'

'You won't come out, Virginia.'

'Dr Stevenson,' said Mother Jerome, 'you have no right to expect the one you love to act against her conscience. In any case, I have had my say. I do not hesitate to add that the order in these changing times needs vocations from women of the calibre of Virginia Pearson. I will leave it to Sister Agnes to decide now. I will wait in the car. My departure without her will mean her decision to leave the order informally.'

'I understand, Mother Jerome,' said Virginia, taking Philip's hand.

'Just one other matter.' The prioress stood up. 'Your dear friend, Mrs Winterbine, has coincidentally suffered a crisis at the same time as you.'

'Oh no,' said Virginia, 'I had an idea that things weren't right with her. What has happened?'

'It may surprise you to learn that her reaction was like yours on hearing of your crisis. She was not surprised.'

'Really? I suppose I couldn't hide it from her.'

'Mrs Winterbine is in the car waiting to talk to you. I asked her to come with me so she could tell you herself what she has been through. She needs your comfort.'

'Please send her up. I'll do what I can for that special girl.'

'No, Virginia— '

'I will give you half an hour to talk to her and to make up your mind, Sister,' said Mother Jerome. 'Do you have your habit with you?'

'Yes, Mother, it is neatly folded to be sent back.'

'Put it on if you decide to return. Good afternoon, Dr Stevenson.'

As Virginia walked to the end of the verandah, conscious of the summer dress brushing against her bare legs, and with Philip following, she realised she was on the point of a decision from which there was no going back. It was a tremendous relief when she flew from the convent with Philip. The distasteful image she constantly had in her mind was that of a long-festering boil suddenly breaking. The poison of the months was suddenly expelled, and she was left to make a clean life with Philip. But, as Mother pointed out, there was an inevitable reality she had to face. Philip knew that, too, despite the uncharacteristic and petulant comments he had been making.

'Here is your fair-haired friend,' said Philip, now at the railing. 'Whatever else can be said, you have a couple of beautiful women as friends.'

'You shouldn't make so much of Aine's appearance. In many ways, it's a curse for her.'

'A curse!'

'Unfortunately, that's a reaction that is all too common,' she said, watching Aine approach along the front path with a cautious smile and a wave. The glamour she had radiated in the fashion magazines, the look that was not her, had gone. 'I'm so glad to see you,' Virginia said, taking hold of her as soon as she had mounted the verandah steps.

A broken and erratic exchange of greetings and retelling of their experiences followed, with Philip looking on. Aine recounted how Margaret had enticed, and Jannie encouraged her to pursue a modelling career with Harry. At first, everything seemed all right, and Charles appeared happy. But without her being aware of it, she was sucked into a mael-strom of mythological euphoria and imagined transcendence.

'I'm astounded you were carried along with it without seeming to resist,' Virginia said after Aine had finished her painful story.

'I know. I have no idea what got hold of me. I'm so ashamed.'

'No, I don't mean that,' said Virginia. 'I mean that the enticement of the Goddess world seems disproportionately strong. In the past, you have turned your back on such enticements without thinking. So there appears to be more than just the talk about professional success and self-fulfilment.'

'I thought I could go along with it without losing touch with all I held dear. I was wrong. The sudden soaring of my spirits overwhelmed me. But it was not just that I had a delusive idea of my own power. The feeling, the aura, had a distinctly anti-Christian spirit driving it. I don't know how I'll ever get over it and how I will make up for it to my husband.'

Virginia stared at Aine.

'I understand your shock,' said Aine.

'No, Aine, it's not shock so much as bewilderment. There is some-thing new here, at least something I've never encountered. Have you ever heard anything like this before?' Virginia said, turning to Philip, who had become interested in Aine's narrative despite his glumness.

'No, I haven't. That stuff about the Aquarian Company is something I'm aware of superficially. Any sort of neo-Gnosticism I've dismissed as the same rubbish as the original Gnosticism, which the Church quite rightly debunked for the anti-Christian nonsense it is. But all this stuff about the earth goddess and the divine feminine, no, I've never heard of it.'

'Mother Jerome said it's a diabolical movement which few people are aware of,' said Aine.

'You can't comprehend how much you have clarified things,' said Virginia, after more reflection. 'Jannie de Kam, under Margaret's direction, enticed you into that morass, but she is deeply trapped in it herself. Her instability has taken a new form, despite the confident veneer.'

One should distinguish between someone like Jannie, warned Philip, and a libertarian like Gemma Greene. The images of the goddess nonsense appealed to Gemma's literary mind. But Virginia was not ready to exonerate Gemma. The literary symbolism had a communal and political function. The theory and symbolism came together.

'This might appeal more to the female mind,' Virginia continued. 'Indeed, you heard Gemma. She said the male mind is incapable of understanding.'

'You may be right,' said Aine. 'I've been trying desperately to understand why I was susceptible. I abhor the very thought of ideas so contrary to Christian belief. Is it Eve's curse?'

'Has Mother Jerome given you any advice?'

'She warned me about its growing influence and advised me to stay well away from it. Unfortunately, she seems to think it will be an ongoing temptation for me. It's frightening to contemplate.'

'Did she?' said Virginia, again reflecting. 'Mother Jerome is not saying as much as she knows.' She looked at her watch. 'Philip, I must go back.' She stood up. 'I must clear up the mess I have made for us.'

'What ...? No, Virginia ....'

'Philip, I cannot start out doing the wrong thing. You know that.'

'Yes, but what do you expect me to say if I risk losing you for a second time?'

'You must trust me, Philip. I love you. That will never change. It'll only be a couple of days.'

'Are you going to put on that habit?'

'Yes ... I must.'

'I won't stay around to see you in it again.'

'I understand. Hold me.'

When they parted, and Virginia had gone inside, Philip walked to the front gate without looking at the car parked on the side road. Joe, appearing and glancing at the verandah, joined him. In silence, they crossed the road to the beach with their eyes on the ground. Philip sat in the sand, his head bent forward. Joe stood beside him and glanced again at the cottage. Ten minutes later, Sister Agnes appeared in full habit, neat, clean, and pressed, carrying her suitcase. She stopped a moment to look at Philip. By this time, Joe was at the water's edge, staring across the Bay. Her eyes lingered a moment, tears brimming, then with Aine following, she walked to the car where Sister Martha took her suitcase and held the door open.

'Hello, Sister Agnes,' said Martha, 'it's nice to see you.'

MOTHER Jerome directed Sister Martha to give Aine lunch in the parlour when they alighted in front of the great wooden doors. Virginia was sent to spend fifteen minutes in the chapel before coming to her office.

'I hope your period of meditation served you well,' said the prioress when Virginia was seated before her.

'Yes, Mother, I needed time alone in prayer to put all that happened into perspective.'

'I have set out a program for you for the rest of the afternoon. You will not come into contact with the other sisters. After Vespers, you will come to my office to give your first decision, that is, on whether you want formalities for a break with the order to proceed immediately or wish to go into retreat for a further examination of your life's desires.'

'My life's desires ... what form will the retreat take?'

'No, Sister, no further discussion until after Vespers.' She handed her a sheet of paper and rose.

'Thank you, Mother,' said Virginia, taking the sheet, 'I will return after Vespers.'

Virginia spent the next few hours either in the chapel or walking around the grounds. Contrary to her expectations, she found the time in the quiet solitude of the chapel beneficial. She went through her usual prayers, those she had neglected during the last few weeks, and reviewed her actions and relationship with Philip as coolly as possible. The walks around the ground brought a different review. The events surrounding Aine and Margaret returned to her as she passed those locations. At the grotto, she looked to see if there were the same remnants of flowers. There were. But now, more were lying around the rocks as if those un-acquainted with the rituals would not heed their significance, whatever those rituals were.

'Well, what is your decision?' said the prioress after Vespers.

'With some reluctance, I have decided it's wise to reflect calmly for a little longer.'

'You will go into retreat?'

'Yes, Mother,' said Virginia, thinking she detected relief on the pri-oress's face.

Mother Jerome regarded her in silence. 'May I ask first why you returned to the convent? On my arrival, you seemed determined to stay put.'

'Yes, my feelings were still running warm, and I was convinced my life was to be with Philip. I still am,' she added. 'But you made me understand that there were irresistible realities attached to my life with Philip, as there were to my life in the convent. Philip realised it, too. We couldn't make a wrong start together.'

'Was that all?'

'No, listening to Aine was deeply disturbing. I couldn't understand how a young woman like Aine—innocent, pure of mind, spiritually inclined—could get caught up in that, that—'

'Diabolical delusion?'

'Yes.'

'Why would that impinge on your decision? On the surface, it does not seem related to your decision about Dr Stevenson.'

'I'm not sure. I suspect it is related somehow, not directly to Philip, but to my decision to leave religious life. I remember Philip saying spontaneously, "No, Virginia," when I agreed to talk to Aine. It was not clear why he said that. It still isn't. But it seems significant.'

'You are right to be disturbed about Mrs Winterbine,' said the prioress, who looked distracted for a moment. 'She was and still is under great temptation. Although she does not fully understand, she came close to breaking her marriage vows, not so much out of base desire as out of an almost uncontrollable yearning to rise above her material existence with a power over all. That includes sexual power. The delusion is demonic.'

Agnes hesitated, struggling to grasp Mother Jerome's words. 'Sexual power … rise above her material existence? She doesn't think in those terms. Demonic? I don't understand.'

'A fervent, somewhat innocent Catholic like Mrs Winterbine is often prey to greater temptation than the ordinary person. Sometimes giving in for a person like Mrs Winterbine means a total surrender to sin, though it is viewed as power and independence rather than sin. There seems to be no half-measures. Indeed, it is complete possession by the devil. I have witnessed some tragic cases over the years. With your time in teaching, you likely have, too.'

'Yes, Gemma Greene.'

'Of course, Gemma Greene was a student of yours. You are still determined to leave?'

'Yes. The ordering of my thoughts has not changed that.'

'Sister, I will now request you to wait outside for a few minutes.'

Virginia had been sitting in a chair outside Mother Jerome's office for a few minutes when Margaret arrived. They looked at each other in surprise but quickly composed themselves. Margaret sat in the chair beside her.

'Would you both please come in,' said Mother Jerome shortly after. 'You have both completed your year at university with success. I acknowledge the pressures imposed on you through study and mixing in the secular world. You need time in recuperative silence to bring you back to reflect on the reasons you chose the religious life. You will be sent on retreat, each to a different destination. You are to spend your time in a balance of recreation and meditation. All other activities are banned, especially study. The study is to be put behind you until you are ready to return to university.' She held up her hand as Margaret was about to speak. 'Sister Agnes, would you kindly wait outside?'

Five minutes later, Margaret left the prioress's office, scowling and without looking at Virginia.

'I have spoken with Mr and Mrs Winterbine,' said the prioress after calling her back in. 'They are more than happy to welcome you. You will stay with them until you make up your mind.'

'Stay with Aine and Charles? Is this the retreat?'

'I gave an undertaking to Dr Stevenson that the convent would not exert its influence. I also want you to be free from the convent's influence. You stand before a critical decision. With the Winterbines, you will be in devoutly Christian surroundings, also free from most of the secular world's influences. It will be an atmosphere conducive to your task. You will wear your secular clothes while you ponder the future. Although the convent has requested that you seek a balance between meditation and recreation, you are free to do what you want.'

'You are placing a lot of trust in me.'

'I know the person I am dealing with.'

'Thank you, Mother,' Virginia said, embarrassed. 'How long do I have?'

'As long as you want.'

'An indefinite period?'

'It will not take Virginia Pearson long to make up her mind, now without the pressure and torment.'

'You consider the torment of the year, and Philip—'

'No, Sister, it's not what I consider. You will decide whether you will confirm your present wish to leave the order.'

'Do you think—?'

'No, Sister.' She held up her hand. 'Mr Winterbine will arrive at around eleven o'clock tomorrow morning. Please be ready. Sister Martha has your suitcase of everyday clothes. She will bring it to the car.'

'May I ask where Sister Catherine will spend her retreat?'

'She will spend time at your old school in Ballarat, not far from you.'

'Does she know where I'll be?'

'No.'

Chapter 47

Aine's vow

VIRGINIA STOPPED talking as the car approached the two peaks. Aine and Charles also fell silent. It was not until the car had passed between them and was on its way down the incline into the town that Virginia spoke.

'What a beautiful little town,' she exclaimed. 'And what a strange, forbidding entrance those two peaks make.'

'Most people comment,' said Aine, lifting her head from Charles's shoulder, where it had lain on and off during the trip up from Melbourne. 'It intrigued Charles so much on the first day he arrived in Binawarra, that he climbed the second larger peak before he drove into town.'

'I should make the climb myself,' mused Virginia after hearing about Aine and Charles's ascent and their declaration of love. 'Perhaps I'll also experience an enlightening moment.'

'I thought you had made up your mind,' said Aine as the car pulled to a stop in front of their isolated cottage.

'I have,' said Virginia, hesitating, 'but there are things to weigh up.'

'What?' Aine continued after they had left the car.

'I'm not sure exactly.' Virginia looked around. 'What a charming country cottage.'

Understanding Virginia did not want to talk about it, Aine accompanied her to the guest room, where Charles had already deposited her suitcase.

'Mother Jerome said I should leave you to yourself after explaining our routine here,' said Aine. 'We shouldn't change our ways or make unusual provision for you. The retreat is for you to be certain you're making the right decision.'

'Did she? She's scrupulous about her promise to Philip, isn't she? It makes you wonder why she suggested, even insisted on, this different sort of retreat to help me decide.'

'Of course, she didn't mean that we should ignore you. She just meant we should give you space to meditate.'

'I understand,' said Virginia, sitting on the bed and fidgeting. 'I do need a little breather. It's one thing to clear out from the convent because of love; it's another to decide where Philip and I are going from here.'

'I imagine you'll get married as soon as you can.'

'I suppose so. Is that what you thought when you and Charles had declared your love for each other?'

'Yes, we both thought immediately about getting married—as soon as possible is what we wanted.'

'You didn't contemplate what lay ahead?'

'No, I was so smitten, so overwhelmed after the terrible experiences in the convent that I wanted to be with Charles all the time—' She put her hand to her mouth. 'Now look what I have done.'

'No, Aine, don't torture yourself,' said Virginia, standing. 'You pulled away from the danger and are now back with your husband. Offer a prayer of thanksgiving that it took you no further than it did. Resolve to avoid the same pitfall. That's what I must do, too—avoid the same pitfall.'

Aine left her to unpack and change.

'You're both embarrassing me,' Virginia said when she finally appeared.

'We're sorry, Virginia,' said Aine, holding out her hands to her. 'We're not used to seeing you like that.'

'You look quite different, Sister.'

Aine and Charles went about their business, including Virginia, when she was around, but did not disturb her when she wanted to be left alone. They had a full routine during the day, Charles with an overload of specialist restoration work from the town council, and Aine with a meticulous organisation of the household.

'I didn't realise how well organised you were,' Virginia said when she and Aine were taking a walk with Estella in the back garden. 'You have the household running like clockwork.'

'That's my vocation. I enjoy caring for Charles and Estella. If it wasn't for the times that— whatever it is, plagues me, I couldn't be happier.'

'You didn't seriously consider doing anything else, did you?'

'No, I couldn't explain to Margaret and Jannie that this was enough.' She stopped and took hold of Estella, who stayed beside her the entire time. 'Why did I suddenly forget that it was enough?'

'I can't answer that if you expect an answer,' said Virginia. 'There is a weakness in us all. Something seems to get at that weakness when we least expect it. Who would have expected Virginia Pearson to take flight suddenly?' She paused. 'You know, in all my reflection this last week or so, I haven't asked myself that question.'

'I wouldn't have expected it. You don't usually hide your feelings, but you're always in control.'

'I'm surprised Mother Jerome is willing to give me another chance. In the past, the convent wouldn't have hesitated to have the bags packed and transport arranged for such a crime. I don't fully understand what's motivating Mother Prioress. I've repeated my decision several times, but yet she persists.'

'She sees something in you. I know that. You have admitted, too, that there are things to weigh up.'

'Why is Virginia Pearson delaying?' she murmured, 'when she knows the man she loves is waiting right now on tenterhooks? Why am I putting him through the same torture that broke me? I'm being terribly unfair.'

'You don't see the way ahead, do you?'

'No, not like you did.'

That evening, she sat on the front verandah with Charles while Aine prepared dinner. Charles had been a little shy and retiring in past meetings, but now he spoke without restraint, content to follow the course she set in the conversation.

'You seem so settled here,' she said. 'Everything's so well arranged. You and Aine work very well together.'

'In our work, we complement each other. And we like being together.'

'Do you mind me asking about the recent upset?'

'No,' said Charles, showing no surprise at the request.

'Were you uneasy about the course Aine was taking into the fashion world?'

'Yes, but I knew Aine would eventually see the illusion it was.'

'That's very trusting. Other men in your position would have been anxious—more than anxious.'

'Every time Aine went down to Melbourne, I offered prayers for her safeguarding until she returned. I was confident my prayers would be answered. And they were.'

'I admire your faith. We should all be so strong. I spent time this year with people who would have scorned your faith as a delusion, not the other way around. Indeed, they would've deplored the superstition now holding Aine back from a brilliant career.'

'I've never met people like that,' said Charles. 'I suppose I've been fortunate.'

'Aren't you anxious about the future that the same temptation—?'

'There's been this thing tormenting Aine for a long time,' said Charles, gathering his thoughts. 'It leaves her alone for a while and then comes back to attack with greater force. I don't understand it entirely. It's something evil. But whatever it is, we will face it together. I will not abandon the vows I have taken or the law of charity the faith has taught me.'

'You leave me speechless, Charles.'

'Why?'

'Your resolution, your conviction—'

'It's no burden, Sister. And you shouldn't make it more complicated than it is. I'm a simple man.'

That same evening, after dinner, Miss Barker arrived unexpectedly. When she saw Virginia, she apologised for her intrusion. 'If I had known you had a guest, I would not have come,' she said, looking Virginia up and down. When Aine reassured her she was welcome, she said: 'Miss Pearson, I'm an old family friend. You will call me Miss Barker, and I will call you Miss Pearson.'

After this fearsome introduction, it became apparent that the sharp, forthright manner was a veneer over a warm character caring very much for Aine and her family. The conversation over a cup of tea went no further than the daily domestic concerns, but Miss Barker's eyes narrowed at length.

'All right,' she said, 'tell me what's going on here. There's more to you than you're saying, Miss Pearson.'

Charles explained that Virginia was a religious sister and an old friend of Aine's who was taking some time out for reflection. They only meant to be discreet about her reasons for being in Binawarra. That reply seemed to satisfy the exacting Miss Barker, although she continued to cast examining looks at Virginia during the rest of the conversation. The following morning, while Virginia sat alone on the verandah with her daily office, Miss Barker reappeared.

'Stay where you are, Sister,' said Miss Barker, shifting one of the verandah chairs next to her. 'I've come to have a short word with you. I'm not a Catholic. So I may only guess the specific reasons you're here for reflection. I am, however, a good judge of character. I understand your type. I like your type. You are open and practical but have strong principles and convictions.'

'Thank you, Miss Barker,' said Virginia, straightening herself.

'I don't want to know your reasons for being here,' she said, leaning towards her and nodding gravely. 'But there is one thing about a person like you. No matter how prudent and practical you are, no matter how firmly you keep your feet on the ground, you must not compromise on the big questions. Mark my words. You will have a life of torment if you do.'

'Why are you telling me this, Miss Barker? And how can you be so sure of my character?'

'The concerns of Charles and Aine are my concerns, is the answer to the first question. Your manner and conversation are the answer to the second. You're here because you must make a critical decision about your life. Am I right or wrong?'

'You are right.'

'I repeat. A person like you must hold to conviction on the important matters.'

'Have you any idea of what the decision is about? Has Aine or Charles said anything?'

'Certainly not, and I don't want to know. My advice will be helpful if I don't know any details.'

It was some time before Virginia said anything. 'What am I not to compromise on? That's the question,' she said, as much to herself as Miss Barker.

'Sister, I'll tell you something in strict confidence, something that nobody in Binawarra knows. I fell unexpectedly and desperately in love with a man of great integrity during the war. We were married for six blissful weeks before the Japanese murdered him in the very act of saving me.'

'Miss Barker, I'm so sorry—'

'No, Miss Pearson, that love I had for six weeks is still with me. I would never betray it and the courage of my husband.'

'That's not exactly what I face.'

'Isn't it? You must decide. And don't dwell too much on the reasons for my intervention.'

'All right ... thank you, Miss Barker.'

Miss Barker slipped away, careful not to alert Aine and Charles to her presence. Virginia stared after her, following her to the front gate. She watched her walk up the street without looking around, then turn left at the first intersection.

'Good heavens, what am I to think of that?' she murmured as she returned to her chair on the verandah. She had to put her breviary away, so preoccupied did she become with the visit of that strange woman.

HAVING finished her errands, Aine made her way through the busy afternoon traffic around the square to a bench in the park. It was her habit to rest a short while and watch the surrounding activity, always greeting people who stopped to say hello and inquire about the family. That afternoon, eyes were on her as she settled to enjoy the square's colour and greenery. In a nearby tearoom, a man looked longingly, a teacup held to his lips. A few minutes later, Harry paid his bill, left the tearoom, and strode across the road, endeavouring to stay out of her visi on.

'No, Harry!' cried Aine, getting to her feet.

'No, what? I just want to see you and talk.'

'No, Harry, go away. It's finished,' she said, grabbing her bags.

'Aine, I can't believe you—when I held you—'

'Stop! Don't say it!'

'Aine, darling, you can't give it all away. I can't let you turn your back on what lies ahead.'

'My husband and family lie ahead of me. Nothing else. And don't call me that!' She walked away.

'You're ahead of your time,' he said, keeping pace with her. 'You're leaving it to someone else to take—to steal the road you and I have opened.'

'You're on the road by yourself. Please, Harry, leave me alone. Leave Binawarra immediately. You have no business here.'

'You can't mean that. When I looked into your eyes, I saw love—'

'No, you did not. You saw pride and delusion—nothing else.'

'Don't be foolish, Aine. Don't fool yourself. I know what I saw. I wouldn't be hanging around here if I weren't convinced of your—'

'Stop it! I won't hear any more!' She dropped her bags, put her hands over her ears, and took off at a run.

'Wait!' cried Harry, standing beside the bags. He watched her take the road to the left at the end of the shopping square and disappear out of sight. 'How could she do this?' he muttered. He picked up her bags, a lone, incongruous figure with the busy rural shopping square as his background.

Aine rushed by the verandah where Virginia sat with Estella and into the workshop. 'Charles, hold me.'

Charles, clasping Aine to his breast, mounted the stairs. Virginia and Estella followed Charles into the house.

'What's happened?' said Virginia as Charles lowered a swooning Aine onto the lounge settee.

'Harry accosted her in the shopping centre,' he said, kneeling beside Aine and caressing her forehead.

'Charles, don't leave me,' Aine murmured, taking hold of Estella. 'I can't bear it.'

'No, I won't leave you, darling. Put it out of your mind. It has passed.'

They heard a car pull up outside, then a door shut. Charles looked at Virginia and put a finger to his lips. He signalled for her to stay with Aine and Estella.

'Don't come any further, Harry,' said Charles, standing at the top of the verandah steps.

'I've brought Aine's shopping bags,' Harry said at the front gate.

'Put them beside the gate and then leave.'

'Charles, I don't mean any harm. I only want to talk. I'll do any-thing—'

'I said leave. We want nothing to do with your plans ever again. I cannot be more explicit.'

'Charles, you misunderstand.'

'I understand only too well,' said Charles, coming down the stairs. 'Let there be no misunderstanding. I'll do all that is legal to protect my family from a predator like you.'

'A predator ...? I've always been kind and considerate.'

'That's the worst sort of predator.'

'Nobody thinks of me like that,' said Harry, taking a step back from Charles on the other side of the gate.

'For the last time, get in your car and go.' He opened the front gate.

'Okay, no need for that,' said Harry, falling back a few more paces. 'I can only hope that you see what's really at stake. I'm always ready to explain.' He got in his car, not waiting for an answer.

Charles watched until Harry's luxury car disappeared among the trees below the two peaks.

THAT evening, Charles helped Aine to the verandah. He looked into the air. 'They have forecast storms, and it does look threatening, but it'll do you good to sit here in the fresh mild air while the rain holds off, and I can fix the dinner.'

'Charles, no, I must do something,' said Aine. 'I can't leave it all to you.'

'You're not leaving it all to me. You must rest and revive your spirits.'

'Can I help, Charles?' said Virginia, who had kept Aine company during the afternoon.

Charles did not need any help. He would prepare something simple. He had done it before. It was best that Virginia kept Aine company. Virginia submitted to the reasonable arrangement.

'Charles is very versatile,' she said when he had returned inside.

'He has had to jump in and rescue the situation many times before,' said Aine. 'I feel so sorry about it. I feel such a burden sometimes.'

'You're not a burden. He understands you can't help it. You must thank God for that.'

'I do, I do. I know the sacrifices he willingly makes. God help me never forget again.' She leaned back and closed her eyes. A minute later, she opened them. 'Will all this help you with your decision? Is this the retreat Mother Jerome had in mind? I don't know if a drama like this will help?'

'No need at all to worry,' said Virginia, reaching across and putting her hand on Aine's arm. 'Seeing how you and Charles battle the demons is clearing my mind. I see how much you and Charles are bound up in each other in organising yourselves and your household. A different dimension to you and your torment has opened. I had little idea of Mother Jerome's precise purpose until now.'

Estella joined them, taking the chair beside her mother. She had been drawing with crayons and was now showing what she had done.

'Look, Virginia,' said Aine. 'She's drawn a picture of the fields around our house with the sun shining brightly on everything.'

'She's a thoughtful little girl,' said Virginia, taking the sheet of paper and perusing the colourful scrawl.

A car coming from the hills stopped outside the house.

'What are they doing here?' said Aine, getting unsteadily to her feet.

Without the wimple and veil, Margaret's face peered through the back passenger window of Jannie de Kam's car. Instinctively, Virginia raised the sheet of paper in front of her face. She hurried inside. But it was too late. It had been an instant, but they had seen each other. She remained just inside the flywire door. Jannie alighted from the driver's side.

'No, Jannie, no,' cried Aine, and she, too, stumbled inside.

'Come back, Aine. I'm not here for Harry,' she called. 'I want you to join us, only women. It's got nothing to do with Harry or modelling.'

'No, go away!' Aine called. 'Charles, please—'

Charles arrived from the kitchen, took one look, and led Aine into the lounge room. 'You have nothing to worry about. I will send them away.' He brushed past Virginia, speaking before the flywire door shut behind him. 'Miss de Kam, you and your friends have no business with us. Please leave.'

A rather plain, bulky young woman who had been out of sight in the front passenger seat joined Jannie at the front gate. She tried to put her arm around her in solidarity, but Jannie pushed it away a little impatiently.

'Charles, I only wish to invite Aine to spend the evening with us,' said Jannie. 'We will be close by, all women and only women. If you have a guest, she can join us, too. It's a special occasion.'

At the lounge room window, Virginia understood Jannie had not recognised her. She marvelled at her audacity. Did she really think Aine still had no idea of her purpose? Or was she convinced she could still win her over? And who was this rather masculine young woman acting in such a familiar manner with her? All this time, Margaret looked on expressionless, making no attempt to hide her face.

'Aine will not join you,' replied Charles. 'I would advise you all to return to wherever you came from. The forecast is for storms, and the weather is closing in.' He pointed to the dark clouds massing over the peaks. 'The storms build up over the hills. They can be fierce. Go home.'

'No, it won't rain. The clouds are passing, and the air is still mild,' said Jannie, without looking up at the sky. 'Please, Charles, let Aine come. She'll enjoy it—revive her spirits. That's what she needs right now.'

'Aine does not need your recipe for reviving spirits. She will not talk to you now or ever. Please go.'

'It's not right that you forbid her this,' said Jannie.

'Go.'

'It's not right—

The plain young woman, who seemed more interested in Jannie than in Jannie's purpose, whispered to her, trying to draw her to the car.

'Wait, Gerda,' said Jannie to the young woman and then turning to Charles, 'I know Aine's still upset over Harry. I won't bother her until she gets it all back in perspective and understands the character-building and self-fulfilment she risks rejecting. Harry's love is a temporary issue. Don't forget I'm always ready to help. Others are, too, in solidarity.'

Charles did not reply. He waited until they had driven away.

'Did you recognise that young woman with Jannie, the one she called Gerda?' said Virginia when he returned inside, 'or anyone else, for that matter?'

'No, I've never seen her before.'

'Neither have I,' said Virginia.

'Why on earth are they here?' said Charles. 'What are they doing organising whatever it is in this sort of weather, and so far away from Melbourne?'

'It's probably for the summer solstice, which is shortly,' said Virginia. 'It's all about celebrating the abundance of the Earth Goddess, the way the pre-Christian pagan peoples did.'

'No ...,' said Aine. 'Why here?'

'It's because of you. They still want you, Aine. I get the impression they want you to be more than part of them.'

'What more?'

'I can't answer that—except to say Margaret sees something in you. They almost had you through Harry. Harry was an unwitting tool to seduce you in more ways than one.'

'No, it can't be,' she pleaded.

'Aine,' said Charles, taking her hand, 'I don't understand what's going on here ... what you have told me about goddesses and Mother Earth and the inner spirit ... but I will protect you from it with the last breath in my body.'

Aine clasped Charles's hand, bowing her head. 'I would like some time in private prayer,' she said. 'Would you give me that time, Charles?'

'Of course, darling, you don't have to ask.'

'I think I do,' she replied. 'I'll be back shortly. No, Charles, I'm all right,' she said, rising. 'I will go by myself.'

LATER that evening, after Aine had put Estella to bed, she appeared in the lounge room in a long white dress, carrying a wooden table. She positioned it in the centre of the room, draped a fresh white linen cloth over it, and then fetched two statues, one of the Sacred Heart of Jesus, the other of Our Lady of Fatima. As Charles and Virginia looked on, she placed a white bowl before the statues and filled it with water. On either side of the bowl, she placed candles and lit them. Her rosary beads and Daily Mass Missal were last to be positioned. These lay in front of the white bowl.

'What's this for?' said Charles.

'I would like you both to accompany me in this brief personal ritual.' She gave them the lit candles and directed Charles to stand in front of the table and Virginia to the side. She turned off the light and gave the missal to Virginia.

'Sister Agnes, I would like you to read the Psalms in the order I have marked.'

'Aine, what are you doing?' said Charles.

'Please, Charles, allow me to do this. After that, I'll do whatever you say.'

Charles gave his assent as the wind rose and thunder rolled over the hills. Aine dipped her hand in the bowl and blessed herself.

'Can any praise be worthy of the Lord's majesty?' she said. 'How magnificent His strength. How inscrutable His wisdom. Lord God, you made us for yourself, but we are full of weakness, which you show by thwarting our pride. We belong to you, and you stir our hearts so that we are restless until we rest in you.'

Virginia recognised a rough paraphrasing of the opening of St Augustine's *Confessions*. Aine had to give a second signal before she fumbled the missal open at the Mass for Passion Sunday.

O God, sustain my cause; give me redress against a race that knows no piety; save me from a treacherous foe and cruel: Thou, O Lord, art all my strength.

The light of Thy presence, the fulfilment of Thy promise, let these be my escort, bringing me safe to Thy Holy mountain, to the tabernacle, where Thou dwellest. O God, sustain.

'Glory be to the Father, and to the Son and to the Holy Ghost, Amen.' Repeating this twice, Aine gave Virginia a further signal. Virginia fumbled again, juggling the candle and the missal.

'There is no corner of the world but has witnessed how God can save: in God's honour let all the earth keep holiday.

The Lord has given proof of His saving power, has vindicated His just dealings for all nations to see.'

Aine said the 'Glory Be' three times and then gave Virginia a final signal.

'I will wash my hands among the innocent, and will walk round Thy altar, O God.

To hear the voice of Thy praise and to tell all Thy wondrous deeds.

Lord, I love the beauty of Thy house, and the place where Thy glory dwells.

Destroy not my soul with the impious, O God, nor my life with men of blood.'

Again, Aine recited the 'Glory Be' three times. Then she knelt, her bare feet showing, and took Charles's hands in hers.

During this time, the wind had risen until it was now whistling around the verandah and window frames, shaking the house in sudden, violent gusts. As Aine took Charles's hands, a violent stream of light crackled across the range in piercing fury, lighting up the framed windows so that they glowed. Charles and Virginia looked up. The rain began beating against the walls and roof.

'It's right over the range,' whispered Charles.

'St Paul said that husbands should love their wives as their own bodies,' Aine continued, appearing not to hear nature's violence. "He who loves his wife loves himself. For no man ever hates his own flesh, but nourishes and cherishes it, as Christ does the Church, because we are members of his body."' She paused and bowed her head. 'I now solemnly repeat my perpetual vow to remain part of Charles's flesh until my death and not to rebel or act in a way that corrupts any part of that flesh.'

Charles and Virginia stared open-mouthed at Aine, who remained kneeling, eyes closed, head bowed, and clasping Charles's hands.

'Aine, what do you mean?' Charles stammered.

'I vow perfect obedience to all your lawful commands from this moment. I will never leave this house without your permission or company.'

'But Aine, this is not necessary.'

'It is necessary. My earthly life is subject to you in Christ.'

Aine's words were lost in a succession of thunderous lightning strikes around the hills and the rain pelting down on the corrugated iron roof.

Chapter 48

Expelling the devil

SOMETIME BEFORE Aine began her personal ritual, two cars and one van drew to a stop in the clearing between the two peaks. Women dressed in long white and black robes, some veiled, some with hoods, alighted from the vehicles and gathered in a circle. The wind had not yet reached its peak, blowing in restraint around their billowing robes. A tall woman in a white robe and veil moved to the middle of the circle. Her handsome face was just visible in the flickering light of the wind-protected candle she held in front of her. She sang a soft, lilting chant, which the others joined in. Then a large, solid woman in a black robe and hood gave a solemn signal. Jannie de Kam moved from the centre of the circle toward the track leading to the sharp peak. In a hood and robe, the young woman, Gerda, quickly moved in behind her. The women slowly made their way along the ridge, harmonising with the wind as it rushed and whispered over them in gusts.

As they issued onto the smooth rocky surface, they formed a circle. Wind-protected candles were lit. Shallow wicker baskets of fruit, vegetables, grains, and other foods were placed on a purple cloth decorated with a white pentagram against a blue background. Bottles of wine and silver goblets also appeared to take their place beside the baskets of food.

All the while, the chanting went on. When all seemed prepared, the large black robe raised a hand.

'Sisters, we are here in this portentous location for the first time, feeling the force and energy of nature's might, to celebrate that great Mother's generous abundance. Let us proceed in joy, happiness, and love. Sister Jannie will now perform a dance honouring the fruits of the earth and harnessing the energy that pours out of the depths into our souls, lighting that divine spark of omnipotence in each of us.'

Jannie twirled forward in graceful movements and spiralled her way around the circle. Then, picking up each object on the cloth, she executed the movements and gestures she had witnessed Aine making in front of her stunned audience. She mesmerised Gerda so profoundly that she rushed forward to join in. As Jannie finished to the applause and cries of her admirers, Gerda clasped her in her arms. After allowing some vigorous embraces, Jannie disentangled herself to give others their turn for enjoyment.

'Sister Jannie has set the tone for our celebration,' said the large black robe. 'Now let us continue with feasting and song and dance and stories that revision our spirit in the energy of Mother Earth.'

The songs and stories proceeded through the rising wind and ample food and wine. Echoing thunder sounded in the distance amid flashes of light. The stories flowed freely, the songs became louder, and the dances more vigorous. Warmth and love overflowed. The embraces were frequent and lingering. Soon, the wind was howling through the cleft created by the two peaks.

'Feel the energy!' shouted Gerda, jumping to her feet. 'Feel the power that rises within us! This is where we belong, in the arms of the Mother's might.' A stream of light flashed across the hills in a deafening roar. 'Mistress of power and might, light the divine spark!'

With a tremendous roar of the wind, the rain pelted down upon them. Another flash provoked more shouts from Gerda, who was now standing near the edge of the rocky outcrop. Black Robe gave the signal to pack up. While the women hastened to the track along the ridge, Gerda remained shouting and waving her arms. The rain-soaked robe clung to her bulky, formless figure.

'Come on!' shouted Jannie through the pelting rain. 'It's dangerous!'

'Dangerous? Have courage,' Gerda shouted back in Dutch, her hair hanging in wet straggles.

Two other women in white robes succumbed to the force of Gerda's performance and remained with her, attempting to copy her movements and cries.

'Come on, I beg you,' cried Jannie in Dutch. 'It's too risky.'

Gerda could not resist such an appeal from the beautiful, desirable Jannie. She left the side of the rocky outcrop and ran open arms to Jannie, who stood inside the track. A blinding flash knocked Gerda over onto Jannie.

'The other two,' said Jannie, struggling from under Gerda, 'are they all right?'

Two figures were lying on the ledge. Jannie stared in horror at the prostrate, rain-soaked robes lit up by the lightning. She could detect no movement. Taking her hand, Gerda tried to draw her to the bush track.

AINE bent forward to wrap her arms around Charles' legs, but another lightning strike toppled her over. She lay moaning, her body crumpled between Charles and Virginia.

'Aine! Aine!' cried Charles, bending down.

She rolled onto her back and stretched her legs out stiffly, moaning in an unearthly tone.

'My God, what's happening?'

'I don't know,' said Virginia, the alarm also registering in her voice. She took hold of Aine's arm as Aine seemed to stiffen even more. 'Let us pray.'

Aine arched her back as perspiration appeared on her face.

'O my God!'

Aine's hair, soaked in sweat, stuck to her head as she moved it back and forth in increasing vigour, her long white dress riding up her bare legs. Then, hideously hissing, she raised herself onto her elbows. Her beautiful angelic face transformed into a snarling feline ugliness. The malevolent eyes that bulged were no longer Aine's.

'Jesus, have mercy!'

'Mater Misericordiae!'

Virginia dashed to her room and returned with the crucifix that hung on the belt of her habit. She pressed it into Aine's shaking, sweaty hands.

'May the suffering Saviour rid you of this torment. May the Holy Mother standing below the Cross come to your aid. Out! Go! Begone!'

With a deep sigh, Aine fell back, her perspiration-soaked face and blue eyes retrieving their natural appearance. 'It has gone out of me. It has passed. It has passed ...,' she whispered.

AS HARRY drove between the peaks earlier that afternoon, frustration began to overtake Charles's warnings. Taking his foot off the accelerator, he let the car roll to a stop in the clearing at the side of the road. A minute later, he turned around and drove back into Binawarra, not knowing what he would do. One thing was sure: he could not leave Binawarra at that moment. With nothing else occurring to him, he settled himself in the saloon bar of the Commercial Hotel. He stayed there, drinking beer and then switching to whisky. The drink did not bring him to any decision; at every point, he realised there was no way of avoiding Charles Winterbine. But if only he could get Aine alone, into a corner somewhere, he was sure he could convince her of his love—and her love for him. He must do it.

Harry, the famous photographer, was not a seasoned drinker. At the end of two hours, he was reeling to the amusement of the hotel's sturdier drinkers. Hardly wanting to humiliate himself further, he wandered back to his car parked under trees at the far end of the plantation. He lowered his seat and settled back to let the alcohol wear off. Some hours later, a furious combination of lightning, thunder, and pelting rain awoke him. He struggled to turn on the car light. He need not have bothered. The successive lightning strikes were enough to show him how late it was. That was the sign for him to give it away. For the moment. Weary and frustrated by his defeat, he set off along the road out of Binawarra.

As he drove up the incline to pass between the peaks, the rain became so heavy that he could scarcely see where he was going. He slowed to a crawl, but it was no good. It was too dangerous to go on. He veered to the left, where he thought the clearing was. Shadowy figures suddenly appeared in the car lights. He jammed on the brakes. But it was too late. Amid muffled cries, he felt the sickening bump of car metal against soft, movable objects.

'My God, what else—!' he exclaimed. He struggled out of the car and felt his way to the front, expecting to see bodies lying everywhere. But he saw nothing in the car's rain-streaked beams. He heard the rustle and scraping of feet at the back of the car. He felt his way to the back, but at that moment, the lightning ceased, and he could see nothing. He heard car engines starting up. Formless vehicles passed him one after the other, disappearing beyond the grey rainy edges of his car's beams.

'What is going on?' he said, relieved there were no injured bodies to accuse him.

'ARE you all right now?' said Virginia the following morning after Charles had settled Aine on the verandah and had gone to his workshop.

'Yes, the worst is over,' said Aine. 'The storm's passing and the return of the summer sunlight symbolise how I feel. The horror has gone, leaving something dark and undefined at the edge of my consciousness.' She shook her head. 'I wish Charles had not called the doctor.'

'It's only to make sure.'

'You know as well as I know a medical doctor is useless.'

'Can you tell me what you were thinking or seeing,' said Virginia, after some moments of silence, 'I mean when you were on the floor ... when you underwent that terrible transformation.'

'I can't describe it. I don't want to describe it. Such horror ... I never thought my mind could imagine such things. How can someone imagine such horrible, degrading things—even feel a longing for them—when faith and reason tell you what they really are, how evil they are?'

'A longing ... is it that man ... Harry?'

'I'm afraid it is ... a part of it, at least ... there were other terrible, terrible things ... the urge for complete mastery ... I can't describe it.'

Sometime later, the doctor arrived and took Aine inside after a brief talk with Charles. Fifteen minutes later, he emerged without Aine.

'Your wife is resting. I gave her a sedative. Can we talk in private?' he asked Charles, glancing at Virginia.

'I would like Sister Agnes to be present,' said Charles.

'Sister Agnes?' he said, raising his eyebrows. 'This is something new. Oh, well, if that's what you want. Mr Winterbine, I have said this before. Your wife has serious psychological problems. There are deep-seated neuroses that must be resolved with the help of professionals. You have no choice if you want a healthy, well-adjusted wife.'

'What opinion do you have of the neuroses' cause, Doctor?' asked Virginia, seeing restraint on Charles's face.

'I will not beat around the bush, young woman. It's that religion of yours. You people have a lot to answer for in imposing such superstitious evil on that delicate young woman. It's criminal.'

'You are not a man of faith, I take it, of any faith?'

'Certainly not.'

'Your opinion is that the cure lies in applying chemicals?'

'That may be the way. I will disregard the amateurish terms and the objectionable implication. There have been great pharmaceutical strides made in recent years—therapies also. Your organisation needs to update itself if it wants to take a responsible place in our modern society.'

'Your opinion is that all illnesses are reducible to material terms?'

'If you mean scientific terms, medicine is scientific. There is no other approach.'

'You do not accept there could be another analysis—that illnesses of the soul exist?'

'If you're trying to pin me down with some Jesuitical explanation, I've no time for that nonsense or this conversation.'

'Your stand, based on science, is philosophical.'

'I am a practical person and know nothing about philosophy, nor is it relevant, as I said.'

Virginia remained silent and expressionless in reply.

'Well, thank you, Doctor, thank you for coming,' said Charles.

'I can write a referral today if you wish, Mr Winterbine. Just say the word.'

Charles thanked the doctor and accompanied him to the car. Aine appeared as he drove off. She frowned and looked at the departing vehicle.

'He said he gave you a sedative,' said Virginia.

'He gave me tablets, and I put them in the toilet. I told him before that I wouldn't take them. He thinks I'm neurotic.'

'How do you react to that?'

'I don't know what he means by that. And he doesn't understand, quite simply. You do. That's why you're always such a comfort. I'm so glad you're here.'

'Aine, I'm returning to the convent.'

'And Dr Stevenson?'

'He knew better than me that I belonged in the convent. He knows I love him and will always love him, but he also knows that, with the best intentions, my actions have only delayed my decision and the resolution he must make. I have work to do. You and Charles have brought me to face it. Why ever did you draw on the opening to St Augustine's *Confessions*? Was it to prod me?'

'No, they were thoughts that stayed in my mind all those years ago. I understood their significance for anybody who wants to meditate seriously about God. The psalms have a special appeal for me.'

'They stayed in your mind all this time, only from my mentioning them once?'

'Yes.'

'Glory be—'

'If you have decided, Virginia, would you please stay with me for a few more days? I'm over the worst of it. I fear there'll be continuing torment, but my vow to Charles will protect me from a recurrence of what I went through with Harry. So please say you will stay. I'll be right after that, I think.'

'Of course, I will. We'll enjoy this time together and celebrate the end of a period—for both of us. We will offer prayers that we can go forward with resolve and stick to our undertakings. We are on the brink of some monumental happening, as Mother Jerome said.'

THAT same day, a brief report appeared in Bendigo's local newspaper about the death of two women from a lightning strike. The newspaper took it upon itself to issue a warning: it is hazardous to be walking unheedingly in the bush during an electrical storm, as these poor women had been doing north of Bendigo, where they were found. The report noted that it was madness to defy the elements at their full natural fury.

VIRGINIA sat in front of Mother Jerome.

'I expected longer,' said the prioress.

'So did I but—'

'Before you say anything, I would like to hear your decision.'

'I have decided to recommit,' she said without hesitating. 'I have a calling. Despite the hurt it will bring, I cannot resist or deny it.'

'Don't say any more,' said Mother Jerome, holding up her hand. 'I would like you to write a letter to Dr Stevenson informing him of your decision and its reasons. We will talk after that.'

Chapter 49

Looking to the future

ON CHRISTMAS EVE, Joe Edelman called on his friend.

'Gosh, mate, how do you live in this place?' he said after Philip had led him into the sitting room.

'It's a bit untidy, I admit, but it'll do. I don't have the urge to clean things up, at least for now.'

'What's going on? I haven't seen you for more than a week. Dodging me, are you?'

'Virginia has decided to stay in her prison.'

'Really?' said Joe, staring blankly. 'You surprise me— Actually, it's more shock.'

'Surprise? Shock? I have other words for it. Do you want a drink?'

'No, thanks, and it looks like you downed enough for both of us.' He frowned at the whisky bottle on the coffee table.

'What's happened? The last time I saw her, she was resolute in leaving the convent?'

'They got their claws into her.'

'It's got to be more than that for her to change her mind so dramatically.'

'Read the letter for yourself. It's on the table there.'

Joe picked up the letter, sat down, read it, and reread it.

'This is a letter from a principled person who thinks she has an important life's purpose, Phil. I don't see any hint of indoctrination or mental coercion.'

'Whose side are you on?'

'Come on, Phil. Do her justice.' He scanned the letter again.

'How do you think I'm supposed to act? Twice she's been taken from me.'

'I've never been in this situation. I can understand your loss, though. But there's no alternative. You must accept it.'

'Stop being sensible. I don't want to accept it. In fact, I'm going straight out to that jail and confront the prison governess.' He stood up, looking around for his car keys.

'You're not serious, I hope.'

'Deadly serious. I'm not giving up just yet.'

'You're in no state to drive or speak sensibly. Leave it until after Christmas.'

'You're right. I'll take a taxi.'

'If you're really determined, I'll drive you. Someone must keep an eye on you in this phase of madness.'

Dr Philip Stevenson struggled out of the car in front of the wooden doors of the Convent of St Augustine. It was just after dusk, and lights were gleaming through the windows. Steadying himself with both hands on the car door, he looked up at the Gothic tower disappearing into the starlit night sky.

'Wait for me here.'

'You won't find me going anywhere here, mate,' said Joe, looking around the shade-enshrouded gardens.

Philip staggered to the great wooden door and knocked. It opened after what seemed an eternity.

'I have been expecting you, Dr Stevenson,' said Mother Jerome, coming forward past Sister Martha and standing in the doorway. 'There is no point to this. Sister Agnes has made her decision, and you have been informed of the reasons.'

'I want to hear it from her, not from a piece of paper. Who knows the coercion she—'

'It will be the same. So please save yourself the unnecessary torment.'

'I am not leaving until I speak to Virginia.'

Mother Jerome regarded him, sympathy appearing in her eyes. 'I will allow you to talk to Sister Agnes on one condition: that you do not attempt to touch her in any way.'

'Allow her? As I thought, she's back in prison.'

'You know that's not true, Dr Stevenson. Such words are not worthy of a man like you. Sister Agnes can walk out of here tonight if she wants. She has freely elected to submit to the Rule of religious life and follow her vocation.' She paused. 'Do you accept the condition?'

'I suppose so.'

Philip pulled himself to his feet when Sister Agnes entered the parlour. She stopped in front of him with her head bowed.

'Look at me, Virginia, and tell me you don't love me.'

'No, I won't tell you that. You will always have a special, unique place in my heart.'

'Then get out of that silly party costume and come with me. Summon the courage to break free from this prison.' Sister Agnes knelt on the floor in front of him. 'No, get up! Get up, I say!'

'Philip, I am so sorry that my weakness, self-deception, and pride unnecessarily prolonged your pain and put off the decision we must both confront,' she said, keeping her head bowed. 'This convent is not my prison. It is the life that has called me. As much as I love you, I cannot turn my back on this calling.'

'No, years of the same rhetoric have persuaded you. A couple more days by ourselves, and you would've been over it.'

'No, Philip, several things you said during those few days made me realise you were aware of the inevitable, that I could not deny the life that was calling me.'

'What, for heaven's sake?'

'If I went with you now and we married, I could not give you all you would want from me as a wife. And the circumstances could not give me all that I am called to. I cannot risk causing regret or even bitterness in both of us. I cannot bear the idea. I can't do it. I want to remember you in the brief final time we had together.'

'I don't believe what I'm hearing. You'll have every opportunity to follow the faith and pursue your studies and a teaching career.'

'No, Philip, you know I couldn't. There are no half-measures with me. I cannot give both. I cannot fulfil the duties of wife and mother, and also the charity, devotion, and tasks I am called to. I want to join those women who surrounded Our Lord, accompanying and ministering to him in his mission. I want to follow in the spirit of Jesus's most Holy Mother, St Mary Magdalene, the other Mary, Martha, Salome, and many others the Gospels speak of. I want to give myself in total submission as they did. I want to devote myself to the service of others.'

'Virginia, get up. Listen to me. It's delusional—'

Sister Agnes got to her feet. 'Philip, you know what I am saying is right. Give yourself a chance to think about it. I wish you all Godspeed and success in your life. You will always be in my prayers and in my heart. Memories of your love will accompany me through my ministry, whatever that will be. Mother, may I retire now?'

'Yes, Sister, you may retire.'

'No, come back!' called Philip as she opened the door. 'Don't be so hard of heart. How can you be so cold?' But the door had shut.

'No, Dr Stevenson, don't say such things,' said the prioress, taking his arm. 'You know she has a soft heart. She is trying to be brave, but that heart is now breaking under the decision she knows she cannot avoid. Don't make it harder for her.'

He sank into the armchair, tears now appearing on his cheeks. 'It's insane,' he said, shaking his head. 'Totally insane.'

Mother Jerome went to the door and beckoned. 'Please bring Dr Stevenson some coffee, Sister.' She waited until the coffee arrived and he had composed himself. 'Dr. Stevenson, I realise it is hard for you. But you must see that Sister Agnes is right. You must face it as she has.' She paused. 'If I may be so bold, resign your position at the university and go overseas, seek a new life in new circumstances, new people. A man of your ability and talent will find something in England. Go and find yourself. Complete your book. Discover Catholic England. Find yourself in your Catholic ancestry.'

Philip put his head in his hands. 'I suppose your advice is as good as any. At this point, I face a big blank as I did six years ago.' He rose. 'Thank you, Mother Jerome. Thank you for your forbearance,' he said with a sigh of resignation. 'I apologise for the upset I've caused your convent.'

'I understand,' she said, accompanying him to the front porch. 'One last word, Dr Stevenson. Sister Agnes requested that you do not resort to excessive drinking. The thought of you wasting your life will be the one thought that will truly upset her.'

'Is it? It's the only thing that keeps me on an even keel.'

'It's not the only recourse you have. You know that.'

'Do I?'

'Remember those humble shepherds out in the chilly fields near Bethlehem, witnessing the heavenly host singing "Glory to God in the Highest and on earth peace to men of goodwill." Enjoy a safe and peaceful Christmas, Dr Stevenson. Give my Christmas wishes to your friend,' she added, seeing Joe standing on the other side of the car. 'Seek solace in your close friends.'

He nodded slowly in answer, then got into the car and waited almost senseless while Joe took him away from the convent and returned him to his lonely bachelor apartment on the outskirts of the city centre. Later that evening, after Joe had departed, there was a knock at the door. He opened it to find Diana's worried face.

'Diana, really, I—'

'No, Phil, I know the whole story. I'm only here as your friend. You must not be alone at this terrible time, especially at Christmas. I know your heartache.'

'I know you mean well,' said Philip, letting her in, 'but it's probably best if I'm left alone.'

'No, it's not. Let me have my way. Please. Go and shower and get into clean clothes. I will take you to my parents'. You need to be distracted in neutral circumstances. Mum and Dad are ignorant of the nun story.'

'Neutral circumstances?'

'Yes, Phil. Trust me. Tomorrow we will have Christmas lunch at Toorak and visit your family in the afternoon. It's already arranged. Joe will be there, too.'

He remembered Mother Jerome's advice to seek solace in close friends. In that sense, nobody was closer than Diana. 'All right. I don't have the will or spirit to resist.'

'ARE you all right?' said Mother Jerome when Agnes sat down in front of her desk.

'Yes, Mother, it's a relief the meeting has passed, and the decision made.' She glanced through the window into the dark of the night. There was a little glow coming up from below.

'You must be sure of yourself. You will not have another chance—no more doubts.'

'I have no doubts. My weaknesses are sure to cause me trouble, but there's no going back. I am committed. The reasons I'm here remain unchanged despite losing sight of them for a while.'

'You must be able to deal with the pressure in the secular world, even the extreme bigotry you encountered this year.'

'I will be more prepared. The thought that I was responsible for destroying Philip's life broke me in the end. I now understand that I can't rescue Philip. I can't give him what he wants. He must drag himself out of it.'

'Was the stay with the Winterbines responsible for clarifying your thoughts and feelings?'

'Yes, primarily, it was there that the proper relations between everything became manifest. When Philip said "No, Virginia" to my desire to counsel Aine, a question was raised that was only answered when Aine passed through the fire of her torment. I witnessed a terrible episode when the spirit of that temptation, that diabolical goddess spirit, took hold of her one evening. Aine's temptation is a threat to all women. I must do something; I feel I can do something.' She did not add that

Margaret turned up one evening among a group of women who wanted Aine to join them in a gathering in the nearby hills. Just then, she could not reveal the conclusions she came to.

'This might develop into an unbearable trial for you.'

'What do you mean ... exactly?'

'We spoke about the La Salette prophecies. I will remind you that the Blessed Virgin said many convents would no longer be houses of God but the grazing ground of Asmodeus and his followers. Asmodeus is the demon of impurity.'

'It's hard to believe it will happen. It's unimaginable at this point, despite the evidence of rot in the system.'

'The La Salette prophecies are not taken seriously in the Church. But you have glimpsed what it may be about. You must be prepared.'

'I'll do my best, whatever happens.'

'Good, Sister. I want now to bring an end to all these conversations. I have been leading you through a period of discernment. We have reached the end. I do not want to discuss it again unless serious matters arise. You are to take your place in the routine of the convent and attend to the duties presently allotted to you. You are to leave all inquiries and investigations about events in the convent to me. Is that clear?'

'Yes, Mother.'

'Of course, there will be a period of penance, you realise?'

'Yes, Mother, I'm ready for it. I await your decision on all aspects of my life.'

'There will be no *mea culpa* session for what's happened. Your action belongs to the confessional and not to a public admission.'

'Yes, Mother. May I ask one last question?'

'What is it?'

'Did you foresee what the stay with the Winterbines would do to me?'

'I had only an idea of what influence it could exert. I guessed there would be meaning for you in Mrs Winterbine's meticulous ways and devotion to her family.'

'You were right. That part of Aine was hidden from me until then.'

'Finally,' said the Superior General of the Order of the Suffering Saviour, 'I want you to consider how you, Aine Winterbine, and Jannie de Kam dealt with a personal crisis. I want you to consider what solution each of you has chosen.'

'Yes, Mother.'

'As a consolation for your decision, you may remember the words of St Paul: "The unmarried woman and the virgin thinketh on the things of the Lord, that she may be holy both in body and spirit. But she that is married thinketh on the things of the world, how she may please her husband."'

IT WAS late January 1963. During the morning, Sisters Agnes and Martha had been tending to the gardens along the upper parapet and were now clearing up. Agnes had taken the wheelbarrow of weeds to the compost heap and was returning to collect the garden tools while Martha remained in the vegetable garden. As she came through the gate, she saw Sister Catherine walking towards her, her black breviary held out in front of her. It was at least what appeared to be her breviary. Agnes's first impulse was to turn her head and attend to her business, but the sight of this woman with her head buried in the Psalms was too much to bear.

'A pleasant day for reading the Psalms, Sister,' Agnes could not help saying as she was about to pass her.

Unaware of Agnes's approach, Catherine slammed her black book shut, lowering it into the folds of her dress. With a frown, she was going to walk on without replying.

Agnes felt her self-control slipping further. 'We know something about each other, don't we?'

Catherine stopped. 'I know something about you, but you imagine you know something about me.'

'Still as slippery as a snake.'

'And you're still unable to control your mouth and emotions, Sister.'

'Why aren't you open about your purposes?'

'About the purposes you imagine I have?'

'I must admire your skill and resolve.'

'To be a good nun—? Thank you, Sister. I'll now leave you to attend to the discipline you've earned from character faults you've not yet been able to overcome.' She turned to walk back towards the main entrance, but hesitated. 'You may consider changing your religious name—St Agnes, virgin and martyr. That's something I'll never have to change.'

'Perhaps it's my turn to say you imagine you know something about me.'

'Just imagine?' Catherine made no effort to hide her smirking confidence.

'The confident card player should be sure he holds a trump card.'

'The confident card player should also be careful about having his bluff called.' Margaret took the book she had been hiding in the folds of her skirt and walked away, holding it out in front of her.

PHILIP looked up from the box where he was putting books to see Vic Brennan at his office door.

'Can I come in?'

'If you must— No, I'm sorry, Vic. Please come in.'

'I won't keep you long. I see you're busy. I'm sorry it has come to this. Is there no other way? You will be missed. Your students will miss you.'

'No, there is no other way. I must make a complete break. Is there anything in particular, Vic? I'm really rather busy. I've got a lot to pack up.'

'You wanted to talk to me about Patricia, and I brushed you off. I've considered it and decided your concern deserved a more polite response.'

Philip straightened. 'All right, take a seat.' He pointed to an armchair loaded with books. He cleared one for himself. He waited, scrutinising Vic, who sat in indecision.

'They say marriage is a lottery,' Vic began. 'There's a jackpot prize if you win. Otherwise, there is a decrease in winnings until nothing. Jane Austen seemed to be making this point, or something like it, at the end of her novel *Persuasion*. Most win nothing. I suppose I am like hundreds of men. I entered the lottery and came up with a fat nil. To be fair, my wife also scored a booby prize. Are you with me, Phil?'

'Yes, Vic. Perhaps that's why marriage vows contain the commitment "for better or worse, in sickness and health," and the rest.'

Vic hesitated and looked down as if gathering his thoughts. 'What was it with me? Was it a pretty face and vivacious manner? Or was it uncontrollable lust, lust I had to satisfy or end up at a brothel? I honestly haven't a clue. But whatever it was—perhaps it was both—I imagined I was in love. Twenty-two, I was, and an immature twenty-two, at that. It did not take long for the tension to rise between the Byronic figure scribbling verses—as I imagined myself—and the little secretarial wife who wanted a clean house, a nine-to-five husband, and a delightful brood of children to show off after Sunday Mass. Are you still with me, Phil?'

'Yes, Vic. I assume there's a point to this rather common tale. Disappointments are in every part of life, to add a banal comment. One has to deal with them. I'm sorry to sound preachy.'

'Dealing with issues of relationships is the point, Phil, as you should now be aware.'

'Point made.'

'I was already at a breaking point, unable to cope with the bitterness, recriminations, and the attempt to squeeze me into a role I was unfit for when a pretty seventeen-year-old made shameless eyes at me during her first tutorial.' He paused. 'Of course, you will say that's a common enough occasion for a university lecturer.'

'It is, indeed. It is a hazard of the position.'

'But, Phil, add a perfect correspondence of feeling, attitude, and interests over time. The age gap dissolved. Two years later, our minds are one. People have probably told you that she is shameless about her love for me. She doesn't care what people think.' He paused again. 'I can't resist that. I don't want to resist it. It's a passion I can't control. That I look like a stupid old goat does not bother me in the least. You understand? You understand how love can take hold of you? I mean a real penetrating, delirious love.'

'I do, Vic. I sympathise. But there are still responsibilities, no matter how burdensome.'

There was a period of silence before Vic spoke.

'Oscar Wilde said, "The Roman Catholic Church is for saints and sinners alone—for respectable people, the Anglican Church will do." That was typical of Wilde's amusing wit, but it's also true. I resign myself to the status of a sinner. I can't do otherwise. I can't help it. The Anglican Church is not for me. I accept that the way ahead will be difficult. I'm a bit like Lord Sebastian Flyte in Evelyn Waugh's *Brideshead Revisited*. I mean, the tragic way he ended up as a helpless drunk at the doors of a monastery in Morocco. Not that I see myself in one or other Muslim country or even helplessly drunk. But as an inveterate sinner, yes.

Philip reflected while Vic stared at him. 'I have never read that book.'

'You should do,' said Vic, standing. 'In fact, while in England, you should supplement your philosophy by reading a brilliant Catholic novelist like Waugh. It will add a heart and soul to your philosophy.' He extended his hand. 'That's it, Phil. You now know what's behind my relationship with Patricia—for what it's worth. I have given a polite answer to your polite concern. I wish you all the very best.'

Philip rose and took his hand. 'Thanks, Vic. I wish you the best in return. I mean it.' He saw Vic to the door and returned to the books strewn over the chairs. He stood contemplating his books for a while before resuming his packing.

JOE Edelman took another piece of cake from the plate Sister Martha offered him.

'I never imagined in my wildest dreams I'd be visiting a Catholic convent,' he said to Mother Jerome, who sat opposite him in the visitors' parlour, 'let alone defending a Catholic nun.'

'You are as welcome as anyone who comes to the convent on business, Dr Edelman.'

'My compliments to your cook,' he said, popping the final piece of cake into his mouth. 'She certainly knows how to bake a cake.' Mother acknowledged the compliment with a nod and a brief smile. 'I hope you'll give consideration to what I've said.' He brushed his clothes and made ready to stand. 'It would be a great tragedy if Sister Agnes weren't allowed to continue her studies because of what's happened. I take some of the blame for the pressure she had to bear. In fact, I need to take a lot of the blame.'

'You were not to know the circumstances, Dr Edelman.'

'If that stupid fellow had told me she had been his fiancée and the one he had been carrying a torch for, I would've acted differently. As it is, I promise I'll do my utmost to respect Sister Agnes's duties and beliefs and to protect her from the malice of others. I give you my solemn word.'

'Thank you, Dr Edelman. Your generous undertaking is appreciated.'

'Then you will allow her to return?'

'It is not usual for us to discuss these issues publicly. However, be assured that your kind action has earned the consideration of being informed when a decision is made. I observe it is not usual for a son of Abraham to be in a position to plead on behalf of a Catholic sister.'

'Alas, I'm more a child of the Enlightenment,' he said with a smile. He stood. 'Philip will be leaving for London later this week. Sister won't need to contend with his presence. That leftist psychopath, Stephen Calder, has been informed that his enrolment is in jeopardy. I've heard he's arranging to transfer to another university. So you see, the way has been made straight for Sister's return.'

'Your manner of pleading is impressive, Dr Edelman.'

As the prioress led him across the vestibule towards the front door, he happened to glance through the archway to the upper level.

'Is it permitted for me to take a look, Mother Jerome?' he asked, stopping.

'Are you so interested, Dr Edelman?' said the prioress, glancing at her watch.

'Yes, few things would be more fascinating for a Jewish boy from New York.'

'That Jewish boy is far from home,' she said, hesitating and then leading the way to the archway.

'I've been far from home for a long time,' he said as he stepped into the sunlight.

'This is where the sisters receive their family on visiting days,' the prioress continued when they were looking over the lower levels to the river and the fields beyond. 'The rest of the convent is private.'

'You say that in anticipation, no doubt? But I appreciate your allowing me to come this far.'

'I have the impression you are a rather candid person, Dr Edelman.'

'I suppose Sister Agnes mentioned that?'

'No, she never mentioned you.'

'Really, she never mentioned me to you?'

'Should she have?'

'That's deflating. I might have caused more interest.' When he saw Mother Jerome would not react, he continued: 'What a beautiful, peaceful scene. I suppose it's conducive to reflection.'

'Yes, most sisters take advantage of the surroundings for just that—and to read the divine office. A selection of prayers and scriptural readings,' she added in response to his inquiring look.

'And study? Perhaps Virginia Pearson walked these grounds reading Descartes' *Meditations*?' he said, just above a murmur.

'Virginia Pearson?'

Two sisters emerged through a gateway at the end of the building. They wore coarse beige aprons over their black habits and carried gardening tools.

'Virginia—'

At that moment, St Agnes looked at them. She stumbled and dropped the fork she held. She picked it up and followed the other sister with her eyes down.

The prioress raised her eyebrows. 'Come, Dr Edelman. We don't want to interfere with the sisters' work.'

'Thank you for showing me the grounds,' he said, following her. 'I'm aware it was a special favour.'

'It was worth showing you—for your understanding.'

'It was,' he said, a little subdued. 'Oh, by the way,' he continued at the front porch. 'Sister Agnes should hear that Gemma Greene organised a very deflating experience for Stephen Calder. He spent a night in hospital. Sister seems to have won the heart of many an oddball.'

With a faint smile, Mother Jerome nodded.

Chapter 50

Departures

PHILIP STEVENSON and Diana Cartwright had checked their bags in at the Qantas counter and were heading to the departure lounge when hailed.

'Hi Phil, Diana, wait.'

'Hello, Harry. How are things?' said Philip. Diana drew back.

'Not great. I'm escaping to Los Angeles. And you two?'

'Off to London.'

'Separately,' said Diana.

They ambled to the lounge.

'What takes you to London, Phil?'

'Adventure. Thought I'd like to discover the opportunities for a philosopher.' He raised a tired, ironic smile. 'And you?'

'I'm sick,' said Harry. He put his hand over his heart. 'Broken-hearted. I'm in love, and the girl won't have a bar of me. It's terrible. I've never had it before. I must get away before I go bananas. Have you ever experienced this?'

'Yeah, I suppose I have.'

'And you, Diana?'

Diana shrugged. They fell into silence.

'Nobody to see you off?' said Harry at length.

'No family. I said my goodbyes at home. I wanted to be left in peace at this point. Diana, too.'

'Yeah, I know how you feel. Jannie brought me to the airport. She's waiting to see me off. She's a good girl.'

'Where's she now?' Philip said, looking around.

'She's with a Dutch friend who's returning to Holland. Not my type. I've left them alone to say their goodbyes. The girl injured herself during her stay—got in the way of a car. Jannie says she needs sympathy. I suppose she'll be on the same plane as you.'

'Probably, if she's going via London.'

'Hi Phil,' an exuberant female voice rang out. 'Are you off today, too?' Gemma Greene flopped in the seat beside him. 'I'll keep you company, soothe your broken heart all the way to London.' Philip gave her an admonishing look. She noticed Diana sitting on the other side of him. Philip introduced them, saying Diana was a close friend.

'Okay,' Gemma said, putting a finger to her lips. 'Hush, hush.'

'You've got women problems, too, have you?' Harry said, but clearly had no interest in taking the topic further or acknowledging Gemma. 'Ah, here's Jannie. All the best, Phil. I hope it all works out for you. You, too, Diana.' He walked to Jannie, who, not paying attention to Philip and Diana, affectionately took his arm and gave him a comforting kiss on the cheek.

'I'm going to take care of you, you poor broken-hearted boy,' said Gemma

'Please, Gemma, give me a break. I can't cope with you at the moment.'

'Oh, poor, poor boy, don't be so apprehensive. I won't molest you. I'm going to look after you for the girl I love. Nothing else in mind. We'll both pray to our gods that she retrieves her senses.'

Philip shook his head. 'Your personality is far too strong for a twenty-three-year-old.'

'What do you expect with someone tall and good-looking besides being too brilliant for words?'

Philip smiled despite himself.

'That's the boy!'

Diana frowned.

Harry's plane took off and deposited him in Los Angeles, where he could not adjust, despite his commercial and professional success. He called Jannie after six months. Jannie flew over, packed him up, and brought him back to Melbourne, where, with her help and encouragement, he became his old self—and could reflect at leisure on his rebuff and what to do about it. Gemma had to give up her undertaking to console Philip all the way to London after seeing him sit next to Diana, who insisted on holding his hand.

END

Select Bibliography

For background reading on the occult and goddess worship, the author relied primarily on these titles:

Occult Feminism: The Secret Story of Women's Liberation, Rachel Wilson, 2021

Goddess Unmasked: The Rise of Neopagan Feminist Spirituality, Philip G. Davis, Spence Publishing Company, 1998

The Inner Goddess, Josephine Robinson, Gracewing, 1998

Women: Why Are You Weeping? Margaret E. Mills, News Weekly Books, 1997

Awakening Your Goddess, Liz Simpson, Barron's. 2001

Also By Gerard Charles Wilson

FICTION

Sixties Series

Times of Distress (Book 1)

In This Vale of Tears (Book 2)

Counterculture Dreams (Book 3) 2024

The Counterculture Goddess (Book 4) 2025

Love in the Counterculture (Book 5) due 2026

Dreams to Nightmare (Book 6) due 2026

The Castle of Heavenly Bliss (Book 7)

A Sense of Loss (Book 8) due 2027

Editing Constancy: A Jane Austen Story

Seeking the Divine Spark: A Satire in the Style of Evelyn Waugh

NON-FICTION

Social History Series

Prison Hulk to Redemption (Part 1)

War Depression War (Part 2)

Me 'n' Pete: Recalling a Fifties' Childhood (Part 3)

Communists, Billycarts and Two-Wheelers (Part 4) due 2027□

Politics and Media Series

Tony Abbott and the Times of Revolution

The Media of the Republic: Who Killed Diana?

The Telecard Affair: Diary of a Media Lynching 2nd Edition 2024

www.ingramcontent.com/pod-product-compliance
Lightning Source LLC
Chambersburg PA
CBHW070534030726
47505CB00001B/32

* 9 7 8 1 8 7 6 2 6 2 0 7 5 *